Beatles

LARS SAABYE CHRISTENSEN is Norway's leading contemporary writer. He is the author of twelve novels as well as short stories and poetry. His international best-selling novel *The Half Brother* has been published in nearly thirty countries. It won the Nordic Prize for Literature as well as the Norwegian Booksellers' Prize, was shortlisted for the 2005 International IMPAC Dublin Literary Award, was longlisted for the Independent Foreign Fiction Prize and was chosen as one of the twenty-five notable titles of 2004 by the American Library Association. *Herman* was shortlisted for the 2006 YoungMinds Award, and *The Model* was shortlisted for the 2008 Independent Foreign Fiction Prize. Lars Saabye Christensen lives in Oslo.

DON BARTLETT lives with his family in a village in Norfolk. He translates from Scandinavian literature and has recently translated, or co-translated, novels by Roy Jacobsen, K.O. Dahl, Jo Nesbø and Ingvar Ambjørnsen.

LARS SAABYE CHRISTENSEN

Beatles

Translated from the Norwegian by Don Bartlett

Arcadia Books Ltd
15–16 Nassau Street
London W1W 7AB

www.arcadiabooks.co.uk

First published in the United Kingdom by Arcadia Books 2009
Originally published by J.W. Cappelen Forlag AS, Oslo 1984

A catalogue record for this book is available from the British Library.

ISBN 978-1-906413-07-1

Typeset in Minion by MacGuru Ltd
Printed in Finland by WS Bookwell

This translation has been published with the financial support of NORLA.

Arcadia Books distributors are as follows:

in the UK and elsewhere in Europe:
Turnaround Publishers Services
Unit 3, Olympia Trading Estate
Coburg Road
London N22 6TZ

in the US and Canada:
Independent Publishers Group
814 N. Franklin Street
Chicago, IL 60610

in Australia:
Tower Books
PO Box 213
Brookvale, NSW 2100

in New Zealand:
Addenda
PO Box 78224
Grey Lynn
Auckland

in South Africa:
Quartet Sales and Marketing
PO Box 1218
Northcliffe
Johannesburg 2115

Arcadia Books is the *Sunday Times* Small Publisher of the Year

Contents

PART 1

I Feel Fine

Spring 1965

I am sitting in a summer house and it is autumn. My right hand is irritating me, stitches everywhere, and my index finger in particular. It is crooked, bent like a claw. I cannot stop looking at it. It is clinging to a ballpoint pen, which writes in red ink. It is an uncommonly hideous finger. It's a shame I am not left-handed, I once wished I were left-handed and played the bass guitar. But I can write backwards with my left hand, just like Leonardo da Vinci. Nevertheless, I am writing with my right hand and tolerate the disfigured hand and revolting finger. There is a smell of apples in here. A strong aroma of apples rises from the old table where I am sitting in the middle of the dark room. It is the evening of the first day and I have taken the shutters off only one of the windows. The windowsill is covered with dead insects, flies, mosquitoes, wasps with thin, desiccated legs. And the scent of the fruit is making me light-headed, my shiny head releases something inside me, shadows dance along the walls in the moonlight which shines in through the sole window converting the room into an old-fashioned diorama. Now I turn around, like Ola's father, the barber of Solli, who on birthdays always put the film the wrong way round in the projector – we watched three Chaplin films from the end – and go backwards in time. And although I don't think about it, the reel behind my eyes stops at a particular frame, I hold it for a few seconds, freeze it, then let it roll, for I am all-powerful. I give it voices, sound, smell and light. I can clearly hear the shingle crunching beneath our shoes as we traipse across Vestkanttorget, I can feel the giddiness after a mega drag and I can still feel Ringo's elbow digging gently into my ribs, and we stop in a line, all four of us, and John points to a shiny, black Mercedes parked outside Naranja pet shop.

George was the first to speak. He said, 'It's yours, Paul.'

Everyone knew that I was the specialist as far as Mercs were concerned. Didn't even need tools for them. Just a question of twisting the round badge to the left three times, letting go and pulling, because the clip had already snapped. We raced up the steps and felt a hot tingle under our sweaters. We took stock.

'Too many people around,' John whispered.

The others agreed. There were two men standing under the apple trees in the corner and an old lady was crossing the street close by.

'No point takin' r-r-risks,' Ringo mumbled.

'We've already got an Opel and two Fords,' George said.

'But it's a 220S!' I protested.

'We'll nick it some other evenin',' John said.

However, there was no guarantee it would be there the following day. And then I felt the rush that I have felt so often since, and I was no longer listening to the others. I sauntered across the street, alone, bent over the bonnet, my heart still beating in a relaxed, unconcerned way. A couple was coming downhill from Berle, the two men standing under the apple trees glanced over, the parrots in the shop window squawked mute shrieks. I twisted the Mercedes antlers round three times, let go, pulled, and stuffed the badge up my sweater. John, George and Ringo were already a long way ahead, they were supposed to be walking as naturally as possible, but from behind they looked like three lamp posts fitted with red bulbs. John turned and waved furiously, I smiled and waved back, and then they broke into a run towards Uranienborg Park. I was still at the scene of the crime, looked around, but no one had reacted. I began to follow the others, slowly, as if to drag the whole thing out, to get a real sensation of how it felt, to give the car owner a chance to catch me. That wonderful warm tingle spread through my body. And no one was following me. I pulled out the booty, brandished it in triumph and ran after the others.

They were waiting by The Man on the Steps corner shop, each with a packet of juice.

'You're c-c-crazy,' Ringo said.

'One day we'll get bloody caught,' John muttered.

He looked up at me, didn't smile, seemed a little resigned, almost unhappy from where he was sitting with a packet of freezing cold juice and a cigarette bobbing up and down.

It was almost nine. Night had fallen without our noticing. The Man on the Steps switched off the shop lights and we ambled down what locals called Farmers' Hill. I gave the Mercedes badge to George, he was the custodian, he kept them under magazines in a box beneath his bed.

'We've got six of 'em now,' he said.

'But no 220Ss!'

'Can't see any d-d-difference,' Ringo said.

'*Seein'* isn't the point, it's *knowin'* that counts,' I said.

'How many Fiats have we got then?' John wondered.

'Nine,' said George. 'Nine Farts.'

'My brother brought back a porn mag from Copenhagen,' John said. We lurched to a halt, looked at him.

'From Denmark?' Ringo whispered, forgetting to stammer.

'He was playin' handball in Copenhagen. Yuk.'

'What's… what's it like?'

'Classy,' said John. 'Have to be off now.'

'Bring it with you tomorrow,' George said.

'You do that!' Ringo shouted, waving a screwdriver in the air. 'Don't forget!'

I joined John. We were going the same way, down Løvenskioldsgate, George and Ringo trudged off to Solli plass. Neither of us said a word. Sand from the previous winter crunched under our shoes and there was congealed dog shit all over the pavement. They were sure signs of spring even though it was still cold and dark, only mid-April. I gazed down at my shoes and was happy that Mum had promised me a new pair in May, the ones I was wearing now looked more like heavy ski boots and were a lead weight. John's shoes were not a lot better as he wore hand-me-downs from his brother, Stig, and he was two years older and one metre eighty-five, John's shoes were always so big that first of all he had to take a step inside them before he could set off.

'Think we may have enough car badges now,' John said, without looking at me.

'Perhaps we should just collect lots of different makes,' I suggested.

'We've got enough,' he repeated.

'We could sell the ones we've got a lot of.'

John stopped dead and grabbed my arm with force.

'Look,' he shouted, pointing to the pavement.

I froze. There was a piece of string in front of us. String. White string on the ground right in front of us.

'Hand Grenade Man,' John whispered.

I did not say anything, just stared.

'Hand Grenade Man,' John repeated, stepping back.

I stood where I was, a metre, perhaps even less, from the cord. It was tied round the bars of a drain in the gutter and disappeared into a hedge.

'Not sure that's the Hand Grenade Man,' I said quietly.

'What shall we do?' John stuttered behind me. 'Ring the cops?'

'Doesn't have to be the Hand Grenade Man himself, even if there is some string,' I went on, to myself mostly.

'Those two boys up in Grefsen rang the cops,' John hissed. 'We could be blown to smithereens!'

At that moment I seemed to melt. I dissolved into nothing. I took a pace forward, bent down, heard John screaming behind me and tugged with all my might.

There was a hell of a racket because six tin cans were tied to the end of the string. John was long gone, on the other side of the street, entrenched behind a lamp post. I presented my catch and he climbed out of his trench. At that moment we heard laughing and giggling from behind the hedge. John was white-faced and his teeth were chattering, and with one leap he was over the hedge and dragging two small brats into the light. He shoved them against an Opel, frisked them, pointed to me and the cord and said:

'D'you know how many years inside you get for doin' this sort of thing?'

The brats swung their heads from side to side.

'Five!' John shouted. 'Five years! You'll be sent to Jæren. You don't even know where that is, right, but it's a helluva long way away, and you'll be breakin' rocks! For five years. Have you got that?!'

The brats nodded.

Then John tied them together with the string and chased them down the street. They ran like lunatics, and everyone was at their windows thinking it was a wedding. We heard the clatter of the tin cans from several blocks away.

'Why don't they take 'em off?' John wondered, scratching his ear.

'S'pose they think it's fun,' I said.

'I s'pose so.'

We ploughed on. After a long pause John said, 'You're mad! You could've been blown apart!'

'What are the pics in your brother's mag like?'

'Big twats. Twice as big as those in *Cocktail*.'

He fell silent. I didn't have the pluck to ask him any more, so I just waited for John to tell me the rest.

'And they aren't even hairy.' It burst out of him.

'No hair?'

'Not one pube. Shaven off.'

'Is that possible?'

'Looks like it.'

'Ringo's dad is a barber,' I said.

'You can see everythin',' John said.

'Everythin'?'

'Yup.'

We parted in Gimle. John went down to Thomas Heftyes gate, I went on to Skillebekk. I couldn't get the shaven twats out of my mind. I tried to imagine them, but it was totally beyond me. The closest I got was the picture of the naked woman in the medical book, but I think the photo had been touched up, at any rate, the twat was just a smooth surface, there didn't seem to be any hair on it, but there wasn't a crack to be seen, either, and I presumed they couldn't show that sort of woman in a family medical book.

As I turned into Svoldergate the rain started, a light, warm drizzle that hardly wets you and you can't see, and I thought it felt just like a lot of hairs touching my face, tiny little dark hairs, and there was a strange smell in the whole street, a bit like the school shower, and no one around anywhere. Down the last stretch I broke into a run because I was already three quarters of an hour late.

But I stopped by the postboxes in the entrance. I saw a brown envelope. Next to it the postman had left a note. There was no one in the block called Nordahl Rolfsen. Could anyone help him? I could. The letter was for me. I shoved the envelope up my shirt, crept upstairs and sneaked into my room. There I carefully opened the letter and sat with my ears on stalks. No one about. What the ad said was true. Discreet and well-packed. From *Alt I Ett*. A dozen *Rubin-Extra*, pink. Eleven kroner. But I didn't need to pay. No one knew who Nordahl Rolfsen was. Cunning. I didn't dare open the smooth package, just held it in my hand, heard the light rain outside, the hairs brushing the window. Then I hid the whole lot in the third drawer, under *Pop-Extra*, Beatles magazines and a Conquest crime magazine.

It was Thursday, must have been because we had an essay for the day after, the last before the exam, and essays always had to be handed in on Fridays so that Lue, our form master, had some entertainment for the weekend. I still hadn't written a word. In fact, the plan had been to start coughing that night, long, barking, despairing coughs that kept Mum and Dad awake till way past midnight. And the following morning all I had to do was heat up my forehead on the pillow so Mum would confirm a temperature of 39.5 and instantly prescribe a day off. But I didn't want to be the last person to see Gunnar's brother's porn mag. I decided to write the essay after Mum and Dad had gone to bed. And all of a sudden my mother was in the doorway with my supper and a glass of milk.

'You could say hello when you come home,' she said. I took the plate and glass.

'We're in the sitting room. That's not so far away, is it.'

'I know,' I said.

'Where have you been?'

'At school.'

'So late?'

'We were playing footie.'

She came a step closer and I knew this was going to drag on. And I knew exactly what she would say and how I would answer so as to be polite.

'Do you *have* to stick all those horrible pictures on the wall?'

'I think they're fab,' I said.

'Are *they* fab?' my mother almost screamed, pointing to a picture just under the ceiling.

'That's The Animals,' I said.

Mum sent me a stern look.

'You need a haircut,' she said. 'It'll soon be over your ears.'

I thought about Dad, who was almost bald, and then I blushed because an eerie apparition, a monstrous head, a crazy hybrid, appeared in my mind and Mum came closer, asked me what was up.

'What's up?' I parroted in a gruff voice.

'Yes. You suddenly went all funny.'

Now the conversation was taking a completely unexpected and dangerous turn. I began to make a show of eating, but Mum stood her ground, leaning against the door frame.

'Have you been out with a girl tonight?' Mum asked.

The question was insane, way off the mark, idiotic, a bolt from the blue and, instead of laughing her out of court, I lost my temper.

'I've been with Gunnar! And Sebastian and Ola!'

Mum patted me on the head.

'I still think you need a haircut.'

Still? What did she mean? What trap was being laid now? I summoned my last ounce of strength and used the argument that always had some effect on my mother because once upon a time she had wanted to be an actress.

'Rudolf Nureyev's got long hair, too!'

Mum nodded slowly, a smile spread across her face and then, so help me, she put her hand on my head for the second time.

'You can bring her home with you.'

I was sure that I had the reddest pale face in the western world, not including Jensenius, the opera singer on the floor above, who drank thirty bottles of Export pils a day and said it was the deposit on bottles and art that kept the world going.

As usual, Dad was sitting in the chair by the bookshelves with a copy of *Nå* and a picture of Wenche Myhre on the front page. He was concentrating hard on the crossword. Then he raised his narrow, pale face and looked at me.

'Have you done your homework?'

'Yes.'

'How's your preparation for the exams going?'

'Fine. I think.'

'You shouldn't think. You should know.'

'I'm well set.'

'Looking forward to going to *realskole*?'

I nodded.

Dad mustered a brief smile and subsided back into his crossword. I said goodnight and, as I turned, Dad's voice was there again.

'What's the name of the drummer in The Beatles?'

He looked very strange as he said that and I think he even blushed. To justify himself, he pointed energetically at the magazine.

'Ola,' I started to say, but caught myself. 'Ringo. Ringo Starr. In fact, his real name is Richard Starkey,' I informed him.

Dad filled in the squares, nodded and said:

'Excellent. That fits.'

I lay awake waiting for my mother and father to go to bed. If I switched on the light now they would come and ask what was wrong, because they could see from the crack under the door whether the room was dark or not. I heard the rain outside, I heard the trains puffing past only a few hundred metres away, between my room and Frogner Bay. I knew exactly where they were going, but then there weren't many railway lines to choose between. Even though they were not going that far and just stayed in Norway they always made me think of distant countries, the ones on the maps behind the teacher's seat. Listening to the trains, I thought about the stars too, and space, and then everything glazed over and I plunged backwards, inside myself it seemed, and if I gave a shriek Mum and Dad would come rushing in, they were tiny dots a long, long way away and they gently pulled me back. But I wasn't screaming now. I heard the trains, and the Goldfish – the tram – screeching its way across Ole Bulls plass. And in the middle of all this there were Mum and Dad's low voices and the radio that was always on, and it was always opera, and it sounded so lonely, sadder than anything I knew, songs from another world, a world that was grey and still, the singing was so cold and dead. On the walls around me were pictures of faces that also sang, but not a sound emerged, the guitars and drums were silent. The Rolling Stones, The Animals, The Dave Clark Five, The Hollies, The

Beatles. The Beatles. Pictures of The Beatles. And I dreamt about Ringo, John, George and Paul. I dreamt that I was one of them, that I was Paul McCartney, that I had his round, sorrowful eyes that all the girls screamed themselves half to death over. I dreamt I was left-handed and played bass guitar. I sat up in bed, wide awake. But I *am* one of them, I thought aloud, and laughed. I am one of The Beatles.

It was half past eleven and Mum and Dad had gone to bed. I set to work. There were three titles. The first was impossible. *My Family*. Dad works in the bank and does crosswords. Mum wanted to be an actress when she was young. My name's Kim. That was no good. The next title was: *A Day at School*. Impossible. Even lying has limits, even for me lying has limits. You can lie up to a certain point and make it sound good. After that it is just insane. I had to take the last one: *Your Plans After Leaving Folkeskole*. *Folkeskole* until sixteen, then *realskole*. I retrieved my exercise book from a pile of sandwiches. I had been given an E for my previous essay, but my father had written that one: *My Hobby*. Of course he thought that I should write about stamps, even though I only had two three-sided stamps from the Ivory Coast. My father got an E. Then I took a risk. I put a new cartridge in my fountain pen and wrote in ink straight on the page. There was no going back. My spine tingled, the excitement seemed to inspire me to greater things. First of all, I would finish *realskole* and afterwards *gymnas*. Then I would study medicine and become a doctor in a poor country where I would spend my life working with sick black people. I stretched it out to three and a half pages and finished with something about Fridtjof Nansen, but couldn't quite get the North Pole to fit with black people, and I realised I should have taken Albert Schweitzer, but by then it was too late. I shut the book without reading through what I had written, and the time must have gone unusually fast because I heard the last train to Drammen thunder by, and the whole world was quiet. The rain had stopped. The trams had stopped running. Mum and Dad were asleep. And I was about to fall asleep myself when a limpid falsetto filled the room, coming from above, but it was not God, it was Jensenius, the nightingale, who had started his nocturnal wanderings, back and forth while singing old songs from the time he had been world-famous.

With Jensenius singing upstairs it was impossible to sleep, even though his voice was nowhere near as sad as those on the radio. Listening to Jensenius was more on the creepy side, but when you saw him it was just comical. He was so colossally big, not so unlike the picture of the man on the IFA salt pastilles, and he was also an opera singer, by the way. That reminded me of something. In the fifth class I had cut out the signature of the man on the pastille packet, Ivar Frederik Andresen, and told Gunnar it was a rare autograph of a world-famous opera singer. Gunnar paid two kroner for it – he collected autographs from everyone from Arne Ingier to Comrade Lin Piao. Gunnar did wonder, though, why it was written on such thick paper. Not paper, I said. *Cardboard.* The finest quality. But why was it so very small? I cut it out of a secret letter, I explained. Three days later Gunnar came over to me and asked if I wanted a salt pastille. And then he took out a packet of IFA and thrust it in my face. He wasn't angry. Just astonished. I refunded his money and since then there have been no further financial dealings between us.

But, well, Jensenius, our block's opera singer, he looked like an airship and from this colossal vessel issued a voice that was so high and reedy and heart-rending that a tiny schoolgirl seemed to be inside him, singing in his stead. I suppose he must have been a baritone at one time. There are several stories circulating about Jensenius and I am not quite sure which to believe, but people say he gave sweets to small girls, and small boys, too, and liked to hug them. He had been a baritone at one time, but they had fiddled with his undercarriage, and now he was a soprano, he drank like a bear and sang like an angel. And I like to call him the Whale because whales sing, too, they sing because they are lonely and the oceans are much too large for them.

And then I fell asleep, the first day.

The essay was handed in during the first lesson, after we had said Our Father with Dragon as prayer leader. But he didn't get any further than 'hallowed be thy name', he fell quiet and reddened and his knuckles were pressed white, and Goose had to take over. Now everything went as smooth as butter and the rest of us stood there, straight-backed, by our seats, mumbling as well as we were able.

Class monitor that week was Seb. He buzzed up and down the lines collecting the exercise books and putting them in a tidy pile on the desk in front of Lue who scanned the class with incredulity.

'All present and correct?' he asked in a low voice.

Seb nodded and went to his seat. He sat at the back of the window row while I sat behind Gunnar in the middle row and Ola sat at the front by the door and was always first out and last in. In fact, it was a good place to be behind Gunnar, his back was broad enough to mask the whole family medical book. He turned to whisper:

'Which one did you write about?'

'Future plans.'

'What are you goin' to be?'

'Doctor in Africa.'

'Seb's goin' to be a missionary. In India.'

'What about you?'

'Goin' to be a pilot. And Ola's goin' to be a ladies' hairdresser.'

'You got the mag with you?'

Gunnar gave a quick nod and faced the front.

Lue was still scanning the class as though we were a new landscape that had manifested itself in all its glory, and not 7A, twenty-two striplings with greasy hair and spots and our hands in our pockets.

'Has *everyone* handed in an essay?' he repeated.

No reaction.

'Who has *not* handed in an essay?' he asked, rephrasing the question.

Silence in the classroom. You could have heard a pin drop. The Briskeby tram clattered past, a long way down in the world, for we were the school's finest and occupied the top floor.

Lue stood up and began to pace the podium, to and fro, in front of us. Whenever he reached the desk he patted the pile of essays and his smile became broader and broader.

'You're learning,' he said. 'You're learning and perhaps my endeavours have not been in vain. You will soon come to realise that *punctuality* is one of the corner stones of the adult world. Now that you are going on to the *realskole* you will be faced with new and much greater demands, not to mention those of you who are aiming at *gymnas* and university, you will soon understand, and the best time to understand this is now. This wonderful pile of essays may indeed bear witness to the fact that you *have* understood if not everything, then at least a part.'

I was sitting in the middle row, behind Gunnar's comfortingly broad back. Lue was marching around up on his stage, speaking with a warm, tremulous voice. No one was listening to one single syllable, but we were content because we didn't have to parse main clauses or read Ibsen's *Terje Vigen*, and after a while his voice faded away, it is a quirk I have, I seem to be able to cut off the sound, as it were, and it can be very pleasant sometimes. Lue became a silent movie, his movements were jerky and exaggerated and his mouth was working with such vigour that his mentally distant classroom audience could guess what was on his mind. Now and then illustrative texts appeared on the board – *When you sally forth into the great wide world, be prepared – Fight for your country and the Norwegian language – Practice makes perfect – Turn your left cheek and always ask first – Bjørnstjerne Bjørnson*. And just before the bell rang, I knew he was happy. He was so happy because for the first time, and the last, we had handed in our essays on time. Lue was happy and he was happy with us. Then the bell rang and everyone raced to the door even though Lue was in mid-sentence and, recalling him now, I see a small, grey figure wreathed in an over-sized smock, with thinning hair falling over his forehead and a face shiny with his exertions and happiness. He is still speaking without sound as twenty-two crazy boys charge out, stampede, and he is still standing there, in his own world, as lonely as Jensenius must be, but he is happy because irony has finally released its grip on him, and he is sincere and warm and likes us.

But that is now and not then. At that time the silent movie came to a sudden end when the bell rang. Lue was gone in an instant, like a technical fault, and I clung to Gunnar. The trail led straight down to the toilet where eventually ten to fifteen boys had gathered, so someone must have had a big mouth and that mouth belonged to Ola, who had the world's worst face for playing poker, his whole mug began to twitch as soon as he had a pair of threes in his hand.

'Where is it!' Dragon hassled.

'This isn't the circus, you know,' Gunnar said.

'You're havin' us on,' Dragon said. 'You haven't got it!'

Gunnar just glared at him, without wavering, and Dragon felt ill at ease. He was fat and sweaty and shifted weight from foot to foot.

'When've I ever had anyone on?' Gunnar asked.

I remembered the time with the IFA pastilles and looked away, for everyone knew that Gunnar would not deceive anyone, and Dragon was slowly but inexorably pushed out of the circle, ashamed, red and breathless.

Gunnar regarded us for a while. Then he pulled up his sweater and shirt and produced a large white envelope. And the circle around him closed in as at last he opened the envelope and took out the magazine. Then, as though he had lost interest, he gave me the magazine without a word and disappeared into a cubicle and locked the door.

So I became the centre of the circle and everyone moved towards me, pushing and shoving, because the break would soon be over. I flicked through it. I could feel the agitation at once, I was agitated myself, it wasn't as I had imagined. The first pictures were close-ups of shaven twats and there was not a sound to be heard, no one laughed, no one grinned, it was as quiet as a burial chamber. I flicked through faster. There were twats from above and from below, whole pages of huge slits spread diagonally from corner to corner. But, at last, towards the end some normality began to return, whole women, huge knockers, loads of hair, but then there was a picture of a guy lying down with his whole face between a woman's thighs.

'What's he doin'?' a voice asked.

'He's lickin',' said another, and it was Gunnar's, he was out of the cubicle and grinning.

Everything went quiet for a while, completely quiet.

'Lickin'?'

'Lickin' the woman's cunt, can't you see!' another voice said.

'Lickin' her cunt?'

Dragon stood on the outer perimeter, his eyes rolling.

'Yup.'

'What…what… does that taste like then?'

'It tastes of grass,' I said, quick as a shot. 'If you're lucky. But if you cop a bitter 'un, it tastes like stale salami and gym shoes.'

Someone was coming down the stairs. A shudder ran through the great flock of white faces. Gunnar threw me a bewildered glance, thrust the envelope in my hand and moved towards the exit with the others. I stood there with my back to the steps and put the magazine in the envelope. The senior teacher grabbed my shoulder and spun me round.

'And what have you got there?' he asked.

For a moment I saw the whole world falling apart, everything fell, and it all fell at the same speed, a never-ending fall. The teacher towered over me like a figurehead on a galleon and I had to lean back to look him in the eye. Everything fell, we fell together, and it was more exhilarating than standing on the edge of the ten-metre board in Frogner Lido just before the big leap, even though I had never dived from such a height.

'My father's magazine,' I said. 'Which I'm going to show herr Lue.'

'What sort of magazine?'

'A travel brochure about Africa. My uncle was in Africa this Easter.'

The senior teacher regarded me for a long time.

'So your uncle has been to Africa, has he?'

'Yes, he has,' I said.

He leant over me for longer still, his breath was unbearable, herring, fish oil and tobacco. Then he took a step back and shouted,'Well, get outside then, boy!'

I ran up the steps into the sunshine. At that moment the bell rang and it felt as though it was inside me, somewhere between my ears. The rest of the skunks were standing by the gym, staring at me as if I had just landed on earth and was small, green and slimy.

'How… how?' Dragon stuttered.

'He likes 'em smooth with cream on,' I said, strutting past them.

And all of sudden I felt drained, absolutely shattered. The gym teacher shouted to us from the door and we shuffled down to the sweaty dressing rooms with wooden benches and iron hooks and the floor that was always wet from the showers. I didn't care if we weren't outside today. At that moment Gunnar joined me. We hung back behind the others. I slipped him the envelope and he rolled it up in the sweater he had just taken off.

'I'm a bastard,' Gunnar mumbled.

We stopped.

'I left you in the lurch,' he went on. 'I'm a traitor.'

'I was holdin' the mag,' I said.

'I left you with the envelope. I'm a shit.'

'You wouldn't've been able to lie,' I said.

Gunnar straightened up, a faint smile spread across his broad face.

'No,' he said. 'I wouldn't.'

We laughed. Gunnar adopted a boxer's posture and punched the air with a fist, then he was serious again, more serious than ever before. He said in a low, almost chiding voice:

'Don't forget this, Kim,' he said. 'You'll always be able to count on me!'

And then he shook my hand, it was quite a solemn act, and his strong fingers squeezed mine as if they were a few sprigs of parsley, and I wondered whether I had seen anything like this in *Illustrated Classics*. Was it *Lord Jim* or *The Last of the Mohicans?* Then I remembered it was in an episode of *The Saint* and I began to look forward to the evening already, because it was Friday and there was an hour's crime programme on TV.

'And then it was six n-n-nil,' Ringo shouted as we turned off by Bislett on our way towards Kåres Tobakk in Theresesgate. He was sitting on the luggage carrier as his bike had no spokes after his brakes had failed down Farmers' Hill and Ringo had stuck his shoe in the front wheel out of sheer panic. It looked like he had trodden in an egg-slicer afterwards.

'S-s-six nil, boy oh boy,' Ringo repeated. '*Six n-n-nil!*'

'If it'd been six against England or Sweden, but against Thailand...' I said.

'Nevertheless! Six g-g-goals!'

Now Theresesgate began to climb even steeper and I didn't have the wind to speak. John and George were cycling slalom in front of us and cheering and shouting, and behind us at the bottom the tram was coming, so now I had to pedal harder to reach Kåres Tobakk before it caught us up.

'Where is Thailand a-a-actually?' Ringo asked.

'Left of Japan,' I panted.

And we made it before the tram. I was already looking forward to the ride down. Then it would be George's turn to have Ringo on the back.

'Wonder if they'll put me on the wing this year,' John said.

'Probably have to count our blessings if we're in the team at all,' George thought.

'If I have to play at the b-b-back, I ain't interested,' Ringo said. 'I get so nervous standin' s-s-still.'

We went en masse into Kåre's dark shop, *Kåres Tobakk*, and it smelt strange inside, of fruit, smoke, sweat, chocolate and liquorice. And we knew that under the counter there were copies of *Cocktail* and *Kriminaljournalen*, but it wasn't a thrill any longer, not after Gunnar's brother's magazine, something had been lost, a shame in a way.

Kåre appeared out of the dark, his good-natured boxer's face with a harelip, and I think he recognised us from the previous year.

'Sub?' he asked.

We nodded and each of us put ten kroner on the counter, he fetched four cards and we dictated our names.

'Born in 51,' Kåre mumbled. 'Boys' team then this year.'

'Have lots of people signed up?' John asked.

'We've got good teams at all levels,' Kåre smiled.

'How's F-Frigg d-doin' in the t-top league then?' Ringo wanted to know.

'We'll win,' Kåre said with conviction.

'And we beat Thailand s-s-six nil, didn't we,' Ringo added with enthusiasm. He couldn't get over it.

'Training starts on Tuesday,' Kåre said. 'Five o'clock on the Frigg ground.'

'Will there be a trip to Denmark this year?' George wondered.

'Reckon so. Train hard and you can go, too.'

We were given our membership cards, split a Coke, but didn't dare buy cigarettes because Kåre might not have liked Frigg boys smoking, and none of us wanted to miss out on the Denmark trip.

Back on the street, Ringo looked at John and whispered:

'What did you do with the m-m-mag?'

'Chucked it,' John answered.

'You've ch-ch-chucked it!'

'Yep.'

And in fact we all breathed a sigh of relief, but Ringo would not give up.

'What'll your b-b-brother s-s-say, eh?'

'My brother thinks it's fine that I chucked it.'

So we jumped on our bikes and flew down Theresesgate. The warm air sang in our ears and our screams of 'I Feel Fine' bounced off the house walls, and George shouted that the needle of his speedo was hovering on eighty, though you couldn't always rely on it, but we were going fast and didn't need to pedal until we came to Bogstadveien.

'Not quite a month to May 17 now,' John said.

'Not long to the exams, either,' George added.

'Or to s-s-summer!' Ringo shouted.

We went quiet for a few moments because it was a bit strange to think about summer. After summer there was no guarantee we would be in the same class, or even the same school. But we had sworn allegiance to each other; nothing would part us and The Beatles would never split up.

First of all, we ran around the pitch, then we did a bit of heading and afterwards we were divided into two teams, eight players in each. We were allowed to use the big goals the seniors and the Police College used, and the goalkeepers felt tiny between the sticks, they could not reach the crossbar however much they jumped. They looked like herrings in an enormous fishing net. John and I were put in the same team, he was centre half, I was right back. My opponent on the left wing was Ringo. George was a central defender and he didn't look very comfortable when John went storming through like a tank sweeping away all the opposition. I stayed in my position and whacked balls to the midfield. George managed to stop John a couple of times, but I wondered whether John wasn't giving him the ball so that we could all be in the same team. Towards the end of the game Ringo intercepted the ball and came roaring up the touchline. When he was close enough he whispered, so that only I could hear:

'L-l-lemme past! L-l-lemme past!'

I held my position, legs apart, didn't move from the spot, could easily let Ringo past because I had already made a few strong tackles and reckoned my place in the team was secure. So I stood rock still. All Ringo had to do was run around me, I was a buoy, and then centre the ball for a clear header on goal. But of course he had to overreach himself, he started with a few crazy step-overs, thinking he was in Brazil, his team were yelling and shouting at him, and then at long last he played the ball forward, lowered his back and ran straight for me. We banged heads and the ball rolled out of play and I got the throw-in.

'Sh-sh-shit,' Ringo wheezed. 'B-b-bloody hell!'

'I didn't even move!'

'H-h-how was I supposed to know. The b-b-back doesn't usually stand b-b-bolt upright, does he!'

I think our team won 17–11, and afterwards there was feedback and a review. A couple of players were down as dead certs, Aksel in goal, Kjetil and Willy in attack. And John must have been in, too, the snowplough. George looked quite exhausted and Ringo was peeved.

'There's a match next weekend,' Åge shouted. 'On Saturday. Against Slemmestad. In Slemmestad.'

No one said anything. The gravity of the situation was apparent.

The trainer continued:

'And we'll win this match!'

We cheered.

'Good lads! Everyone here today meet up at the same place on Saturday at three. We're going to Slemmestad by coach. And the majority of you will get a run out on the pitch. But if any of you don't, your chance will come later, okay!'

The teams dispersed, some boys on their own, some in dribs and drabs. We were left standing in the middle of the huge ground studying each other.

'Reckon all of us'll get a game,' John said.

'That idiot over there wouldn't let me p-p-past even when I a-a-asked him,' Ringo said, pointing to me.

'But I didn't even move!'

'Th-th-that's why! I thought you'd m-m-move left so I headed s-s-straight for you. D-d-dirty trick!'

All of a sudden John went quiet, stared like an Irish Setter in the direction of the Norwegian Broadcasting Corporation building, and whispered in a cracked voice:

'Isn't that, isn't that Per Pettersen comin' towards us?'

We stared, too. It was. It was Per Pettersen. The man himself. He was strolling towards us in white shorts and a blue and white shirt with a bag slung over his shoulder.

'Must have his autograph,' John shouted. 'Any of you got anythin' to write with?'

Of course we hadn't taken a pencil to football training, or any paper. Per Pettersen was approaching and John began to scour the grass in desperation. He couldn't let the chance slip, but all he found was a Zip chewing gum wrapper. He smoothed it out on his thigh and up came Per Pettersen.

'Autograph,' John stuttered, passing him the wrapper.

Per stopped and looked at us with gentle eyes. Then he put down his bag and laughed.

'Haven't got anythin' to write with,' John said.

Per rummaged in his bag, found a biro and wrote his name on the sweet-smelling wrapper, Per Pettersen with two neat Ps. But as he was about to go Ringo pushed forward, he had been hopping from one foot to the other the whole time.

'Could you have a shot at me, like?'

Pettersen stopped and swept back his recalcitrant fringe.

'Okay. You stand in goal.'

Ringo, red-faced, gaped at the rest of us, then sprinted to the goal, positioned himself in the very centre and crouched down like a lobster. Per Pettersen placed the ball on the grass, retreated a few steps and tapped the toe of his boot on the grass.

'Poor Ola,' George said under his breath. 'He's gone soft in the head. If he even gets hold of the ball it'll carry 'im through the nettin.'

Per Pettersen sprinted up and blasted and there was Ringo, sitting on the ground with the ball in his clutches. He hadn't moved from the spot. He looked bewildered, as though he didn't know what had happened. Then he scraped himself up and staggered over to us. Per Pettersen slung his bag over his shoulder, flicked back his fringe and shouted to Ola:

'Great save!'

And with that, Per Pettersen was gone.

Ola looked drained. He could hardly hold the ball. But he was happy.

'Hit it hard, did he?' George asked gently.

'H-h-hardest shot I've ever faced,' Ringo said. 'Gordon B-B-Banks would've had trouble standin' up.'

'Fab save,' John said. 'Perfect.'

'How did you know where he was goin' to shoot?' George enquired.

'I f-f-feinted,' Ola said. 'I p-p-pretended I was goin' to the right. Then I switched to the l-l-left and the ball hit me in the s-s-stomach.'

We strolled towards our bikes in the long grass by Slemdalsveien.

'D'you think Per P-P-Pettersen'll tell K-K-Kåre and Åge?' Ola asked.

'Possible,' John said. 'If they meet up.'

'I s'pose I'll get the goalie's spot then. Regular place in the t-t-team!'

Ola's eyes began to glaze over even more, he seemed to lose sight of us.

'The trick is keepin' eye c-c-contact,' we heard Ola say. 'I focused on the whites of his eyes. And then he l-lost confidence and the b-b-ball was mine.'

We pushed our bikes to the kiosk by the Police College and bought Ringo a Coke. He thought he deserved it and drank the whole bottle in one go. After getting the deposit we had a peep at the crashed cars on the other side of the boarded-up fence, and we thought about the people who had been in them. That was a spooky thought, as if they were still sitting there, bloodstained and crushed, ghosts in smashed-up cars. The Alsatian guard dog growled at us by the gate, its white teeth gleaming in its red jaws. We shuddered and went on to Majorstuen, to the Vinkelgården centre, and pointed at the Durex advert above a clock which showed it would soon be seven o'clock. Then Ringo yelled as loud as he could, he was sitting behind me again, and he was beginning to come down to earth after his wonder save:

'Dew... Dew.... D-D-Dew...'

And Seb responded:

'Rex!'

And Gunnar screeched at the top of his voice:

'Dick-Dick-Dick-Dick.'

And I completed:

'Dick Van Dyke!'

And that wasn't all we could do, we had 'Great Balls of Fire' and 'Country and Western', but then we shut up because Nina and Guri from the C class were standing in Valkyrie plass, and we skidded onto the pavement with screaming tyres and pounding hearts.

'Where have you been?' Guri asked.

'Dance classes,' Seb answered.

The girls laughed and Seb seemed to grow in the saddle.

'Could we have a lift to Urra Park?' Nina asked.

We were going that way anyway, so that was fine, and even if we'd been going to Trondheim it would have been fine, too. But now at least one thing was sure, and that was that Ola would have to get his bike fixed, and smartish, because he was always sitting on the back of mine. Nina and Guri jumped onto Gunnar's and Seb's, and, with that, my chances were ruined. We sped down Jacob Aalls gate with the girls squealing and complaining, and I might just have been a little relieved after all about Ola having scuppered his bike and sitting with me now. Otherwise Guri and Nina would have had to choose between the four of us, and then two would have lost out, and even though we didn't give a shit about little girls with plaits and pouty mouths, it wouldn't have been much fun with no one on the back, whistling and peering into the sunset, pretending everything was normal.

The girls were offloaded in Uranienborg Park, Urra Park as we called it, and we hung over our handlebars again, looking through each other and waiting for something to fall from the sky, as it were, until Ola said in a deep bass voice:

'S-s-saved a Per P-P-Pettersen penalty!'

'Who did?' Nina asked.

'I did! I saved a Per P-P-Pettersen penalty!'

'Who's Per Pettersen?'

Ola looked at us with vacant eyes, begging us for help, but he would have to sort this out himself. He might just as well have said he had saved fourteen shots in a row from Pelé, that wouldn't have made a greater impression.

'P-P-Per Pettersen! Plays for the Norwegian n-n-national t-team, doesn't he!'

'So interesting,' said Guri.

That was the end of the conversation about Ola's miracle save. The girls headed for a bench, we let them go and then followed anyway. And the small green buds on the trees were sticky to hold, the darkness swooped down like a huge shadow and enveloped us all. It was cold standing there in shorts with green knees and elbows. Nothing happened of course. In fact, I can remember better what didn't happen. For what didn't happen but might have happened was a lot more exciting than what really happened one April evening in Urra Park, 1965.

You can say a lot of things about Lue, but he had depths he could plumb. Even while he was coming down the corridor we realised that a fresh disappointment had him in its thrall and was wresting derision and sarcasm from his dry, embittered body. He arrived with the pile of essays under his arm, taking quick, incisive steps like the leader of a janissary marching band. His searing gaze went through us like X-ray beams, an insane smile curled beneath his hair-filled nose, and he said not one word. He locked us in the classroom, sat at the desk with the pile of essays in front of him like a menacing tower and there he remained, as mute as a shoe.

I couldn't restrain myself, I whispered to Gunnar, 'He's lost his voice. Shock.'

Lue was on his feet at once. He leapt down between the rows and stood over me with his hands on his hips, the muscles in his face contorted knots beneath the skin. For a moment I was reminded of Uncle Hubert, poor old Uncle Hubert who was not right in the head, even though he was Dad's brother, and I wondered if Lue was not all there. However, mute he was not.

'*What did you say?*'

I looked up at him. I had never noticed that he had so much

hair in his nostrils before. It protruded like a hairdresser's black broom.

'I asked Gunnar something.'

'And just *what* did you ask Gunnar?'

He seized Gunnar by the neck and yelled, 'Gunnar! What did Kim ask you?'

There was no way this was going to turn out well because Gunnar was the type who was unable to say anything except the truth. If he tried to lie he ground to a halt; he simply could not do it. I watched his neck flush red like a glowing clothes iron.

I spoke up for him, 'I only asked Gunnar for a rubber.'

Lue spun round to me, his lips pinched flat to the point of non-existence, then his mouth re-appeared as a quivering finger pointed straight at my forehead. I was glad the finger was not loaded.

'I'm asking Gunnar now, so *Gunnar* should answer and not you! Do you understand?'

'It doesn't matter who answers if the answer is the same, does it?' I said, almost stunned by my own logic.

Lue's hand loomed larger, it grabbed my shoulder, hauled me out of my chair and dragged me up to the desk. I had to stand there while Lue flicked through the exercise books in his fury. And while standing there I felt some sympathy for Lue because Class 7A was a sorry sight to behold. At last he found my book and waved it in front of my face.

'Since you're so clever at answering questions, you can tell the whole class, all these inquisitive minds, these intelligent, alert and interested peers of yours what your future plans are!'

I said nothing, just looked across the heads in the class and out of the window. Someone was working on the roof on the other side of the street. They had roped themselves to the chimney in case they fell. I would have liked to be up there, balancing without a rope, I felt a tingle down my spine and my brain seemed to be on the point of boiling over, balancing like that, on the very, very edge. Then Lue's voice was there again, a warm puff of air against my cheek.

'You're always the one with the smart ripostes. Now tell them what you're going to be.'

'I wrote in my essay that I was going to be a doctor, but I wrote that because I didn't know what I was going to be. And then I wrote that I would travel to Africa, to pad it out.'

Lue just stared at me, and I could see the fight going out of him. It would not be long now before he gave up. For a moment I felt sorry for him. I would have liked to help him but didn't know how.

'Sit down,' he said. 'And keep your mouth shut unless you are instructed to speak.'

The atmosphere in the classroom was a bit lighter now. All the signs were that Lue was close to surrender. But he bravely fought on, desperate and short of breath. He even had to go into the corridor for some fresh air. With clenched fists he returned, bent over the desk and blinked.

'There are twenty-two boys in this class, aren't there. Twenty-two quick-witted, intelligent, polite, clean, honest and, last but not least, ambitious boys. Do you agree?'

He didn't wait for an answer. Of course we agreed.

'Ten of you are going to be priests. All those going to be priests please raise your hands.'

Hesitant fingers rose in the air. Accompanied by giggles. Dragon was going to be a priest.

Lue pointed a gentle finger at Dragon.

'So you're going to be a priest. You'll have to learn the Lord's Prayer first. By heart! And then you'll have to do a better cleaning job on your teeth, otherwise the congregation will expire at the first hallelujah!'

Dragon looked down at the lid of his desk and the flesh on his neck shook. We knew now he hated Lue, that he could have murdered him on the spot. The other priests didn't look too well, either. I was glad I was going to be a doctor in Africa.

'So, ten priests,' Lue said. 'You can put down your sacred arms now. And then we have five missionaries. *Five*. That's a cut above the norm. Could you give us a sign?'

Five hands went up. Seb's among them.

'You're going to be missionaries. In India. Africa. Australia. Tell me, why cross the brook for water. Why not begin at home? Why not bring Christianity to Norway first? Or this class? Why not begin here and now, with Class 7A, class teacher included?'

None of the missionaries answered. Seb sat with a crooked smirk on his face, leaning back against the wall. Lue had his beady eye on him, he pointed and yelled:

'You! Sebastian! Tell us why you're going to be a missionary! Eh! Speak!'

Seb rocked forward on his chair, still with a grin, that grin wasn't always easy to interpret, didn't know whether he was grinning at you or himself or nothing.

Seb said in a quiet voice, 'I want to travel.'

'And so you have to be a missionary. Do my ears hear correctly?'

'I couldn't think of anything else.'

'Are you taking the mickey?'

'No. I could have been a sailor, too, but couldn't find the words.'

'Are you all taking the mickey?'

Now he turned to the whole class, well, the whole world for that matter. He smacked his hand flat down on the pile of essays and the desk shook. Then he stepped up onto the podium. He stood on the spot where the sun entered the room like a searchlight, but he seemed to have forgotten his lines and there wasn't a prompter around. He took out a handkerchief, but no doves or rabbits appeared, either, and then he wiped his face. His face was small and the handkerchief was large, a cloth, faded, yellow, not quite spotless. Then he moved from the cone of light and stepped down into the room, to the brain-dead, godforsaken audience. Lue stood in front of Ola. Ola crumpled like a punctured football. Lue patted his head.

'Here we have someone who chose a sensible profession, a choice seemingly commensurate with his abilities. But tell me, why a *ladies'* hairdresser?'

Laughter surged like an oil slick across the classroom. Soon Ola was gasping for air. He would not be able to get out of this situation without instant assistance. Gunnar and I desperately tried to think of something, but he beat us to it. The football had regained its bounce. Ola sat up and said in a dry, unfamiliar voice:

'My father says that soon b-b-b-boys will stop having h-haircuts.'

Lue nodded, he nodded gloomily several times. Gunnar, Seb and I heaved a sigh of relief. Ola had coped and the rest of the jessies approved of his answer. They sat pulling their fringes over their foreheads and winding their hair round an ear, and Lue trudged back to his place in the sun.

'And then we have a racing car driver, a couple of pilots, a parachutist and – he settled in his seat – there was one person who wrote about a day at school.'

The class went quiet and everyone stared at Goose. Of course it was Goose, and he was hauled up to the teacher's desk. Lue leafed through the exercise book and read aloud:

'Our class teacher's name is Lue and he is the best teacher in the world.'

A gasp ran through the room. Goose shrank like a woollen sweater in boiling water and everyone agreed that was the boldest statement ever made since Jesus was said to have walked on water.

Lue just surveyed the class, his lips formed a thin, bloodless smile and his eyes became deep wells of despair. He slowly turned to Goose.

'Am I the best teacher in the world?'

7A had never been so quiet. Pulses stopped beating, time lay over us like a huge lid and we were a pot that had to explode at any minute.

'Am I the best teacher in the world?' Lue repeated, calmer than he had ever been before.

'No,' said Goose, and the bell rang.

I got E+, the same as Seb. Gunnar and Ola got a C.

'When we break up for the summer we'll have to buy a present for Lue,' Gunnar said.

'But what?' Ola asked.

'Don't really know. We just have to buy him somethin' to make him a bit happy.'

'We could give 'im a Beatles record,' Seb suggested.

'Not sure he's got a record player,' Gunnar said.

'It's the thought that counts. That's what my dad always says,' I said.

'Then we don't need to b-b-buy 'im anythin',' Ola said.

The atmosphere on the bus was excited and intense. Åge stood by the driver talking tactics. The battle would be won in the midfield. As right back, I saw a long day ahead of me. Fortunately it was sunny. I was sitting next to John and behind us were Ringo and George. George was just staring out of the window without listening. It was always like that with him, he didn't listen, but somehow understood everything all the same, an innate ability, I supposed. Ringo, on the other hand, looked very concerned. The historic save of his was a distant memory now, although it had only happened a few days ago. In fact, he had begun to doubt that it had happened at all – perhaps he had just dreamt it. Besides, Aksel, a mercurial custodian from Hoff, was the regular goalkeeper in the team and no one could threaten his position at present.

Gloomily, Ringo stuck his head between John and me.

'This ain't going to go w-w-well,' he said in a low voice.

'Not go well!' John exploded. 'We're gonna grind the Slemmestad saps into the grass!'

'For m-m-me,' Ringo continued in the same tone. 'G-g-gonna s-s-score an own goal. Can feel it in m-m-my legs.'

'It's not *that* easy to score against Aksel,' I said.

'My legs,' Ringo mumbled. 'They w-w-won't obey me. G-g-gonna score an own goal.'

Ringo slumped back into his seat as we approached Slemmestad, which, for me, after standing on the jetty in Nesodden in the summer throwing tin cans in the water, amounted to no more than white smoke issuing from the cement factory.

It wasn't until we were in the dressing rooms, however, that the gravity of the situation presented itself as barbs in our stomachs. There was a smell of Stone Age sweat and old gym shoes. We sat on the benches with bowed heads staring at our still clean football boots, the long white laces and the knots. Åge stood by the door, notebook in hand, his gaze shifting from one face to the next. On the floor beside him was the box with the blue and white shirts. Silence. It was so quiet we could hear the birds singing outside. At last Åge began to speak. He picked up the goalie's shirt and threw it to Aksel. No one had expected anything else. To everyone's surprise, though, the left back position went to a lad from Nordberg whom many considered a spy and an agent for Lyn. I was right back,

I pulled the stiff, freshly washed shirt with number 2 on the back over my head. George was left wing and John centre forward. Ringo, along with seven others, was left on the bench, but looked almost relieved. He patted us on the back and said everything would be great, all the Slemmestad players were losers and we would win 25–0, at least. Then we ran out one after the other. The Slemmestad dipsticks were already warming up and along the touchline there were eleven fathers yelling and waving.

The grass had not really grown yet, for the most part the pitch was loose earth. We had a bit of a kick-around and took a few shots at goal to get used to the ball. Then a fat farmer blew the whistle and Kjetil and the Slemmestad captain met in the middle, tossed a coin and we had to change ends. It took me a couple of hours to explain to the Nordberg genius that he was standing in the wrong position, in my position. At last we worked out our formation, stood waiting like statues, with the ball in the middle of the pitch, the referee blew the whistle and John kicked off. Everyone slowly lurched into motion. The ball came into our half, the centre half, a beanpole from Ruseløkka, swung his leg and hoofed it up towards the opponents' goal. Everyone stormed up the pitch, but the goalie threw himself into the melee and, with his body at full stretch, pounced on the ball. Clapping of hands and stamping of feet from the home crowd. The goalkeeper would have to be outfoxed, no point kicking up-and-unders. Then the ball came our way again and ricocheted to and fro for a bit. The fat referee was always on the wrong side of the field and every time he caught up, panting, the ball was played back again. John won the ball, accelerated towards the goal, but a Slemmestad lout came in with a late tackle and John went down face first into the wispy grass. Of course, the referee was facing the wrong direction and didn't have a clue what was going on. Slemmestad had possession and launched an attack. The lout sprinted up my side of the field, received a beautiful pass, took it on the run and steamed towards me. Beside the goal, crowds of people were shouting and screaming and nodding their heads. The lout came closer, wild-eyed, and I wondered whether to pull his shirt or elbow him in the nose, but I didn't have time to think the matter through. I met him with my shoulder, pressed my heel down on his boot, rolled the ball backwards with my other foot, turned quickly, rounded the fallen foe, spotted John sprinting down the pitch and sent him a high pass which followed him through the air, landed on his instep and stuck like chewing gum. Though I say it myself, I was pretty impressed. John had an open path on goal. The Slemmestad retards went puffing after him. There was just the keeper left now, but the idiot threw himself at John's feet, both rolled over and the Slemmestad desperado staggered to his feet with the ball in his hands and a very bloody nose. He was treated with cotton wool and a fizzy drink. He would have to be outfoxed, no doubt about it.

The match sank into a slough now. Balls down the middle ended up in free for alls and in-fighting. But then a Slemmestad turkey wriggled his way down the left hand side, leaving everyone in his wake, and made straight for the goal. I ran across to cover the left back. I should never have done that. Realising that I was in his territory, the left back screamed at me to sod off, this was his position and what the hell was I doing there! He completely forgot the Slemmestad turkey, who raced past him. Aksel yelled at us and so I had to come to the rescue after all. I met the turkey in full flight, twisted my body to the right as I dug in my left elbow at kidney height. The bird took wing, the ball landed at my feet and I was about to roll it back to Aksel when our left back hit me from behind. White-faced, he kicked my leg and shoved me aside. And then of course another Slemmestad dipstick moved in, took the ball and ran on goal. Aksel didn't dive at his feet, nothing so silly, he waited for the shot and leapt into the air, parallel to the ground. The ball stuck like glue between his hands. Then he pulled his parachute ripcord and fluttered gently to earth. The Nordberg spy looked perplexed, but kept insisting this was his territory. Annoyed, I suggested he should put up a sign saying private property, and trudged back into position.

There were just a few minutes left of the first half. Aksel rolled the ball out to me. I walked it as far as I could, up to the halfway line, as far as a back could go. I passed the ball to Kjetil. He dribbled past three players. Willy was at his side and they swept through the rest of the defence playing one-twos. One-touch football hadn't come to Slemmestad yet. The goalie did the only thing he could do, dive at their feet, but neither the ball nor the feet were where he threw himself, and Willy was able to nudge the ball over the line with his nose. He had all the time in the world. Totally outplayed. 1–0, a war dance and somersaults. Birdsong drowned the referee's whistle. They were supporting us. Must have been migratory birds from Tørtberg. Obvious, really.

During the half-time interval we gathered around Åge. He wasn't too happy, even if we were leading. The defence was weak, dithery, he said. He took off the sloppy centre half, pulled John back to the midfield and brought in a centre forward from Majorstuen, a sprinter with a PB of 7.6 over sixty metres. George was allowed to continue on the left wing. He hadn't done a great deal, but he hadn't committed any howlers, either. And of course the spy from Lyn was given the heave-ho. Åge scanned the reserves, stopped at Ringo and beckoned to him. Ringo took a step forward, his thighs already on red alert. He was given the Nordberg idiot's shirt and his hands were shaking so much he almost tied it into a knot.

When the interval was over and we were about to run out onto the field, Åge held me back and said in a low voice:

'Not all referees have poor eyesight. Play with your legs and head, not your elbows!'

I trotted after the others and took up my position on the right hand side. I tried to catch Ringo's eye, but he was incommunicado, staring hard at the turf and gripping his thighs. John waved and made the V for victory sign and the second half started. From the kick-off there was an immediate melee. No one saw the ball, but everyone was kicking wildly. Then it flew into the air towards us. John went up for a header, and even though he is not particularly tall he managed to push aside the Slemmestad leeches and nod the ball to Ringo who had moved upfield. Ringo set off, hit the ball as hard as he could, but slightly mishit it and it looped off towards the dressing rooms. Perfect time-wasting. The fathers whistled, but the birds were on our side and out-whistled them. We went back into defence mode, the throw-in led to another mass scramble for the ball and out of nowhere George sped off with the ball at his feet, running along the touchline, sent a cement post the wrong way and curved in a centre. Kjetil met the ball with his head and smacked it against the crossbar. The keeper stood looking at the sky, the ball rebounded in front of him and he dived into a flurry of scything legs. And in some mysterious way he emerged from the mayhem with the ball in his grasp this time, too. He was worse than a kamikaze pilot.

Now most of the game was in the Slemmestad half. John pushed forward, but Åge shouted to Ringo and me to stay in position in case they launched a counter-attack. And that was exactly what happened. I was sniffing around the midway mark when a long ball was kicked into our half. Ringo swung round like a compass needle. Two Slemmestad louts had started on a run, I sprinted for the ball too, it arced goalwards through the air, there were seconds separating us. It happened on the edge of the penalty box. Ringo, with the ball under control, played for time. John and I had cut off the two Slemmestad forwards and the whole thing should have been child's play. We just waited for Ringo to lay off the ball to Aksel. However, instead, he got his whole body behind the ball and powered a perfect banana shot into the top left hand corner – unstoppable. We froze to a man, just stood and stared. Aksel, gaping at the ball careering around the net, was dumbstruck. The Slemmestad poltroons were shouting and embracing each other, and Ringo stood with bowed head banging the tip of his boot into the ground. I couldn't quite see what was going on in his face, but a few weird sounds were coming from it and his back was trembling. The referee blew his rotten whistle and the birds huddled together on the branches and buried their beaks in their plumage.

Then Ringo walked off. He just left the field, walked past Åge, to the dressing rooms. A new man was sent on, a guy from Frøn who was so bow-legged that half the Slemmestad team could have walked between his thighs. We looked for Ringo, but he was gone. There were ten minutes left to play.

The home side had the bit between their teeth now as wave after wave rolled in. John fought like a lion and I didn't keep a low profile, either, because there was only one thing to do now, make up for Ringo's blunder. We had to win. In the distance, George was waving for the ball, but long passes were simply not possible. The game had become stagnant, like curdled milk. It was man to man marking now wherever the ball was. And the clock was ticking. Åge yelled from the sidelines, but no one could hear what he was saying. There were not much more than a couple of minutes left. All the players were in our half. Aksel was like a kangaroo between the posts gesticulating wildly. I managed to win the ball, backed my way out of the ruck and saw that John had set off on a terrific spurt up into Slemmestad's empty half. I put all my power into the kick, leant back and delivered a ball that went through the air like a remote-controlled seagull. John caught it on the run, on his bootlaces, ten men thundered after him, the goalie was ready to throw himself at his feet, but John lobbed him, ten men skidded after the ball, but it was too late, it slipped into the net like a hand in a glove. And there was a rain dance and high jumps and the home supporters were tearing out their hair. The cement-men just managed to take the kick before the referee blew his whistle and the birds alighted from the branches, twittering that victory was ours.

We charged into the dressing rooms to look for Ringo. But no one was there. And the number 14 shirt lay neatly folded on the bench. His clothes had gone. We raced out again.

'P'raps he's sittin' in the coach,' George said.

We sprinted around the building to the car park. The coach was empty. We went back to Åge and asked him if he had seen Ringo.

'Ringo?'

'Ola,' John said.

'Beautiful lob,' Åge said, patting him on the shoulder. 'Worth its weight in gold. I'll put you back into the attack.'

'Have you seen Ola?' George asked impatiently.

'Isn't he in the dressing room?'

'Nope.'

Ringo had vanished into thin air. We searched high and low, but there was no sign of him. In the end we had to take the coach home without Ringo. The mood was not how it should have been. Åge looked nervous. Everyone had some injury they needed to tend. There was a stench of sweat and cement on our shirts, which we had to take home and wash ourselves.

'There's such a thing as a premonition,' Seb said under his breath.

'Premonition?' Gunnar turned to face him.

'Yes. Kind of omen. He said he felt somethin' in his legs on the way, didn't he.'

We thought about this and looked at each other, unconvinced.

'P'raps it was predetermined that he was goin' to score an own goal,' Seb continued.

'Predetermined?' I said. 'By whom?'

'By... by... I haven't a clue, God, maybe,' Seb answered with a blush.

We went quiet again. The idea that God had interceded in the match between the boys' teams of Slemmestad and Frigg was not an easy one to assimilate.

'I s'pose God scored my goal, too, did he!' Gunnar snapped.

'Not at all,' Seb said meekly. 'I was just thinkin' that it was... pretty weird.'

'He was just unlucky,' Gunnar reasoned. 'It could've happened to anyone.'

'*Unlucky*! With *that* shot!'

'He's not used to playin' in defence,' I said. 'He may've forgotten and thought he was a striker.'

We contented ourselves with that. The coach drove past Sjølyst, our stop was Frogner church. We sat locked in our own thoughts about what might have happened to Ola. Either he had started walking or he had taken the train, if he had any money. Or he was still there. Christ.

Åge came to the back of the coach and crouched down.

'I'll ring his parents to find out if he's got home okay.'

We nodded in unison.

'And you make sure he comes to training. Everyone can have a bad day. We'll find him a place.'

'He's good in goal,' Seb said.

'Right.' Åge looked at us. 'It would be difficult for him to oust Aksel.'

'He could be the reserve goalie,' Gunnar suggested.

Åge stood up.

'That's an idea. I'll keep that in mind.'

The coach stopped outside the church and we scrambled out. There was only one thing to do. We walked en masse down to Observatoriegata. But Ola had not come home. His father opened the door.

'Didn't Ola come back with you?' he asked.

Gunnar and Seb looked at each other, lost for words. I cleared my throat and said:

'We had a training session in Tørtberg after the match. Ola went with some others from the class we met in Majorstuen.'

'No, he's not home yet.'

Jensen, the hairdresser, pulled up his shirt sleeve, checked his watch, raised his combed eyebrows and slowly shook his head. 'Do you know where he is?'

'He's probably with Putte or Goose,' I said with alacrity.

Then the mother appeared too, a small, thin lady with lots of curls in her hair and worried eyes.

'Is anything the matter?'

And then the phone rang from deep inside the flat. That must have been Åge, so we backed down the stairs and charged out of the door.

We couldn't walk to Slemmestad. There was nothing else for it but to go home. We hung on in the vague hope that Ola might turn up. He did not. It was strange to think that he might be walking along the road on his own at this moment. He might even have got lost. And soon it would be dark. We shivered, agreed to meet tomorrow at five in Mogens Thorsens Park, Mogga Park to us. Then we each went our own way. The sun was going down behind the red clouds above Holmenkollen Ridge, casting a dark, flat light over the town. Getting home was a priority now because Saturday warfare had started. The Frogner gang could strike at any time. I slunk along a house wall, peered around every corner, thinking about Ola, and about knuckledusters, headbutts, a nose bone which had been smashed into the brain, a boy in the street whose eye went into spasm a couple of years back, the centre of his eyeball quivered while he screamed and screamed.

I ran the last stretch.

I showered, washed the Slemmestad crap off myself and joined my mother and father in the sitting room. I had to tell them about the match and was given sausages, griddle cakes, Pommac and stuff. But I couldn't sit still. Ola might have been kidnapped, put in a sack and dumped in the fjord. Or he might have been sold as a slave to Arabia. That had happened before. I had to ring. My fingers trembled over the telephone dial.

His mother answered.

'Is Ola at home?' I asked. 'Kim here.'

'Yes.'

Ola was alive. I slumped into the nearest chair.

'Can I speak to him?' I whispered.

'He's in bed. He's ill.'

'Ill?'

'That's what he says.'

'Will he be okay tomorrow?' I asked slyly, cringing beneath my clothes.

'Why don't you call and see?' the high-pitched but somewhat weary voice said. And before she put down the receiver I could swear I heard the sound of scissors cutting in the background. It must have been Valdemar Jensen training for the dry cut in Norway's Hairdressing Championship in Lillesand, or perhaps it was just my heart pumping blood in short, furious bursts through my head, like the brash first chord of 'A Hard Day's Night'.

I had arranged with Gunnar and Seb to meet in Mogga Park at five, but the arrangement would be difficult to keep because Uncle Hubert was coming for a meal. At three he stood in the doorway and from then on everything went at half speed. I don't really know what it was with Uncle Hubert, there were these knots inside his head that would not loosen and at times they were tighter than at others, and on this Sunday they were unusually rigid. It started in the doorway. He stretched out his hand thirty-four times without saying a word. In the end Dad had to drag him inside and push him into a chair and both of them were red-faced and sweaty, and Mum rushed out and set another place at the table.

Uncle Hubert lived alone in one of the blocks of flats by Marienlyst. He did the illustrations for weekly magazines and women's novels, so perhaps it was not that strange he was the way he was. Dad was bald, but Hubert had all his hair, and now he was sitting in the chair by the bookshelves. He had regained his composure, his whole body was relaxed and his breathing was heavy and regular. But when he caught sight of me life returned to the bloated body.

'Come closer, come closer,' he called, beckoning to me.

I went over to him. He took my hand in both of his, began to shake it and I was calculating that I would have to stand there for a couple of hours. To my great good fortune he let go after just fifteen minutes.

'Young Kim, the family's hope for the future, how are you?'

'I'm fine,' I said, burying my hands in my pockets.

'Glad to hear that. Do you think I should get married?'

Dad charged over and interposed a quivering head.

'Are you going to get married?!'

'I've been considering the matter, dear brother. So, what do you two think?'

Dad straightened up and said between clenched jaws: 'Kim, go into the kitchen and help Mum!'

There was no alternative. I found my mother bent over a platter of halibut. The steam was rising into her face. It looked like she was crying.

'Uncle Hubert's getting married,' I said.

I had to hold the plate for her.

'What! What did you say!'

'He said he wants to get married.'

She was gone in a flash. I was left with the smoking fish plus the parsley butter, the potatoes and the crème caramel. I heard the intense discussion in the sitting room. Dad's voice was low and vehement, just like when I come home with my grades. Mum's voice was resigned, but Uncle Hubert just laughed.

Some time later Mum returned and we carried the food onto the table.

At first it was fine. We served ourselves and everything was as it should be, except for Dad's face, he was as highly strung as a tennis racquet. When we were about to take a second helping I could not restrain myself any longer.

'Who are you going to marry?' I asked.

Dad's voice truncated the sentence. He snarled my name, the 'i' vanished completely and two distorted consonants were all that was left. Km! Mum flinched and Uncle Hubert looked from one to the next, and as he helped himself to potatoes his brain jammed. I could see it in him. With his spoon halfway over to the potatoes he stopped, he held it there, he seemed to be fighting with himself, he gritted his teeth and his cheeks quivered, then the spoonful of potatoes began to go back and forth across the table, and at some speed, he had to be at the very least a world potato-balancing champion. Dad was on the verge of exploding, Mum fled into the kitchen and Uncle Hubert sat there transporting potatoes to and fro. I wished I knew what had happened in his head. He looked extremely unhappy, yet determined, and when he was finally finished, after forty-three to-and-fros, he slumped back into his chair, exhausted and content. The tablecloth was green from the parsley, Dad's face was purple and Mum came in with more white fish.

As the clock moved towards five, and we still had not started dessert, it was impossible to sit still any longer. I took a chance and asked, even though I knew it was a mortal sin to leave the table too soon.

'I'm meeting Gunnar and Seb,' I burbled. 'At five. May I go?'

To my great surprise, Dad seemed quite relieved.

'That's fine,' he said. 'Don't come home late.'

I leapt up, but didn't dare give Hubert my hand again. Mum issued a few gentle admonitions and everyone seemed happy that I was going. I jumped out of the window, landed softly astride the horse, like Zorro of Frogner, and galloped off to Mogga Park.

John and George sat leaning over the handlebars, each puffing on their Craven A. I freewheeled down to where they were and drew up in a skid on the shingle.

'Have you heard from Ola?' John asked.

'He's in bed. Says he's ill.'

George flicked the butt end in a huge arc over the climbing frame, wiped his chops and said:

'I know how to get him up.'

'How?' John sucked at the glow close to his lips and spat out the bits.

'Wait and see,' George said.

We turned out of Drammensveien and cycled round the University Library in a closed formation. This was a bold plan. It was not easy to heal the sick, especially when parents were at home. Once you had taken to your bed, for the sake of appearances you had to stay there for a while, otherwise, on subsequent occasions, the consequences could be catastrophic.

His father received us.

'We have to talk to Ola,' I said out of breath.

'He's in bed.'

'It's about homework,' I persisted.

Then the mother arrived. She stood at the hairdresser's side.

'You'll have to be quick then,' she determined.

We found Ringo covered with a large light blue duvet. His eyes were barely visible. We closed the door and stood by the bed. There was a smell of camphor.

'What've you done with all the pictures?' I asked, studying the bare walls.

'Dad tore 'em down,' the duvet said. 'The b-b-bugger!'

He sank even lower in the mattress.

'What's wrong with you?' George asked.

Ringo began to cough. The duvet heaved and fell.

'I'm s-s-sick,' he said in a cracked voice. 'I'll infect you.'

We were quiet for a while. This was more serious than we had imagined. There was a pile of Donald Duck magazines and a half-chewed bar of milk chocolate on the floor.

'What got into you?' John asked with caution.

An answer was not forthcoming. We were all nervous, fine-combed our brains to find something intelligent to say. Then Ringo began to speak, he spoke with an old man's voice, it was hollow, dry and bitter.

'The f-f-football field's a thing of the past for me. It's g-g-gone. It's f-f-finished.'

He disappeared completely. We swallowed a lump in our throats, the whole gang, I swear we did. Now the laying on of hands had to start in earnest.

'Everyone can be unlucky,' I said. 'You're not the first person to score an own goal. And since you've gone and done it, it was a bloody fabulous shot!'

We attempted a laugh. Not a sound from the bed.

'Åge talked with us on the coach back,' I went on. 'He'd been talking to Per Pettersen. He wants to have you as the reserve goalie.'

A tuft of hair hove into view. Something spoke under the duvet, soft but clear.

'R-r-reserve goalie? D-d-did he say that? Wasn't he as angry as h-h-hell?'

'We won 2–1!'

'W-w-we w-w-won?'

'John scored,' I said. 'Solo effort from the midfield.'

A whole face appeared. Ringo looked at John.

'Did you s-s-score?'

'Yup. No big deal. Main thing is we won. Those buggers from Slemmestad couldn't even score one of their own!'

The laughter broke the ice and we relaxed. Ringo's bed was shaking, even though he was supposed to be ill. We heard the sound of feet outside the door.

'Come out with us,' I said.

'C-c-can't. I'm not w-w-well.'

George leaned forward, put his hand on the patient's shoulder and kept it there.

'I've got a present for you. There's a… there's a Volvo 1800S behind the Royal Palace.'

A gasp ran through the room. Ringo was out of bed in a flash.

'One like… one l-l-like the S-S-Saint had!' he stuttered, dumbfounded.

'Right. It's yours.'

There was nothing more to say. Ringo pulled on his clothes and four desperate men stomped through the flat. The hairdresser, plus wife, were standing in the hall.

'What are you doing?' his mother exclaimed in alarm.

'I'm g-g-going out,' Ringo said, sweeping all resistance aside.

'You're ill,' his father said.

'I'm w-w-well,' Ringo said.

'Then you'll have to go to school tomorrow,' his mother taunted. 'Just so that you know.'

'I kn-kn-know,' Ringo said.

And so we emerged, slid down the banisters and as Ringo's bike still wasn't repaired he jumped on behind John and we headed for Parkveien.

'How did you get home from Slemmestad?' I shouted.

'Hitched,' Ringo enthused. 'A van. Furniture removal. Got a r-r-roll-up and stuff.'

'Well, I never.'

'Had a copy of *Cocktail* in the glove compartment, he did.'

We cut through the crossroads before the American embassy and slowly pedalled behind the palace.

'It's in Riddervoldsgate,' George said. 'Saw it when I was walkin' with my mum today. Swedish reg.'

'Lots of cops in this area,' John said.

'We'll n-n-nab it, anyway,' Ringo growled from the luggage carrier. 'We'll n-n-nab it!'

There was a hollow in the pit of my stomach that soon filled with anticipation and sweet fear. It grew and grew inside me and felt good. We turned into Riddervoldsgate and there it was, just by the corner of Oscarsgate, a shiny white Volvo 1800S. We jumped off our bikes and stood in a huddle, peering in all directions. A man with a hat walked down the other pavement. We didn't say a word until he was out of sight. Two crows took off from a tree behind us, we all gave a start. Our hearts, red and large, were pounding on this sultry afternoon.

'Let's stand with our bikes on the corner,' I whispered. 'When Ringo has the badge, he can jump on John's and then we'll cycle down Oscarsgate, past Vestheim and on to Skillebekk. No one can catch us on that route.'

The others nodded. Ringo took the screwdriver from George and we pedalled up to the corner. A cat was lying on a stone wall staring up at us with narrowed eyes, but it would not talk, it was on our side. The tram rattled along Briskebyveien, the church bells began to chime. Then everything went still. We pedalled past the Volvo, Ringo stopped again, waited for a few seconds, then went on the attack. There were a few horrible sounds, like when you scratch your nails on the blackboard. Even the King must have heard it. We didn't dare turn around and it took for ever, the whole world was on edge. Blood was cascading down from my head like torrential rain. I don't think I have ever been so nervous before. And I was sure I would not have been anywhere near so frightened if I had been standing by the car instead of Ringo. It was bizarre.

At last something happened behind us. Ringo ran up, we were standing on our pedals, he jumped on the back of John's bike, we raced down to Skillebekk and were sitting on the bench by the fountain before you could say Simon Templar. We dried our sweat, stared, mouths agape, at the Volvo badge and weighed it in our hands, relieved and happy. George took out his packet of Craven A and passed it round.

'Best so far,' John said. 'Christ, I was nervous.'

'How come?' Ringo said, taking a huge drag that made his eyes cross like a pair of scissors.

And so we sat there, it was a Sunday, night closed in around us, turned warm and clammy and before we knew what was going on, the rain was bucketing down. It splashed up to a metre off the ground and the horses behind us whinnied.

'Let's go back to my place,' John shouted. 'My mum and dad are away.' We cycled with the mudguards flapping around our ears and squeezed into his room, soaking wet and tired. John placed the record player in the middle of the room and put the latest Beatles record on. 'Ticket To Ride'. We listened with devout attention, eardrums finely tuned, like bats. We held our breath until the last guitar notes faded and the stylus was scratching across the innermost groove.

Gunnar put it on again. We lay on the floor with our ears in the loudspeaker and our whole bodies throbbing. Our English was good enough for us to understand what it was about and we wondered who the hell would have cleared off like that. The girl must have been pretty stupid. We became embittered and thought nasty things about girls all over the world. The needle skidded into the middle again and we pulled our wet fringes down over our foreheads.

'We should start a band,' Seb said.

We looked at each other. A band. Of course. We could start a band and then Nina and Guri and all the chickens in 7C would be right at the back of the queue.

'What should we c-c-call it?' Ola wondered.

Gunnar fetched an English-Norwegian dictionary and began to flick through.

'What about The Evil-Hearted Devils and the Shinin' Angels,' Seb suggested.

His English pronunciation was a bit rough, but we understood him.

'Too long,' I said. 'Has to be short so that people can ask for the records. Dirty Fingers is a good one.'

'Dirty Fingers 'n Clean Girls,' Seb added.

'W-we don't want anythin' with girls in, do we!' Ola shouted.

'I've got one,' Gunnar said, looking up from the dictionary. 'We should call ourselves The Snafus.'

'S-s-snow shoes?' Ola said, looking at Gunnar in bewilderment.

'Snafus,' he repeated.

'What does it mean?' Seb asked.

'It stands for Situation Normal All Fouled Up,' Gunnar read out slowly and clearly.

'But what does it mean?' Ola queried.

'It means mischief and muddle and mess.'

We considered it and were agreed. No one had any better suggestions. It was snappy, distinctive and we felt we could live up to the meaning. The Snafus.

'I'll go and nick one of my dad's cigars,' Gunnar said. 'We have to celebrate this!'

He returned with a giant poker with a cummerbund, bit off the tip and spat it out of the window. The room was full of smoke after the first drag. We coughed and spluttered and hung over the windowsill, but everyone was agreed it was really great, the best we had ever tasted.

'What songs shall we p-p-play?' Ola said through the fog.

That was a problem. Ola was okay, he played the snare drum in a boys' marching band. We heard him every May 17. Gunnar knew only two chords on his brother's guitar, but on the other hand he was quite good at upping the tempo. Seb played the recorder and I played nothing.

'You can sing,' said Seb.

'Sing! I can't bloody sing.'

'You can learn,' said Gunnar.

'I'm the vocalist then,' I declared.

'You'll have to learn to do a decent *howl,*' Seb said. 'Just like on "I Wanna Be Your Man" and "Twist And Shout".'

I thought about the school singing lessons. 'The Hills and the Mountains'. 'Three Small Drums'. 'Dawn is Breaking'. Perhaps my voice had never had any decent material to work with. Perhaps Jensenius could teach me to sing.

'Alright. I'll be the vocalist!'

Gunnar re-lit the cigar and passed it round. Tears flowed, but no one could see through the smoke. And then we played all the Beatles records, starting with 'Love Me Do'.

In the middle of 'Can't Buy Me Love' the door burst open. Gunnar was so taken aback that he scratched the record. It was just his brother, Stig, but he wasn't just a brother, he was about to start *gymnas* at the Cathedral School, he was one metre eighty-five and his hair came halfway down his ears. He glanced in from the doorway and said:

'Fidel Castro dropped by, has he?'

We didn't understand, but we laughed anyway, that much we did understand. Stig closed the door and joined us, he folded up his long body and sat on the floor. We were mute with awe, hardly dared open our mouths because we knew we would fill our pants as soon as our pained tongues uttered a sound. Gunnar looked a little embarrassed but proud, too. Not everyone had a big brother who could be bothered to mingle with little tubers whose shoots had only just emerged from the soil.

Stig looked at us and took a sudden, deep drag on the cigar. Not a wisp of smoke came out of his mouth. We waited and waited, but it stayed down. That was as bad as anything we had seen.

'You playin' The Beatles?' he asked in a friendly tone.

We nodded and mumbled, yes, we were, The Beatles were great, and especially the latest single 'Ticket To Ride'.

'Have you heard this?' he asked, showing us an LP he was carrying. The picture on the cover was of a gawky-looking kid, stiff curls, huge crooked nose, skinny frame. We hadn't heard it.

'Bob Dylan,' Stig elucidated. 'Best thing ever to have hit this earth.'

He took out the record, carefully placed it on the player, changed the speed to 33 rpm and told us to be quiet, though we were as still as driven snow.

'Listen to this,' Stig whispered. 'Masters Of War'. 'And think about Vietnam at the same time.'

'V-V-Viet what?' Ola burst out. His flushed face stood out like the Northern Lights. Stig had to educate him.

'Vietnam,' he explained. 'A small country on the other side of the planet. Where the Americans are bombin' innocent people. They're usin' somethin' called napalm. Do you boys know what napalm is?'

The record player started up. He held the stylus a millimetre above the grooves. We didn't know what napalm was.

'It's a liquid that sticks to your skin and burns. You haven't got a hope in hell. It burns under water! Listen to me: Napalm burns *under water*.'

He snapped his mouth shut. There was a hiss in the loudspeaker, the hard acoustic guitar followed straight after, chords I will never forget and the voice that lacerated your head like a razor blade. We didn't understand everything, but we understood the gist. It was eerie, and a chill went down my spine. *And I'll stand over your grave till I'm sure that you're dead.* We understood that. And we felt like going out onto the streets and beating up some adult bastards. It was a solemn occasion because now we could never be the same again. Now we knew better.

Stig put the record back in the sleeve and stood up. He towered above us and we would have done whatever he had asked us to do. We longed for him to give us an order, a vitally important, highly dangerous mission and we would go through fire and water for him.

But he just said, from the corner of his mouth:

'Air the room well before Mum and Dad come back, boys.'

I cycled home and tried to sing the new song, but I couldn't get hold of the melody. Every time I started it slipped out of my grasp, as though I had already forgotten it. But it's not true that you forget so easily. You store everything inside yourself and then one day, wherever you are, whatever the time, it appears just like that, just like I could smell wet lilac now, lilac after the rain, even though we were well into autumn. I pedalled down Drammensveien trying to remember the words, the tune and the voice. But as I turned into Svoldergate I was given other things to think about. I pulled up sharp because, coming out of a door, was Uncle Hubert. He stopped, stood still, stared at his feet, then walked back in, backwards, came out, went back and continued like this, and I began to count because there might have been a system to what he was doing, it might have been a secret code. Uncle Hubert went in and out of the front stairway twenty-one times, then he ran off round the corner at full pelt. I stabled the horse, gave it a bag of hay and padded up the stairs. Standing there with the key at the ready I could hear Dad's voice from inside the sitting room. It was loud and hysterical and penetrated the walls like a saw. I stood with my head against the door.

'It's not right. It's simply unacceptable. It's a scandal. Twenty-one years old!'

I couldn't hear my mother's voice. She was probably sitting on the sofa with her hands in her lap looking disconsolate.

Dad's voice continued:

'She could have been our daughter. It's… it's disgusting! Twenty-one years old!'

Then the house went quiet. I breathed in, opened the door as gently as I could and sneaked into my room. And that night I felt I was flying, or falling, falling backwards, with no one to catch me, into a black hole in the sky.

The bombshell fell the day after, on Monday, leftovers day. All of a sudden Dad put down his knife and fork and carefully wiped his mouth.

'My God, Ahlsen, the branch manager, was furious today. At the weekend he had a very important contact over from Sweden, and on Sunday the client's car was vandalised.'

'Vandalised?' Mum said.

'Yes. Some good-for-nothing had broken off the badge at the front and scratched the paintwork. And it was an extremely exclusive car. A Volvo 1800S. The kind the Saint drove, he told me, expecting me to be impressed to bits.'

'Oh, yes,' I confined myself to saying.

'You don't know anyone who does that sort of thing, do you?' he said, turning to me suddenly and looking me in the eye.

'Me? How? How should I know?'

'No. Of course you don't know anything about it.' Dad looked at Mum. 'They reported it to the police of course. They've had several reports of this kind of late. It's a disgrace!'

After the meal I was given shore leave and I cycled like crazy over to Gunnar's. I told him what had happened and we went on to Ola's, dragged him out and panted off to Seb's – he lived just round the corner. His mother opened the door and burst into laughter on seeing us.

'Have you come from the moon?' she laughed.

'It's about May 17,' I said. 'We might have to be flag-bearers.'

Ola gave me a stupified look, but Gunnar poked him in the back to concentrate his mind. There was a little gasp, but then he was quiet.

'Sebastian's in his room. He's doing homework.'

We bustled in with Seb's mother's laughter ringing in our ears and almost scared the life out of him as we burst through his door.

'W-w-we've been caught,' Ola squealed. 'They've f-f-found out!'

'Don't talk so loud, for Christ's sake!' Gunnar hissed.

'What've they found out?' Seb asked.

I told him about the whole business. Gunnar stood by the door making sure that no one was listening.

'But they don't know it was us, do they,' Seb said at last.

'Not yet. But we have to get rid of the stolen goods!'

Seb pulled out the box. We crowded round. On the top there were a few comics, then the glint of metal, polished like my mother and father's silverware. It was pure Count of Monte Cristo stuff.

I took the decision.

'We'll have to dump it in the sea.'

'Where th-th-then?' Ola had the Volvo badge in his hand.

'Filipstad,' Gunnar suggested.

'Bygdøy,' I said. 'Not so many people.'

The others nodded gravely. We admired our hunting trophies in solemn silence, stuffed them into all the pockets we had and stomped out with rictus smiles, like four overweight scrap dealers.

Seb's mother reappeared from nowhere, without a word, and my body seemed to go numb, she had big knockers that wobbled long after she had come to a halt, and her skirt was tight across her hips and it had a slit and stuff.

'Have you done your homework?' she asked.

'Yes,' Seb answered, his hands stuffed firmly down his pockets.

'Hope you get to carry the flags then.'

He looked at her bemused. Ola was about to open his mouth, but I cut in.

'Three people from every Class 7 are allowed to carry the flags,' I said quickly. 'And Ola plays the drums, so he can't.'

And then we were out. We ran down the stairs and raced off towards Bygdøy. We parked our bikes behind the restaurant and went down to the water. We were alone apart from a dog barking in the distance. I could see over to Nesodden, the quayside, Hornstranda beach and the red beach hut. I shivered. Perhaps spring wasn't here after all. It was like being in a warm room when someone opens the door and cold air streams in. It came from the fjord, which was dark and resembled corrugated iron.

'Sh-sh-shall we chuck all of 'em?' Ola asked warily.

'All of them,' Gunnar said with force.

Ola kicked a clump of seaweed.

'D-d-do you think they'll've t-t-taken fingerprints?'

'Fingerprints!' Seb laughed. 'Where from?'

'From the Volvo!'

'They haven't got any proof,' I said. 'Not once we've got rid of these.'

We ran up the beach to the craggy cliffs. There we stopped and scanned the horizon. No one around, the dog had gone, not a boat in sight, just a muddy barge that had been towed into Bundefjord.

'Let's throw stones first,' Gunnar said. 'And then we can chuck a few badges in between.'

A hail of objects fell over the water, Fiats, Mercs, Opels, Peugeots, Morrises, a Vauxhall, Renaults, a Hillman and even a Moskwitch.

'D'you think anyone will find th-them?' Ola mumbled at length.

'The current will carry 'em away,' Gunnar said. 'A long way out. Perhaps all the way to Africa.'

'And then one day my dad'll be sittin' and fishin' on his day off and catch a Volvo badge on his hook,' Seb chuckled.

We cheered and laughed and sprinted to the other side of the cliffs, but stopped in our tracks and stared at something lying on the stones by the edge of the water.

It was a pile of clothes.

'Is someone s-s-swimmin' now?' Ringo stammered. 'Must be bloody c-c-cold!'

We scanned the fjord, but couldn't see anything. The cold wind hit us at full force now that we were no longer sheltered.

'Must be an ice bather, at least,' George whispered.

There was no one in the water, though, or on land. So we walked over to the clothes, slowly, holding our breath, I had never walked so slowly before. Perhaps someone had seen us after all. As we approached we saw there was a suit lying there, a white shirt, a tie and underwear, and a pair of polished black shoes placed neatly alongside. And on top of the suit there was a note held down by a stone. We stopped again. Our hearts were going like cardboard strips between wheel spokes. I went on, picked up the note, with great caution, as if it were an injured butterfly. I read aloud, my voice left me with a terrible taste: 'I have taken my own life. I have no family. The little I have left behind should go to the Salvation Army. No grieving. I have peace now.'

I put back the note and ran to the others, clung to Gunnar.

'Shi-it! He's walked into the sea!'

We turned, legged it up to the restaurant and banged on the door, but it was closed. No one opened up. We jumped on our bikes and cycled furiously to the car park and stopped by the telephone box. We squeezed in and found the police number on the first page of the directory. I picked up the receiver, Gunnar inserted the coin and Seb dialled the number. I was put through at once and went weak at the knees.

'A man has drowned himself,' my mouth said.

'Who am I talking to, please?' I heard.

'Kim. Kim Karlsen.'

'Where are you ringing from?'

'From a telephone box. In Huk.'

'Repeat what has happened.'

'A man has drowned himself. His clothes are lying on the beach and he's left a written note.'

'Stay where you are *and don't touch anything*. We're on our way.'

We cycled back and ran over to the cliff again. The clothes were still there, neatly folded, just like at night when you go to bed. We sat down at a secure distance, kept a lookout across the fjord, but it gave nothing away. I shuddered at the thought of water quickly closing in and hair floating like seaweed as waves broke onto the shore.

'Hope they don't find the b-b-badges,' Ola whispered.

'I'm not gonna swim here any more, anyway,' Gunnar said with a shiver. Soon afterwards the cops arrived. They came in two cars and there was also an ambulance. The constables jogged towards us. Two examined the clothes and two talked to us.

'Was it you who called us?'

'Yes,' I said.

'When did you spot the clothes?'

'Half an hour ago. At least.'

'How long had you been here before?'

'Quarter of an hour or something like that.'

'And you didn't hear anything or see anything?'

'No.'

'What were you doing here?'

The others began to fidget. Ola's left thigh twitched. I looked up at the policeman.

'We were looking for shells,' I said.

Then something else happened. A big police boat arrived on the shoreline. On the deck there were two divers. The uniformed officers strolled down to the water's edge. We followed them, stopped a good way behind.

It didn't take them long to find him. He was close to the shore. They emerged from the water with a blue naked body, as though the colour of the water had rubbed off. It was all stiff and the mouth was large and open. He can't have been so old, younger than my father. They laid him on a stretcher – had to force him into position – covered him with a blanket and pushed him into the ambulance.

It was the first time I had seen a dead person.

Gunnar threw up as we were cycling home. None of us said a word, we just kept ourselves to ourselves. That night I lay wide awake in bed, thinking about death, I was a long way behind my eyes staring into a huge dark void, and I realised, without actually understanding it, that I was already beginning to die, it was a repugnant thought and I cried.

It was spring and we were waiting. We were waiting for Frogner Lido to open. They had already started cleaning the pools. This year I would dive from the ten-metre board, that was a cert, I had the jump in me now. But I had competitors. I cut out a picture of the Russian, Alexei Leonov, hanging in space, a murky, ghost-like photo I didn't quite believe at first. It looked a bit like the first photographs Dad took before he learned how to focus. He floated like that for ten minutes, in the endless blue abyss, tied to his space vehicle by a thin thread, an umbilical cord. And not long after it was the Americans' turn. This time the picture was sharper, more credible, because you could see the earth in the background. Edward White hung outside his capsule for twenty-one minutes. Afterwards he said he hadn't felt at all giddy, it had almost been like swimming. And then I visualised the enormous ocean, I was standing at the bottom of a colossal sea, and far above me, at night, swam goldfish ten times bigger than us, large, golden ships sailing slowly by. Once they had been part of the sun. Perhaps that was also how the suicide victim in Bygdøy had seen it, before his eyes were extinguished. And we waited for the Hand Grenade Man, but the town was quiet, just cycle bells, birds and bands practising.

And, of course, we were waiting for May 17. The day arrived with torrential rain. We met by the fountain in Gyldenløvesgate at three in the morning. It was pouring down and the wind was coming from the west, but that was not important, so long as we could light our matches. Between us we had thirty-five firecrackers, twenty bangers and sixteen jumping jacks. We let off two firecrackers to get into the mood as it were. They sounded a bit feeble, but were loud enough to wake people close by. Then we moved to Urra Park. There was almost no one about, we heard just a few scattered bangs and some cars full of prommers honking their horns in the rain, celebrating the end of secondary school.

'We'll have to find somewhere dry,' George said.

'An entrance to a block of flats,' I suggested.

We sneaked through the nearest doorway. The acoustics were good, a stone floor and stone walls. Ringo lit the match and put it to the fuse, it hissed, then I threw the whole thing towards the stairs and the postboxes. It exploded before we got out, a terrible bang, parting the hair at the back of our heads.

'That'll have w-w-woken them up,' panted Ringo as we sprinted down Briskebyveien, past Galleri Albin Upp. We didn't stop until we were in Urra Park. The clock on the church tower showed half past three. It was still raining. We threw a few bangers at the wall but they were already too soggy. We suspended the bombardment, listened, there was a lorry-load of prommers down in Holtegata. We ran to the railings and caught sight of the red lorry bumping its way up towards Hegdehaugsveien. At the back were a group of soaking wet students shouting at the top of their voices. Then it was just the rain we could hear, continuous, cold rain, falling like stair-rods from the sky, the wind had dropped.

'Let's save the rest for later,' Seb said. 'When the weather's better.'

We lit a cigarette instead, and my empty stomach reacted like a spin drier, I was whirled around, and the others were the same, we banged into each other and spun off in all directions before regaining balance on our way down to Briskeby.

'Perhaps the Hand Grenade Man'll strike today,' Seb exclaimed.

'Shit,' whispered Gunnar. 'In the procession. A hand grenade in the middle of the procession. I'm not bloody doin' the procession this year.'

'Just think about me bangin' the d-d-drum then!' Ola said. 'You c-c-can't just c-c-clear off like that!'

'Of course we'll be in the procession, too,' I said.

And then the tension was back, as though your spine was an electric pylon. My whole being hummed. And in one dreadful flash I saw bleeding bodies, smashed faces, dead children clutching their little flags. At that moment I heard the song in my head, the one Gunnar's brother had played us. 'Masters Of War'.

Then it was back home for breakfast and a change of clothes. It was no use, I looked forward to the time in the future when I could wear the clothes I liked, but it seemed an eternity away, and Mum and Dad's voices were at my ear. At last I stood there wearing, from the bottom up, shiny black shoes, grey trousers with a crease, white shirt and blue tie, blazer with silver buttons, a huge ribbon across my chest, a flag in hand and sailor's cap atop. No, not a cap, but hair plastered down with water like a dishcloth on my skull, yuk, my mother was jigging round me clapping her hands and my father was giving me that man-to-man look. I made for the door before the firecrackers set themselves off.

It was no longer raining as we marched out of the playground towards Stortorget, but the sky was ominously dark. The girls were wearing white dresses and red ribbons in their hair, they were shivering in the cold, and of course we weren't flag-bearers, the creeps could do that, but Ringo was playing drums, we could hear that, he was wearing a blue uniform, knitted cap and almost as many medals as Oscar Mathisen. Lue was strutting alongside, sporting a black suit, see-through raincoat and a student's cap plus tassel fastened to his shoulder with a large safety pin. Behind us walked Nina and Guri and all the plaits from 7C, they were scrutinised, and it would have been better if they had gone in front of us, it was not good to have them at our backs, wily creatures that they were. And then the whole band began to play, more off-key than the previous year, and shouts rang out and flags were waved.

'How much money've you got for ice creams?' George asked.

'Don't wanna buy ice creams today,' I said.

'You don't want to!'

'Want to spend it in Urra Park.'

'My dad sent me an envelope with four tenners in it,' George went on. 'From the Persian Gulf. That's enough for eighteen ice creams, fifteen hot dogs and six Cokes.'

'We can eat ice cream at my house,' John said. 'Dad's put by a carton of nut ice cream.'

In Stortorget the temperature had sunk below zero and there was snow in the air. We went to see Ringo. He looked smart and embarrassed, but then it started to rain again and the band leader was distributing see-through capes like the one Lue was wearing, and so Ringo didn't look smart any more.

'He looks like a johnnie,' George laughed, but Ringo became dangerously annoyed.

'Do I buggery! Look in the mirror and you'll see a real p-p-prick!'

'Wasn't meant like that,' George said to mollify him. 'Got a pack of Consulates for afterwards.'

'And if the Hand Grenade Man strikes, we'll rely on you,' I said.

'Fine!'

John's face went as grey as crispbread.

'Don't, for Christ's sake, talk about the Hand Grenade Man!'

The procession began to move. We took our places and marched towards Karl Johansgate. All the bands were playing over each other, one worse than the next, and hysterical parents stood along the route, screaming and waving, and I pretended to be a victorious soldier returning from war, receiving applause from the crowds. We were heroes, I pretended to limp, the girls were looking at me unable to restrain their tears, waving white embroidered handkerchiefs, blowing me kisses, brave, wounded soldier. And all of a sudden an image appeared to me, crystal clear, it had been in the newspaper, in *Dagsrevyen,* and had been shown on TV: a small Vietnamese girl hobbling along with a stick, barefoot, naked chest, one arm covered in bandages. And behind her what looked like ruins, it is difficult to see, but I imagine dead people there, dead and burned and maimed, her family. The little girl staggers out of the ruins, past me, and she emits a terrible cry, and she is so afraid and desperate, I wonder where she will go and to whom.

'This is where it'll happen,' John whispered.

'Eh?'

'The Hand Grenade Bastard. This is where he'll bung it. In the middle of Karl Johan.'

We had reached the Studenten bar. I heard friendly shouts from the pavement and there were my mother and father jumping up and down and waving. I was happy that at least they hadn't brought the little stepladder with them.

Approaching the Royal Palace, John was pale and quiet. The tension had begun to exert a hold on me too, anticipation of something, of a catastrophe, sweet and repulsive at the same time. There were two ambulances and a Red Cross bus by one of the side streets, but I supposed they were there every May 17. A Chinese firecracker was let off on the lawn, it sounded like a shower of bombs and we clung to each other. Now there were only a hundred metres left. The King was standing on the balcony waving his top hat, Prince Harald was there too with a few ladies, we took a deep breath and crept past. By the guardroom the procession was breaking up like a line of confused ants and we sought safety by the statue of Camilla Collett, sat down on the rock, put our flags on the wet grass and smoked a menthol cigarette.

Ringo ambled along after a quarter of an hour, with the drum over his shoulder and cap in hand. At that moment the clouds parted and the sun embraced Slottsparken, the park around the Royal Palace, and the sound of three cheers rang out.

'You were more off-key than last year,' George said. 'But you were better than the Ruseløkka lot.'

'Someone put a f-f-firecracker down the tuba,' Ringo explained. 'In the qu-qu-quietest p-p-part. Thought it was the H-H-Hand Grenade Man, I did!'

We looked across at the palace. The procession had dispersed now. But he could strike again later, at any time.

The sun disappeared again, taking the colours and shouts with it. A dark cloud encircled us and the first raindrops beat down on our heads.

'Let's go to my place for some ice cream,' John said.

People fled in all directions, charged past us with prams, children and dogs in tow. Trumpets and ribbons were left lying in the dirt with trampled flags and a pair of shoes someone had abandoned. We were already so wet that it didn't make sense to run. We just squelched out of the park, up to Briskeby, bought some sausages from The Man on the Steps, where we met a few giggle-pusses from the C class standing on tiptoe under a large umbrella and drinking Coke through a straw. We walked right past them, down Farmers' Hill, without a turn of the head. After all, we had our pride.

As we rounded the corner, Ringo said:

'Better a plaited twat than a t-t-twat in p-p-plaits.'

We laughed at that for a long time, wedged a firecracker in a dog turd, lit it and ran for cover behind the lake. It was the biggest shower of shit since the time we broke into the school garden and ate three kilos of plums and two cabbages.

At Gunnar's house we ate a boxful of ice lollies and then sat round the record player. Ola placed the drum between his legs, grabbed the drumsticks and hammered away. 'From Me To You' went tolerably well, but he lost the beat in 'Can't Buy Me Love'. He was lagging behind, puffing and panting. In 'A Hard Day's Night', though, he was really in the groove, his nose was twitching like a contented hare's, towards the end he had a go on other things in the room, the lamp, the model boat, the Meccano set, the racquet, the medals on his chest were rattling like castanets, it was the best thing we had heard or seen since the woodwork teacher, Woodentop, had got his huge nose stuck in the lathe the previous year.

We took a breather. Ola was lying on his back. The door burst open and the doorway was filled by Ernst Jespersen, grocer and mild-mannered man in an over-sized suit, tall and rangy 1948 regional 1,500 metres champion.

'You're having a good time,' he said.

'Oh, yes,' we nodded in unison.

'The rain has let up,' he said.

We looked outside. So it had.

'By the way,' he said, his gaze passing round the room and fixing on Gunnar. 'By the way,' he said. 'Do you know anything about a missing cigar, Gunnar?'

Ola began to cough. Gunnar's mien at once matched his white shirt, perfect winter camouflage.

'Do you?' his father persisted, his voice a little sharper at the edges.

Gunnar had already given himself away, the expression in his eyes, in his face, mouth, his whole body, it said everything there was to say, to perfection, nothing less, nothing more. Nevertheless, he made an effort and it sounded pathetic.

'Which cigar?' Gunnar asked.

'A Havana cigar,' his father said. 'A Havana cigar which I had expressly put by for today.'

Gunnar was about to say something. I winced on his behalf, hoping he would tell him the truth, but at that moment Stig came out of his room, behind his father. His hair was longer than ever, he looked a bit like Brian Jones. And he was wearing some dead hip trousers with brown stripes and flares, the lot. He looked at his father, stretched his mouth into a big grin and said:

'Sorry, Dad. It was me. I smoked it with Rudolf and Nag.'

'*My Havana cigar*!'

'I didn't know it was so precious, Dad. There were so many of them.'

Gunnar's father poked the air with a bent index finger.

'You didn't know it was so precious? No. That must have been why you took that *particular* one, was it, because it *didn't* look like anything special. Are you trying to make me laugh?'

'Sorry, Dad. I'll be more careful next time.'

Stig winked at us and the door was shut.

'I can't do it,' Gunnar said, ashamed of himself.

'You gotta either tell the truth,' I said. 'Or you gotta lie. There's no inbetween.'

Gunnar pondered. We heard his father rummaging around in the sitting room. On the floor above someone was playing the national anthem.

'Then I'll have to tell the truth,' Gunnar said. 'I can't lie.'

After the prommers' procession Ringo went to do some drumming outside the old people's home. John, George and I mooched around the town waiting for four o'clock to come because that was when Urra Park opened. We set off a few firecrackers, chucked a banger through an open window, heard a terrific explosion but we were already three blocks away.

We stopped around a corner, leaned against a wall and were covered in sweat.

'Shit,' said George. 'I can't be bothered with this tie any more.'

We tore off the strips of cloth, unbuttoned our shirts at the neck, took a deep breath, and then we smelt it, we were in Pilestredet, the smell of malt from the brewery and tobacco from Tiedemann's, sweet and a bit sickly. We sniffed the air like three anxious deer and then we breathed in again, as deeply as we could, until our blazers tightened round our chests, for like that we could perhaps get merry, with a bit of luck and the wind in the right direction we were bound to get merry.

At four o'clock we stood outside Urra Park, stone cold sober. It was packed with people, the same arrangement as the previous year, the way it should be. Tin cans, hoopla, nails in a plank of wood, tombola, ice creams and Coke. We started with the tin cans, we were each given a cloth ball, three throws and down they came. There we stood with a giant teddy bear, but we couldn't be seen dragging that around, so we gave it to a little girl in a national costume, a good deed, appropriate for a day like this, now we could get up to some devilry.

We hammered in some nails, threw rings, ate sausages and at five o'clock Ringo turned up, in full regalia, with the drum over his shoulder and the sticks in his belt.

'How's it goin'?' we asked.

'A-a-alright. The old 'uns couldn't hear a thing. Clapped in the middle of the numbers.'

He bought himself a Coke, and out of nowhere Dragon appeared, Dragon and Goose. Dragon was wearing the world's smallest suit, looked like he was wearing short trousers, with his thighs and arms bulging out of the shiny, threadbare material. He seemed happy and waved his cap. We looked at each other. Goose looked at us, deathly pale and trembling. Dragon was as drunk as a skunk.

'Sherry, you shee,' he said with his tongue askew.

Goose, shifting feet nervously, was peering around to see if any of the teachers were there.

'He was sitting in The Man on the Steps,' Goose whispered. 'He just followed me. Came after me.'

'You should hop it before Lue comes,' John advised in a kind voice.

Dragon aligned his eyes into a gaze and snarled, 'I'm gonna *kill* Lue!'

We grabbed Dragon between us, dragged him over to somewhere quieter, got him onto a bench and told him to sober up.

'I'm gonna *kill* Lue!' he yelled, forcing his mouth into a cold, malicious grin, the like of which we had never seen before.

'Shall we take you home?' John asked cautiously.

'Not bloody goin' home!'

A smile unfolded over his face. He shoved his hands into his pockets and pulled out a firecracker and matches.

'Not here,' George said, trying to take it off him. Dragon pulled his hand away.

Then he put the firecracker in his mouth, struck a match and lit the fuse. It hissed, the flame advanced on the powder. Dragon closed his eyes, the fuse was half burnt, Gunnar said something, Ola just gaped, Goose retreated, Seb and I exchanged glances. Then Dragon raised his fat hand and was about to take the firecracker out of his mouth and throw it, we held our breath, but his lips were stuck to the paper, I could see quite clearly that the skin on his lips was being stretched, it was glued to the red paper around the powder. Dragon's eyes were wide open, terror-stricken, it only took a second, not even that, then it exploded in the middle of Dragon's face. He was thrown backwards, he sat spread over the white bench with a large blood-spattered hole right under his nose, his teeth were gone, his lips were gone, his whole mouth, he was staring at us, seemingly uncomprehending, as the tears streamed down his cheeks into the red crater. People ran over, Gunnar threw up behind a tree, Seb and I tried to explain what had happened. Not long afterwards the ambulance arrived and Dragon was driven off with a flashing blue light and sirens.

Urra Park slowly emptied. We were the last, all the stands had been packed up and all the prizes taken away. There was blood on the white bench.

'Gimme the firecrackers,' Gunnar exclaimed. 'And the bangers and the jumping jacks.'

We did as he said, put the ammunition in his hand, knowing what he would do. He walked over to the drain and dropped them in one by one. We didn't protest because at this moment Dragon was lying under a white light with his gaping red hole as knives and scalpels flashed.

We headed for Frogner Park. It wasn't May 17 any more. Darkness lay across the sky like a blanket, sausages and ice cream and Coke lay like a dead weight in our stomachs. The flags hanging from the balconies and the windows resembled bloodstained banners.

As we passed Frogner Lido, Ola said, 'I regret all the c-c-crap I've ever said to D-D-Dragon.'

So did we. It was important to have said that. We were glad Ola had spoken up.

'I'll be n-n-nice to him when he comes back to s-s-school.'

That seemed to ease the pain inside, we breathed out all the badness. Ola banged the drum once, Dragon would be fine again, that was certain.

'This year I'm goin' to dive from the ten-metre board,' I said.

'You wouldn't dare,' Seb said.

'Wanna bet?'

'Pack of twenty.'

'Done.'

Almost no one was out now, no old ladies walking their poodles, no one playing football with upturned benches as the goals, no one snogging under the trees, even the poofs had gone, no one breathing hard behind the foliage, the bushes by the patch known as Hundejordet, Dogland, in Frogner Park were unoccupied. Only the dead on the other side of the fence were keeping us company. The wind rattled Ola's medals.

'Know what I think?' I said under my breath. 'I think the man who drowned himself in Bygdøy was the Hand Grenade Man.'

The others gawped at me.

'D'you think so?' Ola whispered. 'How come?'

'He would've chucked a hand grenade into the procession today if he'd been alive,' I said.

'I think so, too,' Seb said.

At that moment fireworks exploded across the sky. Terrified, we looked up. Blood was running in thin stripes over the town.

And in the far distance we heard music.

One Friday, after a week in which we had been well-behaved and hard-working, we went on a class trip. We caught the tram to Majorstuen and from there walked to Vindern, across the fields and up behind Gaustad. We were not alone. 7C was with us, Nina and Guri in the vanguard. It was a hell of a long walk. Lue's face was shiny before we reached the Police College, he was gasping like a fifteen-kilo pike and munching small pastilles. Inkie was with us too, the plaits' class teacher. She always wore brown, today she was sporting large, brown knee-breeches and looked like a cross between Harald Grønningen and Wenche Myhre, Olympic skier and pop star. Another teacher was with us too, a natural science teacher, Holst, a fairly young, weedy type who scuttled around like a lap dog, yapping all the time.

We sat down in a clearing, a green gateway to the forest, and at once Lue started to fuss. First of all, he counted us three times, but no one was missing, except for Dragon, who was still in hospital, there was a problem with his palate as well. Lue's voice thundered across the landscape. Inkie and Holst stood to attention beside him.

'Each and every one of you is to find one *flower* and one *plant*, and you have to show it to Holst. Do *not* wander off. You have fifteen minutes in which to do this.'

The classes got to their feet and scurried off in all directions. We went back the way we had come, furthest from Lue, and when he was out of sight we sat down and poked the grass.

'Should've brought a f-f-football,' Ola muttered.

A beetle wandered past. We let it go. Above us flapped some large birds with long necks, probably geese on their way to Lake Sognsvann. All of a sudden Ringo stood up and stared.

'Funny-lookin' house down there,' he said, pointing.

We stood up and looked in the same direction.

'That's Gaustad,' George whispered. 'Where all the nutters live.'

We saw a high wire fence, the buildings were old and eerie, with almost no windows. A large chimney protruded from one of them, a big smokestack.

'D-d-d'you think,' Ringo stammered. 'D-d-d'you think they b-b-burn 'em?'

There was no smoke. The sky above was clear blue.

'It's just the kitchen,' John said. 'Think of all that food!'

'The nutters eat a helluva lot,' George said.

We sat down. The beetle had climbed up a tall blade of grass. It hung there as the blade bent towards the ground, a black shell on the end of yellow grass.

Something stirred behind a bush and Lue's head hove into view.

'And you have already found four flowers?'

'No,' I said. 'But we've caught a huge beetle.'

'We want flowers,' Lue shouted. 'Let the beetle go this instant and find a flower!'

He turned on his heel and vanished between the trees like a spirit.

We mooched round staring at the ground. There were no flowers in the forest, we would have to go out into the clearing. Suddenly I was on my own. The others were by a bush a long way behind me. Then I was no longer alone, a branch cracked, I spun round and there was Nina.

'How many flowers have you found?' she asked.

'None,' I said.

'I've found two.'

She was standing right in front of me, no more than a metre away and I could feel her breath. And I could see she had blonde hair under her arms, for her blouse was quite loose, and breasts, hers weren't the biggest in the school, Klara probably had custody of those, but anyway, I gulped and looked for the other boys, but they weren't there.

'What did he look like, the man you found in Bygdøy?' she asked.

'Dunno. Didn't see much of him.'

Something was happening in the clearing. Everyone was running back and forming a large circle, staring at something or other. Amid all this we heard the natural science teacher's agitated voice.

'Let's go and see,' I said quickly.

'You can have one of my flowers,' Nina said, stretching out her hand.

I studied her hand. It was small and narrow. Holding a flower.

'That's very nice of you,' I said, carefully taking the moist, green stem and counting four red petals which formed a large bud.

'Poppy,' Nina whispered.

And then we ran down to the clearing as fast as we could. Holst was standing in the centre of the group pointing to the ground. Where a snake lay coiled up.

'Nature provides us with the most essential knowledge,' he lectured. 'Nature is the best book of all!'

We were as quiet as mice, staring in fear at the snake.

'There is only one poisonous snake in Norway,' Holst went on. 'The adder. The grass snake, on the other hand, is harmless. And the slowworm is not really a worm. It belongs to the lizard family. This creature here is a grass snake and is therefore harmless.'

He looked around with an air of triumph. Lue stepped forward, braver now, but Inkie kept her distance, her breeches flapping like pennants.

'Now I'll show you something,' Holst almost sang. 'I'll lift it up by its tail. It's not dangerous because it's a grass snake. And should it turn out to be an adder, which of course is not the case, it's not dangerous to lift it up by the tail either, because an adder can't raise its head and bite at air!'

The circle widened as Holst rolled up his shirtsleeves.

'It looks like an adder,' John said, standing right behind me.

'Yes,' I said. 'It's got to be an adder.'

'Is it wise to hold an adder's tail?' John asked.

'No,' I said.

Holst bent down, grabbed the snake with lightning speed and showed it off with a beaming face. Then the snake twisted in the air, thrust back its head and bit him on the arm. Everyone screamed. Holst screamed, threw the snake away with a howl and the circle dispersed in all directions. The snake slithered into some tall scrub, Holst sank to the ground and Lue stood there, mystified, flapping his arms.

'I'm dying,' Holst rattled, white as sugar. 'I'm dying.'

We carried him to Ringveien and flagged down a car, which took him to the casualty department. Holst survived. Afterwards Lue said that we reap our greatest knowledge through trial and error. He was certain that none of us would hold a snake by the tail in the future.

On the way home John stopped and pointed to my hand.

'What've you got there?' he asked.

'A flower, can't you see?' I said.

'What are you goin' to do with it?' George enquired with a grin.

'Give it to my mum,' I said. 'Birthday.'

'Bloody hell,' said the others.

Nina was walking in front of us. I couldn't take my eyes off her back and her tall, slim neck.

I gently squeezed the giant red tear in my hand.

And someone began to sing a familiar refrain about the local asylum:

'There's a hole in the fence at Gaustad, there's a hole in the fence at Gaustad!'

We had seen death in Bygdøy. Now death was here in a different guise. Exams. Or perhaps it was the waiting time that felt like death, a kind of antechamber, white and soundless. That's what it is, waiting is death. When what you have been waiting for arrives, it is already over, just like the DTP injection, the so-called fork-jab we dreaded for five years, the needle grew in insane proportions over time and in the end we imagined a pitch fork in our backs. However, standing in a line with bared chests in the doctor's surgery and a nurse rubbing our shoulders with moist cotton wool, we were almost disappointed when the doctor jabbed and it didn't hurt. It was as though we had been tricked. And that was how it was with the exams as well. Sitting in the sunlit classroom with the exam sheets in front of me, I felt it was over already, or something new had just begun. The silence was deafening, not even the school bells rang, right up until packed lunches were taken out and the windows were opened wide. Then summer hit us, with bird cries, cycle bells and a whole orchestra of smells. On the first day we had arithmetic and geometry, on the second it was English and finally essay writing. When we finished on the third day we charged down the steps and sprinted into town, to Studenten with fifteen kroner in our pockets and our mouths watering. We started with a chocolate milkshake and followed through with a banana split.

'Which one did you write about?' I asked at last.

'Describe something exciting you have experienced,' John, George and Ringo answered.

Of course they had taken that one, too, and what else could we have written about apart from the man who drowned in Huk.

I swallowed the banana and looked at Ringo.

'You didn't write about us slingin' the car badges in the sea, did you?'

'Are you out of your m-m-mind! Couldn't write about that, could I!'

We finished off with ice cream soda, apple juice and soft ice topped with crushed nuts. Then we strolled down the steps towards the palace feeling replete and tired, past Restaurant Pernille, which was packed to the rafters with crazy folk waving beer glasses. Two guardsmen came towards us, the girls whistled and waved to them, and they both went scarlet under their huge plumed hats. That was living.

And then we met Goose in Drammensveien. Walking with his

mother, he was dressed up in a tie and blue jacket, fresh from the barber's, neck looking like a whetstone. His mother was prodigiously tall. She stooped down and spoke to us with long drawn-out vowels.

'You can stay here and have a chat. Catch me up later.'

She straightened and continued down Glitnebakken.

'Where are you goin'?' George asked.

'Halvorsen's Konditori,' mumbled Goose.

'How did it go?' John asked.

'All right,' Goose answered, his eyes wandering.

'Which essay title did you take?'

'Number three,' he said in a low voice.

'What excitin' experience have you had?' George grinned.

Now Goose refused to look at any of us, made as if to run after his mother but didn't quite seem to manage it.

'I wrote about… I wrote about the man who drowned in Bygdøy.'

We couldn't believe our ears.

'You wrote… you wr-wr-wrote about what *we* experienced,' Ringo stuttered.

Goose gave a series of quick nods. The tight shirt collar cut into his neck.

'But f-for Pete's sake you weren't there!' John spat. 'Hell, it wasn't *you* who had the experience!'

'You can't lie in the bloody exam,' Ringo hissed.

Goose opened his dry lips and gazed at some point in the Palace Gardens.

'It isn't a lie,' he said with solemnity. 'It's *creative writing*.'

Now John thought he was becoming seriously cheeky, he grabbed his shoulder and pushed his face down towards the soft tarmac.

'Don't you bloody know that you can't write about what we experienced?! What the hell d'you think *we* wrote about, eh!'

Goose stood with his head bowed under the pressure of John's hand.

'Everyone in the class wrote about it,' he whispered. 'Everyone!'

John let go and looked at us.

'Did everyone write about what happened in Bygdøy?' I asked in astonishment.

'Yes! Everyone! Except Dragon!'

Then Goose ran after his mother and we were left standing in Drammensveien feeling betrayed and cheated. But the people who marked the essays would probably realise that *we* were the ones who had been there and the others had just heard the story from us. No question. We calmed down and strolled home, picked up our swimming togs and went to Frogner Lido.

'You remember the bet, don't you?' George said as we stood at the diving end. I turned. The tower rose into the air, higher than the chimney in Gaustad. That was when I felt the tingle. I glowed, as though I were an electric eel.

'Yes,' I said. 'Of course.'

I was on my own, atop the ten-metre platform. I could see the whole of Oslo. The heat haze quivered on the horizon. I walked out onto the board. It was a long way down, but it seemed further than it was because you could see through the water, right down to the green floor. John, George and Ringo looked up at me, and they were not alone, all the others down there were also watching. The lifeguard blew his whistle and cleared people away so that I had a free passage. All of a sudden it hit me: everyone is waiting for me. Now it was impossible to cop out. I was caught. There was no way back. That reassured me. I took a deep breath, felt the plunge inside me first, a hundred times ten metres in my head, then I closed my eyes, took off and hit the water at once.

I was pulled up over the side. I brought up chlorine but was otherwise in good shape, just a reddish forehead and a new centre parting.

'You flew through the air like an eagle!' George said, giving me the packet of cigarettes he had obviously bought in advance.

On arriving home, I stuck my sore head out of the window, smelt the sea air from Frogner Bay, and then I heard a few strange noises above me. I looked up and thought I had discovered a new planet, pink with three craters and a big mountain. It was Jensenius.

'Hello,' he said.

'Hello,' I said.

'Would you do me a favour?'

'What's that?'

'Buy me some beer.'

I nipped up to his flat and he was already standing in the doorway, a whale, an airship, he had to walk sideways to get through the door.

'Fifteen Export,' he whispered, giving me a handful of coins.

I went to Jacobsen's on the corner for the beer, they knew me there, paid the Clark Gable lookalike at the counter and lugged the weight down to Svolder. Jensenius was waiting for me and let me in through the door. He took the shopping net and marched into the sitting room. Once there, he sank into a large leather chair and opened the first bottle. He drank half, licked the foam around his mouth and slowly turned to me, standing still by the door.

'Keep the change,' he said. 'You're a good lad, you are.'

The walls were covered with photographs, they had to be from the time Jensenius was young and world famous. There was a bad smell and mildew on the windows.

'Can you teach me to sing?' I asked.

Jensenius contemplated me at his leisure, the bottle close to his mouth. Then he put it down and reached out his hand, a huge smile cutting through the fat like a blunt knife.

'Can I teach you to sing?' he whined.

'Yes.'

I went over to him.

'Why do you want to learn to sing, young man?'

'I want to become a singer,' I said with sincerity.

He pointed me to a chair, opened five bottles one after the other and I sat there for two hours listening to Jensenius talking about singing, about beauty and singing.

'Singing is about letting yourself go,' he concluded. 'Letting yourself go and having control at the same time. You must have control! But don't be afraid of your voice. Everyone has a big voice inside them. Here!' He thumped his chest. The dust rose from the faded shirt. 'Let it go! Scream!' he squeaked.

The last day at school was a big deal. Lue was wearing a dark suit with shiny knees and elbows. He seemed excited, high almost. At first I thought he must have been ecstatic because he was getting rid of us, but then I realised he was just sad and was trying to hide it with wild gesticulations and smiles. He gave a speech, which was not short, and afterwards Goose waddled up to the desk with a somewhat unstable present that made a lot of noise. Lue removed the paper and found himself holding a bowl of water in which a goldfish was furiously swimming around. It was all too much for Lue. He had to go into the corridor where, through loud sobs, he gasped for breath and blew his nose.

Then we clattered down to the film room where the rest of the muttheads were sitting and quaking, the mothers perched along the walls, sporting summer dresses and perms, winking and waving, three-metre long handkerchiefs in their laps. My mother was sitting right by the door and staring at me, burning a scorch mark into my back, and Nina was sitting two rows in front. She turned towards me and showed me a row of white teeth. I was caught in the crossfire and blenched.

Nina leaned towards me.

'You can dive from the ten-metre board, can you?' she whispered.

'Why d'you say that?' I flushed to my roots.

'Saw you.'

The senior teacher's voice boomed out, and he said the same as Lue, and along the walls there were the sounds of sniffling and tutting. These were words we should take to heart, from now on life would be a serious matter, from now on the demands on us would grow, from now on, from now on, bloody hell, on a lighter note he wished us a good summer, if we didn't have a nervous breakdown before Midsummer's Day, that is. And then it was full pelt back to the classroom and Lue distributing certificates and shaking our hands. The goldfish was swimming round and round and gawping at everyone who approached. I got a B in English and a C in maths. And a C in Norwegian. John had the same as me, but a B in maths. George also had a C in Norwegian while Ringo was cursing over a big fat E.

'E,' he hissed. 'I got an E f-f-for essay writin'!'

He turned on Goose who was grinning to himself.

'What did you get for essay writin'?' he shouted.

'B,' Goose answered.

Ringo, nonplussed, was about to go for Goose. We had to stop him.

'How can that be?' Ringo babbled. 'It ain't r-right!'

We were all quite angry, and wondered if we should set upon Lue for a last time, but in the end we didn't care and followed the pack leaving the classroom, and the last we saw of Lue he was standing with his hands round the glass bowl, looking rather confused and bewildered, probably wondering how he was going to get it home.

The mothers were waiting by Harelabben, so we sneaked out into Holtegata and left the school behind us. We celebrated the occasion by buying nineteen rum balls between us at the bakery, the most we had polished off in one go since the dentist died three years ago.

'Got an E in religion,' John munched.

'And I got an E in woodwork,' I said.

And so we compared our grades and discovered that things were not that bad after all. I had only one more E, in handwriting, and a C for behaviour, the same as George.

It was only when I arrived home that I realised that this was going to be a watershed in my life. From now on, my ears rang. Mum had set the table in the sitting room although this was only a weekday, and Dad shook my hand as though we had never seen each other before.

'Congratulations, son,' he said. 'Let me see your grades. And wash your hands.'

I went into the bathroom and upon my return Dad's face was tense and ashen. His index finger hovered over my behaviour grade.

'What does this mean?' he said. 'A C for behaviour!'

'I don't know,' I said meekly.

'Don't you *know*? You must know what you've done, lad!'

I pondered. A was extra good, B was very good, C was good. Wasn't that good enough? I thought.

'Gunnar and I were whisperin' a bit,' I said. 'He sits behind me.'

'Whispering,' Dad corrected. 'He got a C too then, did he?'

And then I went all stupid and honest.

'No. He got a B.'

Dad looked at me with big staring eyes, his mouth agape, but Mum finally brought in the food, and when she had seen the grades she hugged me and smelt of perfume and lemon.

'B in English. That's just wonderful!'

She looked at Dad, Dad nodded and a cautious smile pulled at the edges of his mouth and then he laid a stern hand on my shoulder and rocked me to and fro, and that was when I knew that something really was changing, that from now on it was going to be from now on.

Steamed trout, and Mum and Dad drank white wine, which made their faces go a little shiny. I was even allowed to have a mouthful from Mum's green glass. It fizzed on my tongue like effervescent sodium bicarbonate, but I swallowed it without a grimace. And I wasn't very hungry after all the rum balls. I sat thinking about Lue and the goldfish and how he managed to carry it through the streets. It was a funny thought and I suppose my eyes had a faraway look as I sat there picking fish bones out of my teeth.

'Who was the girl?' Mum asked apropos of nothing.

'The girl?' I spluttered.

'The one sitting in front of you in the film room.'

'In the film room?'

In the nick of time the doorbell rang. I jumped up and opened the door. It was Gunnar.

'They've arrived!' he panted, waving his arms around. 'They've arrived!'

I did an about-turn and ran back into the sitting room.

'They've arrived!' I said. 'I've got to go!'

Dad could not believe his own ears.

'*Who's* arrived?'

'The Rolling Stones!'

The plates were full of fish bones and skin, glasses were half full, there was a slice of cucumber under my chair, the napkins looked like crumpled flowers, marsh marigolds, and I had dirtied the tablecloth.

'You'd better go then,' Dad smiled, and by then I had gone. We picked up Ola and Seb and caught the Goldfish into town.

'They landed in Fornebu an hour ago,' Gunnar panted. 'My brother said. Stayin' at the Vikin'.'

'Thought they were comin' tomorrow,' Seb said.

'To avoid hassle,' Gunnar explained. 'Hardly anybody knows they've just arrived, you know.'

We got off at the Oslo East stop and sprinted as fast as we could to the Viking Hotel. We heard the shouting as we approached, rhythmical shouting and stamping. We were not the first. We were the last. There were hundreds of people there already, screaming and staring. We stopped and looked, too, but saw nothing, just sky and loads of windows.

'They must be in the bathtub drinkin' champagne,' Seb said.

'W-w-with l-l-loads of girls!'

All of a sudden everything went still, dead still, for a fraction of a second, then the din broke loose again, even worse than before, and everyone pointed and stared in the same direction. On the seventh floor a face came into view with lots of long, blond hair.

'It's Brian!' Gunnar yelled in my ear.

It was Brian Jones. I was speechless. The others shouted. A girl in front of us fainted on the pavement, just sighed and collapsed onto the tarmac. The face in the window was gone again. Two cops made their way through the crowd and picked up the girl.

'It's Mick,' someone screamed. 'It's Mick!'

Another figure was standing in the window on the seventh floor, almost impossible to see, but it was obvious it had to be Mick. The screams reached the heavens. I was yelling too, but not a sound passed my lips.

'Now they're all there!' Seb shouted.

Five shadows on the seventh floor of the Viking Hotel. A curtain was drawn to, like the last frame of a film. The screams continued for a while, then the noise sank back into our bodies.

'Well, they've got to rest, haven't they,' Ola said objectively. 'Before the c-c-concert in Sjølyst.'

'Course,' Gunnar said. 'What I wouldn't give for a ticket.'

'The Pussycats are doin' the warm-up,' I said.

'Far out!'

There was someone standing behind us. It was Dragon. It was the first time he had come so close. Gunnar looked away.

'H-h-hiya,' Ola stammered.

Dragon could not grin with his mouth any more. Instead he grinned with his eyes. He had no inhibitions about showing his disfigured face.

He smelt of beer.

'What's goin' on here then?' he asked in a surprisingly clear voice.

'Don't you know!' Seb said. 'The Rolling Stones are stayin' at the Vikin'!'

Dragon looked around. His mutilated face made him seem almost inhuman.

'They're not stayin' at the Vikin',' Dragon said.

'Eh?'

'They're not stayin' at the Vikin',' he repeated. A warm breeze of beer wafted towards us.

'What d'you mean?' Gunnar almost shouted. 'Of course they're stayin' at the Vikin'.'

'We've s-s-seen 'em!' Ola said.

'False trail,' Dragon snuffled. His eyes were narrow and red. 'They're stayin' somewhere completely different.'

'How do you know, eh?' Gunnar asked in a slightly milder tone.

'I know,' Dragon said.

'Where are they stayin' then?' I asked. 'Smart-arse.'

'Can't tell you. Secret.'

That was too much for Gunnar.

'Secret! Are you out of your mind or what!'

Dragon was unshakable.

'Secret between me and Mick.'

We stared at him in silence. His disfigured face did not yield an inch.

'You're bluffin'!' Gunnar shouted. 'You're bloody bluffin'!'

Dragon stuffed his hand in his pocket and pulled out a small notepad.

'Look at this,' he said in what came over as a formal tone.

We gawped at the top sheet. There was a name written there. Mick. Mick Jagger. Flat, loopy writing. Dragon could not possibly have done that himself. He got a Below Standard in handwriting, he could never ever have formed such flawless Gs.

Gunnar's face went green, his chin fell two floors. He couldn't force out a sound.

'D'you believe me now?' Dragon gloated, putting his hand in his pocket again and pulling out something else. 'Got it for keepin' my gob shut.' He waved it in front of our noses and plunged it back in his pocket. It was a ticket to the Sjølyst concert.

'You're bluffin'!' Gunnar said for the last time.

'You can believe what you like,' Dragon said in a low, a spookily low, voice.

Then he turned on his heel and left, larger than life, Dragon who had had to repeat the seventh class, who had tried to kill Lue and later did other, worse things, he was cleverer than we thought, Dragon was, leaving us like that, just staring at a big, fat back, a huge head and trousers which were much too short.

'What do you reckon?' Seb asked after a while.

'Buggered if I know!' I said.

'We saw 'em, didn't we!' Gunnar persisted. 'We saw 'em with our own eyes!'

We raised our gaze to the seventh floor. It was a long way up.

'Might've been someone pretendin' to be the Rollin' Stones,' Seb said quietly.

We shrugged and ambled off, crossed Karl Johan, which was teeming with people. All the restaurant terraces were packed. Girls in bright skirts made of thin, thin material like butterfly wings, everyone was laughing, there was nothing to laugh at, but everyone was laughing anyway, and the darkness was beginning to filter down from the sky, flake by flake, and there was the smell of cigarettes and lilac.

We walked down to Oslo West station. We didn't say a word, just wandered off, out towards Filipstad, past the world's largest banana on Matthiessen's building, and by Kongen Sailing Club we sat down on a bench and looked across Frogner Bay. The yachts were coming in. People dressed in casual clothes were making their way over the bridge to Club 7.

'We're off tomorrow, Mum and me,' said Seb. 'Meetin' my dad in Gothenburg.'

'M-m-me, too,' Ola sighed. 'We're goin' to my grandma's in Toten. Gonna be deadly d-d-dull.'

Behind us a train groaned, dragged sound after it, westbound, disappeared behind Skarpsno.

'We're off to Arendal,' Gunnar said gloomily. 'Stig's not comin'. He's rented a mountain cabin with some friends.'

'I'm off tomorrow,' I said. 'To Nesodden.'

We didn't say any more. But we were all thinking the same, that it was by no means certain we would all be in the same class in the autumn, or the same school. We didn't say a word, but we knew we were all thinking about it and that whatever happened we would never abandon the others.

The darkness was more palpable now. A wind enclosed us, warm and gentle.

And so summer began, first of all with a scream, then with a long, green silence that slowly changed to blue.

She's A Woman

Summer '65

It was the coldest summer since the war. I was lying in my room on the first floor playing records, reading old magazines or doing nothing, just listening to the magpie cackling hysterically in the tree outside and then watching it flutter off like a pair of black scissors in the rain.

These are the things I can recall: plimsolls going green and shrinking in the wet grass, a snail leaving a slimy trail across the steps, the oval shape of gooseberries, with their horrible hairy surface (which reminded me of something I had not yet done), white currants and stomach-ache, the outside loo and a faded photograph of great-grandfather who bought the House in 1920. And the silence. The silence in the rain, under the duvet and beneath my skin, a heavy charged silence. Dad took the ferry to town every day and came back at five on the dot, before he, too, was on holiday. And Mum shuffled around on noiseless slippers with a large shawl around her, she was always cold and bored, just like me.

On one such day, with walls of rain outside the windowpanes, she hit on a crazy idea.

'I'm so bored,' she said out of the blue, clutching her head with both hands. 'It's so dark here. Can't we think of something to do!'

'Won't Dad be back soon?' I said.

She stood up and paced the floor restlessly.

'He's staying in town until tomorrow,' she sighed, staring out at the rain. 'A meeting.'

'We can play cards,' I suggested feebly.

'No, ugh! I hate cards! And you know that!'

I wondered whether to head for the quay and try casting with the new lure.

Mum was ahead of me.

'I've got it!' she exclaimed. 'We'll dress up! Let's play dressing up!'

'Fancy dress?' I mumbled. 'Where would we find the costumes?'

'There are loads of old clothes in the wardrobe in the loft!'

She skipped out of the room and was gone for quite a long time. Most of all I wanted to be outside, maybe go and pick some strawberries in the fields, they would be ripe now, with all that sun and rain. But I didn't move from my chair and Mum returned with a pile of gear over her arm.

'Here,' she beamed, tossing everything onto the large table in the middle of the room.

The clothing had a strange smell, mothballs, dust, dead people, I imagined, something a little sinister. Mum rummaged through the heap, putting aside the things she liked, laughing all the time, she hadn't laughed like that all summer. I found an old double-breasted jacket and hung it over a chair.

Mum undressed. I looked at her in shock and turned away.

Mum laughed behind my back.

'Are you embarrassed, Kim?'

There was a rustle of silk. I spun round and looked at her again. She met my eyes in the sombre room, there was a lot of fear and tenderness in those eyes, the skin on her arms was covered in goose pimples, she stood there naked, the silence lingered, she must have known she was losing me bit by bit now.

Afterwards she strutted around the floor in a straight, tight-fitting raven black dress which reached down to her ankles, and around her forehead she wore a ribbon, also raven black, with a large yellow feather protruding from her hair. She pouted and her lips were bright red. I stood with my legs apart in great-grandfather's old flax jacket and must have looked like a gardener or a deckhand. Then my mother recited verse to me and told me about parts she had rehearsed a long time ago, before she had met Dad, but had never had any use for. And I could see that the line between laughter and tears was wafer-thin, for even though she was cheerful and did a lot of funny things, it was a lonely performance, lonely and frenetic.

I clapped for all I was worth.

That night I had a nightmare: I was lying in total darkness, darker than I had ever imagined. As I struck out with my hand, I hit something hard close by. I struck out again and again and felt blood beginning to flow. Then I heard something outside in the darkness, voices at first, the low buzz of voices but no clear words, followed by music. I struck out against the darkness, screamed as loud as I could, but nothing helped. Then I heard a new sound as I began to sink: the sound of earth falling on boards, three times.

The following day I knew it was time. In the evening, when Dad had come back from town, I took my swimming trunks and meandered down to the beach. The weather was fine, but there was a strong wind coming off the fjord, thrusting the water forward in white, choppy waves. I changed clothes and toddled out to the diving board, hesitated, then hurled myself off. The water entwined me in its cold grey depths. The current and the waves carried me out and I had to use all my strength to resist. For a moment I panicked, was on the point of shouting for help, but no one would have been there to hear me if I had. Then my self-control returned, I swam at an angle to the current and dragged myself ashore.

I was frozen stiff as I emerged, the wind tore at my body, I walked across the slope of bare rock shivering. At a point where I had the wind and the waves facing me I stopped. I breathed in several times, filled my lungs and then I screamed. I screamed until tears flowed, but I was scarcely audible above the wind because it had greater lungs than I. Inside me, things were beginning to loosen, an avalanche was on its way, I screamed and screamed, howled, and in between I sang, stumbled on some lyrics I sang over and over again, tunelessly:

Don't think what might be
Set sail across the sea.
Don't think what might be
Set sail across the sea.

After a short while I was completely worn out. Exhausted and happy, I slumped down onto the wet rocks. I was drained of sound. I had screamed it out for the first time, now my screams, my singing, were on their way into space, like a sputnik orbiting the earth.

One day they would return.

I put on my clothes, staggered home stiff-legged. My father was standing on the balcony, keeping a lookout, he looked furious.

'And where have you been?' he shouted.

'Swimming,' I said.

'You know you're not allowed to swim on your own!'

I didn't have the energy to answer.

Mum came out too, with a suspicious glance at me, she had felt a little awkward all day.

'Now you'll catch a cold, Kim,' was all she said.

And I did. I was in bed for six days with a fever and mild hallucinations while the magpie cackled in the tree outside. And when I got up, gaunt and hungry on the seventh day, the sun was on fire, summer had arrived at long last. We sat on the balcony in the morning and ate, and in walked Uncle Hubert. And he was not alone. He had a girl with him.

Well, well. Dad turned into a lobster and Mum into a canary. And me? I had butterflies. In my stomach. They plodded and groaned their way up to us, sweaty and hot after the walk from the quay. The atmosphere was at breaking point.

She was the most attractive-looking girl I had ever seen.

And she greeted me first.

'Hiya, I'm Henny,' she said, shaking my hand.

And the hands did the whole round, and Mum said something about having to fetch more cups so that they could have some tea or coffee, but Uncle Hubert shouted that he wanted beer and he and Henny disappeared into the bedroom under the stairs.

Mum and Dad stood looking at each other.

'It's nice to have visitors,' Mum said. 'And the girl looked so sweet.'

Dad sat down without answering, found a newspaper to riffle through. Mum fetched a beer from the cellar.

And I carried deckchairs onto the grass.

I counted 123 yachts in the fjord, and sixteen gulls flew over my head, and the ants were extra busy that Saturday, around my shoes alone there were 468 of them and they were all carrying pine needles. And the rhododendron had twenty-nine flowers, but eight of them were withering.

It was a strange day.

The others drank beer. I had Solo lemonade. It was funny to see Dad drinking beer straight from the bottle. Henny looked up at the sky with large, closed eyes. Uncle Hubert was stretched out in the deckchair with a peaked cap over his face. Mum sat with her back to the sun, her shoulders were red.

Henny said, 'We've brought lots of shrimps with us!'

'And white wine,' Hubert added. 'I put the bottles in the fridge.'

'How long are you staying?' Dad asked suddenly. Mum sent him a dirty look.

'We're going tomorrow, my dear brother. Don't you worry.'

'I didn't mean it like that,' Dad laughed, looking very relieved.

'That's fine, brother.'

Red faces in the sun. Empty beer bottles on the grass. I had never seen Uncle Hubert so relaxed, he was like a soft cushion in the chair, emitting noises from time to time, just fair-weather noises, mutterings and contented sighs. All the knots had been loosened, I visualised all the fibres in his head, smooth and silky in tidy lines.

Dad said, 'I think there's going to be some thunder tonight. It's muggy.'

'Suppose there will be,' Hubert sighed. His face was streaming with sweat.

Across the horizon, clouds were building up on all sides.

'I feel like swimming,' Henny exclaimed.

'I don't,' came the response from deep in Hubert's chair. 'Take Kim with you.'

She studied me. From that one look, I got a suntan.

'Would you like to?'

The beach was deserted now. Just paper, empty bottles and orange peel left behind. And a red beach ball bouncing over the rocks. Wind. I dived in, plunged to the bottom, water gushed past my eyes, a wrasse darted away, a jellyfish floated along my thigh. I moved upwards, saw the thin line between sea and sky, broken by the sun.

Henny was staggering through the clusters of seaweed. Bikini. White and scantier than a blade of grass. Her body was lightly tanned and shiny. She had tied her hair up into a blonde bun behind her neck. She lowered herself into the water with a scream.

And the clouds gathered from the horizon, enveloping us.

Henny was beside me.

'Let's swim out,' she said, pulling away from me with long, powerful strokes.

I followed her like a barge, wondering what sort of things you talked about in the water, or whether it was normal to talk in the water at all, but then what would you talk about on land?

'Do you live here all summer, Kim?' Henny asked.

'Yes,' I gulped.

We must have been in the middle of the fjord at least. The wind picked up. Small, choppy waves beat against my face. Above us the sky was becoming overcast. Clouds rolled in dark formations. The air was colder than the water.

'Shouldn't we turn around soon?' I said in a low voice.

Henny stopped swimming, looked at me and laughed.

'I forgot where I was,' she said. 'Of course we should turn back now.'

We swam towards the shore. A multitude of questions lay on my tongue, but I couldn't get them out, my mouth was a barrier net. I would have liked to ask about Hubert, about whether they were, whether they were lovers, whether they were going to marry, and if so, why, when she was so much younger than he, and about what went on in Hubert's head, about the knots, about Henny, about everything.

We were approaching land.

I asked, 'Do you like The Beatles?'

'They're sweet,' she answered.

I almost sank. Sweet. The seawater frothed out of my nose. I watched her. Her profile cut through the waves like a shark's fin.

'Who do you like most?' I stuttered.

'There are so many. Miles Davis. Charlie Parker. Lester Young. And John Coltrane.'

Who was that? I was over moving sands, had swum myself into a corner, my arms withered, my chin sagged in the water.

'Aha,' I said. 'But Bob Dylan is good!' I added.

'Fantastic. And Woody Guthrie. Dylan learnt from him.'

I was a bubble of air and a cork. I clenched my teeth and strained to keep up.

Then we scrambled onto the shore and I ran for our towels. The sun had gone in now. Henny was huddled up.

'It's cold,' she shivered.

At that moment it began to rain. Henny jumped up.

'Let's go in the shed,' I shouted.

She was already off. The rain came hammering down like nails and we found shelter in the ramshackle wooden shed, where the smell from the adjacent toilet was less than welcoming and where there was some writing and drawing on the walls that was not exactly prescribed reading.

Henny leaned against the door, out of breath.

'I'm sure it won't last too long,' she said.

'No,' I said, hoping it would last for the rest of the summer.

'You shouldn't stand around in wet trunks,' she went on. 'You'll be ill.'

And then she took off her bikini and stood naked in front of me. It was only for a second, before she put on some jeans and a shirt. Everything inside me plunged to the soles of my feet. I must have been gawping because she laughed and undid her hair and shook it into place. With a great deal of effort and movement I struggled into my clothes. Everything was pounding, my skin was a size too small, too tight, my blood was throbbing from inside and the rain beat down on the roof.

'Are you starting *realskole* this autumn?' Henny asked.

'Yes,' I managed to utter.

Now it was my turn. Had to say something. Said something:

'What do you do?'

'I draw. For the same magazine as your uncle.'

'Uhuh.'

'But it's just something I'm doing for now, to earn some money. I start at the art academy next year.'

'Are you going to be an artist!' I burst out.

Henny laughed.

'I'm going to paint pictures,' she said.

The drumming on the roof became fainter and fainter. Either the rain was subsiding or I was fading away. Henny opened the door and decided the matter.

'It's let up now,' she said. 'Shall we go back?'

Dad was right with his weather forecast. While we sat peeling the shrimps, the room was lit up by a flame-yellow flash, and at the same time we heard one hell of a bang. We rushed out onto the balcony and up by the flagpole we saw a strange sight. Something on the hill was glowing. Uncle Hubert thought a meteor had hit the earth, Mum thought it was men from Mars, and Dad didn't have his thinking cap on, either. Henny squeezed my arm. After a while the glow died, like a large cigarette. We donned rain jackets and all trudged up to the place together.

The lightning had split open a rock. And it was not just any rock, it weighed a good hundred kilos. Dad told us that his father had carried it up here from the quay with his own hands. It had been a bet. And Granddad had won.

Now the lightning had cracked it open like an egg.

We jogged back down and thanked our lucky stars that the House had not been hit. But the electricity had gone. We lit the fire and lots of candles, sat anxiously listening to the crashes of thunder and counting the seconds to work out where the lightning was. The storm was moving westwards. Those who said anything at all spoke in hushed tones, as though the air around us was highly explosive. Hubert lost control of his left eyelid for a while, had to go into the kitchen to calm down. Henny sat on the sofa with her feet curled up beneath her. Mum cleared the table, Dad stood by the balcony door, looking out.

'Let's go and play some records!' Henny cried, so loud that everyone jumped. She rose to her feet and gave me her hand.

We played my lousy records. Henny sat still, listening, or thinking about something else, must have been doing that, flicking through a Beatles magazine I had brought, *Meet The Beatles*, with pictures of The Beatles in Paris. She said she wanted to go there, to Paris, that was where it was all happening, she said. Oslo was so boring. She smiled. I changed records. Old Cliff. Henny laughed. She'd been in love with Cliff at one time, she confided. 'Summer Holiday'. 'Lucky Lips'. She lit up a cigarette and gave me a drag. The filter tasted of raw skin. And the oblique rain drove past the window.

The lights came back on, our faces were pale and shiny. The stylus scratched on the inner groove. The batteries were on their last legs. I blew out the candle, looked at her, the way I see her now, like a negative on the membrane of my eyes, branded by the flashes of the summer's night.

Henny and Hubert went home, and the days drifted past like on a conveyor belt, the same day all the time, but one day was different, quite different. It was when Dad's holiday was over and he was back at work as usual. And Mum had to sell lottery tickets at Sunnaa's Sykehus, a rehabilitation hospital, and caught the bus as soon as Dad had left.

There I was, with twenty kroner in my pocket and one whole day to myself.

I caught the ferry from Nesodden to town.

I could see if anyone was in, ran past Oslo West station and Ruseløkka, rang the bell at Ola's and Seb's. No one at home. Headed for Gunnar's. Same result. The shop was closed. A sign in the window said: We are on holiday until August 7.

An odd, empty feeling. Everything was different. I mooched down Drammensveien, towards Skillebekk, no one outdoors, no one inside, a new alien smell had invaded the district. It had some similarity with the one in our flat when we returned home in August, sweet, repugnant, it reeked of something dead, of neglect, and it was like we had to start using the rooms anew, breathe life into them, talk to them, repossess them. My street was not what it had been. I stood there, all on my own, not a person around, empty windows, a wind sweeping towards me, blowing sand into my eyes.

I walked into town. At least it was populated. And there was ice cream. I queued for half an hour at Studenten and bought myself a strawberry milkshake. The voices around me were speaking in foreign tongues. I soon left.

All I could do was mooch back and forth. Had a quick look in record shops, but didn't see any of the names Henny had mentioned. I crossed the road, it was better there, in the shade under the trees. The tarmac was steaming. An old lady was feeding a flock of pigeons. A man walking in front of me stamped hard on the ground, the pigeons took off with a squawk, flapped around the woman and disappeared over Wergeland.

And then she, too, was gone from the bench. The man in front of me turned, shrugged and ambled on.

That was not the strangest thing, though.

Below Stortinget, the Norwegian parliament building, a crowd of people stood looking at a picture exhibited in a glass case. *Picture of the Month* I read on a sign. I thought about Henny. Perhaps she had painted it. I made my way through, but it wasn't Henny's picture, not at all. An extraordinary name I could hardly spell was written there. And the picture was weird. I had never seen anything like it. There was a doll in the middle of the picture, almost completely destroyed, just as though it had been melted over a bonfire. And then there was a whole load of red paint, but not as you would expect to see in normal paintings, this was like blood, thick blood that coagulates on the surface of a large wound. And the red paint dripped down onto a flag, the American flag. And behind the picture, yes, it was kind of three-dimensional, not like the flat landscapes Mum and Dad had on the wall, behind the picture someone had written VIETNAM. I read the title, the longest title I had ever read. *A report from Vietnam. Children have burning napalm dropped on them. Their skin burns, leaving black sores and they die.*

Burns under water. That was what Stig had talked about. 'Masters Of War'. The sun stung my neck. My head began to buzz, the doll screamed at me, just like the girl staggering out of the ruins, the blood flowed in front of me, the sun was roasting, the blood clotted into grotesque shapes.

Then something happened. I heard a yell. A hand grabbed my shoulder and pushed me aside. I could not believe my own eyes. A man of my father's age stood in front of the picture, wearing a suit and carrying a briefcase from which he took an axe, an axe, and then he heaved away at the display case. The glass smashed and with one blow he shattered the doll and ripped the canvas. And then something happened which was even stranger. Those standing around watching clapped, they didn't stop him, they clapped. I held my head in my hands, wanting to scream, and moved backwards, scared. And when the man had finally destroyed the whole picture, two policemen came and gently escorted him away.

I went down to the quay and waited for my boat. I did not understand. Something had collapsed. Something had disintegrated. I was frightened.

I said nothing to Mum and Dad. But the man with the axe often appeared at night, he killed small children, he walked round killing small children.

On the radio I listened to reports about bombings, offensives, defeats, victories. I felt so strangely distant and alien sitting on the balcony and eating supper, wholegrain bread, soft goat's cheese and HaPå spread.

The sun was sinking. August had come with a touch of autumn. Signs of departure were everywhere. I seemed to have outgrown myself.

On the last day my mother said I had grown a lot that summer, at least three centimetres.

Help

Autumn '65

'Violins,' Gunnar muttered. 'Violins?'

Mogga Park, the evening before school started. We bent over cycle handlebars examining the LP Seb had bought in Sweden. At first I thought it said *eple*, Norwegian for apple. Then I untangled my eyes. *Help*.

'String quartet,' Seb corrected.

'So you mean *violins*, right?'

'Right. Dead cool!'

We were dying to hear it, but Ola hadn't turned up yet, should have been there half an hour ago. We lit up some evil-tasting dog-ends. Above us a flock of birds was ploughing its way out of the country.

'Where the hell's Ola?' Gunnar said impatiently.

We waited a bit more, until we could wait no longer, and pedalled to Observatoriegata. His mother opened the door, suntanned and light on her feet, but with two wrinkles at the corners of her mouth forcing her lips downwards.

'Ola's had an accident,' she said softly.

We stiffened in our shirts. Accident?

'He's in his room. You can go in and see him.'

Ola was sitting by the window. He had broken both arms. They were hanging in two slings with plastercasts to well above the elbows. He grimaced because inside it itched like hell, and how the hell would he be able to scratch?

'Crashed a tractor in T-T-Toten,' he whispered in a depressed tone. 'H-h-hit the ground with my h-h-hands.'

Gunnar cleared his throat, his voice cracked a little, tried again.

'How... how d'you eat?'

Ola's eyes were narrow and dull.

'My mother feeds me,' he said in a whisper.

We exchanged glances, but turned away immediately because laughter was bubbling behind our serious faces, and Ola was not ready for that yet.

Seb cleared his throat, he cleared his throat for an unnaturally long time.

'But how... how d'you go to the toilet?'

Gunnar's cheeks billowed out like two sails, and Seb stared at his hands and then he opened his mouth wide but swallowed the howl at birth, all that was heard was a tiny gasp, and there he sat with a silent roar of laughter on his face, very red from the forehead downwards.

'You call yourselves f-f-friends!' Ola growled.

'But how d'you do it?'

Ola lowered his head.

'M-M-Mum does it,' he said unhappily, and the room was silent for quite a time.

Seb fidgeted with his cycle bag. We studied the floor. Seb rediscovered his voice.

'We've brought you something,' he said. 'Hope the batteries on your record player are alright.'

Seb took out the record and Ola sucked in his breath with a whistle.

And then we played *Help* for the rest of the evening as the darkness descended from the sky like a grey curtain and inside us the summer seemed to live on. Autumn had already begun, and for the first time we liked violins.

Before leaving, we signed his plaster cast: John, George and Paul.

We had been put in the same school, Vestheim, but we were in different classes. We sneaked past the *gymnas* students standing by the gate in Skovveien, and we wondered when they would initiate us, at least it didn't look as if they would strike today. They didn't look at us, they didn't even look down on us. There were several more pale faces by the wire fence in Oscarsgate. Guri and Nina were in another group, Nina's kneecaps were dark brown, she obviously hadn't seen me.

Then the bell went. We shook each other's hand and parted company: Gunnar with me, Seb with Ola. Slowly the playground emptied as though the broad, dark doors were sucking us in.

Gunnar and I had to fight for places at the back in the middle row. His back was bigger than ever, the teachers would never catch sight of me. Goose was sitting right at the front, hair plastered down and creases freshly pressed. And the girls, there were girls in the class too, sat in the window row, big and unapproachable, and when the sun shone on them their hair looked like candy floss and their faces went soft and white.

Then the door opened and in walked the form teacher, Iversen, known as Kerr's Pink – he had a plot of agricultural land outside his terraced house in Tåsen. He was a shrimp of a man in a factory overall, but he had large, hairy hands and a voice that rose from floor level and oozed out of his mouth like liquid iron.

He called out our names, and everyone scrutinised everyone else, some were familiar, some came from other parts of town, some stared down at their desk lids, some whispered their names as though they were imparting important, dangerous confidences.

Afterwards the other teachers came in and presented themselves. It was a fairly normal collection, no hunchbacks, no clubfeet, noses in the centre of the face and ears on either side of the head. The German teacher's name was Hammer, a plump little lady with lots of square words in her mouth, who sang a couple of impromptu lieder and chattered away in German. And I can remember the gym teacher, Skinke, ham in Norwegian, a real beanpole with a narrow head, thick glasses, a crew cut and three national race-walking championships to his name. He popped in and squeaked that the boys should bring their gym kit the following day, then race-walked out, rotating his hips like a well-greased globe. Last to come was the headteacher, wow, I can remember him, he looked a bit like Hitler, or Arnulf Øverland, the same moustache, the super-compact tuft under his nose, and he rolled his 'r's, it tickled our ears and a round-shouldered boy by the door had a sneezing fit from all the 'r's, it was quite a show.

Then it was over, the first day at *realskole*. We put our new books in our new rucksacks and slouched out. Seb and Ola were waiting by the drinking fountain. They were in the same class as Nina and Guri.

As we stood there making fun of the teachers, a gang came towards us, a shifty-looking lot we didn't know.

Ola began to twitch inside his plaster.

'Now they're goin' to i-i-initiate us,' he stuttered. 'S-s-stick our h-h-heads in the p-p-pisser!'

'They're not *gymnas* kids,' Seb whispered.

They stopped in front of us, seemed pretty full of themselves, tie, chewing gum and cigarette packet in shirt pocket.

'You been feelin' girls, have you?' one said, pointing to Ola.

Ola went bright red and his fringe stiffened.

'Or overdone the wanking?' another asked with a leer.

We said nothing. Those still remaining in the playground came closer.

'What do you do when you have to shit, shortie? Your mummy have to wipe your arse, does she?'

Gunnar dropped his rucksack. This was something we could joke about, but no one else. He placed his rucksack calmly on the ground, stood three centimetres from the bastard, stared into the whites of his eyes and said, 'Say that again.'

The boy fidgeted, was suddenly less sure of himself, the knot of his tie quivered against his neck.

'Say that again,' Gunnar said.

His jaw locked.

'Say that again,' Gunnar said for the third time, went two centimetres closer and the boy had already cracked. He retreated, tried a Parthian shot but it plopped to the ground like a tired spitball. Gunnar eyed them until they were out of sight.

'Pricks,' he said between clenched teeth.

I laughed inside, a big sinister laugh, and at this moment I loved Gunnar, felt like hugging him.

We ran out of the playground and as we reached the steps a small boy brushed past us, to all appearances sidling along the fence, pale, thin, wearing wide grey trousers and an oversized anorak with a zip, even though it was very hot. He walked with his head bent, then shot up the street, as if afraid of someone. He was in the same class as Gunnar and I. I had noticed someone grinning when he had said his name.

I couldn't remember what his name was.
His name was Fred Hansen.

We ambled down to Filipstad, stood on the bridge over Strandpromenaden watching the cars thundering past below.

'When do you think we'll be i-i-initiated?' Ola asked.

'Don't know,' Gunnar said. 'Perhaps they'll wait until winter.'

'I'd rather my head was shoved in the snow than dipped in piss,' Seb muttered.

'Don't think I'll ever figure out German,' Gunnar sighed, sending a gobbet of spit over the railing.

'Dad says it would be better if we were learnin' Spanish,' Seb said.

'Spanish?'

'Lots more people speak Spanish than German. All seamen do. And there's South America.'

Ola sat down on his rucksack.

'How… how d'you think I'll get on with d-d-drummin' now? D'you think I'll be able to play the d-d-drums again?'

'Course,' Seb said. 'Why wouldn't you be able to?'

'Wondered if my arms would be too w-w-weak.'

'Charlie Watts broke his arm ice skatin',' Gunnar interposed.

'Did Charlie Watts break his arm?!' Ola whispered, standing up with difficulty.

Gunnar nodded.

'Ice skatin'?' Seb asked.

'Yeah, fell flat on his face. Twisted his arm as he fell.'

Gunnar was flushed, tired.

'They don't have ice skatin' in England, do they?'

Gunnar looked to me, he was snookered.

'Yes, they do,' I said. 'London has a great ice hockey team.'

'And he was ok-k-kay?'

'Sounds like it, doesn't it,' Gunnar crowed.

'But he only b-b-broke one arm!'

Gunnar was on sinking ground again, sent me a look, but found his way out alone.

'Better to break both arms,' he said quickly, his face hot and red. 'Then it's easier to keep the rhythm afterwards!'

That quietened Ola down. And then we didn't say much for a while. The sun crept back behind a cloud, the fjord darkened, a cigarette did the rounds, a lukewarm Kent Seb had snaffled from his mother.

'This year I'll do home work,' he said. 'Dead cert.'

'Same here,' Gunnar said.

'Same here,' I said.

'Have to be off,' Ola said, his face pinched, legs wobbly.

'What about goin' to the Matthiessen buildin'?' Seb suggested.

'Have to go,' Ola repeated, skipping from one foot to the other.

We all watched him.

'Need a piss,' Ola said.

'Can't you just...?' Gunnar started to say, then stopped.

We looked at each other.

'Let's go,' Gunnar said.

And so we sauntered off towards the centre with the sun on our backs, dragging our rucksacks behind us.

Gymnastics was indoors next day because the rain was pouring down. We were sitting in the sweaty changing room. Skinke peered down at us, flexing his abdominal muscles. All of a sudden he roared in an uncommonly high voice:

'Remember! You can *fail* gymnastics! Do you hear? You can *fail* gymnastics.'

In Indian file we ran into the gymnasium. Skinke directed us into a variety of formations and when he had us where he wanted us, he thundered in his reedy voice:

'And let's get one thing straight. Warm-ups! Warm-ups are the basis of all great performances! Warm-ups are the reverse side of the gold medal!'

He came to an abrupt halt, put a hand to his head, his magnified eyes behind his glasses roaming like planets off orbit. We exchanged looks and some boys put a finger to their temples and stuck out their tongues.

'Now let's run!' he shouted, and we ran, round and round, with Skinke in the middle, as if we were a wheel and he an unlubricated hub.

At last he stopped us, ordered us to the wall-bars where we dangled for a few minutes. Then he pulled the biggest vaulting horse onto the floor, positioned the mat and springboard, pointed to us and said:

'Now let's try a somersault, shall we!'

A groan ran through the acrobats. Skinke came towards us, removed his glasses and flexed his thighs.

'I'll show you first! Watch!'

His feet stormed down, smashed onto the springboard, he swung over the horse in an elegant arc and landed softly on the mat. Then he turned just as quickly and beamed at us:

'That's how to do it, boys! Now it's your turn.'

There was a sort of line. Everyone wanted to be at the back, the bell would ring soon. And in an instant I found myself at the front. I breathed in and ran as fast as I could. I completely forgot where I was, it was like running through a sweat-filled dream, I landed on the springboard with an enormous bang, launched myself at the brown beast, swung myself upwards and pushed off with everything I had, I shot out into space like an astronaut, and straight afterwards, or at the same time, there I was, standing like a fence post on the mat with Skinke shouting in my ear:

'Good! Good lad! What's your name?'

'Kim,' I whispered.

'Good! That was good, Kim.'

Now it was Gunnar's turn. He ran in great bounds across the floor, swung himself over the horse, but failed to get enough air under his legs. He dragged Skinke down with him in the fall. They both lay on the mat, gasping for breath.

'You have to work on height!' Skinke shouted. 'On height! Otherwise it was fine.'

Then they came one by one, all the boys I have forgotten, who have forgotten me: Frode, round-shouldered and fat, landed astride the horse with a hideous scream. Ottar bounded over the horse but seemed to capitulate in mid-flight and performed a belly-landing. Rune, who rolled his 'r's because he came from Ris, managed to land on his back on the horse and slide down onto the floor. But then there was a pause. No one moved. It was Fred Hansen's turn.

'Come on!' Skinke shouted.

Fred Hansen did not come on. He stood down the other end, a wan matchstick in huge shorts. Everything he wore was huge, he must have had a huge brother from whom he inherited all his clothes. Now he was at the front of the queue and luminescent.

'Get a move on!' Skinke yelled.

Fred Hansen stood with his hands down by his side, hollow-backed and a little knock-kneed, his bony legs banging against each other.

'He won't make it,' Gunnar whispered. 'He's scared out of his wits.'

Light thunder on the floor. Fred Hansen was on his way, stiff-legged, his elbows at right angles.

'Good! That's good!' Skinke encouraged.

Fred Hansen dived towards the horse, pushed himself off, looking like an emaciated gull over a shoal of herrings as for a second he hung gangly-limbed in space, then landed on his back with a bang, off the mat.

The silence came just as abruptly. Fred Hansen lay without stirring, his eyes glued shut. He was smaller than ever, and whiter, he seemed ethereal where he lay, like a fallen angel in shorts much too big for him. Skinke knelt beside him, fumbling around, searching for a pulse, he found nothing, looked up at us standing round them in a circle, heads craned.

'What's his name?' Skinke whispered.

'Fred,' someone said.

Skinke pressed the palms of his hands down on Fred's heart and opened his eyelids, but Fred was just staring into space, white-eyed and vacant.

'Fred,' Skinke essayed. 'Fred, can you hear me?'

Not a sound.

'He's dead,' a voice mumbled.

Then Skinke began to scream, he screamed as he shook the lifeless body.

'Fred! Fred! Fred!'

It didn't help. Skinke ploughed a path through us to go for a doctor.

Then Fred smiled, his lips curled on his thin, pale face and he stood up, this was how it must have been when Jesus awoke on the third day, and he crossed the floor as though weightless. Skinke had stopped in the doorway and, scared out of his wits, was staring at Fred as he approached with long, rolling strides. At that moment the bell rang, it resounded through the gym and the atmosphere was pretty eerie and solemn.

In the changing rooms Fred Hansen threw up and was driven home in a taxi, suffering from concussion. He was absent for ten days, and on his return was even smaller than before, his clothes a tent erected around him, and he said nothing, just sat by the wall looking nowhere in particular, faraway Fred Hansen.

Ola and Seb were waiting by the fountain. It was the lunch break and the rain had eased. Ola's arms were covered in names and greetings and drawings, all the girls in the classes had etched something, too. Obviously breaking your arms wasn't the worst thing that could happen after all. Ola had perked up, was excused written work and never tested in class. In fact he was dreading having to go to casualty and have the plaster taken off in a month's time.

'Have you had gym?' he called as we came closer.

'Yup.'

We told him about Fred Hansen. Could easily have broken his neck. Just a fluke he survived.

'The gym teacher's n-n-nuts,' Ola said. 'Thought I'd be let off, I did. Then I had to do seventy knee bends!'

'Have we got enough money for a cake?' Seb wondered.

We ransacked our pockets. Lean pickings every time. It was always me who had the least dough. All I had was twenty-five øre from the deposit on a bottle I had taken back the day before. Gunnar earned money working at the grocery shop. Seb was always sent money by his father. Ola and I were the worst off. But now his pocket money had been doubled after breaking his arms, and he was not expecting his wage to go down once he had recovered. At least *he* wouldn't have to empty a bloody dustbin again. And I was given ten kroner a week, which was enough for a copy of *Poprevyen* and a cinema ticket.

I put the twenty-five øre in the pot. Seb counted up.

'A cake and a Coke it is. And a toffee for Kim,' he grinned.

Behind us something was happening, by the gate to Skovveien. There was shouting and people were flocking around a big crowd.

'Punch-up!' Gunnar said.

We charged down there. It wasn't a punch-up. A few *gymnas* students were holding a huge American flag in the air, and they had another one too, yellow with red stripes. They were shouting: 'Bomb Hanoi! Bomb Hanoi!'

'Hanoi's the capital of north Vietnam,' Gunnar whispered. 'My brother said America has landed 200,000 soldiers in Vietnam.'

The shouts became louder and louder, people were stamping and clapping. I thought about napalm, about napalm burning under water. I thought about the photograph in the summer. I thought about the man with the axe.

'Down with communism! Down with communism! Kill the communists!'

There was a smell of blood in the air. They meant what they said. They wanted to kill. The smell was of blood, blood and aftershave.

'We're off,' Seb said. 'The bell will go any minute.'

We edged past the crowd and raced down Skovveien to the bakery. But it was nigh on impossible to make any progress. Everyone came running towards us to see what was going on by the gate. We had to find a path through, fight our way, almost fighting with those who wanted us to turn round.

It didn't help to have a bank book with 400 kroner when I wasn't allowed to take it out until I came of age. After three tough evenings I took the plunge, got hold of a large cardboard box from Jacobsen Kolonial, strapped it onto the luggage carrier and cycled down to the flower shop in Drammensveien close by the Russian embassy.

Did they need a delivery boy?

'Might do,' twittered the owner, a thin elderly lady in a flowery dress.

That was how I became a delivery boy, cycling round the town with a box full of bundles, a krone for every one I delivered. I earned about twenty kroner a week and fru Eng made tea for me and fed me Marie biscuits. I said nothing about this to the others. I just said that

I had started doing my homework before dinner. What was more, I lied, the caretaker was ill, he was wheezing away in a respirator at Rikshospitalet, so I had to wash the steps and sweep the pavement. Because I did not want Gunnar, Seb or Ola to see me pedalling round the streets with a cardboard box full of flowers. No fear.

So I raced home after school, wheeled out the bouquet express and delivered roses, carnations and tulips to all of Oslo. And it was a pretty good job, for everyone was happy to see me come and I was even given tips sometimes. A woman wearing just a nightdress in the middle of the day and stinking of smoke and beer gave me five kroner and asked me if I wanted to come in and have a fizzy drink.

But I didn't.

Regretted saying that afterwards.

One Friday in the lunch break, with driving rain and the wind from the north, Seb and Ola came bounding over to the shed where Gunnar and I were mugging up on geography. Something seemed to be exciting them, both were giving me sly looks, and then Ola said:

'Nina's got your name on h-h-her hand.'

What was that Ola said?

'What did you say?' I said in a thick voice.

'Nina's g-g-got your name written on h-h-her hand!' Ola repeated, bouncing up and down.

'On her hand?'

'On her hand, and you know what that means!' Seb grinned. He pointed to the back of his hand. 'There. With a big red pen!'

'Really,' I said, trying to read my geography book, but the letters wouldn't stay still, I couldn't have located Africa on the map if I had been asked.

I took the short cut home that day, flung down my rucksack and raced over to the flower shop. There I was given tea and Marie biscuits, and the tea tasted different from the tea at home, smelt different too, of foreign countries and adventure, a thousand and one nights and China. Fru Eng dipped the dry biscuit into the sweet tea and quietly smacked her lips. Afterwards she smoked a long cigarette, and she used a holder with a shiny black mouthpiece.

'I don't think there's anything for you to do today,' she said.

I counted the slips of paper I had collected and handed them over. There were twenty-eight in all, not a bad week all things considered.

She took three ten-krone notes from a pocket in her skirt, two kroner too many.

'Since you're so fast and so nice,' she said, patting me on the head. I looked at the notes. This was big money. You could buy a lot with it.

Fru Eng started tidying up the newspapers and the stalks. I didn't move. My clothes were dripping wet. Fru Eng gave the potted plants a good watering and snipped off any brown leaves. It was steaming like a jungle in the cramped back room.

'Are you still here?' she said, with her back to me.

I was thinking about Nina, about the flower Nina had given me that time.

'What sort of flower is a poppy?' I asked.

'It's a rare flower in Norway,' fru Eng said, turning to me. 'And dangerous. Many poppies are poisonous.' She sent me a strange smile. 'Poisonous and beautiful.'

'I think I'll ask her out to the cinema.' It tumbled out of me.

'You do that,' fru Eng said, going back into the jungle.

The following morning I got up at the crack of dawn, hadn't slept much in the night and was wide awake and tired. At first I wondered whether I should stay at home, feign a heavy cold and stick my forehead under the lampshade. Nope. The others would kill themselves laughing. It was now or never. I crept out into the corridor and found the *Aftenposten*, skimmed through the cinema ads. There were a lot I would have liked to see. *The Dolls* with Gina Lollobrigida, *Loving Couples* with Ann-Margret. Or *The Knack*. It was no good. I would be stopped before I took my hand out of my pocket. The hand. My stomach tied itself in knots like an abandoned gym bag. Perhaps Seb and Ola had gone bog-eyed. Perhaps it was just a note to remind herself to buy something. Or the name of a band. Kinks. Buggered if I was going to fall for that. Would have to see it with my own eyes first. See my name on her hand. But what if she had washed it off? She must have washed her hands! I continued going through the cinema ads. *Donald Duck in the Wild West.* I was out of my nappies. *Mary Poppins* at the Colosseum. I wasn't completely brainless. What was on in Frogner? *Zorba the Greek.* Zorba, I said in a resonant voice, almost tickling myself inside. For adults, but the doorman in Frogner was quite short-sighted. If I combed my hair and stood on tiptoes. Zorba. It sounded good.

'You'll be late!' Mum said from behind me. 'It's gone half past seven!'

But I made it on time. We had Norwegian in the first lesson. Kerr's Pink was as frisky as a colt, read from *Nordlands Trompet* and talked about its author, Petter Dass, while we lay snoring on our desks.

I skulked around the playground on my own in the break. I didn't see Nina. I was beginning to feel relieved. She might have been ill, off school. But there she was in the last break, by the drinking fountain. I strolled over, my insides hollow and my shoes weighing several hundred kilos. I bent down over the jet of water and squinted up at her with my left eye. And I saw her stealing a glance at me, and I suppose she saw me stealing a glance at her, too. I got water all over my face. My name was on her hand. In red letters.

The last lesson dragged, worse than ever before. It was religion with Steiner, St. for short, and he spent three quarters of an hour explaining why Jesus was so angry with the bush that didn't bear fruit, even though it was the middle of winter. At the end he wanted us to sing those insane songs whose texts we never understood. *Jesus, Your Sweet Fellowship To Taste.* But the bell rang and I charged down the stairs, reckless and rich.

I saw Nina in Colbjørnsgate. She was walking home, lived in Tidemandsgate. I followed her for five blocks, did not play so tough this time, was about to give up and escape into a gateway. But she turned round suddenly as if she knew I was there and stood stock still, waiting.

'Hello,' she said when I caught her up and walked alongside her.

I glanced down at her hand. It was in her pocket. After all, I might have misread. The best route was straight down Løvenskioldsgate, but my legs had different ideas. They were following her, past the fountain, soon we would be where she lived.

'Don't you live in Skillebekk?' Nina asked.

'Ye-es.'

She looked at me and smiled.

'Where are you going now then?'

Caught in the act. Exposed and flattened.

'To my uncle's,' I said quickly. 'In Marienlyst.'

Tidemandsgate. Tide and time wait for no man. We stopped at the corner.

'Bloody cold,' I said.

'I like winter better than autumn,' Nina said.

'Have you got the Saint in religion, too?'

'Yes.'

'Would you like to come with me to the cinema this evening?'

'Yes.'

We arranged to meet by the fountain at half past six. My legs were numb. I was about to turn and troll home when Nina stopped me and became quite serious. She said, 'Didn't your uncle live in Marienlyst?'

'Yes, he did,' I said, beginning to walk in the right direction, the vertebrae in my back red hot.

Nina laughed and beckoned to me with the hand she had kept in her pocket, and the red letters shone, blinded me into submission.

Two old men dancing together on the beach! That was pretty mad. Nina walked beside me without saying a word, it was dark after the seven o'clock performance, wet tarmac shimmered beneath the streetlamps. I had another Japp bar in my pocket, but she didn't want it, it was the fourth. Phew, I was so relieved we had been let in, no problems, didn't even have to lie!

Then we were back at the fountain. The water was shooting into the air behind us, a shining column that kept falling but still remained upright. We sat on the edge, quite close together, staring into space.

'I feel sorry for him,' Nina said in serious mood.

'Sorry? Who for?'

'For the old man.'

'Why?'

'He was the one who was unhappiest, wasn't he!'

Zorba, I heard the voice say inside me. As if we had been on a long beach and the sea had come crashing in towards us and there was music everywhere, full blast, and we were dancing, dancing naked! Jesus, my mind was on wings. Suddenly I thought of Henny and went over all giddy. Henny would dance like that, that was a dead cert!

Nina's hand was close to me. I swallowed and said, 'Feel like an apple?'

'Apple?'

'Yeah.'

'Have you got apples with you as well?'

'No, but I can get one from Tobiassen's garden.'

'Tobiassen?'

I was already on my feet.

'On the corner there,' I said, pointing with my thumb.

'Now?'

'Won't take long.'

I sprinted to Farmers' Hill. No one around, so I climbed over the fence and crawled towards the trees. There was light in two windows of the large wooden house. I heard the splashing of the fountain and saw Nina's shadow sitting on the edge.

The apples were so damned high up this year. I couldn't even reach the lowest. I had to climb. I scrambled up the trunk, grabbed a thick branch and pulled myself up. I wanted to go even higher, the best were at the top, of course. I twisted my way through the foliage, searching for the best-looking apple, a big green one which I polished on my jacket and stuffed in my pocket.

Then I heard voices. I sat perfectly still. Tobiassen was a nasty customer. I had heard on the street he kept an air gun handy. But the voices were not coming from the house, they were coming from the fence. Someone was sneaking through the grass. On the pavement someone was standing guard with crossed arms, shifting from one foot to the other.

'G-g-get a move on,' I heard Ola whisper.

'Be quiet,' Gunnar mumbled from the grass.

Seb crept up beside him, carrying a big bag. I didn't think, I just acted. I chucked an apple in the direction of the house. It landed on some branches.

All went quiet on the ground.

'Did you hear that?' Gunnar muttered.

They were crouched down, not stirring from the spot.

I threw another apple, closer this time.

'There it is again!'

'P'raps it's a vole,' Seb said. 'Or a hedgehog.'

They set off again. Then I cupped my hands around my mouth and shouted:

'No apples for thieves! No apples for thieves!'

The grass came alive. They jumped up, screamed at each other, leapt over the fence and ran down Gyldenløvesgate.

I waited for a while, then I carefully climbed down and ran over to Nina.

'You were a long time,' she said, clearly a bit annoyed.

'Had to get the best one,' I explained, giving her the big, green apple.

She sank her teeth into it with a crunch and juice trickled down her chin. Breathing heavily, with the apple held in both hands, she made smacking noises and sucked greedily at the apple. And when we kissed, the taste was of apple, the smell was of apple, everywhere, and the water in the fountain fell and fell.

Ola appeared at school without a plaster cast. His arms were limp and thin and he didn't quite know what to do with them. They dangled down like two bits of string from his shoulders. He looked quite disconcerted. But he reckoned he would be able to get out of writing for another couple of weeks, he could barely raise a pencil and it was obvious he shouldn't over-exert himself.

'You'll have to do finger gymnastics,' Gunnar explained, displaying his fist. 'Like this. That's what Charlie Watts did, you know.'

Ola tried to clench his fist, but it was slow work, he was already worn out after trying his thumb.

'It'll take t-t-time,' he groaned. 'Wait until C-C-Christmas. Then we'll start practisin'!'

The bell rang and we all went in separate directions. Outside the classroom Gunnar stopped me.

'What are you up to at the moment?' he asked.

'Up to? Nothin'.'

'We hardly ever see you!'

'Homework,' I said.

Gunnar gave me a searching look.

'Homework! Don't give me that shit. You didn't even bloody know where Africa was on the map!'

'Bad luck that was.'

'And you weren't at the final trainin' session, either.'

'Forgot,' I said.

'There's not gonna be a Denmark trip this autumn. It'll be in the spring instead.'

'That's alright,' I said.

Then Hammer, the German teacher, came and the minutes crawled by like injured ants. Fred Hansen stood by the board being tested on vocabulary. You could hardly see him inside his large jacket and his haircut was a basin job. The girls giggled and Hammer barked.

'*Head*,' she shouted. 'What's *head* in German?'

Fred Hansen was mute, motionless, behind his lips I imagined him clenching his teeth.

Hammer thrust out her arms in despair and pointed at Fred's lop-sided haircut.

'*Dummkopf*!' she said, pushing him towards his desk.

Then Goose was called to the dais and he knew the rules off by heart and Fred Hansen became even smaller and more cowed in the light of Goose's polished halo.

In the lunch break we went to the shed again. Ola had a bit of zip back in his arms, but the important thing was not to let the teachers see. Fred Hansen slunk along the wire fence with a huge packed lunch in his hands, perhaps another hand-me-down from his brother.

'Everyone takes the piss out of him,' Gunnar said quietly. 'The teachers, too. It makes me bloody sick!'

We glanced at him, he was standing alone, glued to the fence, it was like a picture of a concentration camp in our history book.

'I'd like to see his brother,' I said. 'He must be pretty big.'

'We're off to buy cakes,' Seb said. 'Anyone got any money?'

I pulled a tenner from my pocket and put it in the pot. They looked at me in astonishment.

'You g-g-gettin' *money* from Nina or what?' Ola asked, and they all burst into fits of laughter. Nina, who was standing by the drinking fountain, looked across at us and blood suffused my face as if my skin were blotting paper.

'Let's go before the bell rings!' I said and so we headed for the exit, and Gunnar, Seb and Ola were grinning so much bubbles of froth were forming at the corners of their mouths, and Nina was laughing, too. I was perhaps the only person in the entire playground who was not laughing, me and Fred Hansen.

One Sunday we went to Nesodden to pick apples. I was standing on the deck of the ferry in my windcheater and scarf, even though the sun was shining and it hadn't been so warm for ages, but Mum always said this time of year was tricky, you had to take care and wrap up well. There were still a few yachts on the fjord, dazzling white canvas against black water.

On our way up to the House Dad stopped to wipe the sweat from his brow.

'Indian summer,' he groaned gently.

'What's that?' I asked.

'It's when you get a hot spell in the autumn. As though summer has returned.'

I ran down to the little orchard. The four trees were heaving with apples, the branches were weighed down. The smell hit me like a soft wall, fruit, earth, tree, I ran through it, jumped up and grabbed an apple. And as I sank my teeth in it, Nina was there, in the juicy, succulent flesh, I could hear her breathing.

Then Mum and Dad came with two rakes so that we could reach the top branches. Climbing was forbidden. We put the apples in boxes and carried them to the House. A large table stood in the centre of the dark sitting room. Mum covered it with a tablecloth and clamped it in place with four clips. Then we emptied the apples onto the table and took the empty boxes to refill them. After stripping two trees we ate currant buns and drank tea from a thermos flask, and I spat out all the candied lemon peel, for it was one of the things I hated most, candied peel and the skin on milk and the hard bits in stewed apples. Dad walked around blithely humming to himself, he had even brought his pipe along. Mum was happy too, straightening my scarf, for it wasn't as warm as we thought, Mum always said.

And then we stripped the last trees. On the table in the sitting room there was a mountain of apples. We filled the sacks and string bags we had with us.

'We can get the rest later,' Dad said. 'When we have to shut up for winter.'

We hurried down to the quay. The sun hung over Kolsås, to the west of Oslo, cold and spent. I stood on the deck going back, too. My hands smelt of apples.

One evening I was sent to Uncle Hubert's with a flower box full of apples. He lived on the fourth floor and could see down onto the NRK studio. Cycling through the dark, wet streets I wondered if Henny would be there and my legs went strangely heavy and the pedals began to squeak.

We carried the box into the kitchen and emptied all the apples into the dirty-laundry basket. Uncle Hubert looked exhausted, his right arm was twitching. Henny definitely wasn't there, that was for certain. Afterwards I sat on the sofa and drank Nesquik while Hubert paced to and fro across the floor, unable to find peace. It was always a mess in Hubert's place, clothes, plates, drawings of palaces and women and doctors were strewn everywhere. That was how I liked it, but Hubert's continuous perambulations were making me a bit dizzy. In the summer he had been different, now he was how he had been before, before Henny.

'How's school?' he chatted.

'Fine,' I said.

He didn't say any more. I walked over to the window and peered down at the white broadcasting building, wondering whether it was Erik Bye I could see in one of the windows.

Hubert had sat down in my seat and finished the Nesquik.

'Can't you two come and visit us?' I asked straight out.

Confused, his head rotating, he looked at me.

'Who?'

'You and Henny.'

His eyes were grey and overcast.

'Maybe,' he said, evincing a crumpled smile.

Something was amiss, but I didn't dare ask what. I carried the empty flower box down to my bike and put it on the luggage carrier. I freewheeled down Kirkeveien and the wind inflated my yellow raincoat like a balloon. In Tidemandsgate I stopped and rang my cycle bell. After a pause a door banged and Nina came running along the narrow gravel path.

Mum was right. It was a tricky time of the year. October came and I seemed to go backwards, lying awake at night listening to Jensenius's autumnal song and to the rain that hung heavy in the air and the trains racing against the wind and thundering along Frogner Bay. I delivered flowers to the whole town and fru Eng was in the back-room making wreaths, for autumn was the time when wreaths were in demand. And then there was Nina. Nina was here, there and on my brain. I was exhausted. We mooched the streets every night chewing gum, but for all that I didn't forget the taste of apples, and on one such evening as we battled up Farmers' Hill, heads bowed, we met Guri. She was with a kid from the second year at Maja *real-skole*, and he was three heads taller than me, had a mod haircut and chains round his wrist. Guri's face was stiff with make-up and lipstick, and it soon emerged that they were going to a rave-up in Thomas Heftyesgate. They asked if we wanted to join them and it would have been difficult to say no, so we tagged along. My stomach churned and Nina's hand held mine in a vice-like grip.

'Bjørnstjerne Bjørnson used to live here,' the Maja mod said. 'His great-granddaughter lives in the attic and hasn't a clue where she is.'

It was a large wooden house, dark brown, inside a rather untidy garden. Nina was mute, the Maja mod spat out his fag end and patted Guri's bum, and so we traipsed after them through the gate and down a steep flight of stairs into the cellar. At length we found ourselves in a cold, dark room, but we could see people sitting and lying around. Mattresses were on the floor and there was a smell of booze and smoke and something quite different, wow, I could taste lifeblood in my mouth.

Guri and the mod were gone. I stood there with Nina up against me. Someone lit a match and in the brief flash we saw what some were doing. We stayed where we were – what should we do? – and then slumped down onto the mattress near us, our coats wet and slippery, underneath we were steaming hot, we kissed, Nina opened her mouth and squirmed, our hands criss-crossed each other's body like snowploughs where we lay, Nina's hand firm and clammy, doing things to me, but all of a sudden pandemonium broke loose and everyone stampeded through the darkness. We struggled to our feet and that was when I could feel what had happened to me and I was glad it was pitch black. Someone shouted: 'They're comin'. They're comin'.' I grabbed Nina's hand, dragged her after me, finally located the door and we hauled ourselves up the steps. Flashing blue lights, cops, they had already collared a few people, Bjørnson's great-granddaughter was screaming and shrieking and beating a stick against the window frame. We ran in the opposite direction, jumped over a fence and went into a garden with a denuded apple tree that creaked eerily. We ran faster and sought refuge in the American church. Nina leaned against me and cried and said that Guri hadn't been the same of late, since she had been with the mod, and that she would never go to a place like that again, that she had never been so frightened, and did I think it had been good.

'Yes,' I said, a bit confused, staring at the tarmac. 'Yeah.'

'Could you have lunch with us on Sunday?'

'Yeah,' I said, even more confused, and so it was agreed. It was only when I got home that I realised that the cup final between Frigg and Skeid was on Sunday. Bloody hell! Shit. Shit. Shit!

Nina's father was Danish. He was small and tubby and had lots of beard, so his mouth was non-existent, but it did exist because from somewhere or other strange sounds emerged, fleeting, elongated sounds. Of course they ate early on Sundays, at two, and so I sat in their large, chilly living room, incapable of forcing down so much as a potato because in Ullevål stadium the first half was over and Gunnar, Seb and Ola were screaming from the corner flag, and, there was I, sitting like a baggy-trousered Sunday school pupil, unable to understand a word of what the father said, but I laughed when the others laughed, stained my shirt and kept my ears pricked for a nearby radio or the Ullevål roar reaching Tidemandsgate.

But it was quite formal, too, for I had never eaten lunch at a girl's house before and I had almost forgotten how to manipulate a knife and fork. Fortunately, the mother's laughter was of the soothing variety that rubbed sun cream into red faces. Then, after a while, the atmosphere became quite congenial and the father had the odd dram, so, well, if only it hadn't been cup final day, I had pins and needles all over my body.

Afterwards we sat in Nina's room, the walls were covered with pictures, and we began to argue about bands, she liked The Rolling Stones and The Yardbirds best, gulp, she was well up on music, had an older cousin in Copenhagen apparently who played electric guitar and lived in a bedsit. I was quite tactful and said that they were alright, in their way, but The Beatles were The Beatles, there was no one better, no one even close. Nina had the last word: The Beatles were the best at writing songs, but not so hot at playing.

I was developing an antipathy to this cousin in Copenhagen, he must have been putting himself about and shouting his mouth off. But we had talked so much about Paul McCartney's bass playing that I couldn't be bothered to pick up the threads. Instead I lay on the floor with my eyes closed imagining the green sward in Ullevål, breathing in the smell of camphor, watching Per Pettersen dribble through the centre and lob Kaspar, who stood moon-gazing like a ninny.

Then Nina gave me a deadly serious look and said, 'Can you keep a secret, Kim?'

'Course I can.'

'Promise not to tell anyone?'

'Cross my heart and hope to die.'

'Guri's pregnant.'

I sat up with a start.

'Bloody hell. With the mod from Maja?'

'Yes.'

'What's she gonna do?'

'She hasn't told her parents yet. I'm seeing her this evening.'

'Far out,' I said, lying back on the floor. 'Far out!'

Nina appeared pensive, concerned, seeming to change as she sat there, adding years to her age. I swallowed and said, 'What does the f… father say?'

'Nothing! He's a shit!'

I had seen that at once. A glib bastard. A couple of days after we went to the party, everyone at school was given a letter warning parents about what was going on at the place. Mum eyeballed me and said that I didn't know anything about that sort of thing, did I? Of course not, I answered, and stole into my room with my insides on fire, reflecting that narrow escapes don't come much narrower.

Now the match was long over. I was the last person in the world to know the result. Nina put on a record, The Swinging Blue Jeans didn't quite fit the atmosphere. She placed a hand on my stomach.

'What are you thinking about?' she asked.

'Who won the cup final,' I let slip, and the hand was retracted.

'Really,' she said, looking away. 'It's that important, is it.'

'Not exactly,' I started to reassure her, '… but it would've been nice to know, I mean, erm, who won.'

'Boys only think about one thing,' she sniffed, her mouth a thin line.

There was nothing to say and the silence was becoming quite oppressive. Nina sat like a locked door and I couldn't find the key.

'I'll have to go now,' she said abruptly, rising to her feet. 'I have to go and see Guri.'

I had forgotten to take the flower box off the carrier, it towered up and looked ridiculous. But she didn't want to sit there anyway. The hug I received was quite cold. I pedalled down the bumpy street and it was strange to think that Guri was going to have a baby. But who had won the cup final?

I didn't get any further than Frognerveien. Three villains were standing on the corner and when they saw me they raced across the cobblestones and forced me onto the pavement. They clapped their big eyes on me and the bike.

Ola pointed to the box.

'Been givin' N-Nina rides in the box then?'

'Who won?' I shouted.

'Are you a flower boy now?' Seb grinned.

'Perhaps he's started up a removal business,' Gunnar said.

'Who won?' I shrieked.

Gunnar shoved his hands in his pockets and scuffed the tarmac with his boot.

'3–3 after extra time.'

'A draw!' I roared.

'Yep.'

How lucky I'd been. I'd had my cake and eaten it. Would I be joining them for the replay next Sunday? That went without saying!

At home I met Jensenius on the stairs. He was dragging himself up step by step, and each one creaked beneath his weight, sweat was pouring off his fat skull.

Wheezing like a bagpipe, he stopped when I arrived.

'Don't you sing any more, boy?' he asked.

'I practise,' I said.

'I haven't heard anything!'

'I practise in my head,' I explained.

'You've got to let it out, boy!' Jensenius thumped his chest raw.

And then he launched into an ear-splitting bellow, his face went crimson, the note soared and soared, plaster fell off the ceiling and all the doors were thrust wide open. But Jensenius sang until there was no longer a murmur and the whole stairwell reeked of beer and sweat and minced beef.

'You have to let it out,' he whispered afterwards. 'Mark my words!'

Dad said it was because The Beatles had reduced the English trade deficit that they were awarded MBEs. And Mum thought that 'Yesterday' was very pretty and Queen Elizabeth must have known what she was doing. We went into my room angry and confused and slammed the door behind us.

'There's somethin' not right here,' Ola mumbled. 'Don't l-l-like it when our parents like what we l-l-like.'

We gave the matter some thought and nodded. We agreed. Ola had put his finger on it. There was something fiendish going on.

'They don't mean it,' Seb said. 'They're just sayin' it. They never mean what they say. They just say it.'

We gave the matter some more thought and we agreed. That was how it worked. We had seen right through them. They couldn't pull the wool over our eyes.

First of all, the medals had to be presented. We stuck out our chests and pinned our awards on each other. Ringo got a silver medal in the Holmenkollen relay, which Gunnar's father had won in 1952 with Ready. Seb got the swimming proficiency badge, which I had swum home in Nesodden the year before. Gunnar got a gold medal for prize cows that Granddad had won in Toten two years running, just before the war. I ended up with a Red Cross badge that Seb's mother had received at the local group's annual meeting in 1961. We stood erect in a line, august medals gleaming and rattling, and then we proffered a hand, gave a deep bow and the English queen passed through the room like a spirit.

After the ceremony it was gig time. Gunnar, Seb and Ola had brought along all their records. In total, we had ten singles, four EPs and five LPs. We had to get weaving if we wanted to hear the whole repertoire. I had bought new batteries for the Philips.

We started with 'Love Me Do' and glued our ears to the speaker.

'How's the drummin'?' we asked Ola in the interval.

'Practisin' with pencils. Left hand is worse.'

'Asked for an electric guitar for Christmas,' Gunnar said. 'With a tremolo.'

We turned the record over. 'P.S. I Love You'. Dad groaned from the sitting room. That was more like it. We cranked up the volume.

In the middle of 'Do You Want To Know A Secret' there was a bang on the door. Mum stood there with Nina behind her.

'Hiya,' I said gruffly. Nina came in and Mum closed the door with less sound than Dragon saying Our Father.

She sat beside me on the floor. She looked around.

'Are you playing records?' Nina asked.

'No, we're playin' cards,' Seb grinned. Nina pouted at him, my stomach was leaden.

'We're celebratin' The Beatles bein' given MBEs,' I added quickly.

'Why are they the only ones to get them?' Nina said.

We blinked our baby blues.

'Who else should have got 'em, eh?'

'The Byrds,' Nina said, unperturbed.

'They're American!' Seb bellowed.

'The Rolling Stones then. Or The Yardbirds! Or Manfred Mann!' Nina wasn't giving in. This was a fight to the death.

'Only The B-B-Beatles have reduced the English trade d-d-deficit,' Ola squeezed out and the discussion was over.

We played the rest of the singles and I put on the EP with 'Long Tall Sally' to prove to Nina once and for all that The Beatles could play. Wow, what a guitar solo. Gunnar was wriggling all over the floor like an earthworm and Ola was drumming his fingers on everything within reach.

In the ensuing silence Seb had something he wanted to get off his chest.

'Why's Guri finishin' school?' he asked.

Nina squinted over at me. I looked out of the window. I had not blabbed.

'She's starting a new school,' Nina said.

'Doesn't she like our class?'

Nina turned the conversation to another incident.

'Do you boys know that Dragon tried to kill Lue?'

We jumped.

'My mother told me – she knows the school nurse.'

We were on tenterhooks. Dragon. Murder.

'Lue's got a bad heart, hasn't he. And that's why he needs the medicine he has to take several times a day. He keeps the pills in his jacket pocket, in the right hand pocket, because when his heart is shaky his left arm is almost completely lame.'

'Was that why he used to run into the corridor so often?' Gunnar whispered.

'Yes. Dragon put the medicine in the left hand pocket in one of the breaks.'

'How'd he do that?' Seb could only just articulate the words.

'Lue was found unconscious in the corridor, but they brought him round in the school surgery.'

'How did they find out it was Dragon?'

'He said so himself. He was boasting to everyone.'

'Will he go to p-p-prison now?' Ola stammered.

'He's being sent to Berg,' Nina said.

Things were going downhill for Dragon, Dragon without a face. Our insides froze, Ola putting on 'Help' wasn't much help.

'Would never've thought that Dragon had the intelligence,' Seb whispered.

I accompanied Nina home. We took tiny steps up Løvenskioldsgate. The pavement was steep and slippery.

'Is Guri going to leave the class?' I asked.

'Yes, she's going to have an abortion.'

We walked on a bit. A soaking wet leaf blew right in my face.

'That mod,' I mumbled. 'Isn't it illegal?'

'She won't say who the father is.'

We had reached the fountain. It was closed off now, with solid boards across the pool. We sat on the edge. It was cold to the backside. We didn't move. Nina seemed so strange, somehow distant, that I could hardly reach her.

'There's something I haven't told you,' she began.

Now it was coming. I tried to find somewhere to put my hands. They wouldn't keep still.

Nina's eyes were white in the dark.

'We're moving,' she said.

'Moving? Where to?'

'To Denmark.'

'To Denmark,' I repeated, without losing composure.

'Yes. Copenhagen. Dad has a job at the embassy.'

'When?'

'In three weeks.'

It was autumn. The fountain was boarded up. And my hands were so bloody cold. I put them up Nina's sweater.

'I might visit you in spring,' I said. 'You see, we're going to play football in Copenhagen.'

My hands were so warm and I had her hair all over me.

Things happened thick and fast. I was with Nina every evening, either drifting round the streets, I had never walked so much before, or sitting in her room and playing records and looking at the map of Denmark. It wasn't that far away. If you went through Sweden you would hardly get your feet wet. I knew a kid from Ruseløkka who had sneaked onto the ferry to Denmark, but they found him before they reached Dyna lighthouse and he was given the heave-ho in Horten. But I would go in spring. That was a cast-iron certainty. With number 2 on my back. Oslo's best defender. And after some reflection I wondered whether it was such a bad thing after all. Of course it was hard, but having a girl in Copenhagen wasn't such a bad thing. That was what I told myself as I walked home. I've got a girl in Copenhagen. It sounded pretty cool. A girlfriend in Copenhagen.

Gunnar, Seb and Ola were beginning to send me scowls, wondering whether I had completely gone off the rails. But we went to the cup final the following Sunday equipped with Frigg pennants and chestnuts to throw at the Skeid shites. But the game was another draw after extra time and Seb said that if it went on like that they would soon be playing in snowshoes. The next Sunday we turned up with pennants and chestnuts again, there was frost on the ground and the Ullevål pitch looked like a farmer's meadow, and it was obvious Skeid would win on a ground like that and with such an idiot of a referee, he disallowed a dream Frigg goal in the last minute, obstructing the goalkeeper, Kasper reckoned his toes had been trodden on, for Christ's sake. We shuffled home in dejected mood, looking at the sky and thinking about snow.

'How long till Nina moves?' Gunnar asked.

'Week.'

'You goin' to m-m-move, too?'

'Shut up.'

We squeezed onto the Sognsvann tram and had a bit of banter with some Torshov tossers who had seen the Frigg pennants under our jackets.

'Per Pettersen shoots like a dung beetle,' one freckled face said.

Ola stuck his head forward, his lips aquiver.

'Per Pettersen shoots like a p-p-puma. And K-K-Kasper's a wanker.'

'Piss off!'

'Piss off yourself! No one can play football on a p-p-pitch like that!'

'Conditions were the same for both teams,' Freckles snorted.

'Skeid are better at orient-t-teering! And someone must've g-g-greased the ref's p-p-palm!'

There was a bit of pushing and shoving, but we managed to get Ola off at Valkyrie plass intact and trudged aimlessly through the cold streets with frying smells wafting on the air.

I stopped off at Seb's to borrow an essay on Traffic Safety. It was quite mad. Seb was suggesting that all cars should drive backwards. Then they couldn't go so fast. But they would require bigger mirrors. He would have got an E from me, but after I had got rid of the worst howlers a C should be within my reach.

'Dad's comin' back at Christmas,' Seb said with eyes agleam.

He led me to the hall and stood rocking his thin frame back and forth.

'Give it you back tomorrow,' I said.

'No hurry. You...'

He didn't say any more. I paused and looked up at him.

'Yes?'

'Is it serious? Between you and Nina?'

I didn't answer and sprang down the steps.

'Just jokin'!' Seb shouted, hanging over the banister.

Then he came running after me and held me back. His eyes were suddenly so very sad.

'D'you know... did you know that Guri was havin'... a child?'

'Heard rumours,' I said.

'Everyone's talkin' about it. That's why she left the class.'

Seb's face was white.

'It's terrible for her,' he said and started walking slowly upstairs. 'By the way, I asked her out to the cinema once,' Seb said with his back to me.

Nina was due to leave on the second Sunday of November.

But on Saturday there was the premiere of *Help* and I queued for three hours at the Eldorado to get two tickets at the end of row fourteen. And so there we sat, Nina and I, the auditorium was a cauldron of excitement, I was wondering whether Gunnar, Seb and Ola had managed to buy tickets, but I hadn't seen them in the queue. I was all in, too much was going on at once. I wanted to be with them and I wanted to be with Nina, so there I sat, Nina's hand in my lap, a sticky bar of chocolate in my pocket and a bewildered brain in my head, amid a bedlam of screaming, arm-waving, perfume and boot stamping, sitting there, not taking in one iota of what was happening on the screen.

And then we were on our way home. We didn't say much, we didn't say anything. Last evening. It was freezing, the cold bit into our faces. We approached Tidemandsgate. The house was empty now, the removal men had already taken two big loads. And as we got closer, we squeezed hands harder and harder, until Nina said 'Ow' and pulled her arm away.

'That hurt,' she said.

'I didn't mean it.'

'I know!'

She poked me in the ribs and produced a big apple from her pocket, it gleamed and shone like a red moon. She sank her teeth in it and the aroma was released into the darkness. Then I took a bite, and we ate the apple, each from our own side, laughing and dribbling, right through to the pips, then we were mouth to mouth, the core fell to the ground, it was beautifully staged, and then we kissed for a long time, an apple kiss, it went on and on, eventually we let go, Nina's face was very wet, and I didn't know quite whether it was tears or apple or maybe just me.

'I'll write to you,' she said.

'Good.'

'Will you promise to write?'

I nodded, fidgeted and cleared my throat.

'Do you remember the flower?' I said.

Nina peered up.

'You gave it to me that time Holst was almost gobbled up by a snake.'

'Yes.'

I kicked a stone down the pavement. It hit a hub cap and made a terrible noise.

'Still got it,' I said.

We kissed again, then she tore herself away and hurried down the gravel path, and in the large empty house the windows shone like electric voids in the night.

As I ran home it began to snow.

Rubber Soul

Winter ’65/’66

Mum woke me up to tell me the weather forecast. Forty centimetres of fresh snow in Tryvann. The blind went up with a bang and winter streamed in through the window. I lay in bed with my senses alert, sensed and sensed nothing. Then I leapt out of bed to go to the telephone and call Gunnar, but Gunnar was out, skiing with Seb and Ola. His brother answered.

‘I think they were goin’ to Kobberhaugen. The Americans are comin’.’

‘Eh?’

‘The Americans are comin’!’

I understood zilch.

‘Nordmarka is their first stop,’ Stig said.

‘Kobberhaug cabin,’ I said.

‘Exactly.’

I shot down to the cellar and collected my Bonna skis. The poles were a bit on the short side now. Then I went up to Frognerseteren and set off into the forest, stabbed and clambered my way up, steamed downhill without blinking, took Slaktern standing up, Kandahar bindings squeaking, raced across Lake Blankvann without a thought of whether the ice would hold, it creaked and groaned beneath my weight, someone shouted at me from the shore, but it held, of course it held, and now there were just the last steep paths up to the cabin in Kobberhaug and there they were, covered in sweat, by the fire with blackcurrant toddies and cigarettes.

I joined them and they mustered me from top to toe.

‘Who’s this?’ Gunnar asked.

‘Might live here,’ Seb suggested.

‘Think it’s Ole Ellefsæter’s b-b-brother,’ Ola said.

‘Pack it in,’ I said.

'He speaks Norwegian,' Gunnar established. 'Wonder where I've seen 'im before.'

And so it went on for ages, but in the end they recognised me and Gunnar asked,'Where were you last night? We tried to get tickets for *Help*.'

'I was at *Help*,' I said under my breath.

They were on me at once, red-faced, yelling and carrying on. They made a terrible racket.

'Were you? You've already been to see *Help*!' Gunnar groaned.

'With Nina,' I said.

'Without us! Why the hell didn't you buy tickets for us, too, eh?'

'There were only two left,' I complained.

'Try that one on those that live in the sticks!'

The table went quiet for a moment. I felt hollow inside. This was on a par with high treason. I would be shot on Appelsinhaug ridgetop, burned on the spot and my ashes would be sprinkled over Lake Bjørnsjøen.

Seb said to the others:

'Last evening with his girl, so he can do what he likes. Right?'

Gunnar and Ola gave a reluctant nod, it went even quieter.

'What was it like then?!' Ola burst out. 'What w-w-was it like?'

'Dunno,' I mumbled.

'You don't know!' Gunnar was all over me. 'What d'you mean by that?'

'Don't remember a thing. Word of honour.'

They exchanged glances, and began to laugh. There were no limits to my humiliation. They fell about and their anoraks shook. I made up my mind to leave, but I was restrained by force.

'Don't remember a thing?' gasped Gunnar.

'Zero.'

'But then we'll bloody well go tonight. All of us!'

Too right! A warm flow of blood coursed through me. We piled our money onto the table, enough for tickets and a packet of twenty, and then we jumped on our skis and set new PBs to Lake Sognsvann even though Ola had to lean on his sticks, but we shoved him up slopes and downhill took care of itself, no problem there.

We got front row tickets at the Eldo, sat in line with our medals on our chests and full fringes. The screams from behind were like squalls against the back of our necks and there was a hail of sweet papers and pastilles from the gallery. We sat in the front seats and were no further from the screen than it would take to stand up and touch them.

Snow glinted in the streets as we emerged. We stood admiring the photos showing scenes from the film and were drained, tired and happy.

'One thing is definite,' Gunnar said. 'At least we're better skiers than The Beatles!'

'We'll have to get ourselves some of those t-t-trunks for the summer,' Ola said. 'With s-s-stripes!'

'Do you know what we could do in the summer?' Gunnar suggested. 'Go on a fishing trip in Nordmarka. With tents and all the gear.'

Then we headed home. Talking about all the things we were going to do. About The Snafus. About how famous we would be. About summer, even though winter had barely begun. About all the summers of our lives. We talked about when we would begin at the *gymnas* and when we would finish school for ever. We became effusive and beautiful birds flew out of our mouths. We had a sneak preview of the future and it looked damn good.

The snow lay for three days, then it melted away and all was bare and mild for a week. Then another batch arrived and the snow stuck. It piled up into banks, you had to walk round the whole block before you could find an opening, the mercury quivered on minus twenty, ice covered the fjord allowing us to skate to Nesodden and to jig cod by Dyna lighthouse. And the snow lay deep in the playground. Ola was sure it would happen now, but nothing happened, the *gymnas* students didn't stick our heads in the snow, they walked past us, we were air, nothing, nihil, we sighed with relief, our breath froze around our heads like bands of fog, but deep down we felt a bit cheated, just like with the fork jab. The bike had to be stored in the cellar, now I delivered flowers on foot, with an inclement weather supplement of fifty øre per packet, or I caught the tram, but there was always some fool who had parked on the lines, because you couldn't see them for all the snow, and there was a lot of bell-ringing and shouting and brouhaha, for those were the days when Oslo had real winters.

On just such a day I had delivered a packet of flowers to the plastic surgery clinic in Wergelandsveien, I left, sweaty and nauseous, couldn't stand the sight of all the mangled faces there, faces without noses and chins, without mouths and eyes and ears, it was like being in a field hospital in a Vietnamese jungle. I stood swaying in Wergelandsveien and pumping air into my system when I heard someone shout my name. I followed the sound and saw a figure standing outside Kunsternes Hus waving to me, it was Henny, Henny in a big coat with a hat down over her forehead. I trotted over to her. She was on her way to the National Gallery and asked if I fancied joining her, and I did, because there were no more flowers that day anyway. We strolled past Aars og Foss school and Henny chatted about pictures, about Munch, whether I had been to the Munch museum, I hadn't, I should go, we ought to view the Munch Room at least, now we were there. We wandered up to the first floor, past glistening black bodies, it reminded me of summer, and I dutifully followed her across the creaking floor, feeling weak at the knees. Then we arrived. Horses leapt off the wall. Girls stood on the bridge. Henny pointed:

'Can you see that green face?' she said. Now a face isn't green, is it. Nevertheless it seems to me that exactly that face *has* to be green.

She looked at me. Had I understood?

'Yes,' I said, going green in the face.

'Can you see the *angst*?' she asked.

'Yes,' I said, seeing the angst.

Then all of a sudden I *heard* a picture. It is true. I did hear it. I swivelled round and looked straight at an insane figure standing on a bridge holding her ears and screaming with all her might. In the background the countryside was burning and blood coursed across the sky. I heard it. It's true. I stood rooted to the spot in front of the picture, *Skrik* it said on the frame, my insides froze, the scream grated in my ears and she was not the only one to scream, the mountain ridges behind her did, too, and the sky and the water and the bridge on which she was standing, the whole world was one big scream, it had to be the little Vietnamese girl's mother. A huge yell was building up inside me, it rose like a pillar in my throat, I swallowed and restrained myself, I could not scream here, in a museum, that would not do, I turned away and ran over to Henny, chilled to the marrow.

'I fancy some cocoa,' she said on a sudden whim. 'Do you?'

We schlepped out again and found a narrow window table in the Ritz. Henny bought vanilla slices. We ate with small teaspoons and drank from dainty blue cups.

'Have you seen any paintings like that before?' she asked.

'I saw a painting this summer,' I told her, breathless. 'In front of Stortinget. About Vietnam.'

'What did you think of it?'

'I don't know. It was… it was ugly. Ugly and beautiful at the same time.'

Henny studied me over her cup, with serious eyes.

'That's what I think, too. That's the point. You can't paint a nice picture of something so awful, can you.'

'US bombers drop napalm,' I said in a low voice.

She nodded slowly.

Staring into the empty cup, I ruminated.

'There was an old man there who hacked the painting to pieces. Why did he do that?'

'Because he disagreed with it.'

I didn't understand.

'Disagreed with the picture?'

'Yes, he supported the Americans in Vietnam.'

'But isn't the napalm stuff true?'

'Yes, it is.'

'But how…?'

Henny interrupted me.

'Because he's a reactionary, a fascist. He would kill all the communists if he had his way.'

I scraped the plate clean and licked the teaspoon. The clock over the door showed that I was too late for lunch. And we had piles of homework and the deadline was approaching, and this evening there was a meeting at Gunnar's place where we would discuss the repertoire for The Snafus. But I wouldn't have gone, even if she had sat there for a week.

'I'm going to Paris the day after tomorrow,' she said suddenly. 'I'm going to an art school there.'

'For how long?'

'Two years. But I'll be back for the summer.'

That was why Hubert was so out of sorts when I took him the apples. And I suddenly felt very flat. I also had a girl abroad, to whom I had promised I would write and whom I would visit in the spring.

'It'll be great,' I murmured. 'Paris. Long way.'

She caught sight of the clock too and jumped up, almost knocking over the table.

'I have to be off,' she laughed. 'Had to be somewhere half an hour ago.'

I got a big, wet kiss on the cheek and she made for the door in her huge coat. I sat there dazed, heard someone laughing at another table, stared after her, but she was long gone. Only now did I realise that Christmas decorations had been put up in the streets. It was snowing.

Christmas Eve at home, that was how I had always experienced Christmas Eve, there were no other Christmases to my knowledge. It was us three plus Uncle Hubert, and then there was Mum's mother and Dad's father, because Mum's father was dead and so was Dad's mother, I just remember them hanging over a pram like large trees in which there were lots of birds and sounds, and occasionally a fir-cone fell on top of me. Now they had been dead for a long time, but the others were more than enough. Grandma was a small woman with long, red nails, thin blue hair and a green budgie in a cage. She could breathe with the most tragic sighs I had ever heard and she always held her knife and fork as if they were infected. Granddad was of a rougher hew, Grandma never held his hand after he broke three of her nails on Christmas Eve 1962. He was an old railwayman, laying sleepers at the age of eighteen, a sedentary job in the office when he was fifty, now he sat in the chair by the window in an old folks home in Alexander Kiellands plass flicking through the railway timetable. His ears twitched whenever he heard a train, and he didn't hear it until long afterwards because he was hard of hearing and a bit senile, but it must have been like a song to him, at some point, long after the sound and the train had passed, the song of rails, points, rhythm and journeys.

'That was the express,' he always said. 'It won't be long before they come to fetch me, too.'

It was when we opened the presents that things always went awry for Uncle Hubert. After removing all the paper he would wrap his present again. And he would do that twenty-one times, I counted, unwrapping and wrapping the present. Grandma would have to go into another room and Granddad would slap his thigh, guffaw and say out loud, 'Well, isn't that just like Hubert! Now he's forgotten to wrap the presents again!'

I received mostly soft packages, shirts, sweaters, new hiking trousers. And a couple of hard ones, an old book from Grandma, a Hamsun, a fishing reel from Hubert, an open reel Abu, bullseye. And an ice hockey stick from Dad; as I was opening it my heart was racing, of course I thought it was a microphone stand, because that was at the top of my wish list, but it was an ice hockey stick, and Dad stood there beaming, so I had to swallow hard, shake his hand and look happy, too.

Right at the end it was my turn to tense with excitement. There was nothing left under the tree and Mum gave me the last present, square and flat, there was no mistaking it, an LP. I jumped into the chair and tore off the paper.

'Read who it's from,' said Mum.

I looked at the card and at last Christmas reached my face, too. I couldn't believe my eyes. From Nina.

'Who's it from?' Hubert shouted.

My voice deserted me.

'It's from Kim's girlfriend,' my mother kindly explained. 'She sent it from Copenhagen.'

I was pretty taken aback, but in my confusion there was a solid pillar of pleasure. It was the new Beatles LP. *Rubber Soul.* I held it up in front of me. And then the pillar of pleasure was smashed. The temple it supported was a ruin. I didn't know the reason, yes, I did know, but I didn't understand it. I hardly recognised the four faces bent down towards me, yes, they were standing over me and looking down on me, four hostile, alien faces on the record cover.

Later that evening I stood in my room staring blindly at the record. I didn't dare play it. I didn't dare play it without Gunnar, Seb and Ola being there. Then Uncle Hubert came in puffing on a cigarette, he had bags under his eyes, his face was blue and sad.

'So that's where you are,' he said.

I nodded.

'Aren't you going to play the record?'

'I think I'll wait a bit,' I said.

We said nothing for a while. That was what was so good about Uncle Hubert, you didn't have to talk all the time, even if he was with you. But, despite that, I said, 'Uncle Hubert?'

'Yes.' He looked at me.

'Uncle Hubert. My girlfriend has moved away, too.'

For a second his eyes wandered, then a great clarity came over him, great and pure, we two, we two had understood everything now, and he hugged me. Above us Jensenius, the fattest of angels, was singing a carol, *Deilig er jorden*, and we unravelled, thread by thread, that Christmas Eve of 1965.

It was the day after Christmas and we were sitting in Seb's room gazing at *Rubber Soul*. No one said anything for a long time. We sat bent over the record, silent, almost angry, just as John, George, Ringo and Paul stood over us returning stony looks.

We didn't recognise ourselves.

'What's it like?' Seb asked in a hushed voice.

'Haven't listened to it yet.'

They looked at me and nodded. Now I had made up for the *Help* gaffe. I carefully took the record out of the sleeve, Seb placed it on the new Gerard player, pressed ON and the pick-up rose automatically and sank onto the grooves, as gently as a cat's paw.

We sat around for the rest of the evening playing the record again and again, our ears were large shells and we were lying on the bottom of the sea, listening intently, trying to decipher the songs as they came to us. Gunnar pointed in despair at the picture of John in the spruce forest as we listened to 'Norwegian Wood', and we didn't understand a thing.

'Norwegian wood!' Gunnar moaned. 'Norwegian wood! And what the hell is a sitar!'

Seb had his head in the loudspeaker trying to hear a sitar, had to be a pretty weird thing. But Ola was happy with 'What Goes On', had found a couple of pencils he was tapping, he was on the road to recovery. 'Michelle' was a bit too soppy for me, but 'Girl' hit me like a thunderbolt, made me feel bitter and warm. 'Nowhere Man' passed me by, way over my head. Gunnar was on the verge of tears, sweat was trickling down his forehead, his mouth wide open, speechless.

'What's actually h-h-happened?' Ola mumbled.

At that moment the door was flung open and Seb's father, the captain, stood there with tanned face, white shirt unbuttoned, sleeves rolled up, all the hair on his chest and arms issuing forth like black moss.

'Hello, boys. You look down in the mouth!'

'Dad,' Seb began. 'What's a sitar?'

He came into the room and spread his legs as if the seas were rough.

'Sitar? Well, I'll tell you what it is. Once we were transporting oil to Bombay. And the cook was an Indian. Worked like a Trojan. You need quite a bit of food on board a boat, you know. And that Indian… you see, Indians don't eat meat, because they think their forefathers might suddenly reappear one day as cows or grasshoppers, and hence they don't eat meat. But our Indian had to cook meat every single day and you can't imagine how that must have been for him, to believe that you were serving up your grandfather every day. Well, anyway, there was never any hassle with that Indian.'

Seb cleared his throat.

'Dad, what's a sitar?'

'Don't rush me. There was no hassle with this man, no, that is, there was a helluva lot of hassle because, you see, he played the sitar every night. That was his comfort. A big instrument. Must have had a hundred strings. Sounds like crotchety women.'

'So it's an Indian guitar?' Seb asked.

'Right. Nice to meet you boys.'

With that, the captain was gone. We put 'Norwegian Wood' on again.

Wow. India?

It was a strange Christmas holiday. We did the same as we always did, skied like crazy in Nordmarka, played ice hockey in Urra Park, chucked snowballs through open windows. Yet it was different. More snow fell than ever before, banks of snow grew up to the skies, people had to spend the night in snow caves just attempting to cross the road. That was exactly how it was. Huge piles of snow on all sides. It was as though we had lost something, a part of ourselves. The four alien faces, distorted, were always looking down at us and we avoided their gaze. In the evening I lay looking at the old pictures on the walls, The Beatles in Arlanda each with a bouquet, The Beatles with medals, Ringo on John's back straddled by Paul and George. It was a long time ago now, I longed to be back then, when everything was ordered and great. But at the same time it was exciting, it felt like an electric shock going up and down my spine. And when I closed my eyes *Rubber Soul* spun inside me, and I fell back, further than before, and one night I screamed in my sleep and woke the whole town, my mother and father at any rate. They came rushing in, but by then it was all over.

I sent Nina a New Year's card, spent an entire day toiling over four lines. In the end I wrote everything back to front with my left hand, just as Leonardo da Vinci had done. And the card was a picture of Munch's *Scream*.

New Year's Eve came, we went to Gunnar's in the evening and had ice cream and chocolate sauce. We sat in his room with the same expressions and the same muddled brains and as the gramophone played *Rubber Soul* we began to get quite desperate.

'The sitar is pretty cool,' Seb ventured.

We looked at him.

'I mean, it's pretty hard to try somethin' like that, I mean, no one's ever bloody done it before!'

Stig suddenly appeared at the door with a beer in each hand.

'*Rubber Soul* is the best album The Beatles have made,' he said. 'I prostrate myself in obeisance.'

He bowed to the floor with a huge flourish. We understood nothing.

'Do you agree?' he said as he rose.

'Ye-es.'

'Bloody hell, what kind of drips are you! Compare "Love Me Poo" and "Piss Piss Me" with "Nowhere Man" and "Norwegian Wood"! Eh!'

It went quiet. Stig stared at us in astonishment, then burst into laughter, put the beer down on the bookcase and joined us on the floor.

'Bob Dylan said The Beatles should sharpen up their bloody lyrics! Just listen to "Nowhere Man". That's how it is, isn't it. Everyone walks around wearing blinkers. They don't give a damn about anythin', they don't give a damn about havin' atomic bombs hangin' over our heads, they close their eyes to all the cruelty and only think about plastic and materialism. That's what it's about, isn't it!'

We put the record on again. Stig was well into it.

'Listen to that baroque piano! Swings like crazy! And Norwegian wood does not mean forest or wood. It means tobacco, you know. The tobacco Indians smoke. Peace pipe, folks.'

He sat with us until 'Michelle' slowed and faded, then he snatched his beer and made for the door. We went on playing records, we kept playing until fireworks went off outside the window, big colourful explosions. It was twelve o'clock.

We went out onto the balcony. Gunnar's parents were there, too. The air was cold and good and we felt very warm inside. Happy New Year! Yes. It was on its way. It was great. We were on schedule. Gunnar's father wanted to take a photo of us. We folded up our collars, sucked in our cheeks, lowered our eyelids and crouched down over his brand new flash camera. He told us to smile and not to look so angry. He hardly recognised us.

That was how it should be.

On the last day of the holiday we waded up Thomas Heftyesgate humming 'Norwegian Wood' and pondering the future of The Snafus. It was a year to our confirmation, so we had to get hold of the equipment. It was no good practising with pencils, elastic bands off jam jars or badminton racquets. All of a sudden we heard a loud din in a garage just beyond the English embassy. It wasn't a record player at full blast, it was a band. We stopped dead in the snowdrift, crept closer. A band. They began to sing, it sounded totally out of tune, but it was a band. We stood listening for a long time and while they were playing a guitar version of 'Lappland' someone came behind us and we jumped out of our skins.

'Wanna join the fan club?' bleated a fat tub with greasy hair and a blue double-breasted jacket.

'W-w-we were just p-p-passin',' Ola stammered.

The music stopped and the garage door opened. We peeped in and there stood everything we had dreamt of, electric guitars, microphones, big drums, amplifiers and loads of cables criss-crossing the stone floor. The musicians had red jackets, hair covering their foreheads and ears and were at least twenty years old.

'Found these fans,' said the greaseball.

'Shut the door before our bollocks get permafrost,' the drummer shouted and we were shoved in and the garage door was slammed to.

'Got a gig,' the manager said, lighting a cigarette and blowing fifteen rings up to the ceiling. 'Tutti frutti job with cream. Party night at Vestheim.'

He turned to us.

'Which school do you go to, boys?'

'Vestheim,' I said.

He drew closer.

'Goodo,' he said. 'Goodo with sugar on. You'll be in the front row.'

'Okay,' I said. 'If they let us in.'

'Say Bobby said it was alright, then you'll get in. Just say Bobby said it was alright.'

The band started another song: 'Cadillac'. Bobby was snapping his fingers. The guitarist's solo was very intense, but the singer's voice snapped like a matchstick in the refrain.

'Have to get shot of that catarrh,' Bobby shouted afterwards. 'Otherwise they got into the groove.'

'What's the name of the b-b-band?' Ola asked.

'The Snowflakes,' Bobby said. 'Remember the name.'

'The Snowflakes,' Ola repeated. 'Do you only play in the w-w-winter?'

Now Ola would have to keep his mouth shut before we were pitched out on our noses. Seb was already giving him a poke in the back.

'No, smart-arse. We're called The Raindrops in the summer.'

The Snowflakes started up again, an instrumental: 'Apache'. The solo guitarist moved the tremolo arm and the notes billowed out into the room in slow motion. Bobby trotted to and fro in front of them, crouching down and cupping his ears.

'The sound's good,' he declared afterwards.

There was a hammering on the door. Bobby opened up and in charged three girls who threw themselves over Bobby and then kissed the band, but when they came to us, they stopped dead.

'Fans,' Bobby explained. 'The Vestheim Fan Club committee. Playing there one evening.'

'Cool,' said one of the girls. 'Can't we go out and have a beer?'

'T'rrific idea,' Bobby said. 'Come on, guys. Let's cool it with a few beers.'

He looked down at us.

'We're agreed then, are we?' Bobby said.

We nodded. Didn't quite know what we had agreed to, though.

'Perhaps we could have a bit of a jam?' Seb asked.

Bobby eyed him and had a long think.

'Jam?'

'Just try a bit.'

'That's fine,' the bass player said. 'But take it easy. Sensitive equipment.'

'That's okay,' Bobby said with a frown. 'Take it easy. Expensive gear.'

So they wandered off, the girls had sweaters with 'Snowflakes' written on the back.

Ola pounced on the drums, Gunnar and Seb each grabbed a guitar and I stood by a microphone and we went for it. We screamed and shouted, I moaned and shrieked into the mike and my voice emerged from somewhere else and sounded quite different. Gunnar hammered away at the two chords he knew and Seb did his best to break a string. We kept this up for at least half an hour, it sounded quite awful and quite beautiful.

Then Gunnar shouted 'Stop'.

There was an abrupt silence. We were exhausted. Ola hung over his stool like an old bedsheet.

'We have to *know* what we're playin',' Gunnar said. 'So that we can play *together*.'

'What shall we play then?' Seb wondered.

We deliberated.

'We'll write our own songs,' I said.

Seb agreed.

'Of course! We'll make our own music! Why the hell hadn't we thought of that before?'

'But we haven't done anything yet, for Christ's sake. We have to decide what we can play *now*!'

'"Norwegian Wood",' said Seb.

'Without a sitar?'

'We can try.'

We tried, but we never found the melody. And then we were back at square one. Our stomachs vibrated, we should at least have been wearing a kidney belt, we jumped around, I lay on the floor, screaming wildly, Ola's bass drum was kicking like crazy, Seb was plucking the strings so that it sounded like forty sitars and ten randy cats and Gunnar was striking firm chords to keep the whole thing more or less together.

'Just like in the Cavern!' Seb yelled. 'Just like in the Cavern!'

We shifted into something vaguely like 'Twist And Shout', the sweat was steaming off us, girls in the crowd were tearing their hair and wanted to get near us on the stage, we gave everything we had, everything and the last drop, and a bit more, then the garage door burst open, I was lying on my back and silence fell over me like an avalanche. There stood the girls, squiffy, Bobby, with gaping eyes, and The Snowflakes, with broad grins.

I scrambled up, Gunnar and Seb crept out from under the guitars and Ola put down the drumsticks and appeared from behind the bass drum.

'What the hell was that?' Bobby said.

'We were playin',' I whispered.

'Playin'! Do you call that playin'?'

'What's your name?' asked one of the girls, leaning towards me.

'The Snafus,' I said in an even softer voice.

Then they began to laugh. Everyone laughed. We skulked towards the door.

'Just a sec,' Bobby shouted. 'You remember the gig?'

We nodded.

'So tell everyone you know about The Snowflakes. Got that?'

We nodded.

'Deal's a deal, boys,' he sibilated in Norwegian English.

We left the garage, tired and sweaty, the cold froze our clothes to our bodies.

'Imagine havin' a garage like that to practise in!' Gunnar said after we had calmed down a bit. 'Then we would definitely be better than The Snowflakes!'

'We *are* better than The Snowflakes,' Seb shouted. 'They just play shit.'

I threw a snowball in the air and I could swear it never came down again.

'They don't even know what a s-s-sitar is!'Ola snorted.

School began, Christmas was over. Christmas trees stood in gateways and backyards, brown and bare like fish bones. Stars vanished from windows and re-appeared in the sky on cold, pitch-black nights. A new year. Everything had changed. Everything was the same. Except that Skinke, the gym teacher, had had a new idea. We should swim. On such cold days he announced that it was important and proper that we should swim. For then we would acquire another subcutaneous layer of fat on our bodies, which would protect us against the cold. Viz. the polar bear. And with that we tramped down to West Oslo Baths and jumped into the chlorine. Skinke patrolled the pool blowing his whistle and screaming orders.

'Where's Fred?' gurgled Gunnar, spitting out green water.

I took a gander.

'Here he comes,' I said.

Here came Fred Hansen. His ribs jutted out like the steps of a staircase above the bony hips from which flapped his Tarzan bathing trunks. He hesitated for a few seconds, then strode onto the diving board and launched himself like a contorted seal, jackknifed and hit the water without a splash, without a sound. And there he stayed. Fred Hansen didn't surface. Skinke waved his arms about and yelled. We could see Fred on the bottom like a grey shadow, a skinny deep-water fish. It seemed to last forever and Skinke was on the point of diving in when Fred shot up like a torpedo, almost erect in the water, he really did, Fred leapt like a trout, then he began to swim, front crawl, it was the most elegant crawl I had ever seen, he surged through the water like a transported log, hardly seeming to move, his thin arms driving him forward as though he had a propeller behind his feet.

'That's great!' Skinke shouted. 'That's great, Fred! Keep it up!'

Fred kept it up, back and forth, back crawl, butterfly, front crawl, the rest of us wallowed there, splashing around like disabled hippos, but Fred was a seal, he was a seal!

In the shower afterwards we all stared at him. It was unbelievable.

'You're a bloody good swimmer,' we said.

Fred blushed and vanished in the steam.

Then we sprinted back to school. Our hair was deep-frozen by the time we reached Skovveien and our fringes stood up like peaks on caps. After arriving in the classroom we slowly thawed out and water streamed down our faces, and the girls sitting in the window row laughed.

The day Gjermund Eggen won the gold in the fifty-kilometre cross country event we had the school party at Vestheim. We met at Seb's two hours before the kick-off. His mother had joined his father in Marseille where his new boat was moored. In the meantime Seb's grandmother had moved in and she sat at the back of the sitting room embroidering and didn't hear the clinking in Gunnar's bag as we tiptoed across the carpet.

'Lager!' Seb said after we had barricaded the door.

'Only stuff I could find,' Gunnar said.

'If we do press ups afterwards, we'll be p-p-pickled,' Ola said. We looked at him.

'To heat the b-b-blood. Then it goes to your h-h-head quicker.'

Seb levered open the bottles with his belt buckle and we each had a swig. It tasted of gym bag.

'Pretty good,' Gunnar said.

We nodded and Seb passed cigarettes around. Then we sat there puffing and quaffing lager in blazers with shiny buttons and grey drainpipe trousers. Paul was wailing 'When I Saw Her Standing There' on the record player. That was how life should be, no doubt about it.

At eight we stumbled through the streets, crashed into lamp posts, tripped and grinned and held onto each other, howled at the heavens and sprayed our names in yellow in the snow, as far as it went, it went as far as surname and address, wow, what a night this was going to be.

In the playground people were huddled together in dark clusters. We could hear music from a record player. In one corner a square bottle was doing the rounds. Red faces shone out. Suddenly we were not so mouthy any more, we descended the stairs as erect as flagpoles, hearts pounding behind our shirts and five kroner in our fists. We hung our duffle coats in the cloakroom, which didn't smell of sweat and athlete's foot but perfume, raisins and something else exciting. Skinke, his arms crossed, in a double-breasted silver suit and yellow tie, his hair Brylcreemed, stood guard at the entrance.

'Great somersault,' he said to me as we passed.

In the gymnasium there was no longer a smell of cowshed, it was a new room, with garlands hanging from the ceiling, large fishing nets extended across the walls, balloons, candles and a long counter where you could buy Coke, buns and sausages, and in the corner a big stage with all The Snowflakes' equipment. We calmed ourselves down with a Coke and took a cautious look around. Girls in wide dresses, girls in tight dresses, tall girls with their hair up and black eyes and thin shoes, standing still. And the boys in shiny suits, the *gymnas* students, some wearing Beatle jackets, and we stood there in blazers, starched shirts and knitted ties, feeling pre-shrunk.

People were streaming in the whole time, the place was filling up, some were rowdy and lurched around like overjoyed elephants. Everywhere the talk was of Gjermund Eggen and his gold in the fifty-kilometre, and Bjørn Wirkola's ski-jumping. Names were shouted, balloons burst, girls' laughter. Then the lights were dimmed a fraction and all went quiet. The Snowflakes filed onto the stage wearing red jackets, green trousers and white shoes. Bobby was standing at the side adjusting some cables. They launched into 'A Hard Day's Night', we shut our ears and moved back as far as we could, for this could not be allowed, they could not be permitted to play The Beatles like this.

'Feeble version,' Seb groaned, sticking corks into both ears.

The jungle was alive. Leopards stalked through the grass, scented the wind and moved step by step towards the antelopes. The pumas sat by the wall bars waiting for an unwitting hare to hop past. The zebras frolicked around and the elephants lay down to sleep. Outside in the darkness, hyenas and wolves howled, the ones who had not been admitted.

Some girls from Gunnar's and my class stood close by, overdressed and heavily made-up. They were giggling and their eyes rolled around the room like marbles.

'Aren't you boys goin' to ask them?' Seb grinned.

'Got a girl in Copenhagen,' I answered.

The Snowflakes burst into a Swedish number, '*Där björkorna susa*'. Bobby was on the stage adjusting a few bits and pieces and putting on manager airs. Girls had lined the wall bars and the atmosphere was beginning to pick up. We went to the toilet, taking off our ties on the way, and the toilet was just as crowded. In the midst of the bodies was Roar from the B class, chief hooligan and troublemaker.

'Psst!' he hissed as we entered.

He was holding a fluted bottle, taking immense swigs and wiping the sweat off his forehead.

We stood by the urinal and unbuttoned.

'That Guri,' Roar erupted, his voice unusually high-pitched. 'That Guri who's in the C class, she's as randy as a stoat. Spread her legs for five øre, she would.'

The gang gave a low chuckle. Seb looked down at the dark yellow piss in which brown dog-ends were floating.

'That's why she left. Bun in the oven. Fucks in the fields, she does. Biggest quim in town!'

Seb spun round and stood in front of him.

'Shut your mouth!' he snarled.

Roar looked up in astonishment.

'Didn't quite catch that.'

'Button it, arsehole features,' Seb said.

The toilet went quiet. A circle formed around Seb and Roar. The atmosphere was taut.

'What did you say?' Roar said, passing the bottle to a flunkey.

'Arsehole,' Seb enunciated.

Now everyone knew something had to happen and the circle widened. Ola stood gawping. Gunnar clenched his fists and sent me a look. I closed my eyes. Then a voice boomed out from behind us.

'And what is going on here?'

Skinke. The circle crumbled away, Roar took his bottle and slipped into a cubicle. We sauntered back to the gymnasium.

The Snowflakes were in the groove. They were playing 'Apache', the tremolo arm quivering and shaking. Bobby had organised a chorus of banshees who were jumping up and down in front of the stage, the three girls from the garage. We sneaked past Bobby's gaze and picked up a Coke.

'Watch out for Roar,' Gunnar whispered.

'He can't get away with talkin' that kinda shit,' Seb hissed, sinking his teeth into a currant bun.

'He's p-p-pissed,' Ola said.

'Doesn't help.'

Skinke was back in position at the door, broad-shouldered, puckered brow. A few girls from the gymnasium were sticking close to him and trying to get him out on the floor, but Skinke was unshakable. Kerr's Pink, wearing a blue suit and perforated shoes, replaced him and the girls were all over him and he was dragged onto the dance floor amid stamping and cheering.

All of a sudden Ola was gone. Clean gone.

'Where's Ola?' Gunnar asked.

'No idea,' I said. 'He just went to buy a bun.'

We asked Seb. His head was bowed and he was still seething.

'Isn't he here?'

'Nope.'

'There he is,' Gunnar shouted, pointing.

There he was. Ola was on the dance floor. Ola was on the dance floor with the tallest girl in the school, Klara, from the B class, the goalkeeper in the handball team. We stared, stared so much our eyebrows were perpendicular. Ola almost melted into all of Klara. She swung him round and round to The Snowflakes playing 'Dancing Shoes' and from time to time we saw Ola throw back his head and gasp for air.

We didn't say a word, not a single word. There was nothing left to say.

The music came to an end and Ola wriggled out of her clutches. Klara was holding his head like a handball, but Ola slipped away, good thing he had put on hair lotion before we left, he darted in and out between the couples and came over to us with a look of horror on his face.

'Help,' he said.

'There's nothin' we can do,' Gunnar said with a grave mien.

'Here she comes,' I said.

Klara was on her way.

'Help,' Ola said and we formed a circle around him and smuggled him away to a safer place.

Kerr's Pink had climbed onto the stage and now he was holding a speech. He talked about youth and *joie de vivre*, about fun and seriousness. After a while he got quite hot in his suit and there was the odd whistle from the audience. Bobby motioned to his banshee choir, Kerr's Pink was dragged off and The Snowflakes hammered away at a mindless Finnish folk dance.

Then Seb went missing.

'We'll have to look for him,' Gunnar said with concern.

We trawled the gymnasium, but no one had seen anything of Seb.

'He might've gone out,' I said.

On the way out we met a group of bully boys with Roar at the head, and the mod guy who had been with Guri that time, and the two smooth types who had taken the piss out of Ola on the first day. They banged into us and I felt the rush in my stomach that I was so afraid of, it passed through my body like a gust of wind, and I knew that anything could happen now.

Gunnar raised his shoulders and his head seemed to sink down into his back.

'Come on then!' he said through clenched teeth and we stormed past Skinke and up the stairs.

It was ice cold and dark in the playground. The silence was only broken by hushed chuckles and muffled whispers. We couldn't see a thing.

'Sebastian!' we shouted.

No one answered.

We began to search. It didn't take that long. Seb was in the snowdrift by the shed, face down in the snow. We hauled him to his feet and bundled him over to an illuminated window. Blood was running from his nose, his head, and there was a large wound across his forehead. Gunnar couldn't look, couldn't stand the sight of blood.

'The bastard was wearin' a knuckleduster,' Seb groaned.

I flew down to the cloakroom and fetched our duffle coats, and then we took Seb home. His grandmother wasn't in the least surprised when we turned up with him.

'Tripped down some stairs,' I said.

She produced some iodine, gauze and cotton wool.

'That's what I've always said,' she said. 'Stairs are much too steep nowadays. Much too steep. You'll have to take care in future.'

One evening we couldn't find Ola. He wasn't at home and his mother thought he was with one of us. We shot down the stairs and looked for footprints in the fresh snow. Ola's overshoe with diagonal stripes on the sole pointed in the direction of Drammensveien, but there all the tracks vanished.

'Perhaps he caught the tram,' Seb said.

'Tram? Where would Ola go on the tram?'

Gunnar looked worried, made a snowball and threw it at the statue of Nobel.

'Perhaps he's got mixed up in somethin',' he said.

The Silks, the gang from the posh area of town? The Frogner gang?

We had to start our search again. We went down to Mogga Park, not a sign of Ola, continued up Bygdøy Allé, snow began to fall, now the last of Ola's boot prints would be obliterated for ever.

'Let's try Frogner Park,' Gunnar suggested.

We walked there. We shouted, but there was no answer, just a rustle when the branches could no longer support the snow. We trudged up to Dogland. The wind was blowing the snow through the air horizontally. The cemetery gate creaked and the spruce trees stood like grand old ladies at the side, in black dresses, a whole flock of them, and their singing sounded eerie.

'He's not here. Let's hop it,' Gunnar said.

Then we heard a sound, not so far away, someone sneaking through the snow.

'Ola,' we shouted in hope.

The sound was gone, then it reappeared in another spot, beneath the lamp post right in front of us. And in the cone of light stood a flasher with his pants down and his knob sticking out, his face completely blue. We screamed with shock then packed some really hard snowballs and bombarded him. He leapt off down the path with his pants down and his knob sticking out, whining and yelling.

We crossed towards the Colosseum cinema and Majorstuen.

'Must be bloody cold standin' like that,' Seb said.

'Let's go to Urra Park,' Gunnar said.

The church clock shone yellow like an extra moon. Soon be eight. Down on the skating rink the children were playing tag. Ola wasn't there, of course he wasn't. Where could he be?

We padded down to Briskeby. The wooden walls of Albin Upp Gallery creaked. The Man on the Steps had closed. Time was passing. It was beginning to be critical.

'If they've harmed a hair on his head,' Gunnar said. That was all he said. 'If they've harmed a hair on his head.'

Then I saw something. Halfway down Farmers' Hill. I pointed.

'Look,' I whispered.

We stopped dead and stared. They were coming towards us. One big, broad-shouldered figure and a small, squat one. We stared and stared. It was Ola and Klara.

'It's Ola and Klara!' we all shouted, sped round the corner and hid in the entrance to the butcher's.

It took a while, but then they walked past. Ola and Klara. They were holding hands. Or Klara was holding Ola. And we held our breath.

'He's been kidnapped!' Gunnar said when they had passed. 'We have to set him free!'

We held Gunnar back, waited a little and crept out onto the pavement. Ola and Klara had disappeared in the driving snow.

We let them go.

'I'd never have believed that,' Gunnar said.

We shook our heads and walked home in silence.

And home was a hive of activity. Dad was revising for his driving test, had been swotting since Christmas, in the sitting room with a pile of books in his lap, drawing traffic signs and crossroads, red-faced and very irritable if you went too close and asked too many questions. I enquired when we would have a car, but I didn't even get an answer to that. Mum said 'shhh' and we went into the kitchen and closed all the doors after us. Everyone was being secretive, but as usual I wasn't told a thing, I have always been the last person to twig what was going on.

Fred Hansen's star took another tumble. Fred the seal was forgotten, he was standing by the blackboard mumbling, mumbling through a closed mouth, he had it all there, it just would not come out. Written tests were not a problem for him, but oral tests, that was where the barrier came down. In Norwegian classes Kerr's Pink stalked round him trying to teach him to speak, for we didn't say 'ours's' or 'theirs's' or 'his's', we didn't talk like that. Fred's ears were glowing and he crumpled over his desk lid, feeling so small that he could have crawled into the ink well.

And in the breaks they were after him. A whole gang collected, not only from our class but also all the silks from Skarpsno and further west, and one day one of the spoilt brats kicked his packed lunch into the air showering the yard with cervelat and goat's cheese. Gunnar's jaws began to clench and unclench and we went over to the fence where Fred stood clinging to the wire netting.

The spoilt brat looked at us.

'We're teaching the nigger manners,' said the boy who had delivered the kick.

'Scram,' Gunnar said.

The brat seemed surprised.

'Are *you* telling *me* what to do,' he enquired.

'You've got it,' Gunnar said. 'Scram. Now.'

The brat looked around. Suddenly there was room to move his elbows.

'And if I don't? What then?'

Gunnar is not quick. But he is accurate. His right hand came out of his pocket, his arm stretched out full and the silk collapsed with a sob. The other grubs began to push and shove, but it was half-hearted, they had seen Gunnar's right arm in action. Then we took Fred to the shed and we each gave him a sandwich.

That day Fred waited for us after school. He looked a bit sheepish and asked if we wanted to go home with him. Of course we did, and we trudged after Fred through the town. It was quite a hike because he lived in Schweigaardsgate, the other side of Oslo.

I was the first to put my foot in it.

'What does your brother do?' I asked as we passed Oslo East station.

Fred stared at me for a long time, assuming the wise expression on his face that made him look twenty years older, as though he had understood everything.

'Haven't got a brother,' he said.

'You haven't got a brother?'

He gave a wan smile, looked down at his clothes and flapped a trouser leg.

'Mum buys clothes at Elevator,' Fred said.

'Elevator?'

'The Salvation Army. They sell second-hand clothes.'

There was a strange smell in the entrance hall of the block where Fred lived. I wasn't quite sure what it was. It just didn't smell like home. There was an empty bottle of booze on the letterboxes. The paint hung off the walls like withered leaves. He lived on the ground floor and kept his key on a piece of string around his neck. After a good deal of fumbling he produced it from under his sweater and almost broke his neck opening the door.

There was no one at home. We removed our shoes and had a look around, holding our breath. Everything was different, the furniture, the air, the light. Fred said nothing. He let us look. After a while he said, 'Mum and I live here.'

Now I knew what the smell was. Old clothes, like in the loft in Nesodden.

'Where's your d-d-dad then?' Ola asked straight out.

'Haven't got a dad,' Fred said.

'You haven't got a dad!' Ola looked bewildered.

'No,' Fred said.

Seb tried to warn off Ola, but it was too late.

'Is he d-d-dead?'

'Don't know,' Fred said.

We wandered into his room, a tight fit with loads of pictures of swimmers on the walls. We sat down on the bed, a mattress covered with a faded green rug.

'D'you swim a lot?' Gunnar asked.

'Torggata, a couple of times a week,' Fred said.

We didn't say a lot more, just sat grinning and joking about the teachers. Fred seemed calm and happy, staring at us as though we had done him a great favour. Then, however, the floor began to quiver, the panes in the window rattled and the mattress bounced up and down.

'What's that?' I shouted.

Fred checked his watch.

'The Stockholm train,' he said.

We ran to the window. Right outside, only a few metres away, ran the train lines. Straight after came the Trondheim train, we could see into the carriages, illuminated in the dusk. People sat reading, playing cards, lifting suitcases, just like in a film, lots of yellow images, one after the other, coming to an abrupt end, the sound faded, but the floor continued to quiver.

'I suppose trains go all over the world from here,' I said, impressed.

Fred nodded.

'In our place they only go to Drammen and Sørlandet.'

'They go to Moscow from here,' Fred said with pride.

'Moscow! Is that true?'

'Every Friday. The Trans-Siberian railway.'

The Trans-Siberian railway. My head sang. That was not quite the same as a goods train to Skøyen.

'What does it look like?' I asked.

'It's blue. With loads of carriages.'

All of a sudden his mother was standing in the doorway, a small lady in a large grey coat, thin, transparent hair. She looked at us in surprise, then smiled and we said our names and she put out a hand, a large, gnarled hand that was much too heavy for her small body.

Then Villa Farris sparkling wine appeared, with a bun for

everyone, and she chatted on forever, about Fred who was going to the *gymnas*, he would be the first in the family to take university entrance exams, about how good Fred was at swimming, and if he got even better and did more homework then perhaps he could go to America and study there. America. Fred stared out of the window, his neck thin and tense, staring out into the distance, and his mother told us she would have to wash stairs round the clock, but it didn't matter for Fred was her future, and she talked about the great golden future in such a reedy voice, but there was not a speck of doubt to be detected in her tired grey eyes.

'Rehearsal for The Snafus tomorrow,' Gunnar said as we got off the tram in Solli Plass.

Ola looked away.

'C-c-can't make it,' he said.

'What do you mean by that?' Seb asked.

'C-c-can't make it,' Ola said.

We eyed him up.

'Better be a good excuse,' I said.

'K-K-Klara.'

On my return home Mum and Dad were sitting in the dining room waiting for me. The table was set with tall glasses and heirloom crockery and there were flowers on all the windowsills.

'Where have you been?' Mum asked.

'With a boy from the class. Fred Hansen.'

Dad sat on his chair in a dark suit like a statue with beads of sweat on his nose. Then he took out a small green thing from his inside pocket and waved it in the air. Driving licence!

'Congratulations, Dad!' I said and was allowed to flick through it.

'You can congratulate him again,' Mum said in a formal tone.

'Can I?'

Mum nodded.

'Congratulations, Dad,' I said. 'What for?'

Dad was tongue-tied, Mum had to take over.

'Dad's been promoted to bank manager.'

That didn't mean a lot to me. But it sounded good.

'When will that be?' I asked.

'After New Year,' Mum said.

'Will we get a car then?!'

Dad nodded slowly. He was the King of Svolder now.

'Congratulations, Dad,' I said for the third time and before I knew it I was standing with his hand in mine and it was all a bit too solemn. The King of Svolder arose, Mum shed a few tears and at last it was dinner, a banquet with chicken casserole and wine, and Coke for me. Dad thawed, melted, he was flowing. How far would *I* go when he had achieved so much with *his* modest start in life? My future was staked out there and then, like a world championship skiing race through Nordmarka with a rock-hard piste and red ribbons on every second spruce tree. Business School. Norwegian Institute of Technology. Construction industry. Banking. The seventies would be the decade for practical, realistic men, Dad said. Perhaps I ought to study abroad. England. Germany. America! The heir presumptive of Svoldergate had already begun his career. There were simply no limits.

'What was the name of the boy you were with?' Mum asked.

'Fred. Fred Hansen.'

'Where does he live?' Dad asked.

'Schweigaardsgate,' I said.

Mum and Dad exchanged glances, invisible threads, right over my head.

'Schweigaardsgate, you say,' Dad said calmly. 'That's a long way.'

'Yes, it is!' I said with animation. 'The trains from Oslo East run past there. We saw the Trans-Siberian railway!'

'The Trans-Siberian railway?' Dad gaped.

'That's right. Wouldn't mind living there!'

There was a sudden silence. Dad's eyes fell to his plate. Mum stared at me with a look I didn't recognise.

'Kim!' came the stinging reproof. 'You mustn't say that. You must never say that again!'

I fiddled with my food, feeling the blood rush through my head in my confusion.

'No,' I said meekly.

'And you must *never* go there at night! Do you hear?'

I heard. I studied the tablecloth and the stain that had spread into a bizarre shape, like a disfigured face or a troll, a sinister hybrid. The silence around the table lingered, I thought about Fred who didn't have a brother after all, who didn't have a father either, I thought of his mother's big red hands. And I thought of the future Fred bore on his shoulders, twice as heavy as mine.

'I think I'll go for a Saab,' Dad said.

In the evening we went to the Colosseum and saw *The Sound of Music*. It must have been there I lost my interest in films. We sat in the first row of the Colosseum and saw *The Sound of Music* and whenever I turned round I saw two thousand people with white handkerchiefs. It was like birds nesting on a cliff. Yes, that was where I lost any interest I had in films. I know that now. I should have realised before.

And the days passed with more snow, more homework. On a radio request programme I heard the signature tune of *Zorba the Greek*, my stomach went heavy and I felt the taste of apple on my palate. Mum said that soon I would be allowed to go with her to the theatre. That was obviously a big deal and I was already beginning to dread going. I lay awake at night unable to sleep no matter what. People just pretending, I thought. Fiction. Film. Theatre.

And I delivered flowers all over town. One day I bumped into Guri in Jacob Aalls gate. She looked emaciated, ravaged, a fledgling picked clean, with a gaze that resembled the snow around her. Felt like stopping and having a chat, but she floated by without looking up. I didn't stop her, for there are a great many things like that which you know you should have done but you never do.

That was, incidentally, the day I received fifty kroner from fru Eng, just one fifty kroner note, I couldn't believe my eyes. Because I was never any bother, she said. The best delivery boy in Oslo, she said.

Fifty kroner.

I would save it for the spring, when I went to Copenhagen!

The best defensive player in Oslo.

At Easter only Seb and I were left in town. Ola was in Toten. Gunnar was in Heidalen, they usually rented a cabin there. And Granddad was at the home. We went to visit him. He was sitting by the window with a checked rug over his legs and an unshaven face, watching the cars tearing across Alexander Kiellands plass.

'Here comes the express to take me,' he said giving us an unhurried look and without any particular sign of terror.

'Don't talk like that,' said Mum, fussing around him and putting oranges on his bedside table.

'I can already hear it,' he continued. 'I can already hear it.'

There was an oval picture of Jesus on the wall. A dark cross over his bed. On the windowsill stood an angry cactus.

'I've seen the Trans-Siberian railway,' I said into his ear. Granddad turned towards the sound.

'You don't say,' he said. 'That's wonderful. I've never travelled any further than Sweden. But that was during the war and far enough for those times. Was it very expensive?'

Mum straightened his rug. Dad tried to peel an orange but gave up. Granddad was old, twice as old as he had been at Christmas. I listened for the express, thought I heard singing rails from not so far away.

Granddad cleared his throat. His mouth was dry and small.

'And Hubert's going to Paris! Well, I never!'

Dad jumped up, his bottom lip quivering like a guitar string.

'What did you say?'

'Are you hard of hearing, too, now?' Granddad shouted into his face.

'When was Hubert here?'

'Day before yesterday,' Granddad shouted. 'Or a week ago. I mix up all the days.'

'And he said he was going to Paris?'

'He was all set,' Granddad said, giving us a mysterious look. 'All set,' he said. What did he mean by that?

Dad was busy. Granddad didn't seem to notice that we had gone. We waved to him from the pavement, but he was looking elsewhere, in a different direction.

'We'll have to get this sorted out,' said Dad.

With that he strode off to Marienlyst while Mum and I called in to see Grandma on the way home. She lived in Sorgenfrigate, in a dark room with loads of cushions and a budgerigar that chirruped in its cage and had an embroidered blanket placed on top every night so that it slept well.

I poked a finger through the bars but it got frightened and I could see its heart beating against its green breast.

The Wednesday before Maundy Thursday, Seb and I went to visit Fred. He opened the door with a look of astonishment on his face, then he burst into the broadest grin I have seen and let us in.

We took a seat in his room and chatted a bit about trains and swimming. Schoolbooks lay open on the table. Fred was studying during the holiday. Good grief.

'Have you got a record player?' Seb asked.

'No, but I'm gettin' one when I finish *realskole*. Mum's promised me.'

'You can come back to our places and listen to records,' Seb put in quickly.

'Can I?'

'Course,' Seb said. 'We take all the records to mine and we play 'em all evenin'.'

Fred started to laugh. Think he was enjoying himself.

'Which band d'you like best?' I asked.

He wasn't quite sure and wiped his mouth.

'Don't really know,' he said.

'You don't know!' we said in unison.

'Yes, I do.'

We waited with bated breath. He moistened his lips.

'The Beatles.'

That was it. He was one of us. All settled.

'What do you think about *Rubber Soul*?' Seb asked.

Fred looked at him in despair.

'Røbber?'

'Yes, *Rubber Soul*.'

'What's that?' Fred whispered.

Seb glanced at me. I studied my lap. Fred's breathing was heavy.

'Latest Beatles LP,' Seb said, relaxed. 'Really good. You can hear it at my place.'

'Haven't heard any records,' Fred said quietly. 'Just listen to 'em on the radio. When Mum isn't at home.'

'Why do you like The Beatles best then?' I burst out, and I regretted it at once because it was a pretty stupid question.

'Because they've made it,' Fred said.

'Eh? Made what?'

'Made it. I mean, they're millionaires and world famous and so on. Normal workin' class boys.'

We went dead quiet. Normal working class boys. Made it. My head spun. We'd never thought like that before. Fred Hansen had as good as never heard a Beatles record. I supposed Fred was a working class boy.

'I need the loo,' Seb said, getting up.

'The key's in the kitchen,' Fred said.

'The key?'

We followed hard on Fred's heels into the kitchen. He took down a key hanging from a nail beside the door.

'You have to go up to the first or the second floor,' Fred said.

Seb's eyes widened. Then he smiled a wry smile, took the key and ran up the stairs.

He was away quite a long time. Then he came rushing down, breathless and red-faced.

'Never had a shit so high up before,' he shouted. 'Didn't hear it landin' though!'

'I have to go, too,' I said and was given the key, sprinted up the uneven stairs and found the cubicle.

The smell was dreadful. There were squares of newspapers to wipe yourself with, the toilet roll was finished. Exactly the same hole as in the outside toilet at Nesodden! But in a block of flats? In the town? On the second floor! This was unbelievable. I didn't want to go after all, waited a while, then ran back down.

'Think of the men who have to shovel all that shit!' Seb said. 'Think of that, eh!'

'Shall we go down to the cellar?' Fred suggested.

'The cellar?'

'Got rats there.'

Fred fetched a flat torch and then we crept down the stairs into the darkness and the smell of mildew. He coaxed open a wooden door, it made a befittingly eerie creaking noise. He shone the torch round, but it didn't help much. It was better when our eyes were used to the dark. Then the cellar loomed up, brick walls, sacks of coke, old bicycles, skis, a mattress.

Fred pointed the torch.

'A girl had it off on that,' he said.

We looked at the mattress. Green and filthy with large brown stains. The ceiling dripped.

We ventured in further, on tiptoes, jumped as a train passed, we were beneath the rails, beneath the train. Our bodies gave a strange shudder.

Fred indicated the wall. There were holes in the plaster.

'Bullet holes,' Fred said. 'From the war. They shot a Nazi sympathiser down here. An informer.'

We stared at the wall, lowered our gaze slowly to the floor. Oh, shit, that's where he stood. He fell there. There were holes in the wall from the bullets. Jesus.

Then we saw it. The rat. A fat, black rat with a long tail and a pointed face. It looked at us and seemed to cower. Fred grabbed a broomstick and crept towards it with flapping trouser legs. It darted away. We cheered and ran after it, into another room, we followed it as it zigzagged across the stone floor.

'We've got it!' Fred shouted. 'We've got it!'

We had it. We had driven it towards the wall. We had driven it into a corner. There it turned and stared at us. Its pointed white teeth gleamed. A rat. Seb and I retreated a little. Fred stood with the broom raised ready to strike. The rat hissed. Then it was suddenly gone. Fred looked at us in amazement. Then he screamed. Had never heard a scream like it. The rat was in his trousers. It had run up his trouser leg. We saw the bulge moving towards his thigh. Fred screamed and spun round and round.

'Take off your pants!' Seb shouted. 'Take off your pants!'

The rat was right up by his hip. Fred howled, put his hands to his face and howled. Then he ran against the wall. He ran at full speed and launched himself at the wall. We heard the crunch as his hip struck the wall. Then he sank down onto the floor and lay perfectly still. The bundle in his trousers also lay still. After a while he opened his eyes, looked at us, unbuttoned his trousers and then with great care we removed them. A crushed rat tumbled out.

We manoeuvred him onto his feet and carried him out of the room fighting for breath and trembling. I turned and saw the big bloodstained rat in the light of the torch.

Fred's mother was in the kitchen. Her chin dropped when we arrived, dragging Fred between us, Fred wearing only underpants and with rat blood down his thigh.

'Where are your pants?' she asked.

Fred was unable to answer.

'In the cellar,' I said. 'Fred wanted to show us some bullet holes and a rat appeared.'

She took his arm, pulled him over to the window and took out a sturdy washing-up bowl. We picked up our clothes and wandered home on the day before Maundy Thursday, 1966. Slept badly that night. Dreamt about rats and thought I felt something moving in my pyjamas.

We had expected Gunnar to come home as black as the ace of spades, he usually did after Easter, but his cheeks were only a little caramel-coloured.

'Did you stay indoors all the time?' Seb asked as we sat in his room waiting for Ola, as usual.

No, he didn't, not at all. It was hard work extracting from Gunnar what he had done over Easter, he was distant and giggly, yeah, well, he had done a bit of skiing, listened to Radio Luxemburg, not long to summer now, is it. He sat like that drivelling on for a quarter of an hour. Seb and I exchanged glances and shook our heads.

'Great Easter then,' I summarised.

Yeah. Top notch. Totally wonderful Easter. Already looking forward to next Easter. Wonderful pistes. And good milk. Good milk in the country. Better than in town. Closer to the cows. Straight up.

Gunnar had gone nuts. We tried to tell him about Fred and the rat, but it was like water off a duck's back. He sat there with his rictus smile saying it was terrible, about the rat, terrible. That was all.

Then he went quiet. We waited for Ola.

'Can't've crashed the tractor again, can he?' Seb said.

After half an hour we took the matter into our own hands and sloped over to his place. His sister, Åse, sixth class in Urra with a freckled nose, opened the door. We showed off and patted her head, but that just made her prickly.

'Ola,' we commanded.

'You can't see him,' she said.

We peered down at her.

'He hasn't been on the tractor again, has he?' I asked.

She shook her head vigorously.

'Why can't we see him?'

'He doesn't want to see you!'

'Are your parents at home?' I asked.

'No, but they'll be back soon!'

'Is Klara here?' Seb asked.

'Klara? Who?'

We pushed our way in, stomped across the floor and tore open the door to Ola's room. There was a pungent smell of ointment. He was in bed. Under the duvet. We just saw two clenched fists holding up the cover.

'Hiya, Ola,' we said. 'How's it goin'?'

'Go away!' he hissed. He *hissed.*

'Somethin' happened or what?' Seb enquired.

Not a sound. He lay there motionless. So we started to pull the duvet away. It wasn't easy. There were great forces recumbent in that bed. He kicked out wildly, but we overpowered him. In the end he abandoned his resistance and we folded the duvet neatly to the side.

It was the reddest red I had seen. His face was as red as a Christmas candle. He looked unhappy.

'Go away,' he whispered.

'Was there *that* much sun in Toten this year?' we asked.

He rolled over. His face squeaked.

'Go away,' he repeated. 'I'm never gonna g-g-get up again.'

We perched on the edge of his bed. His hair had been almost burnt off. The tips were curly. One whole-head perm.

'Did the barn burn down?' Seb asked.

His sister stood in the doorway with her hands against her back, rocking from side to side and giggling.

'Ola, Ola, who's Klara?'

He rolled back to face us. It was impossible to blush with your skin that colour. But his eyes darkened.

'T-t-traitors,' he said.

'Necessary evil,' we protested. 'We had to make sure before we invaded your room.'

'Go away,' he whimpered. 'G-g-go!'

We ambled home. It turned out that Ola's grandfather had bought a sunlamp through a mail order firm. On the last day Ola had fallen asleep in front of it and sat there for over an hour. He had burnt through three layers of skin and singed his hair.

'See you at school tomorrow,' Seb said, flicking his Ascot cigarette end over his shoulder. 'Probably be a while before Ola returns.'

Gunnar and I walked on. Gunnar was taciturn and distant. Some way up Bygdøy Allé I stopped him.

'What's happened to you?' I asked.

'Met a girl.'

'What's she like?'

'Unni. Her name's Unni. Lives on a farm. Really nice.'

We continued walking beneath the bare chestnut trees.

'Are you together, proper like?' I asked.

'Yep. Think so. Gonna write to each other. Gonna visit her in the summer.'

'What's she look like?'

Gunnar stared into the air as if he could catch a glimpse of her there.

'Very good-lookin'. Blonde hair. Blonde hair and…'

He didn't say any more. There was a pause. A long pause. He ran ahead. I caught him up.

'Long-distance relationships are okay,' I said.

He looked at me.

'How's that?'

'I mean it's pretty wearin' if you're in the same school.'

Gunnar gave that one some thought.

'Yes, but it could've been a bit closer.'

Paperback Writer

Spring '66

Ola crept out from under the duvet after two weeks, pink and well. He arrived with the sun and the spring. The snow flowed down the drains, everything was flooded and birds flew in from abroad. One night when I could not fall asleep I opened the window and filled my lungs with the night air. There was a noise above me, Jensenius opening his window, he greeted me and the sound of his voice resounded over the town.

Yes, indeed. It had to be spring.

Uncle Hubert came for lunch one Sunday. He looked better, wandered around a bit and rolled potatoes across the table, but otherwise all went well. Hubert was happy, that was the main thing. His eyes had a tranquil sheen.

After we had eaten, I asked, 'Is it true you're moving to Paris?'

Dad was on me like a pair of scissors.

'Weren't you going to the cellar to fix your bike?' he said as gently as he was able.

Hubert found the way to a chair and collapsed in a soft heap.

'Just a little trip,' he said. 'A short visit.'

Dad ushered me out of the room.

'And don't come home late,' he said.

He was brittle, like a hard rubber. One day I would go to Paris, too. I swore I would and slammed the door after me. I trudged down to the cellar and before I could find the light switch I was overcome by terror. Rats. Then the light came on and I breathed a sigh of relief. There weren't any rats here. But Fred had gone to school after Easter wearing the same trousers. The same trousers. His eyes went shifty when he saw me. I had to look away.

I rolled the bike out early that Sunday evening and headed for Gunnar's. A warm wind was swirling up the dust and the sand on the pavement. I whistled cheerfully and found Gunnar in his room, bent over a piece of pink paper with a magnifying glass in front of his face.

'What you up to?' I asked, taking a seat on the windowsill. He cleared his throat and put down the magnifying glass.

'Her handwritin' is so damn hard to read,' he said, desperate.

'Shall I have a go?' I suggested.

He looked at me with suspicion, hesitated for a moment, then passed me the letter.

I read it through quickly, the style was quite stilted, worse than a school essay. I pressed my nose against the ink and peered over at Gunnar.

'Perfume,' I said.

'Read!' he said.

I read slowly, '"Darlin' Gunnar."'

The letters I received from Nina didn't start like that. There was just a 'Hiya' or a 'Hello'.

'What's up?' Gunnar shouted.

I went on.

'"Darlin' Gunnar."'

'I've heard that!'

'"Darling Gunnar. I think about you all the time. At night, too."'

I stopped and looked at Gunnar. He was over by the door, working out with hand weights. The sweat was pouring off him.

'"I'm looking forward to you coming here. I'm counting the days on my fingers. But maybe I'll go to Oslo first."'

Gunnar shrieked.

'Comin' here!'

'"But maybe I'll go to Oslo first,"' I repeated. '"You see, my mother's going to Oslo the second weekend in May."'

Gunnar was lying on his back with his arms hanging down at his sides.

'That's okay, isn't it?'

He closed his eyes.

'Yes. But the mother. They may come here. And see my parents.'

'You could just meet her, couldn't you?'

'Be a bit difficult. Her mother was after us with the hayfork the whole time.' Some kids were playing footie down in the street, smashed a window and ran for their lives.

'Relax,' I said. 'We're goin' to Denmark then.'

He sat up with a start.

'You're right! If we're selected.'

'Of course we will be. We'll go and see Kåre tomorrow!'

He lay back down and all was quiet for a long time. Then he said, 'Bad luck, us bein' away like that. But there's nothin' to be done, is there!'

'Nothing,' I said.

'Go on,' said Gunnar.

'"I think I'm in love with you, Gunnar."'

'You don't have to keep sayin' Gunnar, do you! I know who she means!'

'That's what it says here!'

He folded his hands behind his head and stared at the ceiling.

'"I think a lot about the last evening when you..."'

Gunnar was on me like an elk, tearing the letter away and stuffing it in his pocket.

'Hadn't finished,' I smiled.

'That'll do fine,' he said.

'What were you doin' on the last evenin', eh?'

The door opened, it was Stig, wearing the fabulous waisted jacket with stripes, with hair right down over his forehead and eyebrows like the crest of a wave, and boots that curled at the tip. He stood there, tall and rangy, odd that, that Gunnar and he were so different.

'Lend me a tenner, will you,' Stig asked.

'What you gonna do with it?'

'That's neither here nor there. You'll get it back tomorrow,' he said and added: 'Goin' to Pernille.'

Gunnar took ten kroner from a drawer.

'Great,' said Stig. 'Great! My records are at your disposal.'

He had a badge on the lapel of his jacket, looked like a star.

'What's that?' I asked, pointing.

'Victory to the Front National de Liberté,' he said.

'Are the Americans still droppin' napalm?' I wondered.

'Yes, and how. But the FNL will soon chase 'em out.'

He went into a crouch and sprayed the room with bullets. Then he was gone.

Guerrilla.

We sat for a while looking at the open door. Then Gunnar pulled out the crumpled letter and smoothed it on his thigh.

'Let's read the rest,' he said.

'Let's,' I said, sitting beside him.

We all went, the whole gang. It cost a hundred kroner and Mum and Dad had promised to pay, and I had enough pocket money already, fifty shiny ones. Five o'clock, the first Friday in May, we were on our way. It was a big deal. It was the biggest. The weather had done an about-turn, cold fronts and gales were back. But it didn't matter. We were going south. We went up the gangway in single file with rucksacks, sleeping bags and new football boots. It was a solemn occasion, so solemn that our backs straightened and our heads were held high. But inside smouldered a wild joy, a bonfire of expectations that would set the whole of Denmark alight.

It was half an hour to departure. We were directed to the bottom of the ship where we were to sleep in reclining seats. Åge stood on a chair and shouted:

'Alright, lads, I've said it before, but I'll say it again: this is not your average holiday trip! We're going to play football! We're going to trounce the Danes!'

We stamped in rhythm and sang the Frigg chant. Åge calmed us down.

'And you know all this, too, but I'll tell you once more anyway! Do you hear me?'

'Yes!' we shouted.

'Has everyone got food vouchers?'

'Yes!' we shouted.

'It'll buy you a meal in the cafeteria at the back of the boat. Before seven o'clock! Okay?'

'Yes!' we shouted.

'And all of you, you have to be back down here by ten! By ten!'

'Yes,' came the response, with a little less enthusiasm.

'And alcohol! Alcohol is off-limits!'

A few scattered shouts.

'Anyone caught drinking alcohol will be dropped from the team! Understood!'

The ship lurched. It was approaching five. We charged upstairs and onto the deck. All our parents were standing on the quayside waving like crazy. Then the gangway was removed and the boat slipped away, reversed and turned on a five øre coin.

We leaned over the gunnels with the wind whipping tears from our eyes. *King Olav* cut through the waves. Oslo fjord was a nightmare. Gunnar and Ola were green in the gills before we had passed Nesodden.

I pointed to the shore.

'There's the House!' I cried.

Then we were past it. Ola's head was drooping.

'I-i-if it's rocky here, think what it's g-g-gonna be like after Færder lighthouse!'

Gunnar moaned.

'My dad's been on the sea with waves twenty metres high,' Seb boasted. 'The Atlantic. They were so high they couldn't see the sky when they were in a trough!'

Ola went first, by Drøbak. Gunnar clung to the railing.

The gulls hovered above and below us. You could stretch out a hand and pat them on the beak.

'Let's go and get somethin' to eat,' Seb said.

That was when Gunnar disappeared. He staggered off holding a hand over his mouth. Seb and I looked at each other.

'Landlubbers!' he grinned.

Gunnar and Ola were out of the running. They had been given some seasickness tablets by Åge and were laid out. Seb and I ate red sausages and mashed potatoes and later that evening we found the midfield and strikers up on the sun deck. It was dark, they were laughing and gulls were screaming. They were standing by the wall with five miniature bottles of Larsen cognac and three Tuborgs.

'All Danish girls bang like shithouse doors,' the right wing said. His eyes glowed like redcurrants.

'Do you know what "to have it off" is in Danish?' the centre half said. '*Kneppe*!'

'To button?'

'I'm going to *kneppe* my trousers!' the right wing howled and the laughter spread through the darkness.

We sensed a large shadow standing behind us. Everything went quiet. Åge. White hands and red eyes. Then, so help me, he switched on a torch and shone it in our faces. More and more faces appeared, they loomed up out of the dark, face after face, a luminous white in the beam from Åge's torch. It was more or less the whole team. He didn't want the game against Fremad to be a walkover.

Åge sighed.

'Throw the bottles over board,' he said.

A few seconds passed. Åge switched off the torch.

'I can't see you,' he said. 'I don't want to see you.'

Arms swung through the air. A gull screamed.

Åge switched the torch back on.

'Poor do,' he said.

Then he herded us down to where the deadbeats were reclined, gasping through open mouths, with lifeless pupils and stomachs like barrage balloons. The waves crashed through us. Aksel was the first to throw up. It splashed onto the floor. Then it was the right wing's turn. I held my stomach, but it didn't help. I sprinted for the toilet, stood with the rest of the defence and emptied my guts like a bucket. Seb was the only one to survive. He lay back sleeping and snoring with a tiny grin on his face, and somewhere up in heaven there was dance music and the cries of seagulls.

We arrived in Denmark with our guts inside out, we were driven by coach through Copenhagen and installed in a school. The pitch was close by, green and soft. We limped through the first training session. The match was due to start at five.

Åge paced up and down with a furrowed brow talking tactics.

'Denmark is better technically,' he said. 'They play a Polish game. But we'll outdo them in fitness. We'll wear them down. Long balls. Make them work. Make them run themselves into the ground!'

At twelve there was a break. I asked Åge if I could take a couple of hours off because I had family in Copenhagen and I wanted to visit them.

He gave me a sceptical look.

'Can you find your way around alone?'

'Christ, yes. Been here loads of times.'

'Back by three then.'

I raced down to the changing room, showered and put on clean clothes, a new roll neck sweater, burgundy. Hair didn't look half bad either. When it was wet I could fold it behind my ears and it flipped up at the back. I rushed out into the street, patted my pocket where I kept my money, fifty Norwegian kroner gave you sixty Danish kroner and Dad had got me the best rate at the bank. A taxi drew up, I jumped in, wowee, I was on my way to see Nina.

The driver whistled and ate a Danish pastry.

The taxi meter ticked away like a clock. I had no idea how far it was to Strandvejen.

'I've only got sixty kroner,' I stammered.

He glanced over his shoulder with crumbs around his satisfied mouth.

'Uhuh. Only sixty kroner, sonny Jim. That's enough to get you all the way to bloody Norway!'

I pressed my nose against the glass. Strange to be in a completely new place. Tingle of excitement. Pigeons. Hot dog stalls. Black bikes. I rolled down the window. Bakery smells. Freshly baked cakes and bread.

I leaned back against the seat, closed my eyes and felt happy. Happy and completely calm, couldn't remember ever experiencing that before. I could balance on the tightrope now without a safety net, without a pole, that's how calm I was. For a moment I struggled to recall what Nina looked like, but now she was taking shape, her face was close to mine, her features quite distinct, I could feel her breath and her hair. Apple.That's how she was. I slumped back into the seat as we drove along Øresund with white yachts bobbing up and down against the light blue sky.

It cost twenty kroner. Strandvejen 41 was quite a handsome house with a large garden and a view of Sweden. I wasn't so calm any more. Fear lay like a needle in my stomach. I straightened my hair behind a fence post, took a deep breath and walked through the gate. It was a long way to the house, several hundred metres at least. Perhaps she had seen me from the window already. She must have been waiting. I almost broke into a run and finally reached the door. I couldn't hear a sound. She hadn't seen me yet. Then I rang. Time passed. Someone came. It was her mother. She cast a gentle eye over me. My voice had deserted me.

'Do you want to see Nina?' she asked.

Was she out of her mind? Didn't she recognise me? My heart slowly drained into my boots.

Then she remembered me.

'But aren't you… aren't you Kim?'

I was. I feared the worst.

'Do come in. Nina's in her room.'

I followed her. It was too late to turn round now. Strangely enough, I was calmness itself again, as though I had reached the other side, where I had nothing more to lose.

'Nina's going to be surprised,' her mother chatted. 'Are you here with your parents?'

Hadn't she received my letter? Hadn't she read it? Hadn't she told her parents I was on my way?

I didn't care.

'Football,' I said. 'Here to play football.'

We were by Nina's room. Her mother knocked on the door, opened it and pushed me through the opening.

Nina sat there with big eyes staring at me, bewildered. Beside her sat a herbert with a guitar in his lap and a wry smile. It definitely was not her cousin.

'Kim,' Nina stammered. 'Is that you!'

It was.

'I'll get you something to drink,' her mother wheezed and left.

I stood in the doorway.

'Hello,' was all I said.

'I'd completely forgotten,' she stuttered, ashamed.

I searched feverishly for something to say.

'Can I catch a bus from here?' I asked.

'You can,' the guitarist friend said. 'At the bottom of the road. It goes straight to City Hall Square.'

I got the message. Nina eyed us both at the same time.

'This is Kim from Oslo,' she said, pointing to me. 'And this is Jesper.'

Jesper played guitar for us. His long, blond hair hung over his forehead. Jesper sang in English.

I checked my watch. Inside I was a void.

'Are you coming to the match?' I asked.

Nina stared at the floor.

'I'd completely forgotten about it,' she whispered. 'I can't. Jesper's playing in Hornbæk tonight. He plays in a band.'

We said no more. Jesper played another song. Then he peered up at me.

'Match?' he asked. 'Football?'

'Against Fremad,' Nina explained. I supposed that she wanted to prove that she had read my wretched letter.

'Oooh! Watch out! They're really good!'

I had to leave before the mother returned. I could have left without saying a word, about-faced on the spot. I had every right, but I wasn't in my right mind. Instead, and I hated myself as I did it, I asked, 'What about tomorrow?'

Nina averted her face.

'I'd completely forgotten,' she repeated. 'We're going to be in Hornbæk for the weekend.'

Jesper strummed a chord. Defeat was a reality. All that was left was to drag myself off the field of battle, bleeding, crushed, disgrace dribbling from the corners of my mouth. But my body was so leaden. I had to use force. Having finally managed to turn, I stood face to face with the mother bearing a tray of bottles. I walked past her, found the front door and walked down the front path, walked, didn't run, didn't look back.

And my back burned like the copper roof on Kronborg Castle in the sun.

I took a taxi back. It cost three kroner more. I had ten kroner left. My expectations had turned to blackened ashes. I wanted to murder a Dane.

The Danes were called Jesper and Ebbe and Ib and Eske, the whole lot of them. They thought they were on a dancing course and squealed as soon as you went near them. One strong word and they had their noses in the grass. They had been weaned on pastries and buns and cream. And the referee was a partisan baker and the home crowd stood on the sideline with their beer and sagging bellies.

'Long balls,' Åge yelled. 'Long balls.'

Dribbling was out of the question. They could balance the ball on their tongues if they were of a mind. For us it was all about getting in their way as much as possible. Seb was battling on the left wing but didn't whip in one decent centre. Gunnar couldn't get into the penalty area. Willy and Kjetil's pinpoint passing was deftly broken up by the Danish centre half. But Aksel was a kangaroo in goal. He pouched every shot they made.

We kept the score down to 0–0 going into the break. Åge gathered us around him.

'Well done, lads,' he whispered. 'The Danes are getting tired. Accuracy's on the wane.'

Kåre gave us some juice from a huge plastic bottle.

'We've got 'em on the run,' he said every time he filled a mug.

Round two started with a Danish tidal wave. They flooded the pitch towards the goal. Aksel was a fishing net between the posts, The Flying Dutchman from Hoff. The Danes became desperate. Aksel had pysched them out. Their heads hung at every goal kick, they could hardly be bothered to run after the ball.

That was when it happened. A slippery Dane won the ball in the centre, spun round and came charging towards me. Stop him, a voice said inside me. Stop him. I stopped him. I used an old trick. Instead of tracking back I ran straight for him. I met him with my shoulder, pole-axed him at thigh height and dumped him in the grass like a sack. I passed the ball back to Aksel.

But the referee had blown his whistle. And all the Danish pastries thronged around me. I wondered which one would strike first. The baker forced his way through the melee, stood three centimetres from my face and pointed to the dressing rooms. I left the field amid a shower of invective. Åge greeted me with glowering eyes. I took a seat on the bench beside Ola. The Danish butter-wouldn't-melt-in-his-mouth-boy had got to his feet, limped around and grimaced at the skies.

'Wouldn't even get into drama school,' I said.

'Was Nina at h-h-home?' Ola asked.

'No,' I said.

The match was restarted with a free kick that stuck in Aksel's clutches like a sticky bun. The right wing took my position. Seb trapped a long ball, moved into the centre and sent the ball to Gunnar who raced past him and threaded it through to Willy who made for the dead ball line where he forced a corner.

Finn took it. He had the team's most sensitive left foot and screwed in the ball in front of the goal, Seb jumped highest and headed the ball into the keeper's hands, but the goalie lost his footing and fell on his back with the ball in his lap and over the line. He tried to fling it out, but it was too late. The ball was in the goal. 1–0. The Danes' heads dropped and the crowd hurled beer bottles. 1–0. Twenty minutes left to play.

Now the whole team was back in defence. There wasn't a Norwegian in Fremad's half. Åge ran along the touchline waving his arms. Aksel directed the defensive wall forwards and backwards, the pastries ran like madmen, but this was not cunning tactics, it was blind panic. Then it happened. Ten minutes left, 1–0, and a Danish salami lets fly with a cannon. Aksel is horizontal in the air, like a boa, nudges the ball out for a corner with the nail on his little finger. But he lands awkwardly, lands on top of his right arm and gives a chilling scream as he hits the ground. Åge and Kåre rush over to him with a sponge and Solo. But it's no use. Aksel is taken off. The Danes grin. Beside me sits Ola, the reserve goalkeeper, face as green as a mouldy old tea bag. Åge and Kåre return with Aksel between them. Right arm hanging limp.

Åge points to Ola.

'Your turn,' he says. 'Get ready.'

I help him with his laces, his hands are fluttering like birds' wings.

'Relax,' I said. 'It'll be fine.'

With his good arm, Aksel slaps him on the back.

'Best of luck!'

We push him on his way. He jogs over to the goal and takes up his position between the posts. The corner is whipped in. Ola flies out and, as though standing in the midst of a swarm of mosquitoes, throws a wild punch at the ball. And he hits it. It sails through the air in a wonderful parabola to the midfield, and the Danes have to run again.

'Good!' yells Åge. 'Keep the ball out!'

There are five minutes left. It's the biggest battle in Copenhagen since Napoleon was there. There are at least fifteen men around the ball at all times. It's hand-to-hand stuff. Two minutes left. Then a Danish stork crashes to the ground and the baker whistles and points to the penalty spot. At this point Åge is trying to tear the skin off his face. Ola is alone between the posts, never seen him so small. I sprint around the pitch and stand behind the goal, behind Ola. The Danes take up positions. The captain places the ball on the spot and walks back nine paces. Ola crouches down, looks like a dung beetle from where I am. I watch the captain. He scratches his thigh. I look into his eyes.

'Right,' I whisper to Ola. 'Dive to your right!'

Then he runs up, Ola flings himself to the right, the ball hits his body and bounces off him, nineteen men charge forward, Ola gets to his feet, staggers out and falls on the ball. The horde comes to a sudden halt one millimetre from the crown of his head. Ola holds his arms around his head as if it were the ball. Then he is lifted up, the hero of the hour. Åge does a war dance. Ola stands there with the ball in his hands, not quite knowing what has happened. Then he kicks it out of play. But it doesn't matter for the yeast has gone out of the buns. They have given up. The referee checks his watch, adds a minute, then blows his whistle until his cheeks bulge like red tomatoes. We have won. Norway 1 Denmark 0. Ola is chaired off and thrown into the air, he almost doesn't come back down. Åge falls to his knees with his hands clasped together. I turn my back on everything and stroll down to the changing rooms, sit there with bowed head, feeling I was worth less than a casserole lid.

Gunnar was the first to arrive.

'Ola's greater than Gordon Banks!' he shouted.

He studied me close up.

'Come on, you're not annoyed because you were sent off, are you!'

I finished the Solo.

'Bloody hell, you earned us respect. One sendin' off and the puddin' started to wobble.'

The others carried Ola in. Kåre pulled out a crate of lemonade and everyone collapsed on the benches with exhaustion.

Ola sat beside me.

'Neat save,' I said. 'Class act.'

Ola gave a weary smile.

'I l-l-looked him in the eye,' he said. 'Then he didn't have a h-h-hope!'

In the evening songs and games and food were on the menu at the school. The Danes joined us. The Danes were good losers. I wasn't. At eight I put my boots on the shelf and told Åge I felt poorly, must have been a temperature. He placed two fingers on my forehead and nodded. I went downstairs and lay down. I've got a temperature, I thought. So I lay there, alone in the massive gymnasium with the smell of bodies and sweat and socks hanging from the ceiling like a heavy curtain. Alone in the light blue sleeping bag stuck to my skin. I felt so old and drained. Punished. I couldn't get my mind off Nina and Jesper. I hated him. I hated them both. I had been given the brush-off, made fun of and trampled on. Then I must have fallen asleep, at any rate I woke up to someone shaking me. It was Gunnar. It was darker, I could just see all the sleeping bags scattered across the floor like huge larvae in the night.

'Hi,' Gunnar whispered. 'Are you asleep?'

'I was,' I said.

He rolled closer.

'Are you ill?'

'Temperature,' I said. 'Probably a draught on the boat.'

He came even closer.

'Wasn't Nina at home?'

'Nope.'

'But you'd written, hadn't you?'

'Yep. She was at home. Yet she wasn't.'

Gunnar didn't understand that.

'Cut out the riddles!'

'She was with someone else,' my mouth said.

I woke in a boiling hot swimming pool. I was under water. The surface danced and flickered above me and a crowd of people were standing around the edge peering down at me. I swam up to them and banged my head against the sun.

It was the day after. Don't remember much about it. Didn't even feel like a hot dog. I sat on a bench feeding the pigeons while the others ran up Copenhagen Round Tower. I sat on a bench feeding the pigeons while the others were in the zoo. They managed to get me to board the boat home, but I was not bloody going down to the bottom, not bloody likely. I sat in a deckchair on the sun deck and went to sleep. When I woke it was quite dark and someone had covered me with two thick rugs. Carefully, I felt around. My head was as clear as a mountain stream. I stood up. I saw a knot of people and lights some distance away. Above me, the stars flickered. The boat left a white trail in its wake. A ship passed on the port side. I could hear music and voices.

'He's woken up!' someone said behind me. 'The roughneck's woken up.'

It was Gunnar. He came with Seb and Ola.

'Are you better?' Seb asked.

'Fine,' I said.

'Thought it was best with the rugs,' Ola mumbled. 'So the g-g-gulls wouldn't shit on you!'

'Thanks,' I said. 'They saved me.'

Seb had something in those large pockets of his. Beer cans. They grinned and took a swig each. I didn't want any.

'Åge's in the bar,' Seb said. 'Pretty pissed.'

'With a w-w-woman!' Ola panted. 'Danish b-b-blonde. With knockers a metre long!'

'Looks like Marilyn Monroe,' Gunnar daydreamed, drinking from the can.

Ola tipped backwards, caught himself and leaned forwards.

'Do you know what my dad does?' he grinned. 'Eh? He washes his h-h-hair in beer!'

Ola split his sides and threw his beer can in the air.

'What does he do, did you say?' Gunnar yelled.

'W-w-washes his hair in beer! Promotes g-g-growth!'

He laughed soundlessly with an open mouth, then poured the rest of the beer down his neck and looked totally deranged.

We carried him to the railings where he treated the gulls to some half-digested chunks of red sausage. The waves roared beneath us.

'Bloody hell,' Ola groaned, bringing up some more chunks.

'Best if we stay here a while,' Seb said with a grin and took out another can. He had cans everywhere.

I could feel the fever at the back of my head again, like cold terror now. There was a glass partition between us. I could not reach them. I had been sent off again. Didn't want to lose them too.

'Bet you don't think I dare stand on the railing,' I said.

They looked at me and laughed. Ola raised his head and guffawed, too.

'Don't fart about,' was all Gunnar said.

It was fairly broad, but curved. And slippery, probably. I was wearing plimsolls.

'Shall we join the others downstairs,' Seb suggested, finishing his beer.

I jumped up onto the railing, supporting myself with my hands. There were no lights to be seen on the horizon now, only blackness. The waves beat against my ear drums. Then I found my balance, straightened up with my arms outstretched. I started walking. Gunnar, Seb and Ola recoiled, their eyes white balls. I walked along the railing. My heart was caught between two beats. Time took a break. The waves stood up and froze. The wind fell and died. Then Gunnar ran forward in the dark, grabbed me and pulled me down. We rolled over each other on the deck with Gunnar holding me in an iron grip. Then he slapped me. He slapped me across the middle of the face.

'You silly bastard!' he shouted.

Seb and Ola stared at us, unable to believe what they were seeing.

'Sorry,' Gunnar whispered all of a sudden.

I hugged him. His face was wet.

'Doesn't matter,' I said, feeling the blood flow into my mouth.

I sat in my room swotting. Outside my window, evenings rolled past. I wanted to throw away the dry flower I had kept in the drawer. Poisonous. In the drawer there were a dozen Rubin Extra. Jensenius was singing above me, not so loud now for the spring had been a false alarm. It hailed on May 17. But we saw Wenche Myhre in a prommers' truck roaring up Gyldenløvesgate. My temperature had gone. Spring didn't truly arrive until June. The trees became green machine guns. One such evening Gunnar dropped round. He had a long face. Slumped down on the sofabed.

'It's the end,' he said.

'What of?' I asked.

He produced a letter from his pocket. Not perfumed this time, just a standard sheet of paper ripped out of an exercise book.

'She's found a Young Farmer from Vågå,' Gunnar said, crumpling the letter into a tight ball and throwing it out of the window.

I closed my maths book and sat next to him.

'You can't trust girls,' I said.

Gunnar folded his hands and wrapped them round his knee.

'Best it finished as it did,' he said. 'Can't trust a turnip like that.'

I rested my arm on his shoulder. Bitterness coursed through us.

'They're not worth the shoes they walk in,' I said.

'Wouldn't touch her with a hayfork,' Gunnar said.

'Those Young Farmers probably stink of shit,' I said.

'You can't trust girls,' Gunnar said.

We sat in silence for a while. The street noise tormented us. I closed the window.

'I'll never go to Heidalen again,' Gunnar said. 'Never.'

'Let's nip over to Seb's,' I suggested.

Ola was sitting there with his head between his knees.

'We were just on our way to see you,' Seb said.

We sat down. Ola ratcheted himself up and stared vacantly into the universe.

'Finished with Klara,' he said. 'She's g-g-goin' with Njård's top scorer.'

What a day. What a spring.

'Shit,' Gunnar said and told the others about Unni and the Young Farmer.

'Girls are a bunch of p-p-pricks,' Ola said, punching his fist in the air.

'Not worth the stockin's they walk in,' I said.

'First you and Nina,' Gunnar started counting. 'And then Unni. And then Klara.'

'And Guri,' I added.

Seb averted his eyes.

'And Guri,' he whispered.

We sat without speaking for what must have been over an hour. Outside, the grey gloom settled between the houses and enshrouded the streets. Seb suddenly perked up and rummaged through his pile of records.

'Got this from Dad today,' he gasped.

'Got what?' we asked of one voice.

'The latest Beatles record!'

We threw ourselves at him and put the record on the turntable. 'Paperback Writer'. We played it ten times in a row. It had beat. The B-side was 'Rain'. That was very appropriate.

'What does "Paperback Writer" mean?' Ola asked.

I explained to Ola.

Ola thought this over.

'Could definitely have written a book about us, couldn't they,' he said. 'A b-b-big book!'

Yellow Submarine

Summer '66

One day at the end of June we finally had a book in our hands, green and published by Cappelen, written by Kerr's Pink. But it was not really about us. I was given a C for behaviour and a D for woodwork. Seb got an A for singing and music. Gunnar had a B for behaviour while Ola had an E in German and maths. We couldn't care less now, all we were thinking about was bait. We had to find some earthworms for the big fishing trip in Nordmarka.

We rushed out of the playground but were hooked by Goose standing in the middle of the road, obviously with something on his mind.

'Hello,' he muttered.

'How many As did you get, Goose?' Seb asked.

'Why do you call me Goose?'

'Eh?'

'Why do you call me Goose?' he repeated.

Tricky question to answer that was. Goose had been called Goose all the years I had known him.

'That's the way it is. Like Dragon's called Dragon.'

'The girls tease me,' Goose said.

'Stuff the g-g-girls,' Ola said.

'Couldn't you call me Christian?' he mumbled.

'Sure, yes, of course we can,' Gunnar said. 'But we've got to run. Goin' to dig up worms in Nesodden.'

We charged past him.

'Have a nice summer, Christian!' we yelled down the street.

He beamed all over his face and yelled back, 'You have a nice summer!'

'Funny,' said Ola. 'F-funny.'

'You sure we'll find earthworms here?' Gunnar asked as we plodded up to the House.

'You bet. Behind the outside loo.'

Gunnar stopped.

'Outside loo, did you say?'

'Correct.'

I fetched the spade from the shed and we walked over to the wonky loo with a heart on the door. A strong smell came from the fertile earth. At the top it was quite dry, but a spade's depth down it was soft and moist. I turned a spit over and a worm poked its head out, wriggling and squirming.

'What's that?' Gunnar asked, pointing.

'A worm, you clod.'

'Not that but *that*,' Gunnar said.

I looked where he was pointing.

'That. That's just a bit of toilet paper.'

Gunnar went and sat down on a rock by the apple trees. Ola wasn't exactly ecstatic, either.

'So the fish is s'posed to eat the w-w-worm, is it, and then we eat the fish. Not b-b-bloody likely!'

'You'll have to use a net then, you wimp,' Seb snorted and we were left to dig up the bait. We scooped some soil into the coffee tins and between us we found about a thousand worms. Then we made holes in the lids so that they wouldn't die from suffocation. It was a pretty tight squeeze already.

'Let's go for a swim before goin' home!' I shouted.

I walked round the House to make sure everything was okay. There was a line of ants crossing the kitchen steps. I found an arrow I had lost last year. Then I looked in one of the windows and saw myself sitting inside, I recoiled, frightened by the distorted image in the pane, and ran after the others.

The beach was deserted. We undressed and the sun burned our pale grey bodies. Embarrassed, we scrutinised one other, threw ourselves off the springboard, dived in and emerged with a rock each. Afterwards we lay on the bare boulders and our stomachs went red, and as we walked past the old shed with its protruding boards, peeling white paint and smell of rotting seaweed, I was reminded of Henny in Paris and I knew that what happened last year, last summer, would never happen again, would never happen again.

'What's the tent like?' Seb asked on the ferry going back.

'Stig says it's great,' Gunnar said.

'Don't need a tent if it's good weather,' I said. 'We can lie outside in sleepin' bags.'

Then we traipsed through the town each with a tin containing at least three hundred worms. Reaching the American embassy, we stopped and looked at the flag hanging from the pole.

'My brother says there's a huge trout inside,' Gunnar said.

'Trout? No kiddin'!'

'It's true. In the pool.'

We walked past the guard. He couldn't be bothered to stop us, but then he didn't know what we had in our tins. We entered a large hallway and in the middle of the floor there was a pool with a fountain and lights and so on. We peered down and could only see round pebbles on the bottom. The water was no more than twenty centimetres deep.

'Ain't no trout here,' said Seb. 'There might be an anchovy.'

We strolled round the edge. Then Ola shouted and almost dropped his tin.

'L-l-look there, boys!'

A huge trout was swimming only a metre away from us. It was so big that its back was sticking out of the water. It swam slowly as if it was very old or bored. We followed it, crept after it as quietly as we could, but it was impossible not to make a noise in this tiled hall. The trout approached the edge and lay against it as if its shoulder itched. I bent down and touched it. It let me do that. It was cold and tough, motionless. Then it glided away beneath my fingers, to the slender fountain that perhaps reminded it of some waterfall or other, if it had ever swum towards a waterfall.

'I feel sorry for it,' Seb said.

'Terrible to keep a big fish in such a crappy pool,' Gunnar said.

I flipped off the tin lid and pulled out a nice fat earthworm and threw it to the trout. It couldn't even be bothered to turn, it just swam in the opposite direction. But the guard woke up. He walked over with a gun in his belt and ejected us into Drammensveien.

'Cruelty to animals,' Ola said.

'We should've taken it with us to Skillingen and let it out there,' Gunnar said.

'And c-c-caught it afterwards,' Ola laughed.

In the evening we gathered at Seb's and went through our equipment. Gunnar's father saw to provisions: a whole cardboard box full of wholegrain bread, biscuits, caviar, dried milk, tea, coffee, fruit, cans and 'Dead Man in a Tin' that he had left over from an army exercise in 1956. Ola had a gas stove and a frying pan. We borrowed a tent and compass from Stig. Then we made the final adjustments to the fishing reels. I had been given a rod by Mum and Dad for passing my exams. Gunnar had bought 400 metres of 0.30mm fishing line. Seb had three spinners, two floats and six corks. My mother had got hold of four fine-mesh bags we could put over our heads and use as mosquito nets.

But Seb had something better. He produced a pipe. A corn cob pipe.

'Midges and mosquitoes can't stand tobacco,' he explained. 'Just puff away and they'll be off.'

We laughed at that for a bit, then we unfolded the map and traced the route with a finger and submerged ourselves into the countryside, lost ourselves in dreams.

'We're not takin' watches,' Seb exclaimed.

'Eh?'

'We're not takin' watches. Like Indians.'

We deliberated. We knew the sun rose in the east and set in the west.

'W-w-what about if it's cloudy?' Ola said.

'We'll know when it's dark,' Seb said. 'Stuff watches.'

'Moss grows towards the west,' Gunnar said.

'And anthills to the east,' I added.

'What about an alarm c-c-clock?' Ola ventured.

The doorbell rang. Seb went to answer the door and returned with Fred. He had cut his fringe and sandpapered his ears. And he was wearing new trousers, no doubt about it, new jeans, with turn-ups reaching his knees and a large belt with a luminous buckle. Zorro.

'Take a pew!' we shouted.

He sat down and looked around. Seb fetched a Coke and cigarettes.

'Are you goin' fishin'?' Fred asked.

We showed him our route on the map. He studied our gear, tried the reels and weighed the spinners in his hand.

'They're light,' he said.

'Eight grams,' Gunnar elaborated. 'Almost a fly.'

Seb opened the window and the summer evening flooded into the room. Some girls were laughing up the street, we stuck our heads out but said nothing.

'What are you doin' this summer?' I asked.

Fred's eyes went vacant.

'Holiday camp,' he said. 'Hudøy.'

'Want to listen to some records?' Seb asked quickly.

And so we played Beatles music for the rest of the evening, right up to 'Paperback Writer' and 'Rain'. Fred didn't utter a word, just sat listening with his ears on stalks, his ears were large red flowers and from time to time he looked at us, smiled, almost laughed.

Outside, the sky was drinking blood, the girls had gone home and dogs were barking.

Fred checked his watch.

'Gotta go,' he said.

All of us accompanied him to Solli.

'Have a good summer,' Fred said with a slight blush.

'See you in the autumn,' we said, nudging each other and laughing.

Fred wished us well, *Tvi tvi*, he said, as we Norwegians do, and we all spat on the pavement.

He set off down Drammensveien, Fred Hansen, turned, fell on his face, got to his feet, continued at full speed, and we stood watching him long after he was gone.

There was quite a lot of disagreement about how late it was when we arrived in Skillingen. Gunnar thought it was getting on for six while Seb and I were sure it was only five because the train had definitely been in Stryken at three.

'But the train was late, wasn't it!' Gunnar shouted.

We peered up at the sun. It wasn't there. There were just clouds.

The water lay before us, shiny and still, and warm air caressed our bodies. We could hear a cuckoo in the forest and a river was cascading somewhere we couldn't see.

'It's half past f-f-five,' Ola determined.

'How d'you know?'

'L-l-look at the moss.'

To the south we found a good place to set up camp, there were the remains of a previous fire. The tent had seen better days, but after a couple of hours' hard graft it stood upright. Then we grabbed our fishing tackle, screwed together the rods, took a big handful of worms and headed off. We sat by the water's edge watching the floats. They stayed upright, like eggs, without moving.

'S'posed to be fish here,' Seb said after a while.

'Be better in the evenin',' Gunnar said.

'Must be eight by now,' Seb said, looking around.

The forest on the other side grew murky. The darkness emerged from between the trees behind us.

'H-h-half past eight,' Ola said. 'Can feel it in the air.'

We reeled in and changed bait.

'Beginnin' to feel peckish,' I said.

'If we haven't caught anythin' by nine, let's open a can,' Gunnar said.

All at once it became lighter as though a big lamp had been switched on above us. We looked up. The clouds drifted away even though there was no wind at all. The sky turned deep blue. And right above the trees, at the back of the bay facing west, the sun hung like a bloodstained plum, tinting the water red and yellow. We stared ourselves blind and moaned with pleasure. Gunnar fetched his camera and clicked away.

Then we caught sight of a duck in the middle of the water. It was gliding leisurely along in a strip of sunshine, as if bewitched by the light.

'I'll snap it!' Gunnar shouted, moving the viewfinder.

Then something happened. The duck became restless. It flapped its wings but couldn't get into the air. It screamed wildly and began to sink.

'Jeez,' Seb said. 'It's sprung a leak.'

The duck flapped and flapped, beating the water into froth, but nothing helped. It was caught. Then a huge mouth appeared, straight out of the water, closed over the duck and dragged it down.

A few feathers swirled in the air.

That was the last we saw of the bird.

'I've got it!' Gunnar shrieked. 'Oh, shit.'

Ola was ashen. He started to reel in.

'Are there sh-sh-sharks here, too?' he mumbled.

'Pike!' Seb yelled. 'Biggest pike I've ever seen. Wild!'

'That's why we're not catchin' anythin',' Gunnar said. 'Pikes eat perch and trout.'

We all reeled in. Seb started jumping. He had caught something. The line was zigzagging through the water.

'It's big!' he panted. 'Pulls like a locomotive!'

We stood ready to bring it in. Seb coaxed and pulled. There wasn't much bend in the rod, but it must have been a crafty fish. Sweat was pouring down Seb's nose and he applied the brake harder so that the spool would not slip. Then it came into sight. A perch, maximum fifty grams. But it looked angry.

'There must have been a bigger fish hooked first,' Seb said after we got the beast on land. 'It was pullin' me along!'

Quite possible, but a perch was a perch. The first fish. We collected kindling for the fire, cleaned the littl'un, stuck a skewer through its mouth and fried the body over the flames. It didn't taste bad, there was just a bit too much bone and very little meat. Gunnar fetched a can of baked beans which we heated and feasted on. Then we boiled up some coffee and Seb prepared the corn cob pipe.

'What kind of tobacco is it?' Gunnar wondered.

'Karva Blad,' Seb said, taking a puff.

'Is it s-s-strong?'

'Pretty,' said Seb.

He inhaled deeply, his eyes disappeared inside his head and his hair stood on end. Then he passed round the pipe. We lay on our backs for an hour or two gasping for air. Gradually we recovered and sat closer to the fire.

'Helps digestion,' Seb coughed, and that reminded us of what we dreaded most. Gunnar was the first to have to go. He took the toilet roll and was gone for some time. We waited with keen anticipation. He returned with heather in his hair.

'Loads of animals in there,' he complained, sitting down with care.

We stared into the forest, blinded by the light of the fire. Soon, however, our eyes became used to the dark and trees loomed, uprooted trunks came closer, sinister bushes and anthills and gigantic toadstools as big as pavilions, too. We heard rustling and cracking sounds. Overhead a bird screamed. We started. A cuckoo called. There was something crawling down by the water.

'Let's call it a day,' Seb said.

We peed on the fire and crept into the tent. Gunnar switched off the torch.

And before we knew it, the sun was shining through the canvas. We rose, disorientated, and shook the sleep out of our hair.

Ola was sitting outside waiting, with the coffee made. He was grinning.

'S-s-sleepy heads! It's p-p-past eight,' he said, pointing to the sun with a triumphant expression.

We had breakfast and started fishing. The night had chilled the ground, our clothes were damp. But the sun set over the forest and transfixed us with warm spears. Skillingen lake shone like a huge coin in the midst of all the green. And the floats gave no sign of any movement. Gunnar tried a spinner but when he cast it for the third time it stayed at the bottom and the line broke.

'Let's move on,' Seb said. 'To Daltjuven.'

We packed up, found the forest trail and trudged off in single file. The sun blazed high in the sky and warmed our bones. After a stiff march we spotted the lake between the trees, left the trail and bounded across the heather. Daltjuven. Not that big, but then the fish would be closer. We were lucky and found a good campsite straight away, flat terrain and grassy.

We whacked up the tent, slotted the poles together and tightened the guylines. The worms were keeping well, just hanging their heads a little, or tails. When we got to Katnose, we would change the soil. We ambled over to a rock standing upright in the water. Then we crossed our fingers and cast our lines.

The floats sank right to the bottom.

'Fish!' we hollered in unison.

We reeled in, each with a perch. And it wasn't a bag of bones like the one Seb caught in Skillingen. They were at least five hundred grams, chubby and with dorsal fins like cockscombs. Gunnar went for his camera and a knife. Quite a bit of blood was spilt before the battle was over. We each took a photo so everyone was included. Then we put on more bait and cast and from thereon it was all non-stop. The water was bubbling with fish. Perch, trout and powan. We could have set up shop. The vultures were beginning to circle above. The sun angled into the forest and the colours became intense and distinct.

Then the floats lay still in the pitch black water.

'Think we've got enough, anyway,' Seb said, counting the catch. There were eleven perch, four trout and three powan.

The mosquitoes were beginning to make their presence felt.

Seb and I gutted the fish while Gunnar and Ola took care of the fire. Hunger rumbled in our stomachs. We started with the trout. It wriggled in the pan and the delicious smell wafted all the way to Solli plass. After three trout, a powan each and six perch we could have sprouted fins. We staggered down to the water's edge, shoved our heads in and lay down on the grass.

The mosquitoes were circling around us.

'I'll get the pipe,' Seb said, plodding over to the tent.

The sky changed colour, became more black than blue. A chalk-white gull disappeared over the forest. Seb returned with the pipe and filled it with Karva Blad. Just a question of keeping the smoke over the uvula. We puffed and blew out billows of smoke. Our eyes smarted.

'It's Midsummer's Day today, boys!' Seb grinned, pulling out a fluted bottle. 'Pinched it off my mother!'

'G-g-gin!' Ola mumbled.

Seb unscrewed the top and drank. He coughed violently and passed the bottle on. I pretended to drink. My lips were burning. Gunnar took the bottle from me. He took a huge swig and leaned back with a smile. Ola started to hiccup and had to wash his face in the water. The bottle came round again. I took a deep breath, swallowed a mouthful and it landed in my stomach like a red hot brick.

'This is the life,' Seb said in a hoarse voice. 'Just like Red Indians.'

'Especially in winter,' I said.

He didn't hear.

'People live an artificial life in towns,' Seb continued. 'Dad has told me about South American Indians.'

A golden glow transfused Seb's face. He lit the pipe and passed it round. We blew away the closest mosquitoes.

'Wonder how Fred is,' I said.

'Fred should've come with us,' Gunnar said quietly.

A warm wind set the forest in motion, it breathed and the trees sang. The lake made its own sounds, too. I strolled to the edge of the forest to have a piss. The darkness was closer now, it was a black wall within the forest, blocking the view. A mosquito landed on my dick but before I could shake it off, I heard something.

'Psst,' came a voice from behind a tree.

I looked around, but couldn't see anything.

'Psst,' it said once more.

Then a gnome with a huge beard and eyes that burned through the night crawled out. I was not afraid. He seemed to belong to the landscape, he was part of the tree he had been standing behind. His hair was moss, his arms branches and his voice a coarse rustle.

'I followed the smell,' he said. 'You boys have had fish fortune.'

Fish fortune. That sounded funny.

I nodded.

'Perhaps there's a bit left?'

'Yes, sure. Perch.'

He pointed to the water and poked his moss-head closer.

'The others, have they, have they had clearance?'

'Clearance? They're my friends,' I said in bewilderment.

'Can you vouch for them?'

'Of course!'

He followed me to the remaining embers of the fire.

'Hey!' I called. 'We've got a visitor!'

They tottered towards us. The gnome hid behind me. His eyes went from one to the next.

'He needs some food,' I said.

We fanned the flames into life, brought the rest of the fish and soon the pan was sizzling. The gnome said nothing, just sat with watchful eyes and drool in his beard. He smelt of earth.

Then he could restrain himself no longer. He grabbed the perch with his fingers and stuffed it straight into his mouth. I had never seen anything like it. He just jammed the fish into the right hand corner of his mouth, his mouth rotated like a wheel, and then the bones and skin were expelled on the left hand side and landed on the ground. He was an eating machine, no less. Afterwards he let out a gigantic belch and gave a greasy smile.

'Daltjuven is a fine place,' he whispered. 'But no one has fish fortune here more than once. So tomorrow you'll have to move on.'

We glanced at each other. The fire was casting an eerie gleam across our faces. Then the gnome spotted the bottle.

He pointed with a crooked black finger.

Seb gave it to him. He took a formidable gulp and his eyes glowed even more intensely.

'D-d-do you live here?' Ola asked cautiously.

'The sky is my roof and the earth my floor. And the walls are in the east and west, north and south. Welcome to my world.'

He took another swig and returned the bottle.

'I've lived here since the war, boys. I was in merchant shipping. I walk around in my living room and cannot find peace.'

'In the winter, too?'

'In the winter, too. That's when soldiers rest. The snow is warm.'

The fire died down. The mosquitoes came back with renewed vigour. We shadow-boxed in the air. The gnome sat motionless and allowed them to drink his blood.

Then he rose to his feet and his face became invisible in the dark.

'Say hello to Iris, if you meet her,' he said.

'Who's she?'

'Iris is our angel,' he said. 'She's as beautiful as the sun. If you meet her someone will die.'

Then he left. He walked into the darkness and was gone.

We sat for a long time without speaking. The fire went out. The moon shone in the sky with a dull glow.

Seb unscrewed the top and gave the bottle a good wipe.

'Nutter,' said Gunnar. 'Bloody nutter!'

The bottle did the rounds. I took a swig and spat it out.

The mosquitoes were everywhere. My head buzzed on the inside. Seb lit the pipe, but that didn't help much. They continued to come back to seek out our faces, hands, legs. We gave up. We had to seek refuge in the tent. The bottle went round. I pretended to drink. Soon it was empty.

Ola fell asleep. His head keeled over and the rest of his body followed. His eyes were bloodshot and strange noises were issuing from his mouth. Froth formed at the corners of his mouth. There was only one thing to do. We dragged him outside and then crept back in.

'Can't risk gettin' the tent full of spew, can we,' Gunnar slurred.

Straight after there was a hell of a racket outside the tent door. The sides shook, then the zip shot up, Ola stuck a green mug inside and evacuated the contents of his stomach.

We all screamed at once. Ola looked up at us with contorted eyes, understanding nothing.

'Th-th-thought I was outside,' he stammered.

'You *were* outside,' I said. '*Now* you're inside.'

'Have I chucked up in the t-t-tent?'

We got him out and down to the lake. Gunnar and Seb were convulsed with laughter, on their knees howling. Ola wasn't sure where he was. And the tent stank of toilet, no point sleeping there tonight. We rolled our sleeping bags out around the fire. Gunnar was snoring before he hit the ground. Seb was chortling in the dark.

The mosquitoes kept me awake. I stuffed my head in the net bag and found a shopping list of dreams.

I was woken by Gunnar's scream. He was yelling. He sat erect in his sleeping bag clutching his face. It didn't look good. The bumps made it look like a slalom piste.

I went over to him. He was out of his mind.

'What's happened?' he cried. 'What has happened?!'

'Mosquitoes,' I said. 'You forgot to put the net on last night.'

He screamed even louder. His face was bright red and about twice as big as usual. His nose extended in all directions and his eyes lay far back in their sockets, two terrified narrow slits.

I had to hold him. He was flailing his arms like a windmill, almost tearing his sleeping bag to shreds. I dragged him out and got him down to the water's edge. Otherwise it was a wonderful morning, the air was clear, not a breath of wind, still a hint of the night's coolness. Daltjuven was as shiny as a skating rink. Gunnar squatted down to look at his reflection in the water. He fainted. I had to haul him back onto land. I left him lying on the grass and went to wake the others. They were asleep under their nets with hangovers and bad breath.

'Wash the tent, you pig,' I told Ola, shaking him.

Seb rubbed his eyes and ran five rake-like fingers through his greasy hair.

'Something happened or what?' he coughed.

'Mosquitoes have made a meal of Gunnar.'

At last they got up. Ola stuck two floats up his nose and made a start on the tent. Seb and I went down to fetch Gunnar. He tried to hide his face. His eyes peered balefully through his fingers.

Seb tried to comfort him.

'Healthy to be stung by mozzies. Changes the old blood. Girls have menstruation. We've got mozzies.'

Gunnar wouldn't listen.

I took his legs and Seb grabbed him under the arms.

'Is this how you get when you're drunk?' Gunnar muttered.

'You forgot your mosquito net, you knucklehead!'

He kicked me away.

'Don't you call me a knucklehead!' he shouted with the voice of a madman. 'Don't call me a knucklehead!'

Ola emerged from the tent and announced that it was eight o'clock.

'Did it h-h-hurt?' he asked, bending over Gunnar.

Gunnar hit out all around him. It took all three of us to restrain him. We shoved him into the tent. He lay down without a struggle and stared up at us helplessly.

'You hungry?' I asked.

He shook his head.

'Thirsty?'

'Yes,' came the gruff response.

Seb went for water and Ola lit the gas stove. I took out the First Aid kit.

'Gunnar,' I said. 'Can you hear me? Don't scratch. Even if it itches, you mustn't scratch.'

He started to become feverish. We wondered whether to embalm his whole body in gauze, but gave him three aspirins instead. Seb counted the bites and noted down the number on a slip of paper. He counted eighteen on the nose, forty-three on the forehead and thirty-six on each cheek.

When the sun was at its peak Gunnar began to be delirious. His face was more swollen than ever and he was speaking in tongues. It sounded like Swedish or Nynorsk. He said something about a Young Farmer and a girl with long, blonde hair. We went out and let him rave in peace. Seb hadn't been to the toilet since we had left. His belly felt heavy and he sat in the shade of the tent snoozing. Ola dived into his sleeping bag head first. I tried to do some fishing, but perhaps the gnome had been right. There was no life in the water.

Later that evening I discovered some strange tracks around the tent. One foot was a normal boot, the other an elk hoof. They led into the forest.

I said nothing to the others.

Next morning we woke up to some even worse noises. We jumped up out of our bags, Seb, Ola and I, and stared at the tent where Gunnar was asleep. That wasn't where the din was coming from. We rubbed the sleep out of our eyes. Trumpets. We could hear trumpets. Ola was pointing, his mouth wide open. Over on the other side there was a swarm of scouts. The lake was full of canoes. A brown-clad dumpling with pink knees was blowing a trumpet.

We looked at each other. No more needed to be said. We woke Gunnar, his face had gone down a bit. He had scratched his forehead in a couple of places.

'We have to move on,' I said.

'Don't feel like it,' he whinged.

'Lot of scouts about,' I said.

'Let's go,' Gunnar said.

We rolled up the tent and were off. It was just a question of following the forest path all the way to Katnosa. Ola determined that it was nine o'clock. Could see it from the flowers, he said. Wow, we were impressed. Ola was a wandering cuckoo clock.

And then we were there. We threw our rods in the air and ran the last bit. We could smell cows and coffee. On the doorstep stood a large woman, smiling. She was wearing a blue and white dress, just like the sky.

'Have you come far?' she asked.

We had indeed.

We went into the room and sat round a table.

'Waffles,' we ordered. 'And eight Cokes, please.'

Seb disappeared into the toilet and Grandma took a closer look at Gunnar.

'You've fallen out with some mosquitoes,' she laughed.

Gunnar nodded, would have been stupid to deny it. She fetched a tube of something or other. Rose glycerine, she explained, smothering his face with it. He sat with his eyes closed and his hands folded. Strange smell, had smelt it somewhere before, at Fred's place, on his mother's hands.

'Leave it for a couple of hours,' she said.

She brought over the Cokes and then came the smell of the waffle iron and a little after that came Seb, grinning like Johannesen after his record-breaking run in Squaw Valley, looking ten kilos lighter.

He looked at Gunnar.

'Goin' skiin'?'

'Skiin'?'

'Covered yourself in wax, haven't you.'

We laughed at that until the waffles arrived. She sat with us and we told her about the pike and the duck, Daltjuven and all the fish we had caught, but not about the crazy gnome, don't quite know why not, actually.

'Where are you going now?' she asked.

'Down to the river mouth,' I said. 'Goin' to try the river.'

'You can use the cabin there,' she said.

'Great!' we said in unison and the waffles melted on our tongues and the taste of the strawberry jam lay there for a whole summer and half a childhood. And we changed the soil for the worms. As we left we were given waffles and a loaf of bread so fresh it burned our hands. She stood on the doorstep waving, in a blue and white dress just like the sky, and we followed the path along the lake until we were out of sight.

We edged our way across the dam. Cold water streamed into the river and breathed cold air over us. A host of rainbows arced down to the river flowing into Storløken, where it tarried a while before rushing on to Sandungen.

The cabin was not big, but it was better than the tent. It didn't smell of vomit, more of hay and horse. Gunnar found some shade and fell asleep. Seb, Ola and I tried the worms in the river, didn't get a bite, though. We lit the pipe instead, mixed the dried milk, but it went lumpy. Ola tried it as bait, thought he had a huge bite, but it must have been the riverbed he had hooked. And then the dark rolled in from behind us, thick, over our heads, a bit like in a cinema. We tried the spinners, not a nibble. And then came the midges. They were worse than mosquitoes. They got into your ears and nose and mouth en masse. We puffed on the pipe like demented Indians, but it didn't help. We fled into the cabin, where Gunnar was babbling in his sleep. So we, too, went to sleep and dreamt about horses and waterfalls.

I was up before the others. I was wide awake and starving. I crept out. The weather was clear although I couldn't see the sun. Only now could I hear the roar of the river, a rough, heavy drone. It couldn't have been more than six o'clock.

I took my rod and the tin of worms and wandered down to the bank, found a suitable place where I could wade out barefoot. I stuck on a good clump of worms and cast into the current. The hook floated down, I gave line, reeled it in and cast again. In the meantime the sun had appeared behind me and was warming my back. Birds began to twitter and flowers opened and the rainbows in the river danced and shimmered.

On the fourth throw I had a bite. It hurt my wrist. The rod stood in the air like a paper clip. I let the line run and the fish pulled it along. It had to be a trout. Or a salmon. Several kilos. At least. I started sweating. The reel held a hundred metres and there wasn't much line left. I waded backwards to the bank and eased my way along it, the rod wedged firmly behind my belt buckle. Then the line went even tauter, it sang in the air. I stopped, waited for a few seconds then tried to reel in. Stuck. Nothing doing. Against the current. I waited. I had plenty of time. But then I caught sight of a movement down by Storløken. I couldn't believe my eyes. A naked woman was sitting on a rock, absolutely naked with huge tits and light brown skin. I let the rod slip, the line ran. I stood staring in amazement. She didn't see me. Then she glided into the black water and swam across. At that moment I heard a dog barking.

I ran back to the cabin. They were asleep. I shook them awake.

'Naked woman in the river!' I shouted.

They were out of their bags like bats out of hell and sprinted after me. We found two bushes to hide behind.

'There!' I said, pointing to the rock in the water.

No one there. The river was smooth, without a ripple.

'Where?' they hissed.

I took a few steps forward.

'She was there,' I said lamely. 'Right there. A few minutes ago. Sitting on the rock, without a stitch on.'

The others exchanged glances and rolled their eyes.

'It's true!' I shouted. 'Huge tits she had!

'It's only s-s-seven o'clock,' Ola divined from a flower he had picked.

'Don't you believe me?'

They didn't answer, just shuffled back to the cabin. I went for my rod. Seb was making tea when I returned. Ola was slicing wedges off the fresh loaf. Gunnar looked fine apart from a couple of bumps on his forehead.

'Been up long, have you?' he grinned.

'I did see her. I saw her! Dead cert!'

'Yeah, yeah, yeah,' Seb sighed.

'Hooked an enormous trout,' I said in desperation. 'Five kilos it must have weighed. I was just gonna land it against the current. And that was when I saw the woman and the line ran!'

Gunnar patted me on the back.

'Sure you hadn't hooked her?'

They had a good, long laugh about that.

I walked up to the dam and sat there. Naked woman, I could hear them saying in the cabin. Naked woman in Katnose river! Then there was lots of laughter and whistling.

In the forest I heard a dog barking.

We caught nothing that day so we had to make do with fish balls for dinner. We sat on the doorstep as the can simmered on the gas stove. Seb prepared the pipe in case those pesky mosquitoes and midges came to bother us again. Ola examined the landscape and furrowed his brow, trying to work out the time.

But then he caught sight of something else. He craned his neck and hushed us.

'Someone comin',' he whispered, pointing.

We jumped up and peeped around the corner. She was coming across the dam, a short girl in strange clothes with a dog following – a fat, shaggy Norwegian Buhund.

'That's her!' I said. 'That's the woman I saw in the river!'

The fish balls boiled over. We rescued what we could. Moments later she was standing on the doorstep. The dog sniffed around with its tongue hanging out. She just stood there, for a long time, staring at us, and we became quite frenetic.

'Fancy some food?' I asked with a dry throat.

She nodded, unhitched her rucksack and sat down. I gave her what was left of the fish balls. She shared them with the dog. Then laughed.

'Great catch,' she said. 'Freshly canned.'

She was weird. She was the weirdest thing we had ever seen. She was weirder than the gnome. Her hair was long and very dark. And she had put lots of flowers in it, daisies, harebells and marigolds. She was an entire bouquet. But it was her eyes which were strangest. On the outside they were intense, they stared at you with all their gravity, but behind the blue there was a matt grey, like water that has been trampled in and the sand and mud stirred up.

We made coffee. She didn't move. Seb lit the pipe and cleared his throat. She wanted to try. We were laughing inside. Karva Blad. But she inhaled the smoke with a huge drag and there it stayed. She passed the pipe to me without batting an eyelid.

'Did you catch anything this morning?' she asked.

I instantly went as red as a tomato. All the blood rushed to my head. And it was hot. Blood-red beads of sweat seeped from my brow.

'No,' I whispered.

But she didn't look angry. She was smiling.

'Tonight we'll catch loads of fish,' she said, rolling a cigarette with nimble fingers. The tobacco looked dry and dark. She lit up, sucked in all the smoke, held her breath and closed her eyes. When she opened them, they had changed. The clear blue had receded and the matt, murky sediment appeared. It was as if she couldn't see us. She smelt sickly sweet.

'Tonight we'll catch fish,' she repeated. 'But first of all I have to sleep.'

So saying, she laid her head on the dog and slept on the doorstep.

We went down to the river and each of us sat on a rock.

'She hasn't got a rod,' Gunnar said.

We chewed on that for a while.

Ola spotted an anthill.

'It's half past s-s-six,' he said.

'So you were right after all,' Gunnar said.

'Think she's an Indian,' Seb whispered, blowing smoke rings skywards.

After a good hour she and the dog woke up. They joined us. She looked around and nodded several times.

'Have you seen or heard anyone?' she asked.

'No,' we said, bemused.

'Come on.'

We followed her to the dam. There she stopped and pointed to a large lever. It looked like a lock on a door.

'We have to close the sluice gate,' she said.

'Why's that?'

She smiled.

'Wait and see.'

We had to heave and strain, all of us. The big handle barely moved. But then we got it in an upright position and it slipped down towards the other side. We straightened up and listened. The river dwindled to a trickle. It became quieter and quieter.

'Come on,' she whispered.

She fetched her rucksack and Gunnar took the torch. We went down to the banks.

'We'll have to wait a bit,' she said, sitting down.

It was strange. The sounds from the forest closed in on us now that the roar of the waterfall had gone. I looked at Gunnar. Even in the dark I could see that he didn't like this. He was uneasy.

After a while she stood up and flashed a white smile.

'Now we can fish,' she said.

Gunnar was incandescent. The trout squirmed between the stones in the pools that were left, jammed together like in a can. It was crazy. It was like picking berries. Seb fetched our nets. The Indian woman filled her rucksack.

Gunnar grabbed my arm.

'This ain't legal,' he snarled.

'Course it's not, but it's the first time I've *picked* fish!'

He let go and went up towards the cabin. We filled two nets before we considered stopping. The insane woman had her rucksack full to overflowing. It was jumping about like an octopus.

Then we opened the sluice gate again, pushed with all our might and raised the lever. And slowly the world returned. A murmur at first, then the water plunged down, the roar resounded in our ears and the river flowed into the night with rafts of white foam on its back.

We lit the fire in front of the cabin, gutted eight trout, roasted them on a spit and drank tea. They tasted like waffles with bones. We smacked our lips and slurped so loudly they must have heard us in Skillebekk. Only Gunnar was not hungry. He sat apart from us looking grumpy and cleaning his nails with the knife.

Seb lit up the pipe and passed it round. She rolled one of her own, smoked it for a long time and then began to talk, as if to herself, or to the dog lying beside her with its rough, red tongue spread over its front paws.

'Life is a river,' she said. 'Life is a stream.'

She leaned back and the sky sank in her face. Then she fell silent again. The fire crackled. Behind us, the water flowed.

'Can I have a drag?' Seb asked.

She passed him the cigarette. Seb took a huge drag, his eyes stood out in his face like bandy balls.

'Bloody hell!' he groaned and made straight for the river and drank like an elephant.

She laughed, sucked at the glow until it almost reached her lips, took a flower from her hair and threw it on the fire.

Gunnar was whittling a stick. He said, 'What's your name actually?'

She leaned back again. The dog rolled up its tongue.

'The night doesn't exist,' she said into the air.

'What do you do actually?' Gunnar persisted.

The dog began to growl. The ears on its shaggy head stood erect. A row of teeth came into view in the bared jaws.

She stirred uneasily and stood up. The dog joined her, listened, then growled again and showed its teeth. The animal's body was trembling.

'I have to go,' she said, throwing on her rucksack.

And she left, in the dark, disappeared like the river.

'Wow.'

That was all we could say. 'Wow.'

We sat for a while getting cold. A wall of cold rose from the river. Then the midges came. They came quickly and without mercy. We poured water on the fire, ran for the cabin and dived into our sleeping bags. The moon shone through the small, dirty window casting eerie light into the room. Then it slid away and darkness was all there was. We slept fitfully, talking in our sleep, a strange nervous conversation.

Gunnar was the first up. He returned with teeth gnashing and narrow slits for eyes.

'Sod her,' he said. 'Screw her!'

Ola and I went out for a look. Down by the fire all the fish lay rotting. Flies buzzed in a compact stinking swarm above them. The mesh shopping bags were ruined.

'Forgettin' the fish was our fault,' I said.

Gunnar kicked a stone that went sailing through the air.

It was downright impossible to wake Seb. He was mumbling, talking gibberish and totally incoherent. He was screaming, too. We had to use force, drag him into an upright position and lean him against the wall. Then we packed our things and moved on. We had the longest stretch of the journey in front of us, all the way to Kikut and Lake Bjørnsjøen.

'All those fish thrown away!' Gunnar mumbled. He was furious. 'I knew it!'

'What did you know?' I asked.

'That shit is what you get from messin' around like that. It ain't right to shut the gate. It's no fun. And think of all the people left without water!'

We hadn't thought about that. Ola lost his tan on the spot.

'D'you think they've n-n-noticed that in the n-n-north?'

'Of course,' Gunnar said. 'Lake Maridal. All of Oslo!'

Perhaps it was best to make a few detours. We took a look at the map, but the paths were quite tortuous. We didn't want to end up at Hadeland Glassworks.

I said, 'Wasn't us. We were asleep.'

Seb chuckled.

Gunnar walked at the rear scratching the bites on his forehead.

'Had a wild dream last night,' Seb grinned, rubbing his eyes. 'Dreamt I was a fish.'

'What s-s-sort of fish?' asked Ola.

'Dunno what sort of fish, do I, you puddin'. Just a fish. Swimmin' like mad. And we were talkin' to each other. I mean, we, the fish. Talkin' with little screeches. I know physically what it feels like to be a fish. Mad, eh! And under the water it was totally clear.'

'Was no one fishin'?' I asked.

'Yeah. Spotted a big hook. And I was just goin' to bite when you woke me.'

It was five o'clock when we finally found Lake Bjørnsøen. That was what Ola said anyway. He could see it from the colour of the clouds. We burst into the Kikut lodge and ordered open sandwiches with liver paste on, Cokes and Ascot cigarettes. A huge clock hung on the wall. It was five past five. We looked at Ola. He was tuned in to time.

Footsore, sunburnt and exhausted, we sat there for quite a while. There was an old codger behind the counter and two women in the kitchen. And none of them complained about our lack of activity. Gunnar calmed down a little.

'No one knows *we* did it,' I whispered across the table. Gunnar looked straight at me.

'That's got nothin' to do with it, has it!'

We found a place to camp a bit closer to the mouth of the river, right out on a flat headland that protruded into the water like an index finger. We erected the tent and took out our fishing tackle. The rainworms were beginning to go limp, there was very little resistance when we squeezed them onto the hook. The floats didn't move. Slowly the water turned black as the clouds rose in the sky. A current of cold air blew against the back of our necks. The forest began to sough.

We crept into the tent. It was late enough anyway and we were dead on our feet. The sleeping bags lay end to end. The tent shook in the wind. Far in the distance, perhaps over Frogner, we heard thunder.

'Isn't it a bit s-s-stupid to be outside,' Ola said.

'Worse in the forest,' Seb said. 'A tree could fall on your head.'

We lay listening, heard the wind and the waves beating against the rocks. It was dark. It was very dark.

'Let's count bands,' Gunnar suggested.

Seb kicked off.

'The Beatles,' he said. Obvious really.

Then it was Ola's turn.

'The Beach B-B-Boys.'

Gunnar: 'Gerry and the Pacemakers.'

And me: 'The Rollin' Stones.'

And so it went on: The Animals. The Pretty Things. The Who. The Dave Clark Five. Manfred Mann. The Yardbirds. The Byrds. Lovin' Spoonful. The Kinks. The Snowflakes.

'Who said that?' Seb shouted.

It was Ola.

'Doesn't count. The Snowflakes doesn't count!'

We continued, we weren't asleep yet. The Supremes. The Pussycats. The Tremeloes. The Shadows. Dave, Dee, Dozy, Beaky, Mick and Tich. The Swingin' Blue Jeans.

'The Snafus!' said Seb and then the thunder struck. The darkness was chopped up by blue knives. The ground shook beneath us. The rain hammered down on the canvas. Then it hammered down on us. It streamed in from all sides. The tent leaked like a sieve.

We got up and went out. The sky was grinding its teeth. The thunder rolled down. The wind beat against our faces.

'We'll have to go to Kikut!' Gunnar yelled.

He lit the torch, but it wasn't a lot of use. We packed everything up as best we could and fought our way through the storm, stumbled in the mud, were sent flying by the wind. Now and then there was a blue flash, as if from a huge crackly TV set.

All the windows in Kikut Lodge were dark. We banged on the door, but no one heard us. Seb pointed to another door. It was the toilet. We ran over. It was just as cold there, but it was dry. An unsavoury smell emanated from the cubicles and the tin urinal.

'Let's go home tomorrow,' said Seb.

We tried to sleep, but our sleeping bags were too wet. We tried to light the pipe, but the matches were too wet. We tried to argue, but we were much too wet. Then we must have fallen asleep despite everything, because we woke and were stuffed up and frazzled at the edges. And it wasn't raining. It was just the urinal behind us dribbling. The sun was shining. We staggered out, stiff-legged and sore, bought some broth and rolls and hung ourselves out to dry for a couple of hours in the rising sun.

'D'you recognise that smell?' Seb asked.

'I do,' I said.

The worms. The worms had gone rotten. We went into the forest and emptied them out. A couple of trees instantly lost their needles. Then we hung our clothes and sleeping bags on the back of our rucksacks and started the trek home. We had a rest by Lake Skjærsøen and ate the rest of 'Dead Man in a Tin.'

'Been a great trip,' Seb said.

We could all vouch for that.

Gunnar took out his camera, knelt down, wound it on and squinted. Then an old man appeared on the path and we asked him to take the photo.

So we all were in the picture.

With our last coins we ate hotpot and drank malt beer in Ullevålseter. Now it was downhill to Lake Sognsvann and even though it was nice to be going home to a bed and records and a toilet, we felt an urge to drag the trip out. We took a detour to Lille Åklungen which lay dark and deep beneath the steep scree in the west. We settled down on a green promontory and checked our fishing gear.

'What's the time?' we asked Ola.

He looked around a bit puzzled, counted on his fingers and reckoned it was five.

We put on spinners and cast. Seb's hit the bottom and the line broke. He packed up his things and couldn't be bothered to fish any more. Ola went for a walk in the woods. Eventually Gunnar also gave up.

Seb pointed.

'Look at those pylons over there! They look like huge robots!'

They towered over the trees, hatless, arms outstretched, colossal steel skeletons. If we kept quiet, we could hear the wires singing. It sounded eerie.

'That woman was pretty crazy,' I said.

'The gnome too,' Gunnar said.

'But he was right about us not catchin' any more fish in Daltjuven,' I said.

Ola rummaged through the rucksacks. We strolled up to him. He jumped like a frog as we approached, trying to hide something he was holding in his hand. We forced it open. His watch.

He went a hideous red and developed a twitch in his left ear. It flapped. We just looked at him. A star went out. A cuckoo said goodnight.

'H-h-haven't used it until n-n-now!' he stuttered.

'Oh, no. No, of course not,' we said. 'What's the time now, eh? Can you work that out?'

He stared at his watch.

'It's s-s-stopped,' he said. 'It's not waterproof.'

He peered up at the sky as one ear flapped wildly.

'Think it's h-h-half past six,' he said.

I cast for the last time, swung the rod, the spinner flew in a wonderful arc and landed with a sigh out in the middle of the inlet. I let it sink and wound slowly. Then I felt it jerk my arm. The line quivered and sang like the high tension wires above. It wasn't snagged on the bottom. It jerked.

'Got one!' I shouted.

I let the line run. The fish took it. I gave more. Then it stopped. I reeled in carefully. It wouldn't give in, tried to swim away, but it was too tired and the hook was firmly in position. It surrendered. It came with the line. When it was close enough we saw it glistening in the dark water. I landed it. It weighed at least half a kilo. It was a rainbow trout.

'Shall we eat it now?' I asked.

'Take it home,' Gunnar said, patting me on the back.

We set out on the last stage, trudged past the Gaustad fields. It had been a wonderful trip. Everyone was agreed on that. Some people were coming towards us, a strange procession, ten to fifteen men, all dressed the same, with shaven skulls and deep-set dark eyes and pale blue skin. At the front and rear were two men who did not look remotely like the others, they wore different clothes and looked quite strong, more like guards. They passed us without a word, looking nowhere, their hands grey protuberances and all I could hear was the shuffling of feet.

I stopped and froze from top to toe, impaled by an ice cold pillar. Then I ran after the others.

'Did you see them?' I said. 'Bloody hell!'

'Who?' Gunnar asked.

'Who! The nutters of course. The nutters from Gaustad!'

I pointed up the road. They weren't there. A flock of birds suddenly alighted from the yellow meadow.

'Bet England will win the world championship,' Gunnar said.

'What about Brazil then?' Ola said. 'P-Pelé!'

I turned round once more. The road was deserted.

Ola was in ecstasies. Ringo was the greatest singer in the world. Ringo was the one and only. He sat with his arms and legs round Gunnar's record player, sweat glistening on his neck.

'When I'm called up I'm gonna join the m-m-marines!' he cried.

We pressed Repeat. 'Yellow Submarine', full blast, opened the window and the whole town became a yellow submarine, the sky was the water and we were the crew.

'Have to hurry or we'll be late,' Gunnar harried. He still had a couple of scars on his forehead from the worst of the mosquito bites.

We managed the flip side before leaving at a run. And suddenly the mood was different. The street was metamorphised into a cemetery, for some moments the sun disappeared behind a cloud and autumn stole in. 'Eleanor Rigby'. We sat listening in silence, thinking it strange that everything could change so abruptly inside us, as soon as we flipped the record, just as though we had been split in two: an A side and a B side, happiness and sorrow.

And then we sprinted off to Vestheim. It was the first day at school after the summer. The first day of the second year at *realskole*.

The *gymnas* students stood in Skovveien smoking and showing off, and by the wire fence stood the dwarfs, eyes darting to and fro, only just able to see over their shoes. We ambled past them, recognising a couple of faces from Urra. They tried to say hi and be friendly, but it didn't cut any ice. Had we ourselves not made it through the first year? Exactly. We walked right past them. But one persistent leech with trousers at high tide and a porcupine haircut padded after us.

'What's the initiation ceremony like?' he said, clearing his throat.

We stopped and gave him a searching look.

'Have you got any ID?' Seb asked.

'Eh?'

'This is not a film for kiddies.'

'But what's the initiation ceremony like?' he insisted.

'Don't even think about it,' I said. 'Or you'll never return.'

He went white.

'Is it that bad?'

'Worse,' I said. 'Either they get you now, block the drain in the urinal with bog paper and up-end you until your ears are full of piss, known as the Ernst system, that is, or they wait till the winter and ram your head into a snowdrift and screw you in tight. Take your pick.'

He tottered off to the fence and sat on the ground. The other midgets flocked around him.

The girls had grown. How the girls had grown. We quietly slipped away.

Goose turned up with a crease in his trousers and an apple under his arm.

'Hiya,' he said cautiously.

'Hiya, Christian,' we said and he beamed from ear to ear and stood like that until the bell rang.

The desks were too small now. There was a stale smell after the summer and we opened all the windows. The sponge on the teacher's desk was hard and dry. Goose moistened it. The girls sprayed perfume on him. Yep. Nothing had changed. Except that something was missing. A desk was missing.

Fred was missing.

Kerr's Pink arrived, took a seat behind his desk and fidgeted with some books.

'Sit down,' he said at last.

We sat down.

Kerr's Pink started talking.

'First of all, I have some sad news to announce. Our classmate, Fred, Fred Hansen, is dead. He drowned this summer.'

I don't think I have ever heard a silence like that. And I can't remember anything else until we told Seb and Ola after the lesson. The words were so heavy in my mouth. Seb didn't believe me. He grabbed my shoulders and shook me. Then he believed it.

We walked home. Our brains churned in our heads. Gunnar said what we were all thinking, but couldn't quite think through.

'How could Fred've drowned? He was so good at swimming!'

Not a word more was said. I thought about those old clothes of his. I thought about the rat and his mother's red hands.

Fred was dead.

We went to the photographic shop in Bygdøy Allé where Gunnar had handed in the film of the fishing trip. The assistant found the packet.

'Some light must have got into the film,' he said, taking the negatives from the plastic sleeves.

All that was left of the summer was a strip of black pictures.

Revolver

Autumn ’66

There was a lot of devilry that autumn. We played *Revolver* that autumn. That was the autumn we were confirmed.

Once a week we went to confirmation classes at Frogner church, every Wednesday. The cramped stone room smelt of mildew and wet socks. There were at least twenty of us, each with our Bible and psalm book. The priest was the skier type with a dewdrop hanging from his nose and vertical wrinkles. His voice boomed. He preached about all the things we had promised when we were baptised.

And of course Goose was there. After the lesson he hung around as we lit up a fag in Bygdøy Allé.

‘Do you like the priest?’ we asked.

‘Crap,’ said Goose.

‘Quite a slog to get those presents,’ I said.

‘I’ve asked for a Hammond organ,’ Goose said.

‘Wow. You can play then, can you?’ Gunnar asked.

‘Piano.’ He hesitated. ‘Going to start a band.’

‘Band? Which one?’

The breath caught in our throats.

‘Have to see,’ he said, staring at the ground.

A rainworm was wriggling up the pavement. He trod on it.

‘What did you do that for?’

Gunnar pointed to the mess and grimaced. Goose gave a strange smile.

‘Felt like it.’

He shrugged his shoulders and walked off down the street.

We shuffled up to the fountain. It was out of operation for the winter, even though it was only September. A man rode a horse down the the middle of the avenue, wow, what an impressive sight, a shiny brown horse in the rain.

'How long's your dad goin' to be at home?' I asked.

'Three months,' Seb said, plucking out a Teddy cigarette. He looked gloomy.

'Isn't that alright?' Gunnar lit a match and cupped it with his big hands.

'Ye-es. But he and Mum are arguin' all the time. And he keeps hasslin' me to have a haircut.'

'M-m-my dad moans as well,' Ola mumbled, adjusting his fringe.

We pulled out our combs and tidied our locks. We didn't talk much that autumn, but we had to say something, so we talked about Frigg being fourth in the league with a chance of going top, about the new Stones LP, *Aftermath*, and about the training sessions we had missed. But the thing we all wanted to talk about we repressed. About Fred.

We mooched home wearing yellow raincoats, silent and downhearted.

'Not sure I want to continue with the lessons,' Seb exclaimed.

We pulled up short.

'Stop? Don't arse about,' I said. 'We won't have any instruments for The Snafus if we don't get confirmed!'

The others nodded.

'Right. But why should we go there if we don't believe a word?'

'I told you, you puddin'. The presents!'

We went back to Gunnar's and played *Revolver*. One, two, three, four! Seb was lying stretched out when he heard the first chords of 'Taxman'. And there was 'Eleanor Rigby' again. We pushed closer to the speaker as if we were freezing and the record player were a fire. I was hacked off that Paul had a soppy number on every LP, this time 'Here, There And Everywhere', but 'For No One' went straight to the heart like an arrow and we thought of all the girls, Unni, Klara, Nina and Guri. At the same time we had to listen to 'Girl', we sat there with clenched fists giving the cold shoulder to girls all over the globe. George's sitar penetrated bone and marrow, it was like being at the dentist's. And 'Tomorrow Never Knows' was pretty crazy. Sounded like John was singing with his head in a flowerpot while no one in the entire orchestra in the background could give two hoots about cinema tickets.

'John Lennon's startin' to get fat,' Seb said once his pulse had dropped under a hundred.

Gunnar was annoyed and pinched his stomach to test for excess fat.

'Is he buggery. Just looks like it. It's his shirt that's too big!'

'D-d-definitely want some of those sunglasses for the summer,' Ola said, pointing to Ringo.

Outside, the rain fell, diagonal and unremitting.

September 1966.

'Yes,' we said. 'For the summer.'

And once again we repressed what we most wanted to say and slunk home, each with a heavy stone in our hearts.

Mum was waiting with supper. Dad was reading a thick book with an English title. After Christmas he would be branch manager.

'You'll have to come with us to the theatre soon now,' Mum said.

It sounded like a call to war. I didn't want to go with them to the theatre.

'Aren't you happy?'

'Yes, I am,' I said because Mum looked happy.

Night broke to the sound of Jensenius. He didn't walk so much now, just sat in a chair I imagined, singing. Some evenings he could sing for two hours at a time with a fifteen-minute break. Then I suppose he dreamt applause and stamping and allowed himself to be cajoled into an encore.

Jensenius sang before winter came and snowed on his vocal cords.

I couldn't sleep. A light shone from under the door. Mum and Dad were sitting in the sitting room talking in loud whispers. I held my breath and listened.

'He's an idiot!' I heard Dad say.

Mum was quiet.

'Resigning like that!'

'Taking leave of absence,' Mum interjected.

'And to Paris! To this… this… girl!'

I crept back under the duvet and laughed in the dark. Hurrah for Hubert! Then I had to hold on tight, a dream appeared and launched me through the walls, this was the dream I had that autumn of '66. I dreamt about the War of the Staple in 1962, in the middle of the

Cuba crisis, when I saw my father frightened for the first time, frightened, and when I saw that, fear swept through me with twice the force. Dad bought thirty kilos of canned foods, stored them in the cellar in Nesodden in case, just in case. No one was allowed to touch them, but gradually he calmed down, forgot the cans and did crosswords instead. That's the cans I'm living on now, so thanks Dad, you showed foresight there, we are always at war. But, well, the War of the Staple, the three-day war, in '62, when Skarpsno and Vika met head-on, and we in Skillebekk were caught in the crossfire with fragile hairgrip catapults which were no match for the enemy's canons. But we had one advantage, we knew the battlefield well, we knew about secret doors, holes in the fence and underground passages. It started one Thursday. By Saturday afternoon it was over. When we heard Jakken scream. Jakken was disabled, he had some illness or other, he couldn't walk properly, moved out of the area a long time ago now. Jakken screamed, he was standing in the middle of the street with a metal staple in his eyeball. Blood was streaming out. Jakken screamed and screamed. The war was over. We emerged from the trenches and the bunkers. He lost his sight there and then, in both eyes. Standing in a pool of blood screaming. The war was over. Mum could keep her hairgrips. The cans were in the cellar in Nesodden.

That's what kept me awake at night.

I dreamt about staples and war.

One day, a day like any other that autumn, with a low gurgling sky and rain-bearing winds, we plucked up courage and bought four roses which were so red in all that grey, so dazzlingly red, and we went up to the Nordre Gravlund, to Fred's grave. We dreaded it like the plague and walked in silence down the long road to the cemetery squeezed between Ullevål Hospital and the school gardens.

The graves lay in lines, large stones, wooden crosses, wreaths. Beyond the hedge, an ambulance howled past. Our polished shoes were grey with dirt.

An old man in black came down the gravel path and peered at us.

'Where are you going?' he grumbled.

'We… we're looking for Fred Hansen's grave,' Gunnar said.

The man shivered and pulled the black coat round his neck. Then he motioned us to follow, down a path between the gravestones. There was a smell of wet earth.

He pointed to the corner of the cemetery under the yellow birch trees.

'Down there where the lady is standing. That's his mother. Here every day, she is.'

Couldn't turn back now. We walked slowly towards her. Seb was holding the flowers. The rain came in cold gusts.

She spotted us as we approached, recognised us at once and a slanted smile traversed her face.

'It's you,' she whispered.

We went closer, wiped our hands on our thighs and practised the word in our heads that we had been taught by Kerr's Pink when the class sent her the card and the flowers.

'Condolences,' we said, each in turn, proffering a hand and the lump in our throats grew into a pomegranate, it was good it was raining.

'We've brought some flowers,' Seb said, taking off the wet paper. We looked at the grave, at the inexorable numerals that had been engraved in stone:

14/8/1951 – 25/6/1966.

'You must come home with me,' the mother said suddenly. 'Please!'

We mumbled our thanks and accompanied her across town to Schweigaardsgate and the Trans-Siberian railway.

We took a seat in the sitting room, she made tea. There was still a smell of stale clothes. And the door to Fred's room was open. Nothing was changed, nothing had been moved.

'Fred was the only person I had,' she said quietly.

'We miss F-F-Fred, too,' Ola managed to say. We stole a grateful glance at him. Ola said the right things when it mattered.

'He didn't have so many friends,' his mother went on. 'You don't know what it means to me that you have come here, to talk to you…'

And so she talked about all the things Fred would have been, would have done and she seemed to breathe life into him and now, I thought, now at any rate he would never be able to disappoint her.

'Have more tea,' she said at last. 'I'll get you something to nibble!'

She came back with a bowl full of biscuits.

'Alphabet biscuits,' she smiled.

We chewed the dry biscuits, drank the sweet tea, which was lukewarm. And it seemed to me the only letters to be found in the bowl were F and R and E and D. And I experienced something, it must have been what the priest called holy communion, at least it felt like that, body, blood, and the whole time we were looking at the open door and the room where the maths book lay open at the logarithms page.

On the way home, the weight of the stones in our hearts was too much. The rain cascaded down around us and we seemed to be sinking.

'Fred died on June 25,' I said.

The others, smoking their wet fags, said nothing.

'That was the day we met the woman in Katnose,' I continued.

'So?' Gunnar challenged.

I swallowed the stone.

'Perhaps it was the woman the gnome told us about, Iris.'

Gunnar clenched his teeth in a huge sneer.

'Shut up!' He was right in my face. 'Shut up!'

'The p-p-priest says God has predetermined everythin',' Ola whispered, running his hand nervously through his hair.

'And what kind of God would do that, eh! Who would let Fred drown!'

Gunnar fumbled with a cigarette, gave up and threw the matches at the house wall.

'I'll ask the priest that next time,' Seb said and spat.

'Fred drowned,' Gunnar said in a low voice, as quietly as he could. 'Fred drowned. No one predetermined that! People drown every summer. Fred was one of them. No one can help that.'

'No,' we said.

Fred is dead.

We went home. It was good to have said that. No matter what. It was good to have been there. We felt lighter somehow, as though we could swim away in the rain.

We stood in front of the hall mirror, Mum and I, and it was a bit like the summer in Nesodden when we had dressed up. She was wearing a long dress and gleamed from top to toe, and I, hair trimmed, freshly scrubbed, in a blazer with shiny buttons, ground my teeth.

'You'll get a suit for your confirmation,' Mum said, and there was a hoot outside, for, so help me, she had ordered a taxi as well. And that was fine. I sneaked out of the door, slipped onto the back seat and sat with bowed head, loath to be recognised wearing that outfit.

In the taxi my mother whispered to the back of my neck, 'Aren't you happy? Just think, Toralv Maurstad in *Brand*!'

I was scared stiff.

We hung up our coats and Mum had to stand in front of the mirror again. I wished I were elsewhere, I wished I were infinitely far away, but it was no use. Mum took my arm, held me tight, pointed and showed me how wonderful everything was, told me about Hauk and Alfred and Peer. I tried to calm my pumping heart, at least here I wouldn't meet anyone I knew, that had to be a certainty.

Then a bell rang and people began to make for the entrances. We snaked along our row and found our seats. There was a smell of moths. Moths and perfume and aftershave, it was worse than the church and the gymnasium rolled into one. My tie pressed against my Adam's apple, the elastic was suffocating me. Then the curtain went up, someone started speaking in a demented voice and I passed out.

I was woken by a strong light, applause and stamping.

'Has it finished?' I asked.

'It's the interval,' Mum laughed.

We rushed up to the first floor because Mum wanted a Martini. I had a Solo. There were no seats so we had to stand along the walls. Mum leaned back and gave a sigh of pleasure.

'It's so overwhelming,' she said.

'Mmm,' I mumbled.

'I'm sure you'll be reading *Brand* at school. Or *Peer Gynt*.'

That was when I choked on my lemonade. Right in front of us stood Nina's parents. There was no mistaking them. Sweat was running out of my trouser legs.

'Have to go to the loo,' I said.

Mum looked at her watch.

'You'll have to make it snappy then. It's on the ground floor.'

I sneaked out and passed through the glass doors unobserved. I made my way down the stairs and eventually found the gentlemen's toilet. My heart was doing the sixty-metre sprint. I shouldered open the door. No one there. I gave a sigh of relief. *This* was drama. I stood in front of the urinal and discharged in peace and quiet. But then the door burst open and a short man with a beard took up position next to me. My fountain dried up. It was Nina's father. He rummaged and fiddled and jerked into action, glanced at me and just as I had packed away my tackle and buttoned up, he recognised me.

'Well, if it isn't Kim,' he said in Danish, locating an orifice in the beard.

I nodded, unsure quite where I should look.

'So you've come to the theatre,' he continued blithely, shaking, pointing and holding.

Couldn't argue with that.

'Isn't it dreadful!' he sighed, performing the final adjustments. 'I've already taken three aspirins.'

We both went to a washbasin.

'Well, how was the football match?'

'We won 1–0'.

'That was fantastic. Come with me and say hello to Nina's mother. We're only visiting. Nina isn't with us.'

He dragged me with him and the mother recognised me at once, grabbed my hand, and it was rather embarrassing because I hadn't dried my hands. She got wet and had to take out a handkerchief.

'You disappeared so quickly last time we saw you,' she smiled.

I stared down at the red floor, noticing that I had laced up my shoes wrongly.

'Nina was so sorry,' the mother continued. 'She's coming home for summer.'

And then the bell rang again, twice, the interval was over.

I wandered around for some time unable to find the door to the stairs. All the dresses and dinner jackets streamed towards me trying to take me in the opposite direction. I stood like a salmon before a waterfall, slowly beginning to panic, and eventually found the way to the restaurant where Mum was angrily waiting for me.

We got to our seats as the lights were being dimmed. The curtains opened and it was strange, but it is true, that when I saw the stage set and heard the loud voices making the chandelier above us tinkle, I had already switched off, just like at *The Sound of Music.* I could not understand how anyone could be taken in, be so completely fooled for so long. I closed my eyes, turned down the sound and thought of Nina. Pincers nipped at my stomach. She was alone now in Copenhagen. Alone with Jesper. I almost screamed, but caught myself. Did I give a shit? Yes, I did.

On returning home, I went straight to bed, had hot milk with honey and was absent from school for a week. I was exhausted, dreams played tag with me and I couldn't escape. Images and sounds merged into a red nightmare: Jensenius's singing, the war on TV, an air alarm, a telephone that no one would answer. And on the walls surrounding me: the pictures of The Beatles. I didn't recognise them. That wasn't how they looked any more. We didn't resemble ourselves any more.

And, when I get up now, just as alien to myself after a disturbed but dreamless night, I can feel the same fever in my skull, the pincers in my midriff. My stomach cannot take water from the well, it's brown when it comes out of the tap. I have to go outside to melt snow, to boil it. I wrap up in old clothes and shuffle through the room. On the table are white sheets of paper, like windows in the dark. I go out onto the kitchen steps and am blinded, have to shade my eyes, my head is thumping. And I'm cold, my head is cold, that is the worst of it all because my hair won't grow.

Then I see them: the footprints in the snow. I follow them. They come from the gate. Someone has been here. They lead around the House. They stop by one window where the shutters have been taken off.

Someone has been watching me.

We continued the confirmation classes, sat in the mouldy cellar every Wednesday. We didn't get around to asking why Fred had drowned or whether God had predetermined it. But one evening our appetite was whetted. John had said that The Beatles were greater than Jesus.

Christ, what a stink! It was worse than Luther. Seb wanted to throw that into the priest's face. But Father MacKenzie got his oar in first and asked Seb to reel off the table of contents in the New Testament. Seb couldn't. He got as far as the Acts of the Apostles, but came to a dead halt. The priest's wrinkles tautened and hardened. The girls in the first bench giggled. I covertly took out the holy book and stole a glance. Next were St Paul's letters, the letter to the Romans, the letter to the Corinthians, to the Galatians. Seb was sent back to his bench. Then the priest pointed at me.

'Go on,' said the priest.

I stood up.

'Paul's letter to the Romans. Paul's letter to the Corinthians.'

'First!'

'Eh?'

'*First* letter to the Corinthians!'

I breathed in.

'Paul's letter to the Galatians.'

'Second letter!'

'Eh?'

'Second letter to the Corinthians. Mercy be upon you and the peace of God, our Father and our Lord Jesus Christ.'

'Eh?'

'Go on!'

'Paul's letter to... to the Galatians. Paul's letter to the Ephe... Ephesians.'

I got no further. I was almost halfway. The cellar went quiet. I glanced down at Gunnar. Resigned, he shook his head. Seb sat with a huge grin on his face and could not care less. Ola looked as if he were going to explode with laughter at any moment. Mercy be upon him.

'Haven't you done today's homework, either.'

'Yes. My mind just went blank.'

So the priest tried to elicit it from me. But his skills did not extend that far. He had to turn to one of the plaits on the first bench. She stood erect in her pleated skirt and rattled off the Philippians, the Colossians, Timothy, Titus and Philemon.

After the lesson was over, the priest stopped us and asked us to remain behind. Seb and I were in detention. We were not allowed to leave until we had learned the homework off by heart. We slogged our way through the crazy names, it went fine at first: Matthew, Mark, Luke and John. But the Ephesians and the Colossians finished us off. After twenty minutes the priest told me to have another go. I managed it after three attempts, just got the Colossians and Timothy the wrong way round. But Seb got into a mess again. The hair on his neck stood up like a brush. After the Corinthians his tongue went on strike.

'You can go,' the priest told me.

'I'm waiting for Sebastian,' I said.

The priest looked at him.

'Don't you *want* to learn this?' he asked.

'No!' came the resounding response.

Seb stood up and threw the holy book over to the priest.

'I don't want to be confirmed! Do you think anyone believes what you say! They're doin' this for the presents!'

The priest stared in disbelief. He could not believe his own ears. Seb marched into the cloakroom. I ran after him. Followed by the priest. He was waving his hands.

'Aren't you coming back?'

'No!' Seb said, slamming the heavy door after us.

On the street he had a fit of the shakes, fumbled out a cigarette and then burst into laughter. 'Christ, that was the greatest thing since the resurrection. John Lennon was chicken-feed by comparison.'

Gunnar and Ola were waiting at Gimle.

'Seb got one up on the priest!' I shouted.

They came running over.

I told them everything. They listened with mouths agape and huge eyes. Told them again. They stared at Seb in awe and admiration.

'But w-w-what about the instruments then?'

Seb flicked the cigarette in the gutter.

'I'll get presents anyway,' he said. 'Mum said so.'

He had worked it out in advance! No chance of my mum and dad agreeing. No point even asking.

'So you've asked for an electric guitar!' Gunnar said.

'Yep. Kawai. With a mike and tremolo arm. I can use the radio as an amp. Three hundred spondulicks.'

We traipsed towards Urra. Couldn't go home now.

Seb went serious.

'I mean,' he began. 'I mean it's not right to kneel there and be blessed when you don't believe a word. Is it!'

Gunnar stopped.

'Kneel? Where?'

'At the altar. At the confirmation ceremony. You've got to receive the blessin' and say you believe.'

Gunnar was ashen-faced. He gritted his teeth.

'Do you *have* to?'

'That's the whole point of confirmation! A repeat of the baptism. You skip the water though.'

Gunnar's voice wilted.

'I won't get any presents if I'm not confirmed.'

Seb tapped out four Craven As and passed them round. We trudged on. The Man on the Steps was closing. But there was a corner shop further down the street open till half past eight. We turned into Briskebyveien. It always looked like a Wild West town in the evening with its low creaking wooden houses and the yellow light behind the curtains. All it needed was some whinnying and a bloody duel. All of a sudden someone stood in front of us in the darkness between two street lamps.

Came to a halt.

Goose.

'Hi, Christian,' we said. 'What are you doin' here? Almost midnight, isn't it!'

He came closer. Looked like he had walked through a car wash. Hair plastered down to his skull. He kept licking round his mouth all the time.

'Have you had another lesson with the priest?' he asked.

'Yep,' I said.

'What did he do?'

Seb grinned.

'He didn't do anythin'! It's what we did that counts. Buggered off. For good.'

Goose gasped, his mouth hung open.

'Bloody hell, he didn't!' he said.

We exchanged glances. Goose had sworn.

'Served him right. The prick!' Goose went on.

Ola leaned forward.

'Nothin' up, is there, Christian?'

He didn't hear.

'I can nick a comic from the shop, I can,' he declared.

Silence. No one said anything.

'I can nick a comic from the shop, I can,' he repeated, louder.

'You don't dare,' I said.

Goose came a step closer.

'Don't I?' he whispered.

'No,' I said.

'You don't think I dare pinch a comic,' he shouted.

'You'll have to get a move on then. The shop closes at half eight.'

Goose looked at us all. Then he turned on his heel and crossed the street to the illuminated shop on the corner. We heard a bell ring as he opened the door.

We saw the silhouettes through the window. There was just an old dear behind the counter and one customer. Goose was by the magazine stand. He unzipped his velveteen jacket. We held our breath. Just so long as he wasn't stupid enough to run right out. He had to buy at least some sweets first. Shit. Goose was standing with his back to the counter and sliding a little comic into his jacket. Right. That was okay. Zip up again now.

Then the world stopped. A great lump of a man wearing a beret passed the window. He stared at Goose fumbling with his zip.

Gunnar gave a deep, despairing groan.

'Shit, that's the owner! That's the shop-owner!'

He tore open the door, we saw Goose turn, then he was lost to view in the arms of the giant and hoisted up to the ceiling. We saw him scream. Goose screamed like in a silent film and then the comic appeared, a Davy Crockett comic costing fifty øre.

We began to retreat slowly towards Holtegata, cool, without panic, sprinted round the corner, held our breath and waited for Goose.

'Quite an evenin',' Seb said.

'Shut up!' said Gunnar.

We listened for sirens. The whole town was dead still.

'What did he want with a D-D-Davy Crockett magazine?' Ola mumbled.

Then he appeared. He stumbled out and fell on all fours on the pavement. A voice was cursing and swearing inside the shop. Goose struggled to his feet and teetered alongside the wall like a sick dog. We dragged him into safety round the corner.

'What happened?' we asked.

He just shook his head. Shit, the state he was in. His cheeks were burning after the slaps. His lip was split, a trail of blood ran down his chin. His velveteen jacket was half off.

'What happened for Christ's sake?'

He was crying without tears. Just hiccupping again and again.

'He said he would tell my parents and the school,' he managed to say.

'Did you give him your name?'

He hid his face in his hands.

'Bastard,' Seb snarled. 'Bastard shop-owner!'

'He just said that to frighten you,' I said.

'I might be expelled,' Goose hiccupped.

'For nickin' a Davy Crockett comic! Like hell you will!'

He began to sob again. It sounded bad, as if he were coughing up barbed wire.

'It'll be alright,' I consoled, patting him on the shoulder.

His eyes met mine. He sent me an almost hateful look. Then his eyes drowned in fresh tears, they streamed down his cheeks.

There was a rank smell coming from somewhere. We looked down. The crease was gone from Goose's trousers for good. A big wet stain ran down his thigh.

He left. Goose waddled down the street bow-legged. The sobs sounded like explosions to us. And at some point he stopped under a street lamp, just stood there shrieking, and the light enveloped him, a dazzling, yellow circle.

The day afterwards we met Goose on the way to school. He was coming up Frognerveien. We waited by the bakery.

He walked right past us.

We pursued and surrounded him.

'What happened?' I asked.

He looked at us with vacant eyes. His mouth was narrow and pink. He swallowed. His pointed Adam's apple bobbed up and down.

'He didn't ring.'

'Danger over!' Gunnar shouted, taking his arm.

'Perhaps he'll ring the school,' Goose mumbled.

'Not if he hasn't rung your home,' I said. 'That's for sure!'

'He said he would be in touch,' Goose mumbled. 'That's what he said. That I would be hearing from him.'

Goose had a physics oral that day. He was hopeless. No one could believe their ears except for Gunnar and me. Goose collapsed on his desk.

'Are you ill?' the teacher asked in a friendly tone.

Goose didn't answer.

Then Big Mouth was tested and as usual that took the rest of the lesson. I kept an eye on Goose. He was completely out of it. Kept casting glances at the door as if waiting for the cops to storm in with handcuffs and leg irons.

In the break we took him to one side.

'Nothin' to be nervous about now,' I said. 'If he's said nothin' so far, he won't say anythin' at all.'

'He said *perhaps*,' Goose whispered.

'Well, so what?'

'Perhaps he'll ring tomorrow.'

'Unlikely to w-w-wait that long!'

'Must've forgotten the whole business already,' said Seb.

But it was to no avail. Fear was engraved in his eyes. The next lesson was Norwegian. Kerr's Pink, as usual, used the opportunity to tell us about Petter Dass and read out from *Nordlands Trompet*. All of a sudden Sandpaper was standing in the doorway. We jumped up, straightened our backs and hung our arms down by our sides, everyone, that is, except Goose. He wouldn't stand up. He lay across his desk breathing like a baleen whale. The headteacher entered the classroom, pointed to Goose and said, 'What's up with you, boy?'

Was he crying? There were strange sounds coming from him, his neck was wet. Kerr's Pink was down by his desk and lifted him up.

'Christian, what is it?'

Goose's cheeks were streaming.

'I didn't mean to,' Goose hiccupped.

'What was that?'

'I didn't mean to!'

Sandpaper laid a hand on his brow.

'You're feverish, boy!' He said, rolling his 'r's. 'We'll have to send you home.'

Kerr's Pink packed Goose's rucksack and helped him out of the classroom. We were still standing to attention, no one understood a thing except Gunnar and me. We were just about to relax when Sandpaper swivelled on the threshold and roared from under the steely moustache, 'What I was going to say was: You are forbidden to leave the school grounds in any of the breaks except the lunch break. Have you understood? Forbidden!'

The door was slammed shut after them. We heard Goose sobbing outside in the corridor. Kerr's Pink kept asking him what the matter was, what he didn't mean, but Goose said nothing.

He didn't come back to school that week. And by the following Wednesday he hadn't turned up, either. In the evening we sat in front of the priest collecting mildew. Of course I continued, but Seb dropped out and got his presents regardless. Gunnar also hinted that he might stop, but we convinced him that The Snafus's future was at stake. So we were listening to the priest, he was explaining the miracles, when in came Goose. He was almost unrecognisable, he had shrunk to half his size, he was an apple core, chewed over and spat out. He took a seat near the door without looking at us. His mouth kept going up and down, but not a sound emerged.

'Talkin' to himself,' I whispered to Gunnar.

He sat like that until the lesson was over, chuntering silently, licking his lips, then chuntering again. He was the first through the door. We grabbed our clothes and ran after him. We caught up with him by Norum Hotel.

'Heard anythin'?' I asked.

He shook his head.

'Then you're definitely safe,' Gunnar smiled, offering a Teddy. Goose refused.

'You've been pretty lucky!' I said.

He looked me in the eye. Hardly recognised him.

'He might ring next week,' he said.

'Now just listen here!' Gunnar was beginning to get annoyed. 'If he hasn't rung by now, he won't ring! Why would he wait such a long time, eh?'

Goose moistened his lips.

'To… to punish me.'

Things went downhill for Goose. He came back to school and sat silently at his desk, chuntering. His jaw was going like a piston. We speculated until we were pink in the face about what he was actually saying. One Saturday after school we were at Gunnar's, chatting, it was November and Goose seemed to be lost for ever.

'Think he's gone completely loopy,' Seb said. 'Couldn't take the shock.'

A shudder went down my spine.

Gunnar smacked his hands on the floor.

'He must know that bastard won't ring now! It's over a month ago!'

We sat in silence thinking. I thought about Davy Crockett and the hat I had once had with the long furry tail.

'I'm not goin' to be confirmed,' Gunnar said out of the blue.

'What!' we all yelled at once. 'What d'you mean by that?'

'Can't do it,' he said.

'Can't!' I shouted. 'How come?

'Can't do it if I don't believe a bloody word of it.'

'Will you get the p-p-presents anyway?' Ola enquired.

Gunnar shook his head.

I grabbed his shirt.

'We agreed on this, didn't we. We're not gettin' confirmed because we believe, but because we need the instruments for The Snafus!'

'How are you gonna get an electric g-g-guitar then?'

'Work for my dad.'

'That'll take you ten years!' I yelled.

'Can't help that,' Gunnar mumbled.

'Yes, you can! Why can't you get confirmed like everyone else? Do you think anyone else believes?'

'Can't do it. Can't kneel down. Just can't.'

'So you've decided?'

'Yes. Dad's written to the priest.'

That was that. The future of The Snafus was teetering on the brink.

'Perhaps we'll have to find another guitarist,' I said.

Dead silence. Gunnar fidgeted with his nails. Ola scratched his neck. Seb stared out of the window.

'Perhaps you will,' Gunnar said. His voice was cold and indifferent.

Then we heard a hell of a rumpus in the sitting room. Doors were slammed, feet were stamped, a lamp was knocked over, it was a veritable earth tremor.

'You're *havin'* a haircut and that's it!' shrieked the greengrocer.

No answer.

'D'you hear what I say! You're havin' a haircut! And today!'

No answer.

The father's voice rose to a frightening falsetto.

'Are you tryin' to kill your mother?'

'Relax,' said Stig. 'Jesus had long hair, too.'

Wow. I would remember that one. Better than Rudolf Nureyev.

The father was trying to say something but only noise came out. A door slammed and the room shook. A little later Stig joined us.

'Don't panic, boys. Chief's just blown a gasket.'

He had his hair well down over his ears and the fringe combed to the side so that it reached his cheek. And he was wearing a leather jacket, suede boots and striped flares. Stood with a grin on his face and was in control of the situation.

'Great what you said to the priest,' he said, pointing to Seb.

Seb blushed with pride.

'Bastard American priests bless the troops,' he went on. 'Jesus wouldn't have done, that's for sure.'

We nodded. Of course not.

Stig eyed us, one after the other.

'Weren't thinkin' of wastin' the whole day here, were you!'

We shrugged.

'Electricity workers are on an anti-Vietnam War demo!'

We trotted behind Stig down to Solli. Gunnar walked apart from us, looking grumpy, didn't say a word. I felt such a pull in my stomach, a backwash, I felt a void inside and it hurt. Felt like saying I didn't mean what I had said about looking for another guitarist, but couldn't bring myself to do it. Just couldn't do it.

'Great turnout!' Stig shouted, pointing.

Sommerrogata was packed. There must have been several hundred people, maybe a thousand. Hardly room for everyone. Some carried big placards: VIETNAM FOR THE VIETNAMESE. STOP THE TERROR BOMBING. PEACE IN VIETNAM NOW. The torches flickered in the dark, lighting up faces.

'Have to go,' Stig said. 'Got to carry a banner.'

He was about to go, then remembered something.

'Have you heard The Beatles might be splittin' up?'

We forgot to breathe.

'Pal in my class told me. Read it in English newspapers.'

'Split up? The Beatles?'

'Arguin'. Have to be off. See you.'

He waved his long arms and made his way through the crowd. We stood on the perimeter by the tram lines, unable to say a word, looked past each other. Numbed by the shouts from the crowd. On the other side of the street stood a group whistling and laughing, recognised them, the silk gang from Vestheim, Ky and Anders Lange. The Beatles? Splitting up? Someone started talking into a microphone. We couldn't hear what he said. All of a sudden everyone streamed down Drammensveien chanting in rhythm, chanting in rhythm. Four figures were left behind, us, gaping at the procession meandering ahead, flags unfurled in the wind, banners and placards aloft with the big black letters, torches. We heard the tinkle of glass, a bottle was smashed, someone screamed and fighting broke out near the Chamber of Commerce building. Thick smoke rose from the ground, burned in our nostrils.

We stood in the empty square gawking.

The Beatles.

A thing of the past?

December, no snow, just clear, silvery cold. And the backwash was there all the time, just as when the ferry from Denmark passes Nesodden hugging the coastline and leaving in its wake a load of filth, rotting seaweed, bottles, paper, condoms. I was like that. The backwash had me in its grip. The faces stared down at me from the walls, couldn't get away from them. In the end I could stand it no longer. I tore down all the pictures and put them in a drawer. The bare wallpaper mocked me. Splitting up? Mum appeared in the doorway, broke into wild clapping and called Dad. Eventually he came and was speechless with pleasure, contemplating the walls as though they were the National Gallery.

'Well done, Kim,' said my mother. 'They needed to come down before the confirmation anyway.'

Put them back up that same night, lay awake between the estranged eyes. Sudden flash of Nina. The Danish ferry sailed past and dragged my heart into space. That was certain at any rate. Would never look in her direction again, even if she crawled on all fours, crying and remonstrating, no way, that was over and done with. I heard Jensenius on his nocturnal peregrinations, the shuffle of feet above my head. It could not be true. The Beatles splitting up. Hadn't spoken to Gunnar since that day. Seb was almost never around, nor Ola, who was swotting for German and maths. And Goose, he just got worse and worse. Chuntering on. To himself. He didn't follow in lessons. Couldn't do his homework. Wandered around like a ghost. The girls were almost afraid of him. Like with Dragon. The backwash. If Hubert had been at home I might have asked him. He would know about that sort of thing. But Hubert was in Paris, with Henny.

Sleep.

One day we found out what Goose was saying. In the lunch break Ola came running across the school yard. We were in the shed freezing cold and shivering, not speaking. Gunnar was doing his physics homework, Seb was lost in dreams.

'B-b-boys!' Ola yelled. 'B-b-boys!'

We looked up. Gunnar closed his book.

'B-b-boys! I've been to the bog!'

'You don't say,' Seb said. 'Everythin' alright?' Seb was in sparkling form.

Ola re-discovered his vocal cords.

'I've been to the b-b-bog. And I heard some s-s-sounds from one of the cubicles!'

'Yes?'

'Yes. And it was Goose! He was in there r-r-ramblin' on. And do you know what! He was p-p-prayin'!'

'Eh?'

'Goose was p-p-prayin.'

'To God?'

'Yes! The whole of Our Father. And there was loads m-m-more! He was standin' in the cubicle p-p-prayin.'

The bell rang.

Backwash.

Goose had gone nuts.

Mum and Dad would not give up. They wanted me to take down the pictures. I refused. They wanted me to have a haircut. I refused. Had had a haircut for the first and last time before we went to the theatre. Mum began to cry. Dad slammed doors like Gunnar's father. It was war. It was *Revolver*. Almost refused a meal. But I was just thinking about Goose, that I had to talk to him, and one freezing cold Friday I waylaid him in Gyldenløvesgate on his way home from school.

'Hiya, Christian,' I said, slowing down beside him.

He gave a curt nod. His rucksack looked so big on him, like a hump.

'You're a jammy bugger!' I said quickly.

'Jammy?'

'Yes! The man didn't report you!'

Goose stared at me with that sallow look I couldn't stand.

'What do you mean?' he asked.

I became heated.

'You were lucky he didn't ring!'

I sent him a quick glance.

'He *didn't*, did he?'

Goose shivered.

'Not yet,' he said.

That evening I couldn't sit still. Thought about going to Gunnar's but went round to Seb's instead. He opened the door with a jerk, looking pretty disappointed to see me there.

'Waitin' for Father Christmas or what?'

He took me to his room. From the sitting room we heard low but animated voices. Then a door slammed and someone ran out.

'Everyone's slammin' doors at the moment,' I said.

Seb nodded. He looked dejected.

'Gunnar's father,' I continued. 'My father. Everyone's slammin' doors. Wonder how Ola's gettin' on.'

'Slam doors there, too,' said Seb. 'Ola was given a letter to take home. Have to repeat the year if he doesn't improve in German and maths.'

'Shit on all sides,' I said. 'Piles and piles of it!'

The record player was silent. The sitting room had gone quiet. Could start to snow at any moment. Just two weeks to go to confirmation.

'You think The Beatles'll split up?' I whispered.

'Dunno. Maybe. Don't think so, though.'

Seb seemed a little on edge.

'What'll happen to The Snafus, eh? If Gunnar doesn't get a guitar?'

'Have to work out what to play first, anyway,' Seb said. 'Write our own songs and stuff.'

I swallowed and said, 'Think Goose has gone mad?'

Seb gave a brief smile.

'Looks like it.'

The backwash.

'Think it would've helped if the man in the shop'd rung?'

Seb gave the matter some thought.

'Maybe. He's walkin' around expectin' it. If he rang now, there'd be a huge row, but then it'd be over. Nothin' left to dread at least.'

That was what I had been thinking.

There was a ring at the door. Seb collapsed like a pair of pyjamas. His mother opened up and we heard voices. Seb dragged himself off the sofa.

Then she was in the doorway.

Guri.

I stood up, glanced at Seb, smiled. So that was how he had spent his Wednesdays when we were with the priest accumulating moss. Seb smiled back.

Guri stood there looking happy again.

'Have to be off,' I said with alacrity. 'Haven't started my maths yet.'

'I'm going to write a letter to Nina,' Guri said. 'Should I say hello from you?'

And I said yes.

'Yes,' I said. 'Of course. Just say hello.'

'You're not angry with her, are you?'

And I said no.

'Course not,' I beamed. 'Why should I be?'

I stormed up to Solli. The telephone box was empty. I inserted a coin and dialled Goose's number. In the crime hour on TV they talked through handkerchieves. I didn't have a handkerchief, so I cleared my throat properly and tried to make my voice deeper. I supposed they wouldn't recognise my voice, although Goose would. Signals sparked across Frogner, then there was a woman's voice in my ear.

'Ellingsen,' it said.

'Is herr Ellingsen there?' I asked.

The receiver in my hand was a sponge.

There was a brief pause.

'He's not at home at this moment. Who am I talking to, please?'

I took the plunge.

'It's about your son,' I said. 'I'm the owner of a tobacconist's nearby Uranienborg school. Some time ago I caught him trying to steal a comic.'

Silence at the other end.

I continued, 'I may have been a little hard on him, but you know how it is. It's not the first time I've had pilfering in my shop.'

'A comic?'

'A... Davy Crockett comic. I don't think he was alone.'

'Alone?'

'There was a gang of boys standing outside the shop waiting.'

'I see,' she said.

I doubted that. I had to change ear. The first one was melting.

'I thought you might be interested to know, even though it is quite some time ago now. But I consider the matter closed.'

'Thank you,' she said. 'Thank you very much.'

She rang off. I hung up. I assumed she would be going into Goose's room and slapping him stupid. I staggered out, stood on the pavement, the tram came across the roundabout, and suddenly took on the features of a ship, gliding past me with voices and music. I felt the pull in my whole body, the enormous backwash, I was dragged into the blue darkness beneath the starry sky, I beat Aldrin's record from the day before, when he hovered outside Gemini 12 for two hours, nine minutes and twenty-five seconds.

Then I came back to earth.

Standing in two lines in the central aisle, in white gowns with pale faces and large Adam's apples, we resembled albino bats. The organ washed over us. Ola rolled his eyes looking as if he could throw up at any moment. Goose stood to attention, chuntering occasionally, but his eyes were no longer so full of fear. The organ faded away. The noise from the lines of pews took over, people coughing, clearing their throats and coughing, a sweet falling on the floor, a child's scream. It was worse than in the cinema. Mum and Dad sat by the door with one of my godparents, an old girlfriend of my mother's from the time when she was going to be an actress. She was married to a sports maniac who apparently became the national decathlon champion in 1947. My other godparent was not there. Hubert was in Paris.

The priest came down from the altar and walked among us in squeaky shoes. He stopped right at the back, next to an outsider from Hoff, his gown flapping around him, ready for lift-off. The church went quiet.

'What's the name of the town where Jesus was born?' the priest asked.

Brain seized up. Mental block. Total blank. The silence in the church was nearing bursting point. The priest repeated the question, the red-haired boy in the gown trembled, a man in the congregation was on the point of standing up and shouting something, must have been the boy's father. The boy's knees gave way, all that could be seen was a flame-red head sinking into the gown.

The priest moved on quickly and the answers came in rapid succession. The atmosphere picked up, applause hung in the air. Goose answered that the holy trinity consisted of God the Father, the Son and the Holy Ghost. Ola answered that it was Barabbas who was released when Christ was to be crucified. And I, I answered that Judas was the name of the man who betrayed his master.

Afterwards there was more organ, then we had to go up to the altar and kneel in a semi-circle. The priest walked around the low altar rails and placed his hand on our heads. That was, I supposed, the confirmation. I felt nothing, just knelt there, it wasn't bad, and I didn't scream as Mum said I had done at my baptism. The only thought I had was that there was a fusty smell coming from the railings we were leaning against, from the material they were covered with, it smelt like the black leather bindings of bibles or old clothes in Nesodden.

Then it was over and we raced down to the cellar and changed, just like after a football match. Ola sat beside me and breathed out with relief.

'D-d-did you see my th-th-thigh twitchin'?' he hissed. 'Thought the gown would fall off. The s-s-safety pin under my arm came undone!'

We had a little grin. Goose stood in a corner unwilling to part with the gown, seemed to feel happy in it.

'That b-b-bastard phoned after all,' Ola said.

I nodded.

'Deserves to be sh-sh-shot!'

Then it was the priest's turn again. He spoke softly and said he was proud of us. He shook our hands in turn and we each received a pocket-sized New Testament, a little red book, no bigger than a pocket calendar. And inside he had written a brief dedication to us all and a passage from the Bible to take with us on the way. *Kim Karlsen. Confirmed 1 December 1966. James 2:14. What doth it profit, my brethren, though a man say he hath faith, and have not works? Can faith save him?*

Goose appeared by my side as we were leaving. He was holding the book tightly with both hands.

'Congratulations,' I said.

He stared straight ahead.

'Mum's been to talk to the shop-owner,' he said.

My heart constricted. I almost snapped in two. Ola, right behind us, stuck his head forward.

'Was there any t-t-trouble?'

'He said he hadn't phoned,' Goose said with a perplexed look.

Ola forced his way between us.

'H-h-hadn't phoned! Did he say that!'

'Yes. But Mum had talked to him, so how could he deny it?'

Goose sounded almost pleased and produced a smile on his rumpled face.

'I'm happy about everything that happened,' he declared.

We looked at him. He looked at us.

'That night I found redemption.'

I felt something plummet inside me, deeper than ever before. Redemption through fear, I thought. I really thought that. Redemption through fear.

Then Goose opened the sluggish, heavy door and from the darkness and smell of moths we went out into the winter, which blinded us with all its light.

Soon I was standing there, in my first suit, dark blue, cut in at the waist and double-breasted, all I needed was a sword to take possession of Akershus. I stood there, and everyone looked me up and down while I sent sidelong glances to the gift table without registering anything that remotely resembled an amplifier or a microphone stand.

I started to unwrap the presents. There was a Ballograf fountain pen from my godmother and her husband, a leather wallet with a hundred kroner in it from my grandmother, a compass from my grandfather, and even Jensenius had remembered me: To Kim from Jensenius, congratulations on the big day. A record: Robertino. *O Sole Mio.* Then there was a little present from Mum and Dad. I tore off the paper and held an electric shaver in my hand. Dad grinned and stroked his chin, I did the same and felt nothing, absolutely nothing, I was not there yet. And finally there was something flat. It was a bank book, five hundred kroner had been paid in. Five hundred! I was saved!

'You have to keep that until you come of age and start studying,' Mum said.

That was that. It was an ice age till then. I did the rounds and thanked everyone. Decathlon man squeezed me to pulp and said something about the pole vault, my godmother was all over me with thick lipstick. And Grandma could not restrain the tears.

'You have really become a man,' she sniffled. 'You'll have to remember to shave every morning!'

Granddad was not quite with it, either. He was looking in the wrong direction, but he made a wonderful impression in his old suit.

'Thank you for the compass!' I shouted into his ear.

He turned slowly towards me. Things had gone a bit downhill for Granddad of late. He complained about all the noise the trains made as they raced past his room night and day. So the nurses gave him a box of wax ear plugs. Granddad ate them and had to take an enema for three days in a row.

'They'll have to change the points soon,' he said. 'Otherwise we'll collide. That's what happened in Dovre. In '47.'

Mum came in carrying a tray of sherry, I had to take a glass. I remembered watching a character on TV crime hour pouring a drink in a potted plant so as to avoid being poisoned. Couldn't do that in the middle of the room. I wormed my way out to the telephone, said I was going to call Ola to find out what he had been given. I emptied the glass in a cactus pot in the hall. The prickles went limp. Afterwards Ola was on the line.

'How's it goin'?' I asked.

'H-h-hard work,' he whispered. 'The suit's a bit tight.'

'What did you get?'

'Fountain pen. And a sh-sh-shaver.'

'Same here.'

'Seb got a fountain pen, too. And a m-m-mouth organ.'

We were quiet for a moment.

'Doesn't look as if anythin' will come of The Snafus,' I said gloomily.

'D-d-doesn't look like it.'

We rang off. I had that same unpleasant void in my stomach that just grew and grew. And I wasn't hungry, either. Things looked bleak.

I had red wine with the meal. Everyone kept toasting me all the time and my godmother, she must have thought she had done her job now, made sure I had had a Christian upbringing, she filled my glass and I couldn't keep my eyes off her breasts which bulged out of the top of her dress and bobbed up every time she opened her mouth. I drank the wine and suddenly heard a click, just as though someone had flicked a switch on or off. *Click* I heard and was quite frightened from where I was sitting because I couldn't see properly. Everything seemed to slide away, Mum became two people sitting opposite each other and my godmother was leaning across the table with a split face and four tits.

'I *knew* you would turn out to be a handsome fellow,' I heard her say. 'I saw it when you used to play in the buff in Nesodden!'

'You should've become a *tennis player*,' the sportsman broke in. 'I remember the summer we played badminton. When was that? Seven years ago? Yes, in '59. You were just a toddler then, but you had the *power*, Kim. You had the *swing*. Do you play tennis, Kim?'

I shook my head. I shouldn't have done that. Everything collapsed. A washing machine started in my head. I didn't know what programme it was on.

'I play football,' I whispered.

'Football!' he snorted. '*Team* sport. Individuals don't come into their own there, Kim. Tennis is good. Running, too. Boxing.'

Someone was trying to break a glass. It was Dad. He stood up with someone else. I strained my eye muscles and got him in focus. Dad was standing behind a chair with a small piece of paper in his hand. Everyone went quiet, but my heart was in my throat pecking like a demented chicken at a soft-boiled egg.

'Dear Kim,' Dad began.

Had never heard him be so formal before. Mum was crying.

'Dear Kim,' he repeated.

And then he held a speech for three quarters of an hour. He couldn't have had all that written down on the slip of paper. It had to be a world record at the very least because a man had contrived to write the Lord's Prayer twenty times on the back of a stamp which he sent to China, and Dad had beaten that hands down. I thought of all the speeches I had heard, Lue's, the headteacher's, the priest's, they didn't expect such small things of us, we were their eternal lives. Why shouldn't we be able to become the President of America? Eh? It would be so easy to disappoint them when expectations were so high, when the piste they set up was so steep and so straight that even the slightest deviation was synonymous with a catastrophe, sabotage, the grinding of teeth and a heart attack. I didn't think that then. Not then because my head was a spin-drier full of dirty clothes, loose buttons, combs, chewing gum, tram tickets and dead frogs. I think it now, now that I have already disappointed them. Mum was dabbing her eye with a napkin and, after Dad had talked for such a long time that we could have skated on the game sauce, Granddad stood up and shouted with the powerful lungs of a track-layer:

'Train's coming! Train's coming!'

Dad and the freestyle wrestler had to carry him into the bedroom where he slept in Mum's bed. We finished eating in silence. And afterwards I was unable to stand up. I tried, but I couldn't move. The others gave me a strange look. Mum came over and gave me a hug. Grandma was all over me with her thin, bony arms. Everyone talked at once.

I couldn't move.

'The boy wants more food!' the boxer laughed.

'Come on,' Mum said.

I tried, I did try, but couldn't move from the spot.

'Thank you for all the presents,' I said, scraping the plate of ice cream clean.

The faces took on an expression of concern. Dad grabbed my shoulder.

'Let's go into the sitting room now and drink coffee and eat cake,' he announced.

I took a deep breath and tore myself off the chair. It worked. I jumped up and lurched backwards against the wall, knocking over the chair, and stood swaying.

'Just a bit dizzy,' I said.

While we were drinking coffee, the telephone rang. It was Uncle Hubert ringing from Paris to congratulate me.

'Hello, Uncle!' I shouted.

'You didn't think I'd forgotten, did you!'

'Of course not.'

'I'll bring you something nice when I'm back for Christmas,' Hubert shouted. He sounded happy. No knots in the wiring.

'How's Paris?' I asked.

'You should be here! It's indescribable!'

There was some noise in the background, Hubert's voice disappeared, then there was another voice, Henny, Henny's voice.

'Hi there, Kim.'

'Hiya,' I whispered.

'Congratulations! And *skål*!'

I could hear the clink of glasses in Paris.

'Thanks,' I mumbled.

'I'll see you when I get back,' she said.

'Right,' I gulped.

Then Hubert was back.

'Better ring off. Or we'll be broke. See you, Kim!'

'See you, Hubert!'

We sort of breathed at each other for a minute or two, across Europe, then rang off.

The spin-drier started turning again.

Dad was in the sitting room with a fierce expression on his face. I collapsed into a chair. Everyone looked at me.

'Hubert says hello,' I said as clearly as I could.

'What is your brother doing in Paris actually?' my godmother asked, studying Dad.

'He's working on an advertising project for his company,' Dad said with round eyes.

I looked at Mum. She was pouring coffee.

'And he paints and he has a girlfriend who paints, too,' I said in an unnaturally loud voice as though I was communicating with France.

Dad strafed me with his gaze. Then he proceeded to talk the hind leg off a donkey about something else, don't remember what, don't remember much at all any more, just that more bottles appeared on the table, Granddad was taken away in a VW bus by the Home, the gymnast wanted me to stand on my hands, and to great cheering I did, and I shouldn't have done because after that I was a mess. Henny's voice buzzed in my ear, I thought about The Snafus who might never see the light of day, The Beatles who might split up, Gunnar to whom I had hardly spoken over recent weeks, about Fred who was no longer with us and Goose who was redeemed. And Nina who was coming in the summer. Everything was falling apart. I tottered into the kitchen, picked up a bottle and drank. Soak and Rinse. I ran to the toilet. Engaged. Returned to the sitting room, sat next to Grandma, and she talked about the granddad who had died when I was four. He had worked for a savings company and went round to people's houses to empty their savings clocks. It sounded unbelievable, emptying money from a clock. And the tennis player was desperate to arm-wrestle with me.

Then they all left. Mum and Dad breathed a sigh of relief from their chairs. The spin-drier was no longer in my head but in my stomach. It would soon be time for the drain phase.

'That was an enjoyable evening, don't you think?' Mum said, leaning back.

Nodded gingerly.

They finished their glasses.

'How does it feel to be an adult?' Dad smiled.

I jumped up, raced to the bathroom, managed to lock the door and vomited into the toilet bowl. Mum and Dad rushed after me. It just flowed from my face, flowed and flowed and everywhere in my body ached. It was all the slag that had collected during the autumn, that dreadful autumn of 1966. Now it was coming out. I knelt there as worn out as The Grim Reaper, but for some reason I was almost happy; happy, relieved, empty, while Mum and Dad hammered on the door and called me.

Strawberry Fields Forever

Spring '67

Dad roared. Dad roared as I had never heard him roar before. He waved his mittens and stamped his overshoes. I roared too, banged on the railing and roared. The Swan was on the last lap, his skates flashing like knives in the ice, but it was too late. Verkerk had already hit the final straight. Maier 'the Swan' was way off. But we roared anyway, and banged and stamped, the frozen breath from our mouths like clouds of mist.

'7.30.4' shouted the commentator.

Verkerk and the Swan glided round the inside lane resting on their thighs, without the energy to straighten up. The spotlights made the ice shine beneath them and they cast crouched shadows on all sides.

Dad raised his mittens again and roared like a man possessed. The hot dog man waddled over with his steaming wares pressed against his stomach.

Afterwards we walked through the white streets, across Urra Park and down Farmers' Hill. Dad was carrying a rucksack packed with all the newspapers on which we had been standing.

'Verkerk'll win,' he said.

'Looks like it,' I answered. 'Just so long as he doesn't win the 1,500 metres. Because that would give him three distances.'

'Do you think he'll win the 10,000, too?'

'Depends on the Swan and "Concrete" Guttormsen.'

'And Schenk,' he added.

That was how Dad talked. He seemed to have changed after Christmas, after becoming the branch manager. I didn't quite understand it, thought he would go all bossy, but no, hardly any ranting, no slamming of doors. He smiled. Strange.

'Do you know how much money we had in the vault yesterday, Kim?'

'No. How much?'

'350,000 kroner!'

'Imagine if there was a robbery!'

Dad laughed and slapped my back.

'That only happens in films. And on TV's crime hour.'

Mum was waiting at home with cocoa and rolls, but we were pretty full. We must have eaten at least twenty sausages between us. On the late night news there was a review of the world championships and as Verkerk came down the final outside lane in the 5,000 metres, one arm on his back, his neck tensed, we could see Dad and me roaring and banging on the railing in the background. It was only a quick flash, but we had been on TV. I wondered how many people had seen it. Had to be quite a few, I supposed.

The telephone rang. Mum took it. She returned laughing.

'Ringo Starr wants to talk to Paul McCartney,' she said.

I felt embarrassed and toddled off.

Ola sounded quite animated.

'Session at S-S-Seb's!' he groaned.

'What's up?'

'His d-d-dad's sent the new Beatles r-r-record from England!'

'On my way!' I yelled, jumping into clothes and steaming out faster than Keiichi Suzuki on the home straight, without even leaving any prints in the snow.

The tension at Seb's was at bursting point, worse than at Bislett stadium. He hadn't opened the parcel yet. It was on the table, flat, square, magical. Now we were just waiting for Gunnar. Couldn't he get a move on!

'Dad's been to Liverpool,' Seb said proudly.

At last Gunnar arrived, to drum roll and fanfare, and was just as excited as we were. He stepped into the room, red-faced and white-haired.

'Boys!' he panted. 'D'you know what?'

He sank onto the sofa.

'Yes,' we said. 'We know what.'

We pointed to the record lying on the table.

Gunnar's voice returned to its normal pitch and he got up again. There was a narrow stripe of snow up his back. Must have run here at quite a speed, too.

'Stig told me his friend who reads English papers said The Beatles weren't goin' to break up after all!'

'Is that true!' we screamed with one voice.

Gunnar took a deep breath. His eyes were rolling.

'They've signed a recording contract for *nine years*!'

We danced and cheered until Seb's mother banged on the wall. We sent each other serious looks, stood in a tight circle in the middle of the floor and looked each other in the eyes.

'C-c-course The Beatles aren't goin' to s-s-split up,' Ola said.

'Of course not,' we said.

'The Beatles'll never split up,' I said.

'Never,' said the others.

'Not for nine years and not ever,' Seb said.

'Not ever,' we said.

'No one better, no one even close,' Gunnar said.

'No one!'

We laid our hands on top of each other's in a big clump and stood there in a circle, our piled-up hands between us.

We stood like that for some time and it felt good.

Afterwards Seb put the Gerard on the floor, locked the door and pulled down the blinds. Then we carefully lifted the parcel and with our hearts in our mouths, our eyes and ears on stalks, we unwrapped the paper.

'"Penny Lane",' I whispered. '"Penny Lane".'

'"Strawberry Fields Forever",' Gunnar whispered.

We sat for about an hour examining the cover.

Seb was the first to say something.

'They've got moustaches,' he said.

They had moustaches. We tugged at our top lips. There was not a lot to tug at. There was nothing.

We sat for a while rubbing a finger under our noses.

Then Seb placed the 45 on the deck and pressed ON. The arm crossed the first grooves and when it lowered itself we held our breath, the world stood still, the sounds from the street were nothing to do with us, they were from another planet.

Our ears were as big as umbrellas.

Afterwards we lay stretched out, our ears folded over, with a falling pulse. That was how it felt. That was how it was. Like hearing God say 'Let there be light' on the first day. There was light.

Ola said:

'Just like "Eleanor Rigby" and "Yellow S-S-Submarine". Two s-s-sides of the s-s-same coin.'

Ola had the words.

We lay for a while ruminating.

'Dad wrote in his letter that Penny Lane is a street in Liverpool,' Seb said.

'Like Karl Johan in Oslo,' Gunnar suggested.

'At least the trumpets are better than those off-key attempts on May 17,' I said.

'We c-c-could get summer jobs,' Ola burst out. 'And buy instruments with the m-m-money we earn!'

Of course we could! We all talked at the same time, working out how much we had and how much we needed. Yes. There were plans. We warmed to the topic. The Snafus! They were no limits. We were on our way.

'Perhaps we could have Goose on the organ,' I said.

Gunnar, Seb and Ola looked me up and down.

'What did you say?'

'Would be alright to have an organ. The Animals have an organ!'

'Goose just plays psalms!' Seb said with emphasis.

They continued to talk about guitars, drum kits, mikes and amplifiers, but I couldn't get Goose out of my head. His eyes which had been yellow with fear were matt and closed now, as though they had turned and were staring at the inside of his skull. At the Christmas party he had played organ with fizzes and squeaks and he had sat like a statue in the midst of all this vibrating noise, enclosed, a captive inside his own chords.

'We can practise in the cellar at our place,' Gunnar said.

'Perhaps we can p-p-play at the autumn school party!'

Then we played the record again. 'Strawberry Fields Forever'. Gunnar buzzed around the speaker like a wasp.

'What's happenin' there at the end?'

'Playin' backwards,' I suggested. 'Just like on "Rain"?'

'Groovy lyrics,' Seb said, pricking up his ears and listening with closed eyes.

'What does *strawberry* mean?' Ola whispered.

I explained the title to him.

Let me take you down, 'cause I'm going to.

'Way out lyrics,' Seb puffed.

Living is easy with eyes closed.

'The M-M-Monkees can sh-sh-shove it,' Ola said. 'The Monkees are a b-b-bucket of sh-sh-shite!'

'And Herman's Hermits.'

We studied the pictures again. Moustache. George had a beard as well. Seb scratched his chin.

'Dad says that if you shave every day it grows quicker,' I said.

'Even if you don't have any beard?'

'Yep.'

We considered this for a while. Then we had to leave. Ola flitted round the corner. Gunnar and I walked up Bygdøy Allé together.

'Verkerk'll smash Maier and Guttormsen,' I said.

'Saw you on the evenin' news,' he said. 'Didn't know your dad was crazy about skatin.'

'Neither did I.'

It was beginning to snow. That didn't bode well for the ice.

'You know the shop-owner who caught Goose,' Gunnar said.

Yes, I knew him.

Gunnar grinned.

'He's shut up shop.'

'Why's that?'

'My dad told me. Went off his chump after Goose's mother turned up at the shop and told him he had rung her. Lost his marbles.'

We went our separate ways at the chemist. I watched Gunnar waddle towards Gimle with his hands in his pockets, his shoulders hunched, short and stocky. He turned and waved, shouted something I didn't catch. I shouted something too, I don't suppose he heard it either.

First Goose. Now the shop-owner.

I walked back to Seb's.

His mother was in the sitting room with a man. There were bottles on the table and the room was full of blue smoke. Seb dragged me into his room and slammed the door.

'That bastard comes here every Saturday,' he snarled. 'Gets drunk and shouts and vomits. Fat pig!'

He clenched his fists and slumped down on the sofa. Then he realised that I had come back.

'Did you forget somethin' or what?'

I sat down on the sofa, too.

'The person who caught Goose didn't ring his mother. I did.'

'Thought so,' Seb chuckled.

'Now he's gone barmy too. Closed down his business.'

'It'll pass,' Seb said. 'He'll just be a bit confused. Not so strange. And then he'll forget the whole thing.'

'You reckon?'

'Dead cert.'

'And Goose?'

'Goose has always been like that.'

'How do you mean?'

'What happened that evenin' was just the dottin' of the 'i's and the crossin' of the 't's. Goose is fine now. In great form.'

My heart rate slowed. My stomach settled. I looked at Seb with gratitude. He was laughing without opening his mouth.

'You weren't thinkin' of goin' nuts too, were you!' he grinned.

From the sitting room came the murky sound of laughter and something fell on the floor. Seb gave a start and went to the window.

'How's it goin' with Guri?' I asked.

He stood with his back to me.

'Alright,' he said. 'Haven't seen her for a while, by the way.'

I didn't ask any more questions. Had thought of asking if she had said anything about Nina, but I refrained.

Seb turned to me.

'I hardly dare touch her,' he exclaimed. 'After what happened to her, the abortion and all that. I don't dare. I'm scared… scared of hurtin' her, sort of.'

I pondered, searched for something to say, it was my turn to say something now.

'That's not so strange,' I said. 'After what she's been through.'

Seb just looked at me.

'I mean, perhaps she's scared too. So you could tell her that. Tell her you're scared, I mean.'

Seb smiled, pulled out a drawer and produced his harmonica. He held it in his hands, moistened his lips and closed his eyes. Then he blew, blew and sucked, it sounded like a dog outside howling at the moon or someone sobbing their heart out.

Seb stopped.

'That's all I can do so far,' he said.

'Bloody great!' I said. 'Wow, it's bloody great!'

Then I went home and shaved.

After his return from Paris, Uncle Hubert looked elegant with a black beret, checked scarf and a long coat that swept along the ground. Dad almost turned round in the doorway when he showed up. Hubert had a radio for me, a Kurér, which ran on batteries and when I fiddled with the dial in the evening I could receive all of Europe, all sorts of voices and languages and sounds filled the room. Sometimes I could get Copenhagen too. Then I switched it off. Then I switched it back on again.

One evening I went to Hubert's place in Marienlyst with a pile of cakes, as Mum always had eight sorts of cake until well into February. It was just as messy as before. Hubert was sitting in the middle of a pile of papers when I arrived and it wasn't long before we had eaten all the cakes.

'You can't keep Christmas goodies until March, can you,' Hubert laughed between the crumbs.

Then he brought a Coke for me and a beer for him.

'Does your dad like his new job?' he asked, taking a drink.

'Think so! Last week he had 350,000 kroner in the bank vault!'

Hubert snapped his fingers.

'Oooh! We should've had that, Kim!'

I agreed.

Hubert went for more beer.

'350,000,' he said, returning with a full glass.

'That's a lot of money,' I said.

He leaned back and drained his glass.

'It's almost *too* much money,' Hubert said.

He belched and put on a sad smile.

'Oh dear,' he mumbled. 'Now it's my turn to work again. To earn money.'

'Don't you earn money from your pictures?'

He gave a hollow laugh.

'No, no. Aristocrats. Consultants. Racing drivers. That's the thing now. Beautiful women that wash up on deserted shores. It's enough to make you sick, Kim.'

He showed me a repugnant drawing of a man in a white coat with a stethoscope round his neck. Behind him were two women, one brunette and one blonde.

Hubert was not so well now. His fingers drummed on the arm of the chair, his eyes were locked in a wild expression and his knees pumped up and down.

'It's all lies and nonsense, Kim!' he almost shouted. 'And my drawings are lies, too. People are not like that! Life is not like that, Kim!'

The knots were coming. He was enmeshed in one enormous tangle. I could see that. He could see that I could see. I was beginning to understand Hubert better now.

'When's Henny coming home?' I asked quickly.

And he melted like butter and sank deep into the chair.

'In the summer,' he sighed.

'Nina, too.'

I walked through Frogner Park on my way home. It was criss-crossed with ski tracks but I didn't see anyone. I strolled round Dogland, deserted there too, there wasn't even a dog around. The Monolith was there as always, and the statues were active in the dark. I thought about Nina and Henny, that one day the snow would be gone and that the evenings would be light and warm and almost unbearable. All of a sudden five statues woke up and came towards me from all directions. Their steps were silent, but I heard their breathing and then the movements. I stopped and felt an acrid, burning taste in my mouth. A torch was switched on and shone in my face. I saw nothing. They saw me.

'Out looking for queers, are you?' a voice asked.

The burning sensation filled my mouth and nose. The Frogner gang.

They came closer. They blinded me with the torch. A knuckled fist tapped my head. I felt the pain before it came.

'Aren't you one of those bloody commie bastards?' a voice said.

I tried to shield my eyes. They brushed my hands away.

'Answer me, dickhead! You commie shit! You're the type that goes on those demos for the chinks.'

They shone the light closer.

'Didn't I tell you! He's got slit-eyes.'

I ran forward as fast as I could, found a gap and dived through. They raced after me with the cone of light dancing through the dark. I tripped, fell headlong, my hand hit something, a stone, a stone in the middle of winter! I grabbed it, stood up slowly and swivelled round with my arm raised ready to throw. They stopped too and shone the light on the hand holding the stone. Then they came closer again. I threw. I threw as hard as I could and heard a scream as a shadow held its head and slumped to the ground. Then they were on me. Two held me, one shone the torch and one punched. The fifth was on the ground moaning. I threw up, the one in front of me worked himself up into a fury and kneed me in the balls. Then they let go and I fell in the snow holding my crotch and crying.

The last man had come to and walked towards me. They were still shining the torch, the light hurt my eyes. I was dragged to my feet again, they held me from behind and the one I had hit with the stone stood in front of me, breathing heavily. Then he took my right hand, I didn't have the strength to resist, I gave paw, like a craven dog. He carefully bent back my index finger and when it could go no further he pushed with all his strength. I heard a revolting sound, then everything went black.

When I awoke I was lying in the snow spitting blood. Don't remember how I got home, only that I had lost the keys and Mum let out a scream when she opened the door. It took quite a long time to explain that I had tripped, fallen on my face and scraped it on a block of ice beneath the snow, ending up with my nose in the earth. She cleaned my wounds with iodine, and put on plasters and gauze everywhere. The only place that really hurt was my finger. But I said nothing about it. Lay awake all night feeling the pain in my finger, I couldn't get my mind off it, and in fact there was some pleasure in it for there was so much other shit to think about, but now I was just one big finger, one single swollen finger that hurt a hell of a lot.

Mum spotted it at breakfast one morning. Impossible to hide. The grazes on my face had begun to heal, but the finger was there. I tried to force it into the handle of the tea cup. It wouldn't go.

'What've you done to your finger!' my mother shouted, leaning over the table.

'Sprained it when I tripped that night,' I said.

Dad peered over his paper.

'You should've gone to casualty,' he said.

'Casualty! It doesn't hurt at all!'

But the first week my finger had glowed with pain, I could have used it as a reading lamp in the evenings. Every single night I lay there feeling, just feeling, and it taught me something about pain. Then the pain subsided bit by bit, it was like falling asleep or waking, and in the end the finger stuck out like a question mark, a refugee on my hand.

I said nothing about what happened in Frogner Park to the others, either. Don't know quite why not. Perhaps it had something to do with the stone, that I had thrown a stone. Or that I liked having a secret. I said nothing. But I couldn't get away from the finger. Even if I kept my hand in my pocket somebody would see it.

'What've you done to your finger?' Gunnar asked one day at the baker's in the lunch break.

'Picked my nose,' I said.

'Don't take the piss! It looks like a bent paper clip!'

'I was finger wrestling with my uncle,' I said.

Fortunately the bell rang and we shot up Skovveien. Then it was Kerr's Pink's turn. He refused to correct my essay. *What it Means to be Courageous* was the title and I was very pleased, I had written five pages about how it wasn't possible to be courageous unless you were frightened first.

'A mess!' Kerr's Pink yelled, smacking my essay book down on the table. 'Do you think I'm a trained palaeographer! Eh! The Dead Sea scrolls are easier to read than this scribble.'

'What's a palaeographer?' I asked.

'Now you're stretching my patience, Kim,' he shouted. 'Now you're stretching my patience beyond all reason!'

I showed him my finger. He stared at it in astonishment, held it up to the light. The whole class strained across their desks to stare at my finger.

Kerr's Pink became silky smooth again.

'Why didn't you say that to begin with, Kim?'

I retracted my finger and put it in my pocket. Afterwards I showed it to Skinke and was let off the gym lesson. I decided my finger would hurt until we did gym outdoors.

The finger had its advantages.

But one day Ola came to school with something that outdid my finger by some distance. He came with his hat pulled down over his ears, his eyes barely visible.

He tried to walk past unnoticed.

'Hi, Ola!' we yelled. 'You wearin' a hat, are you?'

He stopped with his back to us.

'Looks like it, doesn't it!'

We crowded round him. It was a terrific woollen hat with a big tassel and a red border with skiers all the way round his head.

'Did you knit it yourself?' Seb asked, trying to goad him.

Ola twisted away with a roar.

'You cold, Ola?' Gunnar asked.

He tried to make off. We ran after him and hauled him back to the shed.

'Isn't it a bit warm to be wearin' a hat?' I wondered.

Ola pointed all around him.

'Still s-s-snow on the ground,' he said.

'Slush,' we corrected. 'No one goes around with a hat on now.'

'*I* do!' Ola yelled.

'Not any more,' we said.

It was not easy taking off his hat. He pulled it down over his face with both hands as we yanked at the tassel. He flailed around him and shouted a lot, but in the end he had to surrender.

We stood there with his hat in our hands.

We stared at Ola, horror pumping through us in furious surges.

We went closer.

'What've you done?' we asked.

'Me!' Ola screamed. 'I've done sod all! It was my dad.'

We gave him back his hat.

'How?'

'Last night,' Ola mumbled. 'W-w-woke up this mornin' and it'd happened. He'd cut my hair while I was s-s-sleepin'.'

An all-over cut. It was worse than a basin cut and a crop at the same time. His skull was shiny round his ears and at the back, and his fringe was non-existent.

We clenched our fists and stood in silence for a long time, it was the worst thing that had happened on the home front since Dragon ate the firecrackers.

The bell rang. We didn't care.

Ola pulled down his hat.

'I'm not takin' it off for the l-l-lesson! I'm not bloody takin' it off for the l-l-lesson. I'll say I've got eczema!'

'You do that!' we said.

'Buggered if I'm goin' home today. Sod 'em!'

Ola forced his hat down further.

We went to my place after school. Sweat was running down Ola's neck, but he kept his hat on until we were safely inside the door. Then he flung it off and breathed a sigh of relief.

Mum peeped in, saw Ola and smiled.

'Hair looks nice,' she said.

She glanced at me.

'You see, Kim. You could have a haircut like that, too.'

We froze her out.

'Parents,' Seb said. 'Parents are bastards.'

'My dad's refused to give Stig any pocket money until he gets a haircut,' Gunnar told us.

'Shouldn't be allowed,' I said.

'They're pissed off because they haven't got any hair,' Gunnar said.

'I'm never g-g-goin' home,' Ola said.

Mum came in with some tea and the last Christmas biscuits, four gingerbread men. Weren't quite sure if we should take food from the enemy, but we relented in the end.

'I'm never g-g-goin' home again,' Ola repeated.

He meant it.

Ola stayed where he was.

Gunnar and Seb looked at their watches. They stayed, too.

Dad came home from the bank, we heard him whistling in the hall.

Mum poked her head in.

'Aren't you going to eat?' she asked.

'Full,' I said.

Ola didn't move.

It was evening.

Then the telephone rang.

'If it's for me, I'm not here,' Ola hissed.

Mum was at the door again.

'Your parents are on the phone, Gunnar.'

Gunnar got up slowly and Mum waited.

'Is there something up?' she asked.

We didn't answer. Gunnar stared at us, nonplussed. Then he left with my mother.

'H-h-hope he doesn't s-s-say anythin',' Ola muttered.

After a while Gunnar returned.

'Gotta go home,' he said. 'Gotta help Dad carry some sacks of spuds. Stig's gone on strike because he doesn't get any pocket money.'

'You didn't s-s-say anythin', did you?' Ola asked.

'What about?'

'That I was h-h-here, of course!'

'Yes, I did. Why?'

'That's what you shouldn't've said!' I pointed out.

'It was only my mum!'

'Yes, and why do you think she asked, eh?'

Gunnar realised he had put his foot in it. He collapsed on the sofa with a bright red face.

Straight after, there was a ring at the door. We sat and waited. If it was Ola's dad, we would barricade the door. We listened. A girl's voice. For a moment my stomach contracted and all my blood raced into my finger. Then it passed. It was Åse, Ola's sister.

Wow. She had grown. Hardly recognised her. We sat gaping at her. Ola stared out of the window, his ears glowing.

'Aren't you coming home?' Åse asked.

'N-n-no!' said Ola.

'It's chops today. We're waiting for you.'

Ola turned slowly.

'Chops?'

'Yes, are you coming?'

Ola didn't answer.

Seb and Gunnar began to put on their coats. Åse stood in the doorway smiling at her big brother.

'There's a letter for you from Trondheim,' she said.

Ola's ears glowed again, his hands fidgeted.

'Trondheim,' he echoed.

Gunnar, Seb and I exchanged glances. Trondheim?

'Are you coming soon or what?'

Ola pulled on the rucksack and pressed the hat down over his head.

'On one c-c-condition,' he said. 'That I don't have to sit at the s-s-same table as Dad!'

Then we wandered out. We were pretty hungry, all of us. Ola repeated the condition in a loud voice.

'I'm not sittin' at the s-s-same table as Dad! That's f-f-final!'

It was a fight to the death, either or. Either Ola or the desperado hairdresser from Solli.

Ola wore his hat for a long time that year. We went out quite a lot, there was a restlessness that drove us out in the evening, even though it was slushy and the record player had new batteries. Outside were the streets. That was where we were.

One evening Gunnar said, 'Beginnin' to get fed up.'

'Fed up with what?'

'With walkin'.'

But we continued. Especially on Saturday evenings when we wandered all over, listening to music from open windows where someone was having a party. Then we stopped, looked up, hurried on. Unpleasant stories about these parties were doing the rounds, about bouncers being struck down with crowbars, TVs being chucked out of windows, walls being painted black, books being burned in the bath. We shuddered. We listened to music from open windows, The Rolling Stones, The Who, The Animals, The Beatles, The Beatles, the echo of laughter, bawling, sometimes crying. We hurried home.

But it was not long before we were out and about again. It was only a sleepy Wednesday evening, there was no music in the streets and the snow lay in the gutters, grey slush. As usual Seb was with Guri, hadn't seen much of him in recent weeks. We walked past the shop where Goose had been caught. *Closed due to illness*. A wooden board had been nailed up inside the doorway. I felt the backwash and for a moment I saw Goose standing in the gleam of the street lamp, motionless in the circle of light, and all around was all the darkness he would have to enter sooner or later.

'There's S-S-Seb!' Ola shouted.

It was Seb and Guri and another girl. They were on their way up to Urra Park. We called and they stopped.

Two girls. Seb looked a bit wild to our eyes. He was holding Guri's hand and the other girl leaning against the railing had long, brown hair, her face was tanned, it seemed to glow like a Red Indian's.

'Hello,' she said. 'My name's Sidsel. I'm in the same class as Guri at Fagerborg.'

We mumbled our names and the conversation ground to a halt.

Guri giggled. Seb whistled. We stood stamping and shuffling our feet.

'I'm cold,' Sidsel said.

And then we continued walking together.

'You must be cold, too,' Sidsel said, looking at Ola.

He pulled down his hat.

'N-n-no, I've g-g-got eczema.'

Sidsel moved over to the other side, next to Gunnar. Ola cursed and gnashed his teeth.

Seb offered cigarettes round. I produced some matches and lit up for Guri. In the light she noticed my finger.

'What happened to your finger?' she asked.

'Got it stuck in a pencil sharpener,' I said.

'Rubbish!'

'Fell in gym.'

Gunnar looked at me, said nothing.

We walked to Vestkanttorget. The monkeys and the parrots shrieked behind the windows in Naranja. Gunnar grimaced and made the monkeys stand on their heads. Sidsel laughed so much she had to lean on him.

Didn't know Gunnar was that funny.

We went on to Majorstuen, did a tour of Valkyrie plass, had a look at the record shop in Jacob Aallsgate. Monkees in the window there, too. Gunnar and Sidsel were lagging behind a little. Ola looked sour.

'Do you know what Dragon's gone and done?' Guri burst out. 'He's gone to sea!'

'How do you know?'

'Someone in the class knows his brother.'

'I will, too,' Seb said.

'You will what?'

'Go to sea.'

'You will not,' said Guri.

'I will. In the summer.'

She retracted her hand. It took Seb quite a long time to regain it. And only after he had promised solemnly that he would not go to sea.

'Word of honour,' Seb said with his legs crossed.

'G-g-gotta be off,' Ola said and just went, rounded the corner and was gone.

'Hang on,' I shouted, but he didn't hear.

Guri suddenly remembered something and rummaged through her pockets. She found a small, pink envelope.

'Nina asked me to give you this,' she said.

I stuffed it into my back pocket without any emotion. Stuffed it in my back pocket and played cool.

Gunnar and Sidsel eventually caught up, with their fingers

entwined. They were not particularly talkative, staring at the ground or at each other.

I felt superfluous.

But my back pocket was on fire.

Seb took Guri home. Sidsel lived in Professor Dahls gate. She came with us, or I went with them. They didn't say a word on the way, shoulder to shoulder, their hands interlaced. I pottered on down to the fountain while they said their goodbyes. I sat there waiting and thinking that it would not be long until the planks would be taken off and the jet of water surged into life.

When Gunnar came, his face was blank.

He walked with me to Drammensveien. Must have needed some fresh air.

'That was quick,' I said.

'Sidsel,' he said. 'Her name's Sidsel. With a "d".'

'Get lucky?'

He set off running, jumped over a fence, vaulted back again.

'Think so,' he said. 'Think I'm in.'

That was as far as he went. Padlock on his tongue.

'There you go, then,' I said, punching him in the stomach.

I'm not saying what was in the letter. Except that she was coming over this summer. Outside I heard the trains pounding through the night. I turned on the radio and searched through Europe until I found Copenhagen and burrowed under the duvet with it.

Gunnar snooped around Professor Dahls gate night after night. Ola's hair grew back. Seb was hardly ever around. My finger didn't hurt any longer, but it stuck up like a curly twig and didn't look like any of the other fingers. I bought new batteries for the Kurér and listened in the evening.

Then came the news. It came via Seb, was whispered in the shed during the lunch break one gloomy Tuesday: Party.

'Sidsel's alone this weekend,' Seb whispered.

Gunnar's eyes grew like plums.

'There are a few from their class coming,' Seb went on.

He looked around nervously. No spies in sight.

'Don't say a word to anyone.'

We each went our own way, letting the news sink in. It was almost unreal. We would be where the music was and others would be walking in the streets listening to us, listening to us inside.

We met at Gunnar's before leaving on the Saturday. Seb smuggled in a half bottle of Bordeaux up the sleeve of a large tweed jacket he must have pinched off his father.

'The beer's under the stairs,' he whispered.

'How will we open the wine?' Gunnar whispered nervously.

'Get a corkscrew, you numbskull,' said Seb.

'Mum and Dad'll notice!'

Ola pulled at his roll neck sweater and breathed out. It was brand new, woollen, burgundy, itched like hell and his chin was sweaty already.

'You can open the bottle, can't you, you being so c-c-clever,' he grinned at Gunnar.

'Eh?'

'After spending so m-m-much time in Professor Dahls gate!'

We chuckled at that for quite some time. Gunnar returned the favour.

'And the letter your sister enticed you home with, what was all that about, then, eh?'

Ola stretched the neck of his sweater to get some air.

'Åse's pen pal,' he mumbled.

'And you read the letters that come to her, do you?'

Gunnar had the upper hand. Ola was on his way back down the roll neck. Two blue eyes were visible. He was speaking through wool.

'R-r-really nice g-g-girl! Two years older than Åse.'

'You've seen her then, have you?'

'J-j-just in p-p-pictures. Bit of alright. Name's Kirsten.'

Seb was becoming impatient. He found a pencil and forced the cork down. The wine splashed all over his forehead. Gunnar was by the door listening to hear if the reptiles were on their way up. They were in the sitting room watching TV.

'*Skål*,' said Seb, taking a swig and passing the bottle round.

When I drank, nothing came, the cork was stuck. I passed the bottle round.

Gunnar put on 'Strawberry Fields' and Saturday had lift-off. We opened the window so that passers-by could hear us. The bottle went round, but I got the cork. We smoked a bit on the window-sill, not saying much, just savouring the feeling, not quite knowing whether we were looking forward to the party or dreading it. The bottle went round without a murmur. When it reached Ola, there was a knock at the door. Gunnar panicked and stuffed the bottle down Ola's roll neck.

It was just Stig.

'Relax, boys. The CIA are in the sitting room eating peanuts. Nice sweater, Ola. Breast pocket on the inside?'

Ola took out the bottle as the sweat poured off him. Gunnar took it and hid it behind a cushion.

'Pre-party's under way, I can see,' said Stig.

We nodded. Pre-party. That's what it was.

'There are rumours going round that the Frogner gang have smashed up a flat in Colbjørnsens gate,' he said.

Bloody hell. Gunnar ground his teeth. Ola developed a twitch in both eyes. Seb went white.

'Got past three bouncers. Rolled a piano down the stairs, shredded a Persian carpet and poured ketchup on the parents' bed.'

Bloody hell. We were unable to articulate a word. Fear chafed at our Adam's apples.

'You know an American battleship has attacked North Vietnam, don't you? And it's dead sure they have nuclear weapons on board. And you know what that means. It means number three, boys. Deep shit. That's why the Vietnamese war against imperialists is our war, isn't it. Do you understand? And it's about bloody time someone started a solidarity committee at Vestheim so that the Young Conservatives can't keep pumping that shite of theirs. Do you hear?'

He stood staring down at us for a while, towering against the door frame with hair tucked behind his ears and bobbing up under his earlobes.

'Where did you get that model?' he grinned, pointing to my finger.

'Steen & Strøm department store,' I said.

He laughed.

'Have to be goin', boys. Off to Club 7. Public Enemies are playin'. The water in Frogner Bay's goin' to be choppy tonight.'

On his way out he turned round again.

'Remember what I said, boys. Après nous the bacteria.'

He slammed the door and trotted through the flat. There was a brief but violent confrontation in the sitting room before he went on his way.

The bottle was empty. Seb snapped his fingers and another one appeared from the other sleeve. And slowly we got into the groove again, forgot the Frogner gang, blood swelled back into our hearts and expectations, expectations which rose like boiling milk.

The girls sat on the sofa drinking Coke. We each found a chair and Seb opened the bottles of beer. The girls scowled. There were four of them. Guri and Sidsel. And two others. Eva and Randi. Randi was a tubby version with a very short skirt. Eva was thin and wore a longer skirt. Seb and Gunnar took charge, searched through the records and put on a Hollies LP *For Certain Because*.

'Won't Jørgen be coming soon?' said Eva and Randi, the first thing they had uttered.

Ola glanced at me and mumbled from the corner of his mouth:

'Jørgen? Who's J-J-Jørgen?'

'No idea,' I whispered.

'I'm sure he'll be here soon,' Sidsel said, drinking through a straw.

'Jørgen's in our class,' Guri explained.

There was a ring at the door. On the sofa Eva and Randi gave a start, went breathless and frantic, pulling out pocket mirrors and eyeliner and busying themselves. Sidsel opened the door and brought in a freshly scrubbed little man who looked a bit like Paul Simon. He gave the girls a brief nod and then blow me down if he didn't shake hands and do the formal bit.

'Jørgen Rist,' he said, softly squeezing my hand and bowing. Jesus.

'Kim,' I said. 'With one "m".'

He didn't laugh. His eyelashes curved in a deep, long arc, as though he had curled them like that. The cheekbones in his shiny face were very prominent and his hair was combed straight back and seemed electric, but the static was probably caused by my acrylic sweater.

Jørgen was not the chatty type. Randi and Eva sat staring chunks out of him, didn't even notice my finger. Jørgen was looking in a different direction and didn't seem to be bothered about anything.

Seb went for more beer. There was a smell of burning cheese coming from the kitchen and the girls were whispering together on the sofa. Jørgen sat staring into the air, Ola peered over his roll neck and all of a sudden Seb and Gunnar were nowhere to be seen. Eva put on a Monkees record, 'A Little Bit Me, A Little Bit You'. My ears shrank like currants and Ola dived down his roll neck.

A confrontation was inevitable.

'Do you know it is actually monkeys singing,' I said, trying to be funny.

Why did no one laugh?

'Better than The Beatles at any rate,' Randi said.

Ola surfaced from the wool. We looked around. Seb and Gunnar had absented themselves and were still absent.

'You can't compare The Monkees with The Beatles!' I shouted.

'"Strawberry Fields" is crap!'

At last Seb and Gunnar returned, a bit unsteady on their legs. A dangerous smell of burning came from the kitchen. The girls flew out and Jørgen trotted after them. Then Seb brought us together and announced under his breath:

'There's a *demijohn* in the cellar! Gunnar and I have found a *demijohn*!'

'What's a d-d-demijohn?'

'Big glass container for making wine, you dope. And it's full.'

They led the way. We crept after them through another room full of books and paintings and stuff culminating in a hall which led down a steep flight of stairs to the cellar.

Sidsel stood in the doorway.

'Where are you going?' she asked.

'To play ping pong,' Seb said gruffly.

'The food'll be ready soon.'

'Won't be long,' Gunnar mumbled, his face glowing like a Northern Light.

We tiptoed down the steps. There was in fact a ping pong table in the cellar. There were also two storerooms. In one there was jam. In the other, wine. A rubber tube was attached to the mouth of the demijohn. Seb grinned, knelt down and sucked. It gurgled and bubbled. Then it was Ola's turn. He got a mouthful down his roll neck and let out a piercing scream. I got nothing at all, must have been sucking wrong, all that came out was foul air.

Gunnar tore the tube off me.

'Don't drink it all!' he grinned, shoving the pipe in his mouth.

Afterwards we staggered up the stairs and found the girls with Jørgen in the kitchen.

The sandwiches were huge and baking hot with loads of cheese and ham. We carried them into the sitting room. Seb opened the last bottles of beer.

Eva put on Herman's Hermits.

'Bubblegum pop,' Seb said, taking a swig.

'Randi and I were at the Edderkoppen gig,' Eva announced proudly.

'And the Vanguards played the pants off them,' I said.

Eva was annoyed.

'Herman's Hermits are much better than The Beatles!'

Seb lowered the bottle.

'You can't compare Herman's Hermits with The Beatles!'

'Why not?'

'Because,' Seb said, scratching his head. 'Because.'

'Because you can't compare the Frogner tram with Apollo 12!'

Ola had a way with words. Cometh the hour, cometh Ola.

We opened the window to air the room, sneaked on a Beatles record, 'I Don't Want To Spoil The Party', and sent the music out in the evening and the streets. That was what it was like to be indoors while others were wearing out shoe leather roaming the streets. Then Sidsel charged in and slammed the window shut, she didn't want any gatecrashers. We were a trifle embarrassed, of course it was stupid to open the window, and then we chatted about the Frogner gang and we seemed to move closer to each other, stirred by a common enemy, warmed by a common fear. Somewhere in Bygdøy they had sawn down a flag post, driven a scooter through a living room and thrown darts at paintings.

'I'm sure they're very nice individuals,' Sidsel said. 'But as a group they're vile.'

'Don't think they're nice in any form,' I puffed. 'Think they're shit-bags through and through.'

The girls and Jørgen cleared away the plates and we sneaked back down to the cellar. Ola and I played ping pong while Seb and Gunnar drank. Then we swapped roles. Couldn't make the tube work for me. Nothing came out. Then we scrambled up the steps bellowing 'Penny Lane' and got lost in all the rooms, but finally found the kitchen. Eva and Randi and Jørgen were washing up. We swayed into the living room, Seb and Gunnar were very loud, put the record player on full blast, dimmed the lights and wanted to dance. They were well gone. Then Eva and Randi and Jørgen joined us, but Jørgen didn't seem to be in a dancing mood even though Eva and Randi were ogling him for all they were worth. Ola and I didn't exist.

The lions of the dance floor collapsed by the table shaking their manes. Some people passed by the fence outside yelling and singing. A bottle was smashed. Gunnar turned off the music and we sat stock still until they had gone. Sidsel went white around the gills.

'Quite mad really,' Seb said. 'Quite mad really that we're more afraid of the Frogner shits than the war in Vietnam.'

The girls looked at him.

Seb leaned across the table.

'Do you know that the Americans have the whole of their fleet just off the coast of North Vietnam! With hundreds of nuclear bombs on board!'

The girls shook their heads, they didn't know.

The room fell silent.

Then Ola said, 'Après nous the b-b-bacteria.'

It was quiet for a while longer. Then Gunnar turned up the volume. 'And I Love Her'. And one couple took to the floor like fused shadows.

'What are you going to do after the *gymnas*?' I asked, feeling so decrepit moss was growing on me.

Eva and Randi were bored.

'Air hostess,' Randi sighed, eyeing Jørgen.

'Finish *gymnas* first,' Eva said.

'Going to be an actor,' Jørgen said with gravitas.

'Eh?' Ola burst out.

'Going to apply for drama school,' he elucidated.

'I'm going to sea!' Seb shouted, but then Guri went into action and he had to promise once again that he would never, never, go to sea.

Seb swore by all that was holy.

'I once played the part of Frans the frog at *folkeskole*,' I said. 'Jumped around wearing a green jersey and green flippers. Ola was Tom Thumb.'

Ola sent me a dirty look from above the roll neck.

'I've played the roles of Jesus and Tordenskiold,' Jørgen informed us.

No more was said about that. Eva and Randi pushed for another round of Herman's Hermits, Sidsel fetched more Cokes and we nipped down to the cellar. The demijohn was bubbling, wouldn't be long before we were bubbling, too. Seb drank. Gunnar drank. Ola drank. Then we heard voices behind us. They issued from the dark, without warning. Sidsel and Guri. Ola waved the tube.

'So this is where you play ping pong,' Sidsel said coldly.

Nothing you could say to that.

'Well, that's dreadful,' Guri said.

Caught in the act. Words were useless. Seb and Gunnar responded with direct action, stifled their protests, and their glowing shadows merged into the dark where the ensuing silence spoke its own unambiguous language.

I looked at Ola.

'Nothing left for us to do here then,' I said.

We staggered upstairs. Eva and Randi were in the living room listening to Herman decrying the lack of milk. Jørgen had gone. Ola slumped into a chair looking worse for wear. I had to pee and crawled up to the next floor. There were lots of doors to choose from, but in the end I found the bathroom. The door was ajar. I peeped in, stopped in my tracks. Jørgen was in there. Standing in front of the mirror with lipstick and eyeliner. He had drawn two black teardrops under his eyes, just like the girls at the *gymnas*. Out of my depth, I held my breath and stepped backwards. Worst thing

I had ever seen. I tiptoed down the corridor, found another room with the door open, had to be Sidsel's bedroom, looked a lot like Nina's room, maybe all girls' rooms were alike. Smelt like it, too. Clean. Sheets that had been hung outside to air. Oranges. And at the same time something heavy, something physical, armpits, scalp. Oh God, I was terrified. Had to make my way downstairs and fast. Too late. The bathroom door opened and Jørgen was approaching. I stood with my back to him without turning.

'All girls' rooms are the same,' he said.

'Just what I was thinkin',' I said.

'Kim's a girl's name, too,' he said beneath his breath.

I turned round slowly, unable to believe my own ears, and stared at him. He had wiped away the eyeliner.

'Who kissed you on the cheek?' I grinned.

'No one,' was all he said.

'You've got lipstick all over your face,' I said.

He rubbed it away with the back of his hand. Weird bloke.

'I'm bored,' he said. 'Do you get bored often? I'm almost always bored. That's why I'm going to be an actor. So that I can be anyone I feel like. And then I'll be spared the boredom.'

He certainly had that one worked out.

'I'm goin' to be a singer,' my mouth said. Instant red face, had no idea why I had said that.

I moved towards the stairs. He followed me.

'Are you?' he said quietly, studying me with shiny eyes hidden behind a soft hedge of arched brows. 'How nice.'

The silence was broken by a scream. I was down the staircase in two bounds and racing into the living room. Total panic. Worse than the *Titanic*. Sidsel was hysterical, the others not much better.

Iceberg on port side.

The Frogner gang.

They were standing by the gate yelling and throwing corks at the window. Five of them, the same as in Frogner Park. One of them had a big bandage round his head.

'They'll smash everything up!' Sidsel sobbed.

Gunnar was ashen but composed.

'We won't let them in,' he said.

'Do you think they'll *ask* to be let in! They'll break in!'

A dustbin lid was kicked down the street, a board ripped off the fence. Jørgen arrived and realised what was afoot. His face contorted with fear.

'Let's ring the police!' Guri said, beginning to cry.

A bottle smashed against the door.

Seb and Ola were ready to run, but there was nowhere to go.

Then I felt the great backwash, the shoreline of my soul was dragged out, my head became clear and sober, I heard the sea in a large conch shell.

I was not frightened. They couldn't do any more to me.

'I'll fix 'em,' I said, walking towards the hallway.

Gunnar leapt after me.

'You crazy or what! They'll kill you!'

I shook him off.

'I'll get rid of them!' I called out.

They all tried to hold me back. The girls were crying. Gunnar was cursing. I broke free.

'You're mad!' Gunnar yelled. 'They'll kill you!'

I went out.

A minute later I returned.

'That's that then,' I said.

No one believed me.

'They've slung their hooks,' I said, taking a seat. 'Danger over.' The girls went back to the window and peered out. Gunnar stuck his face into mine.

'What… what did you do?'

'Just told 'em to sod off,' I said.

After that the party took a new turn. Eva and Randi were not only eyeing up Jørgen, but also stealing glances at me. Seb found some gin in a cupboard, the lights were switched off, the music turned up and I remember dancing with Randi, the plump one, dancing all the time, standing there in the dark and our thighs were soft and hot, we were alone in the room. We lowered ourselves onto the floor and my hand found her breasts, and my hand found even more, but then all of a sudden she was no longer willing, sat up with a start, pushed out her lower lip and sighed up at the ceiling.

'Aren't you Nina's boyfriend?' she said.

Didn't like her tone.

'Nina? Nina who?'

She sneered and left. I sat in the dark. A door slammed. Someone had left. Then I heard sounds above. Someone was in the bedrooms. I assumed Seb and Guri weren't frightened any more.

I found Ola in the cellar. He was asleep on the ping pong table.

'Party's over,' I said. 'Let's go home.'

'Where are Seb and Gunnar?' he slurred.

I pointed to the ceiling. Ola understood.

We dawdled home. By the fountain we rested our legs. There was no one else about. We were the only living survivors in the whole town.

'Fab party,' Ola murmured.

I nodded.

'But that Jørgen was a w-w-wet fart, wasn't he.'

We lit a cigarette.

'Is Nina c-c-comin' this summer?'

'Yes,' I said. 'This summer.'

'K-K-Kirsten, too. From Trondheim.'

He dug a photo out of his back pocket and showed me. It was a booth photo, a girl laughing with big teeth, a centre parting and round cheeks.

'K-K-Kirsten,' Ola said.

That was when we heard it. We heard an organ. A ponderous psalm resounding through the night. There was light in a window in Schives gate, the only illuminated window in the whole town and that was where the sound was coming from.

'That's where Goose lives,' Ola said in a low voice.

'That's Goose playin' the Hammond organ,' I said with a tremble.

The heavy, sluggish chords rolled out into the dark. Soon lights came on in other windows, people stuck out their heads, yelled and shushed, banged with sticks, threw two øre coins, banged lids and all the dogs tried to out-howl each other.

Then the organ tones faded and Goose switched off the light. Afterwards everything was as before, just even quieter.

We flicked away the cigarette ends, strolled on, it was getting cold.

'What did you really s-s-say to the Frogner gang?'
'I told 'em you were there,' I said.
Ola, still a bit shaky on his legs, grinned.
'H-h-hope my dad's not waitin' up.'
'Same here.'
'F-f-fab party,' Ola said.
'Knockout,' I said.

On Sunday evening Seb trolled into my room, stood in the middle of the floor laughing, dived onto the sofa and continued laughing there.

'Bloody hell, you were wasted yesterday,' he said.

'Was I?'

'Out of your head!'

He stopped laughing.

'What did you actually do to the Frogner gang?'

I took my hand out of my pocket.

'Showed them my finger,' I said.

'What did you actually do to your finger?'

I told him about all that had happened in Frogner Park. Seb listened with big, round eyes. I took my time, left nothing out, told him about the one I punched in the face breaking my finger, and that they ran off, shit scared, Seb had seen the one with the bandage round his head, that was the one I knocked down, it was. Seb was open-mouthed.

And then he told me all the things he had been up to, what happened in the room with Guri, about the most fantastic bit of all when the party was over, about the details, about everything. I don't know which of us was lying more, the main thing was we believed each other.

Spring. No doubt about it. Bands were tramping through the streets practising boring marches and runners were training for the Holmenkoll relay race, but the surest sign of spring was Jensenius. The whale was awake and singing in the green ocean. And one day we stuck our heads out at the same time and saw each other.

'More beer!' he shouted.

Then he dropped a heavy purse and a shopping net.

'Export!' he shouted.

He was waiting in the doorway as I staggered up, he waved me in. He followed me into the sitting room where he collapsed in his usual tatty chair and emptied the beer down him as if pouring it down a drain.

'Take a seat,' he said.

I took a seat. The dust whirled up giving off a smell of stale bread.

'You haven't been playing the Robertino record,' he said.

I shifted uneasily.

'Yes, I have. I think it's very good.'

Jensenius was lost in dreams behind the foam.

'An Italian youngster with a throat of the purest gold.'

He expelled a heavy sigh.

'But now destiny has taken his voice. Life can be cruel, Kim.'

'Is he ill?' I asked.

'Voice is cracking,' Jensenius said. 'The devil has polished his throat with coarse sandpaper. Robertino is no longer Robertino.'

He swigged more beer. His stomach flowed over his filthy trousers. His shirt was buttoned up wrong.

'The same thing that happened to me,' he said dolefully. 'Destiny's cruel and fickle musical score. Just in reverse order.'

He fell silent for a few moments, staring in front of him with a gaze that looked backwards.

'Robertino lost his soprano voice and gained the miner's vocal register. I lost my baritone and gained the eunuch's vocal splendour.'

He took a long draught.

'What's an eunuch?' I asked softly.

'Life's slave,' he said. 'Deprived of his virility but left with his desire intact. Sometimes it's unbearable, Kim.'

I studied the floor. The carpet was threadbare from his nightly wanderings.

'What happened?' I asked.

Jensenius opened three bottles. There was a mountain of bottle tops under his chair.

'I'll tell you, Kim. I was due to sing at the University of Oslo Concert Hall in 1954, a sparkling spring day, almost like today.' He pointed to the grubby windowsills. 'I was going to sing Grieg and King Haakon would be present, Crown Prince Olav, the whole of the royal family, Kim! I took a taxi from here two hours before to be in good time. But I never arrived, Kim. King Haakon never heard Jensenius sing Grieg, Kim.'

He drank, his hand trembled around the bottle.

'What happened?' I whispered.

'An accident is what happened, Kim. Where Parkveien crosses Drammensveien. A lorry coming from the left. The taxi driver was killed. I got the front seat in my lap. I was crushed, Kim.'

He emptied the remaining bottles without speaking. That was Jensenius's story. And it was as true as everything that flows from my pen.

But on the woodburner was a bag of sweets, grey with dust and green with mould.

He turned sharply to me.

'But *you* will be something great!' he said.

I was apprehensive.

'Me?'

'Yes, Kim. You will be the greatest of us all!'

'How?'

'Singing, Kim! I've heard you at night. I hear you almost every night, Kim!'

I ran downstairs and rushed into my room. Outside, trees were exploding in green applause and bands never tired of doing encores.

'The radio,' I thought. 'It must be the radio he's heard.'

The first Saturday in May a car in Svoldergate was hooting up a storm, it had to be at least Jensenius trying to cross the road in one piece. I ran to the window. Dad! It was Dad in a new car, a bright red Saab gliding into Svoldergate like a giant ladybird. I sprinted downstairs, Dad had crawled out, was leaning against the warm car roof, having discarded his jacket and rolled up his sleeves, wow, what a spring. Mum came flying down, she fell around his neck and that's how I prefer to remember Mum and Dad, beside the new car, their first car, a bright red Saab V4, arm in arm one May day in 1967.

First of all we picked up Hubert from Marienlyst. He couldn't restrain himself, had to fiddle with various knobs, switch on the windscreen wipers and indicators and Dad became agitated. We had to move Hubert to the back seat to cool down.

'Goodness me,' Hubert said, patting Dad on the shoulder. 'I hope you didn't break into the safe in the vault!'

We laughed and rolled down the windows. Then we drove through the boiling hot town to Mosseveien and towards Nesodden. Dad picked up speed, the engine hummed like a happy bee, not a single car passed us, though Dad had to overtake a lorry by Hvervenbukta, quite close to a bend to the accompaniment of howls and screams from the back seat, but it was fine, Dad clung to the wheel as the sweat poured down over the big smile that I doubt had been there since the time he was a boy and believed in Father Christmas.

Bunde fjord was bright blue. Behind us the town lay bundled into dark green fields wrapped in yellow ribbons of sun.

The road to Tangen wasn't so good, the car bumped and jolted and pebbles shot up round the bonnet. Dad was hunched over the wheel, but coped well with these conditions, and soon we were rolling down to the quay and parked on the headland, Signalen. Dad crawled round the car on all fours looking for scratches to the paintwork, but when he pulled out his handkerchief to polish the car, Mum intervened and took him with us to the House.

It smelt as it always did on the first day of spring in Nesodden, rank and acrid from the rotting leaves on the ground. I always thought the House looked a little creepy with shutters over all the windows, like a dead body, I thought, or maybe a human before it is born because when we removed all the shutters, light streamed through the house as though the walls were transparent and everything inside began to come alive. The flies on the windowsills knocked against the glass, everything rattled and creaked and the dust danced like milky ways in a sunbeam.

I ran up to the place where I knew wild strawberries grew, behind the well, in a damp green hollow. I counted the flowers. Summer would bring an abundance of wild strawberries.

Mum made coffee and we sat on the balcony. The sun was on its way over Kolsås, a shiny aeroplane passed by the golden orb and circled round us.

'How are you enjoying the new job?' Hubert asked, watching the plane as it sped southwards and disappeared from view.

'Very much indeed,' Dad said.

Hubert peered over his cup.

'Kim said you had 350,000 kroner in the vault once,' he said, impressed.

'That can happen. Especially on Fridays when we have a lot of outgoing payments to make. Often have to send out for extra supplies from the main office.'

Hubert sipped his coffee.

'That's a lot of money,' he said quietly. 'Aren't you nervous about having so much money on site?'

Dad laughed.

'You and Kim have seen too many crime programmes, that's for sure!'

And then we drove back to town. There was a gang of long-haired youths playing guitar in Hvervenbukta. They had lit a bonfire on the smooth rock by the sea. Mosseveien was steaming after a hard day. The cranes on Akershus quay were still, like huge dead animals, and the sky over Holmenkollen was blood-red. Dad accelerated and we hurtled into the sunset with open windows and the wind blowing in our hair and bringing tears to our eyes as insects splattered on the windscreen and spread in all directions.

At first I thought I had caught a cold from the car ride, I woke in the night with a constricted throat, gummed-up eyes, and feeling feverish all over. But when I saw myself in the mirror next morning, I had quite a shock. I looked like a confused pelican, my chin bulged down under my face and I could barely speak. The fever had spread to my head, I shuffled back to my room, and when Mum saw me, she screamed.

I spent days on a white carousel. I lay in the desert with cold cloths over my forehead, juice in large glasses and the radio on. My nuts began to ache too, it was just like having toothache in your bollocks. That was when my mother went hysterical and sent for the doctor. He arrived with a stethoscope and did not look at all like the doctors Hubert drew for the weekly magazines. He poked and pressed me from forehead downwards. Afterwards he and Mum talked in low, sinister voices, but I caught occasional words, I heard mumps, mumps and boys, Mum kept going on about boys.

Bit by bit I recovered, the carousel slowed down, the fever was sweated out into my bed, the bulges shrank. And in fact it was quite nice lying there like that, sluggish and listless, listening to old records, Cliff, Paul Anka, Pat Boone, rounding off with the old 45s. I played Robertino too and Jensenius stamped on the floor with approval. Gunnar, Seb and Ola visited me one day, no danger there, they had all had mumps a long time ago. They stood around my bed grinning and telling me about Skinke's shoes, which someone had filled with water, and Kerr's Pink, who had given the whole class seed potatoes. But then they went serious and got to the heart of the matter.

'What about Frigg this year then, eh?' Gunnar asked.

We had been skiving football training all autumn, it would be quite hard to play our way back into the team.

'Don't know,' I said. 'Think we should give it a miss.'

The others nodded.

'There'll be no time for football when we go to the *gymnas*,' Gunnar said.

'No,' we said.

'But we could pop over and say hello to Kåre,' Seb said. 'To tell him we're droppin' out.'

'Of course,' we said.

When they had left, the fever returned and wrung me like a sponge. Mum managed to steer me into the sitting room where I sat, half-dead, waiting for her to change the bedding and air the room. Afterwards it was like lying in the wind, a wind with sun and freshly mown grass and juicy apples. I slept, woken once by some sounds, the rumble of the train, the tram squealing, bombs falling. Then, all of a sudden, it was still again and the next time I woke I was as fit as a fiddle and five kilos lighter.

That was my last childhood illness.

A Day in the Life

Summer '67

We went to see Kåre in Theresesgate. He started looking for subscription cards, but Gunnar stopped him.

'Won't be any football for us this year,' he said. 'There'll be no time for trainin' when we start at the *gymnas*.'

Kåre leaned over the counter and studied us.

'Big lads now,' he said.

We shifted uncomfortably.

'Just wanted to tell you,' Gunnar went on. 'It's been great playin' football for Frigg.'

Kåre gave a sad smile.

'Far too many give up like you,' he said. 'How are we going to keep Frigg in the first division if players keep going?'

We shuffled our feet.

'Don't think we'd've got in the f-f-first team,' Ola laughed with embarrassment.

Two juniors came in to pay their subs, in shorts with plasters on their knees and a key round their necks, only just able to reach the counter with their chins.

After they had left, Kåre said, 'Might be a Petersen or a Solvang in those skinny legs. Who knows?'

No, you could never know, but for us the season was over.

We shook his hand.

Kåre smiled his crooked smile and breathed heavily through his flat nose.

'Good luck, lads,' he said. 'All the best!'

We bought ten Craven A and trogged down to Bislett. Thinking about the team jersey, freshly washed, stiff, blue and white. Åge reading out the names of those in the team. The dressing rooms, the own goal in Slemmestad, the sending-off in Copenhagen. All the pitches: Voldsløkka, Ekeberg, Dælenenga, Marienlyst, Grefsen. Grass, gravel and particularly football in the rain, heavy, sluggish games like in slow motion while the rain bucketed down, that was what I thought about most on the boiling hot day we trogged down Theresesgate leaving Kåre for the last time: football in the pouring rain.

It was all systems go at school. Kerr's Pink was reading from Petter Dass, Hammer was bursting with German verbs and Skinke was a barrel of gunpowder in the sun. The only cool place was in woodwork. I sat filing a teak ring I had thought about giving someone, but one day I dropped it on the floor and it broke. No point trying to stick it together. Couldn't even give it away now. Wondered for a while whether to make a birdhouse, but it was too late anyway, wouldn't finish it before summer. That was, in fact, the day the woodwork teacher brought in a snake skin from Africa, as big as a carpet. His brother had shot the snake while it was lying in the shade of an orange tree disgesting a sheep. We could see the bullet hole, too. The woodwork teacher's brother was a missionary in Africa. Goose stayed behind after the lesson. He had made a cross in woodwork, now he wanted to hear more about the missionary in Africa. Just before the bell rang for the next lesson he came over to us at the drinking fountain and told us that snakes sleep for a whole month after eating a sheep. And the snake was the Devil's Beast. That was why the woodwork teacher's brother had shot it. We could remember what had happened to Holst, the teacher, couldn't we?

'Yeah,' Gunnar said, looking away.

Goose was beginning at the Christian *gymnas* in the autumn. His eyes sparkled. Gunnar flicked through the English course book. I drank water.

'God be with you,' Goose said, he said that and left us.

And he *was* with us, for a while anyway. Norwegian lessons were going well. I wrote about space travel and thought I made a good fist of it. I wrote about humans that are so tiny and space that is so immense and I got something in about a door that has to be opened to enter the blue space. I was in the groove. If there was not enough room for us on earth, we could settle on other planets. When I had finished the rough copy and eaten my packed lunch, sweaty salami and wet goat's cheese, I thought about Goose, he sat behind me and was scribbling away like a madman, I thought that out in space there was perhaps an old God, with a white gown and a middle parting, a bit like John Lennon, and he kept an eye on everything we wrote and knew exactly what we would write and what grade we would get. In that case there was not much point writing at all. Didn't put that though.

Survived English as well. And German. Then came the wall. Maths. The evening before, I sat mugging up on equations and geometry sweating like mad while the summer simmered away and the gulls came in from the fjord with raucous screams and burning beaks and shat on my window. I read about x and y, twirled the compasses, drew triangles and angles and straight lines, while outside the gulls screamed. I thought about the snake skin, that the future was like a snake, a boa constrictor which dropped from the trees, and that we had already been swallowed, zero chance of escaping, we were already in the warm belly of the future and were being digested. Impossible to concentrate with the gull screams right outside the window. Then the doorbell rang. It couldn't be Gunnar, Seb or Ola because they were at home swotting and at least as busy as me. I heard my mother open the door and then nothing because the gulls were screaming. Must have been a perspiring door-to-door salesman. But then there was a knock at my door and when it opened I forgot everything I had read, everything that had existed, everything that still existed.

Nina.

She stood in the doorway looking in at me.

Mum was in the background, she slunk away.

Hardly recognised her with hair down over her shoulders, a flower behind her ear, a long colourful skirt, narrow around the waist, almost like my arm, I gulped, gulped and clung to my mask.

Wished some girl had been with me in the same way that a boy had been with her that time in Denmark. All I had were my maths book and the compasses. Was everything supposed to be forgotten now, as though I had been sitting and waiting for her for a whole year? I was angry, why hadn't there been someone here too, what did she think she was doing, just coming, without batting an eyelid, standing at my door and looking at me with those same eyes, the same smile, which nevertheless seemed so unfamiliar, for she had changed, and yet she was the same, she was Nina.

I was angry. I was confused.

'Hello,' I said.

She came in.

She went straight to the point.

'Did you get my letter?' she asked.

'Yes.'

She closed the door.

'Are you studying for an exam?'

'Maths.'

'Are you mad at me?' she asked.

'Mad? Why should I be?'

'I could sit quietly,' she said. 'So that you can study.'

She had brought a parcel with her. Flat. Square. I didn't want to ask, but couldn't stop myself.

'What's that?' I pointed to her hands.

'For you,' she smiled, putting the package on my maths book.

I felt her hair on my face. There would be thunder tonight.

'For me?'

'Yes.'

I unwrapped the paper, my hands were sticky with sweat.

Sergeant. Sergeant Pepper. Sergeant Pepper's Lonely Hearts Club Band.

'The new Beatles LP,' she whispered behind me.

Caught. Bound hand and foot. The new Beatles LP. Why weren't the others here, Gunnar, Seb and Ola? Everything had gone topsy-turvy. And yet everything was as it should be.

I just stared. The faces stared back at me, a whole collection of heads, and at the front, in uniform between exotic plants they stood there expecting something from me, expecting me to do something, right now. The four faces when I opened the cover, close up, insistent, were forcing me to do something. On the back, with the lyrics in red, John, George and Ringo stared at me while Paul had his back to me. I was sitting with my back to Nina, could sense her behind me, I turned.

'Thank you,' I mumbled, eased the record out of the sleeve and put it on the turntable. 'Thanks,' I mumbled again, blew the dust off the needle, prayed to Goose's God that the batteries would hold out.

Think something changed at that point, in my room, the night before the maths exam with summer like a green, throbbing pulse outside the window. Nina beside me, and the music which, at first was unfamiliar, in the same way that Nina was unfamiliar when she first stood in the doorway. Then I got to know them, Nina and the music. And then I had to change, too, to let the music flow inside me like water, to open myself completely like a door that had been jammed shut for a long time, that is the only way I can express it. Like raising yourself or carrying each other. Our hands crept across the floor, groping their way forwards. 'A Day In The Life'. A day like this, of which there is only one, and I could swear her mouth still tasted of apple.

I took her home. She would be in Norway until autumn. Everything was different, the streets, the trees, the windows, the people we met, they smiled, just smiled. And Nina walked barefoot on the tarmac, which was cool in the night air. We sat by the fountain, felt the spray on our necks.

'Jesper's nothing,' Nina said.

Didn't answer.

'Don't think any more about it,' she said.

As if I had been thinking about it.

I gave a harsh laugh.

'You must've met other girls, I suppose,' she said, without looking at me.

'Might've done,' I said, lighting a cigarette.

Then we said nothing for a good while. The apple trees in the garden on the corner were lit up in white and all the dogs in the whole town gathered in Gyldenløvesgate, panting and wheezing, and, gently growling, they came over to sniff us, must have scented something.

Behind us, the column of water rose in the air.

The class followed me with their eyes as I smacked down the papers on the teacher's desk in front of the cross-eyed invigilator and it was barely quarter past twelve. I raced out of the airless torture chamber, took the stairs in three bounds and ran straight into the arms of Nina, who had been waiting in the school playground.

'Have you finished already?!' she laughed.

'Yup. Straight onto paper. From Gunnar's draft. The invigilator couldn't see further than a metre.'

We went back to my place to get our swimming togs and *Sergeant Pepper*. Nina carried the record player under her arm, and we cycled to Huk, Nina on the luggage carrier, the sun like needles in our faces.

Lay there all day, until the last bathers had gone home, until we were alone. Ate strawberries out of a green punnet and lay with our ears against the speaker and our faces close. Our stomachs and shoulders were burning. She rubbed in some Nivea for me. I did the same for her. She had brought along sunglasses, two pairs, one round, one square, with blue and green glass. We lay on our backs staring at the setting sun with open eyes.

Then we were all alone.

Yachts leaned against the horizon.

A sandal had been left at the water's edge.

'Wait here,' I said to Nina, running onto a rock, breathing in and diving. The water was black to my eyes, a cold current pulled at me. For a moment I panicked, saw floating figures with undulating hair, bodies in slow, weary, almost beautiful movement, like astronauts. I was about to give up, my head was exploding, but I fought my way down and touched the bottom. I rummaged around in the sand, and between stones and seaweed felt something round and rough, got a foothold and launched myself upwards to the green sky.

Nina was sitting by the record player. I held my hands behind my back and dripped water over her.

'Which hand do you want?'

She pondered and chose the right one.

I gave her the rusty Mercedes badge. She laughed and asked what it was.

'A fallen star,' I explained.

She lay in the grass and pulled me down to her. I switched on the record player. India. It was magical. It was unbelievable. I was caught, laughed at Paul's 'When I'm Sixty-Four', listened intensely to the groans on 'Lovely Rita' and was woken by the cocks crowing on 'Good Morning, Good Morning'.

'The batteries are flat,' Nina said.

She was right. The music played in waves, getting deeper and deeper, it sounded terrible.

'No problem,' I said, using my finger, getting the right speed again, thirty-three and a third revolutions per minute.

'What did you do to your finger?' Nina asked.

I lay down beside her, the music jarred again, played in fits and starts.

'Got it stuck in the lathe,' I said.

'The lathe!' she laughed.

'Yep. I was making a ring.'

She bent over me.

'Who for?'

I pulled her down and whispered in her ear.

'But it works fine now. My finger, that is!'

'Prove it,' Nina whispered.

So I started the music again, with my finger, until the rhythm throbbed inside us like the boats chugging across the fjord, harder and harder, higher and higher, my finger was on every revolution, until the final scream, almost inaudible, pushed her head back and 'A Day In The Life' came to an abrupt end and slipped into the silent grooves.

Afterwards we sat back to back listening to the silence, a few birds, a few waves, a wind, the boats that had gone.

'We'll have to go back soon,' I said. 'They're waiting at Seb's.'

'Who are?'

Nina leant her head back over my shoulder and beamed.

'The others of course! Gunnar and Sidsel! Seb and Guri! Ola and Kirsten!'

A warmish shower fell as we cycled home but we didn't take off our sunglasses. Nina sat at the back talking about someone she knew in Copenhagen who had been to San Francisco and was going to India. Didn't catch everything she said. Kept thinking, kept thinking that everything had taken such a long time and yet it had gone so damned fast.

PART 2

Hello Goodbye

Autumn '67

I was in my seventeenth year, scrambling through an autumnal forest, tripping over twigs, branches whipping into my face, the compass needle quivering on the north-south axis, but Skinke's hand-drawn map didn't match the terrain, I was getting lost, now I think, now that the footsteps are closing in around me, the footprints around the house in the January and New Year's wet snow, someone has been here again, they must have looked in, now I have to get out of this chaos, but the compass I received at my confirmation gives absurd readings, invisible birds scream above me, I plough my way through, time is getting short, I am beginning to panic, time is running away from me, I am the last man to return, I push the branches to the side and at last I see Cecilie, she is sitting on a rock beneath Ullevålseter, feeding a goat.

'How many control points did you find?' I asked.

'None,' she says.

'I found the third down by Lake Sognsvann. That was all, then I lost the trail.'

'Orienteering is the most stupid thing I know,' Cecilie said, continuing to feed the goat with slices of bread.

I sat down on the rock an arm's length from her, trying to think of something smart to say.

'Thought I'd got lost,' I said. 'It's an absolute jungle.'

'I came straight here,' she said.

'Went fishing here a couple of years ago. With Seb. And Gunnar and Ola. They're in the B stream. Sciences.'

Cecilie didn't seem particularly interested. Cecilie didn't seem particularly interested in anything. The goat was sucking her fingers and she was looking in any other direction but at me, just like in the classroom. Cecilie sat next to me in the second last row, I saw her profile against the window, I couldn't get over her profile, erect and soft at the same time, and her eyes, brown I think they were, brown, but they never looked in my direction, they looked at the ceiling, out of the window, down at the desk, across the dark green forest where the autumn sky let a cold, transparent light fall to earth.

'Shall we have a beer at Setra then?' I asked quickly, blowing a persistent ant off the back of my hand.

Cecilie just got to her feet and left, I followed her up to the house, where we found a window table. I ordered a beer, Cecilie wanted a blackcurrant toddy.

'Think we've veered a bit off course,' I said.

'Why's that?'

'You seen any of the others from school?'

She shook her head. Her hair came undone, and I liked it when the knot in her hair loosened and strands pointed in all directions, wow, my stomach turned to lead.

I drank my beer.

Wondering what to say next.

I rolled a cigarette. Cecilie didn't smoke.

'How do you like the class?' I asked stupidly.

She chuckled – I didn't quite know why – and looked out of the window. An old man came plodding up with a rucksack and walking stick. The goat was standing with its head in the grass.

'Don't really know,' Cecilie said.

'Sphinx is a bit on the slow side,' I said. 'Could be one of the statues in Frogner Park. Hasn't blinked since we started. Strange his eyes don't dry up.'

'I like French best,' Cecilie said.

'I know a girl in Paris,' I boasted.

'Do you?' she said, warming her hands round the cup.

'Not exactly,' I crumbled. 'It's a woman. Colleague of my uncle's. Paints pictures.'

Cecilie seemed bored out of her mind. I was getting desperate, drank some beer and it went up my nose. I coughed and spluttered until foam came out of my nostrils.

That was when Cecilie looked at me, right then, straight at me, and laughed.

'Went down the wrong way,' I said.

'There's a class party next Saturday,' she said.

I cleared the beer from my sinuses and swallowed.

'Wow! Terrific!'

Cecilie looked grumpy again.

'It was my parents' idea,' she said.

Cecilie lived in Bygdøy and her father apparently sold watches, binoculars and jewellery, wowee, I was excited already, but that didn't seem to be the case with Cecilie.

She pulled a long face.

'They think you *have* to have a class party so that everyone can get to know each other,' she said.

'Will they be at home?' I enquired anxiously, detecting a tiny fly in the ointment.

'No, they're going out.'

'Next Saturday?'

Cecilie nodded and some strands of hair fell across her face. Something happened in my stomach and my fingertips went numb and goose pimples screamed down my back. Cecilie's dark eyes brushed past me like a radio scanner, she picked up the signals and switched over to another frequency at once.

'Dreading the maths test,' was all she said, looking bored again, and so time passed.

I heard a loud noise behind me and there stood Seb, trousers soaked to the knees, hair like a haystack and the hood of his anorak filled with spruce needles and twigs.

'So this is where you are,' he panted. 'Half the school is out searching for you.'

We looked at our watches. Getting on for five. We should've been at the finish by three at the latest.

Seb sat down.

'Sphinx's eyelid is twitchin'. Doesn't bode well.'

'We got lost,' I said. 'Couldn't help gettin' lost.'

'I'll say I found you in a bog,' Seb said, and off we trudged.

'Skinke's flyin' round with a walkie-talkie up by Skjennungen,' Seb went on. 'Sphinx is waitin' at HQ.'

'Who won?' Cecilie asked.

'I don't know. We got lost by Lake Bånntjern and then Ola fell in.'

'How did he manage that?' I smiled.

'He didn't exactly fall. Dropped the last beer and jumped in after it. Came up with a bone.'

'A bone?'

'They used to dump children in the lake in olden times, you know. Ola got the shakes big time. We carried him to the station and then Hammer took him home. Gunnar is searchin' for you in Gaustad.'

Sphinx was not best pleased when we arrived at the HQ by Svartkulp, but I suppose he must have been happy we were alive. It wasn't easy to know where you were with Sphinx, our class teacher, he had big hands and a big head and he moved once every century. He moved now. Twice. I was given a real rollicking – tried to blame the compass, but to no avail. Cecilie wasn't told off at all and Seb was awarded a medal for finding us.

Afterwards we caught the tram to Majorstuen, but Sphinx had to get out and look for Skinke because Skinke was the only person with a walkie-talkie and it wouldn't make any difference how much he fiddled and shouted, he might be talking to a radio ham in Japan, in fact I felt a bit sorry for Skinke.

We sat in the smokers' compartment, lit our roll-ups and grinned. I had never been so close to Cecilie before. I felt her thigh against mine. She wasn't listening to what Seb and I were nattering about.

'Didn't think Ola would resurface,' Seb said.

'Didn't he take off his boots?'

'Yes. But that was all. Gunnar was on the point of jumpin' in, too. But then he shot up like a rocket-borne sputnik with the bone in his hand. It was the biggest leap I've seen since the pike in Skillingen.'

So stupid that Gunnar and Ola were doing sciences, I thought. Now they wouldn't be going to Cecilie's party.

'Cecilie's havin' a class party next Saturday,' I said.

Seb snapped his fingers three times and leaned across me.

'Great stuff!' he said, patting her on the shoulder. 'When shall we come?'

'Seven,' Cecilie said, sitting stiffly beside me and staring into the distance, and I cursed Cecilie for being such a hard nut to crack, but

I would manage it, I would, perhaps I shouldn't have had the beer in Ullevålseter.

Uncle Hubert was drawing aristocrats and medical consultants for weekly magazines. Didn't see much of him that autumn. Henny was in Paris. Jensenius was singing less and less, must have already felt the winter in his bones. When I bought beer for him, he just stuck a limp hand through the door crack and retreated. Sometimes he went out for a walk too, the stairs made almighty creaking noises, he must have walked a long way because he always came home by taxi, once he had tried to break into the Concert Hall. There was something up with Jensenius. Everyone said Granddad could die at any moment, but he didn't, he never died, just went on living, sitting in the chair by the window and laughing at something no one understood, stamping with his foot. Grandma's budgerigar disappeared one day, flew out of the window, and she hung notices on all the trees in West Oslo. She put an advertisement in *Aftenposten* too, but the bird had flown. And Mum and Dad went a bit hysterical about the old jacket I had taken from Nesodden, Granddad's drab, grey-white linen jacket, double-breasted and threadbare. Every morning there was grumbling and nagging. Why didn't I wear the tweed jacket Mum had bought me for my birthday? She had obviously forgotten the dressing-up party we had had, that summer a long time ago. But otherwise they tiptoed around and thought it was brilliant to have a son at the *gymnas*. But once you were there, it wasn't that difficult after all. You just changed building, a couple of the teachers and you were in a new class. Just like with the fork jab, we felt a bit cheated again. It was always like that. The waiting time was best, or worst, it all depended. Once it had happened, when you were there, it was already over and there was something harder or better or grimmer or worse beckoning in the distance. And so it was just a question of getting on with the waiting, the anticipating and the dreading again.

It was a hassle.

But now I didn't know what was awaiting me.

Yes, I did.

Cecilie's party.

And I have closed the shutter on the last window.

It started off nicely enough with tweeds and mini-skirts and a thimble of sherry for everyone. We stood in the largest living room I had ever seen, a hangar with clocks everywhere, seven, all set at the same time, with Cecilie's father holding a deadly embarrassing speech, wishing us luck and so on, quite what for, we didn't know. Her mother stood three steps behind him in a full-length dress and pearl necklace and Cecilie waited with head bowed. Seb and I were dying to go to the toilet because we had knocked back a few beers beforehand to get a flying start, and we needed it because there were sixteen boys and six girls and it was going to be dog eat dog. I had a sneaking suspicion that Slippery Leif was hovering over Cecilie, but with his double chins and myopia I didn't see him as the greatest threat. Peder was altogether another matter, the 400-metre runner, sailor and winner of the orienteering, still suntanned after the summer. He was not to be trusted. He had already found himself a seat perilously close to Cecilie while I stood with legs crossed, desperate for the clockmaker to tick to an end.

At long last he stopped, retreated with the diva and the herd began to stir. Seb and I made a dash for the toilet, there were three to choose from on the first floor, marble and gold taps and Greek statues in niches and inset clocks. Hell, we hardly dared piss. Seb swung out the last beer from his jacket sleeve, he was a specialist, I never quite worked out how he did it. We drank at a rate of knots.

'We've come to the wrong place,' Seb said. 'This is Drammensveien 1.'

We raced down, afraid to miss the opening manouevres. There were a few scattered bottles on the tables, cigarette smoke was floating through the hall like blue cirrus clouds and some people were balancing plates on which there was a steaming mass of meat. We were sizing each other up, making fun of the teachers and keeping a headcount on the girls. They were all there and we sniffed out a group standing in the hall with a hipflask: Leif, Crutch and Ulf. We scrounged a drink and Leif looked at me through metre-thick glasses, blinked, as if wondering where Cecilie was, not to mention Peder, as though I knew. I dashed back into the hangar and surveyed the scene: five girls on the sofa with eleven bulls at their backs. I ambled into the kitchen and of course they were there. Peder was helping Cecilie with the pans.

A boiling hot plate was shoved into my hands.

'You were unplaced in the orienteering,' Peder said, grinning to both sides.

'Right,' I said. 'Slipped on Ullevålseter.'

'Got to have your navigation in order, you know. And your speed.'

Couldn't be bothered to listen to the sailor, cleared off again and now there was a bit more life in the place. The sound system was on full peg, some old-time jazz thing, three couples slipped across the parquet and a few others were negotiating. Seb lay on the floor rummaging through the record stand, shaking his head in desperation. I couldn't get Peder and Cecilie out of my system and in my annoyance I made a grab in the air and caught Vera on the hoof. She was so shocked she clung to me and her breath was hot and her eyes were framed by black eyeliner. A damned tango wailed from the speakers, I held her tighter, bent her backwards and stuff, and people were cheering. Then Peder and Cecilie came in with more food, Cecilie stopped and met my eyes, not for more than a second, but it was the first time, the first time we had *looked* at each other. I let go of Vera, sat down on a chair and lit up. Vera was left on the floor, alone, like a little child, abandoned in a large crowd.

Peder brought me some food.

'Close your eyes and point west,' he said.

'Not hungry,' I said, blowing smoke past his parting.

He sat on the edge of the table.

'Nice jacket you're wearing today,' he said, feeling the tweed between his fingers. 'Brand new?'

Ears pricked up in the room.

'Inherited it from Jesus's uncle,' I said.

Peder continued to rub the lapel. His blue jacket was blinding me.

'That's what I thought,' he said. 'Because you buy your clothes from the Sally Army, don't you.'

I hadn't thought about Fred for a long time. Now he stood in front of me as clear as day, in his wide trousers, and the rat, I saw the rat in the torch light.

It all happened very fast. I punched him on the nose. He fell back with blood spurting like a fountain over his mouth and chin.

The girls screamed, Cecilie came running in, Slippery Leif and Crutch held me from behind and Cecilie took Peder up to the bathroom. I was too common for him to be bothered to retaliate.

There was a bit of a hubbub, the nation split down the middle into those for me and those against. The girls took Peder's side. Slippery Leif tried to arbitrate, smooth things over, Crutch was grinning so much he was foaming, Vera was sending me glares of contempt.

Seb took me aside.

'What happened?' he asked.

'The bastard was makin' fun of Fred,' I said.

'Of Fred?'

'Takin' the piss out of the Salvation Army,' I said.

Seb nodded several times.

'Got what he deserved,' he said.

Peder and Cecilie were in the bathroom a hell of a long time. Was she having to sew his nose back on or what? My stomach was churning. I smoked until my palate felt like a fakir's mat. The couples were beginning to take shape: Vera was deep in a chair with Morten, Astrid was in a clinch on the floor with Torgeir, Trude was glued to the wall with Atle hanging over her like a banana. There was feverish activity among the last mini-skirts and *The Sound of Music* crackled through the air like a doped-up swarm of bees. Peder came across the floor with cotton wool in one nostril. Cecilie stood in the doorway watching. The room fell quiet. He stopped five centimetres from me. The top of my head was level with the knot of his tie.

Peder stuck out his hand.

'My apologies,' he said.

I couldn't believe my ears.

He repeated it.

'My apologies. We're quits.'

Shook his hand, our hands bobbed up and down.

'My apologies,' I said tamely.

The atmosphere seemed to explode. Peder turned on his heel and went back to Cecilie and I was left standing looking perplexed, just like Vera a moment before, and I realised I had lost, Peder had won,

I had been hammered down into my shoes, I was beneath my own soles.

A few hours passed of which I have no memory. I sat smoking and watching for Cecilie. The couples were clear now, one or two adjustments had taken place at the last moment. Vera could not deride me enough with her eyes. Cecilie was not there. Nor Peder. Seb came over.

'Dull fare,' he said. 'We're goin' to see if we can get in Club 7.'

I shook my head.

'It's only across the bay. Could swim there.'

'Nothing doin',' I said. 'I'm stayin'.'

'Seen the record shelf, have you? Frank Sinatra, Mozart and Floyd Cramer.'

'I'm stayin',' I said.

'I got you the first time,' Seb said, waddling over to the other corner on his long, thin legs.

I went for a tour of the palace. There were corridors and rooms everywhere, stairs going up, stairs going down, needed a compass at least, I smiled, tried anyway, face was set in concrete. This was a house in which you could be lonely. I began to understand Cecilie a little. I began to hate Peder. I walked down a long corridor with doors on both sides and lines of family portraits. Beneath me I could hear music, voices, laughter. Then I heard another sound, coming from behind one of the doors, a door that was ajar. I tiptoed over, my heart bulging beneath my shirt, took a cautious peep, opened the door wide and my heart sank like a lift. Cecilie was in bed, and for a moment I thought she was with someone, Peder. My blood drained away. Then I discovered she was alone. She turned slowly towards me, her face swollen and red, not looking like the Cecilie I knew.

'Anything the matter?' I stammered.

She sat up, dried her eyes, that took a second, then she was the old Cecilie, her armour was back in place.

'No. What could be the matter? Just a bit tired.'

There was nothing I could do. I followed her down. Peder was standing with Slippery Leif and Crutch, discussing something or other. Seb was sitting in a chair, bored out of his skull. Cecilie went over to Vera and Atle, turned her back and left. I was barely worthy of her back.

I bummed a smoke off Seb.

'Low gear,' he said. 'Almost in reverse.'

'Think we'd get in Club 7?'

'Maybe. Gunnar and Ola were goin' to try. But they left with Stig.'

Slippery Leif waved to us and we shuffled over to their corner. Didn't have a lot to lose. Peder was smoking. Rare sight. 400 metres. He scowled at me with the plaster on his nose.

'Drinks cabinet,' Leif whispered, rolling his eyes. 'We have to find the drinks cabinet, boys!'

That wasn't such a bad idea. We agreed to meet in a quarter of an hour in the same corner and each went our separate ways. The expedition returned empty-handed.

Seb had left. Probably going to try and find Guri.

'He must have the booze in the safe,' Peder said.

'I'm no safecracker,' Crutch said.

'Fridge,' said Leif.

We trooped into the kitchen. Empty, too. Just milk. Loads of milk. We sat round the table. The prospects were gloomy. Gradually more people came, all the remnants. In the end it was quite a gang sitting there racking their brains.

Then Slippery Leif had it. He snapped his chubby fingers and smiled.

'You see the speck in your brother's eye, but not the beam in your own!' he said.

We leaned across the table.

'Eh??'

'Haven't you been confirmed yet? My dad's a doctor. It'll take half an hour.'

He left and we waited for three quarters of an hour. Then Slippery Leif breezed in with a bulging jacket and placed two lab jars containing a transparent liquid on the table.

'96,' he said. 'Medical alcohol. Quality merchandise.'

We distributed glasses and the atmosphere was electric.

'What shall we mix it with?' wondered one of the drinkers.

'I'll take it neat,' Crutch said, sticking his tongue in the jar.

Crutch didn't say much more that night. He lay in a corner making hissing sounds.

'Milk,' Leif said.

The milk bottles appeared on the table and we mixed some real bombshells.

'Can't see it!' Pål grinned, raising his glass.

We drank. Looked at each other. Drank again.

'Doesn't taste of anything,' Ulf said.

We tasted, smelt, drank again.

'Won't get drunk on this,' Tormod said.

We mixed a new round. Drank and smacked our lips.

'Tastes of milk,' Peder thought.

We were agreed. It tasted mostly of milk.

'Sure it's 96?' Leif queried.

Slippery Leif pointed to Crutch lying under the tap. Yep, had to be 96. No doubt about it.

The door opened and Cecilie peered in.

'Are you drinking milk?' she said.

'We are indeed,' Leif said. 'Milk's *in*.'

Cecilie laughed and went.

'I definitely won't get drunk on this,' Peder said.

Leif poured another round.

We drank and smacked our lips, smoked and drank.

Then Ulf got up, a generally solid type, a flatfooted person of regular habits, he swivelled round three times and banged his head on the wall. That was where he stayed.

We looked at each other. Then we slowly got to our feet and the party actually started, or finished, there. We stumbled around, crawled on all fours, crashed, fell on our faces. Pål swore he was walking on the ceiling. Tormod tried to walk into the fridge. We searched desperately for the door, Kåre disappeared into the pantry, Otto opened a cupboard, rubbish poured into the room. In the end someone found the handle and we charged into the halls like a flock of paralytic calves with St Vitus's dance. There was a bit of a commotion in the living room. I remember seeing Cecilie's face as a white, luminous oval of fear, then I remember nothing until I was standing on the roof. I stood on the roof of Cecilie's house and the night was starlit and the wind was blue. Down in the garden people were running around shouting and screaming. It was a long way down, long, steep and dark. I balanced on the slanting roof tiles. Someone was crying down there in the dark green garden. I danced across the roof of Cecilie's house. Then I heard someone right behind me. I turned sharply, almost fell, one foot slipped and I fell forward. A howl like a wild bird's cut through the night. I got to my feet again and stood still. The voice was nearby.

'Kim, for Christ's sake!'

A light was switched on and I saw Peder's face emerge from the roof hatch.

'You'll kill yourself!' he shouted.

Shit, not again, he won't walk away with the victory this time. I clambered up onto the ridge, straddled it and looked out on Frogner Bay, Nesodden, the lights over the fjord, all the flickering dots of the night as if the starry sky was being reflected onto the earth. Then I stood erect on the pointed edge, and I had never felt so steady on my legs. Peder had left the skylight and there was total silence in the garden. The darkness swallowed all the sounds, only my heart was beating like furious palms against the kettledrums of the night.

Then I wriggled my way down to the skylight and into the attic.

Only remember the party was disintegrating, girls were crying, boys were vomiting, Cecilie was stuck to a blue wall with her hands down by her side.

'Shall I help you to clear up,' I slurred.

'Go,' she said and her glare deep-froze me.

I went.

Had no idea where I was going, just knew that I was in my seventeenth year and I was scrambling through Kongeskogen, having been turned away from the palace, tall swaying trees loomed menacingly on all sides, and I arrived at the sea, lay down under a bush and slept like a rotating rock on Paradisbukta beach.

I was awoken by the frost, I was freezing like a mangy, furless dog and my teeth were chattering. It was a grey dawn, grey light, the choppy waves beat against the shore. My shoes were drenched, my jacket full of vomit, my head at half mast, I was the only person in the world and not to be trusted.

Then I did the most stupid thing of all.

The idea lodged itself in my crazy, jumbled brain.

I found the way back to Cecilie's house.

It stood like a colossus in the dawning day. The curtains in Cecilie's room were drawn. I sneaked across the lawn. The door wasn't locked. I slipped in, stood in the huge living room where the party had left its all too visible marks. I crept up the stairs. The corridor with all the doors seemed endless. I tripped, crawled on all fours on the soft carpet to Cecilie's door. Listened. Heard her sleeping. I did. Heard her breathing and her dreams and her turning between the sheets. I was about to haul myself up to the door handle when I felt a fist haul me up even higher. A cold voice assailed me.

'What the hell do you think…?'

Cecilie's father twisted me round and at that moment two doors burst open. Cecilie's mother was standing in her dressing gown with her mouth open. Cecilie looked at me, I imagined she wasn't happy. Then I was dragged outside like the dog I was, into the garden and tossed over the gate. I didn't hear everything he said.

Then it was a case of staggering home to another father. He was sitting on a stool in the hallway with an exhausted expression and white knuckles.

'Where have you been?' he yelled.

I had nothing to say.

I stumbled past him.

'*Where* have you been?' he repeated, brandishing his arms.

'At a party,' I whispered.

He lashed out. He slapped me and was just as terrified as I was, pulling his arm back as though he had burned himself.

Now Mum was there, too.

Three was a crowd.

'Now you *are* getting a haircut, Kim!' was all she said.

We stood there puzzled, looking at each other. Dad hid his hand behind his back and put on an odd smile.

'I'm tired,' I said, walked into my room and locked the door.

First came fear, belatedly, too late. My kneecaps melted and I threw up in the waste paper basket. At that moment sunlight flooded through the window. It was going to be a beautiful Sunday, the last this year with what was left of the summer, an Indian summer.

I lay in bed and was suddenly afraid of the fear, the fear that came too late.

Was that everything? Yes. I'm an elephant and never forget anything.

And as I lay there, ill and awake, Mum and Dad drove to Nesodden to collect the apples, the apples.

After the party quite a few people were impressed. They called me Karlsen-on-the-roof. But they had not seen the finale. Cecilie had. And now she not only stopped looking at me, she also stopped talking to me, and the worst thing was that she changed her desk, too, moved further away so that I could only see her neck, which was as taut as two steel hawsers. There was no point even getting close to her, she disappeared, slipped away, and I felt like a rotten apple while the others thought I was terrific and wondered if I had a propeller on my back and the party was talked about for the rest of the year, to the exclusion of everything else.

I was left wondering how I could approach Cecilie again, but it seemed to be impossible. The bell rang every time I took a step in her direction. I was a leper and insane. The only consolation was that Peder had also been excluded from her royal court. At least that was how it appeared. But Slippery Leif was on good terms with her and allowed to enter her domain, even though he was the one who had brought the damned firewater. There was no justice in the world.

We sat at my place in the evenings because Gunnar, Ola and Seb were being subjected to rows and scenes in their houses. In Bygdøy Allé, just down from Gimle, they were erecting a large building which was going to be a supermarket with self-service and so on. Gunnar's father turned grey and developed a stoop overnight thinking about his tiny greengrocer's and how it would fare. Stig's hair, the longest in Frogner, had not been cut since New Year and the Cathedral School headmaster was threatening to expel him if he didn't change his hairstyle, but Stig let it grow, it was quite a to-do. Ola's father's customers were all balding pensioners now, unless boys began to have their hair cut again he was bound to go bankrupt. He went home to his sitting room to get in some practice with his scissors, the only thing that could save him now was a good performance at the Norwegian hairdressing championships in Hønefoss. And Seb's father, home on three months' leave, was arguing with Seb's mother and had apparently thrown a teapot against the wall one night, so no peace was to be had there, either. We sat in my house. Mum and Dad had calmed down after my early morning return, we sat in my room smoking, drinking tea and pulling at our beards.

Didn't talk about The Snafus much now, not after *Sergeant Pepper*, didn't make any sense. After 'Lucy In The Sky' and 'A Day In The Life'. We laughed at 'Love Me Do' and had taken the pictures down from the wall long ago. Sat up till the early hours discussing the lyrics, they were the best texts that had been written since the Bible and the sagas.

We went into great detail.

'"Lucy In The Sky With Diamonds"', Seb said, 'means LSD.'

And the BBC refused to play 'A Day In The Life'.

This is where it all began.

And so the evenings passed. With tea and smoking and music. Ola talked about Kirsten. In the summer Ola would go to Trondheim, dead cert. The groove between Seb and Guri had developed a scratch – she had met a slalom creep from Ris and Seb was dreading the day the snow arrived. Gunnar and Sidsel saw a lot of each other. I imagined that once you had experienced the security of Gunnar's back, it was hard to leave. And I received a letter from Nina. She wrote that it had been a wonderful summer, the best she had ever experienced. She wrote that she had smoked cannabis and had had such a strange dream about me. But I had almost forgotten the summer and didn't answer.

Then one evening Gunnar turned up with an LP he had borrowed from Stig and Stig had said the LP was a bomb, we would need a safety belt and a parachute to survive the grooves. Intrigued, we peered at the cover. The Doors. Never heard of them. We put on the record and turned it up full volume. Then something happened. Afterwards we lay in separate corners screaming and covered in blood. It was bad. We picked up the pieces and gathered round the speakers again. We were fish on the quayside with flapping gills. You didn't find this organ in a church. It was quite different from Goose's stuffy chords. And the voice was from another planet.

Jim Morrison.

'Great,' Seb said. That was all he managed to say. He was lying on the floor bathed in sweat.

The End.

Then I felt the backwash. My lungs were inflated like huge balloons. I waited for the scream. I thought about the corridors in Cecilie's house, the row of doors, the portraits.

Father, I want to kill you.

Afterwards, when Seb, Gunnar and Ola had left and Mum and Dad had gone to bed, I opened the window and sang into the autumn night. I sang as loud as I could, like the time on the beach, but no one heard me, not Jensenius, not Mum, not Dad, not even Cecilie, although the wind was blowing towards Bygdøy and the night was as still as a cremated oyster.

The day the Barber of Solli was snipping away at the Norwegian championships in Hønefoss, we were sitting in Ola's house. Winter and exams were on the way and the new Beatles' single was out. It didn't set us alight, we tried to get each other worked up, but *Sergeant Pepper* cast a shadow over the grooves. Didn't measure up. 'Hello Goodbye'. Life after *Sergeant Pepper* was not easy. The B-side was the craziest thing since 'Tomorrow Never Knows'. Gunnar gave up. He covered his ears. 'I Am The Walrus'.

'Sounds awful,' he mumbled.

Ola agreed.

'Listen to the *words*!' Seb urged and was already translating the text into Norwegian. '*Listen*! That's how we dream, isn't it!' he said with emphasis.

'Gotta go,' Gunnar said. 'I'm stuck on an equation.'

Ola flicked through his maths book.

We played the A-side again. I thought about Nina, went dizzy for a moment, then thought about Cecilie, couldn't sink the fishing line, couldn't get it out either, it was all entangled. She still hadn't spoken to me. Then I thought about Nina again, and was afraid because now I had forgotten her, forgotten what she looked like however much I tried, I couldn't visualise her face. It was strange. It was eerie. Then I thought about the dance. The school dance after Christmas where The Public Enemies were going to play.

I was going to break the sound barrier there.

Goodbye.

Hello.

Revolution

'68

My heart was in my mouth, but that was all I had there, I was as sober as a mummy, at least Cecilie would not be able to hold it against me that I had got plastered twice in a row. I stood alone in the gym, the others were in the smoking den in 1D. The student council had dug up a military cop as the doorman. It was war. Couldn't see Cecilie.

Then the band arrived, The Public Enemies, straight from their caves, they occupied the stage in the corner, wow, they were a different breed from The Snowflakes, they stood up there in the worst clothes I had ever seen, my old jacket from Nesodden was a flash blazer by comparison. They peered around as if they didn't quite know where they were, the organist knocked a bottle over the keys, the bass player belched into a microphone. Then they stepped up, all of a sudden, all at once, and we were blasted sideways and nailed to the spot, it was wild, what a noise! Seb was already lost to the world, he made his way to the stage and stared at the harmonica player and didn't move, Guri turned away, piqued, and sat in a corner, Gunnar and Sidsel were dancing, Ola took it easy, after all he had a girl in Trondheim, so no stress there.

And in the chaos, the chaos of dancing, happy, thronging people, in the labyrinths of the wild music, I cleared a way, as if it were a forest, a Norwegian Wood. I had to find Cecilie, but wherever I looked, Cecilie was not there. I bought a Coke and stood drinking, lifeless, powerless. It could not be true that she hadn't come. I had waited a whole winter, it was a new year, 1968, the Americans had deployed 15,000 more soldiers in Vietnam, Che Guevara was long since dead, The Doors had brought out a new LP, *The Forsyte Saga* would soon finish, the first person in the world had been given a new heart and had already died, North Vietnam had launched the Tet Offensive, and she hadn't come.

Slippery Leif tapped me on the head.

'Karlsen-on-the-roof,' he said. 'Are you looking for someone?'

'My mother's pickin' me up at ten,' I said.

'Very wise,' said Slippery Leif. 'Because the animals on the stage are not on a lead.' I left. He followed.

'The committee is meeting in the bog in ten minutes,' Slippery Leif said. 'We've voted unanimously that the Coke's too weak.'

He winked three times with his right eye and was gone.

The music wound its way through my auditory canals like rusty barbed wire. 'Little Red Rooster'. Seb was by the stage staring himself blind. Cecilie was nowhere. I wanted to go to the toilet, but not right now. Guri appeared by my side wanting to dance. We danced. It was nice holding her.

'Seb's fun to go out with,' she said.

'Seb's got things to learn tonight,' I said.

'You, too,' she said.

'Me? How come?'

'Why don't you write to Nina?'

My eyes were roving, an over-nervous falcon with its wings in slings. We danced for a while without saying anything, that was for the best, yelling to each other all the time was painful.

'Why haven't you answered her letters?' Guri repeated.

'I will do,' I said lamely, and at that moment Cecilie appeared. She was not on her own. She was with Kåre, the editor of the school newspaper, the class above me. I let go of Guri and dragged myself over to the bar to order a Coke with a straw. Might just as well have given the dance a miss. I was finished, it was over and out for Kim Karlsen, Kim's game where the cards didn't match, I was washed up, down the drain. Should write to Nina after all, should bloody do that tonight, a long, hungry letter to Nina.

The Public Enemies took a break and slunk off the stage, the room was deafeningly quiet. I escaped before the bar was invaded by the wolves, roosters and hens.

Seb wanted to go home and get his harmonica, but Guri restrained him.

'Got to use your tongue, lips and hands!' he panted. 'Did you hear "Little Red Rooster"! What a blast, eh!'

I was a bit unconcentrated, watching Cecile who was sitting among the editorial staff and being ministered to with laughter and compliments. The editor was standing on a chair, holding a speech, and I had never seen her laugh like that before. Weeping ulcers. My heart fell out of my right sleeve, my body rejected my new heart, I was left holding the bleeding, beating mass in my hand, I was worth nothing.

'Are you with us?'

Seb snapped his fingers in front of my nose.

'Yes and no,' I said. 'My soul has left my body.'

'Good,' he said. 'Death to materialism.'

Sidsel dashed over, agitated and frightened.

'Gunnar's got into a slanging match,' she gasped.

She pointed to the door. Gunnar was hemmed in by a crowd thronging round him, there was tension in the air.

We cleared a path through them.

'Bloody commie!' was the first thing we heard. Some beanpole said that, he spat in disdain over his shoulder as he spoke. 'Bloody commie!'

Gunnar was onto him.

'What the hell have the Vietnamese done to you, eh? Have they done anythin' to you? Have they spread terror in America? Eh? Has a single Vietnamese or Chinese harmed anyone in America?'

The beanpole leaned over Gunnar and flicked his tie in his face.

'This is a fight between freedom and repression, you prick! Move to Russia if you don't like it here!'

Gunnar roared with laughter.

'Russia! Did you hear that? *Russia*!'

Gunnar continued to laugh at Beanpole.

I don't know why, but I just lost my temper at the whole shiny band of blue jackets, their polished faces, they were identical, a multi-headed monster.

I thought about the man with the axe who had launched himself at the picture. A picture!

I thought about napalm burning under water.

I thought about the photograph of the girl crying and the bombed village.

I thought about Cecilie.

'So you defend bombin' villages out of existence, do you?' I said, and I must have said it pretty loudly because everyone turned towards me at once. 'Eh? Villages of women, children and old people, you defend that, do you?'

'It's war,' said the Beanpole.

I froze.

'War? Between whom?'

'Between the free world and communism.'

'And the free world drops napalm on young children?'

'It's war,' he repeated. 'We're defending ourselves!'

'We! We! Defending! *Ourselves*!'

Think I shouted.

'Après nous the b-b-bacteria,' Ola said behind me, and then The Public Enemies started up again, the floor vibrated and the zoo was open.

Cecilie was dancing with the editor. Cecilie was dancing with the chairman of the student council. I was finished. Wished I could start the propeller and float out of the room. But I wasn't dreaming of flying any more. Not after Cecilie's party.

Gunnar came over to me.

'We got 'em there,' he grinned.

'What?'

'What! Don't mess about! We had 'em against the wall, man!'

'Of course, we did,' I said, and Cecilie danced past without so much as a flicker of the eye or the mouth.

Gunnar went off with Sidsel.

Ola was talking to Guri.

Seb was sitting by the stage, beyond redemption.

I bought a Coke and went to the toilet, met Slippery Leif and Peder on the way.

'Still on the ground?' Peder smiled, spreading his breath over me like mustard gas.

'Lost my propeller,' I said, retaining the imagery.

'We've got a spare here,' Slippery Leif whispered, patting his inside pocket.

'Nothin' doin',' I said and went to the toilet.

Had a smoke in the doorway. The sky was black. There were voices in the dark. It smelt of night.

Stooged down to the cloakroom again. Put down my Coke bottle, went through my duffle coat and found a packet of Teddy.

'Been to the flea market,' Peder smiled, pointing to my jacket. Slippery Leif chuckled and straightened his tie.

Ignored them, took my Coke and all of a sudden Cecilie was there. She looked at me for the first time since the party. I was so taken aback that I stuck the bottle in my mouth and took some hurried swigs. Cecilie seemed frightened, then she was dragged into the zoo by the school newspaper editor. Behind me Peder and Slippery Leif were laughing. The music from the gym was doing my head in. I fell forwards and at that moment I knew, I had been duped again, the flames were licking up my throat and the carousel began to turn.

I staggered into the gym, it went round and round and I had to grab support from all sides. I trod as carefully as I could, like a cat, but a sick cat with glass in its paw. Reached the bar and ordered a lemonade, tiptoed back again, past Skinke and into the open air. I put out the fire and inhaled the night, the carousel braked. For a brief instant my head cleared, it was transparent, angry and logical. Then the moon passed into a new phase and I no longer knew where I was and my hands were doing things I didn't instruct them to do, and my head was a diorama, just as the natural science teacher had talked about, and the shadows were dancing their witches' frenzy along the walls of my skull and I was unable to read the warnings. Ascended the floors, the empty corridors with hooks on the walls like a desolate slaughterhouse. My footsteps echoed on the stone floors. Far away, beneath me, I heard the music throbbing like a frog's heart and I danced my solitary dance. I reached the loft, pulled at a door, locked, pulled at another and it opened, a revolting smell hit me. Went in nonetheless, fumbled around the door frame and found the light switch. I almost fell flat on the floor, then laughed. A skeleton was hanging on the wall, the cranium smiling at me. On the shelves were jars of frogs, snakes, pig foetuses preserved in alcohol, must have been the kind of jar I had drunk from. I walked along the shelves feeling nauseous yet calm. Revolting, disgusting, as disgusting as life can be, prepared, eternal life, which Goose longed for, foetuses in alcohol, postage stamps, pressed flowers, Latin names, insects on a windowsill, relics of a hot, boring summer.

Heard the music reverberating through the floors, through this floor, through the floor of my stomach.

Dancing.

No one was going to be a wallflower here! I unhooked the skeleton and carried it under my arm. The bones rattled, its head hung. I carried the skeleton downstairs to the cloakroom, someone screamed, girls clung to the boys, the boys laughed, Slippery Leif and Peder clapped. I got past the military guards. There was an uproar. I danced. With the skeleton in my arms. I wanna be your man. Then it was over. Over for me. They came at me from all sides. Skinke. Kerr's Pink. Sphinx. The doormen, the MPs. I didn't see Cecilie. Everything went so fast.

Remember they talked a lot, then I was given my duffle coat and discharged into the night. It was dark and silent. Snow. Fresh snow. It was eerie. You could tiptoe over it, you wouldn't be heard, but you left footprints. Footprints.

The music behind me faded.

I threw up under a street lamp.

I staggered along. Then I heard someone. I have ears like a bat.

'Kim,' a voice said.

I stopped.

Someone came closer.

'Yes,' I said.

'I saw what happened,' the voice said.

It was Cecilie.

She was wearing mittens.

'It was a lousy trick,' she said.

'I know,' I said. 'I wasn't nice to the skeleton.'

Cecilie came closer.

She had wound her blue scarf three times round her neck.

'I didn't mean that,' she said calmly. 'They poured alcohol into your Coke bottle. I saw them.'

I said nothing.

She had followed me. She had left the dance.

'I tried to stop them, but Kåre wouldn't let me.'

'The editor,' I said.

'He's stuck up,' Cecilie said. 'They're all stuck up.'

'I was chucked out,' I said, as though that was anything to worry about now. I almost toppled over, banged into a wall.

'I'll take you home,' said Cecilie.

She took me home.

And in Svoldergate she kissed me, even though my mouth must have stunk of guts and vomit.

I think the moon came out.

Then she walked on alone.

That was how we got together, Cecilie and I.

On Monday I was standing on the carpet in the headmaster's office, legs apart, hands behind my back. It smelt of tobacco in there, a musty pipe. On the wall there were pictures of all the headmasters before Sandpaper, they looked the same. I couldn't quite take my eyes off the moustache under Sandpaper's nose, it was like a hedgehog's spine. He was sitting behind a large table on which lay papers, pencils and files lined up in rows. He observed me for a long time, much too long, then the dry, gravelly voice issued forth from under his moustache:

'This is serious,' he said.

I heard.

He stood up, walked around me, stopped behind me, stayed there. I stared at his empty chair. I wondered what he would have said if I had sat in it.

Sandpaper said, 'Kim Karlsen, you were drunk. You broke into the natural science lab.'

I listened.

His breath against the back of my neck. The empty chair. The fear that would come too late.

'Have you anything to say for yourself?'

'No,' I said.

It went quiet behind me, then he re-appeared in his chair, looked at me with a grey expression and I instantly felt I had not been completely condemned, there was something conciliatory about the way he raised his hand.

'Good,' he said, straightening a piece of paper. 'You definitely will not be allowed to take part in any future excursions.'

He flicked through a few papers, taking his time. I heard the clack-clack-clack of a typewriter outside. People were walking to keep warm in the playground.

Sandpaper peered up.

'I could suspend you from school for two weeks,' he said. 'But I don't want to.'

Contrary to appearances, a heart of gold. Basically decent. The moustache is deceptive.

'You will be banned from watching the Olympics for two weeks,' Sandpaper said.

I smiled. I was almost beginning to like him. I think I did like him a little.

'I'm not interested in sport,' I said.

'But I have written a letter to your parents,' he said.

I started disliking him again.

Sandpaper pointed to the door. I responded.

'I don't want any more trouble or misconduct from you,' he said, seated in his chair. 'Is that understood?'

'Yes, it is,' I said.

'Are you aware of the gravity of this?'

'Yes, I am,' I said.

I pressed the door handle. My hand was shiny with sweat.

'Is that the only jacket you have to wear?' he asked.

Now I didn't like him at all. Or I felt sorry for him. In his grey suit, with the grey tie, the grey moustache. He was an object of ridicule.

'No,' I said. 'But I like this one best. I inherited it from my great-grandfather.'

I thought I should tell him about the rock, but I refrained.

Sandpaper began a new sentence, but didn't complete it.

'We would like to keep our school…'

He broke off with a sudden hand movement.

'You can go,' he rasped.

And I left.

In the break Peder and Slippery Leif slunk over to me with green faces and swollen eyes.

'Did Sandpaper issue a press release?' asked Slippery Leif, resorting to his usual grandiloquent humour.

'He's drafted a missive to my parents,' I parried, quick on my feet.

Peder ran his fingers through his thick hair.

'You didn't say… you didn't say anything about the alcohol, did you?'

I didn't lose my temper, but still couldn't believe they could think that of me.

'Arseholes,' I said and the bell rang.

I wasn't Karlsen-on-the-roof any more. I was Skeleton-at-the-dance. The whole school already knew. The dwarfs from the *realskole* surrounded me. The editor of the school newspaper wanted to interview me, the teachers tested me every bloody lesson, and three days later the letter arrived. I was called into the sitting room, Mum was on the sofa with a tear-stained face and Dad stood with the letter in his hand, his whole body shaking.

And still the fear was not there.

Dad could not control his voice.

'What is this supposed to mean? What have you done? How could you do this to us?'

To them?

'It had nothing to do with you,' I said.

Dad yelled even louder.

'Are you being rude as well?'

His hand was glowing, Mum's crying rose like the sea at high tide, Dad lowered his arm.

I realised I was going to have to lie to make them understand.

'It was a bet,' I said. 'I won.'

'You were drunk!'

'Everyone was drunk,' I said. 'It won't happen again.'

I thought that sounded quite professional.

'No, that's for certain and make no mistake about it!' Dad bellowed.

Mum was sniffling on the sofa, dried her eyes with the back of her hand and looked at me.

'A bet?' she said. 'Did you win?'

'Yes.'
'What?'
'A girl.'

The carrot and the stick. Mum and Dad were the stick. They were somewhat upset after receiving Sandpaper's letter. It was important to keep a low profile for a while. I wore the tweed jacket and grey trousers for a whole month, and the atmosphere improved a bit when I came home with a B+ in English, I was a specialist on the Magna Carta, at least so long as Sphinx didn't sniff out the crib I kept hidden under my bockwurst. And the carrot was Cecilie. At school she was the same, sat three seats in front of me with stiff neck muscles and didn't speak to me in the playground. But she had kissed my foul, stinking mouth without hesitation and we sometimes met after school, walked together, further and further, I had accompanied her all the way to Olav Kyrres plass, but that was the limit for a heathen like me.

Ola was slogging away at maths, shrinking over logarithms and square roots like a shrivelled up missionary in the deepest jungle. He was better at writing letters, the postman in Trondheim had a busy winter that year. Gunnar and Sidsel went out together if they didn't have any homework, they were good like that. Sidsel was studying natural sciences at Fagerborg, but couldn't understand how I had dared to touch the skeleton. It was plastic, I said. Ye-es. Hard times. Evang moved to our school and taught us all about hash. Uproar. Only Seb was a bit at sea. As musically confused as a black man in Telemark. He sat in his room blowing the harmonica, not knowing whether to go for Mayall or The Doors. The Beatles were not the thing, not for a man with a harp, and The Snafus were over and out. In addition, he had tuned himself into The Mothers of Invention and Vanilla Fudge, sat with his legs crossed, and his head, too, confused, trying to meditate, but that didn't work with all the racket going on in the sitting room, his father was on leave and the slamming of doors was like castanets.

'I'm movin' out,' Seb sighed. 'It's like this all the time.'

That didn't sound good.

'Mum looks forward to him comin' home like a child. And when he *is* at home, it's non-stop noise and rowin'. Can't live in this house.'

'Play The Doors,' I said.

Seb played The Doors.

Strange Days.

They certainly were.

He calmed down a little.

'Greatest thing since *Pepper*,' he said. '"When The Music's Over". Just *listen* to the nerve of the guitar, the soul of the organ! And the voice from the guts!'

We listened with eyes lowered. The silence afterwards was overwhelming, even in the sitting room they had taken a break.

Seb straightened up.

'Wrote a poem in the French lesson yesterday,' he said, unfolding a piece of paper. 'Wanna hear? Inspired by "The Walrus".'

'Go on,' I said.

Seb read with the sweat running down him:

> Have you climbed up the City Hall while you think like a
> venomous cobra and laugh yourself to death?
> Sitting on the top of a flagpole, believing your head is
> attached to the sky.
> Dying all the time, trying to find the words, but you have
> forgotten how to read, can't see through the wall in front of
> your brain.
> We're all going to die, we're all going to die one day!
> Staring at the shop windows where glucose covers plastic
> souls.
> Rats and bats fly out of your eyes and acid runs down from
> your dead ears.
> We just smile, we're all going to smile one day!
> The picture on the screen chases you, the shadow turns
> in front of the mirror, suddenly you are lying in a heap of
> animals, but you cannot see your friends, you shout, but your
> voice is alien.
> They have gone, we're all going to go one day!
> Meet subterranean creatures, bury yourself in a rock, plastic

> hearts beat 380 times a minute, patients die like beautiful blowflies while slalom skiers race through the woods like shaven elks.
> You are alone, we're all going to be alone one day!
> Fake advertisements blow your mind, blood donors queue at tram stops, you can hear the screams when the brain police come and arrest the innocent.
> We're all in prison, we're all going to prison one day!

I gave it some thought. The rowing had resumed downstairs. Seb folded the piece of paper.

'It's about Guri really,' he said.

'Guessed as much,' I said.

'If I sort out the rhythm, rewrite it in English, insert a few cool rhymes, we could do a blues number with it. You sing. I play the harp and tap my foot!'

He blew a minor key on the mouth organ.

'Seb and Kim the Bluesbeaters,' I said.

'Wow, yes!'

'Would sound good to sing the blues in Norwegian,' I said.

'Yep, of course it would.'

Of course it would. Seb, musically confused and warped, would end up with the blues no matter what. It was still winter and Guri had a monthly ski pass and the Slalom Prince was beginning to make serious inroads into Seb's pastures. Seb was a bit down.

'How's it goin' with Cecilie?' he asked.

My head shot up. Seb understood most things.

'Don't really know,' I said.

'She's a tough nut.'

'Yes,' I said.

'Patience,' he said, sounding like one of the wise men from Oslo Observatory, patted me on the head and flipped Mayall's 'Broken Wings' onto the turntable.

Well, I was patient. We continued to meet, Cecilie and I, as though we shared a secret, something forbidden and dangerous. And in some strange way it appealed to me. Night-time activities, deserted streets, a gateway, the harbour front one dull afternoon, or in the middle of a bridge. One day when we were stealing around Bislett, we met Goose, I was carrying Cecilie's schoolbag and we were on our way south, going down quiet, narrow streets where few people were about. He was walking towards us and at first I didn't know who it was, just knew there was something familiar about him, and my stomach went queasy, as though I had been caught in the act. Then I realised it was Goose in his blue poplin coat buttoned to the top and a leather cap with flaps tied under his chin.

He stopped. His eyes were blue and calm beneath the fleece rim.

'Hello, Christian,' I said.

He looked straight at me, straight into my pupils. It hurt.

'Long time, no see,' he said, as if we were pensioners.

'Time passes,' I said sagely. 'How's it goin' at the Christian school?'

'Fine,' he said. 'I've found my path in life.'

There was a pause. Cecilie regarded us with curiosity.

'Sounds good,' I said.

'I can thank you for that,' he said.

'I beg your pardon?' I answered in shock.

'You led me along the right path,' he said. 'You were God's instrument.'

Didn't want to go down that route. But his gaze was serene now, even though it pained me, like water where there were no fish. And no waves and no wind.

'Must be off,' he said gently and went.

'Who was that?' Cecilie asked after a while.

'Pal from *realskole* and *folkeskole*.'

'What did you do to him?' she continued, as grave as grave could be.

I tried to laugh it off.

'I have a good influence on people,' I said. 'Didn't you hear that? I'm God's instrument.'

I held Cecilie's hand. I thought of the passage in the Bible, I knew it off by heart, I know it off by heart: *What doth it profit, my brethren, though a man say he hath faith, and have not works? Can faith save him?*

I knew a huge backwash was on the way, spray would splash

through my head and the moon would draw up the sea like an eagle sucking an egg dry.

Cecilie said, 'You tell too many fibs, Kim.'

Snow covered the ground for ever that winter. Seb was unhappy, played the blues on his own. After Håkon Mjøen sniffed gold in Grenoble, no one could get Guri and the Slalom Prince off the slopes. Cecilie and I went skiing in Nordmarka on Sundays. I chased after her in her tracks, she set out to torture herself, or me, and I hardly had the energy to peel an orange when we arrived in Kikut.

The smell of hot broth and ski wax.

We sat in the warming sun.

The roof was dripping.

We had to remove our anoraks and sweaters.

I asked her straight out: 'Are we a couple?'

Felt pretty stupid. Would have swapped places with the jigger standing on Lake Bjørnsøen pulling at nothing.

Cecilie laughed, a rare sound from her.

'Of course we are.'

Then she leaned her head against my shoulder and I put my arm round her, and a moment like that was worth quite a lot of lapses, scandals, threatening letters and deranged parents.

Yes, we became bolder and bolder. Cecilie seemed to soften, slowly, like the frozen ground after a long hard winter. The sun rose higher in the sky every day. The light became stronger. Water murmured and trickled around us. But I didn't venture out to the palace in Bygdøy, it was out of the question, Alexander the Great would have turfed me out like a sack of rubbish. But we went to the cinema, sat in the blue auditoriums with hot, moist hands. We saw *Bonnie and Clyde*, Cecilie squeezed my hand to jelly, but films did not do it for me, I just sat wondering why people ooohed and aaahed and jumped in their seats, it was all fakery. No one could trick me after *The Sound of Music.* Walking home afterwards, she could talk and talk about the films, I tried to respond, to say something, but it all seemed so unreal, as though we were talking about shadows, talking about our own shadows, just like the man who attacked the picture with an axe, a picture! It was hard to believe. It was hard to understand.

After the seven o'clock performance at the Colosseum one night I suggested nipping down to Valka, I had earned a few tenners and could afford a treat. We found an unoccupied booth and the atmosphere was cosy with grey smoke and laughter in the darkened room. I spotted a few celebrities, nudged Cecilie in the ribs and nodded discreetly over to Harald Heide-Steen and Rolv Wesenlund. We almost killed ourselves laughing. It was cool to sit in the same pub as the Wesensteen duo, just like being in the TV programme. Cecilie wanted a Coke and I ordered a beer. Cecilie sent me an angry look.

'We won't be a couple if you drink,' she said. I had been drunk twice.

'Spirits is quite a different matter,' I said.

The drinks arrived. I liked Cecilie's mouth when she drank from a glass.

I rolled a cigarette.

'Won't touch Leif's medicine again,' I said.

Cecilie started chatting about the film and I was bored. What happened on celluloid meant nothing to me. I wanted to talk about Cecilie, about us, but she wanted to talk about the film.

I interrupted her.

'Is your father still angry?' I asked.

She seemed taken aback, then her face stiffened and retreated into the hard features that frightened me.

'Don't know,' she said, obviously not interested.

'Do you think he would give me the heave-ho if I visited you?'

She just hunched her shoulders as though it were irrelevant whether I was dragged out on my face or not.

I drank some beer. My heart clawed in my chest. Someone at a table was laughing hysterically.

'I hate my parents,' she burst out.

And at that moment Uncle Hubert came in, stood in the middle of the floor squinting in all directions and nodded. He had been there before, no doubt about that.

'Hate?' I managed to get out before Hubert was upon us, his eyes softened by the sight of beer, his coat hanging around his shoulders like a tarpaulin.

'Kim,' he said. 'What a surprise.'

He looked at Cecilie. He looked at me. I began to feel nervous.

'This is my Uncle Hubert,' I explained, sweat forming on my brow. 'And this is Cecilie.'

I pointed in all directions.

'I'll take a seat here,' Hubert said, sitting down. There was a short silence. Cecilie's words were burning in my brain. Hate?

'We've been to the cinema,' I conversed. 'Very nice.'

Cecilie smiled.

'He didn't like it at all. Kim hates going to the cinema.'

So she had known. I tried to laugh.

Hubert gave a kind of gurgle.

'Say what you think, Kim. Don't be afraid.'

'The film was crap,' I said. 'All films are the same.'

Another silence. The glasses were empty. Hubert treated us. I had to go to the toilet, the pressure on my bladder was terrible, I couldn't wait, but I was reluctant to leave Cecilie on her own with Hubert. What if he had a fit and started throwing beer over her? But I had to go to the toilet, wriggled my way out and while I was standing there having a sprinkle, another thought struck me: What if he started chatting about Nina? Panicked, gave it a last burst, it sprayed back, I scrambled through the banks of mist and there was Cecilie with her head thrown back, laughing with abandon, I wondered what Hubert had said or done to make her laugh like that.

Squeezed in and sat down.

'I was talking about Granddad eating his earplugs,' Hubert chuckled.

I drank and laughed. Everything was fine.

But still it rankled, the thought about Nina, suddenly remembering her like that, having a guilty conscience. But then hadn't she been knocking about with Jesper Salami? Anyway, I had already forgotten her.

Hubert talked about Paris, about the restaurants and bars, about warm nights, colours, fruit, trees that caressed the river, green cardboard boxes and a woman called Henny. His shoulders twitched, but the spasms subsided. The memories had been so strong and clear, in his mind he was still there and was almost happy.

'When is Henny coming back?' I ventured to ask.

Hubert didn't answer. He said, 'When I have some money I'll go there and settle.'

Hubert was dreaming.

'Where will you get the money from?' I enquired.

He looked sheepish.

'I do the pools,' he said. 'And the lottery. Every month without fail. The draw's tomorrow.'

'Here's to you winning,' we toasted.

Cecilie looked at her watch and had to go.

Hubert sat with his bock beer, huge coat and red scarf, and a distant look that penetrated the wall and crossed Majorstuen and Europe.

'Was *that* your uncle?' Cecilie said as we waited for the bus.

I nodded.

'I liked him,' she said gently.

'He's an okay uncle,' I said.

'Is he like your father?'

'They aren't identical twins,' I said.

I was reminded of what she had said.

'Do you hate your parents?' I asked in a hushed voice.

Cecilie looked at her watch.

'He'll be sitting there timing me,' she answered.

That unsettled me.

'Does he know you're with me?'

Cecilie looked me in the eye.

'I say I'm with Kåre,' she said, straight out.

I was punctured.

'Kåre? The editor!'

She nodded.

The bus drew up in front of us.

'By the way, he wants to interview you for the school newspaper,' she said quickly, jumping onto the footboard. The bus roared off towards Bygdøy, leaving me behind like a flat tyre jettisoned in the gutter.

But on the way home I found the repair kit. In fact, Kåre was the loser, Kåre with the straight parting down the middle and the round glasses, the class above me, the coat hanger shoulders, the intellectual snob from Ullern, the spotty pseudo. He was the one left with egg on his face, he was the whipping boy for our clandestine meetings.

I felt on top of the world.

The bad news was that something came of the interview. The following Friday Kåre the Editor swanned over to me in the last minute of the break and asked if I would mind doing a pupil-of-the-week feature for the school newspaper. Of course I didn't mind. I turned up in the newspaper office after school, on the top floor, slanting ceiling, cramped, empty bottles, typewriter and papers everywhere. The beanpole Gunnar had argued with at the dance sat on a box squinting, the layout manager, fidgeting with Letraset; the photographer was in the top class, he smiled and kept pulling lengths of pink bubble gum out of his gob. The editor sat behind the only table with a pencil behind his ear and a cap over his skull. They had all rolled up their sleeves. This was the editorial team of *The Wild West*.

They gave me a Coke, drew up a chair and lit a cigarette for me, this was heavy, print run of 600.

'Let's get down to business,' Kåre said, whetting his pen.

'Fire away,' I said.

'Born when and where?'

'51 Josefinesgate.'

He looked me up and down.

'Special characteristics? Club foot or hunched back?'

'One arm has a limp,' I riposted.

Kåre wrote.

'Hobbies?'

'Collectin' elephants.'

'Which subject do you like best?'

'Needlework.'

The photographer grinned.

'The man's a wit.'

'Which dancing school did you go to?' Kåre continued.

I smelt a rat.

'No comment,' I said diplomatically.

'Shall we ring for a solicitor?' Beanpole grinned.

The photographer snapped away.
'Favourite writer?'
'John Lennon, Jim Morrison and Snorri Sturluson.'
'What would you do if you were headmaster for a day?'
'Sack all the teachers.'
'Dream woman?'
Kåre removed his glasses and rubbed the bridge of his nose.
'Hasn't stepped out of my dreams yet,' I said.
'Ooooh,' the photographer intoned. 'The man's on the ball.'
Kåre replaced his glasses.
'Do you support the USA in Vietnam?'
'No.'
'Explain.'
'Imperialism,' I said. 'A nation must be allowed to determine its own fate without outside interference.'
Heavy.
Beanpole stood up, almost hitting his head on the ceiling.
'Can we print that lie, boss?'
Kåre peered up.
'This is a democratic newspaper in a democratic country. Everyone has a right to express their opinion.'
The others nodded. The photographer zoomed in.
'Do you support NATO?'
'Not as long as NATO supports the USA in Vietnam.'
Wow. Logic.
'Favourite group?'
'Beatles.'
'There are persistent rumours that you climbed onto the roof of a certain house in Bygdøy. Any comment?'
'No comment.'
'Solicitor's on the way,' Beanpole smiled, opening a Coke.
'Do you think long hair's attractive?'
'Especially under the arms.'
'Why do you wear the ugliest jacket in the school?'
'Disapprove of the question.'
'Wow,' said the photographer. 'He's a pro.'
That was all there was to it, well, apart from having a few more

pictures taken, and the photographer persuaded me to strip off, just the chest. Everyone was photographed like that when they were interviewed in *The Wild West*. Except the girls, of course, raucous laughter. I leaned against the wall, tensed my biceps and the camera flash swept across me, from the front, then the back.

'I'd like to check through the interview first,' I said to Kåre.

'Impossible,' he said. 'It goes to press this evening. You can trust us.'

He stared at me and even though he was quite friendly and jocular, I think he hated me somewhere, and I think I would have done too if I had been him. I had a nasty feeling that he was up to something sneaky, but I couldn't work out what. And anyway, I was pretty high after being interviewed with photos and so on. I raced down the steps and met Cecilie at Dagmar Café. We had enough for a vanilla slice and I told her everything I had said. Then she had to go. Alexander the Great was waiting for her return, on pain of death, I have a feeling spring's on the way, I told Cecilie.

It was not. I knew that now. Kåre the Editor was out to cause trouble and he got it too, but he created more of a stir than he had bargained for. Needless to say I was the last to see the school newspaper, came back from the gym lesson, sweaty and sore, and from the moment I entered the classroom I knew that something was brewing, something big. Everyone stood with their noses in their copy of *The Wild West*. There was stamping and clapping when I arrived. I grabbed a copy and flicked through. Kåre the Editor had really gone to town. There was a picture of me from the rear and the front, and one where Beanpole, the layout manager, had mounted a model propeller on my back. Very smart. And that was not all. They had incorporated a skeleton too and written underneath: *Kim Karlsen's girlfriend in Copenhagen*. What the hell! I caught sight of Cecilie. She was standing by the blackboard, a white, ice-cold silhouette. I read. The interview was fine. But in the lead-in Kåre from Ullern had disassociated himself from my demagogic opinions. I was confused rather than corrupt, he wrote. My addled brain was due, he presumed, to the fact that I had been in a long-term relationship with a girl from Copenhagen, and Copenhagen was the axis of evil and immorality in the world, as everyone knew, at least in Scandinavia. I looked at Cecilie. Black board. White face. Sphinx had written something on the board that had not been cleaned off: *I think, therefore I am.* I headed for the door and found Ola wandering round with a maths book. I swung him round.

'Ola,' I said, keeping my composure. 'What the bloody hell did you say to that creep Kåre?'

He was engrossed in an equation.

'Say what to wh-wh-whom?'

'Have you seen the school newspaper?'

He shook his head.

I showed him the page. It began to dawn on him.

'He just wanted some p-p-personal information,' Ola stuttered.

'Right, yes, and so you told him about Nina?'

'Was that so b-b-bad?'

The bell rang. It was a hard path to tread. Seb met me outside the door.

'I would advise against suin' for defamation,' he whispered. 'Let the editors drown in their own shite!'

Cecilie's face was granite, her eyes ground me to sand and a small, insignificant snort blew me onto the mountain plains, abandoned for ever.

Slippery Leif and Peder proffered their sincere congratulations, Peder not without *Schadenfreude.*

And, God help me, I had to roll up my sleeves yet again to prove that I didn't have a propeller.

Cecile turned away in disgust.

It was French with Madame Mysen, Madame Squint, a thin Parisian baguette with blue nails and an aquiline nose. She translated Sphinx's words: *Je pense, donc je suis.*

After precisely ten minutes I was hauled before the headmaster. Kåre was there, too. His glasses had steamed up. He didn't grace me with a glance.

Sandpaper sat behind the desk, leafing energetically through *The Wild West.* I wondered whether he had combed his moustache. Or whether it just grew like that. I ran my finger under my nose. Soft down. Fluff.

Sandpaper peered up.

'As editor of the school newspaper you should know about press ethics,' he rasped, making the room vibrate.

Perspiration was dripping off Kåre.

'And you, Kim Karlsen, you should have kept the skeleton business quiet! I thought you had understood that!'

Kåre spoke up.

'This is my fault, sir. Karlsen knew nothing about it.'

Honest. Kåre was an idealist. He looked at me out of the corner of his eye.

Sandpaper flicked through the pages, shaking his head. The stakes had been too high for Kåre. It ended with him having to resign in disgrace as editor and the student council had to appoint a new one. I was disgraced, too, I lost Cecilie, but no one appointed someone new for me.

I didn't have a snowball's chance in hell of getting close to her, she slipped away again, shut her eyes to me, but saw me nevertheless. I could just enjoy myself with my girlfriend in Copenhagen. I tried to use Seb as a go-between, but he didn't know the password, either. Gunnar thought Kåre was the slimiest bastard that had ever walked the earth. What about if we ran an anti-Kåre sticker campaign and hung him out to dry once and for all. Ola was unhappy and said that he would never speak to the press again, that was for sure. Peder and Slippery Leif went back on the offensive, but Cecilie seemed impregnable to one and all, like a bunker.

Seb and I stuck together, both despondent, again and again we told each other how unhappy we were and tortured ourselves even further. We sat at my house playing The Doors. We sat at Seb's playing Bob Dylan and The Mothers of Invention. *Freak Out*. Seb took out some sheets of paper with lyrics on them. He reckoned he was well on the way with a great blues number, because this was the time for blues.

He read the first, and hitherto only, verse while coughing into the harmonica from time to time.

I was born down by Vika,
That's what I was told.

Mother scrubbed steps
Father's soul was sold
To the yard for forty years
Before he worked his lease.
Got a watch from the Boss
Priest wished him peace.
They know nothin', no siree
They know nothin', can't you see
Don't know nothin', no siree
Ain't got nothin' to do with me

'Your mother doesn't scrub the steps,' I said. 'And your father's at sea!'

Seb studied me for a long time, then shook his head.

'When you write, you've got to lie, too,' he said. 'Just like Goose did that time when he wrote about the suicide in Bygdøy.'

'Ye-es,' I said. 'Of course. But the secret is to lie well.'

'Well, you would know,' Seb smiled. 'You're the best liar of us all.'

Then we played *Sergeant Pepper* and I started to unravel because Nina was in those grooves, and Cecilie was, too, in negative form, an absence, and we each sank into our own gloom and said nothing for several hours.

Then Seb said, 'I fought for Guri once. D'you remember?'

'Course I do. How's your grandma by the way?'

'Alright. She shows up when Dad's away.'

We played 'A Day In The Life' again.

'Any progress with Cecilie?' Seb asked.

'I'm a fetid sausage on her platter,' I said.

'Oh, boy,' Seb said. 'I'm gonna use that one.'

He jotted things down in a little book till the sparks flew. Then he grabbed his harmonica, flicked the hair off his forehead and hollered away.

'I'm a fetid sausage on her platter
I'm a fetid sausage on her platter'

He stopped.

'What rhymes with platter?'
'Matter,' I said.
'Jeez.'
He blew up a seventh.

'And she don't care 'cos I don't matter.'

We took it again, and I sang. I really went for it, roared the moss off my lungs. Seb was red in the face, stomping with his stockinged foot. Seb and Kim, the Blues Howlers.

'We'll have to write more verses,' he said afterwards.

'About slalom snobs,' I said.

'And sneaky school newspaper editors and lousy girls.'

They were in for it now. No one was safe now.

'Heads will roll,' Seb pronounced prophetically.

On the day I saw Kåre suck up to Cecilie and inveigle her into a conversation that lasted a whole break I decided to write a letter to Nina. I had received four and sent none. I sat in my room writing all evening while thinking about Kåre and Cecilie; childhood friends, ex-sweethearts, that's what they were, I was sure, she knew I had seen them together. I wrote a letter to Nina. About how boring school was, about whether she had heard The Doors, if there were lots of hippies in Copenhagen. Wrote until my ears buzzed. But said nothing about why I hadn't replied earlier.

Folded it up and popped it into an envelope. My mother was at the door.

'Are you doing your homework?' she asked.

'Yes,' I said.

I was into monosyllables.

Mum tiptoed in and took a seat behind me.

'You're not still depressed about the letter from the headmaster, are you, Kim?' she said, and I loved her for that, but couldn't show it, just couldn't bloody do it.

'No,' I said.

'It's all forgotten now,' she said.

Kind words.

I slipped the letter under a book.

'The girl... the girl you... were talking about... who is she?'

Would have loved to talk too, relieve some of the pain, but there was a padlock on my mouth, a Jubilee clip round my larynx. I coughed and squirmed. Couldn't tell her the whole story about the school newspaper, either, on the contrary, I was desperately hoping they would never get their hands on a copy of *The Wild West*, I think Dad would have expired on the spot. And that's how it was, there was no conversation, as though we could not talk to each other any more, and the only comprehensible sounds to human ears came from Dad in the sitting room as he yelled, 'Tell him to get a haircut. Tell him to get a haircut *now*!'

'Jesus had long hair,' I said.

The next day I sent the letter to Nina.

In April a new Beatles single came out. I wended my way down to Bygdøy Allé and bought it at Radionette. They had got quite a long way with the new building down from Gimle where the supermarket was going to be. I went home and played the record in peace and quiet. I was pretty enthusiastic. 'Lady Madonna'. Yes. It was up to scratch. I gave Seb a call and played it over the telephone. He was pretty enthusiastic, wasn't hanging from the ceiling, but the music held up, a pro job, resting on their laurels, they had every right. The piano swung. We discussed whether it was Paul or Ringo singing. It was Paul, might have had a cold. Dank climate in England in the winter. Anything else? Seb was working on a few new texts. He had borrowed Jan Erik Vold from the library.

'The snow's meltin',' I said. 'Won't be able to slalom in Kleiva now.'

Seb sighed down the line.

'Have you turned meteorologist or what? Heard of water skis? The creep's got a homestead on Hankø in the fjord with fifty horses. Nobody loves you when you're down and out.'

He was quiet for a moment.

'What rhymes with homestead?' he asked at length.

'Dead,' I replied.

'I'm slowly losin' the will to live,' he said.

'What about bread?' I suggested.

'That's more like it.'

We rang off. I gave the disc another spin. The B side. 'The Inner Light'. I was depressed, it was another useless Tuesday, crappy, boring, one of the days you could give a miss, drop completely, a grey hole in time. A Tuesday in April, 1968. Leftovers for dinner and a couple of jibes across the table about hair and clothes, pathetic they were, too. Homework. English. French. *Passé simple.* Kipling. If. Norwegian. Sagas. Filthy windows, nasty smell from Frogner Bay, sore balls, impossible to concentrate on anything. Lying on the sofa, staring at the ceiling. Not a lot to look at. Strange the silence coming from Jensenius. A door slams somewhere. Squeals of a car braking. But nothing has anything to do with me, one boring Tuesday in April, 1968.

The doorbell rang, but I couldn't even be bothered to shift my carcass, probably just a salesman trying to palm off some Tupperware on Mum. I heard someone come inside and then there was a knock on the cell door. I leapt to my feet. Cecilie was standing there. Cecilie. It was incredible. That such a Tuesday could bring Cecilie. Mum was standing in the wings peering in, Dad's head was there, too, I quickly locked the door, had no idea what to say.

'Cecilie,' I said.

She looked around as if she had come to rent the room. Looked at the records. The books. The clothes on the floor. The slippers, my idiotic slippers, looked like two ducklings with a red ball on the beak.

I padded around barefoot, socks were full of holes. Would have to cut my nails soon. Embarrassing situation.

Say something.

'Are you hungry?'

She sniggered quietly and sat down.

'He's explained everything,' she said, looking up at me.

'Explained what?'

'About you and the girl in Copenhagen, that it's been over for some time.'

'Who has?'

'What?'

'Who has explained what?'

'Ola, of course.'

'Ola?'

I sat beside her on the sofa.

'Seemed it was sort of his fault,' she said. 'But now he's explained everything.'

She looked at me. With gentle eyes.

'Ola,' was all I could say.

She laughed again:

'It's taken quite a long time, but I've got there!'

Ola, my Ola! Comes in with a whimper and goes out with a roar! We caressed each other, ended up in a passionate embrace. She let me go for a moment, leaned back and tidied her face.

'It was a rotten trick Kåre played on you,' she said.

I felt the time was ripe to be fair to the enemy. Could afford to be now.

'At least he admitted his guilt,' I said. 'Over the skeleton business.'

She nodded.

'I thought you were cheating on me,' she said, not mincing her words.

'Course not,' I stammered, raising my hand.

'So it was over a long time ago then?' she said with eyes cast down.

'Yes,' I said, suddenly remembering the letter I had sent, and my stomach started to churn.

'Yes,' I repeated, as if the words could change anything at all.

Cecilie looked at me.

'Lies and dishonesty are the worst things I know,' she said in a serious tone.

'But you lie to your parents,' I suggested gently.

She sniggered.

'That's not the same. I've always done that. It's best for them.'

Always done that. My stomach gave a new lurch. Must have lied about many more before me, a whole bunch of them, I'm going to see Kåre, I'm going to see Kåre, and then she had gone somewhere else, to secret assignations, the back row in the cinema, in an out-of-the-way park on the other side of the town. I started to touch her, my hands ran wild, she pulled away with a laugh.

'Yes,' I said and had no idea why I was saying 'yes'.

'Are we friends again then?' she asked, simple as that.

Friends.

'Yes,' I said again, leaning across her.

Afterwards I played her the new Beatles record. She listened without much interest, talked about a singer who was even better than Simon and Garfunkel, Leonard Cohen his name was. Had never heard of him. She could play a few chords on the guitar.

I played the record again. It was a run-of-the-mill letter I sent, nothing dangerous, like a postcard you sent to friends and family on holiday, to prove you were still alive, a weather report, wouldn't cause a problem.

I calmed down.

'Lady Madonna,' I said.

'What?'

I had my head in her lap.

'Lady Madonna,' I said. 'You're my Lady Madonna.'

Thought that sounded cool. But I'm not sure that she liked it.

She was quiet for a while, then looked down at my face.

Stroked my eyebrows.

'You're sweet,' she said.

Not sure that I liked that.

'Lady Madonna,' I repeated.

Then she lowered her mouth and her hair fell over me like a thin, freshly washed curtain.

Spring arrived with a vengeance, worse than ever before. I bought twenty bottles of Export for Jensenius and he held a damned concert until late in the night when the cops had to come and restrain him. After that Jensenius was quiet. But the sun continued, ripped up the winter by the roots, and bikes and bands streamed into the streets like animals emerging from hibernation. Cecilie and I kept the pot boiling with clandestine, stolen trysts on misty, sultry evenings that were not as warm as you thought, which necessitated closeness and initiative. She visited me sometimes, out of the blue, without warning, and one evening I went to hers in Bygdøy.

Alexander the Great and wife were at the opening of an exhibition in the Trade Fair Hall and the palace was unoccupied. We sat in the hammock in the garden, swinging and drinking orange juice. I peered up at the roof, went weak at the knees, it was steeper than the landing section of the Holmenkollen ski jump. Otherwise the garden wasn't bad, the grass had been manicured with nail scissors and the lawn was the size of a golf course. The apple trees stood on the horizon like white ghosts and my knees went weak again. Apples. Hadn't heard anything from Nina after I had sent the letter, not so strange though, it was a pretty stupid letter. Cecilie told me about the gardener whose name was Carlsberg. He had *green fingers*, Cecilie said. Carlsberg is Danish beer, I said. I shouldn't have said that, that's obvious. Cecilie was offended and immediately got off the hammock. So I was forced to perform resuscitation, after half an hour everything was fine again as a rule. It was quite strange really because she wanted to hear about this Nina, as she called her, she would beg me to talk about her, she was curious and scared at one and the same time, and I did talk, but it didn't do to tell too much, to warm to the topic, tricky area, a fine line, worse than walking on her roof. But this evening she didn't want to hear about Nina. At first we had to do some homework together and afterwards we could play records. Quiet evening. We lay in the grass with our English and French books, testing each other on vocabulary.

'What do you think of *Victoria*?' she asked after some time.

'Boring,' I said.

She looked disappointed.

'I think it's beautiful,' she said to the sky.

'Would never have thought Sphinx would choose schmaltz like that,' I persisted.

'Would have liked to know the miller's son,' Cecilie sighed.

'They make it more difficult than it needs to be, don't they,' I said, and caught myself feeling stupid. 'Anyway, it's only a book,' I added.

Cecilie lay daydreaming, the spring murk was on its way, a light cloud scudded across the sky.

'I'll fetch the record player,' she said, running in.

She brought her guitar as well. And Leonard Cohen. She couldn't get enough of Leonard Cohen. And the whole time she was staring at the picture of this dark, tragic man with the spiritual resonance that girls would queue up for.

I was pissed off.

'Don't you like Leonard, either?' Cecilie asked with resignation in her voice.

On Christian name terms.

'Schmaltz,' I said. 'The same old schmaltz all the time.'

She turned her back on me and played the B side. I couldn't hear the difference.

'You only like The Beatles, you do,' she said.

'True,' I said.

I was in that mood.

We didn't say any more. When the record had finished she took the guitar in her lap and strummed. I liked her better then, well, I liked her best of all then, when she tried to play the guitar, because she couldn't, and that gave me a bit of a frisson, watching her do something at which she was completely hopeless.

She strummed with her nails, moved her left hand into contorted positions with her fingers sticking out in all directions and pressed the strings. However, as far as fingers are concerned, I can't talk, my index finger stuck up in the air like a misshapen question mark, and I was glad Cecilie didn't ask about that.

Then she began to sing in English.

It sounded forlorn.

Loved her at that moment.

After finishing, she stared vacantly into the distance as though listening to an echo.

I hugged her.

'That was great,' I said.

'You're lying,' she said.

'I mean it! It was great!'

'You're lying,' she said, and continued to play and sing 'Suzanne', and I really liked the song when Cecilie sang it, 'rags and feathers from Salvation Army counters', it had something that stirred my heart.

Behind us stood the enormous palace, the garden stretched out in all directions, the sky moved slowly above us and there was the smell of freshly mown grass. Cecilie sat with her Levin guitar playing folk songs, and it was odd that Cecilie, uncompromising Cecilie, liked these songs so much. Not Bob Dylan but Donovan, not Barry McGuire but Cohen, not John Mayall but Simon and Garfunkel. She played her whole repertoire of five songs. 'Donna Donna', 'Catch The Wind', 'Suzanne', 'April' and 'Yesterday'. When she had finished and it had actually turned a little cold, I snuggled up to her and took the place of the guitar. But then there was a buzz at the gate and footsteps crunched up the gravel path. Cecilie scratched me through to my shirt, she was so afraid, we sat there as quiet as mice, it was too late to escape anyway. But it was not her parents, it was an old man with a straw hat and wide trousers flapping in the gentle wind.

Cecilie breathed a sigh of relief.

'It's just Carlsberg,' she whispered.

He caught sight of us and came across the lawn, walking with care, as though he might be hurting the grass.

'Hello,' Cecilie said.

He stopped, doffed the yellow straw hat and took a deep bow.

'Good evening, frøken Almer,' he said with quiet humility.

He gave me a brief nod. I could see that his fingers were not green, they were brown, thin, elegant, almost like a black man's hands.

'I must have left my pipe in the kitchen,' he explained with some embarrassment.

Cecilie went in with him. They soon re-emerged, Carlsberg disappearing with another deep bow and meandering off almost without a sound.

'That gave me quite a shock,' said Cecilie, sitting next to me.

I was speechless.

'He won't say anything,' she continued. 'Carlsberg's loyal.'

She giggled. I didn't think there was much to laugh about.

She gave me a fleeting kiss.

'You'll have to go now,' she said.

Walked along Frogner Bay, heard jazz coming from Club 7, the water was rippling around the boats, a motor bike was revving up. Couldn't get Carlsberg off my retina, humble, bowing, a metre's distance: frøken Almer! It was almost spooky. I strained to remember the chords instead, especially her clumsy fingers which kept fumbling and missing. That was how I wanted to remember her.

Stig finished *gymnas*, had the red graduation cap pressed down over his mane, wrote *Mao* on the peak and on his prom card it said: *Norway out of Vietnam*. Not everyone understood that, we were given one each and we chuckled. It was obvious that Stig did not take the exams to have the cap put on his bonce, proms were middle class inanity for the sons and daughters of the Holmenkollen wealthy. Stig joined the prom celebrations to infiltrate the enemy. And on May 17 he and three other long-haired rebels from the Cathedral School were thrown head first out of the prom procession for unfurling a long banner in front of the American embassy: USA = STATE MURDERERS. Beer bottles rained down over them, furious fathers with graduation caps on their heads and a tassel attached to their padded shoulders clenched their fists and screamed and spat, but Stig was well pleased, a successful operation. The element of surprise had caught them out. The shock burned like a corrosive negative deep into the middle class's wrinkled retina. We had an audience with him in his room, Bob Dylan crackling in the background, Stig sat in the lotus position on the divan while we lay scattered around the floor. Things are brewing, Stig said. Soon they will explode, Stig said. Before the summer is here, the world will no longer be as it was. Paris, Stig said. There, it wasn't just slinging mud at embassies, but barricades, weapons, strategy and spontaneity! There, they didn't only have Finn Gustavsen, they had Sartre and Cohn-Bendit. Workers and students stood shoulder to shoulder. De Gaulle could just go and dig a hole for himself in the ground like the corrupt mole he was. We sat listening in awe. It sounded heavy. It will spread, Stig said. Today Paris. Tomorrow Oslo. Or the day after. He looked a bit tired. But he was glad he was experiencing these times. Right, comrades? The fanfare announcing the evening news sounded in the sitting room and we piled in, just caught the off-kilter globe twirling round. Gunnar's father was sitting on the sofa, head bowed, black bags under his eyes, grey thinning hair. He had great plans about expanding his shop, mounting some opposition, moving into the cellar, making a market in the yard, building upwards, no limits to his plans. But no banker would lend him the money when they heard his little shop was situated right next to where Bonus would be. Gunnar told me that one evening. And I thought about Dad. Dad could probably loan him money, so I asked him one day. Then Dad explained to me the whole business about profitability and security, staring reality in the face and not overstretching your means. I understood little to nothing, but I knew that something was crack-brained, seriously crack-brained. But now we were standing in front of the TV, our eyes widened in disbelief. The drama that was unfolding on the screen did not seem to concern Holt the greengrocer. We leaned forward and stared: *Paris*. Unsteady, jumpy images as if the camera man was running or being chased. It was taking place in a large square. Now and then we spotted a fountain in the background, some animals spouting water. People were running in all directions, there must have been a fire somewhere because there was a lot of smoke and most people were covering their faces with their handkerchiefs. The commentator was calmly reporting on the clashes between students and police. And workers! Stig shouted. Another vanful of cops was disgorged, armed with glass visors, big shields and long batons. They slashed around, hit out at anyone who came near them as if it were all some insane game, but this was not a game, this was the vile reality that materialised from the thousands of dots which form the TV screen: blood flowing from heads, people fainting, people screaming in blind terror, blood streaming down faces and batons raining down blows, and that was when I saw it: a blow to Henny's head.

It was the sort of moment when you are suddenly and ineluctably drawn in as a participant, not as an observer, when the threads of chance weave you into a new reality, like taking a step to the side, like relinquishing a dream, like seeing yourself in the mirror without recognising the image. I saw Henny being beaten by clubs, she held up her arms to protect herself, but to no avail, they hammered away and in the end she just covered her ears and screamed, as though unable to stand the sound of her own piercing cries. Then she was lost from the screen, but the images kept rolling inside me.

I ran as fast as I could to Marienlyst. It had begun to rain, a vertical, quiet rain that made the hot tarmac steam and smell, and the lilac trees shone like polished domes. I raced through the peaceful rain, through the sleepy streets and found Hubert in a wretched state. He had also seen it, no doubt about it, it was Henny they had been attacking.

'I have to go there!' Hubert shouted. 'I have to go!'

He paced up and down the floor, trod on picture frames, kicked at papers and canvases and magazines. His face was grey, his eyes were filled with horror, longing and indignation.

I tried to reassure him, felt at once so adult sitting and trying to ease my uncle's mind.

'You could try ringing,' I said.

'I *have* done!' he shrieked. 'Can't get through. It's impossible to call Paris. I've rung the embassy. I have to go there!'

He slumped into a chair, exhausted.

'You *saw* it?' he groaned.

'Yes.'

He hid his face in his hands.

'They *smashed* her! Her head. Her nose. Her mouth.'

He stood up, sat down, stood up.

'Hubert,' I said. 'She must have lots of friends in Paris. She'll get help. She'll be taken to hospital.'

He sat down.

'She'll be fine,' I continued. 'I'm sure it looked worse than it was,' I said, not believing myself for a moment.

Hubert just stared at me.

'And when she's better, she'll ring you. It won't help if you go there now.'

'No,' he said. 'Yes, it will.'

I fetched two bock beers from the kitchen.

We drank.

'Thanks,' Hubert said. 'Thanks for coming, Kim.'

We sat for a while and felt the sweet, heavy taste of the beer seep through our bodies.

'It'll be alright,' I said.

'That's the worst thing I've ever seen.'

'Same here.'

I went for two more beers. Fear came in sharp stabbing pains, as if someone were throwing darts and I was the board.

'How's it going with Cecilie?' Hubert asked.

'Fine,' I said, no longer sure whether I believed anything I said.

Exams were approaching and the world was beginning to fall back into place. Stig was exhausted after his exertions, things had turned rough and now he was lying with swollen eyelids, waiting for the military police. Naturally he had declared himself innocent. De Gaulle was gaining the upper hand in Paris and Cecilie and I were swotting together. We worked at my place or on a bench in Frogner Park when the weather was dependable. She wasn't very interested in what had been going on in Paris, but she was good at French and taught me a few tricks. I didn't tell her about Henny. Hubert still hadn't heard anything from her. Cecilie was interested most of all in her guitar, she talked about the new chords she had taught herself, the diminished and the seventh, she was following a guitar course in a women's magazine. She had bought an LP by the Young Norwegians. I chatted about the band we had thought about starting once, The Snafus. At school it was the same old stuff. Cecilie was distant and indifferent towards me, and Peder and Slippery Leif snooped around to see what was actually going on, but no one was trying to revive Karlsen-on-the-roof or Skeleton-at-the-dance. I had my feet back on the ground.

One evening we were at my place poring over German, chewing bread and regurgitating subjunctives, datives and bloody rules. Cecilie tested me on prepositions and would not give up until I had them. It took quite a long time and there were so many other things I would rather have done. Outside, the rain kept falling, gentle, warm, just right for running around naked in, I thought, and my eyes locked onto Cecilie, I lost concentration, mixed up genders and couldn't make anything agree. Cecilie became desperate, flicked through my pile of records, but couldn't find anything that caught her interest. She liked the early Beatles, particularly Paul's ballads, as she called them. In fact, 'Yesterday' was in her repertoire. But she didn't like 'I'm The Walrus' or 'Lucy In The Sky'. However much I tried. I was happy to settle for her folk songs, and that night she sang for me without the guitar. She sat on my sofa in a red blouse, concentrated, singing for me while tapping the beat on her French book. 'The Sound of Silence'. I said I thought it was wonderful, but she didn't believe me and sang it once again. That made me feel calm and happy. That was how life should be.

It was afterwards that it happened. A full house. I was going to walk her part of the way home, along the sea front, the rain was right for walking girls home in. I shot down the stairs ahead of her and opened the heavy door, Cecilie was standing in the dark hallway as I stepped onto the pavement and felt the first drops on my hair. At that precise moment Nina appeared. She raced towards me with that same long dress stuck to her lean body, her hair over her face and a big white smile. She held her arms open wide and threw herself on me and was everywhere.

'Thanks for your letter!' she sang in my ears and her voice had a Danish twang.

At that moment Cecilie came out of the door. Nina was hanging off me. Then Nina noticed Cecilie and her arms slowly released me. They looked at each other, sized each other up, without a word, yet without any misunderstandings. I didn't even have a chance to think of something to say, I didn't even raise a finger before each went her own way, and I was left standing in the cold torrential rain until I was drenched, unwell, mortally ill. Abandoned, I thought, the word sounded harsh and sickening. I tried to roll a cigarette, but the tobacco and the paper floated away. It just kept raining, I stood there and my heart turned inside out like an old, black umbrella.

Everything around me went quiet, as if I lived in a sound-proofed room with a burning sun in the middle of the ceiling. The raining had stopped. Everything had stopped. Cecilie had donned her armour and I was less than nothing to her, a ridiculous moth. Her back was as steep as a Lofoten cliff and just as cold. I had to study alone for the exams, they went badly, and I didn't give a shit. Slippery Leif and Peder were horning in on her while I hit my head on a glass wall every time I tried to approach. But I followed their every movement, and the day Slippery Leif and Peder were holding long discussions with Cecilie in the lunch break and I was standing by the water fountain watching arrangements being made amid gales of laughter, I could stand it no more. My brain went click and after school I followed them. I really did follow them, a hundred metres behind, sneaking from gateway to gateway, hiding behind cars, lamp posts and old ladies, like in a lugubrious TV crime film, for I was sick at heart and hardly knew what I was doing. They walked a long way. They walked through Frogner Park, Peder and Cecilie side by side, close, Slippery Leif tripping around them like the drooling lapdog he was. I leapt from bush to bush. They ended up in Heggeli, where Peder lived, entered a white doorway and were gone. I sat down and waited. I waited for an hour. I felt sick to my stomach. Then they came out. Peder was carrying a bag of racquets. Everyone was laughing. I huddled up. I followed them. To the tennis courts in Madserud. They disappeared into the clubhouse and after a quarter of an hour Peder and Leif came out wearing white shorts, their pockets bulging with tennis balls. They fooled around laughing while waiting for Cecilie. She appeared ten minutes later in a tight, white top and a white, postage stamp-sized skirt. Slippery Leif and Peder gawped, stupid expressions on their big, stupid faces. I sank back behind the rose bush. They wandered onto a free court, Peder flexing his brown thighs so that his muscles shone in the sun while lethargic Leif tried to hide his gut and jogged after them with his tongue hanging out.

Peder adjusted the net. He hit a few serves. Red sand whirled up into the baking, yellow light. They began to play. Slippery Leif was the ball boy. The ball went to and fro in pat-a-cake fashion. I heard Cecilie breathing heavily. I ate a rosehip. Peder was practising his backhand. A smash made Cecilie give a little scream. Peder laughed. It was Cecilie's serve. Tossed the ball in the air and lunged after it, lunged into space as if she were going to hit a planet, her short skirt crept up and her panties came into view, her narrow hips, it lasted almost an hour, she stretched out, stretched out the time, Slippery Leif had to polish his glasses, Peder's racquet hung expectantly in the air, he twitched, then Cecilie struck and it was an ace.

I ate another rosehip. It was Leif's turn to show his mettle. Peder was sitting on the bench drying the sweat off his face. My back was beginning to ache and I shifted position. Then Cecilie looked straight at me, through the thin foliage of the bush, through the orange rosehips, straight at me, and there was no surprise detectable in her eyes, she had known the whole time I was lurking there. She held my gaze while returning Leif's ball, then she released me, the way you let a fish off the hook, threw me back. Uneatable. I packed my rucksack and crept away, from the red dirt, the tennis strokes and Cecilie's white skirt. Humiliation was a fact.

That night I dreamt of sounds. The silence was broken in my sound-proofing and I longed for the silence. I dreamt about sounds, they were near, right inside my ear, and I awoke with a scream, a scream that even Cecilie must have heard, at any rate Mum was sitting there when I opened my eyes, and she had laid a cold cloth on my forehead. I dreamt about the tennis match, about the sound of ball on racquet, the dull, dry thud of the tennis ball against the taut strings, like a heartbeat. Straight after I dreamt about Paris, about the square where all the people were running in all directions, where the police attacked as though they were more frightened than those at whom they lashed out. I dreamt about sounds, the sound of batons hitting skulls, some cracking open, and then the soundless explosion of blood blacking out the world.

I dreamt about batons and tennis strokes.

I squeaked through the exams. Ola had brought the biggest packed lunch in the school with him, he had scratched mathematical formulae in the goat's cheese. It worked fine and for one very tense day our heads buzzed and then we had finished our first year at the *gymnas*.

'What do we do now?' Gunnar said.

'We won't go to Studenten, that's for sure!' Seb said.

We chucked our revision notes in the nearest litter bin and wended our way home holding only our pencil cases. Mum gave me fifty kroner as a reward and rang Dad to tell him that their son had taken his first step to heaven. The others landed a nice sum too and so we went down to Drammensveien and fought our way to a table at Pernille.

We ordered a round of beers and put the pack of Teddy in the middle of the cloth. Gunnar adjusted the parasol. The waitress brought the glasses. We drank them and ordered another one straightaway. We were thirsty.

'At last,' Seb said.

We were right behind him on that.

'Only two years left,' Gunnar said.

'Shut up,' we said.
The beer came.
'I'm h-h-hungry,' Ola said.
We ordered four shrimp smorgasbord.
The place was heaving. They were queuing between the tables. Old people were sitting and sweating beneath the trees in Karl Johan. The beer settled like a blue grotto at the back of our heads.
The shrimps arrived.
We ordered another round of beer.
We ate the shrimps and the woman with the white apron came with a tray of beers.
We lit up and blew four rings, which lay above the table like a secret signal.
'Snobsville,' Seb said. 'All blazers and the Royal Norwegian Yacht Club.'
He pointed behind him with a discreet thumb.
'I can hear Kåre's dulcet tones from here,' he went on. 'And Slippery Leif's athleticism.'
I craned my neck. They were sitting in the far corner, fifteen – twenty of them round a table. Kåre, Peder, Slippery Leif, Beanpole. A whole gang of white shirts, Conservative badges and canned laughter. And Cecilie.
'How's it goin' with Cecilie anyway?' Gunnar asked.
'What do you think! Bloody great! We've decided to sit at separate tables and only meet at weekends.'
'Pack it in.'
'It's gone tits up,' I said. 'It went tits up some time ago.'
I told them about Nina's unexpected appearance.
'That's the blues,' Seb said. 'That's pure blues, man. I got two women, nobody loves me no more.'
He pulled out his harmonica and produced a high-pitched wail.
The other tables listened. Even the Ullern roll necks in the corner shut their gobs. Seb put the harp back in his pocket and drank his beer.
'All over with Guri too. Can't compete with water skiin'. Dishonourable discharge.'
We ordered more beer and carried out a lightning check of our finances. There was enough.

The beer arrived.

'But you two are happy lovebirds,' Seb smiled, looking at Gunnar and Ola.

'Goin' to T-T-Trondheim in July.'

'Got a date with Sidsel in two hours,' Gunnar said.

We drank beer and looked at the stream of people passing us, all types, all colours, all smells. Girls' tanned thighs, creased suit jackets, screaming kids with soft ice all over their faces, beer guts, perfume, the odour of sweat. We drank in the shade under the parasol and had finished the first year at the *gymnas*.

When we had drunk our beers, Ola said, 'G-g-gotta piss.'

All our bladders were full.

Seb leaned over the table and whispered, 'Let's go to *the park*, boys!'

We watered a bush and went up the steps to the hill in Slottsparken. Quite a lot of people were there, sitting in clusters on the trampled yellow grass. Some wandered around peering, others stood up erect staring with narrowed eyes as though waiting for some great event. They had long, greasy hair, longer than Stig's, flared trousers, frayed at the end, long coats, headbands and sallow skin. It was like going to a party not knowing a living soul. Feeling a bit like four reps from the Salvation Army junior division, we sat down by a peeling tree trunk and fiddled with the grass.

'What do we do n-n-now?' Ola asked.

'Relax,' said Seb. 'We wait.'

A hundred metres away, Cecilie was sitting with the poker faces and the sailor boys. We sat with our legs crossed among those who had turned their backs on everything, who had swum in the fountain, who didn't give a piss about royalty or a shit about the cops.

Our heads buzzed with all the beer.

Now we were here.

An emaciated type strolled over to us and bent down. His eyes were close together, it was almost only one eye, long, narrow and yellow. He fidgeted with a leather pouch hanging from his belt.

'Peace be unto you, folks,' he chanted in a strange voice.

We sat as quiet as mice, as though the party host had taken pity on us and said we could stay.

The Cyclops spoke under his breath:

'The vibes of spring,' he said. 'Feel the grass growin' under your feet. It tickles, folks.'

He was barefoot. He began to snigger.

We sniggered, too.

He bent closer. His face smelt sweet.

'*This* is the dream, you know. There is no reality. But we're not dreamin', either. We *are* the dream. Dig? Do you dig? It's others who *dream* us. Dig?'

'Dig,' said Seb.

The man knelt down.

'Resources are tight,' he whispered. 'But I have two reefers ready, Moroccan, quality guaranteed. David Andersen hallmark.'

He had a coughing fit and rolled over in the grass three times.

He recovered, put his hand in the leather pouch and took out two thin sticks.

'Fifty spondulicks,' he whispered.

We looked at each other. Seb produced a few tens and gave them to him.

He placed the reefers in Seb's hand, slowly got to his feet and moved away as the money disappeared into his trouser waistband.

And as Seb lit the cigarette, I heard the Cyclops shout: Siri! An equally emaciated girl with thin, greasy hair got up from a group of people and went over to him. She whistled and a dog loped over, a bone-bag of an elkhound, mangy and pink, its fur almost all gone and its ribs protruding like an insane harp.

The seller pointed to us and the girl turned.

Seb took the first drag, closed his mouth and kept the smoke down in his lungs.

He passed the reefer on to me.

The three skeletons wandered up to the palace.

Siri was the dog.

I said nothing. I thought about the gnome in Daltjuven: Who would die this time?

Then I inhaled as hard as I could, swallowed the burning smoke as my eyes watered.

Gunnar puffed, blew the smoke out through his nose. Ola sucked and howled.

Afterwards we sat upright in silence and waited. A tape recorder was switched on behind us. Jefferson Airplane.

Seb lit the next reefer. It did the rounds. The music became louder and louder behind us, seemed to be coming from all sides as though the trees were full of speakers.

'Don't f-f-feel a thing,' Ola said.

We sat there for a while. I could hardly stand the music any longer. My head was pounding as if I had the world's biggest headphones stuck to my ears.

'Can't stand the music!' I hollered as loud as I could to drown it. 'Put it down!'

The others sent me a strange look.

'Eh?' Ola said.

'The music, for Pete's sake! I can hardly hear what you're sayin'!'

Seb patted me on the shoulder.

'They switched the music off ages ago,' he said. 'They've gone.'

I turned round. No one was there.

Straight after Gunnar and Ola got up at the same time, staggered over to a tree and puked green vomit. They tottered back with a line of sweat round their forehead like a filthy headband.

'I'm off,' Gunnar slurred, trying to locate his watch. He stood there pulling at his trouser leg.

Ola followed him.

I felt like going, too, but I stayed. An insane thought had lodged itself in my brain. That it was Cecilie's fault I was moping, off my rocker, I was doing this because of her. Now she could enjoy herself with the sailing fraternity's sons, all the rackets and backhanders.

Strength of will was draining from my spine like water from an open tap.

Seb lit up the reefer.

'How d'you feel?' he asked.

'Dunno. Heavy. Limp.'

Seb lay back in the grass.

'Nirvana,' he said. 'We're on our way to Nirvana.'

I pulled at the glow by my face until it burned, and spat out the bits. My lungs throbbed in an irregular rhythm. I placed my hand on my heart, but couldn't find it.

A psychedelic crowd came over to join us. They burned some tobacco in silver paper, packed it into a chillum and fired up like pyromaniacs. Seb was passed the pipe, put his hand over the mouthpiece as they did and sucked. Sweat covered his face like a sheet. I tried it too, it burnt all the way down and I gasped for air. Someone smiled and smacked my back. I unbuttoned my shirt to see if there were burn marks on my skin. Someone put a hand on my stomach and the smell of incense tickled like straw in my nose. I started laughing. And I couldn't stop. I laughed as I had never laughed before. The others around me laughed, too. I was sitting amid a concert of laughing, a stomach orchestra, a mouth symphony, I laughed louder and louder, and while laughing I heard laughter exploding everywhere like mines, I lay writhing on the grass and then I noticed that everyone was watching me with closed mouths, I was the only person laughing, I stopped laughing.

The girl with the incense bent over me.

'You tickled my nose,' I said.

Her hand lay on my stomach like a cold shell.

'Your shirt's hideous,' she said.

I ripped off my shirt and threw it up into the tree.

'Your trousers are hideous as well,' she said.

I yanked off my trousers and slung them away.

Another pipe was passed around and after that I remembered nothing until I woke up and it was pitch dark and I was freezing cold. Not far away four candles were burning. Incense hung in the air again. Someone was playing guitar. I heard Seb playing harmonica.

I didn't understand why I was wearing just swimming trunks. And suede shoes. My head worked maniacally. My neck and chest hurt. Then it struck me, with slow inexorability. Nina. Of course, I had to go to Nina's. I didn't have time to say goodbye. I rushed across the grass, past the guardsmen, past wide-eyed evening promenaders with poodles and giraffes on a lead. Had they never seen a person in swimming trunks before? I began to wonder. The ducks lay in the grass like oval statues. I ran through Briskeby, Urra, my old school, past the shop under new management, past The Man on the Steps, down Farmers' Hill, round the corner where the apple trees shone like electric lights, passing a fountain that surged into the night like a gentle haemorrhage.

I found Tidemandsgate, I found her house, rushed down the path and rang the bell.

I waited for ages. I rang once again. At last I heard footsteps, the door was torn open and a smoking jacket with a shiny chest stared at me.

'Nina,' I said. 'Nina.'

Several others appeared. Their eyes were so strange, like uncut jewels.

I stood up on my toes.

'Nina!' I shouted. 'I have to talk to Nina!'

'No one lives here that you would know! Please remove yourself!'

I got a foot inside the door.

'Nina,' I cried.

'Go away!' the man at the front roared.

I lost my temper.

'You're tryin' to hide her!' I shrieked. 'I know she's here! Nina! Nina!'

I was grabbed. They bundled me into the street. I felt a knee in my kidneys and they twisted my arm behind my back. I thought I heard them laughing.

'Nina,' I said meekly, standing in the dark street as the smoking jackets returned indoors, swearing.

I started walking again. I was sick and threw up in Gyldenløvesgate. It flowed as if from a hippo. Nina, I sobbed. Cecilie. Then I heard rain falling close by. I had an insane thirst and ran towards the rain. It was the fountain, the good old fountain flowing in the dark. I could have cried with happiness. If I was going to Cecilie's I would have to have a bath first. That was self-evident. I jumped over the edge and landed with a splash in the lukewarm water that reached up to my thighs. I began to swim, swam into the spray of the fountain like a lonely trout. I stood up, looked up at the black sky and let the cascade of water wash over me.

A crowd had gathered. They were standing around the edge watching me. Soon afterwards, a car with a blue light on the roof arrived. Two constables conferred with the assembled people and then they turned to me.

'Come here,' one said.

I didn't want to.

'The game's up,' the other one said.

'You're disturbing people's sleep,' the first said.

'Come on, get out of the pool now,' the second said.

I didn't.

The constables wandered round the perimeter. But I was standing in the centre by the fountain and they couldn't reach me. All the windows were lit now. I imagined I could hear the organ in Goose's room. The square was crowded. I stood by the fountain and the constables circled me.

Then they lost their patience. The taller of the two took off his uniform and jumped in. There was quite a commotion and a bit of splashing before he could grab me and drag me ashore. I was carried horizontally into the car and dumped on the back seat.

'Fun's over now,' the uniformed officer said.

'Where do you live?' the lifeguard said.

I reflected on that.

'Bygdøy,' I said.

And then I gave them Cecilie's address.

They became a little gentler when they heard where I lived.

'Prommer, are you?' the driver asked.

'Yes,' I said. 'Got my grades today. Two As and two Bs.'

'What a to-do,' said the second officer, who was fully dressed now.

'Couldn't take my booze,' I said. 'But I'm fine now. Thank you for helping me.'

'It doesn't do to behave like that, you know.'

'Of course not,' I said.

'What have you done with your clothes?' the driver asked.

'Left them at a girl's,' I said.

They chuckled to each other, then it was a hundred kph out to Bygdøy. The palace stood there with all the ground floor windows illuminated. At regular intervals a lawn sprinkler burst into life.

I walked down the long drive with a constable on each side. They rang the bell. I was as calm as a dead lemming. The door was opened.

The constables touched their caps.

'Your son was detained after a bit of a disturbance of the peace, so we had to bring him home.'

Cecilie's father stood in the doorway gaping in amazement.

'A student with such good grades has to celebrate, but there are limits,' the second officer said.

They saluted one more time, bowed and set off down the shingle.

That was when the fear came.

Cecilie's father stood with his mouth agape.

The police car started up with a roar.

'Are you out of your mind?' he said.

I stood there in my trunks, freezing cold.

'It's a misunderstanding,' I ventured.

'You've got five seconds!'

'I fell in a pool. I wanted to talk to Cecilie.'

No chance.

Cecilie's father was counting. He had reached three.

At four I turned and ran.

The day after, Henny returned home from Paris.

I don't know if I had been hoping for rain. Clouds hung like black boards over Nesodden and gulls formed white letters in the air. But it didn't start to rain. With heavy strokes, I slowly swam ashore, dipped my face in the waves and through streaming eyes saw Henny sitting on the mound in a green military jacket with a big bandage round her head. She was pale, her face was hard.

I stumbled over the seaweed and sat beside her.

'Put some clothes on or you'll catch cold,' she said.

'No hurry.'

She dried my back with the towel and hung it over my shoulder.

'Great that you came,' I said. 'Gets a bit boring after a while.'

She crouched down with her chin between her knees and looked across the dark water.

'Think it's going to rain?' she asked.

'Don't know. Maybe.'

I put on my shirt, flipped out two cigarettes.

'It gave me a helluva shock when I saw you on TV,' I said. 'It looked terrible.'

Henny gave a thin smile.

'The reality was worse.'

'Is it over now? I mean, there's no more trouble in Paris now, is there?'

Henny looked at me.

'It's only just begun, Kim. This was just a rehearsal. To show our strength. The same thing's happening all over Europe. And in the States.'

She scanned the water again, adjusted her bandage. I pointed towards Bygdøy.

'Know a girl there, I do,' I said. 'But her parents don't appear to like me. The father chucks me out every time I turn up.'

Henny laughed.

'Does *she* like you?'

'Not entirely sure.'

'Don't think your parents like me that much, either,' she said.

I fidgeted with my cigarette, burnt my fingers.

'Are you going back to Paris?' I asked quickly.

'Yes. After the holidays. Going to share an atelier with a French girl in Montparnasse.'

Wow. That sounded cool.

'Will Hubert be joining you?'

She shook her head carefully: 'Don't think so.'

'Unless he wins the lottery,' she added with a smile.

Clouds leaned over us. Gulls screeched through their shiny yellow beaks. A shoal of mackerel made for the middle of the fjord.

'What's actually wrong with Hubert,' I asked, 'when he does all these crazy things?'

Henny said nothing for some time.

'He gets nervous,' she said at length. 'He doesn't fit in here. Just like me. The middle classes crush him. When he's in Paris, he's fine. Hubert was never meant to be here drawing all that flimflam for weeklies!'

Considered that for a while.

'If he wins the lottery, will you get married then?' I asked, immediately feeling an oaf.

Henny laughed.

'No, we're just friends. Good friends.'

She used the word in such a strange way. Friends. Not the way that Seb and Gunnar and Ola and I were friends. A sort of inbetween thing. Not lovers. Not pals. Something in the middle. Neither the one thing nor the other.

It struck me that Cecilie had used the same word.

'Friends,' I repeated.

'I'm cold,' Henny said, slowly rising to her feet.

We walked past the old shed and I was not quite sure if I hoped it would rain. It didn't. We walked past the shed, the stinking ramshackle shed where names and hearts had been scratched into the paint and words were written that were more distinct than the gulls' Japanese symbols in the sky.

And so I went home, leaving summer, another summer in my life. Now the heat has gone, cold rises from the images I draw. The diorama has been transformed into a room of mirrors, a chamber of horrors. It is not dried up, dead insects I see now, but mutilated, humiliated dying people. It is no longer a Charlie Chaplin walking backwards through my brain, but cold, clear images blown up on the walls around me. The Vietnamese girl, she is screaming without making a sound. The young boy with his heart cut out in a triangle. My Lai. An infant from Biafra with its stomach extended like a drum, an elderly man's face with eyes covered in flies. Newborn, born dead. An arm covered with needle marks and a vein protruding from under the skin. I write and the luminescent stitches running across my hand ache, my head with the shorn-off hair that will not grow aches: the images. They have nothing to do with me. The words sparkle with lies, like my hand. I can't lie that much. The images on the walls around me grow. And just like the time when I saw Henny being beaten up on TV, I am forced to get involved with the images. The images surge over me, just as a photographer in a war zone is forced to be involved in his motif. There are no more Beatles pictures on the walls. My hand can hardly control this writing.

Today I switched on the radio for the first time since I have been here. They talked about a volcano in Iceland and a town being reduced to ashes. They talked about 500 seabirds dying in an oil slick. They said the Workers' Communist Party had been founded in Oslo. I switched off. I was frightened by the voices. Afterwards I stood at the window looking out through the crack between the shutters. Winter dazzled me. The snow lay even on the ground, no human tracks.

Mum must have been here. Mum.

I went back to the table and the papers, still blinded.

Things are restless inside here. The images move.

In three months' time it will be spring.

I don't have much time.

The fence had to break in the end. The crowd poured forward in an uncontrollable wave, a police horse went berserk, it stamped its iron hooves on the pavement and reared up with a foaming whinny over the terrified people trying to escape. At the same time a VW went amok, lurching backwards and forwards in the crowd, behind the wheel a sweaty gabardined figure with his forehead on the horn. Panic was total.

And in the overgrown garden the Russian embassy stood locked and blacked out.

We pushed as far as the house wall on the corner. This was the biggest battle in Skillebekk since the War of the Staple in 1962. But gradually tempers cooled. Those washed up against the fence got to their feet, the VW threaded its way down Drammensveien and the police horse stood shitting in Fredrik Stangs gate.

'Look who's here,' Seb whispered.

Peder and Slippery Leif with Kåre and the editorial team in tow. A broad grin above their ties.

'Hello, hello, hello,' smiled Slippery Leif. 'So this is where the lefties hang out.'

We kept our mouths shut, feeling that we were on the defensive. The wall behind us was cold and uneven.

Peder pulled some gum from his mouth, let it hang from his forefinger.

'And you've been to the USSR this summer, have you? Looking a bit on the pale side.'

Guffaws spread through the ranks. Peder was taking cheap shots today. He could indulge himself. People would buy anything.

Slippery Leif took over.

'You Hanoi, Vietcong and socialism sympathisers, bet you'd like to be living in Czechoslovakia now, wouldn't you, eh?'

Gunnar stepped forward.

'You misunderstand. You always have done, you and all the other bloody flunkeys. We condemn the invasion of Czechosklovakia just as much as you and all the others. Get that clear. Okay? We don't support the USSR. What they have there now isn't socialism. We support the 1917 revolution, we support Lenin's teaching, but since Lenin the USSR has become a socialist-imperialist superpower!'

Wow. We were as dumbstruck as Slippery Leif. Peder stuck his forefinger in his gob.

'You've got better at talking, haven't you,' he whispered between clenched teeth, and so they drifted off with their honour semi-intact and their grins at half mast.

'*Have* you been to the USSR this summer?' Ola smiled.

'Did you see that?' Gunnar hissed. 'The flunkeys were as happy as pigs in shit. They're *happy* the Russians have invaded Czechoslovakia. It was what they needed. This is their lucky day.'

Gunnar had surpassed himself. We could only take a back seat, everyone took out a cigarette and while we puffed the crowd dispersed, the tramlines in Drammensveien reappeared and in one of the windows in the Russian embassy a curtain was carefully drawn to the side and a sleepy face peered out.

'Probably just a stand-in,' Ola said. 'Like that time at the Vikin' with the Rollin' Stones.'

We went back to Gunnar's place. In the sitting room his father was walking in circles thinking up new moves to counteract the supermarket opening in Bygdøy Allé in three months' time. The whole shop was plastered with posters displaying special offers. This week's price for carrots was ten øre a kilo. He was giving potatoes away.

'You really took them down a peg,' Seb said.

'Been readin' a bit this summer,' Gunnar mumbled.

'The frogs were turned into tadpoles,' Ola declared, lighting a cigarette on the windowsill.

There was a knock at the door and Stig poked his head in. He had undergone a major change over the summer. Cut his hair, grown a beard. And there was a host of badges on his cord jacket. We took a close look and Stig stuck out his chest. Front National de Liberté. Mao. Lenin.

'The rabble are enjoyin' it,' he said. 'Best thing that could have happened to them. But do not lose focus. We're fightin' against both superpowers. Don't forget the dialectics!'

He threw a single into the room.

'The Beatles are finished,' he said. 'Crap A side. Revisionist B side.'

The door slammed shut after him.

'Stig's been to Tromøya,' Gunnar said, sending us an embarrassed glance. 'Socialist Youth Front's summer camp.'

In the middle of the floor lay the new Beatles 45. We gathered around the record player. Gunnar put it on the turntable. I had to have a closer look. Apple. There was an apple on the record. I had to go to the window to get some air. My stomach groaned. Would I never be able to play a Beatles record without having an apple thrown in my face?

Hadn't heard a thing from Nina.

It was the longest single we had ever experienced. At least a quarter of an hour. 'Hey Jude'. It hit the mark, built up to a fantastic scream. There was a huge howl and we waited for the innermost groove and then it was over. I liked it. It was one of their best.

No one said anything. Gunnar flipped it over. 'Revolution'. John sang. Eight large ears flapped. Four pounding hearts. The stylus floated across the grooves. John Lennon sang calmly about the revolution. Gunnar's forehead became as low and furrowed as an expanded accordion. Ola tapped the beat with a Teddy.

Afterwards it was quiet, all we could hear was Gunnar's father's footsteps in the sitting room.

'Revisionist,' Gunnar whispered. 'Worse than Finn Gustavsen.'

We were silent for a while yet. It had started raining.

I cleared my throat.

'Paris was just the beginning,' I said. 'Now it's beginning to happen!'

The others gave a nod. We played both sides again.

I thought about apples.

'Don't like Yoko Ono,' Ola said. 'Think she's goin' to mess things up.'

'I've split with Sidsel,' Gunnar said suddenly and gazed out of the window. 'Happened in the summer. Couldn't agree on anythin'. Didn't seem any point.'

'It's over with Guri, too,' Seb mumbled. 'That slalom creep turned her head round three times.'

That seemed too much to take in at once. Russia and Czechoslovakia. Gunnar and Sidsel. Seb and Guri. John Lennon and Yoko Ono. The Beatles and *Revolution.* I thought about Cecilie, who had reduced me to a vacuum, and Nina, who had run down Svoldersgate as fast as her arms and legs could carry her that dreadful night in June.

'How's it goin' with Kirsten then?' I asked. 'Was it good in Trondheim?'

Ola was one big smile.

'Goin' so well sparks are flying,' he grinned and did a drum solo with the remaining Teddys.

At that very moment we realised that something had definitively changed, something was different now, as it had never been before.

We stared at Ola.

'Ola,' said Gunnar, inclining towards him. 'You're not stammering!'

He bowed his head in a cloud of red.

'No,' he said. 'I don't stammer.'

'But how did it happen?' we shouted.

Ola took a deep breath.

'Well, I was in Trondheim this summer,' he said. 'At Kirsten's place. And I woke up one mornin' and I didn't stammer any more.'

'You just woke up?'

'Yes. Well, it was Kirsten who realised in fact. She was lyin' beside me and…'

'We understand!' we yelled. 'We've got the point!'

And then we crowded round Ola and were as one, almost like in the old days, like before the revolution.

Crown Prince Harald got Sonja. Bob Beamon jumped like a giraffe through the thin Mexico air and Black Power clenched coal-black fists against the light blue sky. Frigg was relegated to the second division and Uncle Hubert didn't have anything accepted for the

Autumn Exhibition, following which he doubled his stake in the lottery. Rebellion was simmering at Manglerud school, the teachers were on the point of being chucked out and the FNL flag was hoisted in the school playground. Stig skulked up and down with leaflets under his arm and a suspicious expression, must have had his finger in every pie that autumn. And we all went to the Chinese embassy to receive our Mao badges from a rotund Chinese man in national dress. We didn't pay any attention to John Lennon not attaching Chairman Mao to his lapel. We were given Mao's red book as well, a handy little number, not much bigger than the Bible we received from Father MacKenzie for confirmation. There was a picture of Mao himself first, under a thin leaf of tissue paper. He had a wart on his chin, which irritated the hell out of me. And this time the dedication was easier to memorise by heart. *Workers of the world unite!* There was quite a bit of booing at school, but Cecilie couldn't even be bothered to turn round. Peder and Slippery Leif dubbed me Kim Il Sung on the spot, it sounded quite good. But Cecilie was deaf and blind to my whole existence. She had begun to frequent Dolphin, and a number of folk singers had come into her life. They knew more than forty chords, had beards and bedsits and picked her up from school every Friday.

That was autumn that year, an invasion, an Olympics, a revolution, a long spell of rain that turned to snow and wrapped November in a white cover, like the Beatles new LP, a double album, *The Beatles*, white, bare, with four pictures of John, Paul, George and Ringo inside. We sat at Seb's quietly listening to the four sides. His father was at sea again and the sitting room was quiet. We puffed on Peterson pipes and listened, looked at each other, unfolded the lyrics sheet and slowly nodded. 'Yer Blues' sounded suitably grim, fitted the mood. 'Don't Pass Me By' made Ola blush, we skipped that one in silence. I hated 'Obladi Oblada', but I dug 'Black Bird' and thought about the black fists being raised in Mexico. Gunnar thought the words of 'Back In The USSR' were near the knuckle, you don't make jokes about socialist imperialism.

We cleaned our pipes, opened the window, the snow was fluttering down in huge flakes, winter was early that year.

Sat in the cold for a bit without speaking.

Refilled our pipes.

Seb said, 'It's not like The Beatles. Doesn't *sound* like The Beatles. I mean, they each seem to be doin' their own thing.'

We chewed on that. Seb was right. It didn't sound like The Beatles.

The photographs on the inside. One each. Touched up. They looked a bit old and lethargic.

Ola had to go, had private maths lessons, he was hanging on by the skin of his teeth. Gunnar went straight afterwards, had to help his father do up his grocery shop. He still believed he could be a match for the supermarket.

Seb and I were left and listened to a couple of tracks. 'Happiness Is A Warm Gun', yes, had to give them that one, a belter. And the guitar solo on 'While My Guitar Gently Weeps', that one wept. They were the bright spots. Otherwise things looked pretty bleak.

Someone had come, there was talking in the sitting room. Seb's face went black and he clenched his fists.

Then the door burst open and a fat face peeped in with a golden-toothed grin.

'Hello, Sebastian. Just wanted to ask you to turn the music down a bit.'

Seb raised his head and sent him a hate-filled look:

'Learn to knock first,' he said.

The grin vanished.

'What did you say?'

'You heard. *Knock* first!'

The door closed again. Seb thumped his fists on his thighs.

'The prick can go to hell,' he snarled. 'Comin' here and playin' boss.'

'Is he often here?' I asked cautiously.

'When Dad's away.' He hesitated, gritted his teeth. 'They're goin' to get divorced,' he said at last. 'Mum and Dad. They're goin' to separate.'

It sounded incredible. I thought of my mother and father at home. Divorce. The word didn't exist.

'I'm not goin' to live here if that arsehole moves in and that's definite,' Seb said.

We lit the curved pipes and Seb took out a record I hadn't seen before. There was a big picture of a pretty tired-looking negro, reminded me of a country pancake, with a terrible scar between his eyes.

'Little Walter,' Seb whispered. 'Dad sent it to me from the States. *Confessing The Blues*. Plays the harmonica like a guru. He can play with his *nose*!'

Seb put on the disc and set the volume to max. There were some nasty scratching sounds first. Then came some thunderous drumming, a bass pounded in and a harmonica turned the room upside down and sandblasted our brains. 'It Ain't Right'. And, shit, how it rocked and grooved. Seb took out his harp and added a few howls, I launched myself into it with a few throaty moans and we were no longer blowing a long march, we were blowing a long, dirty blues.

Couldn't even puff on the pipe afterwards.

'The guy's name is actually Walter Jacobs,' Seb enthused. 'Died a year ago.'

An idea was beginning to form in my mind. It was a good idea. I would sing Cecilie back. And Seb would play.

I sat up.

'You know,' I said. 'You know Cecilie's runnin' around with folk singers, don't you. Perhaps we could perform at Dolphin, do a raspin' blues, and blow the Young Norwegians off the stage.'

Seb gave me a long, hard look, curled a faint smile and sucked a wail from between his hands.

'Alright. This is what blues is all about. Women. Women and cash.'

We practised intensively for a week and one day we went for it. Walter and Jacobsen. I knew the words off by heart and my throat was like a rusty saw after all the screaming. I had checked that Cecilie would be at Dolphin that night, I was on tenterhooks. But before we even got going Seb was suffering from serious nerves. His teeth were chattering, and he couldn't play harmonica if his teeth were chattering, he said. He had a fifty-krone note on him, and next to the underground we hailed a psychedelic junkie who had ready-made joints going cheap. Seb said he didn't think he could stay outside in the cold smoking – the feeling in his fingers and lips would go. So we dropped by Kaffistova in Rosenkrantzgate, ordered a glass of milk and a bowl of stew to share and sat there. Seb lit up, inhaled, his eyes closed, I took a toke, swallowed, passed back the joint. We sat in Kaffistova until it was no longer Kaffistova but an evil-smelling den in Chicago or New Orleans. Seb told me about all his dreams. We stayed there until the music from the speakers in the ceiling no longer played Ole Ellefsæter but a stomping blues number that blew our diaphragms apart, until the ashen old men with rustling newspapers were sweaty black men knocking back beer and whisky after a day in the slaughter house or in the cotton fields. Then we, Walter and Jacobsen, left for Dolphin.

I spotted Cecilie straightaway. She was sitting in a corner, her face shiny and yellow in the light of the table candles. A bearded wonder was all over her like a rash. A girl with long, greasy hair and sandals was singing a folk song. All around her there was silence, and complete darkness. The place smelt of carrot juice and steaming bodies.

We squeezed onto two unoccupied chairs by the door. The song the girl was singing had a lot of verses. Seb's nerves were beginning to fray again, he had forgotten that he was a black man, the colour was running off him like shoe cream. I was ice cold and raring to go. The girl finished, received generous applause, blushed, walked to a table and sat down. Then the boss folk singer guy stood up and announced that there would be a break before Hege Tunaal sang, but if anyone wanted to get something off their chests, they could come up on stage.

We had something on our chests.

I led Seb to the stage where the girl had stood.

I saw Cecilie watching us. Her mouth fell open with surprise and she looked a bit gormless.

I killed myself laughing inside.

The chatting subsided in the room and soon it was absolutely quiet. A few scattered claps rose into the air like birds from the snow.

Seb pulled out his harmonica, covered it with his hands and took several deep breaths. I started stomping the beat with my snow boot.

Seb wailed from between his trembling fingers and I began to howl:

I once had a girl. She had some skis.
I once had a girl. She had some skis.
I fell on my nose. She skied with ease.

The slalom prince was waiting at the lift
The slalom prince was waiting at the lift
Greasing his hair and holding his gift.

I once had a girl. She gave me the push
I once had a girl. She gave me the push
I liked her a lot. All I heard was whoosh.

Afterwards it was quiet for a long time. Then the crustaceans began to clap. But by then we had already started the next number. Seb was one big harmonica and I was a boot and a howl.

I'm a fetid sausage on your platter
I'm a fetid sausage on your platter
But she don't care 'cos I don't matter

I live in a tent, she lives in a villa
I live in a tent, she lives in a villa
She's got diamonds but I'm a gorilla

No one understands a thing but I know it all
No one understands a thing but I know it all
She thought I was cream and found I was gall.

I looked at Cecilie. She stared at the candle melting over the cloth and solidifying in a red clump. I didn't hear anyone clapping, but I saw palms hitting each other. Seb was already on his way out. I ran after him, someone tried to stop us, but we had done our bit. We fell down the steep steps and into the ice cold, ferocious, biting winter which froze us into submission.

Then I saw it. There were gravestones piled up right outside
'It's a cemetery, isn't it!' I smiled and burst into laughter.
Seb hadn't caught his breath yet.

'Stonemason's, you moron,' he panted.

And then I vomited, stew and milk, vomited over one of the monuments which had not yet had a name engraved, one waiting for a body and a grave.

That was the first and last performance by Walter and Jacobsen.

The next day Cecilie spoke to me. In the lunch break she came over to the shed where I stood swotting French, pale and sickly, freezing like a dog in my reefer jacket.

'How did the English test go?' she initiated.

Had almost forgotten what her voice sounded like.

'C,' I stuttered. 'Forgot my crib.'

She looked me up and down, gave a cautious smile, her hand hovered.

'Are you ill?' she asked.

I didn't answer. Wasn't sure where this was leading. Best to stay on my guard.

'Seb was great on the harmonica,' she continued.

She held my eyes and giggled.

'But your singing was vile!'

The nausea shot up from my stomach and hit my palate like a harpoon.

'Was it?' I said without blinking, swallowing all the crap.

She nodded. My ears were frozen stiff. She was wearing a hat. A brat was caught throwing snowballs by Skinke.

'Grim,' Cecilie said, suddenly snuggling up to me without a word. We stood like that until the bell rang.

I went straight home after the last lesson. Now I was going to ask Jensenius to teach me a few decent techniques, he would be given the chance to make a silver-tongued nightingale out of my howling ape. I think I had a temperature. Cecilie's imprint was still on my body. I ran down Gabelsgate. I was freezing and had a temperature. But in Svoldergate there was a rumpus and a blue flashing light outside the front door. People were standing on tiptoe, peering and whispering. I walked over, dread in my heart. Then I heard it, not a howl, not a scream, but a long ululation, the way whales call in the middle of the Atlantic as they send up a skyward column of air and water. It was coming from the stairs. Then it went quiet save for the sound of footsteps slowly descending.

They brought him down strapped firmly to a stretcher. He lay with his eyes wide open, they met mine, pulled at me like a magnet. There must have been five people carrying him.

Then they pushed Jensenius into the ambulance and started the engine.

I ran upstairs. Mum was standing by the window.

'What's happened?' I shouted. 'What've they done to Jensenius?'

'He couldn't live on his own any longer, Kim. They've taken him to a home. He'll be fine now, Kim.'

Jensenius had gone.

Cecilie was back.

The evening before, Dad was relaxing in the sitting room as though nothing was about to happen. He was doing the crossword with a gentle, thoughtful expression on his countenance. Mum was knitting. On the front of *Nå* there was a shot of John Lennon and Yoko Ono stark naked, taken from the rear.

Dad must have noticed I was observing him, he raised his eyes. The knitting needles stopped.

'Another word for change?' he wondered.

'Revolution,' I said.

'Revolution,' he repeated, counting on his fingers, bent over the squares. Mum went on knitting as though nothing was about to happen.

The day after, Bonus was opened in Bygdøy Allé, Nixon was elected President and Dad came home from the bank in a police car. Three men accompanied him, two in uniform, the last one in a long, grey cloak with gimlet eyes and pendulous cheeks. Dad looked at Mum and me, and said in a voice I didn't recognise and one he didn't seem to trust:

'Robbery. The bank was robbed today.'

The detective tried to cheer Dad up.

'We apprehended the Homansbyen Post Office robbers within

twenty-four hours. Oslo is hermetically sealed. They won't get away, you can be sure of that.'

'There was only one man, I think,' Dad said in the same voice.

'Inside the bank, yes. He must have had accomplices outside.'

The detective sat down opposite Dad with his head close to Dad's face as he flicked through a loose-leaf notepad.

'Try to remember. Any details, even though you may consider them immaterial. Everything is relevant.'

Dad rested his chin on his hands and spoke through his fingers.

'I've told you everything. He came into my office. Threatened to shoot unless I gave him the money.'

'You didn't *see* the weapon?'

'No.' Dad removed his hands from his face. 'I had no choice!' he shouted. 'I had no choice!'

Brief silence. Dad's shouting resounded in my ears. Mum was crying.

'300,000,' the detective mumbled. 'Unusually large sum of money.'

'It's pay day today,' Dad said wearily. 'Friday. It's quite normal for us to have that sort of amount.'

'You didn't *see* the weapon,' the detective continued. 'But you felt *threatened*?'

Dad had obviously been through the same questions several times before.

'Yes. He meant it. Meant what he said. To shoot.' Dad raised his voice. 'It's my duty to think of my staff. My employees come first.'

The detective nodded. His cheeks shook.

'You did the right thing, herr Karlsen. Quite right.'

'He seemed,' Dad started, staring at the floor, 'to be full of remorse.'

'Yes?'

'He seemed,' Dad looked away, 'he seemed a little mad.'

'Mad?'

'Yes. I mean abnormal. Of course it isn't a normal… situation, but he seemed… mad.'

The detective became animated, flipped over a new sheet in his notepad.

'Could he have been on drugs?'

Dad just shook his head.

'I don't know. Possible.'

The telephone rang. Mum went to take it, but the officer was quicker, as though he lived there.

He listened and put down the receiver.

'It's ready, boss. The rogues' gallery.'

The detective rose to his feet. Dad stayed where he was.

'I'm afraid you'll have to come with us to Victoria again. To see if you can identify any faces.'

'I've told you I didn't see his face! It was covered with a scarf. And his hat was pulled down over his forehead.'

'We always know more than we think we know,' said the detective.

Dad looked up at him, frightened. His hands fell towards the floor like two weights.

'What?'

'We have to go now,' the detective said impatiently, and Dad followed him like a sleepwalker.

There was a report on the TV news. One of the cashiers was interviewed. He had noticed the robber as soon as he entered the bank, he had a distinctive tic, the cashier exulted: 'He kept tossing his head. Obviously nervous. That's the sort of thing we bank employees notice,' he said. 'Anyway, it wasn't so cold outside that it was necessary to wrap your scarf all the way round your face.' A blaze of camera flashes greeted the cashier. Subsequently Dad came on the screen. He was looking away. The detective was walking beside him. It was better the time Dad and I were on the news together, in Bislett. It seemed an eternity ago.

Dad didn't come home until midnight. He didn't speak to us. He went straight into his bedroom and to bed. The day after he didn't get up and didn't want to read the papers. Mum rang the doctor. He came with his stethoscope and bottles of pills, spent a long time with Dad and talked to Mum in a low voice afterwards. One of the bank directors came too, consoled Mum and said that Dad had taken the only possible course of action: he had kept his composure. Hubert rang. But Dad didn't get up. Dad stayed in bed.

Carry that Weight

’69

In the January draw Hubert won first prize and travelled to Paris. Dad still hadn’t got out of bed. The robbers still hadn’t been caught and the newspapers were no longer writing about it. Hubert rang the same day and said he had won and was on his way to France, Mum told Dad. An hour later he was standing in the sitting room in his pyjamas, thin, grey, with black stubble like a shadow across his ravaged face. His eyes were sick and watery, they stared at us and he said nothing. It was the first time I had seen him since the historic day when Bonus was opened and Nixon was elected President. I hardly recognised him and he didn’t seem to know who he was, either. I was frightened out of my wits. He just looked at Mum and me with those sick eyes of his, as though we were strangers in some deserted boarding house. Then he slumped into his chair, took the magazine lying on the little table beside him with the photograph of John Lennon and Yoko Ono, which had not moved since the day before the robbery. He flicked through to find the crosswords and continued where he had left off, holding the bank biro as if clinging to an anchor.

But Dad was not completely lost to us. He could dress himself, the suit hung off him, so thin had he become. He shaved, but could not remove the shadow that had fallen across him. He went back to work, to the bank, one cold morning and came home with flowers from the staff. Mum put the bouquet in water and it stayed there for three weeks. Dad solved more crosswords, the doctor dropped by one day and they had a friendly chat. Dad was on the way up, slowly, out of the nightmare he had had since the previous year. But he could not shave off the shadow. It had taken root and he never managed to fill out his suit again.

He began to be himself, but there was one strange thing. He didn’t seem to be bothered about anything any more. He didn't mention my hair, he said nothing about me coming home late and he didn't ask how school was going. He didn't even talk about Hubert, who had gone to Paris for good.

However, if things were moving slowly for Dad, they were going much faster for Gunnar's father. Bonus glittered like a funfair in Bygdøy Allé with eight tills, self-service and offers on products all year round. Grocer Holt was about to throw in the towel. His customers disappeared one by one, only the oldest were left, the ones who bought least and had the most time. It was the same with Ola's father, only those with the least hair went for a haircut.

One evening we were at Gunnar's listening to his father pacing up and down in the room below, Stig came in and took a seat. He was studying philosophy at Blindern and spoke way over our heads.

'Dad's a Norwegian citizen, right, but he's lower middle class and he doesn't exploit anyone, does he,' Stig said, looking us in the eye.

We listened.

'You have to make a distinction between the lower middle class and monopoly capitalism, right. Bonus is killin' off the lower middle class. Bonus is monopoly capitalism. It's not just Dad who suffers as a result. Small shops keel over all the way down the line. Soon there is only the supermarket left. And what happens then? The prices soar sky high! Do you think that's chance, eh? Bonus. Irma. Domus. They entice you with low prices. Crush the small shops. And then they go for the kill with the customers. Simple as that.'

We listened.

'That tells you where the struggle is, boys! Down with monopoly capitalism! We're gettin' a taste of it first-hand, aren't we!'

Stig rose to his full height, stroked his beard and peered down at us.

'Dad's not the enemy. Dad's one of the victims. It's the workin' class and the lower middle class that have to suffer!'

He darted through the door and was gone.

'He's right,' said Gunnar.

We chewed on this for some considerable time. That was how it seemed. He was right. But beer was cheaper at Bonus.

However, things between Cecilie and me were in neutral gear. That was fine with me. Cecilie was my anchor that winter and I was pleased that Slippery Leif, Peder and Kåre and the rest of the gang were being neglected. We met in the evening, somewhere or other, because I did not want to take her home with my father in the shape he was. And going to her house was out of the question, I was excommunicated and would never be allowed to cross Olav Kyrres plass. We roamed the streets, the snow-covered streets, went to the cinema where I was bored out of my mind, but was permitted to hold her hand and that was enough. We were in neutral and I was happy. But sometimes I was frightened. She had left off going to Dolphin, didn't talk any more about guitar chords and didn't mention the din Seb and I had made at the folkies' head office. It was as if she had grown tired of a toy and chucked it out of the pram like a spoilt child who gets everything she points to. That was what I thought in my darkest hours. It was not that often. But when I was under the thrall, I considered myself one of those toys she might chuck out at any point. Nevertheless, I was happy, we were together in the evenings, sat on benches, went skiing, watched the snow melt and the sun grow stronger, heard the snow drip and trickle. Cecilie and I were in neutral until the badgers came onto the scene.

It all started with the dustbins. Every morning they lay on their sides and refuse was scattered everywhere. The first suspects to be questioned by furious janitors were the young kids. But they swore they hadn't touched the bins, why on earth would they have done, the time was past when you could find jewels and postage stamps in the dustbins, and no one could be fagged to collect beer caps any more. But the bins were up-ended every night and after a while watchmen were stationed in backyards. The news came as a shock. Skillebekk was almost evacuated. Beasts had been spotted. Rumours spread as the snow melted. It could have been anything from a rat to a bear. It was the sole topic of conversation in shops, at the tram stops, people stopped each other in the streets, people who had never exchanged a word before, theories were aired, everyone racked their brains as to what kind of creature could be preying on Skillebekk. Even Dad had pricked up his ears. The flood of rumours streamed on, dinosaurs and crocodiles, no creature was exempt, until a vigilant hunter in Gabelsgate was able to lay the facts on the table: a badger. There were badgers afoot.

It was the start of spring, or the end of winter. The snow ran in dirty rivulets down the streets, skis were stowed in cellars, cycle chains were lubricated, snow boots put away and new shoes brought into the house. The badger hunt was on. It didn't rummage through the rubbish any more, it had been frightened into hibernation, but it had to be found. It was not right and proper that there should be a badger in Skillebekk.

One evening Cecilie came to my house. It had been the warmest day so far that year, one great river of a day, and the hunters were out in force on the streets. I wanted to join the hunt, too.

'Let's go out and find the badger,' I said.

Cecilie gave me an old-fashioned look.

'Badger?'

'That's right.'

She followed me out. We walked up Gabelsgate. People were standing and peering into gateways, crawling along hedges, climbing up trees. Cecilie was at my side.

'A badger?' she repeated.

'That's right.'

'How did a badger get here? In the middle of the town?'

This was a question that had vexed many people's minds. Some thought it had swum into Oslo fjord. The most stupid claimed it had come through the sewers. The hunter in Gabelsgate said it had come from Nordmarka in the autumn and found itself a place to hibernate and slept there all winter.

'Doesn't matter how it got here,' I said. 'The fact of the matter is that it's here. We have to find it.'

We trekked down Drammensveien and I knew where to search. We should search the land in Robsahmhagen, between Gabelsgate and Niels Juels gate, where the old wooden house was, with the storeroom and the stable. If it was a badger, it would be there.

We met the hunter. He was coming out of a gateway and looked frenzied, walking as if he had lead between his toes and this was not too far from the truth.

'Have you found anything?' I asked.

'We're on its trail,' he said. 'We've observed droppings. The dogs have its scent.'

He was pulling a couple of dogs, he was not the only one, dogs were sniffing everywhere, they were dragging their tongues along the ground and wagging stiff tails.

He looked at my feet.

'You don't go out on a badger hunt wearing casual footwear,' he jeered.

I had my new boots on, suede, pointed, quite high heels, iron tips, didn't take a step without them.

He pointed to his boots.

'See! Rubber boots! With coke inside! If the badger bites, it'll make his jaw crunch, my lad! Hence the coke. It'll let go as soon as it hears the sound of coke!'

He cast a contemptuous glance at my boots and waddled down the street with the dogs panting behind him.

I knew the way to Robsahmhagen and would find the badger first. We crept through a few gardens, clambered over a fence, and there we were, in the filthy slush, in the middle of the reserve, in the middle of Oslo, a little ridge, tall trees, the large wooden house, the stable and the storeroom on pillars.

'Where are we?' Cecilie whispered as though we were somewhere sacred.

'The badger has to be here,' I mumbled into her ear, she smelt good, had to grab her, she wriggled out of my grasp with a smile.

'What will you do if you find it?'

I hadn't considered that.

'Come on,' I said.

We crept this way, then that, no one saw us from the house, we didn't see anyone, either. Darkness began to settle. We could barely see each other and I switched on a torch.

Cecilie stood in the light.

'Is it dangerous?' she asked.

I didn't know much about badgers.

'Dangerous? A badger! It's no bigger than a frog!'

I shone the light around me. Snow, brown grass, trees, branches. We stood still and listened. Only heard the tram in Drammensveien.

Then the light caught a wire netting door that had been ripped through and some steps leading down into the ground.

Cecilie clutched my arm and pointed.

'It's bound to be there,' she said.

I shone the torch away, lit up a fence.

She guided my hand back to the door.

'It must be there,' she repeated, pulling me along.

We stopped by the old air-raid shelter.

'You'll have to go down,' she said.

'Badgers don't live in houses,' I ventured. 'They build lairs.'

Cecilie looked at me.

'You go first,' she said.

I tried to hold the torch still, but had to use both hands. I shone the torch down the steps. They were steep. At the bottom there was a half-open door.

'Come on then,' Cecilie prompted, impatient.

Didn't she know, wasn't she aware, that no one in the whole of Frogner would have dared go down? Some had gone as far as the door. They had never been the same since. Even during the War of the Staple, despite being surrounded on all sides, no one had dared hide in there. It was said there was a German in there, a German who hid there when the war was over.

I shone the torch down the steps.

Cecilie nudged me forward.

I started to walk. The steps in front of me jumped in the torch light. Cecilie was right behind me. I stopped at the half-open iron door.

'Go on,' urged Cecilie.

I opened the door. The creaking sound was terrible. I shone inside. The beam lit up a pitted wall, pitted with bullet holes, a pile of planks, a box, another door.

Cecilie pushed me. I went on. It was quiet, as if the world around us no longer existed. I gripped the torch tightly, stood by the next door.

I held my breath. I held my breath and my heart pounded inside me. The veins throbbed in my hand, pulsated in my neck. Fear washed through me, red and burning.

Cecilie was right behind me.

I cast the light into the next room.

I went in.

Cecilie stayed where she was.

The smell hit me at once. An acrid stench that stung my nose. My hand went walkabout, the light floated round and when I finally had it under control I found myself looking into the eyes of a furious badger. It was lying across the floor and stabbed its pointed features in my direction growling feebly like a sick dog. I stood rooted to the floor, the foul stench in my nostrils, then I slowly retreated, but my back didn't meet the door, I backed straight into the clammy wall and was stuck there.

I shone the torch at the badger.

It glided towards me as if it had no feet. It flashed its teeth, red and white, I slid sideways along the wall, tripped over something, screamed, but was unable to utter a sound. The badger crawled closer, the stench became more and more overpowering. I was trapped in a corner. The badger came closer. Sweat poured down my back. The terror came from below, like a precipice. I was in a corner. The badger came closer, black, white, with bristles protruding from each cheek like antennae. I flashed the torch at it, I didn't dare do anything else, didn't dare let it lie there in the dark, didn't dare stand in the dark. We exchanged flashes. Then it rushed towards me, scraping along the floor. I squeezed into the corner, felt the rough, clammy angled walls against my shoulders and head. It crawled towards my legs, the stench made my eyes water, then it came to a sudden halt. It stopped, got its foul-smelling mouth into position and ran its snout across my feet. I was jammed in a corner with a badger smelling me. It sniffed and snuffled for an eternity with its revolting pointed snout, it seemed to be smiling, grinning, then it turned its backside to me, sat on my boots and rubbed for a good long time, never seemed to finish. I was shaking, I shone the light on the crazy animal rubbing itself clean on my immaculate boots. Then, satisfied, it crawled into another corner from where I heard squeaking and whimpering. I followed the badger on the floor, up onto some twigs and leaves, and there lay four furless carcasses with pink heads and gummed-up eyes. I stood watching. The smell rose up my nostrils like a putrid column. Then I heard Cecilie's voice, she was shouting to me from somewhere in the dark. I pointed the torch and followed the sound.

We scampered up the steps.

'You found it,' Cecilie said.

I shone the beam on her.

I could hardly breathe.

'You bastard,' I said.

Her eyes went strange in the light.

'You bastard!' I shouted.

She looked straight at me, she didn't understand what I was saying.

I had blood in my throat, I was bringing it up, acidic and grey. My voice was slurred.

'I'm not some plaything!' I shrieked. 'You can't just get me to do whatever takes your whim! D'you understand?'

I walked down Gabelsgate. She followed. My ears were pounding, as though my forehead was too small, too tight. I stopped again and shone the beam on her.

'I'm not your servant!' I yelled.

Cecilie stood stock still. The torch shook. I hurt, right out to my extremities, right out to my mangled finger.

'What did you do to it?' she asked, touching me.

And before I could answer, I was surrounded by furious dogs. They came from all sides with evil, gleaming eyes and drooling jaws, they growled and groaned and gnashed their teeth, and their coats bristled. That was too much for me, I ran, but they came after me, an army of dogs, and in the end they were all over me, barking round my feet, biting at the leather, pulling and tugging. In the end I peeled off one of my boots and threw it over a fence. The dogs bounded after it, howling.

Cecilie was standing at the top of the street.

I limped home.

The next day, my boot was returned. Cecilie brought it with her to school. She had repaired and impregnated it.

'Almost as good as new,' she smiled.

It was not. It looked like a biscuit someone had chewed and spat out.

She gave me back the boot and I stood in the playground feeling like a mentally deficient shoemaker.

Cecilie just laughed.

'I'm not angry at you,' she said.

I looked at her in amazement. *She* wasn't angry? At *me*? Didn't understand.

She picked some strands of tobacco off my jacket. Peder and Slippery Leif were standing by the fountain scowling with incomprehension.

'Don't give it another thought,' she said. 'I'm not angry.'

A host of thoughts whirled around my head, but the foremost image in my mind was Carlsberg: the distance, the subservience, the loyalty, the manicured lawn, the black servant's long fingers.

She had stunned me into silence.

'Aren't you going to try it on?' she persisted.

I whipped off my slip-on and stuck my foot in the boot. Didn't fit at all.

With a resigned laugh, she said, 'Wrong foot!'

I forced my toes in, the big toe cracked.

'Perfect,' I said. 'Perfect.'

After the badger, of course, nothing could be the same again. My boot lay at the back of the wardrobe, bitten to pieces and disfigured, unwearable, like some hidden shame lying there in the dark, and I had to wear slip-ons for the rest of the spring and felt very flat-footed. But Cecilie came to school with her thin legs in red high-heeled shoes as if she was keen to humiliate me even more, she strode around like a wading bird in the pond, all the frogs drooled in the reeds, and me, I splashed after her with webbed feet and a snorkel and a diving suit that was much too tight, I began to get low on oxygen, but I followed, it seemed almost to amuse her, I didn't really understand everything that was going on that spring. My mother, nonplussed, wondered what had happened to my boots, I said I had tripped over a barbed wire fence when we were hunting the badger, it would have been impossible to retell the whole story, about the German hiding in the air-raid shelter in 1945, she would never have believed me. But I told the story to Granddad at the old folks home one afternoon when I was alone with him and a bag of oranges. He chuckled for three quarters of an hour and told me badgers' bristles were used to make shaving brushes in the old days. He stroked his rough chin and nodded for a long time. Didn't get brushes like that any more. Badger was the best. But I had an electric razor and zero beard.

One day Cecilie wanted me to go with her to town after school to buy clothes. It was April, the snow was gone, there was the faint smell of spring in the air, patches of green.

Cecilie grabbed my arm.

'What happened to the badgers?' she asked, straight out, as though nothing had happened.

'They were put in a zoo somewhere in Sørland,' I answered, ruffled.

We walked past the American embassy. I spat on the pavement three times.

'Pig,' Cecilie said.

We stopped in Universitetsplass. Someone had erected a huge tent there and it wasn't the scouts. We took a closer look. The square was packed with people. A horrible sound locked itself onto your ear, it was like an impaled heart, beating and throbbing without end. It was the counting mechanism by the entrance. For every heartbeat a number rose with a clock-like tick. In luminous letters the sign said: *The population of the earth has increased by 100,054 people since nine o'clock today.* While we read, there were forty-three more. We looked at each other. Wow. We went into the tent.

There were large photographs on all the walls showing pollution, the population explosion, cars, motorways, factories and coffee plantations. We walked in silence and took it all in, it was not very cheerful viewing. We were living on a time bomb. We were living in a sewer. We were shitting on our own food. We were digging our own graves. The earth we had inherited and for which we should be so grateful was just a dirty tennis ball smashed out of court in the first set. There were new images for my darkroom, for my cabinet of horrors. The photographs burned a stronger pessimism in my eyes than the optimistic messages the texts tried to convey. They said we could do something about the situation, about the crisis. The whole thing was a political question, a question of economics, distribution, power, profit, solidarity. All the time I could hear the throb of the counting mechanism, another heartbeat every second, several times a second, adding to the global choir of screams.

Cecilie beckoned me over to another wall. It was an overview of contraceptive devices. It looked like cutlery for a big meal. Condoms, coils, pessaries, the pill. I discreetly felt my back pocket, my wallet, where I kept my Rubin Extra, pink, purchased some time at the beginning of the Stone Age, ordered in the name of Nordahl Rolfsen and never paid for. The pack of twelve was still complete.

48,246 people were born while we were there. The Band of the Royal Guards came down Karl Johan and drowned the heartbeats.

'Would you like to have children at some point?' Cecilie said.

'No,' I said, hearing my heart beat in my ear. 'Never.'

It was a strange spring. It arrived without Jensenius. There was something missing that spring, it was like a spring without birds. May 1 was around the corner and Stig harangued every one of us, the meeting place for the Red Front procession was outside the electricity station at two thirty, the main slogans were *No to VAT, Oppose the TUC's class co-operation policy, NATO out of Norway, Full support for the triumphant Vietnamese people!* Gunnar would be there, naturally, Ola had to study maths, Seb promised to come too, but it was never easy to know what Seb would get up to, life jumped the rails that spring for Seb after his parents got divorced. He put his harmonica on the shelf, it was The Doors now, *Waiting For The Sun*, did nothing but quote Jim Morrison, turned up zonked for a couple of lessons and was skiving school big-time. Seb couldn't give a shit that spring. But he would try to come. Yep. If they let him in. Seb grinned from under his wispy moustache. Stig interrogated me. But it was difficult because I had received an invitation, I was pretty taken aback, an invitation from Cecilie to dine at her house on May 1. I told Stig that I would make every effort to turn up, but when May 1 came and the Internationale boomed out from Solli plass, I was making my way towards Bygdøy in freshly pressed cords and a tweed jacket wondering what the hell the purpose of this was.

Cecilie was standing at the door when I arrived. Her hair hung in a loose knot behind her neck. That was enough for me. I forgot the slogans on the spot. I would eat grass if she asked me. I plodded towards her while keeping an eye open for Alexander the Great.

'Hiya,' said Cecilie, administering a hug.

'Is it just us?' I enquired.

'Mummy and Daddy are waiting inside.'

'Eh? Is this your idea?'

She just shrugged.

We ambled across the golf course, Cecilie holding my hand. I certainly needed it. Her mother appeared on the first floor balcony and waved down to us. The father made a surprise entrance from behind a sliding French door.

We walked towards him. He was standing with his hand at the ready. Cecilie let go of mine and I took his. He shook my hand warmly.

'Nice that you could come, Kim Karlsen,' he said.

I mumbled and stammered and then the mother came out too, wearing an elegant dress and jewellery on every patch of bare flesh, all that was missing was a regal coronet in her hair. She beamed a gleaming-white smile and took me away from her husband.

'Here you are at last,' she said.

I understood zilch. Sweat was flowing into my socks.

'And now you young ones can go for a walk in the garden while Daddy gets changed,' she said, nudging us onto the green expanse.

We strolled towards the apple trees. I lit a cigarette.

'What the hell's going on?' I whispered.

Cecilie moved away. She didn't answer.

I held her back.

'Is there something wrong with their memories or what? Don't they remember who I am?'

She just shook her head as if she understood just as little herself, and the knot behind her neck loosened and her hair cascaded over her shoulders like a river.

And at that precise moment I could have sworn I heard footsteps marching down Drammensveien and slogans being hurled in the air because it was half past three and time for the departure from Solli plass.

A bell rang at the palace. The meal was ready.

The table in the enormous dining room had been set. I was bewildered by all the glasses and knives and forks, and sent Cecilie a discreet glance to see where she would start. The father had put on a sailor's blazer and a silk cravat. He clapped his hands and the double doors at the back of the room opened and two ladies in black entered with steaming dishes and green bottles of white wine. There was prawn cocktail and trout and bombe glacée. Were we getting married? Alexander the Great sat at the end of the table peering happily at his watch and when several clocks struck four, he raised his glass and said with a broad, sincere smile:

'Well, now that one's scuttled, *skål*!'

It was quite evident that he had gone mad. Cecilie's father had gone mad.

A halting conversation spluttered into life. The mother wanted to hear a little about school and I gave laconic answers. Cecilie was not very helpful. My voice sounded hollow and resonated in the vast room. The serving lady stood behind me with another bottle at the ready. A fish bone got caught between two of my teeth, it stuck out at the corner of my mouth, I couldn't loosen it, it was enormously annoying. I took a sip of wine and coughed into my napkin. Conversation across the table was extracted like teeth, the father shovelled down the trout and seemed almost bored by what was going on. The mother looked embarrassed and I praised the food and said the fish tasted better than the rainbow trout I had caught myself in Lille Åklungen a light year ago.

Cecilie's father lit a big cigar and appeared to come to life.

'Fly?'

I stared through the banks of fog rolling towards me.

'Pardon?'

'Fly?' he repeated.

I had to be extremely cautious not to say anything that might irritate him. I deliberated, feverish, sweat bubbled on my scalp, my collar was wet around my neck.

'Mosquito,' I said. 'There were loads of mosquitoes.'

He blew away the smoke hovering between us with one snort.

'Fly!' he roared with laughter. 'Did you catch it with a fly?'

I flushed from my chest upwards. Cecilie giggled and received a kick from her mother under the table, I saw her, I hated all of them.

'A spinner,' I said.

The conversation over dessert died a death. The serving ladies went round as if they had been wound up mechanically and released onto the floor. I was frightened. I glimpsed Carlsberg through the double doors, his long, dark fingers. I was scared stiff.

'What are you going to do after your final exams?' the mother asked.

'Not sure yet,' I answered in a clear voice. 'Maybe study languages.'

'That's what's wrong with you young people,' the father broke in, blowing out all the candles in one breath. 'You can't see *ahead*. You don't have *perspectives*! I started off with two empty hands!'

He showed us them. The palms were sweaty and his life line stretched a long way down his forefinger. I was depressed.

'Have you any hobbies?' he continued, smacking his hands down on the table.

My head was like a swarm of bees. Answers flew in all directions. I caught the first to come to hand.

'Stamps,' I said.

He gave a nod of acknowledgement.

'That's good. That's an *investment*!'

Then, suddenly, it was over. He rose to his feet. In a second we were on the terrace in the unusually cold evening wind blowing off the fjord. It was 1 May 1969. Cecilie and her mother had to go in and fetch more clothes. I remained with her father. He gave me a cigar and lit it. We each stood in our cloud of smoke without speaking. On the lawn Carlsberg was busy sticking hoops into the ground. He looked grouchy and offended.

And then we played croquet. I lost. Cecilie's father saw to that. He pursued my ball and knocked me miles away every time he had the chance. I seemed to be stuck in a corner of the garden on my own smacking the ridiculous yellow ball with the idiotic mallet.

'Conditions are the same for everyone!' the father yelled to me as encouragement.

I thought I could hear shouts coming from Stortorget.

I took shot after shot and never hit the peg.

After I had lost five times in a row, the mother and father went in and Cecilie and I were left in the green, damp darkness.

I lit a cigarette as soon as they were behind locked doors.

'Was it you who set this up?' I asked without wasting any time.

Cecilie started to walk.

'It was Daddy's idea.'

'But what's the point?' I would not let go. I didn't understand.

'Trying to be nice perhaps.'

I ran after her.

'Didn't you say once you hated your parents? Didn't you say that?'

She just shrugged. I became annoyed.

'And what did he mean by *now that one's scuttled*? Has he gone nuts or something?'

Cecilie didn't answer.

At that moment I saw it all, the whole context, I stopped and had to draw breath. He was not mad. He was cunning. He had led me up the garden path and back again. He had feared I would drag Cecilie along with me on the May 1 procession, her first. That was why he had got me out here. We were being supervised. Jesus, how could I be so utterly bovine!

I caught up with Cecilie, who was standing with her back to me. I said nothing. She would have to work it out for herself. I plaited her hair and was filled with a tenderness I had only known once before, when Fred died. Inside, I smarted, I was one big smarting graze throughout the length of my body. I placed my hands over her breasts. She gently pushed me away.

'I have to go,' I said.

She stood still.

I walked past Carlsberg, who was removing the hoops and smoothing down the grass with his black man's hands.

I went to Gunnar's place. Heavy scene there. Stig was sitting with one gummed-up eye, swearing. Seb was on the sofa asleep. Gunnar tried to explain to me what had happened. The explanation came in fits and starts. I couldn't make much sense of it. But they had definitely been to Somewhere To Go and then they must have occupied a house. The cops had come and run riot. Gunnar's voice went into falsetto. A beer was put into my hand and I pointed to Seb.

'Stoned,' Gunnar said. 'Can't see land.'

There was a ring at the door and Ola walked in. He had his maths book under his arm and looked pale and worn. Stig held his hand over his black eye as he stared around wildly at us with the other.

'Where the hell were you while we were fightin' the police lackeys?' he groaned.

'Private lesson,' Ola said meekly.

'Alright, alright. And where were *you*?'

He was pointing at me.

'Bygdøy,' I said.

'On May 1! Who the hell do you think you are?'

'Infiltration,' I said with a forced laugh.

Soon after Seb came to. He poked up his dishevelled head and then began to cry. He cried like a baby and the tears came in floods.

'For Christ's sake!' Gunnar said and went into the kitchen.

I sat at the end of the sofa and Seb leaned against my shoulder sobbing.

'It'll be alright,' I said, stroking his greasy hair. 'It'll be alright.'

Ola ran the bath, we steered him there, undressed him and put him in the hot water. He was still crying. I poured in bath salts. Seb brightened up and asked for a beer. Stig put on Dylan and Gunnar read aloud from all the leaflets he had been given.

Then we dressed Seb, and Ola and I took him home. His grandmother was waiting for him there and we were reminded of another time when Seb had been carried home with his head under his arm and his heart askew.

That was the spring. But there was something missing. Uncle Hubert. Jensenius. Birds. The promise of summer.

Dad walked around in his shadow world, silent, closed, buttoned up inside his suit. But sometimes I caught him when he thought no one was looking, standing there with clenched fists, a pain seared across his face that made me cover my eyes. He gasped for breath and crumpled up. I was terrified, backed silently into my room, it reminded me of Goose, when Goose freaked out. Mum became more and more tired, I could see the hysteria growing as she fussed over him as if he were a little child, when he came home from the bank, in the morning over the breakfast table, where he sat mute, not even reading the paper. Mum got wrinkles around her mouth, which she tried to conceal. All of a sudden she looked old. I longed for the times when Dad ranted and raved and nagged me about my hair and what I would do after I finished school or what I was going to do that evening. But Dad was sealed with seven seals and bore the shadow of a catastrophe on his brow.

Granddad lived in the home. He had let his beard grow.

Grandma bought another budgerigar. She embroidered another night cover for the cage and put the old one at the bottom of a drawer.

Cecilie and I studied for the exams and tested each other on vocabulary. She still hadn't twigged that her father had led us up the garden path.

We didn't talk about badgers any more.

Clouds billowed up. They came from all sides, floated up into the sky, the same way as the diaphragm on a camera lens closes. That's the photograph of spring 1969: blurred, not enough light, sloppy development. Seb, Gunnar, Ola and I are sitting on the harbour front shivering, a bottle of beer in hand. The exams are over. Ola has failed. The rest of us passed by the skin of our teeth. Vestheim school is going to be closed and in the autumn we will be scattered to the winds. Ola can't be bloody bothered to take the second year again and will try to find a job. Seb has been accepted for the final year at the Experimental School. Gunnar has applied to attend the Cathedral School and I was going to start at Frogner. We open another round of beers and have just enough feeling in our fingers to light cigarettes. There was a huge mouth behind us blowing gales against our backs.

The train roared past.

We chuntered on about the latest Beatles records 'Get Back' and 'The Ballad Of John And Yoko'.

The Nesodden boat in the distance was specked with foam.

I visualised a summer with colds and unending days. The sightseeing boat chugged towards Bygdøy.

'Goin' to try to find digs for autumn,' Seb whispered. 'Not goin' to bloody live with that fat fascist.'

Something had unravelled, the foundations had been torn away, as though someone was toying with us, a cold-blooded demon.

'The whole capitalist system is rotten,' Gunnar said in a loud voice. We were right behind him and opened another bottle.

'Let's try to get into Club 7,' Seb suggested.

We just had to drink up our beers and have a piss.

Then we noticed. It was unbelievable. It was beginning to snow. In June. Large flakes fell and melted on the tarmac. We got up and stared into the sky, speechless. It was snowing.

'It's hailin',' Gunnar whispered.

'It's snowin'!' Seb shouted. 'It's bloody snowin'!'

We cavorted around. The cars in Sjølystveien skidded into an enormous pile-up. The Drammen train derailed. The royal yacht went aground and planes crashed over Nesodden.

Then a spear of sunlight shone through and the air melted.

We shaded our eyes.

The storm passed, this time.

But a cold snap lay in the air that we could not escape: chaos, divorces, hysteria.

We didn't even get into Club 7.

On the Sunday the Eagle landed in the Sea of Tranquillity, Mum and Dad were going to a bank party in town and they were not due to return until the day after. Dad had pulled himself together and the sun had coated his face with a golden tan, but his eyes were the same, they looked through everything, he kept himself to himself and his conversation was limited to 'yes' and 'no'. Mum was more unrestrained. I found a half-full bottle of red wine in the cupboard when they had gone, drank the contents and strolled down to the quayside, sat on a bollard and lit a cigarette. The muffled sounds of summer could be heard around me: a motorboat in the middle of the fjord, a young lad fishing for whiting, the song of the fishing line. Some people jumping into the water, laughter. A gull circling high in the light blue sky and homing in on a shoal. I sat feeling loneliness wrap itself around my body like clinging seaweed. Then I made my decision, and I always marvel at how quickly you can decide, that it is so easy, like a landslide in your brain, as if time no longer works. So I made my decision and went to see Fritjof at Signalen, the Nesodden headland, and found him in the shed hammering a brand new lure into shape.

'Rare visitor,' he smiled.

I could concede that. Fritjof had taught me to cast a line with tin cans, swing it over your head keeping your thumb on the line like the trigger of a six-shooter. No one beat Fritjof. They could turn up with an open reel Abu, a glass-fibre rod and the best bait, it wouldn't help if Fritjof came with his tins and lures. He cast furthest. And caught most.

He showed me the little marvel, a bent piece of iron painted silver with a red speed stripe.

Fritjof was pleased.

'Have you lost your lures?' he grinned.

'Nope.' Kicked at the gravel. 'Could I use your phone?'

He showed me into the room, stood polishing and filing while I dialled the number.

Cecilie was at home.

Afterwards Fritjof stared at me with a mischievous smile on his tanned face.

'Your parents went on the six o'clock ferry,' he said. 'Are they goin' to be away long?'

'Until tomorrow night.'

He punched his fist into my back.

'Good luck, boy! I know nothin'. I've neither heard nor seen a thing!'

We emerged on the front step.

'I owe you a krone,' I said.

'Forget it,' Fritjof said.

I sauntered back to the quayside, by the wire fence and the hedge, thinking of all the evenings I had played hide and seek here, thinking about Cecilie, thinking about all the underground passages, what was left of Signalen Hotel, thinking about Cecilie.

I heard Fritjof filing and singing.

I turned and waved.

Cecilie arrived three quarters of an hour later. She raced through the sounds of summer in a hundred horsepower boat and swerved into the quay.

'Where can I moor?' she shouted up to me.

I directed her to the hill face where the steps led down. She jumped ashore and made fast. We kissed and almost fell in the sea. Cecile was in a good mood, mmm, her hair smelt of saltwater and she had red nails.

'Didn't think you would be at home now,' I whispered.

'Mummy and Daddy are in Italy. They come home the day after tomorrow.'

My heart rejoiced under my T-shirt. We had a whole day to ourselves.

And the Eagle was on its way to the Sea of Tranquillity.

We walked hand in hand to the House. Summer was a springboard for many things. The air was full of birds, the bees buzzed in the rose hedge and the squirrels nibbled away in the trees.

Cecilie wanted to see everything. I followed her from room to room. We walked through the orchard and tasted the unripe apples and the acidic rhubarb, picked a handful of wild strawberries by the well and fed each other. And summer embraced us in friendly arms, a transparent, living darkness. Spray foamed around the bows of a ship.

I sliced the bread and slapped on the marmalade. We sat on the balcony with lukewarm milk and the Kurér between us on the table.

'Did you bring your guitar?' I asked.

'Shhh!' Cecilie whispered.

The voices on the radio spoke quickly and with enthusiasm. It would soon be nine o'clock. The Eagle would be landing at any moment.

The halyard beat against the flagpole. The huge rock lay split into two, black and gnarled.

'Hope the welcoming committee is ready,' I said.

Cecilie sat with her head bowed over the radio.

'Such daring,' she mumbled, turning up the volume.

I went down to the cellar and fetched more milk. When I returned the Eagle had landed. Cecilie clapped her hands. I lit a cigarette and peered into the sky. Couldn't see the moon.

'They've pulled it off!' Cecile yelled and flung her arms around my neck.

It was a strange time. Men on the moon. Cecile here. I held her tight. My heart was in my throat and I couldn't swallow.

It began to feel cool. I fetched blankets to cover ourselves up in. The hours slipped by in the dark. We didn't speak. The radio chattered. It wouldn't be long before Armstrong would leave the Eagle. Even the birds were quiet. We kept each other warm with nervous hands.

At twelve I went in search of more red wine. I couldn't find anything. Mum must have hidden the bottles well. I couldn't find the johnnies, either. I was sure I had left them in my wallet, they had to be there, but the wallet was empty.

When I returned to the balcony the moon was visible. It hung in the sky, pallid, as though it had been pinned on.

The voices on the radio were becoming excited.

'We'll see each other even if you're starting at Ullern, won't we?' I said.

Cecilie didn't answer.

I went back in to search for the Rubin Extra. They weren't in my wallet. I felt my pockets. Not there.

Cecilie sat hunched over the radio. Just like before. Her hair was lighter in the dark and surrounded her face like two petals, I thought. I ran a finger through it and the moon shone in her eyes. An animal snorted in the darkness outside.

'I love you,' I whispered, not knowing whether I had said it before or whether I meant it.

There were minutes to go. There were seconds. It was half past three, one summer's night in 1969. Dawn was beginning to break.

'I love you, too,' Cecilie said with her ear glued to the radio and her hand on the antenna.

I went inside again, ran up to my room and searched feverishly through my books and records and clothes. They were gone.

Then Cecilie shouted and I dashed out. The door of the Eagle was open and Armstrong was on his way down the ladder. We sat with our ears to the radio in a deep wet kiss. It was unbelievable. Then the membranes crackled and hissed and a slurred American voice rasped above us. I didn't catch what he said. Then someone clapped and Cecilie's tongue was licking the inside of my mouth.

'Come on,' she said.

I followed her. She walked with high, slow steps through the wet grass as though walking in an airless landscape, swaying, firm, playful movements. Her hair seemed to defy gravity, undulating up and down in gentle, coruscating arcs. I ran after her, but was unable to catch her. It was strange, even though she moved slowly, danced, I was unable to catch her.

Cecilie stretched her arms in the air and laughed.

The smell of sap wafted down from the birch trees.

I stopped, out of breath. I thought without really understanding: this is as far as we can go. Cecilie and I. We can't get any higher.

But I would catch up with her, that was sure. She seemed to be moving in slow motion. Birds were singing in all the trees. It was already morning and a kitten darted across the shingle.

I would catch her up.

Then Mum called out. I turned slowly, infinitely slowly, saw Mum and Dad coming up the garden path. I closed my eyes and opened them again.

Mum was standing beside me.

'Aren't you in bed?' she said.

'Been listening to the radio,' I whispered. 'Didn't think you would be here until tomorrow.'

'Dad wanted to come home,' Mum sighed. 'We came in the Saab.'

Then she noticed Cecilie. Cecilie was standing under the plum tree. I started to explain and before I was finished, Cecilie had joined us.

Dad didn't notice a thing. He just padded round the House and was gone.

Mum looked at us both. I thought it was odd that everything could go smoothly on the moon while the tiniest things on earth came to grief.

'You can sleep on the divan in the sitting room,' Mum said to Cecilie, going inside to find bedding.

'Bloody, sodding hell,' I said.

Cecilie held my head between her hands.

'Bloody, sodding hell's bollocks,' I said.

She laughed and closed my mouth with hers.

I lay there, suddenly awake, as the room became light and some magpies screeched outside the window. I heard my mother's voice.

She was whispering hysterically although Dad must have been asleep because he wasn't answering. In the end, Mum went quiet, too. Then I crept down the stairs and into the sitting room. No one was there. Cecilie was not there. I panicked, found my jeans and gym shoes and rushed out. She wasn't in the orchard, either. I ran down to the quayside. The motorboat was gone. Fritjof glanced sideways at me, he was standing on the edge, circled the line over his head, let go and the lure flew out into the fjord.

I ambled over to him.

'Left half an hour ago,' he said. 'She almost cut my line.'

I sat down beside him and bummed a roll-up.

'Mornin's are best,' Fritjof said. 'There's nothin' like mornin's. Before six. The noise starts at six.'

'Happy landin' last night,' I said.

He glanced down at me, winding in the lure.

'Which one?'

'The moon.'

'Oh, that one.' He cast out. 'Not interested in that sort of thing. We've got no business there.'

Then Fritjof went silent, let the lure sink, wound back in jerks, stopped, pulled, held his arm still, jerked again, and there it was.

Fritjof beamed with pleasure and rested his brown hand on the taut line.

'The hardest part comes now, you know,' he chatted. 'Anyone can get a bite, but not everyone can get it up.'

He pulled carefully, let the line run.

'First you have to get to know it, gauge its strength, see through its tricks.'

He let the fish go. It didn't swim out but across.

'No two are the same, you see. They have their methods, all of them. Some go straight to the bottom, others come up, some go along with you until you reckon they're home and dry and then tear themselves free at the last moment. But one thing they have in common. It's always a fight. Isn't that right? Always a fight.'

Fritjof held the can tight in his right hand, started to turn the reel gently, felt the resistance with tiny jerks, listened to the line, let it glide between thumb and forefinger.

'It's already lost,' he said, looking almost sad.

With strong sorrowful movements, he reeled in.

Then it came out of the water, a smooth, glistening mackerel, almost a swordfish. Fritjof hauled it over the edge of the wharf with care and as he broke its neck and the thick, red blood flowed over his hands, the sun rose above the ridge behind us and shone on the fish's dead, vacant eyes.

First day at school and I contrived to be late, thinking I had plenty of time strolling around the fountain, sitting on the edge and letting memories of various kinds pulsate through my brain, wondering if a letter would soon be appropriate, a letter to Nina.

I liked the regular sound of water falling behind me. I ought to write a letter, wouldn't have to be that long. Could write something about fountains. A sparrow hopped round my feet and was not in the slightest bit intimidated. Anyway, I wasn't dangerous. I wondered if Dad would ever be the same again. Wondered what the Experimental School and the Cathedral School and Ullern were like, and Ola's job. He had started as a bell boy at Norum, wondered what this autumn would bring. Then the bell rang at the bottom of Gyldenløvesgate and it sounded angry. I sprinted down the avenue and the caretaker had to show me the way to the classroom. I was the last to arrive and everyone stared at me with curiosity, and the teacher, a beehive hairdo with American glasses, greeted me with a dry handshake and pointed to my desk. My pulse was at an even 150 and everyone glared at the stranger who had burst in. I slumped down on the much too high chair and it was then I spotted him, Jørgen, he was sitting in the window row, bathed in sun with hair like a halo round his head and he was distant and transparent. I had the seat right in front of him, turned sharply, happy to see a familiar face.

'Great party at Sidsel's that time,' I whispered.

The lady banged her pointer on the desk and the lesson began.

In the break Jørgen came over to me, shook my hand and was decorum in person.

'Recognised you at once,' he said. 'Nice to see you again.'

'Nice class, isn't it.'

He shrugged.

'How's the singing going?' he asked.

'Badly,' I grinned. 'My voice isn't up to it.'

'Fancy joining the drama group?'

I certainly did not.

'What are you performin'?' I asked.

'Tolstoy's *War and Peace*,' Jørgen said.

The bell rang and we made our way to the classroom. Jørgen went to the sink and washed his hands. A flock of girls I had never seen before sized me up.

'Are you the boy who beat up the Frogner gang?' one asked.

I could hardly believe my ears.

'And danced with a skeleton at the school party?'

Before I could utter a word, they were on their way into the class and another crazy teacher entered with seven-league boots and a stopwatch.

Jørgen caught my arm and pushed me into the classroom. For the rest of the lesson I felt all eyes were on my body.

Jørgen passed me a note. I heard some of the girls giggling.

'Don't forget the drama group,' he had written.

I already had a clear idea of how the autumn was going to turn out.

In the evening Cecilie rang to say she had two tickets for the premiere of *Heaven and Hell*. And so we sat there in the blue darkness in Klingenberg while Lillebjørn Nilsen dragged his body across the canvas. Cecilie just *had* to pinch my arm every time a face she knew appeared, and that was most of the time because half of West Oslo were extras. My arm was aching all over when the show was finished and we stood waiting for the Bygdøy bus.

'L was fantastic,' Cecilie said.

I lit up.

'Worst gunk I've ever seen,' I said. 'Have we got time for a beer at Pernille?'

'I have to go home.'

'What's Ullern like?'

'Good,' she said, looking past me. 'And Frogner?'

'Good,' I said, flicking the fag-end onto the tramlines.

'Are you going to Pernille?' Cecilie asked, her eyes hanging on me for a few seconds and then letting go.

'I'll pop by to see Seb,' I said.

We gave each other a half-hearted hug and she jumped on to the running board, hesitated for a second, but did not look back.

Stood watching the bus. It was belching black exhaust fumes that mingled with the cool, gentle late summer air. It would be a long time before I would see Cecilie again, almost two years, and somewhere in my bones I knew, I knew it was all over.

Seb had moved away from home when the fat bastard had wormed his way into Observatoriegata for good. His grandmother had fixed him up with a student room in Munchsgate, next to the Experimental School. His grandmother took care of everything for him. There was nothing like it this side of fiction.

There were a couple of hundred postboxes on the wall in the hall entrance to the block and on one of them was the word Seb, just Seb. All the boxes were green apart from Seb's, his was black and red. And that was not all. There were only girls' names there. Seb was the sole male in the whole caboodle. I took the lift up to the fifth and was accompanied by a chubby girl who grinned from ear to ear and stared at me without any inhibitions.

'Are you visiting the new guy who's just moved in?' she asked.

'Goin' to Seb's,' I said.

She just kept smiling and jumped off on the fourth.

'See you,' she said.

'See you,' I said. The metal grille slid shut and the lift continued on its way. I was beginning to envy Seb in a big way.

The corridor was dirty yellow and lined with doors to student rooms. A bizarre smell of a mixture of foods met me, it was like sticking your head in a rucksack filled with uneaten packed lunches on a hot day. Not so hard to find Seb's room. He had painted the door in psychedelic colours and you only had to follow the noise. He was playing 'Soft Parade' at full blast. The door wasn't locked and there was no point knocking. I strode straight in and saw a motley group of people sitting in lotus position with mugs of peppermint tea and currant buns. A Jim Morrison vocal cut through the fug like a steel comb.

I dropped down beside Seb. He passed me the spliff.

'Been to *Heaven and Hell,*' I grinned.

'Bourgeois crap,' he said. 'Alcohol is more dangerous than drugs. Have you ever seen anyone get aggressive on shit, eh?'

A freak called Pelle with a centre parting leaned forward and drawled, 'Half a million people and not one damn fight. Not one damn fight!'

'Where was that, did you say?' I shouted.

'Woodstock, you retard. Got a chick who has a cousin who was there. It was Peace and Love, man! Half a million!'

He took a swig of tea, staring at me over the cup.

I turned to Seb.

'It's all over with Cecilie,' I said.

'Dreamt about Guri one night,' he whispered. 'Dreamt about the abortion. That it was me she was abortin'.'

He was passed a chillum and clasped his hands around it.

'Stopped playin' harmonica, have you?' I asked.

He sucked and closed his eyes.

'Listen to it. *Listen* to it. Sharman's blues.'

He slumped into a smile and sat like that until the stylus scratched to the end. Pelle and the rest of the gang stood up like gangling calves.

'Goin' for a walk in the park,' Pelle said. 'You comin'?'

'Goin' to groove,' Seb said.

They hurried out, Seb turned over the record and lay back on the mattress. I opened the window and had the town right in my face, looked across the rooftops, wondering how many lonely people there were, how many crazy, stoned, stupid, confused, angry people there were living in this steaming town. The music was hammering me black and blue from behind, I was standing in the firing line, and I remembered a time when we cruised the streets longing to be indoors, that seemed to put a damper on my thoughts.

'It's gone quickly, in fact,' I said.

'What has?'

'Time.'

Seb stood up and shook his hair.

'Time doesn't go,' he said. 'Time just *is*. Watches are for materialists and social climbers.'

He showed me his thin, bare wrist.

'It's all about livin' *now*,' he said. 'No point reminiscin'. No point plannin'. Life's about *now*.'

There was a knock at the door and in walked Gunnar. He was carrying a pile of leaflets under his arm and wandered over to the window to get some fresh air.

'The crap you buggers smoke,' he grumbled.

'The oxygen you're inhalin' is full of lead and radioactive shit,' Seb said, pointing to the sky. 'You'll die of cancer if you keep this up.'

'I know that,' Gunnar said calmly. 'But I've got no choice, have I. I have to breathe, right. But shit is somethin' you choose.'

Seb groaned and sat down on a stool.

'That's true, Gunnar. I moved to a room to get some peace.'

We boiled some more water and night settled over the town like the tea infusing in our mugs.

'Don't like your postbox,' Gunnar said.

'No socialism without freedom. No freedom without socialism,' Seb recited.

Gunnar produced another stencilled leaflet.

'The fight is against rationalisation now. School bureaucrats want to introduce the five-day week. And who the hell profits from that? The state and monopoly capitalism. The pupils lose out. The pupils and the teachers.'

Seb didn't have any sugar. The tea tasted bitter. He switched on a red lamp.

'Anyone spoken to Ola?' I asked.

'Got all the suitcases for an American travel company mixed up yesterday,' Gunnar grinned. 'Good revolutionary field work.'

'On purpose?' Seb gurgled.

'Makes no difference, does it. Action is action!'

And some time later the man himself turned up, exhausted, with an armful of beers. We flipped off the caps and toasted to the end of summer and the start of autumn.

'Have you been fightin' with the chambermaids?' I asked, pointing to the graze on his forehead.

'Oh, hell,' Ola hissed. 'The lift got stuck today, so I had to carry things up and down the stairs. One of those steep spiral staircases with iron steps. Fell headlong with five suitcases from Kuwait. Rolled down two flights. The sheik was beside himself. Threatened to turn off the oil pipelines. Had a suitcase full of porn magazines. Scattered everywhere. Shit, hangin' by a thin thread there, I was.'

We opened the other bottles of beer and Seb put on *Waiting For The Sun*.

I don't know if we knew then that we were sitting and toasting to something that was nearing its end, something that had started at some point and was already at the beginning of the end. The Beatles would split up, Jim Morrison would die and we would be searching for each other all over Europe.

We toasted with lukewarm beer as the open window brought in the sounds of Oslo city centre and a wilder world outside, waiting and ready, in the frenzied blue light of our planet.

I wrote a letter to Nina. The autumn reminded me of *Revolver*. A storm was brewing. I thought about Fred and the Trans-Siberian railway. Death came again that autumn, first of all to Grandma. She died in her sleep in September. I had never been to a funeral before. As the coffin was lowered into the ground, I recalled something I had read in The Illustrated Classics a thousand years ago, that when sailors died on board ship they were buried at sea. Don't know why that of all things came to mind. I thought about Fred. And Dragon. Now Grandma was gone. The wind picked up, shook the heavy branches and swept slowly across the ground, lifting shiny yellow leaves and releasing them again. A storm was brewing.

Mum didn't cry, she went round in a fragile silence that could crack at any moment, the surface of water, an eggshell. Dad was in his own world, locked in an insoluble crossword. We inherited Grandma's budgerigar. It was put in my room, but I didn't want the green creature with me at night. It sang and flapped its wings inside its cage, pecked at the swing and I saw its tiny heart beating under its plumage. I didn't dream about flying any more. I carried the bird into my father's room one night and for a second he seemed to wake, it was me, his son, I was bringing him a bird. He smiled, accepted the cage and poked a finger inside, in which Pym instantly pecked a hole. From that day forward Dad was lost to us. He forgot his crosswords, he forgot us, he forgot everything he had forgotten. From now on it was just him and Pym. He experimented with seed mixtures, bought a new cage, made swings and a house, cleaned its beak, served biscuits, he was on hand twenty-four hours a day for that budgerigar. And Mum walked around in her brittle silence observing everything as if we were natural disasters she could do nothing to prevent.

Then one day her silence cracked and the autumnal storm closed in. I was to be carpeted in the sitting room, Dad had his nose between the bars of the cage and Mum had her nose in a handkerchief.

'Are you taking drugs?' she sobbed.

'Drugs? Of course I'm not. Why?'

'Do you smoke hashish?' she continued, drying her wet cheeks.

'Have you gone completely loopy?' I shouted.

Mum looked at Dad, but Dad couldn't follow, and it turned out that she had read some insane article about drugs in *Nå* and it had listed all the symptoms of drug addiction. It was full of crazy things, but after *Heaven and Hell* people were quite hysterical. It took a lot of earnest explanation to get Mum back on an even keel, and I realised that it was the first time we had spoken for many years. The budgerigar cleaned Dad's nails, that was his latest trick, and I tried to persuade Mum that she had nothing to fear.

'Don't have to be a drug addict just because I pick my nose once in a while, do I,' I said calmly.

Mum just looked at me. I got a sudden itch in both nostrils, but I didn't dare stick my finger up, she would only have thought the worst.

'It says here,' she said, patting the magazine, 'that drug addicts often pick their noses and have sores.'

'Everyone picks their noses, don't they!'

She bent closer and lifted my eyelid.

'I think your eyes are red,' she said, horrified.

'I'm just a bit tired,' I said.

Mum went hysterical.

'That's what it says here! Tiredness. Listlessness. Kim, what is going on in Seb's bedsit?'

'Nothing,' I said. 'We play records and drink tea and chat.'

'Are there lots of addicts at the Experimental School?'

I couldn't be bothered to answer. We had been through this before. My mother imagined the Experimental as some sort of Indian opium den. My father was imitating one of Pym's throat sounds. Mum took a deep breath.

'You smell so strange,' she said.

'If there's any strange smell here, it's from that zoo over there!' I shouted, rising angrily from my chair.

Dad turned round.

'Don't raise your voice. Pym gets scared.'

I think Mum could have flown at him. She was gripping the sofa tight.

'You go to the toilet such a lot,' she burst out.

I started laughing. What else could you do but laugh! The laughter thundered in like a locomotive.

'Don't have to be an addict to have a crap, do you!'

'Kim!'

Mum had stood up, too.

I went into the hall and flung on the military jacket I had bought at the Urra Marching Band flea market.

'Where are you going?' Mum said.

'Out for a walk.'

She came up close and only now could I see how frightened she was, petrified, her hands were trembling and her pulse was throbbing in her neck like a runaway metronome.

'Trust me,' I insisted.

I left to the sound of crying and birdsong behind me. Outside, gusts wrapped themselves around my legs, auguring stronger winds, a storm.

I headed for Norum and Ola. His bell boy uniform was better than the school band's, burgundy with gold buttons and a flat hat. Could see his reflection in his shoes. He smuggled me into the kitchen where a stalwart girl served us coffee and cakes.

Ola sighed with contentment and leaned across the table with crumbs round his mouth.

'Goin' to the cinema with her on Saturday,' he whispered. 'Name's Vigdis.'

'Well I never. Small world. She lives on the floor below Seb.'

Ola's eyes flickered and the furrow above his nose grew into a roadworker's trench.

'Does she?' was all he said

'How's Kirsten then?'

Ola cast wild glances in all directions.

'Shhh, for Christ's sake!'

Vigdis returned with the coffee pot and flicked a speck of dust off Ola's shoulder. He sank beneath the weight of her fingers. I was seriously concerned that he would start stammering again. Vigdis looked at me, smiled, didn't recognise me.

'Any news on room 23?' she asked, laughing behind the words.

Ola shook his head, sending her an arch smile.

Then Vigdis went to the kitchen. A gaggle of chambermaids burst in. We wandered off to the reception desk.

'What's 23?' I asked.

'A room,' Ola grinned. 'A couple from Fredrikstad. Honeymoon. Haven't left the room for four days.'

A bell rang and Ola had to lend a hand, a taxi packed with fat Germans.

'You goin' to Seb's tonight?' I asked.

'No time,' Ola panted carrying four leather cases and a protective suit cover over his shoulder.

'Say bye to Vigdis,' I said and headed for town.

Seb was not at home. I strolled up to the school and found him in the art room. He looked like a full-blooded Red Indian, he had painted his face and plaited his hair.

'Greetings, Red Fox,' he intoned, flourishing a brush.

Two girls were busy at the lathe, water and leather flying everywhere. An old man sat carving a piece of wood.

'Your smoke signals have been received, Yellow Peril,' I said.

'Outta sight!' Seb bleated. 'Outta sight!'

We shuffled down to the common room where the bridge club was in session. Seb poured cold tea into two grubby mugs.

'Point of no return,' he grinned. 'It was in the *Rollin' Stone*. The Beatles have split up.'

The tea lay bitter under my tongue.

'New LP coming out in a couple of months,' I said.

'Oh, yes. It's all on tape. But there's nothin' after that.' He swallowed the slop. 'And that's fine. Should pack it in when you're at the top. They should've stopped after *Sergeant Pepper*. Fab funeral. Do you agree, Green Eagle?'

'Seen anythin' of Gunnar?' I asked.

Seb pulled a grin and rolled a magical mystery tour.

'Busy man. Been made big chief of Cathedral School.'

I took a plug of Mac Baren's.

'Apparatchik,' I said. 'That's like Gunnar.'

'Stig was here yesterday lecturin' on anarchism. A belter.'

'Wow. Has he shifted course?'

'Fell foul of the party line. He's worried about his little brother now. Stalin has blood on his whiskers.'

Seb blew four rings in the air.

'Gunnar knows what he's doin',' I said.

'And God won't forgive him,' Seb grinned, mashing the dog-end.

Pelle came in and was on an upper. I didn't like Pelle. There was something about his eyes you couldn't quite work out. He had black nails and acne. He ignored me.

'Meetin' in the park,' he whispered to Seb.

I walked with them to the Royal Palace. I thought of my mother and my head ached. They stood in groups under the trees, thin, black figures. The wind howled across the bare landscape. A match lit up a yellow face. Pelle went over to someone standing alone by a bush.

'Sweetie shop's open for tonight,' Seb whispered, the paint burning on his face.

'Dope?'

Seb chuckled.

'Nothin' special,' he said. 'Nothin' special. No point goin' to Bogstad if you can have a free trip to Katmandu.'

Pelle returned with a cupped hand. He nodded to Seb and they began to walk down the steps. I hesitated. Seb turned.

'Are you comin' or not?' he called.

I deliberated. The wind was blowing through the trees, making an unpleasant dry sound.

'Gotta be off,' I said.

Seb and Pelle disappeared from view. I stood in the weather-ravaged park. The terrain was hard and rugged. The wind tore at my hair. I saw the lights down Karl Johan, the neon signs, Freia, Idun, Odd Fellow. Behind me matches were lit like staccato fires. I already knew that this autumn had gone off the rails, we were off the rails, I knew that, and what the hell could I do about it?

I went home and wrote another letter to Nina.

All mothers loved Jørgen, except his own. There was a strange atmosphere at his place in the dark flat in Jacob Aallsgate, heavy, gloomy vibes, as though the whole house was guarding a secret that must never be revealed. It smelt of moths and misappropriated funds, the doors creaked and the curtains were always drawn. Deep in despair Jørgen's mother paced to and fro, with protruding eyes and white knuckles, and in felt slippers. The father was a toiletries sales rep and almost never at home. The first time I went there, it was the Saturday Beate held a class party, but I had decided once and for all that this year I was going to keep a low profile, I didn't want to risk any more rooftop walks or dances of death happening, so I didn't go to the get-together, and neither did Jørgen. Instead we stayed at his place sipping strawberry liqueur and getting quite merry and playing The Mothers of Invention. His mother glowered at me with hateful eyes when I arrived, didn't even shake my hand, just gave me the once-over as though I had come straight from the lab and was radioactive. Now she was padding outside the door releasing tiny whimpers and sighs from between pursed lips. Days were pretty tough at home with my mother in accelerated mode and my father going to seed, but, wow, this was worse, Jørgen should pack his things before he became environmentally damaged. And I told him so.

'It'll pass,' Jørgen smiled.

'Don't be so sure,' I said. 'The only solution is to get away in time.'

'Sounds like you're thinking of making a break for it as well,' Jørgen joked.

'After our final exams. Not stayin' a second longer.'

Jørgen laughed and leaned back, then his mouth tightened and he sat staring at the ceiling.

'One day they'll realise,' he whispered. 'One day they'll understand.'

'Understand what?' I asked, pouring more pop.

Jørgen didn't answer. He closed his eyes and took a deep breath. Behind him there was a large poster of Rudolf Nureyev. He didn't have such long hair after all. He was perched on the tips of his toes and under his tights his balls bulged out like a cabbage. Jørgen sat under the light from the blue lamp on the desk and for the first time I noticed how handsome he was, the lines of his face were clean and graphic, his cheekbones prominent, the narrow cheeks were in shadow as though he had applied make-up, I couldn't take my eyes off his face and I understood why the girls were disappointed when they heard that Jørgen wasn't going to the class party.

Jørgen must have been aware I was watching him. I spilt my drink on my trousers. He wiped it off with his handkerchief. Outside, his mother was pacing the dark corridors.

'Why didn't you want to go to the class party?' Jørgen asked.

I lit a cigarette. It was a funny evening. When he asked like that, I knew I would lay all my cards on the table. It seemed so easy to be frank with Jørgen, in the flat with the dark and hideous secret honesty was not an issue.

'Tend to get plastered,' I said. 'My brain misfires and I lose all sense of proportion. Don't seem to be myself any more. I'm not in charge. It's pretty annoyin'.'

'Does it only happen when you're drunk?'

'It's definitely worse then. Have mild attacks when I'm sober, too. Especially at night. Used to scream. Screamed so much I couldn't speak the day after.'

'I get frightened sometimes,' Jørgen said. 'Sudden attacks. Dead frightened. And I know there's nothing to be frightened about. I know that, but I'm still scared out of my wits. Lasts a couple of hours. Then it passes.'

'Sounds nasty,' I said.

'That time at Sidsel's party,' he went on, 'when you chased the Frogner gang away, I was certain you would be my pal and I would never have to be frightened again.'

I held up my hand. The forefinger was an eyesore, a sweaty hook with a nail on it.

'This is what sorted that out,' I laughed. 'They'd broken it a few weeks before after I'd hurled a stone at one of them. Hit 'im in the face.'

Jørgen looked at me bewildered, then he laughed and poured red wine into the glasses.

'At any rate, I'm fine now, Kim. Haven't been frightened since the day you entered the classroom.'

'Why didn't *you* go to the party?' I asked.

'I get bored. Parties like that bore me.'

I needed a leak and crept out into the chamber of horrors. The mother was there in an instant, my smile was not contagious, she just stood there keeping me in check with her festering suspicion and ominous secret.

'Loo?' I slurred and she pointed to the door next to me. She was without language and voice, her eyes were dead, there was something she had seen which had reduced them to ashes.

I went to the loo and emptied my bladder. Afterwards I happened to see my face in the mirror. It was pale and unhealthy-looking. But I had washed my hair and it crackled all the way round my head like black electric wires. I combed it and heard it crackle in my comb as though visions were on their way out of my skull.

Jørgen was sitting on the windowsill flicking through an acting copy.

'Thought any more about the drama group?' he asked.

'No.'

He threw the pages over to me. *War and Peace*.

'We've got a role for you,' he said with enthusiasm.

'Me? Nothin' doin'. Hate the theatre. Went to see *Brand* with my mother once and almost had a haemorrhage.'

Jørgen laughed.

'The theatre is the truth,' he exclaimed, in all seriousness. 'Isn't it? We're acting all the time, with each other. It makes us lie. We fool each other and pretend not to notice. But on the stage everyone is clear about their role. Only on the stage are we truly *honest*.'

'Last time you said you wanted to be an actor because you were bored.'

'I'm bored with lying,' Jørgen said. 'I'm bored with people talking at cross purposes.' He sent me a quick glance. 'And you wanted to be a singer!'

'Because I wanted to drown out all the bullshit,' I laughed.

Jørgen sat down beside me.

'We need to fill one more role,' he said, flicking through the manuscript. 'The messenger. We need a powerful voice!'

'How many lines?' I asked.

'One,' Jørgen said.

'I'll think about it,' I said.

As I trundled home that night and the wind swept across Vestkanttorvet and the moon crossed the sky like a football, I thought that Jørgen, Jørgen was going to be my fixed point in the time to come, Jørgen was the anchor, Jørgen was the eye of the storm: the circle of calm in the midst of all the chaos.

Gunnar dropped by one evening, with a pile of leaflets as usual. He smuggled them into my room and started sorting them. I had to distribute *No To Rationalisation* the day after. There was no urgency about the solidarity committee's reaction to the lie that American troops were being withdrawn. It was fine if I handed them out on Saturday in the lunch break.

Gunnar spoke fast, in a staccato way, didn't even have time for a cup of tea. Was on his way to a student council meeting.

I started perspiring at the back of my knees.

'Is there no one else who could distribute them?' I asked cautiously.

Gunnar's eyes bored into me like harpoons.

'What do you mean?'

'I agree with the content, no question, but I don't quite get the standin' in squares and holdin' speeches.'

Gunnar shuffled the piles of leaflets.

'I don't reckon that's what's botherin' you most,' he said.

'Why's that?'

'Think you've yelled in squares quite a few times,' he went on. 'At the school dance. At Dolphin.'

'Right. That's why I'd been thinkin' of keepin' a low profile this year. Takin' things easy.'

Gunnar's glare didn't waver.

'That's a pretty weird attitude. It's fine that you don't want to make a prat of yourself, but political work is not the bloody same, is it.'

'Didn't say it was, but you're still in the spotlight, aren't you.'

'Spotlight, yes. Aren't you joinin' the drama group?'

He had me.

'Ye-ah. One line.'

'And so you don't want to hand out leaflets?'

'Didn't say I didn't want to.'

'What are you sayin'? Do you think the revolutionary movement has time for such trivialities? Monopoly capitalism is earnin' fat profits on that crap. Are you gonna distribute leaflets or not?'

'Give me them, you bugger.'

He counted a hundred of each and grinned.

'Good, comrade Kim. You'll get another pack next month.'

I put the leaflets in the drawer where I used to hide pornographic films in the old days, and Gunnar was already on his way out. A wild sound came from the sitting room. He stopped and looked at me.

'It's just Pym,' I said.

'Pym?'

'Dad's budgie.'

In fact, he had taught it to whistle on command now. He coaxed the notes out of the poor green creature by chirping himself. Sometimes I wondered who had the upper hand, wondered whether it might be Pym who was making Dad sing. It was beginning to get on my nerves.

We stood listening for a while, Gunnar and I. Now Dad was whistling.

'Not havin' a great time, our fathers, are they,' Gunnar whispered.

I shook my head.

'Dad's on the point of packin' it in. And Mum's joined a Christian sewin' circle.'

That was when I noticed Gunnar was trying to grow a beard.

'Can lend you my mower,' I grinned, stroking his chin.

He blushed and hurried out of the room. In the hall my mother was staring at the badges on his jacket. He had the full complement: Marx, Engels, Lenin, Mao, Ho Chi Minh, FNL. Gunnar puffed out his chest and then scooted off.

Mum held me back.

'Is Gunnar a Young Socialist?' she said.

It sounded so comical. She said it as though it were a venereal disease, worse than syphilis, incurable and contagious for many generations to come. I think she felt she ought to wash her mouth out with turps after saying it. *Young Socialists*. Her lips were cracking.

'What are you laughing at?' she shouted.

'Nothing.'

'You didn't answer. Is Gunnar… a Young Socialist?'

She rubbed the back of her hand across her mouth.

'Don't know,' I said.

'Are *you*?'

Pym and Dad were whistling in unison.

'*Are* you?!' Mum repeated, sounding demented.

'No,' I said.

'They do weapon training, you know! In Nordmarka. They've got supplies of arms!'

'I don't know anything about that.'

'They said so on TV!'

'If you believe everything they say on the box, things are in a bad way.'

I made a beeline for my room.

Mum stomped after me.

'Are you suffering from nerves, Kim?'

'Nerves? Why?'

'You walk so fast. I've noticed that for a long time now. You walk… as though someone's after you!'

'Take it easy now, Mum. There's no one following me, is there!'

'Are you sure you're not taking drugs?'

'Have you read that somewhere too? That addicts walk fast, eh?'

'Answer me honestly, Kim!'

'I've just been elected to the Supreme Soviet and I've been a junkie for nine years.'

I slammed the door behind me. Mum tore it open.

'Don't you dare talk to me like that, Kim! Don't you dare!'

'And you keep your hands off my wallet. From now on I want my contraceptives left alone!'

Her face fell, all her strength seemed to ebb away, she slowly closed the door.

Then she ran into the sitting room and I heard a medley of her sobs and Dad and Pym.

Those were the days.

After the class party which I did not attend I was met by glares everywhere I went, I became agitated, I was unable to take a step in peace, felt the eyes all over my body, like suckers. In one break Beate ambled up to me and stood there with that vinegary smile of hers and faced me down.

'Shame you couldn't come to the class party,' she said.

'Yes,' I said, staring beyond her. Over by the rubbish bins there was a group of girls grinning and whispering.

'You're such fun at parties, aren't you?' Beate continued.

I scented a crisis looming and began to look for a way out.

'False rumours,' I said.

'It was in the school paper,' she cooed.

'The editor got the boot,' I parried.

'But you and Jørgen had a cosy time, did you?'

My voice stuck in my throat. Beate tossed back her hair.

'There he is by the way. I won't disturb you.'

She wiggled back to the circle, they stood watching Jørgen and me.

'What the hell did the bitch mean by that?!' I said.

'Nothing to worry about,' Jørgen mumbled. 'Have you learned your line?'

'Napoleon's comin'! Think she's got it in for me. Why's Beate so bloody pissed off with me, eh?'

'You have to put more feeling into the words, Kim. You have to make the audience quake!'

The bell rang and we trooped off to class. There was a suspicious silence when we arrived, a gasp ran through the rows. Jørgen took his seat, distant, condescending, superior. I stopped, stared at the blackboard. Dick was there, a strapping lad from Smestad, close-set eyes, he had drawn a large heart and written names inside. Jørgen + Kim. Something hot and painful descended into my stomach, my head burned. The laughter exploded and Dick stood there, grinning proudly, the laughter washed over me, sticky and sour like mildewed syrup, wet sugar, I had to fight my way out of the laughter lava streaming from their gaping, red, slavering mouths.

'Wipe it off,' I said.

The class went quiet.

Dick wrote on the board: Please leave!

The laughter burst out anew, I was drowning in the laughter, gasping for air and I knew I was on the point of losing control.

Dick walked back to his desk. I stopped him. He peered down at me. Then I spat into his face, a magnificent, thick green gobbet.

It went quiet again. A squeal of surprise emerged from Dick, he raised his hands.

Then I struck. I hit him with a force I never knew I possessed. My arm was a bomb, a canon, my fist an iron ball, and Dick folded in the middle like a french loaf. I grabbed him by the scruff of his neck, hauled him up to the board and wiped it with his face and hair.

The room was stunned into silence.

Blood and fury raged through my veins.

I let Dick go and sat down. Jørgen was white, motionless. No one looked at me.

The teacher burst in as Dick was crawling along the floor. I had to keep a firm hold on my chair. The backwash was on the point of dragging me through the window.

'What's going on here?' Klausen whined.

No one answered. There was a two-fold silence. Dick lugged himself onto his chair. Klausen tapped with her pointer and then she began to talk about case and conjugations.

So I no longer had a low profile, I was as visible as a rose-painted monolith. But strangely enough I was not pestered any more, they directed their suckers elsewhere now, Jørgen and I were left in peace. I was allowed to go in peace in the way a leper is: everyone avoids him. Everyone knows what he is like. Jørgen was the only person who wanted to know anything about me. He didn't once make any mention of the drawing on the board.

Things continued like this until I lost my self-confidence. I quite simply lost my confidence and couldn't bring myself to distribute leaflets at the gate, it was like putting yourself in the firing line, I couldn't do it. I lied to Gunnar's face and accepted more leaflets about rationalisation at school, VAT, class cooperation, Vietnam, the pile grew in the drawer, my bad conscience grew in my stomach, I had the same feeling I had when I didn't eat the packed lunches my mother made and they swelled in my school bag, green and foul-smelling. I couldn't bring myself to throw away the leaflets, either. Every day I put it off. Soon I would be wading in leaflets and I still hadn't received an answer from Nina, the only letter I had received was from the army, I would be summoned to a call-up medical in April next year.

My mother was overjoyed when she heard I had joined the drama group. She changed from that very instant, as though she had snapped her fingers and decided to trust me in the future, not a word about Young Socialists or drugs, she just talked about the theatre and said something very similar to what Jørgen had said, that the theatre was the truth. I didn't quite understand that, but I was relieved that my mother had calmed down and would not be having a nervous breakdown every time I went to the toilet or picked my nose. But the truth they had talked about, I couldn't see that. Sometimes I lay awake at night thinking about what truth was, I did, and I tried to list a few examples. Dick is a shit. But Beate certainly didn't think so. She was positive I was the shit. The Beatles is the best group in the world. But my mother and father definitely did not agree. I compressed my thoughts: I am me. My brain was steaming. Who the hell was I? Who was I in others' eyes? Jørgen's? Gunnar's? Was I just as many people as there were eyes? In Nina's?

Didn't sleep a lot on such nights.

There were many such nights.

And I didn't discover the truth in the drama group, either. That was for certain. We rehearsed in the gym every Thursday. The coach was a huge woman with a bosom that projected into the room like the Alps. Her name was Minni. She insisted that *War and Peace* was about people today even though it had been written in the previous century. Tolstoy was ahead of his time, like all great artists. As background music she had chosen Jan Johansson's *Jazz in Russian*, she almost went weak at the knees at the brilliance of her own idea: it would give the audience a hint that the play was also about our time, wouldn't it. I suggested projecting pictures from *The War Game* on a big canvas in the background, but that didn't meet with approval, on the contrary, it was a pathetic idea. One must not frighten the audience, alienate them, it was a balancing act, a balancing act between war and peace, between the performers and the audience, as Minni expressed it. That sounded impressive. And I was searching for the truth, but I could not find it. Tolstoy's brick of a novel had been planed down to a one-act show. Jørgen played someone called Pierre. His counterpart was a girl from the second class, Astrid, she was to bring Natasha to life. There were nine others plus me, the messenger with one fateful line. In Tolstoy's novel there were a good five hundred characters.

But we all looked forward to receiving our costumes from the National Theatre.

Seb's place was jumping and I didn't want to be part of it. A grotty clique sat there smoking spliffs and drinking tea, hookahs were gurgling and chillums puffing, and incense hung in the room like the smoke spewed out of a perfume factory chimney. I dropped by some nights but soon gave it a miss, don't know quite what it was, I was bored with them sitting there, wasted, not looking at each other, just picking fluff out of their navels, putting on mystical smiles and rolling their eyes. Solo sprints in their heads, ego trips on package tours. But one evening Seb had swept the Slottsparken crew off the floor, it was going to be the great night, it was set up to be the greatest night for many years. Gunnar was there, without his leaflets, Ola was there, didn't bat an eyelid when we called him Gigola. And Seb was compos mentis and freshly scrubbed. We were all there and on the turntable was the new Beatles LP *Abbey Road*. We passed the cover round, scrutinised it minutely, ran our fingertips over it. The silence was pregnant with hot anticipation, it was now or never. We pinned back our ears, Seb started the record player and we didn't say a word for forty-six minutes and twenty seconds. Then we lay on the floor, burnt out, staring at the ceiling with eyes closed, and each of us, every one of us, wondered for how many years, how many LPs, we had lain like that, a whole century rushed through our brains, a pile of calendars flipped their pages through our hearts. We were drained and happy. Then we lit the goodies, Capstan laid a smoke-screen around the room and comments were fired off from all sides. Seb's two songs were the best he had ever done, he had surpassed himself, produced two pearls from the oyster, the tunes sat like silver coils in our ears. Gunnar rocked his socks off on 'I Want You' and was pretty heavy on 'Come Together'. Even Ola had knocked together a groove that was up there, 'Octopus's Garden', he lay on his back with a proud smile winding round his face.

'I'm gonna join the navy after all!' he shouted. 'I'm gonna join up!'

And I loved the singing on 'Oh Darling!', the voice was on the point of breaking, but it didn't, it hovered and quivered towards the impossible, on the brink, on the brink. And on 'Because' all the voices intertwine, they were the best harmonies we had ever heard, the Beach Boys and Sølvguttene could pack up their larynxes and start tap dancing instead. We put it on again and didn't say a word for forty-six minutes and twenty seconds. Then we played the B-side again and there was no doubt. It was the best. It wasn't necessary to say anything. It was the best. It was The Beatles. We dispatched all impure thoughts into the cellar, about splitting up, about arguing, and we worked ourselves up into a state of extreme optimism: this was just the beginning. We were on the threshold of a new calendar: from 28 October 1969, one bitterly cold evening between autumn and winter. We began to talk about The Snafus again, perhaps it wasn't too late after all, the hell it was. After sailing through our final exams we could soon find a job to earn some cash for instruments and amplifiers. Ola was already there. Fantastic. Seb had a pile of songs already written. Neat. That was how we spoke, we raised each other's spirits and held them there, we had a bedsit in heaven, it was late at night and the sun was shining all around us, we were floating in light and music and the vibes were as gentle as a kitten's paws.

Then the door creaked and the comedown started. Pelle and the gang burst in with bloodstained faces and torn jackets. They stood there swaying and were way off course.

'The pigs cleared the park,' Pelle groaned. 'Shit. Went berserk. Must have had fly agaric soup for supper.'

The boss had spoken and they collapsed on the floor. Scattering earth from their hair and clothes.

'They arrested at least twenty of us,' whispered a white-faced jessie.

'Did you have anythin' on you?' Seb asked nervously.

Pelle gave a little smile and pulled out an oval tin.

'The gods are with me. I sought shelter behind Camilla Collett. Said I was her grandson.'

He put the tin on the table and the others crowded round it, went down on their knees as if it were a damned altar. Gunnar looked annoyed, Ola tried to put a record on.

Pelle pointed to the cover with a filthy finger.

'A con,' he scoffed. '*Abbey Road* is utter junk.'

He fiddled with the tin and removed the lid.

Now Chief Sitting Bull had gone too far.

'What do you mean by that?' I demanded to know, and pronto.

He squinted at me, screwing up his face as if it were a dishcloth.

'Paul McCartney's dead,' he said. 'He isn't on the record at all.'

I couldn't believe my own ears. They froze to ice. They fell off. Ola and Gunnar inched closer.

'Dead? When?'

'Four years ago. Car accident.'

'Four years! He wasn't on *Sergeant Pepper* either, then! Or *Revolver*! Come down to earth, you flyin' Dutchman!'

Pelle rolled his eyes and held a pill in the air.

'Got a cousin in the States who knows a chick in the Midwest.'

'Last time it was a chick who had a cousin!' I yelled.

Pelle interrupted.

'It was in the papers, pea-brain. He died in a car accident in '65. So they got hold of a guy who looked like the guy and used him instead.'

'Who could sing just the same as Paul too! Are you a complete idiot or what!'

'The boys in the studio fix that, you know, you turnip. Distortion and so on.'

Pelle's composure was getting on my nerves. I could see that he had the ace of spades up his sleeve.

He placed the LP sleeve in front of him on the floor.

'Look here, mister. McCartney's left-handed, isn't he. D'you think a left-handed person'd hold a cigarette in their right hand? And McCartney isn't walkin' in synch with the others. Eh? Is he! Now keep up, brother. He's *barefoot*. And that's an ancient symbol of death. Right from Vikin' times, man.'

Pelle looked around with a triumphant expression. My eyes were burning like dry ice. Couldn't get a word out.

Pelle snapped his fingers.

'And look at his clothes. John's dressed in white like a priest. Ringo's dressed in black, mournin' clothes. And George's in workin' gear, he's the gravedigger.'

Pelle rolled a pill in his hand.

'Can you see the VW there? Have a good look at the number plate, man. 28IF. Black on yellow. Paul would've been twenty-eight, if he'd lived. What about that?'

I had to counter-attack.

'Why are they showin' that now, eh?' I stammered. 'When he's been dead for four years!'

'Because The Beatles are washed up, anyway. The Beatles have split up, man. Can't you get that into your skull?'

I could have strangled Pelle on the spot, grabbed the broad leather belt he swanked around in and strung him up from the lamp.

'Not only that,' he continued. 'Not only that, this isn't the first time they've presented him in this way.'

He eased *Sergeant Pepper* out of the pile, turned it over and pointed.

'Can you see the badge on Paul's shoulder? OPD. You know any English? Because that stands for Officially Pronounced Dead.'

I crumbled. The pipe was cold. My head was a blasted plain. My blood crept through my body like an earthworm.

Pelle grinned.

'Think we need some brain food, folks.'

'What's that?' Seb mumbled.

'Amphetamines,' Pelle whispered. 'Keeps you clear-headed and in a good mood the whole day through.'

He swallowed one himself, the other Red Indians munched too, Seb tried, Ola wasn't interested, Gunnar just glowered at Pelle and turned away, I took a capsule and washed it down with flat beer.

Afterwards there was a long silence in the room.

The death notice lay on the floor.

After a while Gunnar left. Ola followed him. I stood up and it was as if I had left my head behind, I had to lift it up, but couldn't get it into position.

I ran after Gunnar and Ola. They were waiting in the lift. There was a mirror on one wall. I saw myself step into the iron room. Gunnar pressed the ground floor button and as we sank I flowed out through walls, poured in all directions, disappeared from the mirror's matt surface.

Fear slashed at me like a blunt axe.

'Am I here?' I asked.

Gunnar and Ola could only stare at me.

'Am I here?' I screamed.

Gunnar dragged me onto the street. The cold wind kneaded my face and gave wings to my fear. I began to run. They followed me and held me.

'You're a bloody idiot!' Gunnar hissed close to my ear. 'Why did you have to swallow that damned pill.'

Ola looked jumpy, at any rate he couldn't stand still, he was running round me.

'Throw up,' Gunnar said. 'Throw up for Christ's sake!'

I stuffed my finger down my throat and brought up the beer and tea. I tried again until I tasted bile on my palate.

Gunnar thumped me on the back. I slid down round the lamp post. They dragged me to my feet.

I went home between them.

'Have to put an end to the drugs at Seb's,' Gunnar kept saying. 'Pelle's a reactionary prick!'

The town and the wind swept across my skin, everything around me seemed so close, so well-defined. It was like waking up, we approached Skillebekk and the world came towards me with a new clarity, as if I could see through anything. Throwing up helped, I thought. It was as if my head had been washed, my eyes scrubbed. I almost became religious. Everything felt so strong, as though the volume in the world had been turned up and someone had brought the image into focus. Jesus.

We stopped in Solli.

'How d'you feel, you prat?' Gunnar asked.

'Fine. Very good.'

I hugged them, gave them a big squeeze.

Then I wandered home alone. Dad was in the sitting room with Pym. He wanted to teach Pym how to speak.

'How did the drama group go today?' Mum asked.

'Super,' I said.

I couldn't be bothered with any supper and went to bed. Clocks were ticking everywhere, I could hear Mum's and Dad's wrist-watches ticking, too. They were mincing time into minute pieces, I had to hold my ears, buried myself in the pillow and wound the duvet round my head.

But the sounds just got louder and louder.

And I became more and more awake.

I felt like a sleepless old mattress from which the springs kept popping one after the other, singing with a rusty, ripping noise. I ran around myself, around a large inconceivable emptiness: insomnia. In the gym lessons I flew over the vaulting horse, but in mid-flight I forgot what I was doing and fell astride the box. Then I clambered up the ropes like a terrified monkey, but when I hit my head on the ceiling I forgot where I was and slid down burning the skin on my hands. I couldn't sleep and was in constant activity. I did my homework like never before, but when I had read half a page of history I couldn't remember a thing, my mind was a blank, and then I started another book, and so it went on. Springs pinged out everywhere, from my eyes, ears, nose, mouth, rusty piercing music that kept me awake, wide awake, night after night. I didn't even sleep in lessons. Life steamed ahead at 78 rpm, and one night I lay with the weight of the world on my body, a stinking, sweaty, revolting world, when I remembered the dream I had had in the summer of '65 when Mum had been playing fancy dress and she had stood naked and frightened on the cold floor. I dreamt I was dead. That I was in a coffin and felt myself being lowered. I pushed the world aside and jumped out of bed, soaking wet, rusty, with fear like a fishing spinner in my heart. I started to search for more signs, and I sank deeper and deeper into the unreality that was wrapped around me like a dirty sheet.

I played all The Beatles records I owned, and that was all of them. I examined them from top to bottom, copied down the lyrics and fine-combed them, studied the covers under my philatelist's magnifying glass, filled a whole album with pictures of Paul before and after '65. I searched and I found. I was standing in a rampant river with a sieve and found the coffin nails. On *Sergeant Pepper* Paul stood with his back to us. And a left-handed bass guitar was placed on a grave. A wreck of a car burst into flames. A priest held a hand in benediction over him. On *Magical Mystery Tour* John, George and Ringo had red carnations in their jacket lapels, but Paul's was black. On *Revolver* Paul was the only one who was photographed in profile. John sang 'one and one and one is three' on 'Come Together'. One 'one' was gone. One 'one' was missing. I stood for hours in front of the mirror studying my face. I had pictures of Paul McCartney everywhere. That was how that autumn passed. Black frost paved the streets and windows were draughty. Sweat froze to ice crystals on your skin, the cold slowly permeated me and put me into deep-freeze mode.

Gunnar popped by on lightning visits to deliver more leaflets. The piles grew in my drawer, soon there would be no more room. One evening, on his way to a meeting as if propelled by some kind of rubber band motor, I stopped him.

'How's Seb?' I asked, could hardly speak, my teeth were chattering like a penguin's.

'Okay I s'pose. Have you got a cold?'

'Is he still takin' those pills?'

'Shit knows what he's up to. But I do know for certain that he should stop, and right now. Pelle's an arsehole.'

Gunnar was on his way to the door again. I creaked after him.

'D'you think they're dangerous, those tablets?'

He held my gaze.

'They're not exactly liquorice!'

We smiled at each other, fleetingly.

'D'you still collect autographs?' I asked.

'Won't give up until I have Mao's,' Gunnar said.

We stood shuffling our feet and thinking about the IFA salt pastilles and porn magazines.

'I can get Lin Pio's autograph,' I grinned.

'I've got it, you bugger,' Gunnar screeched. 'You're not gonna trick me twice!'

He put his hand on my shoulder, then withdrew it quickly as if his hand had frozen.

'You can't even take booze, Kim. Keep off that gunk. D'you promise?'

I looked at Gunnar.

'Yes,' I said.

'Get those leaflets handed out before Saturday!' he shouted and was gone.

I couldn't rest, I was as busy as Gunnar, but Gunnar was achieving something, he was turning out stencilled leaflets and had a goal, I was just going in circles, I was a carousel round the mirror, insomnia, the record player and fear. In the school breaks I couldn't stand still, wandered up Gyldenløvesgate, tried to find peace by the fountain, by the covered, frozen fountain. One day Jørgen happened by as I was sitting there.

'You're skipping rehearsals,' he said quietly.

'I don't have time,' I said.

He ruffled my hair and smiled.

'You have to come next time,' he said, suddenly serious again. 'We're going to run through the whole play.'

I lit a cigarette and started to speak.

'I've written a letter to a girl,' I said. 'Nina. Her name's Nina. We went out together a few years ago. But she hasn't answered. But she sent me loads of letters I didn't answer. Think it's revenge, don't you?'

A doleful expression fell over Jørgen's face, a shadow that dissolved slowly.

'I'm going to England in the Christmas holidays,' he said.

'Great,' I said. 'Liverpool?'

'London.'

He folded his hands and leaned across to me.

'I'm nervous,' he said.

'She could bloody answer me, couldn't she. I've written *four* letters!'

'Nothing wrong with being happy and sad at the same time,' Jørgen said.

'Yes,' I said. 'Of course. That's what it's all about.'

'Do you love Nina?'

'Yes.'

'She'll write. If you love her.'

'Are you goin' to England?' I asked.

'Yes,' Jørgen said. He almost sounded glum.

'Napoleon's comin'!' I shouted.

The bell rang and we ran back to the chalk and wet sponge.

One Friday I skipped the last two lessons and raced down to the Experimental School. I had meticulously gone through the texts on *The White Album* and a line in 'Green Onion' reverberated in my brain: *The walrus was Paul.* I had leafed through all the dictionaries in the Deichman library and discovered that the walrus was an ancient symbol of death. I was in a state of permafrost. I was full of fossils and solidified energy. The only living thing in me was fear. I sprinted down to Akersgata and found Seb in the common room. A girl was standing in front of him screaming.

'You're a bastard! A bloody bastard!'

Seb tried to calm her down. The girl banged her fists on the piano keys and swung her scarf round her neck.

'*You're* the one who destroys things!' she raged. 'You destroy everything for the whole school.'

'I can do what I like,' Seb said.

'Not here you can't! Here you're part of a community. And when you bring shit in here, you destroy everything for the rest of us. Don't you understand? You're the kind of person the Ministry of Education and Kjell Bondevik are after!'

The girl turned on her heel and stormed out of the room. Seb stood by the piano which was still ringing from the angry, biting chord.

He spotted me and traipsed across the floor.

'You great lout,' he growled. 'Fancy a game of pinball?'

I manoeuvred him over to a stained table. A record player was thumping out Led Zeppelin a floor above. Seb rolled a loose cigarette.

'Stressed?' he asked, lighting up. The tobacco sizzled round his lips.

'Who was the girl?'

'The chief salamander,' Seb grinned.

All of a sudden she was there again, red-faced, pointing at Seb with a clenched fist. But her voice was calm and precise.

'At the general meeting we passed a motion that our school will be drug-free, Seb. You know that very well. If you go to the park and dope yourself up and murder your brain cells, that's up to you, even if it's a very stupid thing to do. But what you do *here* concerns all of us. Have you got that, Seb?'

Seb flushed behind his wispy beard, a touch of colour lit up his wan face, he forced himself to look up.

'You're right, Unni. Hell, you're always right.'

She smiled, her fist melted and she stroked Seb's hair, gave him a hug and slipped away.

'Tells it like it is,' I said.

'Unni's the boss here,' Seb said, hunching over the table. 'Somethin' comin' off? Premiere nerves? You're up and down like a yo-yo.'

I began to talk.

'What that Pelle character said the other night about Paul bein' dead, dyin' four years ago, that was just a con, wasn't it? Or what the hell was it?'

Seb unfolded a king-size grin and laughter rippled out of his mouth.

'You don't mean to say you fell for that hogwash, too, Kim, old chap, did you!'

I put on a grin too and placed one hand over the other like two sandwiches in a lunchbox.

'Of course not. Just thought it was a bit far-fetched.'

'And have you been sittin' at home lookin' for Paul's death notice on every damned record since *Help*? Eh?'

I shrugged.

'Not exactly. Had a look. Some very weird things.'

'At the school there's a committee that's trawled through the whole lot. Now they've discovered that George must be dead, too. They're gonna start on John next week. The hardliners think Ringo is the only one who was born.'

'You don't believe it then?'

'Come on, Kim. D'you think they can conjure up some joe, give him a facelift and distort his voice? Just advertisin', man. Money in the bank. Surely you didn't *believe* that?'

I laughed out loud.

'Are you crazy?'

Fat cheeks peered round the door and spotted Seb.

'You comin' to the Norwegian class?'

'Went there last week.'

'Bjørneboe might be on the agenda, you buffoon!'

Seb clattered to his feet and was on his way.

'You comin'?' he called out to me.

I flew after him. In the corridor the walls were painted all over with psychedelic figures, quite different from the slaughterhouse corridors at Vestheim and Frogner.

'Haven't got the time,' I said.

Seb stopped.

'Will you be droppin' by one evenin'?'

'The pill,' I started. 'The pill Pelle had. Have you come down yet?'

Seb stared at me, took a closer squint, turned up my eyelids and examined my pupils.

'Come down?' he said.

'Had a tough time last week,' I mumbled.

He gave me a searching look.

'You talkin' about the tablets Pelle had?'

'Right. I've been trippin' ever since.'

He stifled his laughter.

'That was just quinine, man. Pelle was bluffin'. It was *quinine*. You can get it at the chemist. Without a prescription.'

Seb shot off down the corridor and a door slammed. My head was spinning. Four girls with their hands covered in wet clay came towards me giggling. They could have kneaded me into whatever they liked. They could have made teacups or jars or candlesticks out of me, put me in the kiln and burned me into eternity. I could see from their eyes that they would have liked to. They came towards me with dripping fingers, bent, ready to attack.

'Napoleon's comin'!' I shouted and ran home, frightened, angry, furious and frightened.

Mum was standing in the hall when I burst in.

'Jørgen rang,' she said before I had taken off my military jacket. 'He said you mustn't forget the rehearsal tonight.'

'I know,' I said. 'I know!'

'Are you nervous about the premiere?'

'Premiere's not takin' place till after Christmas!'

'You'll have to articulate when you're on the stage, Kim.'

'Not gonna be on the stage. The big moo says I have to stand in the auditorium and shout the line.'

I set a course for my room. Mum followed me.

'There's a letter for you,' she said.

The blood drained from my brain. It was too much for one day. I was almost on my knees.

'Letter?' I gasped.

'It's on your table.'

I dragged myself in. It lay beside my books, a big, thick envelope with Danish stamps. My name was typewritten. I already knew something was up. Blood was coagulating, clotting in my mouth.

I opened it.

Out fell all my letters. There were several of them. They were unopened. Eventually I found a typewritten sheet. In the top corner it said: *The Royal Danish Embassy, Copenhagen.* At the bottom was her father's name. I read slowly. It wasn't long. He wrote that Nina had gone abroad early that summer, to Paris, with some friends. She still had not returned. They had received a letter from Turkey in which she had written that she was thinking of going east, to Afghanistan. That was two months ago. They had not heard from her since. They would ask her to write to me when she returned or when they found out where she was.

I sat on the floor. The withered Virginia creeper banged against the windowpane. When I closed my eyes, I could see her, thin, smiling, teeth gleaming behind big, red lips. I could visualise Nina and now she was somewhere else in the world and no one knew where.

I closed my eyes again, the wind shook the panes, I had already forgotten what he looked like, Paul McCartney, I knew that time was over, The Beatles had gone their separate ways, everything was clear now, I would never stand in front of the mirror again, relax my eyelids, arch my eyebrows and pretend to be left-handed. That was over. That was over.

I opened my eyes and could feel that I was tired, desperately tired as though I had not slept all my life, tired to the marrow of my bones.

Mum woke me. She was on her haunches shaking me with a scared expression on her face.

'Did you fall asleep on the floor! Are you ill, Kim?'

I jumped up. The letters. I picked them up and opened a drawer. There was no room, it was crammed full with leaflets. I put them in another drawer.

Pym and Dad were talking in the sitting room. Mum sat beside me.

'You'll have to hurry,' she said. 'The rehearsal begins at seven!'

It was strange weather outside. The sky seemed to have been tinged by an alien light, the air seemed explosive, it quivered in the odd blue light from above. Now and then a gust of wind swept through the streets with a howl, like a jet plane. Then it was still again. It was like crawling through a canon while the fuse was burning.

I was the last to appear in the gym hall, and big-titted Minni began to tell me off the moment I showed my face through the door.

'Do you think it's right to keep the whole cast waiting for you?!' she shouted.

'No,' I said. This day was seriously beginning to be more than I could take.

'May I ask whether you intend to come to the premiere?'

'I'll try,' I said.

She spread out her hands and put on a sarcastic smile.

'Well, I am truly relieved, Kim Karlsen.'

And then we were off. She broke in after about every second line, chalked positions on the floor, directed, articulated, groaned, cut out parts, added, shouted, scolded, cried. A couple of girls broke down and ran to the dressing room howling, I think that was something they had seen in the cinema by the way. They were enticed back with Cokes and flattery, and then it all started again. At least I roared my one line in the right place, but the big moo was not happy with my intonation, I had to feel the whole history of the Russian people, the horrors of war, Siberia's freezing temperatures and the mothers' fears; the century-long sufferings should be compressed into my two words. After roaring *Napoleon's coming* twenty-three times, I didn't give a flying fart, grabbed my jacket and trudged off. They must have thought I would return, so the cast was quite laid back. But I didn't return. I went into the streets and now the wind had picked up with a vengeance, it hammered through the town, I was literally thrown back into the entrance, crawled out on all fours and only just managed to struggle to my feet. My eyes smarted, my ears howled, I tensed my stomach muscles, held my hands in front of my face and walked head down into the wind.

It took me at least half an hour to reach the fountain. There I found shelter behind a low wall and, after sixteen matches, succeeded in lighting a cigarette. There was no one around, just a poodle blew past me like a black ball of fluff. The trees in the avenue were bent to the ground. The street lamps swung in all directions, casting their beam around wildly like a drunk with a torch. Somewhere a windowpane tinkled. The air was one huge howling wind.

I dragged myself up and staggered on, I tripped and was blown onto a lawn, grabbed a clump of grass, crawled for a while, found my footing and stood upright. A newspaper flew between the trees like a prehistoric bird. I lumbered over to the avenue and fought my way from trunk to trunk. It was half past nine by the time I was standing in Tidemandsgate. I called her name, but the wind smothered all sounds. I yelled again, but no one could hear, I couldn't hear myself, just felt the rasping in my throat and the painful throb in my eardrums.

I sank to the pavement, a gust of wind spun me round, I could hardly breathe, lay with my mouth open gasping for air. A tree fell across the street, crushing a wooden fence. Something sailed past and smashed against a wall. A roof tile. Tiles were sliding off house roofs. A splinter hit me on the forehead and I felt something wet run down my nose. I forced myself off the ground, protected my face with my arms, was about to walk into the wind when I saw him coming, Jørgen was walking in the storm with his hands in his pockets, whistling as if nothing had happened, as if nothing had happened. He stepped into the wind without any difficulty, jumped over the tree and ran up to me.

'Thought I would find you round here,' he said.

A roof tile sliced past him.

'Careful!' I shouted, pulling him to the side.

'This is where Nina lived, isn't it?' he said, peering at the large wooden house that stood darkly in the overgrown garden.

'Worst weather I've ever experienced!' I bellowed. 'Think the electricity has gone all over town!'

Jørgen looked at me.

'You're coming back, aren't you? To the drama group.'

I nodded and felt the wind trying to tear out my eyes.

He patted my shoulder, spoke through the storm as though it had no effect on him.

'You always come back, don't you, Kim?'

My eyelids stung, I could no longer see. My head fell forward and I leaned my forehead against Jørgen's chest. He settled his hand against my neck and held me tight. Then I felt his cheek against mine, his mouth, I put my arm around him, we were in the middle of the storm and I cried on Jørgen's breast.

Let It Be

Spring/summer '70

The coarse Russian uniform itched all over, it was worse than bathing in rose hip seeds. The sweat piled down my back, my heart palpitated and my nerves began to jangle. I sat forlorn in the dressing room waiting for my cue because, of course, big-titted Minni had decided that I would appear from behind the audience, run up the central aisle, roar my momentous news and disappear behind the stage. I heard Jørgen speaking in the auditorium, his voice was clear and articulate and the audience was hushed. Then Natasha answered, the stuck-up snob, I could hear the swish of silk. I looked through the keyhole, saw all the stiff heads lined in rows. The stage went dark, someone tripped, then the spotlights came back on and there stood Napoleon, in the circle of light, a fat, pasty-faced boy with colourless eyes who had been given the role because he was the smallest in the school, one metre fifty-nine. He stood with his hand on his chest and the insane hat on his skull like a ship, and in the background Jan Johansson was playing 'The Volga Boatmen'. I went back to the bench. My nerves were stretched to the limit. Fortunately I had brought along some beers for the job. I opened an Export and drank it. It didn't help. I knocked back another. It was still a long time before I had to make my entrance. I opened the third and it began to hit the mark. My nerves were settling. Just the woollen material itched. Then I needed a leak. The beer had only bubbled up in my head, the rest went straight to my bladder. I had plenty of time and slouched off to the toilet. There, I had quite a job unbuttoning the Russian fly, there were at least twenty metal buttons to undo, and it was worse putting them back, much worse. Panic took hold of me. I grabbed the material and forced the buttons in, my skin itched, my crutch too, the heavy leather boots were like lead. At last I did up the fly and raced back to the dressing room, stopped, heard nothing, no one was speaking inside, there was just a low whisper, a hollow mumble sweeping along the rows of seats. I peeped through the keyhole. The whole cast was standing there waiting, sending each other nervous glances, waiting, waiting for me. My heart jumped like a salmon making its way upstream, then I breathed in, grabbed the sabre and tore open the door.

From that moment on I don't remember much, but I must have made quite an impression, because the whole audience screamed as one and there were signs of panic in the back rows. I shrieked my grim news and ran for cover behind the stage. Terje, the lighting manager, slipped me a beer and insisted that my one line must have shown up on the seismograph in Bergen and that I already had my Oscar guaranteed for best male supporting role.

'That's for films, you pillock,' I said under my breath.

'Same difference, Igor. You'll get the Eli statuette anyway!'

Then Jan Johansson played 'Moscow Nights' and the gym went dark as the stage slaves carried in the pink sofa, fell flat on their faces over a cable, got up and staggered back. The lights went up, Pierre talked about his great love and Natasha cried and people in the audience began to sniffle too, especially one person, had to be my mother, and I cringed over my beer. And then it was all over, the lights dimmed over Pierre's body, the silence held for a few seconds, then the deafening applause broke out, and we threw ourselves around each other's necks, the corpse managed to wriggle off the sofa before the lights came back on, and we stood on the stage in a line, holding hands, as the stamping and clapping thundered in our faces and the flashes from the international press corps went off. I spotted my mother in the first row, she was beaming, I hadn't seen her look like that since *Brand*. And Seb and Gunnar and Ola were sitting at the back grinning and whistling. We had to return to the stage five times before the cossacks would relent.

And afterwards there was the premiere party at Minni's, a huge house in Bygdøy Allé. I tried to hide in the forest undergrowth, trod carefully with the leaden weights on my feet and the bottle of beer, and I concentrated, just as if I was continuing in a new role, I paid attention to what I said, *thought* about my own thoughts, it was crazy, but I was scared stiff of turning somersaults or running amok. So the evening passed uneventfully, some slept in a corner, Natasha whispered something in my ear which I didn't catch, but she had a fit of giggles and went off into another room wearing the large, rustling dress as though she were part of a painting from a previous century. I saw Minni press Pierre up against the wall, then she turned all of a sudden and was gone. I sat in a chair, found a half-full bottle of beer, lit a smoke and stared at Pierre, who was still attached to the wall. Then he smiled and came over to me.

Had hardly spoken to Jørgen since the night of the storm, and Jørgen seemed to change after the Christmas holidays when he was in England. Now he perched on the arm of the chair and placed a hand on my shoulder. Wanted to chat to him now.

'Went off well,' I said.

He nodded. Someone was banging away on a piano.

'You're gonna be a pro,' I said.

He didn't answer, just rubbed my shoulder with his hand.

'How was it in London by the way?' I asked.

He looked around as if scared someone might be listening.

'Fine,' he said quickly. 'Great.'

He sat there for a while, looking down at me.

'Got myself a lover,' he whispered.

I aimed a soft punch at his stomach.

'Terrific!' I said. 'What's she look like?'

His sad eyes swept across me, then he stood up and went into the other room. I remained in the chair with the empty bottle and suddenly felt sick.

I was asked to sing. I refused. The girls begged on their knees. I refused point blank. Napoleon wanted me to climb onto the roof, all I had to do was grab the gutter from the balcony. I began to tremble. They wanted me to do things. I knocked over a lamp and went to the toilet, locked the door and rested my forehead against the cool wall tiles. Then, behind me, I heard the sounds of waves and summer. I turned slowly. The bath was full of water and foam. Then I saw her, Minni, lying there with a broad smile and closed eyes, her breasts bobbing around like beach balls. She hadn't drowned. She spoke to me.

'You're a good friend of Jørgen's, aren't you, Kim?'

I fiddled with the door lock, it had jammed. The woollen uniform seemed to shrink and itched.

'Ye-es,' I said. 'We're pals.'

There was a splash as she raised her arm from the foam.

'Come here,' she said.

I didn't.

She opened her eyes and locked them onto me.

'Come on,' she said.

I did as the drama coach said. She grasped my hand and held it tight. Then she pulled it towards her, downwards, and she was strong, I could feel the lukewarm water over my fingers, I could feel her soft skin, she pulled harder, pressed my hand between her legs.

Then she let go.

I slowly retrieved my arm. The uniform was wet and heavy.

She smiled.

'You should have had a bigger role, Kim. I realised that this evening. You should have had… a bigger role.'

I scooted off in a hurry. I was petrified. I peed in the kitchen sink and crept into the living room. A jazz tune drifted across from the record player, couples on the sofa in the dark. There was the sound of clothes rubbing. I took a drink from a bottle, it burned, vodka, and the moment I decided to leave, Natasha was behind me.

'Are you looking for Pierre?' she whispered.

'Was thinkin' of goin' home,' I said.

'He left ages ago,' she mumbled close to me.

I found a sofa. She followed, sank down beside me.

'Your arm's all wet,' she said.

'Dropped my cigarette in a bottle of beer,' I said.

She sniggered and leaned closer.

'You're not as crazy as they all say,' she said.

I tugged myself free and fell onto the floor.

'Who says that?' I gasped.

She looked unhappy.

'No one,' she stammered. 'No one.'

I left. In Bygdøy Allé the windows of Bonus gave off the garish gleam of a brothel. I didn't want to go home. I plodded through the snow to Norum Hotel and rang the bell. Ola was on night duty three times a week. He opened the door and stared at me with a condescending air. Then at last he recognised the messenger and waved me in.

'It's three o'clock,' he yawned.

'Got any beer?'

Ola trotted down to the cellar and fetched two beers. He had unfolded a camp bed behind the counter. We sat down in the lounge. He took a packet of Camel out of the machine.

'Worst thing I've seen,' he said.

'What?'

'The play, you ass! The only time I was awake was when you stormed in.'

I chortled in my uniform, lit another fag.

'How's it goin' with Vigdis?' I asked.

Ola cast sideways glances, frightened of being caught red-handed, in the middle of the night in a hotel, by Kirsten of Trondheim.

'Alright,' he whispered. 'Alright, but Kirsten's my girl. There are clear lines drawn.'

'Good,' I said. 'Clear lines. That's what Gunnar says, too.'

We sat in silence for a while. I knew that I was drunk. Nothing would stay still. Fear rushed in on me although there was nothing to be afraid of, fear was paid for up front now and I had no idea why I was paying.

I stubbed out my cigarette in the ashtray.

'Better get my head down,' Ola said. 'Day before yesterday I forgot to wake an Indian who was flying to Madrid. He tried to burn me alive.'

'What d'you think… what d'you think will become of us?' I asked in a soft voice.

Ola looked at me in astonishment, closed one eye and smiled from the other edge of his mouth.

'What d'you mean?'

'How will we make out in life?'

He was smiling from both sides now.

'Fine,' Ola said. 'How else?'

The switchboard buzzed and a red light came on. Ola padded

over to the counter and picked up the receiver. It was a CIA agent wanting a Coke.

I dragged myself out into the snow again. The town was as silent as the grave. I stood in the middle of Bygdøy Allé wearing a Russian uniform and high black boots. I drew my sabre, yelled and ran towards Bonus, and fell flat on my face in a snowdrift.

Gunnar dropped by with more leaflets, concealing them on his person in cunning ways, inside newspapers, magazines, Bonus carrier bags, record sleeves. In general, Gunnar had become pretty cunning, cunningly fired up and suspicious. He walked with one eye over his shoulder all the time, seldom or never spoke on the telephone. But he seemed content, in all the political hatred that steamed off him there was pure and obvious happiness, politics was Gunnar's sauna, I think Gunnar was happy. He spent his evenings at meetings in Ytre Vest, went to the Young Socialist study circle, manned FNL stands and was on the students' council. When he came by it was to drop off leaflets, and this time they were about the Americans' plans in Laos. Soon I wouldn't have any room left for any more leaflets. The drawer was full. Thinking of all the leaflets I had not delivered turned me into an instant insomniac.

He sidled into my room, made sure the door was locked, drew the curtains and pulled out a pile packed in greaseproof paper.

'Best tomorrow,' he whispered as if there were a special agent lying under the bed with a telephoto lens and a tape recorder.

'Okay,' I said, feeling corrupt, telling lies was one thing, physical deception was quite another, even I understood that.

Gunnar stayed for a quarter of an hour, then he had to move on, had to write an article for the school newspaper about the five-day week and sick leave.

'How's Stig?' I asked.

He didn't want to talk about that.

'You remember Cecilie from Vestheim?' he said instead, getting up. I looked at him blankly. Did I remember Cecilie?

'Think so,' I said.

'She's in the same study circle as me. She's the editor of the school newspaper at Ullern.'

'Cecilie?'

He pulled out a magazine and showed me. *Ulke Hulke*. Editor: Cecilie Ahlsen.

'She's in the study circle too?'

Gunnar nodded and flicked open the newspaper.

'There's a good article about the Young Socialists and Mao here,' he said. 'And the Norwegian *Gymnas* Association. The best damned school newspaper in town.'

Then he had to leave. And Gunnar did not leave the usual way. He took the kitchen stairs, climbed over the back garden fence, swung down holding the rotary dryer and was gone.

That night I was feverish. Cecilie. Cecilie the editor. Cecilie in a study circle. My head was swirling. And the leaflets in the drawer were burning.

Three days later Gunnar returned. One eye observed the other and he had ten copies of *Class Conflict* with him, wrapped in the *Aftenposten*.

'Could you sell *Class Conflict* in Frogner?' he asked.

I hesitated, I hesitated a long time, there was no more room for any more, I had come to an impasse, the situation was out of my control.

Suddenly he grabbed my shirt and pulled me closer.

'You haven't delivered one bloody leaflet, have you,' he hissed. 'Eh? Have you!'

He let me go and I slumped down on the sofabed, holed beneath the waterline. I was about to say something, but Gunnar didn't give me a chance.

'Where've you put 'em?'

I pulled out the third drawer. It jammed. Gunnar raked the leaflets into his bag. Vietnam. The Kiruna strike. The five-day week. Rationalisation. The Ministry of Education. Laos.

'And you thought you could trick us!'

'Didn't try to trick anyone,' I insisted.

'Is that so? What d'you call this then? Filin'?'

'I'm right behind what they say. I just couldn't bring myself to deliver them.'

It sounded tame. I was at the end of my tether.

'That's sort of the point about leaflets, you know. If you only wanted to *read* them, you wouldn't need fifty of each! Would you!'

Nothing you could say to that. I was an idiot. I accepted the rebuke.

Gunnar emptied the drawer.

'You angry with me?' I asked meekly.

'It's the *masses* who are angry with you,' Gunnar said. 'The *masses* are *disappointed* with you.'

As he left, I said something that turned me into a complete lackey, that would make me an eternal laughing stock.

'Please don't say anythin' to Cecilie,' I said.

We suddenly realised that our final exams were approaching. But I was unable to concentrate that spring, couldn't do it, thinking about Nina, thinking that no one knew where Nina was, thinking about Cecilie the editor, Cecilie in the study circle, my brain was too small to contain such thoughts, I didn't have the space, if she had married Kåre the Creep or played mixed doubles with Peder in the Norwegian championships I would not have been able to say a word. Now my brain did not have the capacity. Cecilie and Nina. Sometimes I dreamt that Nina was running across a desert. It was a silent dream and I could see from her face that she was close to dying of thirst. On such nights I occasionally had to get up and drink water. And Jørgen seemed to slip away from me, didn't see much of him. And the mess with Gunnar. My eyes smarted at the very thought of it. I had been humiliated and ground into dust. I walked and yearned for The Great Revolutionary Feat, which would restore me, raise me from the dead, cleanse me. The Great Sacrifice. I dreamt about great things, not trifles like playing in goal for Norway, one up against Sweden, the Swedes getting a penalty and me flying through the air like a banana to the top corner and tapping the ball down with my forefinger. Not at all. I dreamt that I washed ashore in Vietnam, became a soldier for the FNL and led the final and decisive battle against the Americans. That was how I dreamt. Or that I kidnapped Nixon and made him admit that he was an imperialist, fascist pig, whereupon he signed the capitulation papers unconditionally. That was how I dreamt. But the opportunities never came, even though I did my best at the national service medical, but that did not seem to be taken into account, for in the end Gunnar didn't want to be a conscientious objector.

The evening before the medical, I sat in Seb's room, it was just us two with Jim Morrison whispering in the background. On the table there were 160 Teddys, on the floor three bottles of home-made white wine and Seb had a big, fat spliff in his pocket.

'But for Christ's sake,' I shouted. 'Wasn't Gunnar supposed to be a conscientious objector?!'

Seb shook his head.

'New line. Boys have to enter the forest. Work from inside.'

I lit a Teddy. My fingers were dark yellow already, my hideous forefinger was brownish and smelt acrid.

'Beginning to get a sore throat,' I groaned.

Seb poured some wine. It was turbid and tasted of sand.

'No good *pretending* your hands shake,' he said. 'They weren't born yesterday even if they are generals.'

I looked at my hand. It did shake a bit. That was not enough. We had been practising this every evening for ten days. My head was swimming. Seb looked as though he had hepatitis and migraine and double pneumonia.

'Be easier to put on female underwear,' he slurred. 'You'd be rejected on the spot.'

'Not bloody likely. Not bloody likely. Rather say I was a bed-wetter.'

Seb forced down the wine with a gulp and a bulge of his eyes.

'Won't work,' he wheezed. 'They'll take you on just to see if it's true. Follow you to the train, too. To see if you pee your pants.'

We sat in silence for a while. Seb played 'The Unknown Soldier'. I thought about Gunnar who was going to join up after all. I drank wine and felt nauseous and empty.

'Gunnar's changed,' I said.

'You think so? I don't. He's how he's always been.'

He put on 'Morrison Hotel'. I peed in the sink. Seb assembled the bong.

'Met Guri last week,' he said.

'How'd it go?'

'So so. Just stood gapin' at each other and had nothing to say. Crazy, isn't it.'

'Still with her slalom pal, is she?'

'Damned if I know. Didn't ask. Doesn't interest me, either. But it's crazy that you can't talk to people, isn't it.'

'Yeah.'

'And when people talk, they talk such superficial crap. The weather and the price of milk and TV. My mum, for example. Since that piss artist broke into the nest, she's gone all plastic and TV. They sit there with drinks and peanuts gettin' plastered, Jesus.'

'Heard anythin' from your dad?'

'Have you seen *Easy Rider*? Cool film. Once I've finished my apprenticeship I'll get myself one of those low-slung motorbikes and head south. Have you seen it?'

'Nope. Don't do cinema any more. Worst thing I know. Had a surfeit of it when I was with Cecilie.'

Seb lit the water pipe, sucked and it made a gurgling sound, a bit like when you step into a bog wearing high boots. He passed it to me and for a while we were inside ourselves.

'Understand Cecilie's become a Marxist-Leninist,' I said.

Seb grinned, ran a yellow finger through the sparse blond moustache hanging from the corners of his mouth.

'They can hold a summer camp in Bygdøy this year then,' he spluttered.

We sat gurgling while Morrison sang 'I'm A Spy In The House Of Love'. We washed the smoke down with white wine. My stomach felt like a tumble dryer, a rusty tumble dryer in an abandoned launderette in a damp, musty cellar. That was how I felt. It was the evening before our medical.

'D'you think we'll carry it off?'

'Christ, yes,' Seb said, getting up, staggering around and corkscrewing down.

'Sure?'

'Mustn't start messin' up now, you know. Don't take a towel with you. Don't take the draft papers. Give weird answers to all the questions. Ask to have a psychologist present at once. Easy as wink, Kim.'

'D'you think they'll believe us?'

Seb opened his eyes wide.

'*Believe?* The point is they won't *want* us.'

'When you lie, it's a good idea to stick to the truth,' I declared.

Seb didn't say another word for the next hour. We lit the pipe and drank the wine.

Then he said, 'You're damn right.'

I tottered home at about two. The town was chilly and grey. The streets stretched into the distance, they had a different tinge to them now that there were no people around, almost as if the sky were hugging the tarmac. I was alone in the streets and it went through my head that I could wake the whole town with a scream, at the top of my voice, and watch the lights coming on in window after window, hear the roller blinds shooting up, doors slamming, men yelling, taps running. I could have done that. I could have screamed this town into life. I did not. Instead I found Svoldergate and crept indoors. Mum and Dad had long gone to bed, but Mum was not asleep, I could hear her turning in her room, I could hear her eyes staring in the dark.

I didn't go to bed. I opened the window and finished smoking the rest of the Teddys. I looked at my hands. They were yellowish-brown, filthy, they trembled. If I could have poked a pipe cleaner through one ear to the other, I would have discovered that my soul was black and stained. My greasy hair hung over my face. At four o'clock I threw up over the pavement. At five the light on the other side of town arose, a yellow breath of wind, or white, it ascended behind Ekeberg and leaned across the sky. I stood at my window watching and it struck me that I had never seen anything to match this. The day came like a shining, transparent fan gently blowing away the night. My aching head was overwhelmed. But that was how it must have been every morning.

I went up to the loft and fetched Dad's gas mask. Then I left. There were three hours left before I was due to appear in Akershus.

I sat on the harbour promenade and put on the mask. It was difficult to breathe. I saw my reflection in the water. I looked like a deformed ant-eater. Sitting like that, I examined myself for traces of fear. But there were none. I thought about the time I had walked on Cecilie's roof, danced with the skeleton, done battle with the badger. I had been fearless. It was at that point that I became scared. I spewed up my stomach contents, they were grey-coloured.

The traffic behind me was becoming heavier.

Cranes swung on the skyline.

I was a quarter of an hour late. A green-clad idiot pulled the mask off my face and pushed me into a room where a film was being shown, and beside the screen stood a crew cut with a pointer, talking about the training opportunities in the forces. The pictures showed some slick types sitting in an office or operating radar or tinkering with a jet plane. Then the lights came on and I spotted Seb. He resembled a sickly ghost. Behind him were Gunnar and Ola. They just shook their heads.

Then we were given a pile of papers with questions and crosses. It was mad. Car A goes from Drammen at four o'clock and car B leaves Oslo at five. Car A does fifty kilometres an hour. Car B sixty kilometres an hour. When will they meet? They crash in Sandvika, I wrote in the margin. And then there were shapes that were supposed to interlock, word association tests and other bright ideas. *Inspection*. What do you associate with it? Examination? Investigation? Torture? I went for 2, an away win. I went for away wins all the way down, it looked nice and tidy. Can you swim? No. Hobbies? Will people ever stop asking me that? No. I put the sheet to the side and lit a cigarette. A sweaty gorilla appeared above me and whipped the fag out of my mouth. There was quite a commotion, then they chased us out into the corridor. A general asked where my towel and call-up papers were. I showed him the gas mask. He ground his teeth. The sparks flew in my direction. Gunnar and Ola disappeared down the corridor. Seb's shadow fell into one room. I was thrust through a different door, where there stood at least twenty lethargic bodies from before. I grabbed one that was dressed, he reeled backwards as my breath hit him.

'I need the psychologist!' I whispered. 'I need the psychologist!'

He calmed me down and gave me a friendly pat. I went all weak inside – there were humans here, too. He measured me with his eyes and appeared truly concerned. Then I was led out again and told to wait. I smoked four roll-ups one after the other. The smoke stung my eyes. Tears poured forth. The soldier came back, he can't have been more than a second lieutenant, maybe just a private, perhaps he was the caretaker, but he was kind.

'Are you crying?' he asked.

'Yes,' I said.

'Come here,' he said, gently taking my arm.

I was shown into a large office where a highly decorated bear of a man was sitting behind a desk. I slunk onto a chair and stared at the floor.

'What's up with you?' he asked, and his voice was surprisingly soft, I had been expecting an electric drill, but this was children's hour.

I was unable to answer.

The general leaned across the polished desk.

'You smoke too much,' he stated.

A long silence followed. I began to scratch my scalp. I scratched, clawed like an eagle. He just looked at me.

'Don't worry,' he said. 'This is just a formality.'

The door opened and my second lieutenant showed me into the doctor's waiting room. Three of the candidates from before were standing in a corner. I sat in the middle of the floor.

A quarter of an hour later I was hauled in. The doctor scrutinised me with cold eyes.

'Do you smoke hashish?' he asked.

I didn't answer.

He felt my pulse, squeezed my kidneys. Then he jotted something on a slip of paper and gave it to me.

'Give this to the psychologist,' he said and shouted another name into the Dictaphone.

The second lieutenant followed me through. I read the slip. *Drug problems*, it said. *Clear neurotic features.* Wow. I began to feel really nervous. Right there, in the stinking corridor, with the kind second lieutenant at my side, I registered that I was no longer pretending, now it was deadly earnest, I had crossed a threshold, from my room to theirs, I wanted to get out of the room, out of it as fast as possible.

'Everything will be alright,' the second lieutenant said.

The psychologist was quite young and eager. He read the note and stared at me. I looked past him. A bird crashed into the window. He took his time, walked around the room, tied his shoelaces, straightened a picture, stood behind me and at last sat down.

'When were you born?' he asked.

I began to talk, it made my throat hurt.

'1951. Autumnal equinox. On the cusp between Virgo and Libra. Some horoscopes make me a Virgo. Others a Libra. I was born on the autumnal equinox, you see. It's just dreadful.'

The silence hung in the room like an echo. Then the shrink started clicking his nails.

'Tell me a bit more about yourself,' he said.

And my voice was like an avalanche, a landslide, my body was talking for me. I told him about Cecilie's roof, the skeleton, the badger, that I had been a bird before, that I could fly at night, I told him about the fear that opened inside me like a knife wound, I told him I bled when the police beat up the demonstrators in Paris, that I screamed every night, I told him I was guilty of a bank robbery.

The psychologist sat with a pen between his fingers. He wrote something on a sheet of paper. It made a rustling noise. Suddenly he stopped, blew on what he had written and scratched his armpit.

'Is there anything you would like to ask me?' he said.

'Why do you click your nails?' I asked.

His eyes burned holes into my forehead. I felt instant remorse. Then he continued to write, blew again, folded the paper and put it into an envelope, which he licked with a grey tongue.

Then he flashed me a smile.

'Because sitting here is driving me mad,' he said.

He accompanied me to the door and gave me the letter. I bowed and scraped.

'Give this to the doctor you saw before,' he said, pushing me out.

The second lieutenant was at hand and accompanied me back downstairs. I was worn out. I noticed there were knobs on the hand rail, just like at school. So that the generals would not be able to slide down. I thought about saying that to the second lieutenant, but refrained, think that was a wise move.

The floor below was teeming with people. I looked for Seb, Ola and Gunnar, they weren't there. But right at the back was Jørgen. A green-clad bastard came and led him away.

Then I was with the doctor again. It was never-ending. He stood with his back to me and read the psychologist's letter. He swivelled round, folded the letter round his forefinger like a banknote.

'Have you got bad guts?' he asked.

'Yes,' I said.

He nodded several times and glared at me. I held my hands over my stomach. Then he picked up the military service booklet and wrote – I could read it upside down: UF. UFCD. I asked what they meant. Unfit, it meant. Unfit for civil defence even. Unfit was my middle name thereafter. And still I wasn't finished. I was given the military service booklet and my valet accompanied me back to see the general. I gave him the booklet, he slowly flicked through it, stood up, his eyes were sad, sad, and he came around the table.

'Oh dear,' he said. He said that. Oh dear.

Now fear washed through me like a tidal wave and slapped against the red cliffs of my heart. I almost fell to the floor. He held me up with a steely hand.

'The nerves business is the worst,' he said with sorrow in his voice. 'We don't really know what nerves are.'

He half-carried me to the door and opened it.

'Good luck,' I heard as I left. 'Good luck, Kim Karlsen!'

I stood in the corridor. It smelt of chlorine. The second lieutenant came over to me with the gas mask, put it in my hand.

'You can go now,' he said and left.

It smelt of chlorine. So I toddled off. And in the sunshine, in mid-relief, a wild thought struck me: the letter. The letter the psychologist had written. What was in it? What was in it that made them drop me on the spot? I had only told them the truth. What was in the letter?

I walked home through the rotten town. Mum was all over me before I had taken out the key. The questions were stacked up in a queue. She ran a hand across my filthy hair and looked frightened.

'Where have you been?' she stammered.

'Medical.'

'Last night! This morning!'

Her hand was shaking.

'At Seb's,' I said. 'Left before you got up this morning.'

She followed me. Pym was singing in the sitting room.

'When will you be called up?' she asked.

'They didn't want me.'

I showed her my finger.

'Do you think you can shoot with such a twisted finger?'

I dashed into my room and slept like a log.

I was woken up by Seb. All of a sudden he was standing there with the broadest grin of the year. My mother was keeping watch behind him. I closed the door and Seb was beside himself with excitement.

'How did it go?' he panted. 'How did it go?'

'Fine in the end,' I said. 'But it took a bloody long time.'

He threw himself down on the sofabed and punched the mattress.

'Gunnar was declared fit for combat duties. And Ola's joinin' the navy!'

We grinned for a long time. Seb stretched out and flipped half a bottle of wine from out of his sleeve. Could do a stint at the circus with that one. We each took a swig.

'How did *you* wangle it?' I asked.

He laughed and tapped my forehead with a dark yellow finger.

'Just followed your advice,' he said. 'About lyin' and stickin' to the truth. I said I was in fine fettle and was lookin' forward like mad to joining the army. They didn't bloody believe me. Was kicked out after five minutes. They didn't bloody believe me!'

The Great Revolutionary Feat was slow in coming. I was a superfluous spoke in the Wheel of History. There was no use for me. It was as if Gunnar had forgotten the leaflets in my drawer, for the Wheel was rolling on regardless. It rolled through Norway in the spring of 1970 leaving ruts everywhere. The workers were on strike. The trams were silent. The workers at Norgas were on strike. The cops were beating up the pickets. The workers continued to strike. Gunnar was rattling a money box. I put two tenners in. That's more like it, Gunnar said. On April 22, on the centenary of Lenin's birth, the struggle was crowned with victory. The Wheel of History rolled towards the finishing line and I was no more than a rusty, superfluous spoke.

But on May 1 I did not want to stand, cap in hand, on the sidelines. I turned out at Grønlands Torg ten minutes before the start and saw Gunnar waving a large placard in the wind. NO TO THE FIVE-DAY WEEK! He grinned on seeing me, asked me to hold the placard and disappeared into the crowd. There must have been several thousand people present. I stood in the middle of Grønlands Torg, in a cauldron, swaying with the placard in the wind. Some began to sing the Internationale, elsewhere a chorus was chanting: USA OUT OF VIETNAM! Behind me there was the rattle of tins. In front of me stood a girl with a screaming infant in her arms. A megaphone crackled through the ether. The crowd began to move. I hung on tight to the placard and looked around for Gunnar. He had gone. I was in the middle of people moving forward slowly, purposefully, finding their positions. Gunnar had disappeared. I couldn't see Seb, either. The wind almost sent me flying. A man with a red armband said I should pick my way over to the schools section. He pointed to the back of the procession. Obediently, I staggered that way. I could hear music. Hands clapping. A bruiser with a drooping moustache held up a large picture of Stalin. I struggled onwards. Those at the front had already started to move off. I was walking in the wrong direction. I was dragged into the ranks and found myself standing beside a man carrying a portrait of Mao on the beach.

Gunnar was not there, either. A girl asked me to stand still. And then it was our turn. Shouts from various sections mingled, formed themselves into a higher unity, into a shout that merged all the slogans and thoughts into one, the revolution's Esperanto, just like the orchestras on May 17, Constitution Day. This sounded much better. I joined in the shouting, could not hear my own voice, I shouted with the others, as loud as I was able and still couldn't hear my own voice.

Then something happened. Just as we were leaving the market square. The cops formed a chain and forced a scattered bunch of demonstrators onto the pavement. They were hollering and screaming and waving red and black flags. One of them broke through, ran across the street with a big poster above his head: STALIN=MURDERER. It was Stig. Stig at speed. Two stewards tackled him from behind, brought him down and tore the poster to pieces. Then the cops dragged away what was left of Stig. The mood was turning nasty. Red Front stewards closed ranks to keep out the anarchists. I saw Seb, too. Then we were past them. I understood nothing. I stuffed the pole of the placard into the hands of a man behind me, skipped out of the line and ran to the head of the procession. I had to find Gunnar. I thought I caught a glimpse of Cecilie, but was not sure. I ran on, was soon at the front, by the flag-bearers. Crowds lined the pavements. Shouts resounded down Storgata, were cast to and fro between the house walls. I found Gunnar in the anti-imperialist section.

'What the hell happened to you?' I panted.

'Had to take over here. What did you do with the placard?'

'Gave to it some bloke. See what happened?'

'No, what happened?'

'The anarchists were chased away. The cops kicked them out. Along with the stewards. The cops workin' with the stewards!'

'No place for anarchists here!'

'This was Stig, though! And Seb. Seb and your brother!'

Gunnar looked straight ahead. I was the seventh in the row and out of step.

'The revolution's no vicarage tea party,' said Gunnar.

I stopped. The procession streamed towards me. Then someone pushed me to the side. I started walking back, I jogged, back again, headed down towards the square. Those at the end passed me and the square was empty. A red flag rested against a post, abandoned. The sand crunched beneath my feet. The square was deserted. Leaflets and hot dog wrappers fluttered in the wind. I stood in the middle of Grønlands Torg and looked all around me.

Four students were mown down at Kent University. I remember the picture of a girl in tears collapsing beside a bloodstained body. It has left a scar on my eyes. I remember Gunnar's father, the runner, standing in the vegetables section at Bonus in his blue coat with a name tab on his chest. He had had to give up his grocery business. I remember him standing there the day I went to stock up on beer after the exams were over. I was unable to meet his eyes, did an abrupt about-turn and saw in the mirror over the meat counter a stooped, beaten man weighing lemons, potatoes and tomatoes. I hurried out with the crate of beer and got stuck into the mammoth booze-up I had been looking forward to for twelve years, for the exams were over and the sluice gates were open. Yes, I remember the exams too, a sweaty affair, a clammy funeral in the gym where we sat dotted across the freshly polished floor. The teachers tiptoed around in black suits and ironed ties, and the superannuated invigilators who accompanied us into the toilets, they sat there with their creaking shoes and sweets individually wrapped in sandwich paper, I remember all that. I had to write about Nansen again, but this time I didn't mix up Nansen and Schweitzer. I wrote about what Nansen had said about living in a town, and it was pretty wild. The exercise was entitled *People in Boxes*, and Nansen compared people with animals living in boxes, sleeping in boxes, eating in boxes, not sure if I quite caught the point. And he wrote about those societies where people just sit in big communal boxes and drink themselves stupid. 'I understand they're called parties,' Nansen wrote, and I added that when we die we end up in another box, but to be frank I doubted whether the North Pole had anything better to offer, I wrote in *Nynorsk* and was reasonably satisfied with my effort. And I wrote in *Bokmål* about a poem by André Bjerke, *The Adults' Party*, it made me think about opera on the radio, which I always listened to in years gone by, lying with the door ajar and my ears on stalks, and there was a world out there that became alive after I had gone to bed, something mysterious, something that was intended to be kept hidden from me. Now I knew it was just a bluff. And I wrote that. In English I guessed correctly. I had a miniature version of the Magna Carta under a Kvikklunsj wrapper, and the Magna Carta came up. In the history oral I was tested on the Napoleonic wars. I rounded it off with my line: *Napoleon's coming*! and was awarded a solid B. Then I tore down to Bonus and ran into Gunnar's father, pretended I hadn't seen him and rushed out with a crate of beer feeling more or less like Armstrong when he landed on the green cheese.

I didn't see much of Gunnar, met him on May 17 when he was handing out leaflets condemning prommers' celebrations, he didn't ask me if I wanted to give him a hand. Ola was doing double shifts to save up money for the navy. One night I dropped in at the hotel to have the last or the first beer of the day when I detected a gloomy expression on his rotund face.

'I'll try and take my final exams next year,' he whispered, looking away.

'How's it goin' with Vigdis?' I wondered, idiot that I am.

He put a finger to his lips.

'Not Vigdis. *Kirsten*.'

I nodded sagely.

'You do know Vigdis lives in the same block as Seb, don't you?'

An ugly twitch developed across his forehead.

'Even if I did drop Nina's name to Kåre the Creep that time, that doesn't mean you have to exact your revenge now!'

'Take it easy,' I reassured him. 'Take it easy. I have no idea who Vigdis is. I've never heard anythin' about her.'

Ola unfurled a smile and slumped back on the camping bed behind the counter. I leaned across.

'You alright?' I whispered.

Ola gave a wry grin and we clinked bottles and drank.

'What's it like bein' a prommer?' he mumbled.

'Dunno,' I said. 'Haven't noticed much.'

Then Ola went to sleep at his post. I went out into the May night thinking about all the things that were in the past now.

Seb had his orals at the Experimental School and he flew through them on Buddha's back, the time of miracles was not over. I lay in his room sweating my way through the hot days, drinking beer and tea and planning nothing. Mostly I thought about Nina and when I dreamt about her, I always dreamt she was somewhere in the world where it was winter now, and night-time when it was daytime here in Oslo, June, 1970.

One morning I asked Seb, 'Are you sure you're goin' to sea?'

He tried to scratch away the sunlight that burst through the window and landed on his navel.

'Yep. Just waitin' for a letter from Dad. And where I should meet him.'

'Alright if I use your room while you're away?'

'Course it is, man. Of course.'

He stretched out a hand and grabbed a half-full bottle of Export.

'Got the feelin',' he mumbled. 'Got the feelin' somethin's about to happen.'

And we shared the rest of the beer and a new day had started.

A few days before the results were announced I nipped home to put some food in my system and report in. My mother was like a cat on hot bricks wondering where I was staying at the moment and Dad was in the sitting room with Pym on his shoulder. I went for a snooze in my room and was woken by the telephone. Jørgen was on the line. We agreed to meet for a beer at the Herregård in Frogner Park. So I was off again. Mum ran after me with a fresh shirt and trousers with a crease, but those days were gone. I went as I was. I had been doing that for three weeks.

Jørgen was sitting at the table with the most sun. He was leaning against the yellow wall with a foaming glass of lager in front of him, it was a world of orange light. But soon the sun would sink behind the ridge and turn into a red blood orange. Jørgen waved to me.

I took a beer too, we toasted, squinted at the prom blazers scattered around, the geese waddling down the lawn, heard the monotonous fall of water through the buzz of conversation, didn't know quite what we should say, it was a long time since Jørgen and I had talked, there seemed to be a barrier.

'How's it goin'?' I asked.

'Yeah, fine.'

'Have you been to Denmark?'

He shook his head.

'Haven't done anything special. You?'

'Alternative celebrations,' I grinned. 'Stayin' away from bars.'

We ordered another round and the sun crept behind a branch. A group of exhausted merry-makers in crumpled outfits and green caps staggered through the landscape. We were served beers and drank in silence.

'What are you going to do now?' Jørgen asked at length.

'Don't know. Try to find a summer job. Earn myself some bread. And you? The military?'

'No. I got out of it.'

'Terrific! Me too! Said I was crazy. How did you wangle it?'

'Told them the truth,' Jørgen answered.

The beer tasted flat on the palate. I was beginning to feel I had had my fill. I was beginning to be run down. I was tired to the core. I ordered another half litre.

'Going to England when the results are out,' said Jørgen. 'If I pass.'

'Course you'll pass! Will you be spendin' the whole summer there?'

'I'm going to live there. In London.'

There was a barrier between us, a bar. We finished our beers. People were leaving. We shuffled off as well. We stopped on the bridge and looked down into the water. It smelt of sewage. We went on. I had nowhere else to go, so walked with Jørgen some of the way.

'Did *War and Peace* give you a taste for more theatre?'

I laughed.

'Not at all. The stage is not the place for me.'

'I'm going to apply for a place at a drama school in London. Where my friend is a student.'

The Monolith towered over us. I thought it seemed luminescent in the pitch dark. Couples were frolicking on white benches, there was the sound of activity behind the trees and bushes, the whole park was steaming, it was almost impossible to breathe.

We crossed over to Dogland and were suddenly alone. I needed a pee and stood by a post. Jørgen stood behind me scraping his shoes on the shingle.

'Like to come and visit me in London?'

'Course I would. If I'm passin' that way.'

'I'll send you the address.'

We mooched onwards. And then we were not alone any more. They came from behind us, we turned and they encircled us. There were seven or eight of them, and I recognised some of the faces, from another time when I was crossing Dogland and it was winter.

I showed them my finger, but it didn't work.

'Bloody bum bandits!' hissed one of them, grabbing Jørgen. 'Filthy buttfuckers!'

Jørgen stood mouth agape, his arms down by his side. One of them slapped him. Jørgen didn't react, he stared into the distance with dry, terror-stricken eyes. One of the others jabbed me. Their faces shone. They had dog-eyes.

'And you do the Nordic combined, do you, sweetie? Which do you like best, cross country or ski jumping?'

I thumped him even though I knew it was useless. I got a knee in my back and a ringed fist scraped across my nose.

Jørgen tried to run for it. They caught him like a lobster in a trap. He lashed out in all directions, just swung, without aiming, without hitting anyone, he was like a windmill. They laughed and kicked him backwards and forwards. Then I heard an ugly sound. The ringleader stood there with a flick knife in his hand, the blade shot out, long, thin, pointed. The others retreated a little. Jørgen stood crying with his hands over his ears. I didn't react until it had happened. Blood gushed from Jørgen's face and his cheek opened like a caesarean section. Then I tasted an iron fist and kissed the grass.

Someone was shaking me. Someone was sniffing at me and whimpering. I thrust open my eyes and stared into the black face of a poodle. Above me, an old man stood shaking his head. Then he poked me with his stick. I rolled over and caught sight of Jørgen. He was lying on his stomach with his arms outstretched in the grass, motionless.

'Ambulance,' I snuffled. 'Ring the hospital!'

I crawled on all fours across to Jørgen, turned him carefully. His face was slashed from temple to chin. My hand was drenched. Blood was pouring out of his fly.

Seb's room smelt freshly washed and clean. His grandmother had been there to tidy up, chuck out all the mouldy crusts and empty the bins. The results were out. We had passed. Ola had received his pay and holiday money and laid on Upper Ten Scotch and bock beer. The new Beatles record lay on the windowsill. 'Let It Be'. But it was not new, it had been recorded long before *Abbey Road,* it was over a year old.

We toasted each other.

'How's your snitch?' Gunnar asked.

'Can feel it's there,' I said, carefully feeling it with my hand, pain shot through my head like a scimitar.

'Why did they go for Jørgen with a knife then?' Seb enquired.

'Christ knows,' I said.

I had been to hospital to visit him, but I hadn't been allowed in. I had not been allowed in. Jørgen did not let anyone in. His mother stood outside crying. He had been given fifty-one stitches. I had to leave. I was not allowed in to see Jørgen.

Seb put on 'Morrison Hotel'. We mixed lukewarm water with the whisky. We didn't say much. It was as though we knew it was the last evening we would be together for a long time.

'When are you goin'?' I asked Seb at length.

'When I get a letter from my dad.'

'What will you do when we've gone our separate ways?' Gunnar asked.

I hummed and hawed, I had no idea.

'Start studyin' or somethin.'

'Are we goin' to play 'Let It Be' then?' Ola said.

We opened a few beers, couldn't be bothered to go into the corridor to pee, took turns to have a leak in the sink.

'What's your brother goin' to do this summer?' Seb asked.

'Goin' to Mardøla,' Gunnar said. 'Would've gone there myself if I could have.'

'Bloody great talk he gave about anarchism, by the way. Got to agree with a lot of what he says, haven't you?'

'Well, some. But the basic thrust is wrong. You think monopoly capitalists are good boys who will release the production means without a fight.'

'That's not true,' Seb interrupted. 'We just think that the socialism you support is so bloody authoritarian. Isn't it. People should be able to choose. What did Stalin do, eh? Smashed the faces of all those who disagreed. How many was it he buried, Gunnar? Ten million or thirty million?'

'Stalin had good and bad sides,' Gunnar said. 'And how many Russians fell in the battle against Nazism, eh? If it hadn't been for Stalin we'd be lyin' in ovens, the whole lot of us. Wouldn't we.'

But this was not the night for confrontations. We drank slowly and stayed cool. We talked about May 1, when Stig and Seb were booted out of the procession. We sat reminiscing and became a little sentimental and grinned into our beer.

'Put The Beatles single on now, will you!' said Ola.

'Vigdis asked after you the other day,' Seb said.

Ola cowered and looked like an angry bull.

'Shall we go and get her?' I suggested.

'Don't arse about, boys!' Ola shouted. 'Don't arse about! I can't help it that Kirsten lives in Trondheim, can I. I'm gonna visit her when I'm on leave!'

We patted him on the back and served him some bock and Upper Ten. He calmed down. Then we were quiet for a long time, it was a strange evening.

'Dad had to give up his shop,' Gunnar said apropos of nothing. 'Workin' in Bonus now.'

He said no more than that. I didn't say that I had seen him. Gunnar mixed a red-coloured drink and knocked it back.

'Have you heard McCartney's solo album?' Seb asked.

I shook my head.

'And you who thought he'd snuffed it!'

'I bloody did not!'

Seb grinned and leaned against the wall.

'You bloody did! You were on your knees.'

Ola and Gunnar chortled.

'Did you believe it?'

'I'm not a complete bonehead, am I. Course I didn't think McCartney was dead!'

They contented themselves with that. The hours ebbed away. It was dark, but not completely dark. Seb closed the window.

'My dad's goin' on about my taking the final school exams,' Ola said. 'One-year course. Do you think that'd work?'

Of course it would. Nothing was impossible. Then we talked a bit about all the pressure on us to be something, all the plans that were being made for us, we were going to be bank directors, shop managers, hotel proprietors and ship owners if our parents' dreams were to come true.

We chuckled and drank a toast to the future.

'Put "Let It Be" on before we fall asleep,' Ola said.

But we fell asleep anyway, all four of us, each in a corner while the room went blue and the town beneath us became quieter and the alcohol in the brain relaxed its grip and goldfish swam in front of our red eyes. And so we slept on the last evening, the last night, for a long time.

We were awoken by banging and shouting. It was Seb, who had

fetched the post. There was a letter from his father. He stood among the bottles and read aloud while we straightened our hair, swallowed bad breath and peered around for cigarettes and beer dregs. Seb was supposed to meet his father in Bordeaux where the *Bolero* was moored for unloading. He just had to pack his kitbag. Seb's face shone with pleasure. Then he turned the sheet over, went all serious, sat down on the floor and stared at each of us.

'Listen here, boys. *Listen* here! Dad's written about *Dragon*!'

We were awake at once and leaned closer.

'Dad's written about Dragon! Wow! Listen here! Dragon was on board a ship sailin' round South America. Christ. And some prick of an American officer kept takin' the piss out of him because of his face. And do you know what Dragon did! Dragon stabbed 'im. Stabbed and killed the bastard. And then he jumped overboard! Dragon jumped into the sea and was gone!'

'Must've drowned, I suppose?' Ola whispered.

Seb went quiet.

'Says here there are loads of sharks in the waters. Must've been eaten by a bloody shark.'

We thought about May 17 when the firework had exploded in Dragon's face. We didn't utter another word for a long time. Then Gunnar said, 'Wonder if his Mick Jagger signature was genuine.'

And then they departed, the seaman and the soldiers, while I was left behind in the hot, stinking town where the tarmac melted beneath your feet, June 1970, when the cinemas were the coolest places to be and the beer was never cold enough.

I moved my things down to Seb's, namely, a few records, a few books, a change of clothing. My mother asked whether I was going to Nesodden, I doubted it, and she cried a little as the taxi drove off, I sat in the back seat with a sleeping bag and cardboard boxes, went down Svoldergate without a care. I bought a cold chicken and white wine for the evening, celebrated the occasion on my own, considered going to see Vigdis, but changed my mind, this evening was mine. I hung my clothes in the wardrobe, put away my records, propped my books against the wall, Mao's *Little Red Book*, *The Anarchistic Reader*, *The New Testament*, *Kykelipi* and *Victoria*, didn't quite know why I had brought that particular one, had to be a huge mistake, was given it by Grandma at Christmas 1965, old edition, smelt a bit of Bible when I sniffed it. It said 'A Love Story' on the cover and inside there was a faded drawing of a man sitting with bowed head crying while flowers and blood rained down over him, pretty slushy, I hadn't even read it. Then the book opened at some random page and out fell a flower, a flower, a pressed red poppy, I was sure that I had thrown it away, it fell to the floor and disintegrated, turned to dust, it was so dry. I collected the remains as well as I could, put them in a cup, and I was sure that if I made tea in the cup now, a spirit would emerge in the room, and if I drank it, I would go wherever Nina was.

I was a bit dismayed when I woke up the next morning, woke up alone, sweating from the heat, in my own room for the first time. I opened the window and heard the City Hall clock strike eleven. It was a pleasure and a delight. I was free. I let out a huge howl across the town, a mating cry, a call for mischief. Then a window shot open beneath me and a girl peered out. It was Vigdis from the lift.

'Hiya,' she said.

'Is that an invitation?' I said.

She laughed and looked up at me.

'Are you livin' there now?'

'Yep. Old Seb has gone to sea.'

'Is Ola in the military?'

'Madla naval base. Yellow Submarine.'

Then we retreated to our respective rooms and a problem announced its presence with undreamed of potency. Money. I didn't have any money for breakfast. I gave the matter some deep thought over a coffee. When I had finished cogitating I went out to find a telephone box and rang City Parks and Gardens. I could begin the following day.

And so I became a gardener. I planted tulips in St Hanshaugen Park and drank lukewarm beer at Friluften. I watered the grass in Frogner Park and threw a Frisbee with a dozy bunch high on booze and spliffs. These were days on a slack leash. I was on nodding terms with all the bums and freaks in the whole of Oslo. But one morning I was sent to Slottsparken with a hoe and a fork to turn the soil. The sun spread like a crushed plum across the blind, light blue sky, there was not a breath of wind and life passed in slow motion. I dug the earth and turned it over for about half an hour, then I reckoned that was enough, knotted my shirt around my head and sat behind a tree. I must have fallen asleep. For when I awoke Pelle was there with his piglets behind him. The park had come to life, people were lying all over the scorched grass, a record player was playing a warped Fleetwood Mac LP, a thin guitar sound competed with a couple of sleepy birds, smoke from pipes of peace rose into the air.

'Horizontal council worker,' Pelle grinned. 'Got any bread goin' spare?'

Hard to refuse anyone on a day like this, even though Pelle was an uncouth bastard. I forked out a couple of tens and they made their way over to another group. They were sitting and blowing smoke skywards. I closed my eyes to recharge myself for another spell with the fork. Then Pelle was there again, a smoking joint hidden behind his cupped fingers.

'Forget your packed lunch, did you?' he wheezed, offering his hand. And I accepted it, smoked the Moroccan kif, in my lunch break, in Slottsparken, in the summer of 70.

That was probably the moment my career as a gardener came to an end. I worked slowly through the flower bed, dozed off again and dreamt about Afghanistan and Nina, and when I was awoken for the third time, it was the last time. There was pandemonium. The fuzz had arrived with three black Mariahs and were running around with truncheons and slavering Alsatians. Suddenly I was staring into steaming red jaws and I got to my feet very smartly. A bloody cop was hitting out at me with his erect baton. I ran over to the flower bed and held the fork in the air. He bounded after me with the beast on a tight lead.

'I work here!' I shouted.

They were slinging people into the paddy wagon. I saw a truncheon hit Pelle over the ear and glimpsed blood spurting from his nose before the animal sank its teeth into my trousers and tore off a chunk of material

I swung the fork aloft.

'I'm a gardener!' I yelled.

There was a sudden scrum around me. They stood in a semicircle and approached with stealth. I held the fork in front of me and retreated towards a bush. The Alsatian lay flat on the ground and its saliva shone in the sunlight. Then they were on me and I don't remember anything else until I was lying on my stomach in the black Mariah, my arms shackled behind me. The floor hit my face, we drove off.

'He threatened us with a fork,' a voice said.

'He? You sure it's not a girl?'

I was yanked over, a boot kicked me between the legs. I screamed, but the sound was strangled by the vomit that spewed forth. I saw blood. I saw only blood. My eyes were red balloons.

'Boy,' grinned the man. 'Reckon that's a boy alright.'

'Tried to kill us with a pitch fork, didn't he,' another voice said. 'Very dangerous individual.'

I was given a kick in the ribs, then someone stood on my back and ground my face into the jolting, lurching floor. Don't know how long it was before the van came to a halt, and a furious head came close to mine, his spittle flew as he roared, 'You're getting off lightly, you long-haired homo. We could report you for police assault.'

'I'm a gardener,' I said meekly. 'For City Parks and Gardens.'

He was deaf in that ear.

'And you were in possession of cannabis!' he shouted.

'Was I hell!' I said.

He smiled. The policeman smiled, but it was not sincere.

'Right, sweetie pie. We found this on you.'

He produced a dark brown slab.

'Didn't we, boys. We found this on our missie here.'

The others were in total agreement.

'But we'll turn a blind eye this time. Just want to teach you a lesson.'

Chortles and chuckles all round. Then I was held from the back and the bastard policeman conjured up a pair of scissors. His stinking yellow teeth moistened with saliva. Four sweaty hands twisted my head into position. And then he hacked at my hair from all sides. I screamed, I yelled, but to no avail, my hair flew around the van and their grins grew wider and wider.

'Now he looks good,' the pig sang. 'I was right, see. It is a boy.'

'You cocksucker!' I howled and spat a juicy gobbet into his face, it ran down his cheek, thick and yellow.

Now they came to life, they assaulted me from all angles, in the end I didn't feel the kicks and punches, I was outside my abused body and the pain was only a dream.

Then the door was opened and I was rolled out, heard the engine roar and saw the black Mariah race down a path between tall trees. I lay on a path in the middle of a forest and had no idea which. Was it Kongsskogen or Norwegian Wood? It was neither. I stayed on the ground until my soul had regained its place in my body. The pains launched themselves over me anew and into the dry earth I cried bitter and burning tears.

I tried to walk, to walk the way the pigs had driven. My legs buckled beneath me like grass. I had to rest on a rock. The sun looked like scrambled eggs gone stiff. The forest floated in a haze. I forced my legs to go on. They carried me for a while. Then I spotted a river, crawled down to the edge and stuck my head under the water.

When I emerged someone shouted at me.

'Hey, you gnome, you're frightening the fish!'

I looked around. In the middle of the rapids stood a fly-fisher in wading boots with a cap covered in hooks.

'Where am I?' I shouted back.

'Can't you see I'm fishing, you troll! Clear off!'

'Where am I?' I repeated.

'Are you a complete idiot? You're in Åborbekken.'

He must have had a bite, he fought with the huge rod and the long line, cursed and swore, until finally he got himself tied up in a huge tangle with a pile of twigs on the hook.

'That's your doing!' he screamed. 'Everything was going fine until you arrived on the scene! You hobgoblin!'

'Which way to town?'

He couldn't point, so he had to nod. He nodded eastwards, or southwards, pulled at the line as the water poured over the top of his waders. I gingerly picked myself up and continued on the forest path.

I walked for several hours without seeing a single person. Then I came to a large expanse of water. At first I thought it was the sea, but I realised that it was fresh water. I was alongside a lake in Norway and walking along the bank. Walking there, exhausted and sore, battered and bruised, I began to hate all the parks in Oslo. Parks just caused disasters, parks persecuted me, ever since I went to the ski-training school in Frogner Park, parks had been after me. I would never go to another park again. I would ask the foreman to put me on churchyards instead, that would suit me better, I would apply to do that. All of a sudden a rock-hard ball hit me in the forehead and I almost went down for the count. At the same time I heard a cry, it didn't come from me, and, some distance away, behind a sandbank stood a weird-looking type in checked trousers, tearing his hair. Beside him there was a little person with a trolley full of clubs.

'Watch out, you idiot!' I shouted.

He sank to his knees and began to pull at the grass.

Then, of course, I knew where I was.

'Is this Bogstad golf course?' I asked, relieved.

The man stood up with whitened knuckles around the club.

'Where do you think you are, you halfwit? At the circus? At a funfair? Do you think, do you think I was *trying* to hit you? Do you think I was aiming? Are you out of your mind? Are you mad!'

'You should be a bit careful with that ball!' I responded. 'You could have smashed my head in.'

He changed clubs and tried to hit me. I had to take to my heels. He followed me while shouting something about the eighth hole. I pulled out a couple of flags as I sped past and emerged through a gate into an elegant road of detached houses. I sat down on the kerb and felt my forehead. Another bump was on its way. I was being persecuted. But now at any rate I knew roughly where I was. I wandered around until I found the direction, over Røa, past Njård sports hall, across Majorstuen, straight into town as the sun lit the forests in the west and the light let the darkness in. And I met Vigdis in the lift again. She let out a squeal of fright when she saw me, I was unable to meet my own gaze in the lift mirror.

We went up to the fourth floor.

'What happened to you?' she exclaimed.

'Long story. You would never believe it.'

I followed Vigdis into her room. It was traditional with embroideries on the walls, photographs of her parents on a bookshelf and oranges in a woven basket on the table, felt at home immediately.

She patched me up with plasters and gauze. Vigdis's hands were chunky and red and light as feathers.

'Your hair,' she laughed. 'What have you done to your lovely hair?'

I glanced at a mirror. There was nothing to laugh at. I looked worse than Ola had the time his father ran amok with his scissors. Ola had been elegant in comparison with me. I was a marked man.

'Could I have an orange?' I asked.

'As many as you like,' Vigdis smiled, clearing the operating table.

Then something strange happened. But I was not very surprised, for the whole day had been against me anyway. I peeled the orange and there was nothing inside. It was empty. I peeled and peeled and there was no orange. I said nothing to Vigdis. I just put the peel on a plate and wiped my mouth.

Vigdis turned.

'That was quick,' she said.

'Oranges are a speciality of mine,' I said.

'You can have another.'

'Only eat one a day.'

I got to my feet and took a step towards the door. All of a sudden Vigdis was holding a full bottle of gin in front of her.

'Would you like a drink?' she asked mischievously.

And for once I was sensible, for nowhere was it written that this day could not throw up any more disasters.

I swallowed hard and did not tempt fate.

'No, thank you,' I said. 'Another time. Another time.'

And then I was given the sack. When I turned up for work on the following day I received a real rollicking and they refused to give my story the time of day. I had abandoned my tools and cleared off during working hours, I was scum, I only had to look in the mirror, there was nothing to discuss. I was given the sack and my wages, three hundred kroner, which were burning a hole in my pocket as I stood in the middle of Oslo wondering what the hell to do next. I went to Pernille. Later I rang Jørgen. His mother answered and said in a hazy voice that Jørgen had left for London two days before. She didn't know when he would be back. She slammed down the phone. The day after, I was broke again.

I lay on the mattress with a thick head, listing badly. My brain cells clung together like sticky rice. But one of the grains was fitter than the others and transmitted a brilliant message: Go to the bank and empty your account. I soaked my head under the tap and trudged off to St Olavsgate, to the bank where Dad was the branch manager, the bank that was robbed by someone who was never apprehended. It was many years since I had been there, but the smell was the same, mint and a freshly waxed floor, and the sounds, the crackle of banknotes, as though there was a little fire alight the whole time. And it was dark. I was almost blinded as I entered from the white light outside, into the crackling, clean darkness. Dad used to sit at the counter, I remember he was always very careful to cut his nails every morning. Now he had an office at the back of the building. A lady led me through. Dad was not in the least bit surprised to see me. He just looked friendly and a bit tired, his slowness was almost the worst thing of all, he didn't notice my clothes, or my hair, he didn't even see my crazy haircut.

'Is that you?' was all he said.

'How's Nesodden?' I asked.

'Fine. Not a good year for apples though.'

'Redcurrants?'

'I think the redcurrants will be okay. And the gooseberries. But the plums don't look at all good.'

The office was cramped and oppressive, the walls dark, papers filed in binders on the desk in neat piles. Dad looked up at me, rested his chin in his hands.

'What are you doing?' I asked.

Dad smiled.

'Nothing.'

I sniggered. It struck me that it should have been him asking me that question and I would have answered the same way he had.

'I need money,' I said. 'Thought I might withdraw some from my account.'

Dad nodded and stood up.

'That should be alright,' he said.

Then he went to speak to a cashier and a quarter of an hour later I was standing on the pavement with 850 kroner in my back pocket and the world, or Oslo at least, lay before me like a swing door. I stocked up with white wine at the *vinmonopol* and carried the goods back to my room. But another surprise was waiting for me there, a handsome bill for Seb in the postbox, he hadn't paid the rent for ten months. I would be evicted if the money was not paid within three days. There was no option but to pay up and as a result I was left with seventy-eight kroner. I wondered whether to catch the first boat to Nesodden, but heroically I resisted. And so the summer passed, I was broke and living on crusts and lukewarm water, but one day I met Vigdis in the lift again, she saw how the land lay and took care of me, feeding me with thick vegetable broth and full-fat buttermilk and waffles. Vigdis took care of me for the rest of the summer, kept me alive for some reason and I realised that The Great Revolutionary Feat was not meant for the likes of me, I wasn't cut out for that sort of task. I realised that one evening, leaning back against the windowsill, satiated after having eaten thirty of Vigdis's waffles. It was Dragon who had accomplished the Great Revolutionary Feat, I saw him swimming through foaming water, a knife between his teeth and sharks on all sides. Dragon, I thought, you have avenged Fred, you have avenged Jørgen, Dragon the Avenger!

Golden Slumbers

Autumn/winter '70–'71

Standing on the auditorium steps with my matriculation papers in hand, I was aware that autumn had already begun, even though the sun was hanging over the National Theatre and filtering through the trees, it was an Indian summer, just as Dad had said once when we were going to pick apples, it was September and I thought that soon they would probably be nailing down the boards over the fountain again. I stood on the auditorium steps as people ran past me. I didn't see anyone I knew. Some wore black hats. Some were in traditional costume or suits. Some turned up in denim, like me. I peered around for familiar faces, but saw none. I wondered what to do now. I walked down the steps over to the bench where Mum and Dad were sitting. They squeezed my hand and were proud, had needed to hold the stiff diploma with the red stamp, one after the other. Mum glared at my clothes, but refrained from making a comment. She said, 'Are you going to stay in your room, Kim?'

'Thought I would.'

'But isn't Sebastian coming back soon?'

'Don't know.'

'Are you coping on your own?'

'Oh, yes.'

The conversation stalled. We smiled at each other, but at that moment Dad woke up, as though he had found his old self in his suit.

'And you're sure you've chosen the right subject?' he asked in loud, clear tones.

'Think so. But I have to take the prelim first anyway.'

'Philosophy,' Mum said slowly. 'What sort of job can you do with that?'

We stood shifting feet again, then Dad took out a crisp hundred note, hot off the press from Norges Bank.

'To celebrate with, in moderation, though,' he said, nudging my shoulder.

'Wow,' I smiled. 'Wow.'

Stood there with the crisp banknote while Mum and Dad walked arm in arm under the trees, didn't quite know what to do with myself, sat down on the bench and lit a cigarette. A girl walked past distributing anti-EEC leaflets. Afterwards a boy from the Action Committee gave me another. I stuffed them in my pocket, looked around, no familiar faces. So I took the tram to Blindern, browsed around in the bookshop, examined a few set books and felt weary. It was better in the record shop, self-service, could listen to whatever records I liked. I flipped through a few jazz LPs, Davis, Coltrane, Mingus, but couldn't somehow find my rhythm. I strolled over to Frederikke, bought myself a cup of toxic coffee and sat alone at a table in the huge barn. No familiar faces there, either. I smoked too much and had to go to the loo. On the floor below there was a line of student stands. The students launched themselves at me, stuffed me full of paper. Eventually I found the toilet, there was a man standing at the urinal, and he began to speak the moment I appeared, asked whether I was a member of the People's Movement or the Action Committee. I beat a retreat, ran past the stands and emerged between the red tower blocks. People were sprawled over the grass, I walked past, slowly, but I didn't know a soul. I headed for town again, via Tørtberg, some young lads playing football in blue and white, stood watching them, Åge was on the sidelines, yes, it was Åge, he had filled out a bit, but it was Åge, recognised his yells. The leather ball seemed so comical among the thin legs. I trudged on, chuckling, and then I was back in Karl Johan. What to do now, I wondered. I went to Pernille and had the last beer of the year. The glass in my hands was cold. That was when I realised. I had lost my matriculation papers. Must have left them in the record shop. Couldn't be bothered to go back now. I sat until my back became cold. No one I knew in Pernille that day. I mooched around again, down to the quayside and watched the Nesodden boat reverse out and turn. On the way back, I stopped by Klingenberg cinema. Long queue and excited atmosphere. *Woodstock*. Had nothing else to do, queued, and then I sat in the auditorium, the lights went out and the images and the music assaulted my senses. Soon the whole room was illuminated by lighters, rows of them burst into flame and the thick, sweet smell wafted through the air. My neighbour nudged me and passed a glowing spliff. I accepted. There were four pictures on the screen at once. From behind I was given a chillum. A few guards patrolled the sides scratching their heads. A girl gave me a lozenge. Country Joe sang. The rain. The rain at Woodstock. I will never forget it. Then it was over and we shuffled into the streets. I ran a hand through my pockets. I was broke. The darkness reflected off the tarmac and I didn't like the film that was crossing the sky, didn't like the images at all. I ran home, to Munchsgate. The lift took me up. I stood with my back to the mirror. I exited on the fourth and rang Vigdis's bell. She was at home and let me in. Afterwards I could only remember that I woke up in her tiny bath in my underpants, my head a quarry. I dragged myself up to my full height and when I saw my face in the mirror, I screamed, I screamed, for there was a stripe of blood across my face, my face was divided into two, it was ripped open, I screamed, and then Vigdis was there, chubby and naked, with pendulous breasts touching my back.

'You're weird,' she said.

I ran my hands across my face, turned on the tap and bent down. I had to rub damned hard, it wouldn't all come off, a dark shadow across my face remained.

'You owe me three things,' Vigdis said.

I looked at us in the mirror.

'What?'

'A bottle of gin.'

I nodded cautiously. Couldn't complain about that.

'Lipstick.'

The empty tube was on the floor. We looked at each other in the mirror.

'And the third?' I asked.

Vigdis ran her finger down my spine.

'I don't want to say.'

She had to work and I had to go home. I went up a floor, stumbled into my room, vomited into the waste paper basket and dived onto the mattress, as though from the ten-metre board, ten metres into an empty pool, and slept for nine months.

PART 3

Come Together

Summer '71

It was overwhelming. There were thousands, tens of thousands of people, had never seen so many in one place before. We were standing in Youngstorget, it was the beginning of June and the height of the afternoon, and Gunnar and Ola were on leave.

'Now let's have some fun with the middle classes!' Gunnar yelled through the din of stamping feet, clapping hands, slogans, crackling microphones, rattling money boxes, music and wind.

I just smiled in return. People were pouring in from all sides, we were squeezed together tighter and tighter, it was like being on an enormous dance floor where everyone was dancing with everyone.

'Where's Seb?' Ola shrieked into my ear.

I shrugged. I had no idea where Seb was.

'Hasn't he come home yet?'

Gunnar looked frightened.

I shook my head, for it was impossible to speak in this chaos. Big placards and banners and Norwegian flags were raised over the massed turnout. ALL ROADS DO NOT LEAD TO BRUSSELS. EEC MEANS INCREASED LIVING COSTS! NO TO EEC – YES TO DECENTRALISATION. And then those at the front began to move towards Karl Johan and the City Hall square, and it took at least four hours from the time the first ones set off until the last. You might have been forgiven for thinking some were walking in circles, but they weren't, it was the nation that had taken to the streets in Oslo that June in 1971.

The town was green and red, and smelt of lilac and exhaust fumes, sun and clenched fists.

In the City Hall square it was even more cramped. A speaker's platform had been rigged up on the back of a lorry and Norwegian flags fluttered against the sky. We were standing roughly in the middle of the crowd and being pushed from behind. Ola was becoming paler and paler. He seemed to be sagging suspiciously close to paving height.

I dragged him up.

'You unwell?'

He rolled an eye, sweat streaming down his forehead.

'Claustrophobia,' he whispered. 'Gettin' claustrophobic.'

He started gulping and we steered him out of the crowd, found refuge by the National Theatre.

'How d'you manage in the submarine if you can't even stand it here?' I grinned.

Ola's spirits were reviving.

'I didn't manage,' he groaned. 'Almost ruined an entire NATO manoeuvre. Became a cook at Madla naval base instead.'

That made us laugh for a good long time and we headed for Saras Telt, ordered a round and sussed each other out. It was a long time since we had seen each other, we looked for changes, wondered if we were the same as before.

'So you haven't heard a peep from Seb?' Gunnar asked.

'Zilch. Zero.'

I hadn't heard from Nina, either, nor from Jørgen. My mother would have had to re-address any post that came, but the postbox had been empty every single bloody morning, a black well, no sign of life, not even so much as a garish postcard.

'Funny,' Gunnar mumbled, looking concerned, he drank, rolled a Petterøes cigarette. 'Have you spoken to his mum?'

'Nope.'

'What've you actually done this year?' Ola asked. He was back on top form.

I took my time.

'Not a lot. Slept.'

'Haven't you taken the prelim?'

'Didn't apply.'

Another round was carried to the table. We clinked and drank.

'Strange that Seb hasn't dropped a line,' Gunnar repeated.

'You haven't exactly had writer's itch, either,' I burst out. 'Didn't you have any leave or what?'

They were embarrassed and I regretted speaking out of turn. Ola had spent all his leaves with Kirsten, Gunnar had been working with a team in Bodø.

I laughed it off.

'It was dismal here without you,' I said, knocking back the glass.

Gunnar looked straight at me, his eyes didn't deviate by one millimetre.

'That was bad of us, Kim. Very bad. We accept the criticism for that. But now we're here, anyway. Though Seb isn't.'

He didn't manage to say another word as Stig crashed down at our table holding a pile of anarchist newspapers in his arms.

'Greetings, kinfolk. This is where you sit poisonin' yourselves of your own free will, is it?'

He snapped his fingers at the beer glasses.

'And you, too, brother. Thought ML'ers were united in their fight against alcohol.'

'Drunkenness,' Gunnar said. 'We are against drunkenness. But workers are damn well allowed to have a bloody beer of a warm summer's evenin', aren't they?'

Stig shaded his eyes and peered around.

'Workers? Where did you say they were?'

'Been in the procession?' I asked, to lift the lid off the pressure cooker.

'Sure thing, boys.' He slapped Gunnar on the back. 'Shame you couldn't have joined us, brother.'

Gunnar slowly turned towards him.

'I bloody did.'

'Did you? Thought the action committee considered mass demos bourgeois crap. Thought the action committee had its own slogans.'

Before Gunnar had a chance to come with a riposte he stood up and stretched out his arms as though he were the pope and was going to bless us.

'Pop by Hjelmsgate one day, lads. We have a book café and biodynamic food. See you!'

He shuffled over to another table. Gunnar didn't say anything for the next three quarters of an hour. Then he said, 'Damn it! We have to find out what's happened to Seb!'

I slunk home later that night. The postbox was empty again. I took the lift to the fourth and rang Vigdis's bell. A girl I didn't recognise opened the door and I could see that there was a new name on the door, too. Vigdis had moved a long time ago, several months before. She gave me a strange look. So I didn't manage to give her what I owed her after all. I clambered up the last floor and let myself in. It didn't look good. I would have to tidy up. It was time I did. I opened the window. I emptied the stinking waste paper basket, stuffed clothes into the wardrobe, tidied away books, stacked the records, blew fluff off the stylus, poured away rancid milk, chucked out the rock-hard, green crusts, washed and cleaned. Seb would have a nice welcome if he came back, and if he didn't, we would have to go and look for him, by Christ we would.

The following day we visited his mother, and she confirmed our worst fears. Seb had never reached Bordeaux. His father had waited and waited until in the end he had had to leave without Seb. Something had happened to Seb on the way. He had sent one card, just after New Year from Amsterdam, saying he was going to Paris and was fine. His mother looked unhappy and frightened.

'And how are you?' she ventured with a smile, appraising each one of us.

'Fine, getting by.' We shuffled our feet and made for the hall.

'Tell me if you hear anything!' she begged, wringing her hands.

It was raining outside so we held a pow-wow at Krølle. The situation was critical. We would have to go to Paris and search for Seb.

'We can hitch down there,' I said. 'Take a couple of days. Cinch.'

'I'm flat broke,' Ola said.

'There was a bloke in the military who used to have a summer job in Majorstuen Transport Office,' Gunnar said. 'They need loads of people all summer.'

'And when we get to Paris, I can touch up my uncle for cash!'

We batted to and fro what could have happened to Seb, there were quite a number of things, we huddled round the table, whispering, freezing, it was urgent now, there wasn't a day to lose.

On Monday morning we turned up in Aslakveien in Røa with a herd of others smelling of booze and rolling red mix with trembling yellow fingers. A man with a peaked cap, Cap'n, noted down our names and then someone shouted and the hired workers trudged off after the drivers. Gunnar got a job, Ola got a job, and at last my name was called out, too. I was sent to the warehouse for six straps and took them back to the Bedford where five big lumps with hairy arms were waiting. I had minor palpitations. I had been assigned to the piano van. They must have confused me with Gunnar. They measured me up with cold smiles and exchanged glances. My thighs were thinner than the driver's upper arms. I could just about carry the straps.

'Chuck them in the van,' one man growled, 'and sit on them.'

I did as I was told. The others grinned. Then we set off. It bumped and jolted, I was suddenly reminded of the black Mariah and cold sweat began to form. I peered out of the filthy van window, behind me came the Bedford lorry. We drove towards Majorstuen and stopped outside Mayong in Slemdalsveien. The others piled out to eat breakfast. They had forgotten me. They left me to sit in the cramped, stinking van. I pushed and pulled at the door, but it would not open. I was an incarcerated dog, and I hated them. Then one of the men came out and opened the door. I scrambled out and gorged myself on oxygen. He patted my back and gave a rough guffaw.

'Sorry, pal. We forgot the luggage.'

The heavily muscled gang was sitting behind the window chuckling over their burgers. I wished Seb was home. I took a seat at their table with just enough money for a coffee.

Feverishly I rolled a cigarette.

'You know that in fact you've got to wear a hairnet on this job, don't you?' said one beefcake tensing his tattoos. 'So that you don't get your hair caught in the straps. Worse than getting your dick caught on a hook, that is!'

The laughter rippled around the table, and I laughed with them, had at last stopped fiddling with the roll-up.

'We've got to carry a piano, have we?' I asked before the laughter had subsided.

It quickly died and everyone looked at me. They shook their ample heads.

'Nope. Not a piano.'

I was relieved and my confidence grew.

'Concert grand,' said the driver.

It had to be taken to the large music room in Chateau Neuf, the student house and concrete block that had blighted Tørtberg. The legs had been unscrewed, so it was on its side, wrapped in a tarpaulin and lashed to an iron frame with six holes for the straps. The whole thing weighed half a ton. There were six of us. Or five and a quarter.

I couldn't manage the knot in the strap and had to have help. They rolled their eyes and I felt a bit like the time when my father used to stand behind me to knot my tie. Then we adjusted the strap lengths, put the hooks in the holes and at a signal from the foreman we stood up. It was like having your spine pushed down one leg. Blood and head parted company and I staggered giddily through the door and to the stairs with the entire world on the hook. We stopped and put it down. The strap burned my neck and shoulders, the knot cut into my kidneys.

'You go at the front,' said the foreman, pointing to me. 'Adjust your strap so that it matches Kalle's.'

Kalle was the one with the tattoos and the biceps. I took off the strap, loosened the knot and looked Kalle up and down. He just stood staring at me.

'What the hell are you doin'?' he yelled.

'Makin' an adjustment,' I said meekly.

'But for friggin', freakin' Pete's sake you don't need to take off the strap to adjust the length.'

'You don't?'

'Are we the same height?'

'I reckon you're taller than me,' I said.

'Right, brains. So your bloody strap should be shorter than mine if we want the piano to be level, shouldn't it!'

A blush descended over my head like a tight, hot helmet. I slipped the strap on, then we bobbed up and down until all the hooks were at the same height. I was having trouble with the knot again, but didn't dare ask for help. At length I managed to tie it and it felt fairly secure.

Then we took the strain, lifted at the same time and began to climb up the stairs. It was heavier than carrying your own body. Your heart seemed to be pushed down into your stomach, your brain sucked into your mouth. But then something happened in the middle of the staircase leading to the first landing, it began to feel lighter, as if I had become used to the weight, as though it didn't seem to affect me any more. It was a miracle. I felt light, uncannily light, I felt like whistling, telling a joke, it was like floating. However, Kalle's face was getting redder and redder, sweat was pouring off his brow, his eyes were narrow and turbid and his mouth was twisted into a demented grimace.

'Down!' he bellowed and we lowered the grand piano onto the landing. He leaned across the tarpaulin gasping for breath, wheezing like a bagpipe. I felt nothing and smiled at the others.

Then Kalle stood up, unhooked himself, came round to me in a furious temper and measured my strap. It was at least ten centimetres longer than his.

'Tryin' to be funny, are we?' he rasped. 'Givin' me the whole weight?'

'I didn't mean to,' I stuttered.

He examined the knot, looked at me.

'For Pete's sake, you can't use a granny knot to lift a grand piano!'

The others groaned and cried out, smacking their foreheads.

'The whole thing could tip, you plonker!'

So he had to knot my tie again and we carried the piano over the last stretch, up to the music room, I carried until I cried, I felt like a dwarf when we eventually sat down, I had blisters on my back and water on my knees, I was bruised, bent and ashamed of myself.

Afterwards Kalle came over to me, gave me a proper cigarette and patted me on the shoulder. Then they drove me back to base and I was given the job of stacking cardboard boxes in the warehouse.

At half past three Gunnar and Ola were back, too. We handed in our timesheets at the cash desk, were paid, caught the tram to town and it was hard to cross Majorstuen with our pockets weighed down. We found a table at Gamle Major.

'Buggered if I'm gonna keep doin' this shite job,' I said. 'I was on the piano run and made a complete tit of myself.'

'You'll fare better tomorrow, you see. Ola and I had cushy jobs.'

'Almost broke my back carryin' that bloody piano. Should've had bloody knee pads. Buggered if I'm gonna queue tomorrow!'

'So you don't want to stick with it because the piano was heavy or because the blokes took the piss?' Gunnar asked.

'Another job like that and I definitely won't be goin' to Paris.'

The atmosphere was fraught. Gunnar was het up too, he leaned across the table and shoved the bottles to the side.

'The trouble with you, Kim, is that you're a coward. You've always done crazy things, but when it comes to the crunch, you're a coward and touchy with it. You can climb onto a roof and dance with skeletons, but you can't take it when an older workman laughs at you because you can't tie a knot!'

Did Gunnar say that? Don't remember, and it doesn't matter. In any case, I turned up the following day, of course I did, and was sent to empty an elegant detached house in Persbråten, and was given beer and overtime. It was Gunnar's suggestion that we should just spend the money we needed to live on so that we didn't drink our travel money up at Gamle Major. No sooner said than done. We were drivers' mates and criss-crossed the whole of Østlandet, getting to know every café and grocer's in Oslo and surrounding areas, just like we had once known every grass pitch and football field, and later every park. Ola met the man who had given him a lift from Slemmestad on that fateful day and the reunion was heartfelt, he became a permanent fixture on that lorry. Gunnar took my place on the piano lorry and I shifted and carried, packed dank underwear and dirty crockery, manhandled freezers crammed with food that melted and stank in the heat, I piled up books, rolled carpets, opened cupboards and pulled out drawers. I saw behind the façade of half of Norway and I didn't really like what I saw. I saw dust and crap and a multitude of useless things. We went to people who were splitting up, they scrapped over every bloody plate and teaspoon, I saw hatred, I saw love, a photograph under a pillow someone had forgotten, a slip of paper between books, and after stripping an apartment I knew everything about those who had lived there, there were no secrets left. We moved stuff from the apprentices' college in Bogstadsveien, carried foul mattresses covered with wank stains down from the third floor and drove them all to the dump in Skui.

I remember standing there, it was a hot day, the sun was baking, I stood there wearing sandals on the decomposing landfill site, unloading crap while giant flies as big as helicopters buzzed around my head, gleaming white seagulls circled and screamed and glistening rats ran in all directions. That day I had to go to Gamle Major no matter what.

But then one day I got the top job, the crème de la crème, we had to move The Doll's House at the National Theatre, the company was going on tour. We whizzed down, a driver and two driver's mates, parked by Pernille, wandered into the spooky house behind the stage, in the wings with wires and ropes and all sorts of things hanging down. The caretaker showed us what had to be taken. It was just a question of getting started, and we did, and it occurred to me then and forever afterwards, that films, theatre, books and poems were just a fraud. It's only music that doesn't deceive, it doesn't pretend to be anything else except what it is. Music. All the others are empty shells, lies. We attached straps to a piano, heaved and it came up easily, weighing no more than a few kilos. The caretaker grinned and opened the lid. There was nothing inside. The guts had been removed. When Helmer played on the stage it was a recorded tape. We carried it out on our little fingers and customers at Pernille stood up from their tables and stared at us wide-eyed. We exited the rear door of the National Theatre and received a standing ovation, three removal men carrying pianos, tiled stoves and trunks on outstretched arms. I wished my mother had seen that.

And so the days passed, they sped by happily, I hit the pillow, fell asleep at night with tired muscles, slept well, buttered sandwiches and was picked up in Pilestredet every morning at seven. The days floated past, and one night I was strolling home in filthy work clothes with calloused hands when I bumped into Cecilie in Grensen. I didn't recognise her immediately, her hair was short and her back erect, had to dig back through my memory, then I knew, of course, it was Cecilie.

'Hiya,' we said.

She gave me a look of acknowledgement. I produced a mini-cigarette from my pocket and lit up.

'Are you working?' she asked.

'Yep. Removals. What are you up to?'

She told me that she had specialised in sciences and was going to study medicine in Iceland from that autumn.

'Iceland?'

'In Reykjavik. Couldn't get in here.'

'Long way away,' I said, to say something. 'And damned cold, isn't it?'

She laughed.

'You can come and visit me,' she said.

And then Cecilie wrote her address in a notebook and tore out the page.

And we each went our separate ways.

The money in our kitty was growing. But one day Cap'n asked Gunnar if he had a driver's licence. He did, and he didn't need a HGV licence to drive the Bedford. And so Ola and I were assigned to him as driver's mates and we had to move a NATO general from Kolsås to Blommenholm. We cheered, all three of us sat cheering and shouting as the lorry banged its way to NATO headquarters. The coot lived in a terraced house, it was a pushover of a job and the crew-cut pig served us duty-free Tuborg on the steps at twelve, spoke with a freaky accent and was over-friendly. Gunnar walked around on the lookout for secret papers and weapons, but the only thing we found was a sizeable stack of porn magazines and an arsenal of sealed whisky. He waved us off with a cheerful smile as we left for Blommenholm and was desperately fair.

'Bloody imperialist bastard,' Gunnar snarled as we drove to Sandvika. 'Must've been in Vietnam!'

'The old fella was great,' Ola said.

'Druggin' us with beer in the mornin'! Fancy bloody workin' for such a pig!'

Gunnar stepped on the gas and turned off to Blommenholm. We were approaching a tunnel under the railway. Gunnar slowed down.

'Will we get under it?' he asked, coming to a complete halt.

It didn't look very high. We jumped out, had a look at the vehicle and clambered back up.

'Think it'll be alright,' I said.

'Don't think it will,' Gunnar said.

'Not sure,' said Ola.

'Are there any other routes we can take?' Gunnar asked.

'It'll be fine,' I said.

'D'you think it'll be alright, Ola?'

'Ye-eah.'

'You'll slip through like butter,' I said.

Gunnar revved up and we raced down the underpass. Then we heard the terrible sound of the roof scraping, we were thrown forwards and the general's furniture gave an infernal groan behind us. We had come to a standstill.

Gunnar was pale.

'No good,' he said.

We wriggled out and examined the mishap. The Bedford was stuck. It wouldn't budge. We were jammed under the bridge with the NATO load.

We scratched our heads.

'What about if we take the stuff out?' Ola suggested.

'Then the van'll be even higher, you twit!' Gunnar bawled.

'It was just an idea,' I mediated. 'Anyway, NATO is a rotten alliance.'

We stood for a while staring at the snarl-up. Quite a queue was building behind us.

There was only one thing to do. We found a grocer's a hundred metres away and rang base. Half an hour later they arrived with sandpaper and a specialist driver. We had to crawl into the back to put weight on the wheels. It didn't make a nice sound as the Bedford was coaxed out. And Cap'n was none too pleased. But that didn't matter much. It was the end of July, we had earned enough cash and NATO's aggressive imperialism had been set back three hours. We had worked enough in this line of business.

We received our wages and raced to Gamle Major. We were loaded. During the first and last half litre Gunnar said, 'Great action we pulled off today! The people's war has started! And tomorrow we're off!'

We toasted, finished our beer, went home and packed our sports bags.

I was not the only living creature in Place St Michel. People were scattered about as if Slottsparken had been dug up and moved to Paris. I felt at home sitting tired and happy on the edge of the fountain peering through the exhaust fumes, the pigeons and the sun, didn't reckon I would see Gunnar and Ola for a few days at least. I had been lucky. We had been standing in Mosseveien at seven o'clock on Thursday morning. After three quarters of an hour an Opel occupied by a fat couple skidded to a halt, they were going to Copenhagen, but only had room for two. Gunnar and Ola took the lift.

'See you in Place St Michel!' I shouted, waving them off.

'Last man there buys the wine!' Ola yelled.

They disappeared over the horizon and I waited for several hours, but the cars were giving me a wide berth and my thumb was beginning to droop. Perhaps it was right what Gunnar had said, that I should have had a haircut, no one would go out of their way to pick up a long-haired tosser, he had grinned. Damned, damned if I was going to let any bloody motorist with plastered-down hair determine how I had mine. So I stood there in Mosseveien, time passed and cars zoomed past, Gunnar and Ola must have been in Gothenburg by then. Then it came, like a gold-bearing galleon down from the sky, the articulated lorry from Transport Office, I cheered and waved, the long vehicle braked and I ran after it. It was Robert, a decent type, but a go-getter to his fingertips. I jumped into the cab, for I was sure he didn't have much time, he slammed it into gear and we were on our way.

'Where you goin'?' Robert mumbled as we passed the slip road to Drøbak, he wasn't the talkative kind.

'Paris,' I said.

'Lucky for you.'

'Where are you goin'?'

'Paris,' said Robbo.

And when we arrived in Svinesund he turned to me and said a whole sentence, and more, 'And now you've got a job to do, see, keep me awake. Got that? I want to break the record for the Paris run. Matisen holds it at thirty-four hours.'

And so I tried to keep Robbo awake for the rest of the trip. We drove through Sweden, on the ferry to Denmark Robbo drank fourteen coffees and two Aquavits. We ploughed through Denmark as darkness settled over the fields. We raced down through Germany. In a lay-by south of Hamburg we slept for two hours. Robbo had three alarm clocks with him, one after the other they went off in our ears, and then we swept onwards, on the autobahn, at night, in the cab high above the road, in the dark, with all the lights well below us. Every time I nodded off I got Robert's elbow in my ribs and a mouthful of abuse. In Belgium the sun rose above the mud heaps, in France we stopped to fill the tank. I peeled my eyes for the Eiffel Tower, but the first thing I saw in Paris was vast clusters of corrugated iron shacks, shanties, boxes, rubbish, slums, people living there, then we were past them and the Eiffel Tower came into view in the blue haze, far away, like a weathered fountain. Sweat was pouring off me. I was in Paris. Robbo accelerated and grinned. He pulled into the first post office and sent a telegram to base. Exactly thirty hours. He didn't need any help with unloading, so he drove me straight to Place St Michel. The tiny French cars veered away in fright as we thundered down the windy, narrow streets, and at five o'clock on Friday I was sitting on the kerb peering at passers-by and a crazy thought burst into my brain, that Seb would appear from nowhere. Seb and Henny and Hubert. Don't know how long I was sitting like that, but it was certainly dark and I was homesick. The lights on the ground took over. I felt the big city pressing against my chest, my body was still in motion, the lights from the restaurants, the shops, the windows, the cars, raced towards me, passed me, disappeared behind me with runny red eyes, at breakneck speed. I was starving, but didn't know where I could get some food. I could go to Henny's address, but I had to wait for Gunnar and Ola. I sat there on the edge of the fountain with the winged lions spouting brown water. The Seine flowed somewhere close by, some people were playing the guitar, whistling, some were singing. The square was crowded, big bottles of wine were being passed around, a cop car trundled by, I was nervous, thinking about what had happened to Henny that time. It would soon be night. I was hungry, alone in Paris. Then a girl came over and sat beside me, staring at me with swollen brown eyes.

'Are you new in town?' she asked in American English.

'Arrived a few hours ago.'

She produced a bottle of wine, a baguette and a powerful cheese from her shoulder bag, nibbled and drank, passed it to me, I followed suit. Then she lit a cigarette, which we shared. I told her I was Norwegian. It was the strongest cigarette I had ever tasted. She laughed and stroked my back. I knocked back the wine. The hours passed in seconds. I was in Paris and had forgotten my sleeping bag. Joy – that was what she called herself – rolled out hers and invited me to join her. I produced two blurred passport photographs and showed her, asked if she had seen anyone resembling them. She shook her head and went to sleep. I lay awake, in the sleeping bag of an American girl on speed, in the middle of Paris, staring at photos of Seb and Nina. It was such a ridiculously long time since they had been taken and a thought, like a furious lobster, struck at my heart, if we found them they would not look anything like the photos, we wouldn't recognise them, we wouldn't recognise each other.

Joy slept and there was not much room. At some point the city was absolutely still, for a few seconds, then ten million people stirred. I wriggled out of the sleeping bag, froze, tugged on a sweater. There was some wine left in the bottle, I drank half. Water trickled into the gutters. Black men dressed in blue and Arabs swept the pavements. The cafés opened, tables and chairs were carried out, the sun crept up over a house and its rays caught the back of my head. I took off my sweater. The creatures in Place St Michel woke up. A girl sang 'Blowing In The Wind'. Joy rolled up her bed.

'See you,' she said.

'Where are you going?'

'Mediterranean,' she said and began to move in that direction.

At ten Gunnar and Ola arrived. Their astonishment at seeing me there was immense. Then we hugged and jigged in a circle.

'How the hell did *you* get here?' Gunnar shouted. 'Catch a plane or what?'

'Robbo from the Transport Office picked me up,' I said. 'How did you get on?'

They both groaned.

'The old fart in the Opel was a complete idiot,' Ola recounted.

'We were goin' to Copenhagen and ended up in Stockholm. I kept tellin' him, you're goin' the wrong way, mister, but he was deaf in that ear. And so we were in Stockholm, and he almost took the ferry to Finland.'

'And if that wasn't enough,' Gunnar picked up. 'His fat wife thought Stockholm looked nicer than Copenhagen and so they stayed there and we had to hitch again. Didn't get to Copenhagen until yesterday.'

'And then we took the train,' Ola said.

I mock-punched each of them in the stomach.

'Come on, let's find a table!' I said. 'You owe me some wine!'

Gunnar wiped off his sweat and reviewed our situation.

'Can't bloody stay here, can we.'

'Any better ideas?'

'There must be a hotel nearby.'

'Loaded with cash, are you?'

'Didn't you say we could borrow some money off your uncle?'

'Of course,' I said. 'Let's find a hotel.'

We found one in Place Odéon. The room cost eight francs each and was on the fifth floor. Ola was bundled off to stock up with wine and came charging back with his arms full. He unscrewed the cap of one bottle, took a lengthy swig, shook his head, screamed and dived for the sink. We smelt the contents, it stung our nostrils.

'You bought vinegar, you clown!' I grinned.

'Vinegar?'

Ola's face was parchment colour, he slumped onto the bed.

'*Vinaigre*,' I read out to him. '*Vinaigre*!'

So I, being the language specialist, had to go out and exchange the sustenance, I brought home a basket of *vin de table*. We opened the window, raised the bottles over Paris, caught a glimpse of Notre Dame and drank greedily.

Then all three of us fell asleep in a line on the soft beds. We were woken by the rain coming in onto the floor. I closed the window and opened another bottle of wine.

'Now it's time we went to look for Seb,' I said.

We started with a few beers at a bar across from the hotel, Le Ronsard. It had stopped raining and a carnival of smells arose from the adjacent market stalls. Large women were all shouting at the same time and grinning, displaying rotten stumps of teeth, mangy dogs slunk along the pavements, fat sparrows rolled around like swollen tennis balls, there was the sound of a pinball machine behind us, but what I remember most is the smell of strawberries, big, gleaming, bright red strawberries, they reminded me so much of Nina I had to go over and buy some, managed to blather myself a punnet and shared them with the others, strawberries, wine and beer.

And then we wandered all over Paris, nosed around the Latin Quarter, ate Tunisian bread rolls and almost burned our palates, strolled along the Seine, chatted to a few Dutch freaks, we hadn't met any Norwegians, watched the old boys fishing in the brown river as black barges and gaudy *bateaux mouches* glided by. We went to Pont Neuf, but Seb wasn't there, either, just a bunch of idlers moping around under the chestnuts and the weeping willows, we stood watch at Place St Michel, once I thought I saw Jørgen there, my nerves had sunstroke.

We arrived home at the hotel exhausted every evening, or night, and rounded off the day with a dark beer at Le Ronsard.

'Aren't you goin' to visit your uncle soon?' Gunnar enquired.

I dreaded it and kept putting it off. I dreaded it like the plague.

'Ye-es,' I said.

I went to the bar and ordered another round.

'Pretty ropey plan, in fact,' Gunnar said.

'Why's that?' Ola mumbled.

'Thinking we could find Seb in this anthill. Shit, we aren't even sure he's *here*!

Our heads dropped, we trudged back to the hotel and crashed out to the sound of chirruping cockroaches.

But the next day we sallied forth again. We searched the Jardin du Luxembourg, we took in the right bank and wandered down the Champs Elysées, but saw only snobs and shops, we clambered up the steps to the Sacré Coeur, just Japanese, mooched round Pigalle, whores, live shows and sleazy doormen, we found our way back to the Seine and sauntered by the green boxes of books. It became clearer and clearer to us that we were off course, way off course. Ola reckoned it was time we started using the metro, he had blisters on his knees, but Gunnar insisted, for Christ's sake, that we couldn't look for Seb underground.

'I'm starvin' anyway,' Ola moaned.

We found a grubby restaurant down a side street and ordered croque monsieur and beer.

'But what the hell is he *livin'* off?' Gunnar said.

'Christ knows. Must be takin' on odd jobs.'

None of us believed that, though. The food arrived on the table, three burned slices of bread with cheese and ham. There was a terrible smell, but that was probably the foul water in the gutters. The waiter lit a cigarette over our heads, and we got stuck in. In fact, it tasted good. We scraped up every last crumb and wondered if we should order another round. Then I felt something chafing and rubbing against my leg. I lifted up the tablecloth and looked into the whites of the eyes of the ugliest animal I had ever seen. I stood up, knocking my chair over sideways, Gunnar and Ola jumped up and the crossbreed came out, a crazy, scabrous mongrel, poodle at the rear and wolf at the front. It sprang up at me and licked my face with its rough, stinking tongue. I heard someone roar with laughter and it could not have been Gunnar or Ola. Then I caught sight of its dick protruding between its rear legs, stiff and red and thin, saliva dripped onto me and the dog was banging against my trousers like a mad thing. Gunnar came to my rescue and dragged it off. I got to my feet again, but the mongrel wouldn't give in, it leapt on me, smacked its front paws down on my sweater. I kicked as hard as I could, there was a crunch as my clogs made contact and the furless beast rolled over and crawled along the floor of the restaurant on its stomach. Then something else attacked me, I felt a sweaty, hairy hand on my neck, I twisted round, it was the waiter, he was cursing me in no uncertain terms and spit was flying in all directions. But enough was enough. Gunnar came over with his lifting tackle, raised the little man off the ground and sent him flying into the bar. And then we ran off leaving the bill and the swarthy latino howling. We didn't stop until we were at Le Ronsard where we collapsed at our regular table, and never was a beer more deserved.

'There's rabies in France,' Gunnar said.

The beer stuck in my throat.

'Eh?'

'Learned about in the military. If you've got an open wound or a cut and are near a rabid dog you can be infected.'

'Bloody hell! D'you think the mutt had rabies?'

'Don't know,' Gunnar said seriously.

I began to panic, felt dirty and leprous, relived the animal's revolting smell, searched feverishly for wounds, found a cut on my hand, but it had almost healed, I itched everywhere, I scratched, lice, scabies, I had the whole lot, all at once.

'How does rabies work?' Ola asked.

'You get thirsty,' Gunnar explained. 'Hellish thirsty, but you daren't drink for fear you'll drown in what you drink. In the end, you're scared of drowning in your own saliva. And then you die.'

I leaned on my elbows and tried to remain composed.

'If you're thirsty and drink like buggery, you don't have rabies. Is that right?'

'Exactly,' Gunnar said.

I went over to the bar and began to drink. It flowed down. I drank until the taps were dry at Le Ronsard. Then Gunnar and Ola guided me to the hotel. I remember dreaming I was a stray dog.

I woke up alone next morning with a dome bigger than the one on St Sophia's Church in Istanbul. It was late in the day and the din from the traffic in Boulevard St Germain rose five floors and hammered on the windows and my eyelids. I was thirsty. I had never been so thirsty before, not just in my mouth, but in all of me, one burning drain from my soul to the balls of my feet. I crawled to the sink, turned on the tap and at once remembered the warning about drinking water in Paris. But there was nothing else to drink in the room, I was half-demented, so I stuck my head under the tap, swallowed, spat, fear came with its suckers, the cockroaches grinned, a wild thought settled around my neck and tightened, that no one would notice if I metamorphised into a dog right here, no one would try to stop me if I padded down the stairs with a mangy coat and slobbering jaws, they would just kick me out head first, and I would be another dog in Paris. I tried another time and after a few swallows I got it down, I drank and drank the horrible sewage water, I recovered my equilibrium, my head began to function, I sat on the floor thinking this was going well, gingerly felt my stomach and swore that this would be fine. Then I threw up. I vomited in an arc into the basin, water and soft pommes frites, I was a fountain. Afterwards I found the note from Gunnar and Ola. *Meet you at Ronsard at four.*

The waiters clapped when I arrived. I had thought of slowing the revs with Vichy water, but they served me a big beer before I could utter a word and they refused to take payment, just stared at me in awe, almost asked me for an autograph. I drank my beer and it stayed down.

'What shape are you in?'

'Poor. Back's gone all hairy and my arms are growin.'

We chuckled quietly. Then Ola said, 'We'll never find Seb here. Even if he is here. While we're lookin' in one place, he's in another. We're just circlin' round each other all the time.'

We pondered that. Ola was right. It was the least successful search party of the century. I had two passport photos in my back pocket and it all seemed so ludicrous. Not even the prospect of going to the market could cheer me up. I saw a huge maggot in the punnet of strawberries.

'And now you've got to shake your bloody uncle out of your shirt-sleeves,' Gunnar hassled. 'We're almost out of funds.'

I was aware of that.

'Let's move to Le Métro,' I said. 'I'm gettin' edgy sittin' here. The waiters are starin' holes into the tables.'

We pootled over to the other corner, stood at the bar and were given three glasses brimful with wine. The waiter, with a yellow cigarette between his front teeth, grinned, added a dash more, until they were filled to overflowing, and we had to bend forward and suck like mammals.

'French humour,' said Gunnar.

We were getting stale. On the first day we would have laughed ourselves silly and asked for full glasses. It was time to go home. I had to visit Hubert and Henny.

Then we heard it, through the hubbub at the bar, through the wall of traffic noise, a blues, a rasping blues, a howling harmonica, a tortured wolf, coming from the ground, from the metro station just outside, everything went still around us, the traffic slowed and we heard it, more and more clearly. We stared at each other, eyes as big as plates, then we charged out, ploughed our way through, skated down the steps to the station. There we came to a halt. We couldn't believe our eyes. Seb was leaning against the filthy yellow tiles beside the green metro map, in the draught from the corridors, in a cloud of stinking piss, he was hardly recognisable, we could only just make out old Seb, he was there somewhere, a long way away. And he could not believe his eyes either, if they were still his. The harmonica fell from his mouth and his lips were full of sores.

'You here?' he stuttered.

'Do bears shit in the woods?' Ola asked. What would we do without Ola?

We raised a few grins. And then Seb began to smile, turned away and banged his head against the wall as the few onlookers picked up their coins and slunk off.

We got Seb up to our hotel room and put him to bed. He trembled like a flame, in the end we had to hold him, Seb was in a mess, just like his long, greasy hair and dirty, spindly beard.

'Where've you got your things?' Gunnar asked, straight to the point.

Seb pointed to his little green shoulder bag.

Then he said, lying stiffly in bed and waiting for the next convulsion:

'Boys, I've gotta have… I know where you can get it… a fix.'

We were not that surprised, but nevertheless it was dreadful to hear. Gunnar, ashen-faced, jumped astride Seb and shook him like a match that would not go out.

'You little bag of shit! Don't ask us for that! D'you hear me! D'you hear me!'

Then Gunnar peeled off Seb's jersey and we saw the sailor's tattoos on his arms, not an anchor and a heart, but a pattern of brown needle marks.

We poured a liqueur into Seb to calm him down. Grimy sweat poured off him. We stuck a cigarette between his lips and lit it, hauled him upright and held him against the wall.

'What happened?' I whispered.

And so Seb told his story, in fits and starts, it took a whole bottle of Calva and two packets of Gauloises. Seb sat with bowed head and talked through spasms.

Things had already gone awry on the boat to Denmark. On board he had met a dopehead, a chick from Tåsen who was going to the Isle of Wight. When the chick told him that Jim Morrison in person was going to bless the multitudes, that had been too much for Seb to resist. Seb joined the girl, they hitch-hiked to Calais, caught the ferry and found the wind-blown island where there were already a couple of hundred thousand mind-blown Red Indians.

Seb took a break. We sat with sweaty eyes and ears on full alert.

'Was… was Jim Morrison there?' I managed to stammer out.

Seb nodded. Ash fell on his bed.

'He was there. Out of his brain, tall, with a Jesus beard, direct line to the gods. Jerkin' off the mike like crazy. Greatest thing I've ever seen, boys.'

The memories alone were exhausting him. We poured in sustenance and lit soul food.

'Go on,' Ola whispered.

When the battle on the Isle of Wight was over, Seb had a week left to meet his father in Bordeaux. The chick from Tåsen persuaded him that he had time to nip over to Amsterdam, it was just over the channel, so Seb joined a multinational gang of freaks to Tulip Town, and there things went wrong big-time. The days passed, but Seb didn't notice and the first time he caught a haze-free glimpse, it was autumn. The Tåsen chick was over and out and he found himself in a shanty by a stinking canal with twenty other muddle-headed junkies.

'The worst thing I've ever experienced, boys. Head was blown apart. I'd missed the boat. I was skint and stuck in Amsterdam. What the hell d'you do then?'

'Go to the embassy,' Gunnar said in a matter-of-fact tone.

'Stand barefoot at the embassy office with eyes like cannonballs and arms full of holes? Great idea. Next stop, the nick.'

'But what did you do?' Ola whispered.

Seb didn't go to the embassy. He stole a harmonica and played blues in the streets of Amsterdam. The coins came in, but he couldn't move on or go home. Kicking the habit was too hard. Seb was hooked. He stayed in Amsterdam until the New Year.

'Know who I bumped into one day, Kim?' he exclaimed. 'Nina.'

'Nina?'

I crumpled, tasted the apple flavour of the liqueur, the essence, the blood of the apple.

'Nina?'

'Right. Nina from Vestheim.'

The room went quiet. It was dark outside the window. The pigeons were cooing on the ledge.

'How was she?' I asked slowly.

'What d'you think? She was on dope. Just like all the others.'

Seb stared vacantly through the smoke.

'Thought she was in Afghanistan,' I said.

Seb chuckled, a hoarse, jerky laugh.

'That's what they all say. That's what all the hopheads say. That's what all the mind-blown, broken-down blood-fuckers say.'

He hid his face in his hands and shook. I was petrified. Fear had paralysed me, it was a poison dart in my back, couldn't even smile.

Seb looked up.

'But they never get there, you know. She'd been to Paris. Didn't get any further. Had to go home to the canals.'

I threw up in the basin, the apple blood spurted out and sprayed my face. No one said anything. I didn't have the energy to ask any more questions.

'I never saw her again,' Seb continued. 'And then I came to Paris. Brought my harmonica and came to Paris.'

'Where the hell have you been then? We've been searchin' everywhere!'

Seb squeezed the cigarette out, burning his fingers without noticing.

'This summer I've been to the cemetery,' he said. 'Père Lachaise.'

'Eh? In a cemetery?'

'By Jim's grave.'

'Jim?'

'Jim Morrison.'

Then Seb went out like a light. We kept watch over him. He was as thin as a nail and rusty. Not even the cockroaches noticed him. They crawled across the ceiling. And outside the sun rose through the blue Paris air.

I went to see Henny while Gunnar and Ola kept an eye on Seb. I was too tired and hungover to dread the meeting. I gave the note with the address to a taxi driver and he drove me to rue de la grande Chaumière in Montparnasse. I remembered another time when I was sitting in a taxi in a foreign city on my way to see a girl. I was composure itself. I was foolish enough to believe that after all that had happened, things could not get any worse.

I looked up and down the narrow street until I found the number, a big green door with glass and bars, and a marble slab on which was written in gold letters: *Ateliers*. Three baguettes had been left at the bottom of the door. But the door was locked and there was no name on it. Abutting the house was a little bookshop with art books and reproductions in the window. Inside some clod was looking out at me with curiosity. I entered, managed to stammer something about a Norwegian girl, pointed to the address on the paper and he beamed the broadest smile I have seen. His hands danced above his head and he kept nodding and jabbered away. It was all Greek to me, but I think he was asking if I was Norwegian, too. I said yes and he went even wilder. He started rummaging around in a crammed drawer and pulled out a card which he pushed into my hands. I looked at it and a blunt knife was turned round in my heart three times: Munch. *Piken og døden*. The girl and death. Then he led me outside, pressed the button for the second floor, opened the door and waved.

I dragged myself up to the second floor and rang the bell. It was a long time before anyone came, long enough time for me to have cleared off ages ago. But I was standing there when Henny opened up, semi-naked. Then she threw herself around my neck and dragged me inside, stepped back a bit and examined me carefully. She was a bit fatter, there was a softness about her, she was even more attractive.

'Hope I didn't wake you,' I said.

'Yes, you did,' she laughed.

She stood studying me, in the huge room with the large window and several green plants winding across the walls and ceiling.

'You've changed,' she said.

A door opened and I expected to see Hubert. But a girl came out of a bedroom, she undulated across the floor, naked, and embraced Henny, they kissed lovingly, for a long time, right there, in front of me. I turned slowly and averted my eyes, my cheeks burning.

'This is Françoise,' Henny said at length. 'And this is Kim.'

Françoise kissed me on the cheek fourteen times and retreated into a corner.

I had to speak.

'Where's Hubert?' I asked.

Henny found herself a chair and lit a cigarette.

'Hubert lives on the Ile de Ré,' she said. 'An island on the Atlantic coast.'

I slumped into a chair, too. My hangover was receding.

'I have to get hold of him. Is it far away?'

'You'll have to take the train to La Rochelle and the ferry from there,' Henny explained.

I told her about Seb. I told her we needed cash for the train tickets home.

'Come with us to Coupole!' Henny said.

Françoise and Henny disappeared into the bedroom and were gone for some time, I sat there in the greenhouse sweating, my brain in a whirl, then finally they emerged and we walked to Coupole, a hangar-sized restaurant, and as soon as we had sat down, the table was surrounded by smooth types with water-combed hair and crumpled, double-breasted suits and white shoes. Françoise and Henny ordered eggs and tea, I ordered a beer and all the greasers wanted to say hello and spoke close to my ear. Then Henny prattled away in French and the snails each put a banknote on the table and patted me on the shoulder and I no longer thought they were so greasy, in fact I have never been a good judge of people, in fact I'm a bit dense.

'Françoise and I are broke, you see,' Henny said, pushing the money over to me.

I was embarrassed and drank up my beer.

'I can easily hitch,' I said.

'Take the money,' she insisted 'And say hello to Hubert.'

She jotted down his address and explained to me where the railway station was. Three quarters of an hour later I was sitting on a train westwards in a compartment full of sleeping Frenchmen. I just had to sit quite still and allow my thoughts to settle, but my head was a dustbin and I was unable to empty it. Instead I fell asleep, too, and perhaps that was the best thing that could have happened. But at twelve I was awoken by a terrible noise. The other passengers in the compartment were opening bottles of wine, wolfing down blood-red tomatoes, eating ham and chicken, putting rotten cheese in their laps and I escaped into the corridor, yanked down the window and let the wind double-cleanse my head. Villages. Fields. Vineyards. Over a river, on a sudden impulse, I threw out the photos I had been carrying in my back pocket.

I trekked onwards from La Rochelle by bus and ferry and docked on the Ile de Ré at the onset of night. There, I had to take another bus and jumped off in Le Flotte half an hour later, a tiny harbour where the breeze came in off the Atlantic. I heard fishing boats rolling on the waves and saw the lights of two bars. I entered one and showed them the address. They knew where it was, I was given a beer on the house and then a young lad accompanied me over the last part. He stopped outside a gate, pointed and went on his way. An old woman came out and subjected me to closer examination. I showed her the slip of paper and said *Norvège*. She clapped her hands and nudged me into a courtyard where there was a low wall with a veranda in front.

'Yber!' she bawled. 'Monsieur Yber!'

And then out he came, leaned over the balustrade and peered down at us. I ran up the stairs. Hubert was standing there in his belted dressing gown seeming quite unsurprised. He had a beard.

'You've hidden yourself well,' I said.

He laid his hands on my shoulder.

'Come in,' he said softly.

It was a fairly spartan room. In the middle of the floor there was a table. In the corner a pile of canvas stretchers. The walls were bare.

In the harsh light I could see the fear. After such a long time, I was suddenly unprepared.

'That was not a great move,' I said.

'Life here's cheap, Kim. I can live here for the rest of my life.'

He went into the kitchen and poured mussels into a saucepan. He stood with his back to me. I could hear the crashing of the sea.

'Do you get any painting done here?' I asked.

Hubert didn't answer. He poured white wine over the mussels, chopped onions and took a swig. He stood with his back to me. I spotted a picture of a man with a bloodstained bandage round his head. I smelt the aroma from the wine and the mussels.

'That was not a great move,' I repeated.

'Has your father forgiven me?'

His voice sounded like one of my mother's old records.

'Yes,' I said.

We sat up for the rest of the night eating mussels and drinking white wine. Hubert told me that La Flotte meant the sea, and when he was a bit drunk he said that *moule*, mussel, also meant pussy. I couldn't face any more mussels.

'Regards from Henny,' I said.

Hubert stood up to fetch another bottle.

'It didn't work out for us,' he said quietly.

'I need money,' I said. 'Four train tickets to Oslo.'

Then we polished off a *Prince Hubert de Polignac* and the sun arose again, as though nothing had happened. We went onto the veranda and heard the fishing smacks chugging out to sea, heard the sea and the wind and people.

'They caught a shark last week,' Hubert said. 'A shark.'

He walked with me to the bus stop by the harbour. There was a smell of fish and salt and seaweed.

'Sure you've got enough money now?' Hubert asked.

'Plenty enough,' I said.

'Say hello to everyone.'

'Think you should come home soon,' I said. 'You can come home now, no problem.'

He took my hand and would not let go. He shook me and his beard moved from side to side. He could not let go and his eyes were full of saltwater. The driver hooted. He did not let go. All the faces on the bus were turned towards us. So I had to tear myself away.

I sat at the back and watched Hubert standing alone at the bus stop, and as my mind sped back over a whole life he disappeared behind masts and seagulls.

At Hôtel Odéon there was mayhem. Seb had done a runner. He had gone to the toilet and had not returned. That was twenty-four hours ago.

'You should've gone with him,' I shouted.

'We're not bloody nannies, you bonehead! And where the hell've *you* been, eh?'

Ola stepped between us.

'Don't quarrel now, boys. We don't want any bloody quarrellin.'

We went to Le Ronsard but didn't get much further. Evening was drawing in and Paris twinkled and screamed at us and snarled bad breath into our faces. If I started counting people I would go mad. They trudged past, line after line, they stood in big groups at all street corners, they filled shops, cars, houses, bars, they were everywhere, I was reminded of the time we played hide and seek in Nesodden, I had found the perfect place, a little hollow behind a bush, I lay on my stomach, closed my eyes, thought I would be even more invisible like that. Then I felt my legs itch and I realised I was lying in the middle of a path of ants, they were all over me, I didn't dare move a muscle, I lay still as the ants covered me, and I thought, while I was lying there, about the adder I had seen, the dead adder in the anthill by the fence, as someone far away was slowly counting to a hundred.

Gunnar unfolded the map on the table. Seb was an addict. Seb had hopped it to get a fix. A girl played 'Light My Fire' on the jukebox. Then I knew.

'The cemetery,' I said. 'Morrison's grave.'

We found Père Lachaise on the map and hailed a taxi.

'If we find him, let's catch the train tonight,' I said.

Père Lachaise was a whole town, a windswept ruin, where stray cats ran between graves and there weren't only common-or-garden gravestones, there were houses, statues, staircases, temples, pillars. I felt ill just being there, it was the other side of Paris, the realm of the dead, just a taxi ride from the tumult of human life.

We searched up and down, saw women dressed in black standing among the trees in silence, heard cats howling, saw withered flowers and smashed stained glass, smelt the stench of rotting foliage and cellars, we walked our legs off, were scared of getting lost, standing in the middle of an insane labyrinth. Ola was grey-faced and silent, Gunnar searched with vacant eyes, the wind tore right through us, heavy clouds hung in the sky and the first drops fell with a rumble of thunder. Then we heard another sound, coming from the graves close by, an electric piano, bass, drums, thunder, rain and then Jim's voice. 'Riders On The Storm'. We ran down the path. *Morrison Hotel* was written on a wall, we followed the arrow beneath, heard the music clearly, the echo, the rain, the thunder, clambered past a few imposing stones, and there, on a bedraggled piece of land, sat a scattered band of freaks, one of whom was Seb.

We were struck dumb by the solemnity of the occasion and quietly sat down beside him. A dark-haired, pale girl clung to the cassette player, crying without making a sound. On a wooden board was written *Douglas Morrison James*. A wine bottle containing a flower protruded from the ground. A circle of mussel shells surrounded the grave.

'We've got to go,' I whispered to Seb. 'We're catchin' the train tonight.'

He stood up without a word and followed us, without offering any resistance, a substantial, unreal calm seemed to have settled over him, his eyes shone beneath his wide central parting. We returned to the hotel and collected our things, took the metro to Gare du Nord and I bought four tickets to Oslo via Copenhagen. The train left at five minutes to eleven, that was still a couple of hours away. We stocked up with beer at the station buffet and sat down to wait.

Then Seb started talking. He spoke slowly and clearly as though frightened we would not understand him, as though he were a priest and the capacious arrivals hall his church.

'Jim is not dead,' he said. 'Jim is not dead.'

We bent closer.

'Isn't Jim dead?'

'He's just pretendin' to be dead. He's gone his own way. To Africa to live with his new soul. It's his old soul which is buried in Père Lachaise.'

'What are you on about?' Gunnar enquired.

'No one's seen the body,' Seb continued. 'Pamela was in on the whole thing.'

'Pamela?'

'His woman. Met them at the Rock'n' Roll Circus and tripped out with Jim for a week. He said he was goin' away soon.'

All of a sudden Seb became nervous, cast covert glances in all directions and waved us closer.

'This is a secret, boys. Not a word to anyone else, alright? The FBI's after him!'

We drank beer and our train appeared on the electronic information board.

'What've you actually got in your shoulder bag?' Gunnar asked.

Seb hugged it without answering. There were twenty minutes left to the train's departure. Gunnar wouldn't let the matter drop. He grabbed the bag and opened it. Inside was a syringe and a box of matches.

'So you thought you'd take this shite home, did you?'

'Christ, boys, I've gotta have a fix before we set off!'

Gunnar held the bag and sent him dark looks.

'No,' said Gunnar. 'We're chuckin' this down the bog!'

He stood up. Seb leapt after him. He screamed.

'Gunnar! For Pete's sake! You're killin' me!'

'I'm not, this is!' Gunnar said, pointing to the green bag.

'This is not firecrackers and bangers you're playin' with now!' Seb shouted, suddenly clear-headed.

But Gunnar was on his way down to the toilets. Seb couldn't believe his eyes.

'He's doin' it,' he murmured. 'He's doin' it.'

I bought three bottles of brandy from across the road and we jumped on the train at the last second. Then we chugged out of Paris, on our way home, all four of us, through a stinking Europe that lay on our skin like grey dirt.

Sentimental Journey

Autumn '71

It was autumn. Gunnar started at Oslo University and found himself some digs in Sogn. Seb calmed himself down with milk and honey at his grandmother's. I turned twenty, was granted a study loan, bought books for the prelim and continued to live in Munchsgate. Ola stayed with his parents in Solli and was accepted at Bjørknes School. Everything in the garden seemed to be rosy until the telegram from Trondheim arrived. That put an immediate end to Ola's future plans. Kirsten was in her fourth month and a man of honour did not run away from his responsibilities. Ola bought rings and a train ticket and the evening he was due to leave I arranged a big stag night in Munchsgate. The study loan was still hot, so I served up a ton of shrimps, champagne, white wine, beer and gin. And so we sat there, and it was hard to lift the mood. We were chucking it down our necks and Seb, who had been sober since Paris, had obviously cracked big-time. I carried the shrimp shells to the refuse chute and on my return I found Ola crying. He was smoking and drinking and crying and trying to talk at the same time.

'Shit, boys,' we heard. 'Shit! Now of all times when we're together again!'

'Calm down,' Gunnar said. 'You're not goin' to Alaska.'

Ola cried even louder.

'This wasn't how I'd planned it,' he sobbed. 'Gettin' into Bjørknes and all that. Shit!'

Gunnar shook him with a gentle, but firm hand.

'Listen, bridegroom. You can do your exams in Trondheim, too. And you'll be able to live with Kirsten. Haven't you always wanted that, eh?'

Ola dried his tears and smiled. I passed him a killer cocktail.

'What the hell would I do without you boys!'

We pounded him on the shoulder and Ola waggled his head.

'Hope it's a boy,' he whispered.

The atmosphere picked up. Ola looked as if he was already the proud father of four and knocked back the drinks at a furious tempo. Then his expression changed, he hunched up, terrified eyes receded into his head.

'Imagine it's not my child,' he breathed.

'Now you bloody well pull yourself together!' Gunnar shouted. 'We'll pretend we never heard that.'

Ola was counting desperately on his fingers, counting and recounting, and with a little sigh and a lightning drum solo on his bottle of booze he slowly fell to the floor.

'June, July, August, September,' he chanted. 'It must've been the mornin'...'

'Spare us the details,' I grinned, mixing him a chainsaw of a drink.

Seb had not exactly been garrulous, but now he made a suggestion and opened a fat black book he took from his pocket.

'Since we won't be able to join you at your weddin', I think we should perform a trial ceremony here,' he said.

And, so help me God, Seb was sitting with the Bible in his lap and flicking through it.

'Now he's really gone bonkers!' Gunnar shouted.

Seb was not listening.

'Please rise,' he said to Ola. 'Kim can be Kirsten.'

'He's not gettin' married in Nidaros Cathedral for Christ's sake!'

Gunnar was aghast.

'All the more important that we perform this symbolic ceremony,' Seb said calmly.

Either he was clean out of his mind or this was a monumental piss-take. But we were with him all the way, we were not going to stand in his way.

Gunnar sat in his corner, shocked, while Ola and I stood swaying side by side and Seb read slowly and clearly from some chapter in the black book, then we promised to love each other in good times and bad, fumbled with the rings, split our sides laughing and rolled over the floor.

Seb maintained his mask and we roared even more. However,

Gunnar didn't seem to think it very funny. He took Mao's little red book off the shelf and found some solace in 'Dare To Fight, Dare To Win'. Ola and I regained vertical posture, poured ourselves a drink and hiccupped in unison. The ceremony was over, the priest slammed the book shut and then Ola began to cry again, and this time he seemed inconsolable. The days with the boys were over, now it was nappies, debt, mother-in-law and nagging. No more Snafus, no more gatherings around the grooves and wild drum solos. We sniffled a bit, all of us. Then he fell asleep.

We transported Ola and his suitcase to Oslo East station in a wheelbarrow we found in the backyard, carried him onto the train and hung a sign around his neck. *Silent Homecoming*. Then the train departed. It puffed out of the station, past Fred's window, and we waved as though it were necessary, stood there with empty hands, waving.

Working Class Hero

Autumn '71

Didn't see much of Gunnar after he had moved into the student village, and things were quiet for me now that Ola had left and Seb lived like a monk at his grandmother's. I popped into a couple of lectures about logic, but never really got the point. One day there was a huge hullabaloo in front of the Frederikke building. A fanatical mob stood there waving their fists and screaming at each other, and in the midst of this melee was Gunnar, yelling. I sneaked over, it was the solidarity committee stand for striking pilots. 'I suppose you think pilots don't earn enough, eh!' a guy at the table snapped. 'You'd probably go around rattling a box in the aid of bosses striking at *Aftenposten* too, I wouldn't wonder!' I think Gunnar was standing on tiptoe, at any rate he seemed taller than I remembered him. 'We support wage disputes! Wage disputes are a blow against the capitalist state!' 'The bloody pilots would do better to give a few thousand to the low-paid!' 'So it's up to individuals to make up the gap between rich and poor in this country, is it! What sort of politics is that, eh!' And so it went on for almost an hour, then the crowd dispersed and Gunnar was left, sweaty and cheerful, behind the table, rattling the box.

Then he caught sight of me.

'Long time, no see,' I said, putting five kroner in the box.

'Think the bridegroom arrived?' he grinned.

'Haven't heard a thing.'

We each rolled our Petterøes.

'How are the studies goin'?' I asked.

'Badly. Don't get any time for lectures. But a girl in the flat lets me borrow her notes. How about you?'

'Mmm,' I nodded, 'goin' alright.'

'Feel like droppin' by one day?' I wondered.

'I'll see. I'll see. Got loads of things to do.'

A week later he was on the phone.

'Be at Universitetsplassen at three!' he shouted.

'Is somethin' comin' off?'

'Now get a grip on yourself! The government's tryin' to cripple the university. Catastrophic budget. Can only just afford invigilators.'

But when I arrived at Universitetsplassen a few minutes before three, the square was deserted. I checked my watch and discovered that the second hand was not moving. I sprinted down Karl Johan with the cold November rain in my face. The clock over the garish Freia chocolate advertisement said half past four. There wasn't anyone in front of the government building, either. I was freezing. Thought about the time I had deceived Gunnar over the leaflets. I stamped the ground, could hardly light a cigarette. I followed the road around the corner to Stortorget. That was where I spotted him, too late for me to snake out unnoticed. He was staring straight at me. I ambled up to the table where he was sitting with some other people I didn't know.

'Any room?'

Gunnar looked up at me. The others resumed their heated discussion.

There was room on the bench. I squeezed in.

'You didn't make it after all, I see,' Gunnar said in a flat tone.

I wondered whether to spin a long tale about a sick mother or about feeling indisposed in Munchsgate, but decided against it, couldn't be bothered. I tapped my watch.

'Stopped,' I said.

Gunnar broke into the discussion, I was brought a beer. When I had finished it, the others stood up and trooped off. Gunnar was left sitting on the bench. We sat facing each other, didn't say anything for a while.

Then Gunnar said, 'We've started on a mission, haven't we. We have to pull up the whole villainy by the roots. We don't give a shit about reforms and Storting. We hate capitalism. We despise this so-called social democracy which has hoodwinked workers. We abhor the ruling party's claptrap and can see through it. Two thirds of the world's population suffer from starvation and oppression. Hence, we do not believe promises, we do not believe words. We prioritise *action*.'

He paused to take a swig, but without his eyes deviating for a second.

'And where the hell do you stand, Kim? You have to choose which side you're on. Whatever you do, you're makin' a choice! The way you're goin' now you're just an errand boy for Bratteli and Nixon.'

I don't quite remember what my answer was, but I think Gunnar was satisfied with it. At any rate, he ordered another round and leaned over the stained tablecloth.

'We're from the lower middle class, okay, but they also suffer under the yoke of capitalism. We have to learn from the workers, put ourselves at their service.'

'My grandfather was a tramp,' I said.

'And then he became a white collar worker. Yes, that's the ideal in the social democracy. Bein' a worker is not good enough. You're a retard if you're a worker.'

We drank. Gunnar continued talking.

'Our parents've had to suffer under capitalism, haven't they. My father was crushed by monopoly capitalism and had to sell rotten potatoes at Bonus. And your father became a victim of the bank, so the right-wingers could blacken the name of revolutionaries even more!'

Didn't understand.

'How was that again?'

'It's obvious, man. Didn't you see what the bourgeois newspapers wrote afterwards?! Young drug addict robs bank. More severe punishments. More cops. More surveillance. They consider us criminals, Kim! Are you tellin' me the bank didn't have secret lists of Young Socialists!'

'You don't believe that the bank robbery… that the robbery was a set-up?'

'Course it was! If it'd been a junkie, he would've been nabbed in no time. The town was hermetically sealed. But *no one* was arrested! And so the bourgeois press could have a field day bangin' on about dreadful young people and buildin' more and bigger prisons. Bloody hell, Kim, it stinks.'

Didn't know quite what to say or where to look. I set to work on a roll-up.

'Seen anythin' of Seb?' I asked.

'Nothin'. Didn't like that priest stuff of his, by the way.'

'It was just a joke!'

'Not so sure about that. The boy's got the predisposition.'

We were interrupted by a girl coming over to Gunnar. She was wearing a red raincoat and carrying a shoulder bag full to overflowing. She bent down and gave Gunnar a quick kiss.

'Merete,' he said when he could, 'lives in the flat in Sogn.'

'Kim,' I said, raising my glass.

Gunnar began to pack up his things.

'He's teeterin' on the edge,' he said, and he must have meant me. 'But he's a bit slow. Needs a good kick up the arse.'

Merete came a step closer, I was afraid she was going to have a punt. Instead she clenched her fist.

'Never too late,' she smiled. 'You're always welcome!'

Then they left. To go to the Action Committee meeting. I sat over the foul-smelling ashtray, and while I tried to get my watch working I caught myself longing for something to happen, anything, something wild and big.

The second hand started to move round.

My Sweet Lord

Autumn '71

One evening in mid-November Seb made an appearance. He looked dazed, but was off drugs and steady. He put down his bag and breathed out heavily. Seb was back in Munchsgate.

I boiled up a few litres of tea and we talked at cross purposes for a while, couldn't find the right tone straight off. Seb's face was thin and serious, and I went to find us a nice cold beer, but realised that things might get out of hand. Seb was standing by the window sweating.

'I'm gonna try to find another room,' I said. 'There might be a place in Sogn.'

He turned round quickly.

'No point doin' that, is there? You can live here. With me.'

'D'you mean that?'

'Of course I mean it. Shit, you mustn't move, Kim.'

We stood there smiling, Seb with the black window behind him, the town and the hard frost. I took a step towards him and hugged him.

'This'll be great, won't it,' I mumbled.

I saw that the tattoos on his arm had almost gone.

Seb tidied the mattress and I unrolled the sleeping bag alongside the other wall. He was asleep before I had turned off the light. I lay awake until dawn. Then Seb woke up, dressed and stole out quietly. He didn't return until the evening and didn't say where he had been. And I didn't ask.

One thing was certain. There was not a lot left of the old Sebastian. I wanted to talk about Paris, about his drugs, about Jim Morrison, about Nina, but Seb seemed to have drawn a line under it, didn't mention it at all. He just lay on the mattress, deep inside himself, brooding, or else he was out. I didn't have the remotest idea of what he was up to. The atmosphere was beginning to be ominously heavy in Munchsgate. I was scared he was back on drugs, and after mature reflection I carried out a blitz on his things one day when he was out God knows where. I didn't find any drugs. I found a pile of papers written by Moses David. So that was how the land lay. I went out and bought a bottle of red wine and sat down to wait for Seb while reading David's letters. The countdown to doomsday had already begun. The earth would be powder by New Year. He returned at ten o'clock. By then the bottle was empty and I didn't feel like hiding the fact that I had found his Jesus certificates.

'Where d'you get this crap, eh?'

'From a guy,' Seb said, sitting on the mattress.

'Don't tell me you've gone all religious!'

He sat still for a long time, flicked his hair behind his ears, rested his chin on his hands. He didn't answer.

'You of all people, after wiping the floor with the priest in the confirmation class! Eh!'

I tried desperately to remind him of his heyday, but Seb didn't react. I was really frightened. Then he began to talk.

'I've learnt,' Seb said in a low voice. 'I've tried booze and dope and smack, but I didn't find what I was lookin' for. Now I've found the path. I've found the path, Kim.'

'Where in hell are you goin'?'

'We have to have somethin' to hold onto,' he went on. 'Everyone has to have a fixed point, a light, a meanin'.'

'That's word for word what it says in these papers!' I shouted.

'Otherwise we're empty shells and life is a wasted second. Gunnar has *his* path, Kim. Ola has a family and is a father-to-be. But you, Kim, you're still moochin' around not knowin' what you want to do with your life.'

I couldn't believe my ears. Then I felt my blood boiling beneath my skin, I could see it, could see my blood. I tried to speak as calmly as I was able, my voice caressed my tongue like sandpaper.

'You're not waitin' for Jesus,' I said. 'You're not searchin' for Jesus. It's Jim Morrison you're waitin' for. You're still high, Seb. You haven't bloody come down yet. Your eyes are as opaque as sauerkraut, Seb. You don't know what you're sayin'.'

'I may be blind,' Seb said, with the same accursed composure. 'That's why I've put my fate in His hands. He'll see me through.'

At that, I crept down into my sleeping bag, and when I awoke Seb was gone again. Beside the mattress was the old, black Bible.

I made breakfast and there was not a great deal to do. Another day lay before me, but I didn't have any clean paper or anything to write with. I tried to read, but was too unsettled and leafed aimlessly through Schjelderup's psychology book. I ploughed through a section about Kretchmer's constitutional types and had to smile, couldn't help myself, tried to categorise us, it was pretty crazy. Ola was the pyknic type, that was definite, and Gunnar was the athletic type, Seb was a clear case of the leptosome build, and me, I was dysplastic, one of those with some kind of unpleasant physical abnormality. My crooked finger followed the lines in the book making me feel nauseous, so I put it away. There was nothing left to smile about. The day was grey and leaden, a restless heap of hours. I remembered another day, a Tuesday too, sluggish and slow like this one, but it had turned round, a metamorphosis into heart-throbbing pleasure, this Tuesday could never provide the same, it was and would remain a Tuesday, abject, stillborn.

I went for a walk. That was not a great deal better. Oslo was bleak. The trees in Karl Johan stood like scarecrows in a tarmac garden. People walked with heads bowed, struggling against the wind and the high cost of living. Freaks shivered in their Afghan coats. Afghanistan! By the National Theatre the Salvation Army sang from the bottom of their hearts. A Jesus tripper stood perfectly still and erect with a large placard: The World Will End In Thirty-Nine Days. I went for a coffee at Frokostkjelleren and what Gunnar and Seb had said to me gnawed at my innards. I had to sit there screwing up my courage, telling myself that I was not lost yet, it was just a question of taking the first step, in one direction or another, and I could be where Seb and Gunnar were, just a question of saying one word, the word. But something in my body, in my hands, in my legs, in my chest, fought against it. It was not so simple. But I was wrong. I had to begin somewhere. Here. Now. I stubbed out my cigarette and went straight home to Munchsgate to get my life into shape. That was where I hit the wall. Seb was sitting on the divan beside a sunken-cheeked individual with a headband and a cap. He turned slowly to me and said, 'God bless you, Kim.'

I didn't recognise him at once, the hairy Jesus freak. Then he stepped forward, came towards me like a photograph and came into focus. It was Goose.

'Christian?' I whispered.

'You can call me Goose, that's alright.'

Goose stayed until the evening telling us about his stay in a collective owned by the Children of God near Gothenburg. But now he had been sent to Oslo to gather souls there. Then I spotted his sleeping bag. I looked at Seb.

'It's alright if Goose stays here, isn't it?' he said.

What could I say?

And Goose stayed. During the day they went out with their placards. In the evening they sat by candlelight leafing through the Bible. I had to buy food, for they were both dead broke. But the morning Goose tried to make further inroads into my moribund study loan things boiled over for Kim Karlsen.

'Think I'm goin' to give you cash for your mafia, do you?'

'You don't need any money,' he said.

'Reckon the ticket prices will be pretty high on doomsday,' I said. 'Thirty-two days to go now, isn't it?'

That didn't cut any ice. Nothing cut any ice with Goose. He was composure in person. He just turned his shiny eyes on me and advertised for eternity.

I tried another approach.

'*You* don't need any money. No, you scrounge off others. You come and go here like a holy parasite and send me the bill.'

Not a spark.

'I share my beliefs with you,' he smiled.

I understood the point. We were one too many.

I just had to get away. But I couldn't face going back to Svolder, it was so long since I had been there, I didn't have the courage to answer all their questions. The night I found myself locked in the Palace Theatre I had made the decision to visit Cecilie in Iceland.

I had gone out for a whole evening, trying to make myself as small as possible in Munchsgate. At twelve I was coming down Karl

Johan when I needed a pee. I nipped into the entrance of the Palace Theatre and took a leak there. In mid-sprinkle I heard some iron grating hit the ground. I packed away my tackle and ran out. Didn't get very far. I was locked in and Karl Johan was deserted. I shouted, shook the bars, but no one could hear me and the grille was unmovable. I panicked, my spine a fuse hissing towards my brain. Then I forced myself to think clearly. And, as I did, snow began to fall outside, big white flakes fluttering down onto the street and turning it white. I thought coldly and clearly, then looked at the film posters. The next performance was the following day. *Donald Duck Goes West*. In other words, that was as long as I would be stuck for. Again I shook the grille and shouted. It didn't help. I was locked in. I lit my last cigarette, I was beginning to get cold. The yellow piss was frozen into a map of Norway. Then I spotted a crack in the door to the cinema, I tentatively pushed the handle and the door slid open. I stood still, my pulse a wild bronco, then I entered the empty auditorium, sat down in the middle, put my feet on the seat in front and stared at the black screen. And slowly images began to move in front of me, all the images I had stored and from which I cannot escape. There was a smell of sweat, melted chocolate, perfume and clothes. I heard a full house breathing. I sat like that all night, in the blue room at the Palace Theatre, film after film rolled across the screen, and I decided to go and see Cecilie, she had invited me, I had her address.

Wild Life

Autumn/winter '71

I had done it. I was going to Iceland. The aeroplane rose into the sky, the world outside the window tipped over and Nesodden fell away. Then time stopped, a bubble burst in my head, I was flying across Norway, through the crystal-clear, translucent winter air, a few metres from the sun. The North Sea came into view, I saw an oil platform, the Faeroe Isles were beneath me, then it clouded over and before I had finished my drink and begun to collect myself, I was jerked downwards towards Keflavik and landed with a bang on the runway as the squalls roared against the fuselage. I retched into a bag, a stewardess accompanied me out between the glaciers with a smile and later the bus took longer to reach Reykjavik than the plane had taken to fly to Iceland.

I was dropped off by a closed petrol station and night had settled over the capital. The wind battered your face with the force of a knuckleduster and what seemed like sleet and shingle hit the back of your head. I looked around for people, but everyone in Iceland must have gone to bed. I took a swig of duty-free and began to walk in a random direction. I tried to keep to what appeared to be a pavement, but the wind was of a different mind and I was forced out onto soft ground. In the end I was standing in the middle of wasteland, up to my knees in mud, and the only things I had were a bottle, a toothbrush, a return ticket and Cecilie's address.

I took a few swigs and struggled on. My boots squelched. Then I found myself walking on what to all appearances was a football pitch, on gravel. I could make out two goals. I dribbled my way through the wind and found a path. There, at last, I caught sight of some people, ran after them and showed them my piece of paper. They were two couples and they pointed in four different directions before deciding and sending me north, into the wind, with the hail coming from the side and a lurking fear at my heels.

It was well past midnight when I finally chanced on Cecilie's street and house number. She lived on the first floor. The entrance was green and smelt of stale eggs. I rang the bell and she took a long time to appear. Then she opened up, wearing a dressing gown, sleep-befuddled and grumpy. And the moment she clapped her eyes on me and they slowly widened and her mouth became an empty hole in her face, I knew this had to be just about the most stupid thing I had ever done.

'Kim,' was all she said, softly, terrified.

'I happened to be passin',' I ventured.

We stood there, on either side of the threshold, mute, confused, her a sleepy galleon figurehead, me a dripping marsh troll.

'You'd better come in,' she said at length. I tugged off my filthy boots and padded in on stockinged feet.

Cecilie was practical and efficient. She lent me dry clothes and hung mine up to dry in the bathroom. I poured myself a dram and sat in the sparsely furnished sitting room, a couple of posters on the wall, EEC, NATO, a narrow bookcase with thick volumes, crumbs on the table after supper, an Icelandic newspaper, a radio.

'What have you done to your boots?!' Cecilie cried.

I crumpled. Didn't she even remember? The badger. I should never have come here. I was a misunderstanding.

'Got lost in a bog,' I said.

After a while she came in and sat down, pulling her dressing gown tight. She was wearing yellow slippers. Her eyes lingered on me. I fumbled for something to say.

'How's it going in Norway?' she asked first.

'Alright. Gunnar's moved to Sogn, Ola's married a girl in Trondheim and Seb's become a Child of God. Otherwise things are fine.'

'What about you?'

'Me? I'm the same old idiot. Tryin' to study.'

'You've stopped working?'

'It was just a summer job.'

'And now you've used your study loan to come here?'

'Right.'

'To visit me?'

'Yes.'

'That all?'

My head was beginning to ache. It had to be the flight. The air pressure was still there.

'Thought I could buy a few Christmas presents at the same time,' I said.

At last she smiled and gave me a squeeze.

'Wouldn't you like a dram, too?' I asked quickly.

Cecilie stood up.

'There's an important lecture early tomorrow morning that I *have* to attend.'

'Of course.'

'But afterwards we can take a little trip. You'd like to see the Great Geysir, wouldn't you?'

'Yup.'

Cecilie brought me a blanket and I had to sleep on the sofa. I didn't sleep because I was still flying, just like in my earliest childhood, I was hovering, had to hold onto the cushions. And all the time I had a strange smell in my nostrils, burnt matches, something singed, it had to be a damaged undercarriage, there was going to be a belly landing, I had lost contact with the tower, a disaster was imminent.

I woke up a wreck and on the table was a hastily written note: *Back at twelve. Cecilie.* I staggered into the bathroom to repair the damage, but as I approached the water I almost about-turned. Either the sewage system had gone to pieces or I had the worst mouth odour of the century. I tried the tap in the kitchen, but it was just as foul. It was the same odour I had smelt in the night, scorched rubber, sulphur, I was standing on a volcano, it would not be long before lava surged upwards like steaming red porridge, the ground beneath my feet shook. I found a bottle of beer in the fridge, Skallagrimsson, had to be strong mead. Tasted of flat lager, lay like a lead weight in my stomach. I had to go to the bathroom again and pee, dabbed some water under my arms and put on my dry clothes. While I was standing there in the burning sulphur smell, curiosity got the better of me. I had a peep in the cupboard over the basin, an extra tooth-brush, eau de cologne, I should have bought some on the plane, damn, tampons, guitar strings, I was gripped by a serious longing, so serious that I had to bring up some Skallargrimsson. Afterwards, I felt pangs of guilt and carefully closed the cupboard door. Of course they were not guitar strings but dental floss. But her guitar was in the bedroom, I could see it through the crack. I did not go in. I sat down by the window and waited. There was an hour left until twelve. First of all it rained. Then there was a grey period before the sun burst through in its full glory. Then a wind blew up, a covering of sleet was released, the rain took over, the wind came inland and moved the clouds along, a tornado sent a couple of dustbins flying through the street, then it was quiet and suddenly the sun was back in full force. Then Cecilie came. She sailed up in an immaculate Land Rover and hooted the horn. I rushed downstairs and patted the bonnet.

'We're going now,' said Cecilie, 'so that we can get home before it's dark.'

'Classy set of wheels,' I said, and was unable to restrain myself. 'Alexander the Great piss in the pot, did he?'

'You can walk if you like. Fine by me!' Cecilie snarled and gave it full throttle. I sprinted after her. She stopped at the corner.

'Didn't mean it like that,' I grinned.

She let me in, did a U-turn with screaming tyres and roared off.

'The upper classes have exploited the workers for years, haven't they. And when my upper-class daddy wants to buy me a Land Rover, I say yes and exploit *him*! But he can't buy *me*, if that's what you think.'

'Course not. By the way, the water at your place tasted of athlete's foot.'

'Same everywhere. The water in Reykjavik's like that.'

'Thought I'd entered the lowest circles of hell. The sulphur stung my nose.'

'That's where we're going,' Cecilie said.

'Where?'

'To Hell.'

She put her foot down and it was not long before we had left the town behind us. On a hillock stood a huge spectacle, an unfinished church, the frame resembled the skeleton of a dinosaur. Then we were in the wilderness and in the far distance I espied some snow-white mountain plateaux and shining glaciers. I saw a small, sturdy horse walking across the rotting fields in search of fodder. It started raining again.

'The meteorologists must get pretty frustrated here,' I said.

'Just so long as it doesn't snow,' said Cecilie. 'We could get stuck on a mountain pass. People have been trapped inside their cars because of snow there.'

'Isn't there anythin' excitin' to look at in Reykjavik?' I ventured.

But Cecilie drove on. I lit a cigarette. It stopped raining. A flock of sheep leapt off the road in fright. The wind shook the high-sided vehicle. We reached bizarre terrain – rugged, reddish, wavy forms like a petrified sea and that is precisely what it was.

Cecilie pulled into the kerb and stopped.

'This is lava after an eruption,' she told me. 'Can you see what it resembles?'

'A petrified sea,' I said.

'A moon landscape. The American astronauts trained here before they went to the moon for the first time.'

I looked at her. She said it as if it were the most natural thing in the world.

'Is that true?' I whispered.

I opened the door to get out. Cecilie stopped me.

'You can't walk in those boots!' she laughed.

She produced a pair of robust safety shoes and I changed. Then I trotted off, but Cecilie didn't want to join me. She stayed in the car while I walked on the moon, alone, wearing heavy shoes. I had to tread carefully, slowly, balancing on jagged rocks. There was a smell of sulphur and smoke rose from the ground. I staggered across the moon and space was silent and windswept.

'You're a child,' Cecilie laughed as we drove on.

'I'm a tourist,' I said.

We climbed the mountain pass and drove to the white plateau. I thought the snow had started and was nervous, but it was just odd snowflakes flaying the windscreen. Cecilie gripped the wheel tightly and the needle registered 130. She snarled, bared her teeth, squeezed the accelerator, coaxed out a few more horses, cracked the whip, I could hardly take a swig, the bottle rattled against my teeth.

'We won't get snowed in, even if you slow down a bit!' I shouted.

But she just summoned her last ounces of strength, and the windscreen wipers went berserk. It's me who's wrong, I thought. I've been running at the wrong speed. I've put an LP on 45. It's been like that all the time. It's going too fast. Then we came down to sea level. Cecilie turned to me with a proud smile. A cool wind caressed the car. I rolled down the window. The föhn. Sudden sun. The smell of salt. I saw the sea. The ground was green and rolled towards the mountain like an upright carpet. The hot springs simmered and smoked. There were big greenhouses by the farms. Two horses ran across a field. A small white church stood surrounded by a stone wall.

Cecilie flung the Land Rover onto a new road and tarmac turned to gravel. The brown-green expanse spread towards a chain of mountains in the east. I still hadn't seen a tree.

'Living in Iceland, you get to know what imperialism is,' Cecilie started to explain.

I studied a few enormous rocks scattered down a slope. A jet black bird sailed through the air with an animal in its yellow claws.

'The government keeps saying it's going to run down the base, but the fact is that they're making Iceland more and more dependent on it. Jobs. Foreign currency earnings. They lick the USA's boots.'

We drove over a river of green water. A bank of fog rolled towards us and for some minutes I couldn't see a metre ahead.

'Do you know that the Americans have their own TV and radio programmes here? And they're transmitted to the whole of the Icelandic population! It's brainwashing pure and simple!'

When we hit clear weather again, Cecilie stopped and jumped out. I followed suit.

'Are we there?'

She shook her head.

'Come on,' she said.

We scrambled up a hill. The air was cold and pungent. Then we reached the peak. Our lungs contracted with a gasp. Blood took refuge behind knees. I was staring down the mouth of a volcano, a crater, several hundred metres in size, greyish-white ice floes floated on the brown water a long way down, like a crushed eye.

I crept backwards. Cecilie laughed.

'It's not dangerous. It's been extinct for ages.'

I ventured forward again, threw a stone as far as I could, but didn't hear it fall.

'Imagine all that power,' was the only thing I could say.

'Yes. One day it might erupt again. Just like the people.'

'Thought you said it was extinct.'

She started to walk back to the car. I needed a leak. I peed into the volcano. It gave me a sense of superiority.

I ran down to join Cecilie.

'You really *are* a tourist,' she said. 'All men absolutely have to pee into the crater at all costs. You should've seen an American coach-load here!'

She laughed out loud. I was piqued. We drove for an hour. There wasn't a road any more, just two wheel ruts. The snow lay strewn in filthy clumps. The fog hindered any views. I was frozen.

Then we were there. We got out and the stench hit me. Sulphur. I had to cover my nose, I almost retched again. I followed Cecilie into the area. The soil was red and brown, deep vents bubbled and gurgled, the steam coiled around my legs. I began to lose a sense of orientation. It was like walking through a dream with someone who was fully awake. Everything trembled around me. I heard a bang and a few metres away a glistening column of water shot into the air, it stayed there for ten seconds, twenty seconds, half a minute, a howling pillar of boiling water, then it slowly subsided and disappeared down a crack. I was stunned, crept closer with care. The earth was breathing, small bubbles simmered around the rim, the water rose, inflated itself into a glass bell, a transparent membrane, an embryo, a pulse, it was beating, then it exploded and the fountain spouted forth again. I ran back to Cecilie.

'Never seen anythin' like it,' I whispered.

'This is not the Great Geysir,' she said. 'It's Strokkur. Geysir's up there, but it's dormant now.'

She pointed to a steaming hillock behind us.

'Strokkur is just the younger brother,' she smiled. 'The only way to make the Great Geysir gush up is to empty green soap into it.'

'Eh?'

'They usually do that when there are loads of tourists around. It increases the pressure.'

'So that's what you learn at university. To give an enema!'

Cecilie laughed.

'Come here,' she beckoned and I went with her to see a puddle.

'That's the descent to Hell,' she said.

The little pond was utterly still, green, I felt with my fingers, scalded myself.

'Hell?'

I didn't understand what she meant.

'Can't you see the descent?' Cecilie smiled.

Then I saw it. Beneath the calm surface was a black hole, an abyss, right down into the earth, inside the earth.

'They threw people down there in the old days,' she told him.

I began to sweat.

'And no one… no one knows how deep it is.'

'Mmm.'

I was standing there staring hell in the eye as something exploded behind us. I almost fell face first into the hole and felt sulphur smack against the back of my neck. We turned and an incredible fountain surged towards the heavens, a water rocket, it rose and rose, it was unending. Strokkur was a mere bag of juice by comparison. Hot rain showered us, I bent my neck backwards trying to see the tip, fifty metres, a hundred metres, holding its position with a power that had blown me to the ground. Cecilie hauled me to my feet and danced round me.

'It's the Geysir!' she shrieked. 'It's the Geysir!'

I joined in her jig, and for some time, while it was at its height, we were close to each other, an old intimacy was breathed back into life. Then the Great Geysir disappeared into the ground and the heat and the sulphur were all that were left.

'It hasn't erupted for years,' Cecilie said, exhausted. 'It gushed for us, Kim!'

I didn't dare light a cigarette. I was frightened the whole country would be blown into the air.

It happened on the way back. We had only been driving for about a quarter of an hour when the front wheels suddenly buried themselves in mud and we tipped forward like a short-circuited dodgem. Cecilie tried to reverse, but then the rear wheels became stuck. Cecilie tried to turn. We sank even deeper. Cecilie tried everything. Even that didn't help. I thought Land Rovers could go under water. It wasn't true. The crate was up to its doors in mud. Cecilie was becoming hysterical. She ordered me to push, but I didn't think much to being a mud flap. The wheels spun deeper and deeper. I looked around. The flat landscape melted into grey fog. An icy wind stroked my back and I laughed. I was becoming hysterical.

'We'll have to wait in the car,' I said. 'Then at least we won't freeze to death.'

'Just a moment,' Cecilie bawled. 'Wait, who for? Father Christmas?'

'For people.'

'No one will come this way for at least a week! Don't you know it's Christmas Eve the day after tomorrow?'

In fact, I didn't. But she would never have believed that.

'Yes,' I said. 'Of course I know.'

'And there was you perhaps hoping to celebrate Christmas in Iceland. You have your wish fulfilled now! Cosy here, isn't it?'

'Be a trifle difficult to find a Christmas tree,' I said, trying to be humorous.

Cecilie staggered out of the car. And I followed.

'I have to be home tomorrow,' I said. 'Day before Christmas Eve. Aren't you goin' home?'

'No!'

She was close to bursting into tears. I wanted to console her, but I suppose there wasn't much comfort in me.

'If people won't find us, we'll have to find them,' I said objectively.

For some reason she followed me. We plodded along the bumpy wheel tracks and neither of us could remember having seen a house on the way to the geysers.

We must have been wandering around for at least an hour and were near collapse. The wind pursued us from all sides. Visibility was getting worse and worse. Then Cecilie spotted something by the edge of the road like a sort of bird house for sea eagles. But it was a postbox. It gave us fresh heart and we left the wheel tracks and followed a trail into the fog and wasteland. We had been lumbering along for quite a long time, hand in hand, it wasn't the most pleasant countryside to go for a walk in on the day before Christmas Eve. And the moment we saw a farm, a narrow walled box and two byres, a snarling Norwegian buhund leapt forward and rounded us up with well-practised growls. We were rooted to the spot as the dog's jowls came closer. At last an old man appeared on the doorstep of the house and yelled: *Seppi*! At that, the tyrant lay flat, wagged its tail and the master himself waddled towards us with a face covered in grey beard and an unkempt circle of hair around his knobbly bald pate.

He said three words in Icelandic, I assumed he was introducing himself, so I stuck out my hand and shouted 'Kim Karlsen'. He gave a broad grin, spat sideways and dislocated my shoulder.

'Gisle Tormodstad!'

Cecilie took over, it was strange to hear her speak Icelandic, she seemed drunk, or else I was, I was on a direct route out of reality, I just let things happen and that suited me fine. We followed Gisle and Seppi to the farmhouse, he conjured up an ancient jeep from under a tarpaulin, and after a lot of to-ing and fro-ing and kicks he got it going, and we rumbled off across the desolate plain and saw the Land Rover buried in mud.

We attached ropes and chains and Gisle coaxed it out, it was as easy as taking a splinter out of your finger. Cecilie gave thanks in Icelandic, and Gilse uttered a short sentence.

'He's invited us for coffee,' Cecilie translated.

Gisle's house was narrow, with all the rooms in one line. We sat down immediately, it was chilly there, stone walls, raw. Seppi started to like me and warmed my legs. On the bookcase there were big leatherbound volumes with gold writing on the spine. Gisle served us some dynamite coffee and schnapps from a shiny bottle with a black label.

'Black Death,' Cecilie whispered.

Gisle poured and we drank, it burned all the way down. Gisle poured again. There were tears in Cecilie's eyes. The wind battered the windows. Gilse turned slowly and looked out. Afterwards he said a few words. Cecilie's face went white and she dried her tears.

'What's up?' I asked.

'We'll have to stay here. He says there's a snow storm coming. We can't drive over the mountains now.'

'Did he say all that?'

Gisle added a sentence.

'You'll have to help him get the sheep inside,' Cecilie interpreted.

I trudged after Gisle and Seppi across the farmyard and down to a hollow where I was surrounded by bleating. The wind was blowing the wax out of my ears and I could barely stand. Gisle had the sturdy gait of an elephant. Seppi went wild when he caught the scent of the sheep, ran round in big circles and gathered them until they were as tightly knit as a sweater. Then Gisle found two shaggy horses, which looked pretty weary, swung himself up on one and I deduced that I was supposed to do the same. I assumed I would be thrown straight off, but the beast was easier to mount than a ladies' bike with balloon tyres. I let the wind blow through my hair, grabbed the mane and we rode home on either side of the flock while Seppi doubled back to pick up the stragglers. Cecilie was standing on the step when we arrived, with a telephoto lens, snapping away. I gave the nag a kick with my safety shoes, something happened, and I found myself on my face among the sheep. They trampled over me, pulled me along, I stared into matt, dry eyes, smelt the strong, pungent stench of sticky wool, and there was a lot of bleating. I heard Gisle laughing, the horse whinnying and Seppi growling, crawled to my feet and Cecilie took me into the house while Gisle saw to the animals.

I had to have three rounds of Black Death before I was myself again.Then Gisle and Seppi came in. He said three words. Cecilie smiled and looked at me.

'He asked if you were Danish,' she said acidly and rewound the film.

I gave a good, long shake of my head.

It began to snow.

Seppi lay by my legs and licked my shoes clean. Otherwise nothing happened. Outside, it grew dark. The storm hit the house. Gisle looked at us, nodding towards the bottle. I took a shot and passed it to him. He drank without shifting his gaze. His eyes were slow and deep. Seppi settled down in a corner and slept with one ear cocked. Cecilie put on more clothing. Then Gisle brought in some food. He placed a large piece of meat on the table and I remembered that I hadn't eaten since I had arrived in Iceland. Cecilie turned away, looking ill. Then I saw what it was. It was a sheep's head with the eyes still in. Gisle cut off a slice and gave it to me. I put it carefully in my mouth and chewed for a long time. It tasted of plimsolls. He cut off another piece. I took it. He looked at me while I was eating. I wanted to say something. I had a tongue in my head. I remembered what Sphinx had chiselled into our brains in the second year.

I recited in Old Norse:

Cattle die,
kinsmen die,
you too will soon die,
I know one thing,
that will never die,
the reputation of all the dead.

A beautiful smile spread across Gisle's face. He passed me the bottle, trotted over to the bookcase and pulled out a big book. *Egils Soga* was printed on the spine. And then he read aloud to us for the rest of the evening, slowly, but with a clear, child-like voice. I understood nothing and had understood everything.

Gisle went to bed early. He led us to a room on the first floor and went on his way. There was a narrow bed alongside the wall. We could hear the storm. Cecilie sat down in the corner. I lay on the bed. Cecilie remained sitting. We could feel the storm.

'Don't you want to lie down?' I said. 'Room for two here.'

She didn't answer. The rug under me was as stiff as a cactus and smelt of sheep.

'Aren't you tired?'

She didn't answer. She just looked at the bed with disgust. And then some devilry got into me.

'If you mean to fight for the workin' classes, you should be prepared to sleep in their bloody beds,' I said.

She didn't even meet my eyes, she just got up and reclined on the bed with her back to me.

I put a hand on her head.

'I'm having my period,' she whispered.

And so we lay there until the light transfixed us and Seppi barked the cock's clarion call.

Cecilie didn't want any breakfast. Gisle stood on the doorstep as we drove off into the white countryside. Seppi ran after the car yapping. We could see Hekla in the east. The storm was over. Everything was deserted and quiet. The car engine. We drove for two hours to Reykjavik without uttering a word. After parking outside her house entrance, she said, 'We can catch the plane if we hurry.'

'Are you goin' home, too?'

'No.'

She ran up and collected my few possessions and I put on my boots. And then we left, out of town once again, into the American zone, past the soldiers with machine guns at the ready. Cecilie rolled down the window and spat.

'When are you comin' to Norway?' I asked.

'In the summer. Maybe.'

We approached the airport and I was reminded of an old film we had seen together, in black and white. Parting of the ways beneath the wing in atmospheric fog.

I got out of the car and received a hug through the window.

'Have you got your ticket?'

'Yes. Don't wait until the plane has taken off. I'll be on it. You can be sure.'

She drove off at once. I was left standing in a cloud of exhaust and snow. A bus full of American soldiers rolled past. A fighter jet screamed above my scalp.

I stumped into the transit hall, over to the bar. People laughed out loud, held their noses and pointed. A Christmas carol was being played on the loudspeakers. I found a shop with souvenirs.

At first she began to cry, clung to me and sobbed, then she backed away with a sniffly nose and the questions came so thick and fast that I needed a queue number.

'What's that smell on you?'

'Think it's sheep,' I said, putting my gym bag down in the hall. Dad was in the sitting room decorating the Christmas tree and sent me a quick nod as if I had just been downstairs to collect the post. Pym was sitting on the Christmas star.

'Where've you been?' Mum shouted.

'Iceland.'

'Iceland? What were you doing in Iceland? Why don't you tell us anything? Have you completely forgotten about us? Last summer you didn't say anything when you went to France, either! What's got into you?'

I almost about-turned in the doorway, but I was broke and from the kitchen I could smell pork ribs and all the Christmas baking that my mother always did.

Dad appeared with cotton wool in his hair and glitter down his shirt.

'Where have you been, did you say?' he asked.

'Cold country, six letters.'

'But what were you doing there?!' Mum shrieked. 'What has Iceland got to do with you?'

'I visited Cecilie. She's studying in Reykjavik. Thought of starting there, too. Geology.'

The atmosphere changed in an instant. The future shone from her eyes and Mum was all over me again.

'But you could've told us, Kim. We've been so frightened for you. You have to promise us you won't go anywhere without telling us.'

'Okay.'

'Do you promise?'

'I promise, Mother.'

I disinfected myself in the bathtub, then sampled a foretaste of Christmas food, after which, exhausted, I dived between freshly ironed sheets, lay there listening to the train going round the bay and the tram in Drammensveien, took out the Kurér to tune into Europe, but the batteries were dead. I lay there counting sheep, in my boy's room, on the night of 23 December 1971.

It was well above zero when we trudged over to see Granddad in the home. Someone must have mixed up the dates. The thermometer was hovering on plus ten. Winter was not what it had once been. Father Christmas was wearing a raffia skirt.

'Indian winter,' I said.

All three of us laughed, a family on their way through the warm, wet Christmas streets.

'You could've had a haircut,' Mum teased, tugging my hair.

'I *have* had a haircut. The year before last.'

It was fun. But now and then I felt like a tightrope walker. The pole bobbed and the wire vibrated. This could not last, it was impossible. I decided to hold out until next year.

Granddad sat by the window as usual, he had shrunk, become ancient, his face was so thin there was no room for his dentures. They gaped open in a glass of water on his bedside table. But Granddad laughed, his spirits didn't seem affected. He leaned forward and produced a picture from the drawer to show me. He spoke indistinctly, it was like listening to Gisle. But I caught the gist. It was a photograph of the railway workers on the Dovre line in 1920. Granddad stood in the middle of the gang with a moustache and a glint in his eye. Mount Snøhetta towered up in the background.

Granddad waved away Mum's oranges.

'I've been to Iceland,' I shouted.

'Iceland? By boat?'

'Aeroplane!'

'Haven't they got any trains in Iceland?'

'No. They haven't got any trees, either.'

'Sleepers,' said Granddad. 'Sleepers.'

He beckoned me closer.

'They've been carrying beams in and out all week, Kim. Is there going to be a war?'

'Not at all. They're just measuring ceiling heights.'

Granddad nodded for a good long time. Then he was given his presents. He was astonished. I had bought him a mug with a picture of the Great Geysir on it. He put it down on the windowsill and looked at us.

'It isn't my birthday!'

'It's Christmas Eve,' Mum explained.

He looked at us. His eyes had sunk deep into his skull. He pointed to the door.

'When I go out of that door, there's going to be a party!'

And then he laughed, he roared with laughter, shook, the tears poured down.

Mum and Dad went to the four o'clock service in Frogner Church while I went home and drank Black Death. The presents lay under the tree. I took a peep at the labels. Hubert hadn't sent anything. Nor Nina. I slumped to the floor and at that moment music sounded from the flat above. It gave me a start and instantly I remembered all the things I had been missing. It was the new family who had moved in, children singing a Christmas carol with squeaky voices.

Mum and Dad returned from the church and as we were eating they asked me to tell them about Iceland. I told them everything I could remember, about the volcanoes, the lava, the hot springs and the Great Geysir.

'And you've thought about studying geology there, have you?' Dad enquired.

'Yes,' I said. 'Has to be the place for it.'

'You're not studying philosophy any more?'

I was in trouble, I lost my balance and had to grab the wire tightrope. Then Mum suddenly asked, 'Did you visit Hubert this summer?'

'No.'

'I can't understand why he doesn't get in touch!'

Dad sat huddled over his plate. It was empty. The silence impaled us, as if with a harpoon.

Mum went to the kitchen to fill the dish.

Dad and I looked at each other.

'I said you'd forgiven him,' I breathed. 'I asked him to come home.'

Dad continued to look at me.

'Think that was generous of you,' I said.

Pym landed on his shoulder, the green crow, Dad smiled briefly and Mum returned with more food.

Afterwards we opened the presents. For Dad I had bought a true-to-life model sheep. I think Pym became jealous, it fluttered round the room wildly and would not stop until Dad put the fleecy wooden model in the pile of paper. For Mum I had a plate with Hekla volcano on it. I didn't get a microphone, but new skis. And so Christmas Eve, with its glad tidings, faded out as the Christmas holidays brought slush and bombs. I dragged myself across the slopes and the Americans dropped their presents over Vietnam. The angels were burned, baby Jesus experienced the world in a dank air-raid shelter. Mum served cakes and Dad did crosswords. One evening when I could hear the explosions and the screams close by, I had a peek at one of his magazines. The crosswords were finished, but there weren't any words, just letters. He had been scribbling letters into the boxes at random. We were alone in the sitting room and he looked away.

'Don't think any more about it,' I said in despair. 'It's over now!'

Don't know if he heard me. Pine needles were falling from the tree already.

'I admire you, Dad!' I said quickly, and I meant it. 'I admire you!'

Mum brought in the seven kinds of Christmas biscuits and on December 30 it was announced on the news that the bombing would stop. New Year was round the corner. It was a time for resolutions. I had none. I hadn't done anything wrong.

Revolution 9

Winter/spring/summer '72

I stuck out living at home until February. The nest was too small. It was either Pym or me. It was me. When Nixon went to China I packed my gym bag and strolled up to the university. To my great surprise, there was a study loan waiting for me. Four Ibsens and the basic grant. I went to the record shop, listened to some heavy stuff, but it didn't do anything for me, instead I bought a record by Little Walter, went for a beer at the barn and counted the money on my fingers. Then I took a taxi to Munchsgate.

It wasn't Seb who opened the door. It was a girl. It was Guri.

'Wow,' I said. It was all I could say.

'Hiya, Kim. Come in!'

I did just that, had a squint around, things had changed. There was calm and orderliness, the aroma of tea and soap, a blanket on the mattress, green plants on the windowsill, two freshly washed pairs of pyjamas drying on a clothesline.

'Wow,' I said. 'Where's Seb?'

'He'll be here soon. He's out buying something for lunch.'

I sat down. Guri filled the kettle. I was so glad to see her, she looked so strong, her body seemed to radiate with health.

She pre-empted me: 'I live here,' she said.

'Nice.'

She looked at my gym bag.

'How are you doing?

'Makin' progress. And you?'

'Started law.'

'Wow. Cool.'

The water boiled and Guri scientifically infused the leaves. It was quiet as the tea brewed. I wondered what to do now.

'Terrific plants,' I said, pointing to the windowsill. 'Brighten the place up.'

'Those are Seb's,' she smiled. 'His new hobby.'

She poured the tea, golden brown, sat opposite me. I was beginning to find my bearings.

'How's Sidsel?'

'Think she's training to be a secretary.'

The tea went down like a glowing peach.

'Have you heard anythin' from Nina?'

Guri put down her cup.

'She's come back home,' she said in a soft voice, and the tea spilt over my hands, scalding me. 'To Denmark. She's at… at a rehab clinic.'

'Where… where'd she been?'

'Her father found her in Afghanistan. Through the embassy… he works at the embassy, you know.'

I had to put down my cup. My hands were burning.

'So she did go there,' I mumbled.

The door burst open and there was Seb with a big cod fish on his arm. He looked down at me and broke into a huge grin.

'Been out jiggin', have you?' I essayed, but my voice seemed to get stuck, my vocal cords got entangled.

He offloaded the fish into the basin and sat astride a chair looking very happy and freshly-shaven.

'Thought you'd fallen down a volcano! How was Iceland then?'

'Alright. I might start studyin' there. Geology. Gotta be the right place.'

'Have you heard about Nina, by the way?' He glanced at Guri. 'Deep shit, but she'll manage, Kim. She'll be as right as rain. A couple of months off dope and her skin will be as smooth as a baby's bottom.'

Seb was on form, hadn't seen him like that since the day he left to go to sea. Hoped the passage would be better this time.

'What happened to Goose?' I asked.

Seb grinned and averted his gaze.

'That was a dead end, that was, Kim. Well, you know, he thought the end of the world was nigh and he was countin' and crossin' the days off the calendar and so on. When there was one day left, he was on his knees all night mumblin' furiously. You got a mention too, by the way. And the old fella in the shop. Pretty gruellin' night. And when morning came he crawled over to the window and took a tentative peep outside. Christ knows what he was expectin' to see. Enormous hole maybe. But everythin' was as you would expect it to be. And then he lost the plot. Went mad, packed his bag and scooted off. Haven't seen 'im since.'

We chuckled and Guri poured more tea.

'And then I appeared on the scene,' she said. 'Met Seb in town on New Year's Eve.'

They gave each other a lingering kiss. It was time to make tracks. I pulled out the record and passed it to Seb. His face lit up.

'*Hate To See You Go*!' Wowee. Little Walter!'

'Keep it,' I said, standing by the door.

'Thanks, Kim. Far out. Drop by one evenin' and we'll ride the grooves.'

Guri looked at me.

'If you hear anythin' from Nina… or write to her, say hello from me,' I said.

'Right.'

'Say hello from me. Will you do that?'

'Yes, Kim.'

I stumbled down to Gjestgiveriet wrapping a lukewarm compress round my thoughts. Don't know what I felt, I was empty, inactive like the volcano I had pissed in. It was too much for me, in the end it was too much for me, the doorman dragged me outside, gave me the usual bollocks about long-haired chimps. Stortorget was a dark hole with scaffolding round it. The cold was turning my pores inside out. I took a taxi up to Gunnar's in Sogn. He was mildly surprised and invited me into his digs, twelve square metres, lamp, sofabed and books.

'Long time no see, comrade. How's it goin'?'

'That's the thing, Gunnar. Reckon I could stay here for a while?'

He immediately called a general meeting in the kitchen and four others turned up, two blokes and two girls, one of them Merete, whom I had met before. Gunnar explained the situation and said it was fine if I kipped down in the hall, provided that I took my turn washing up, put fifty oncers in the kitty and kept a beady eye open for the cleaner. Passed unanimously. The others drifted back to their rooms, Gunnar and Merete stayed. Gunnar grabbed a beer and poured, even though it was only Wednesday, and Merete showed me the washing-up roster. Already I felt at home. Mao was hanging over the kitchen table, I never understood why he hadn't had that revolting wart removed.

'What are you up to now?' I asked.

'Political science. And you?'

'Goin' to try to bag the prelim. Might start studyin' in Reykjavik by the way. Geology.'

'You can borrow my philosophy notes,' Merete offered.

'That's very kind of you.'

Then we went to bed. Shortly afterwards five alarm clocks went off. I was a student.

And so the winter passed. I sat in Gunnar's room reading while he was at university. Merete had weighed me down with folders and I sat taking notes from notes with an alert mind, counting lines and jotting down the time of the day in the margin. I made spaghetti and washed and scrubbed. Everything went well. The only thing I didn't like was the view. Above Sognsveien, behind the allotments, across the green forest dotted with white I could see the spire of Gaustad and the tall chimney.

I drew the curtains.

One day news came from Trondheim. Ola had a son and they were going to call him Rikard. We thought that was very moving and had to nip down to the restaurant to crack open a bottle, even though it was the middle of the week. Usually we went to Samfunnet in Chateau Neuf on Saturdays and I could never enter the bunker without thinking about straps and blushing at the thought. I sat at the back, at the top, with a beer, and could feel the weight of the concert grand while the political speakers murdered each other on the rostrum. Afterwards we crunched home on the snow through the cold of the night via Tørtberg, Gunnar, Merete and I, Gunnar talked about the debate, reviling the anarchists, he talked all the way, past Blindern, we crossed Ringveien, he talked about his brother who lived in the agricultural collective in Gudbrandsdalen, they refused to use a tractor, it polluted the potatoes, a sidetrack from the workers' struggle, Gunnar said with contempt, he talked about the referendum in September, said that Bratteli had already dropped a clanger, Gunnar disappeared in a cloud of icy breath, talking about impatience, the revolution, Gunnar and Merete, I felt a little left out, a gooseberry, a spanner in the works.

On nights like this I usually borrowed Gunnar's bed. And on Sundays I went to see my mother and father, if I had time and didn't have to study, shovelled down a hamburger and was off. They had a colour TV and watched *Ashton*, talked only about Ashton, even my father was wondering how Ashton was getting on. I took my leave after watching two minutes of the lurid faces. They didn't seem to notice that I had gone. I slammed the door. On occasion I walked down to Munchsgate, but then changed my mind, dithered for a while and slogged all the way back to Sogn, slowly.

Everything went fine. I read Merete's notes and took more notes, got through the syllabus, put money in the kitty and hid from the housekeeper. The only thing I didn't like was the view. The spire. The chimney.

Drew the curtains.

Winter thawed, Easter, the world melted. Something was up with Gunnar. He was beating round the bush. I was the bush. Him and Merete. They had meetings, people came, one by one, left later that evening, one by one. Gunnar didn't ask if I wanted to take part, didn't even breathe a word about it. But he was thinking about something, about giving me another chance. It came on the day before May 1.

'Comin' to the workers' party tonight?' he asked.

'Party?'

'We're goin' to do a bit of hammerin' and paintin' for tomorrow. And knock back a few beers. West Oslo.'

'Don't know if I'll have time. Got to read a few chapters.'

It took him ten seconds to persuade me. And at seven o'clock we turned up at the house in Ekely equipped with wooden boards and paintbrushes. Work was already under way. The various sections had each occupied a room. Gunnar and Merete disappeared into the cellar, I was left standing in the third world. A girl gave me a hammer and I banged. Later there was stew and beer. I could feel it inside, I was being sucked along by the mood, the optimism, the community, the devilry, the fight, the glow, the happiness, there was a sudden rush to my head, I felt it, I was being dragged along, I think my face was shining, for Gunnar and Merete were laughing at me. A guy was standing on a crate of beer and reading Brecht's *Questions From A Worker Who Reads*, a girl strummed a chord and everyone sang 'Move Aside, EEC, You're Standing In The Sun'. The walls swelled, my heart was under a ridge of high pressure, the roof rose, the heat, the solidarity, I must have lost control, I clambered onto a table and the gathering fell hush.

'Comrades!' I shouted. 'I've just been to Iceland and bring greetings from our comrades there. The people are fighting against the American base, brainwashing and suppression. The reactionary government has dropped its mask! They kowtow to the USA and have committed Iceland to worldwide American imperialism. They are making Iceland dependent on the USA, they're forcing Icelandic workers to work for the Americans, but the fight has only just begun! And it is the same fight we are taking to the EEC! One day I went into the countryside and met a farmer called Gisle. He read to me from *Das Kapital* and asked me to pass on his greetings to the Norwegian nation. Our struggle is their struggle. Their struggle is our struggle!'

I almost fainted. Sweat was pouring off me, then the cheering broke out, I fell off the table and was met by pats and embraces, soft cheeks and clenched fists.

It was past midnight when the paste group had finished stirring five buckets of flour and water. The placards were covered in glue and rolled in newspapers, and the company was divided into nine pairs to cover West Oslo. I was entrusted with Skillebekk and district, a dangerous area, crawling with cop cars circling embassies, it needed someone with local knowledge. Gunnar sent me an appreciative nod, and together with a little red-haired number I set out into the May night with five bags of *No To Selling Norway.* We cycled past Hoff and up to Bygdøy Allé, parked our bikes by Thomas Heftyesgate and continued on foot.

'Where shall we begin?' asked Little Red Riding Hood.

I stopped outside Bonus.

'Here,' I said.

I unfurled the placards and plastered the windows. It was a terrible mess. I had paste all over me. But it looked impressive when I had finished. There was no room for advertising any offers. It would take years to scrape them off.

'We can't stick them all here,' Red Riding Hood whispered.

'Right,' I said.

We worked our way down towards Skillebekk, from lamp post to lamp post, Red Riding Hood was calculating and systematic. We crossed Drammensveien, Red Riding Hood wanted to head for the Russian embassy, I managed to point her towards Svolder. There, I pasted every lamp post and gateway, my flesh tingled when I saw Dad's Saab. Then we made our way back to the tramlines.

'Important area,' I whispered to Red Riding Hood. 'A lot of floatin' voters. I know that. Grew up here.'

'The petite bourgeoisie are a stubborn lot,' she said.

We had three bags left and pasted our way out of Drammensveien. Red Riding Hood had the knack. She could stick the placards without spilling a drop. I looked like a tube of Karlsen's glue. But all went well. Up to the moment we saw the cop car gliding down Fredrik Stangsgate to bear left.

Red Riding Hood took command.

'Let's split up!' she shouted and was gone, like a red wind.

I swivelled and ran, dragging the bags after me, hurtled up Gabelsgate, felt the sour breath of the law on my neck and panicked. My legs were like wheels beneath me. Sirens. The scream of tyres on a bend. I shot into a backyard, jumped over a fence and was in the country. The brown grass was wet. Pale green trees in the cool darkness. The storehouse on pillars. The stable. I heard brakes and reversing and car doors being slammed. I had no choice. I groped my way towards the air-raid shelter and crept down, not completely, halfway, sat on the steps. I heard voices. I listened for dogs and held my breath. Don't know how long I had been sitting there. I heard nothing, just my own staccato pulse. The steps were cold and dark. I thought I could see eyes down there, at the bottom in the dark. I couldn't stand up. I was sitting in a quagmire of glue and placards and newspapers. I thought I saw something move. I thought I heard the sound of a gate locking. I shouted. My voice zigzagged between the musty walls as if there were a line of people screaming back at me. I shouted, I summoned all the powers, I shouted to the badger and Mao, to Jesus and Marx, to Lenin and Mum and Dad, I shouted in terror, sitting in the glue, but it was not a prayer, it was not a prayer.

It was early morning when I reached Sogn. Gunnar and Merete were sitting up waiting for me, they had set the table for a big breakfast in the hall. They were ecstatic, thought I had been chucked into the clink and was being given the third degree. Then they started laughing. And when I saw myself in the mirror I understood why. I was a mobile advertising pillar. The others were woken by the laughter and the history student said I looked like a cubist collage-sculpture and wanted to enter me for the Autumn Exhibition. I took off my rags and put on the only clean clothes I had left. Then I packed my gym bag and carried my books under my arm.

'I'm off,' I said.

'Aren't you stayin' for breakfast?'

'Don't think so.'

The table was covered with red flags and the Norwegian flag.

'Great speech you gave about Iceland,' said Merete.

Gunnar came over to me.

'See you soon,' he said. 'Good luck with the exam!'

Then he shook my hand.

'You shouldn't have done that,' I said.

He gave me a strange look. Then he understood. Our hands were glued together. We pulled and pulled, we tugged from all angles, but it didn't help.

'Good glue they make in West Oslo,' Gunnar grinned, and we had to put our hands under the tap.

Then I left Sogn's student village. It was spring and a gentle fragrance of perfume wafted through the air. Large red flags hung from windows and there was music everywhere.

It was all change at Seb's again. It took him three quarters of an hour to crawl from mattress to door, and there he stood, swaying, two metres of stained underpants and pigeon breast. I was relieved.

'Right bloody time to come visitin'!'

We stepped inside and Seb wrenched the window open. There weren't any green plants on the sill any longer. Pyjamas were hanging out to dry.

'Where's Guri?'

He dropped onto the mattress and lit up.

'She's gone and left me,' Seb said in English with a sigh.

'Looked pretty lovey-dovey last time I was here.'

'Exactly, hawkeye. Remember the botanical garden I had on the windowsill, do you? Well, Guri thought it was hyacinths and bulbs and stuff, but then one day she found out it was hardy cannabis from the high plains. Got 'em off a guy in the park at Christmas. She took the whole crop with her and slung her hook.'

'You were growin' hash on your windowsill?'

'Course. Had the oil-fired central heating on full blast and was just waitin' for the spring sun. South-facin' window. Greenhouse conditions, Kim.'

'You're out of your mind.'

'Bloody hell, Kim. People brew their own moonshine, don't they?'

He put on some water for coffee, gave me his smoke and burrowed down into a pile of clothing.

'Have you moved out of Sogn or what?' I heard.

'Yep. Too much naggin'. Thought I might stay here and study for my exams.'

He reappeared with frayed denim jeans and a faded sweater.

'Don't think much of this exam trip of yours, Kim. Your eyes are like two slits! But stay here. As long as you like.'

We drank instant coffee. It tasted of fungus.

'Have you got anythin' to drink?' I asked.

'Good idea, professor. Let's go and see Grandma. She's got a cellar full of booze from Grandpa.'

She lived by Sankthanshaugen and was eating breakfast when we arrived. There was a smell of toast and marmalade. She gave us both a hug and wanted to open a can of Norway-famous snurring when she saw how thin he had become, but Seb went straight to the heart of the matter.

'Could we borrow a few bottles of juice from you, Grandma? It's May 1 and the shops are closed.'

She sent him a sceptical look, winked with one wrinkled eyelid and fetched the cellar key.

'Don't take much of the blackcurrant juice, boys, because there's only a little left.'

It was dog eat dog. We trundled down and opened her storeroom. The long wall was covered in bottles, each in their own slot.

'Grandpa was a collector, and Grandma drinks 'em,' Seb grinned. 'Fair deal. She won't be able to knock all this back before she dies.'

We took ten bottles of white wine and an excellent cognac with us. Grandma gave us a few general warnings when we returned the key, but she could rely on us, we wouldn't spill a drop. And then we made our way back, past the Cathedral School and Vår Frelsers cemetery, and people were in the streets. The janissary bands could be heard round the corner and we speeded up. At the Experimental School it was all go, banners hanging from the windows and carnival atmosphere. We pressed down a cork and treated the midgets and the religion teacher to a sip. Then we padded home and put the provisions in the freezer.

We started on the cognac to ensure a solid base.

'You goin' to the procession?' I asked.

'Nope. Been thrown out before. I'm goin' to Hjelmsgate.'

'D'you know how Nina is?' I asked quickly.

'Think she's gettin' better. But she was well gone. Worse than me.'

'She made it to Afghanistan,' I said softly.

'She did.'

We opened a bottle of chilled white and the town beneath us was in ferment.

'Dad's back home,' Seb said. 'He's stayin' with my mum.'

We shut up for a while, mulling things over.

'Heard anythin' from Ola?' I asked.

Seb grinned and lay down flat.

'Rikard's growin'. Was born three weeks late, you know. Had a fringe and front teeth when he finally arrived!'

We smiled at that for a while and dived into the wine.

'Have to visit him,' I said. 'Hell, let's go to Trondheim. After the exams!'

'Terrific idea! We'll surprise the Jensen family with a lightnin' raid from the urban guerrillas!'

We drank to it and opened another bottle.

'What the hell are you learnin' at that dated university, eh?'

'That we've got to the oral phase. Talkin' and drinkin'.'

All of a sudden I was utterly exhausted. Seb faded in the mists and my brain ceased to exist. He bent forward and shook me.

'Comrade Kim! We're hittin' the town!'

'Don't think I can be bothered,' I mumbled.

And that was the last thing I can remember before he returned and it was a new day.

He dragged me out of my slumbers.

'Don't tell me you've been asleep since I last saw you!'

I didn't know where I was, I was everywhere, in all the rooms I knew of, and people were sitting in each of them trying to wake me. At last I caught sight of Seb.

'Somethin' happened?' I mumbled.

'The whole town was out, Kim! Standing room only! We set up darts games in the university square. With Stalin as the target! There was a real buzz in the atmosphere.'

He stretched out on the mattress as I was getting to my feet.

'Met Stig by the way. We're invited to the farm. When are we goin'?'

'After the exams.'

'You're completely hooked on that dope, aren't you!'

Then it was Seb's turn to sleep, and I sat down to do some studying. It was a good arrangement. We were never in the same rhythm. When I was asleep Seb was busy somewhere in and around Oslo. When he was asleep, I was sitting over my books and one morning in the middle of May it was finally exam time. My nerves were as calm as Mum's balls of wool and my brain was on full alert. Seb walked in the door with nine bottles of wine he had picked up at his grandmother's, wished me luck and passed out on the mattress. I wandered through the weightless rain to Blindern, found the gym hall and took my seat by the wall bars. Around me sat groups of fringes with knotted brows. I was Buddha. I was the wind and the sea. I laid newly sharpened pencils, rubbers and biros in front of me. I knew everything by heart, had it all at my fingertips, apart from one, the crooked finger, the ugly one, that was my only gap.

Then a door slammed, an ill wind ran through the room, and the superannuated teachers distributed the exam questions. But before I managed to read them, another old man came up demanding to see my student card. He took it. I read on. It looked easy. It looked ridiculously easy. No pencil necessary here. I grabbed my biro and felt a hand on my shoulder.

'Your name's not on the list,' the man whispered in my ear.

'Which list?'

'The exam list. Did you register?'

'Register?'

I had to accompany him to the invigilator at the desk. There the matter was quickly and ruthlessly clarified. I had not registered for the exam. They regretted to inform me. Kim Karlsen was obliged to capitulate after four minutes. Everyone stared at me. I couldn't be bothered to collect my pencils. I went to Frederikke and bought myself a beer. It was the finger's fault. I hated the finger, banged it on the table, felt like stamping on it, chewing it to bits, tearing it off. Three girls in the corner were watching me. I scurried out, ran down to Munchsgate and woke up Seb.

'How did it go?' he gurgled.

'Got chucked out. Had forgotten to register.'

He stumbled to his feet with a grin splitting his face.

'Nice one, Kim. Nice one. The best thing that could've happened. This has to be celebrated!' He pulled the white wine out of the fridge and filled half-litre glasses.

'Afterwards we'll go to the harbour and buy shrimps and lie under the trees in Akershus. Does that sound good or what, Kim?'

'And tomorrow we'll go and see Ola!'

'Exactly.'

But we didn't leave the day after, we didn't get our fingers out until mid-June, but then one warm morning we were standing on the Trondheim road with our thumbs aloft and our heads pretty fuzzy. Gunnar couldn't join us, he was on an agitprop tour in Sørlandet. To compensate, he had furnished us with a pillowcase full of leaflets and folders.

'Weird,' I said to Seb. 'Recently, time, the last six months, just seem to have flown by. Haven't had time to put two thoughts together.'

'That's what it was like in Amsterdam when I was goin' through the mill. Another time. You blinked with your right eye and a week had gone.'

'Makes me bloody nervous! It's like you're losin' control.'

'Cool down now, Kim. We're on holiday.'

Cars tore past us to the Sinsen intersection. The town lay wreathed in mist. The fjord was like a blue floor. Nesoddlandet was a green slope leading to the sky.

'Sure we shouldn't ring and say we're on our way?' I said.

'Take it easy! There'd just be organisin' and panic. The boy has a *family*! Don't forget that.'

A throaty car skidded onto the pavement in front of us and a door flew open.

'Hop in, lads! I'm on my way to work.'

We scrambled onto the back seat and the man had left the outskirts of Oslo before we closed the door.

'Going to Trondheim, are you? Guessed as much. With you standing in Trondheimsveien. Ha ha. Met a bloke thumbing in Stavangergata, in the city centre, once. You're lost, I said. Way off course.'

We laughed politely and he watched us in the mirror.

'Did you get it?' he asked.

We laughed even louder and the Brylcreemed fatty performed a wild overtaking manoeuvre, slinging the car between a bus and a trailer with a second to spare.

'Usually comes off,' he grinned, and Seb took out a big roll-up and we lit up.

'Don't know that tobacco, lads. New brand?'

'Pakistani menthol,' Seb said.

'That's what I keep saying. These foreign workers are sneaking in everywhere. What's wrong with Teddy, lads? Tell me that! Can't walk through town without bumping into a horde of bush men. I'll tell you something, boys. I was in Lillesand last week and met an Arab who spoke with a perfect Sørland accent! What d'you think about that then? Can I have a try by the way?'

He leaned back and snatched the joint out of the air, sucked, inhaled and spluttered over the steering wheel. The car swerved into the left lane, he yelled and swung it back with a scream.

'Tastes terrible,' he coughed. 'Menthol did you say? There you go! They call it menthol and it's absolute shite. Donkey shit. I know all about that. And when we're in the EEC, the dagoes will invade the country with their rubbish. What do you think the Espagnolos and the Eyeties know about soap and perfume and make-up? Nothing, boys. But they sell their crap cheap and ruin everything for us, the honest guys. It'll be a disaster. All Norway will stink of sweat. Agreed?'

'You a rep?' I asked.

'Hole in one. I make women more beautiful. *Pedersen's Pretty-bags*. That's me. Perfume, polish and powder. Plus, plus. That's me. Got any more of those cigarettes by the way? Run out of baccy.'

Seb gave him a spliff, he puffed away, rolled down the window and whistled as he barrelled along at 120. Mjøsa lay to the left. The clock on the dashboard was going as fast as the speedometer. We approached the mountains. He rolled up the window. I looked at his face. It had turned black since we left Oslo. He groped around in the glove compartment for an electric shaver and it buzzed across his face.

'My heat-seeking missile,' he smirked. 'That's another thing women like. Especially the single ones. You get my meaning?'

Seb had fallen asleep. Pedersen's eyes were popping out of his head. The road was his. He just hooted and cruised past if anyone was in his way. By a hair's breadth. The hours and kilometres behind us mounted up. I watched Pedersen's beard grow, I *saw* it, the black stubble sprouted out of his face and the machine droned across it as we zigzagged through Norway and hit Trondheim right in the navel coming to an abrupt halt. Seb awoke with a gasp.

'Here we are, lads.'

We were in the middle of a bridge. Nidaros Cathedral cast its shadow over us.

We thanked him for the lift and opened the door. He stopped me with a smooth hand.

'No one can say that Pedersen is tight-fisted,' he slurred.

And then he produced two packets from the box on the front seat and gave them to us.

'*Pedersen's Pretty-bags*,' he said. 'There you are. You both look absolutely dreadful.'

We stood on the bridge over the river watching him drive away in the dusk. There was a smell of scorched Brylcreem. At the first crossroads there was a collision. The cop car came from the right and Pedersen accelerated. The uniforms surrounded the car and dragged out a ranting Pedersen.

'Think we'd better scram,' said Seb.

We did. We ran as far as a park. There we sat on a bench and opened our make-up bags. Seb had an attack of the giggles and started powdering his sallow face.

'Have to glam ourselves up!' he whinnied.

And we did look quite glamorous as we rang the Jensen family doorbell. Mascara, powder, lipstick, perfume and hairspray. Suddenly Ola was in the doorway, his mouth agape. We were men from the moon. We threw ourselves on him and he sank to the floor. He wrestled himself free and staggered back against the wall.

'Who is it, Ola?' we heard from the sitting room, must have been the wife.

Ola was unable to utter a word. We opened the door wide and there were three people sitting in the room with lamps and embroideries on the wall, coffee and cakes on the table. Their mouths dropped. They stiffened like statues over their coffee. Ola arrived behind us gesturing with his arms.

'This is S-S-Seb and K-K-Kim from Oslo,' he explained maniacally, pointing in all directions. 'And this is K-K-Kirsten and her p-p-parents.'

'Where's Rikard?' Seb screeched.

We shuffled into the bedroom and there lay a chubby body in a Moses basket. The moment I saw him, the pink sleeping head, I was as clear and transparent as glass and a diamond carved fear right through me.

'He's wonderful,' I whispered. 'Wow, he's wonderful.'

I placed a finger on his forehead and Rikard began to scream. Kirsten charged over and lifted him up, rocked him quietly and gently. I couldn't stop myself gulping. Ola stood there, proud and frightened and unsure what to do. Kisten unbuttoned her blouse and Rikard put out a hand for her breast.

'Think we should go into the s-s-sittin' room,' Ola said in a low voice.

That was where things went downhill. Every time the mother or the father opened their mouths Seb howled with laughter. He sat bent double in his chair spluttering cake everywhere. The atmosphere was taut. Ola crushed a cup between his fingers. In the end, Seb was rolling around on the felt carpet, holding his stomach and laughing till the tears came, smudging the powder on his face. I wiped off the make-up and the sweat and Kirsten came back, her face hardened. Ola sat on the sofa like a mussel.

I felt obliged to give an explanation.

'We've just come from a carnival,' I smiled weakly. 'At Oslo university. The semester's over. That's why we, that's why we… are like this.'

Noticed all of a sudden that I couldn't do it any more, that I was unable to lie. They didn't believe me. I picked the guffawing Seb off the floor and dragged him to the door. Ola followed and we were alone in the hall.

'Sorry,' I said in a soft voice. 'Sorry. Hope we haven't ruined anythin'.'

'Should have s-s-said you were comin'.'

Ola looked away.

'I envy you,' I said. 'Baby and all that.'

'What are you g-g-gonna do now?'

'Go home. All the best from Gunnar.'

I gave him the pillowcase with the leaflets. Seb was vertical again and leaned over Ola.

'Good thing you're only stammerin' again,' he grinned. 'Trondheim dialect really cracks me up! Ever heard an Arab speaking with a Sørland accent, have you?'

I shoved him into the stairwell and patted Ola.

'Say hello to Rikard,' I said. 'In fifteen years' time he'll be playin' the drums for The Snafus!'

Ola didn't say anything, but his eyes spoke volumes. I pushed Seb down the stairs and heard a child crying as we stepped out into the sobering June night.

'For Christ's sake! Did you have to piss about when the in-laws were there!'

'Couldn't help it, Kim. It was too much for me.'

'You twat!' I shouted into his face. 'You twat!'

There was nothing else for us to do in Trondheim. I had enough money to buy a ticket home. The train left at ten and we caught it.

'Are you comin' with me to see Stig?' Seb asked, standing in the corridor and watching the lights whiz past like shooting stars.

'Nope.'

'Hell, you're not angry with me, are you?'

I pressed my face against the window and felt it vibrate. I leaned harder. The jolts banged against my head.

'Goin' to Nesodden,' I said.

Seb jumped off in Oppdal. I went on to Oslo. I saw Fred's mother standing in the window. I had early morning dew in my eyes.

In Munchsgate the heat was unbearable. The town awoke like a listless lion. I was broke. I couldn't even afford the Nesodden ferry. I lay on the mattress thinking things through. Later I went out. The sun was high in the sky. Up the street, outside the bakery, a few young shavers were playing football. I ran over to them and latched onto the ball intending to show them some tricks. They were annoyed and dribbled circles round me and shouted at me. I slouched off. I had to get some cash before I could go anywhere. I had a plan. I ambled back to Svolder and let myself in. The smell of holiday. Curtains filtering the light. The dust. Rugs over furniture. I collected all my Beatles LPs, put them in a bag and hurried out. The street was empty. A wind blew sand past me. A gull screamed behind me. I went down to the shop in Skippergata and showed the greedy old hag what I had to offer. With bony fingers, she pulled out the discs, squinted at them and blew.

'They're worn,' she whispered. 'Scratches. Stains.'

I didn't answer.

'Ninety kroner,' she snapped.

She already had the money in her hand. I took the notes and ran out, stopped for a few seconds, hours, then I walked up Karl Johan. My conscience began to prick. I had sold myself. There was a table free at Sara. I ordered a beer, rolled two tenners together and stuffed them in my back pocket so that I would be sure to be able to get on the boat. I didn't need to go until the evening. I scanned the restaurant for familiar faces. I finished my beer and went back into Karl Johan. People streamed towards me like slanting, toppling columns, dressed in black in the heat, with white dusty faces. I reached Studenterlunden Park. Someone put a leaflet in my hands. It was Peder with Slippery Leif. HAVE YOU SAID NO TO THE EEC? read a big poster. I threw the paper away and ran on, then came to an abrupt halt. They were all sitting together on the yellow benches under the trees with the green light casting its rays over them like silent rain. My guts rose into my mouth. There was Nina with a syringe in her arm. There was Fred, dripping wet, thinner than ever. There was Dragon with his imploded face and the bleeding remains of a devoured arm. And Jørgen, fat, thinning hair, with a blue cut down his cheek and lifeless eyes. I ran as fast as I could. I heard a car slam on the brakes. The park was deserted. I knelt down in the grass and threw up. The palace was being redecorated. Scaffolding. I sat in the shadow of a tree. A guardsman woke me up and told me to clear off. I walked slowly back down to Karl Johan. No one was sitting on the benches. The green light had turned darker. The parasols at Pernille looked like over-sized amanita mushrooms. Then they came towards me again, the crowds, slanting, toppling columns. I turned on the spot, sprinted towards Club 7. Closed. I had to go down to the harbour. The clocks on the City Hall tower struck. I walked across the concrete graveyard, stopped, looked around, noticed the sky. I remembered the old Vika district and felt a sudden steel-like spasm in my back. I screamed, I screamed, it was the scream I had been waiting for, it had returned, I screamed, and the windows around me broke, I stood in an avalanche of glass, and in every shard I saw the gleam of a red sunset.

Love Me Do

Summer/autumn '72

I awoke slowly from a pain searing up my arm and settling in my chest. A woman in white laid a cloth on my forehead. Further back was another woman who resembled my mother. She came towards me, stooped over my bed.

'Does it hurt, Kim?' I heard weakly.

'Where am I?'

The woman in white raised my hand with care and placed it over the duvet. That was where the pains were coming from. Bandages. Mum was still there.

'What happened?' I whispered.

'You smashed a shop window,' she said softly. 'They had to stitch you up at casualty.'

I was given a glass of water. The nurse supported my head with a strong yet gentle hand.

The room was small with bare, light green walls. Some clothes hung in a wardrobe by the door. My tweed jacket. Confirmation suit.

I looked at my mother.

'Where am I?'

She turned away.

'Gaustad.'

I smelt turpentine and went back to sleep.

The next time I awoke several people were there, Dad had come, Mum, the woman in white, and a small, dark man sitting on a chair by my bed. He held his hand inside his jacket, his face came closer, burning eyes, glistening black hair. It was Napoleon. I screamed. I heard lots of voices and Mum stood over me telling me fairy tales. The doctor took my pulse and the woman in white brought me a glass. Dad stood with his back to me. Think the sun was shining through the window. I heard a bird.

'Why am I here?'

'Now you just rest, Kim,' the small man said. 'You're here to rest and we'll help you, all of us. Do you understand?'

There was something else. I could feel it, there was something about my head. They had done something to my head. I felt with my good hand. Bald as a coot. Smooth. Noticed the bump where the skull had healed.

'What've you done to me?' I shouted. 'What've you done to me?'

'We'll talk to you later, Kim,' said the small doctor. 'You're too tired now.'

The nurse rolled up my sleeve and the people disappeared. I was tiny and sat in a keyhole. On one side of the door it was pitch black. On the other, a white sun moved across the floor.

I heard the sound of keys.

Mum was with me almost every day. My hair would not grow. Asked her to bring me a hat. The cold corridor outside the room. The footsteps. The canteen with all the grey faces and the revolting, tasteless meals. I couldn't eat. Pills in the morning. And in the evening. The visitors' room with the old radio, the magazines and the tin ashtray. The visitors sitting stiffly clutching their terror and disgust. Someone running amok. The solitary confinement. The muffled screams. A boy who threw himself out of the window. And lay bleeding on the brown earth. The bathtubs, the green chipped enamel. Getting undressed while people in white ran the water and made jokes. Standing there, an emaciated carcass, a laughing stock. Refused to remove my woollen hat. Refused point blank. They had a good laugh. I was not allowed to lock the toilet door. The door to my room was locked from the outside. The view: a dark spruce forest nearby. The other side: the main building. Straight ahead, over the fence and across the road: a field and a clearing, green, open, sun-dappled.

Mum: 'How's it going, Kim?'

I looked at her. She had braced herself. I couldn't detect any weakness in her eyes.

'Do you talk to Dr Vang?' she went on.

Napoleon. I called him Nap. In my cremated mind. I had to go up to his office in the other wing every third day.

'How do you like it here?' he always asked, as if it were some tourists' hotel in the mountains.

Never answered.

He soon lost his patience. A hyper little man.

'You're not very cooperative, Karlsen,' he said with a smile. 'You don't even talk to your mother.'

I became more and more convinced that he wore a wig. It lay flat on his head and the parting was one woolly line.

He was always the first to get up.

Didn't dare say anything. Couldn't lie any more.

The nurses were decent enough. They discussed the EEC and one of the oldest nutters stood on a chair and screamed that the EEC was the beast in the Book of Revelation, the Treaty of Rome was the work of the Antichrist and the winds of doomsday were already blowing around our ears. What a palaver there was. For the most part I stayed in my room. It was quiet there. I looked out of the window. Summer. Had only one thought: Will I be here for ever? Didn't know why I was there.

Sometimes I watched TV. The clock. The white second hand going round. If I closed my eyes and had a daydream, I timed the dream, and when I opened my eyes, only half a minute had passed, and I could swear I had been sitting there for several hours. A nutcase who played patience the whole day, of all things, the Idiot, could never finish a game, he sidled up to me.

'Don't let the TV fool you,' he whispered, shuffling the cards quickly and nervously peering round. 'Have you seen the sports programme? When they replay the goal? The goalkeepers always save it then. In the replay!'

Went to my room. Night always came without my noticing. The line between sleep and day was slowly eroded by a remorselessly conscientious nurse.

Mum: 'Why don't you say anything, Kim? We were able to talk together before.'

'Were we?'

This was hard to take, she tensed the muscles in her face, but in her eyes there was no weakness, only sorrow.

'What did we do wrong!' she burst out.

She clung to my arm for the rest of the visiting time.

'I miss Nesodden,' I said. 'I long for Nesodden.'

Nap wanted me to speak. He walked around me with his hands against his back and was pathetic. His room smelt of sweat. In his dark eyes I could see another, a more dangerous, Napoleon than the one he purported to be.

Kept my mouth shut.

Had no appetite and became ever thinner. A doctor arrived to remove the stitches from my hand. There were scars everywhere. My mangled finger was the worst. During the evening the anaesthetic wore off, it burned itself out. It was good to feel some pain. Then they arrived with supper. The pills. Chlorpromazine. Phenthiazine. I don't remember all the pet names they had. Don't remember all they said. But it was all for my own good, they kept saying.

Mum: 'Uncle Hubert's come home!'

Couldn't understand how she could drink the coffee.

'He's had a picture accepted for the Autumn Exhibition!'

I turned to the window.

'Do you think crime pays?'

She immediately got frightened.

'You haven't done anything bad, have you, Kim?'

'Why am I here?'

'They want to help you, Kim. You'll soon be well again. You'll soon be out.'

'Will there be a lot of apples this year?'

'Yes,' said Mum.

Sleep.

One day I was allowed to go for a walk. We were a scruffy lot trotting up to Lake Sognsvann, past the fields. Two orderlies walked at the front and two at the rear of the pack. Summer was in its last phase.

Weary. Worn out. Had to be August. Legs were leaden. We dragged ourselves along the road. Then I saw them. They were coming towards us. Four boys with rods over their shoulders and big fishing bags. They slowed down and were quiet as we passed them. I turned. They were whispering and looking at us.

That night I couldn't sleep.

The wind rose, rattled the windows.

Shadows on the wall. Processions.

Close by someone was playing a tune on a saw.

The following day I had visitors. Gunnar and Seb sat in the visitors' room chain-smoking. I went to see them with my hat pulled well down. They didn't try to tear it off.

Sat down on a wobbly chair.

They were shitting themselves, didn't know what to say.

'How was it at Stig's?' I asked.

Seb was tanned and had acquired biceps.

'Alright,' he whispered. 'Been diggin'. Gonna move there this autumn. You can have my room,' he added quickly.

'Don't think I'll need it.'

We went into my room.

'Been searchin' for you all over town,' Gunnar said. 'Your mum said you were here. We didn't bloody believe her!'

Didn't say anything for a while. They rolled cigarettes and smoked.

'What happened?' Seb asked, studying the floor.

'Don't know. Got rabies.'

They tried to laugh. Sounded terrible. Couldn't look me in the eye.

'What are they doin' to you?' Gunnar asked abruptly.

'Dopin' me up.'

'Shi-it!' Gunnar leapt to his feet and stood by the window. 'Christ! Spit the crap out! Spit it in their faces!'

'Can you hear the shouts?' I said.

They were silent and listened. Screams. As if someone were screaming with a muzzle over their mouth.

'Solitary confinement,' I said.

Visiting time was over. I accompanied them to the exit.

'George wasn't playin' the solo on "While My Guitar Gently Weeps",' I said. 'It was Clapton.'

Seb gave me a strange look, nodded. Then they had to go.

Sat as quiet as a mouse for the rest of the day.

Rain.

Mum: 'I wanted to be an actress once. I had lessons. Have I told you that, Kim?'

'Why didn't you continue?'

'Life doesn't always turn out the way you imagine. You'll have to realise that some day, too.'

My hat made my forehead itch. Took it off. Mum liked seeing me like that. She caressed my shiny skull and smiled.

'Can I trust you?' I asked.

'Yes,' Mum said. 'Always.'

'Whatever happens?'

'Yes, Kim. Whatever happens.'

Rain. Pills. Water.

Nap wanted to talk to me again. I sat in his room. I studied his hair.

'It's a shame to have to say this, but you are treatment-resistant, as we say. You would like to stop taking the medicine, wouldn't you. But of course we can't let you do that, if you won't cooperate in other ways.'

He thumbed through some papers on his desk.

'And we can't keep you here for an eternity, can we.'

I thought about those senile apparitions in the canteen, they no longer had an age.

'How long is an eternity?' I asked.

His face shot up with a look of surprise at hearing my voice.

'When you got up to these stunts, Kim, had you been drinking or smoking? Or did you just decide to do it of your own accord, of your own free will?'

My mouth dropped. Napoleon stared at me.

'I have plenty of time today. Take all the time you need, Kim.'

'What stunts?'

'You know very well. The skeleton, for example.'

Mum must have told him. Mum. Now there was no one I could trust. I kept my mouth shut. I would never open it again.'

Nap waited.

Then he couldn't wait any longer.

'Don't you feel any shame for robbing your father's bank?'

I was feverish, yet I was clear, clear and cunning and wary like a hunted Red Indian.

I saw it. The letter I had carried around myself when I was called up for the military medical.

It lay open on Napoleon's desk.

At first I was happy. Mum hadn't told tales.

Then I made my decision. I leaned forward as if I were going to tell him something in confidence. Nap sent me an expectant look. But instead I swept his reading lamp onto the floor, snatched the letter and made a leap for the door. He followed me down the stairs, I tried to read as I ran, but I was too weak, I didn't have the strength, I was seized from behind, lashed out with my left hand, just caught sight of his wig falling off before I fell myself, with incredible speed, down into a white, imageless darkness.

Late summer sun. Clear, crystalline air. Could count spruce needles at a distance of ten kilometres.

Mum: 'I've knitted you a new hat.'

I tried it on. It was a good fit. Soft. Black.

'Thank you.'

'Dad sends his love.'

'Why didn't he come?'

'You mustn't do things like that any more, to Dr Vang.'

'What do you all know about me?'

She put the old hat in her bag.

'Isn't it time we got to know each other better?' she said slowly.

Strange words.

'Yes, it is,' I said.

The bell rang.

Couldn't keep up with the days. Couldn't keep up with the nights. A line of marbles. The view from the window. It had to be getting on for autumn. Glass. A yellow leaf.

Then I remember one day after all. Never forget it.

There was a visitor for me in my room.

Nina.

She was sitting on the chair with big heavy eyes, thin, scrawny, long black dress. Mouth.

Sat on my bed, hid my face in my hands, felt alive for the first time for ages.

She sat down beside me.

'Kim,' she said, one shoulder close to me.

'When did you come?' I asked. 'To Oslo?'

'Yesterday.'

'Yesterday?'

'Yes. Going to stay here now. We live in Tidemandsgate. Do you remember?'

I covered my eyes.

'Are you clean now?' I whispered.

'Think so. It's over. There are other things to live for. Aren't there, Kim?'

'Yes, but not here.'

'You'll soon be out.'

We fumbled into each other's arms, somehow, our gaunt bodies, I leaned over her, she was under me, crying or laughing. I pulled up her dress and she held me tight around the neck.

'Be careful,' she said, she begged.

'Don't be frightened,' I mumbled. 'I've had mumps.'

It happened so fast. We were two grindstones rubbing against each other, she helped me into position, it hurt her and she cried, then we were frenzied, and the moment I felt a searing pain in my dick, the door opened. I twisted my head round and yelled, and there was Cecilie, paralysed, in the doorway, Cecilie, she spun round and was gone, like a dream and an alarm clock.

I rolled over, fell, crawled over the floor. Nina was mute, crying without a sound, pulling on her clothes. A nurse charged in. I could hear more footsteps. Then I just remember I was in an avalanche, dogs were barking, I felt sticks poking me all over my body, but no one started digging where I was.

The woman in white came with a photo for me one morning, when I was up, when I had been found.

It was of me. I was lying in the middle of a flock of sheep and thrashing around with my arms and legs.

New days. Old days. Ballooning nights.

I was given permission to go for walks in the area. An eye in every window. Cold. Time had disappeared. Hair hadn't grown back. I saw the chimney close-up. The fence. I followed a path, downwards, someone was coming towards me, a huge figure, a slow-moving mountain of a man. I wanted to turn back, but it was too late. My mind began to buzz, my thoughts dissolved, one by one, a field of flashing lights.

He stood directly before me.

He blocked out the view. He was larger than ever.

'Jensenius,' I said, removing my hat.

His gaze fell on my skull.

He opened his mouth, but no sound emerged. His eyes were pools of old fear. His tongue hung over his lips, big and motionless. He trembled.

Jensenius was a mute.

He pointed over his shoulder, towards the main building.

The green spire.

Then he produced a stump of a pencil and a slip of paper, wrote, gave it to me, turned round slowly and waddled back.

I read the note.

Get away. Before it is too late.

That evening I stopped taking the medication. I was terrified. I was ready. I was scared to death and dangerous.

September.

The sign of Virgo. I was Libra.

Mum: 'Kim, you have to cooperate with them. You must get well for our sake.'

'Can I trust you, Mum?'

'Yes, Kim. Of course you can. But why don't you want to talk to Dr Vang? He only wants to help you after all.'

'What picture did Hubert paint for the Autumn Exhibition?'

Mum giggled.

'A mussel.'

I chewed on a cigarette.

'Mum, one day, could you bring me a stack of paper and something to write with?'

She looked at me in astonishment.

'No problem. What are you going to do with them?'

'And an envelope and a stamp.'

Yellow leaves gusting through the air.

Sat down in Napoleon's office. The wig was immaculate. He looked at my hat and gloated with satisfaction.

'Would you have preferred to go to prison?' he asked.

'Yes,' I said.

Conversation over.

On my return downstairs, Gunnar was sitting in the visitors' room puffing away.

'Let's go to my room,' I said.

The corridor.

I closed the door and listened.

Gunnar watched me.

'The most recent opinion poll shows forty-three per cent against and thirty-six for,' he said.

I sat by the window and lit up.

'You know it's exactly ten years since The Beatles recorded 'Love Me Do', don't you?' I said. '11 September 1962.'

'Bloody hell. We were so young!'

Gunnar seemed to perk up, his muscles relaxed.

'D'you remember the autograph I flogged you that autumn?'

'The salt pastilles. You bastard! But you didn't bloody manage to trick me over Comrade Lin Piao!'

We grinned. I thought of the leaflets in the drawer.

'D'you remember that porn mag Stig brought back from Copenhagen?'

'After the handball tour? Yes.'

'Exactly.'

Gunnar seemed happy that he could talk so easily to me. Jesus!

'Muck,' he chortled.

'And d'you remember that I got you out of a fix while you were on the bog?'

'I'll never forget that, Kim.'

'And you shook my hand and promised me you would be there for me if ever I was in any trouble?'

'Of course, Kim. Gunnar doesn't forget that sort of thing.'

I fell on my knees before him, clenched my fists and beat the floor with them, stopped, listened.

'You have to get me out of here! You have to get me out of here, Gunnar!'

Indian summer.

I sat in my room waiting.

Lukewarm slop on a plate. Everyone was talking about the killings in Munich.

Lying awake at night.

Mum: 'What are you going to do with all this paper?'

I put it in my bag in the wardrobe.

'The envelope and the stamp?' I asked.

She passed them to me, too, and the biros.

'Are you going to write a letter to Nina? She's been here, hasn't she?'

Yesterday I took the shutters off the window. The light surged into the House like a wave. There were dead insects on the sills. I was blinded, staggered around with my hands in front of my face. Spring came at me from all sides. May. Everything was transparent. The paper shone. The writing disappeared in the burning sun. I crept onto the balcony. My eyes adapted to the light, as though I had been blind for years and was slowly regaining sight. The fjord was full of boats. Sails. A cruise ship. A motor boat. Then I heard the sound. Someone was there. I slowly rose to my feet. She was sitting on the rock my great-grandfather had carried up from the quayside. Astride the two uneven black halves, with a big stomach bulging out from under her flowery dress.

Nina looked at me.

'Hiya, Kim,' she shouted with a gentle wave.

She ran with light, wary steps towards the gate.

I wanted to run after her, but had no strength.

She turned and smiled, holding her bulky stomach.

I waved with my injured hand.

'I'm waiting for you!' she shouted.

And then she was gone, down the steep path.

Behind me the apple trees were in white blossom.

It was the night of the referendum.

25 September 1972. I was twenty-one years old.

I sat in my room. An excited orderly burst in gesticulating with his arms.

'The noes have it!' he yelled. 'The conservatives are looking down in the mouth already!'

He left just as quickly. Heard the noise on the TV. Clapping. Cheering.

Drowned the solitary confinement.

Looked out of the window. Soon be night. Bed. The bare walls.

The woman in white brought in supper. She put the tray of pills on the table and rested her hand on my shoulder.

'It'll be a Yes, anyway, Kim. The votes from the towns are coming in now.'

'Can I be excused the pills tonight?' I asked. 'I wasn't allowed to vote. I would've voted for No.'

She was impatient and tense.

The noise from the TV.

'It's my job,' she said quickly.

'Go and watch the box,' I said. 'I can swallow them on my own.'

She gave me a squeeze and scurried out.

Heard the door lock.

I crushed the pills and scattered them under the bed.

Heard the shouts and the groans from the room where the white coats were sitting round the TV set.

The weather was unsettled.

The wind outside. Shadows on the wall.

Then she was back again.

'Aren't you in bed yet?'

I sat on the sheet. She took the empty tray.

'Bratteli's been on TV. It's going to be a Yes.'

I lay on my back and she tiptoed out. The key. The lock. Footsteps.

Woken by gentle taps. I looked around in the dark. The tapping continued. The window. I peered between the curtains and saw Gunnar's mug in the light of a torch. I waved and he switched it off. I got dressed. Took out the bag with the pens and paper and the letter. It surprised me that it was so easy to open the window when the door was locked from the outside. I wriggled across the windowsill and Gunnar caught me. We ran half-bent over the slippery ground, climbed the fence, for there were no holes in the fence round Gaustad, and there, at the side of the road, was a Volvo PV with the engine running.

Gunnar pushed me in, Ola pressed the accelerator to the floor and we sped round the bends.

Seb was sitting at the front and passed a bottle of white wine back to me.

I was on the verge of tears.

'Bloody hell, boys. Shit!' That was all I could say.

'We won!' Gunnar shrieked in my ear. 'We won!'

'Eh?'

Ola sat over the wheel like a goalkeeper.

'Drove down from Trondheim when the arrow was on Yes. Six hours. A record!'

'Was it a No?'

'Yes!'

It was party time in the car, Seb played a happy blues on the harp, Gunnar sang, we raced towards the city centre and Norwegian flags had been hoisted in the wind. Some retard with a Europe sticker on the rear window was in our lane. Ola passed him on the outside and forced him into the ditch. We stuck out our heads and gave him three straight fingers and one crooked one.

'Stick that up your arse, you clod!' Seb yelled, and he was left way behind.

Ola parked in the middle of Karl Johan. The university square was crammed with people. They were dancing and jumping around with flags and bottles and fireworks. The clouds in the sky cleared and we threw ourselves into the mayhem, we were carried away, delirious with happiness. We turned cartwheels and were the conquerors of the world.

Then I turned my back on the euphoria and the chaos and left them to it, posted a letter to my mother in the box next to Hotel Continental and continued on down to the quay. The City Hall clock struck six. Soon the first ferry from Nesodden would arrive.

I stood on the deck all the way there.